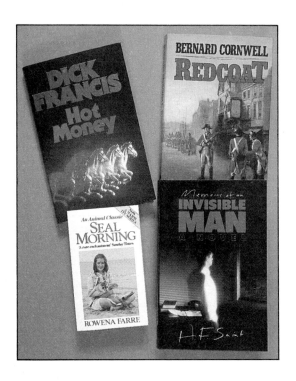

THE READER'S DIGEST ASSOCIATION LIMITED
25 Berkeley Square, London W1X 6AB
THE READER'S DIGEST ASSOCIATION
SOUTH AFRICA (PTY) LTD
Reader's Digest House, 130 Strand Street, Cape Town
Printed by Petty & Sons Ltd, Leeds
Bound by Hazell, Watson & Viney Ltd, Aylesbury
Original cover design by Jeffery Matthews FSIAD
For information as to ownership
of copyright in the material in this book see last page

Reader's Digest

CONDENSED BOOKS

HOT MONEY
by Dick Francis

When he's buying and selling gold, Malcolm Pembroke truly has the Midas touch. But neither his fantastic wealth nor his fabled luck can help him elude the killer who has murdered his fifth wife, Moira, and who is now stalking *him*. Where can he run to? Whom can he trust? He finds he can turn only to Ian, his amateur jockey son from whom he has been estranged for three years. As the plot thickens, Malcolm makes some unexpected discoveries about Ian—and some even stranger, more frightening ones about the rest of his family. It is a time when family skeletons suddenly become all too real . . .

A tantalising new mystery from this ever popular author.

MEMOIRS OF AN INVISIBLE MAN
by H. F. Saint

After a scientific accident at Micro-Magnetics, Inc., Nick Halloway, a young securities analyst, disappears—*literally*. Finding himself utterly invisible, Nick has to make a momentous decision. Should he hand himself over to the American government or try to escape their control?

He decides to escape, but how can he survive in today's busy world, pursued by a relentless government agency? Where will he live? How will he earn money if he can't, visibly, do a day's work? How can he shop for food—in fact, need he still eat at all?

H. F. Saint's first novel is a gripping read and enormous fun, with a wry, wise look at modern-day life.

SEAL MORNING
by Rowena Farre

For young Rowena, life in a remote Scottish croft is a succession of long walks in the wildly beautiful countryside, evenings spent reading by the light of a paraffin lamp, occasional visits from friends. But all is not peace and quiet, thanks to a collection of unusual and highly entertaining animals.

The star among them is a young seal called Lora. When not delighting audiences with her unique vocal rendition of "Danny Boy", she might be found helping to unpack the groceries, or demonstrating her superior swimming skills to a pair of boisterous otters. Her antics, and those of all the members of this lively household, have made Rowena Farre's charming animal story a classic of its kind.

REDCOAT
by Bernard Cornwell

In the winter of 1777 the allegiance of the citizens of Philadelphia is sharply divided between the occupying British Redcoats and the routed American Patriots.

Caught up in the crossfire of loyalties is Sam Gilpin. A Redcoat who took the King's shilling for adventure, Sam is proud of the uniform he wears and prepared to die for his country. But on the battlefield, and in the streets of the captured city, he soon finds out what his red coat and his patriotism really entail—and he has to make a heart-rending choice between duty and love.

This powerful and moving novel evokes all the bitter conflicts of the American War of Independence.

HOT MONEY

A CONDENSATION OF THE BOOK BY

Dick Francis

ILLUSTRATED BY LEN THURSTON

For Malcolm and Ian Pembroke, "like father, like son"
could not be further from the truth. Malcolm is rash,
oft-married and blessed with a talent for making deals
that has made him millions as a gold speculator. Ian, his
son, is prudent, single, unemployed and uncertain of his
future in the racing world.

Yet, despite their differences, they come to share
rather more than a love of horses and memories of
happier days at Quantum, the family's Victorian
mansion. For suddenly, someone is after Malcolm—
someone desperate enough to murder. And when the
large and clamorous Pembroke clan gather, father and
son find the lines between family and foe blurring with
alarming speed.

Chapter One

I intensely disliked my father's fifth wife, but not to the point of murder.

I, the fruit of his second ill-considered gallop up the aisle, had gone dutifully to the next two of his subsequent nuptials, the changes of "mother" punctuating my life at six and fourteen.

At thirty, however, I'd revolted: wild horses couldn't have dragged me to witness his wedding to the sharp-eyed, honey-tongued Moira, his fifth choice. Moira had been the subject of the bitterest quarrel my father and I had ever had, and the direct cause of a nonspeaking wilderness which had lasted three years.

After Moira was murdered, the police came bristling with suspicion to my door, and it was by the merest fluke that I could prove I'd been geographically elsewhere when her grasping little soul had left her carefully tended body. I didn't go to her funeral, but I wasn't alone in that. My father didn't go either.

A month after her death he telephoned me, and it was so long since I'd heard his voice that it seemed that of a stranger.

"Ian?"

"Hello, Malcolm," I said.

"Are you busy?"

"In general," I said, "fairly." I had that day quit my job and put on idleness like a comfortable coat.

He sighed down the line. "I suppose you know about Moira?"

"Front-page news," I agreed.

"If you want me to apologise," he said, "I'm not going to."

His image stood sharp and clear in my mind: a stocky, grey-haired man with bright blue eyes and a fizzing vitality. He was to my mind stubborn, opinionated, rash and often stupid. He was also financially canny, intuitive, quick-brained and courageous, and hadn't been nicknamed Midas for nothing.

"Are you still there?" he demanded.

"Yes."

"Well . . . I need your help." I couldn't remember his asking anyone for help ever before.

"What sort of help?" I said uncertainly.

"I'll tell you when you get here."

"Where is 'here'?"

"Newmarket," he said. "Come to the sales tomorrow afternoon."

He rang off immediately, and I thought of the last time I'd seen him, when I'd tried to dissuade him from marrying Moira, describing her as a bad misjudgment on his part and as a rapacious bloodsucker. He'd knocked me to the floor with one fast, dreadful blow, which he'd been quite capable of at sixty-five, three years ago. Striding furiously away, he'd left me lying dazed on my carpet and had afterwards behaved as if I no longer existed, packing into boxes everything I'd left in my old room in his house and sending it on to my flat.

Time had proved me right about Moira, but the unforgivable words had remained unforgiven to her death and, it had seemed, beyond. On this October evening, though, perhaps they were provisionally on ice.

I, Ian Pembroke, the fifth of my father's eight children, had from the mists of infancy loved him blindly through thunderous years of domestic infighting. In a totally chaotic upbringing, I'd spent scattered unhappy periods with my bitter mother, but had mostly been passed from wife to wife in my father's house as part of the furniture and fittings.

Only with the advent of Coochie, his fourth wife, had there been peace. Coochie had been different. She had been my only real mother, the only one who'd given me a sense of worth and identity, who'd listened and offered good advice. Coochie produced twin boys, my half-brothers Robin and Peter, and it had seemed that at last Malcolm Pembroke had achieved a friendly family unit, albeit a sort of sunny clearing surrounded by jungle thickets of ex-wives and discontented siblings.

I grew up and left home but went back often, never feeling excluded. Coochie would have seen Malcolm into a happy old age but, when she was forty and the twins eleven, a hit-and-run driver swerved her car off the road and downhill onto rocks. Coochie and Peter were killed outright. Robin, the elder twin, suffered brain damage. I'd learned the meaning of grief on that drizzly afternoon, and still mourned them all, their loss irreparable.

On the October evening of Malcolm's telephone call, I glanced at them as usual as I went to bed, their three bright faces grinning out from a silver frame on my chest of drawers. Robin lived—just—in serene twilight in a nursing home. I went to see him now and again. He no longer looked like the boy in the photograph but was five years older, growing tall, empty-eyed.

I wondered what Malcolm could possibly want. Newmarket, I thought. The sales. Newmarket was all very well for me because I'd been working as an assistant to a racehorse trainer. But Newmarket for Malcolm? Malcolm never gambled on horses, only on gold. Malcolm had made several immense consecutive fortunes from buying and selling the hard yellow stuff, and had years ago reacted to my stated choice of occupation by saying merely, "Horses? Racing? Good Lord! Well, if that's what you want, my boy, off you go."

Malcolm and Newmarket bloodstock sales simply didn't mix. Not the Malcolm I'd known, anyway.

I DROVE THE NEXT DAY to the isolated Suffolk town whose major industry was the sport of kings, and among the crowd found my father outside the salering building, eyes intently focused on a catalogue.

He looked just the same. Brushed grey hair, smooth brown vicuna knee-length overcoat, charcoal business suit, silk tie, confidently bringing his City sophistication into the country.

It was a golden day, crisp and clear. I walked across to him in my own brand of working clothes: cavalry twill trousers, checked wool shirt, padded olive-green jacket, tweed cap. A surface contrast that went personality deep.

"Good afternoon," I said neutrally.

He raised his eyes and gave me a stare as blue as the sky. "You look older," he said.

"Three years."

"Three years and a crooked nose." He observed it dispassionately. "I suppose you broke that falling off a horse?"

"No . . . You broke it."

"Did I?" He seemed only mildly surprised. "You deserved it." I didn't answer. He shrugged. "Do you want some coffee?"

"OK."

We hadn't touched each other, I thought. Not a hug, not a handshake. Three years' silence couldn't easily be bridged.

He set off not in the direction of the regular refreshment room, but towards one of the private rooms set aside for the privileged. I followed.

The Newmarket sales building was in the form of an amphitheatre, sloping banks of seats rising all round from the ground-level ring where each horse was led round while being auctioned. Underneath the seating

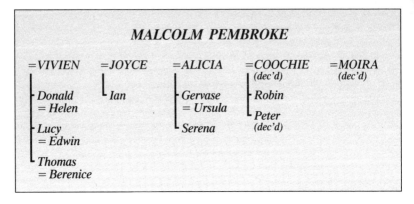

MALCOLM PEMBROKE

=VIVIEN	=JOYCE	=ALICIA	=COOCHIE (dec'd)	=MOIRA (dec'd)
⌐ Donald = Helen	⌐ Ian	⌐ Gervase = Ursula	⌐ Robin ⌐ Peter (dec'd)	
⌐ Lucy = Edwin		⌐ Serena		
⌐ Thomas = Berenice				

and in a large adjacent building were rooms used as offices by auctioneers and bloodstock agents, and as entertainment rooms by commercial firms, such as Ebury Jewellers, Malcolm's present willing hosts.

Ebury's space was decorated as an expensive showroom, with well-lit glass display cases shining with silver and sparkling with baubles.

A smooth young gentleman welcomed Malcolm and offered drinks and goodies from a well-stocked buffet. We took cups of coffee and sat at a long, polished table, I, at any rate, feeling awkward. Malcolm fiddled with his spoon.

"What sort of help?" I said.

I suppose I expected him to say he wanted help in some way with horses, in view of the venue he'd chosen, but it seemed to be nothing as straightforward.

"I want you beside me," he said. "All the time."

I frowned, puzzled. "I don't understand."

"I don't suppose you do," he said. He looked up at my face. "I'm going to travel a bit. I want you with me."

"Why now, and why me?"

"You're my son." He stopped fiddling with the spoon. "I trust you." He paused. "Can't you get some time off from work? Have a holiday?"

I thought of the trainer I'd just left, whose daughter had made my job untenable because she wanted it for her fiancé. There was no immediate need for me to find another place, save for paying the rent. At thirty-three, I'd worked for three different trainers, as an assistant. The natural progression was towards becoming a trainer myself, a dicey course without money.

"What are you thinking?" Malcolm asked.

"Roughly, whether you would lend me half a million quid."

"No," he said.

I smiled. "That's what I thought."

"I'll pay your fares and your hotel bills."

I looked at Malcolm's face, and surprised there an expression that could only be interpreted as anxiety. I was unexpectedly moved. I'd never wanted to quarrel with him: I'd wanted him to see Moira as I did, as a calculating, sweet-talking honeypot who was after his money, and who had used the devastation of Coochie's death to insinuate herself, turning up constantly with sympathy and offers to cook. Malcolm, deep in grief, had hardly noticed when she began saying "we". I had for the whole three silent years wanted peace with my father, but I couldn't bear to go to his house and see Moira smirking in Coochie's place.

"Yes," I said. "All right. I can take time off."

His relief was visible. "Good! Good! Come along then, I may as well buy a horse." He stood up, full of sudden energy, waving his catalogue. "Which do you suggest?"

"Why on earth do you want a horse?"

"To race, of course. Everyone should have a hobby," he said briskly, though he'd never had one in his life. "Mine is racing." As an afterthought, he added, "Henceforth," and began to walk to the door.

The smooth young man begged Malcolm to come back any time. Malcolm assured him he would, then wheeled away from him and marched across to one of the display cabinets.

"While I was waiting for you, I bought a cup," he said to me over his shoulder. "One rather like that." He pointed. "It's being engraved."

The cup in question was a highly-decorated and graceful elongated jug, eighteen inches tall and made of sterling silver.

"What's it for?" I asked.

"Mm. The Coochie Pembroke Memorial Challenge Trophy. Rather good, don't you think?"

"Yes," I said.

He gave me a sidelong glance. "I thought you'd think so." He retraced his steps to the door. "Right, then, a horse."

Just like old times, I thought with half-forgotten pleasure. The sudden impulses which might or might not turn out to be thoroughly sensible. With Malcolm it was always a toss-up.

I called him Malcolm, as all his children did, on his own instructions, and had grown up thinking it natural.

Outside, he said, "How do we set about it then?"

"Er . . . This is the first day of the Highflyer Sales."

"Well?" he demanded, as I paused. "Go on."

"I just thought you ought to know that you'll be lucky today to get a top-class yearling for under a quarter of a million."

He was not noticeably deterred. "Come on, then, Ian. Let's go and start bidding."

"You need to look up the breeding first," I said.

"Ian," he said with mock sorrow, "I don't know anything about the breeding, I can just about tell if the thing's got four legs. So let's get on and bid."

It sounded crazy to me, but it was his money. We went into the sale-ring where the auction was already in progress, and Malcolm asked me where the richest bidders were, the ones that really meant business.

"In those banks of seats to the left of the auctioneers, or here, in the entrance, or just round there to the left . . ."

He looked and listened and then led the way up to a section of seats from where we could watch the places I'd pointed out.

"If you buy ten yearlings," I said, "six might get to a racecourse, three might win a race and one might be pretty good. If you're lucky."

"Cautious Ian."

"You," I said, "are cautious with gold. You're fast and flamboyant, but you wait for the moment."

He merely grunted and began paying attention to the matter in hand, intently focusing not on the merchandise but on the bidders on the far side of the ring. The auctioneers in the box to our left were unimpressed by the fortunes passing. "Fifty thousand, thank you, sir; sixty thousand, seventy . . . eighty? Shall I say eighty? Eighty, thank you, sir. Against you, sir. Ninety? Ninety. One hundred thousand. Selling now. I'm selling now. Against you, sir? No? All done? All done?" A pause for a sweep round to make sure no new bidder was frantically waving. "Done, then. Sold to Mr. Siddons. One hundred thousand guineas."

"Selling now," Malcolm said. "I suppose that means until the fellow says 'selling now', it's safe to bid, knowing you won't have to buy?"

"Yours might be the bid that reaches the reserve."

He nodded. "Russian roulette."

We watched the sales for the rest of the afternoon. He looked around the amphitheatre at the constantly changing audience of breeders, trainers, owners. "Whose judgment would you trust most?"

I mentioned several trainers and the agents who might be acting on their behalf, and he told me to tell him when someone with good judgment was bidding, and to point them out. I did so many times, and he listened and passed no comment.

After a while we went out for a break: a Scotch, a sandwich, and fresh air.

"I suppose you know," Malcolm said casually, watching yearlings skittering past in the grasp of their handlers, "that Moira and I were divorcing? And that she was demanding the house, half my possessions and half my future earnings?"

"Could she?"

"She was going to fight for it."

I refrained from saying that whoever had murdered Moira had done Malcolm a big favour. I said instead, "Still no clues?"

"No, nothing new."

He spoke without regret. His disenchantment with Moira, according to his acid second wife, my own mother Joyce, had begun as soon as he'd stopped missing Coochie; and as Joyce was as percipient as she was catty, I believed it.

"The police tried damned hard to prove I did it," Malcolm said.

"Yes, so I heard."

"Who from? The three witches?"

I couldn't help smiling. He meant his three living ex-wives, Vivien, Joyce and Alicia. "Yes, them. And all of the family."

Malcolm's alibi for Moira's death had been as unassailable as my own, as he'd been in Paris for the day when someone had pushed Moira's retroussé little nose into a bag of potting compost and held it there until it was certain she would take no more geranium cuttings. The police still clung to the belief that Malcolm had arranged for an assassin, but even Joyce knew that that was nonsense. Malcolm was a creature of tempest and volatility, but he'd never been calculatingly cruel.

We returned to the scene of the action, and again found seats opposite the big-money crowd. Malcolm became particularly attentive to the flickering electronic board which lit up with the amount as each bid was made, not only in English currency but in dollars, yen, francs, lire and Irish punts at the current exchange rates. He'd always been fascinated by the workings of money.

He considered that the best years of his talent had been wasted: years when, for political reasons, gold bullion couldn't be bought by private Britons. Always large, Malcolm's income, once the controls were lifted, went up like a hot-air balloon, and it was at the beginning of that period that he'd first been called Midas. Since then, he'd ridden the yellow roller coaster several times, unerringly buying when the price sank ever lower, selling as it soared, but before the bubble burst.

The amphitheatre had filled to capacity while we'd been outside: the blood of Northern Dancer and Nijinsky was on its regal way to the ring.

A hush fell at the entrance of the first legend-bred youngster, the expectant hush of the knowledgeable awaiting a battle among financial giants. A fat cheque on this sales evening could secure a Derby winner and found a dynasty, and it happened often enough to tempt belief each time that this was the one.

The auctioneer cleared his throat, managed the introduction without a quiver, and asked for an opening bid. Malcolm watched as he scanned the faces for the drop of an eyelid, the twitch of a head, the tiny acknowledgments of intent. ". . . against you, sir. No more, then? All done?" The auctioneer's eyebrows rose with his gavel, then came smoothly, conclusively down. "Sold for one million seven hundred thousand guineas . . ."

The crowd sighed. Then came rustling of catalogues, movement, murmuring and rewound expectation.

Malcolm said, "It's a spectator sport."

"Addictive," I agreed.

He glanced at me sideways. "For one million . . . five million . . . there's no guarantee the colt will ever race, isn't that what you said? One could be throwing one's cash down the drain?"

"That's right."

"It's a perfectly blameless way of getting rid of a lot of money very fast, wouldn't you say?"

"Well . . ." I said slowly, "is that what you're at?"

"Do you disapprove?"

"It's your money. You made it. You spend it."

The following lot, a filly, fetched a more moderate sum, but the hush of expectancy returned for the next offering. Malcolm, keenly tuned by now to the atmosphere, watched the bidders, not the nervous chestnut colt.

The upward impetus stopped at a fraction over two million and the auctioneer's eyebrows and gavel rose. "All done?"

Malcolm raised his catalogue.

The movement caught the eye of the auctioneer, who paused with the gavel raised, using his eyebrows as a question, looking at Malcolm with surprise. "You want to bid, sir?"

"And fifty," Malcolm said clearly, nodding.

All round the ring, necks stretched to see who had spoken.

"All done, then?" the auctioneer asked again, and with no further replies, said, "Done then. Sold for two million and seventy thousand guineas to . . . er . . . the bidder opposite."

The auctioneer consulted with his colleagues and one of them left the box, carrying a clipboard. He hurried down and made his way to Malcolm, handing him the clipboard and politely requiring him to sign the bill of sale, in triplicate. He then invited Malcolm to his office, and we went. They computed what he owed and Malcolm wrote them a cheque. They politely suggested proof of identity and a reference. Malcolm gave them an American Express card and the telephone number of his bank manager. They took the cheque and said that although Mr. . . . er . . . Pembroke should arrange insurance on his purchase at once, the colt would not be available for removal until . . . er . . . tomorrow.

Malcolm said tomorrow would be fine, and in high spirits told me I could ferry him back to his Cambridge hotel, from where he'd come that morning in a taxi, and we would have dinner together.

After we'd called in at an insurance agent's office and he'd signed some more papers and another cheque, we walked together to the car park. Night had fallen, and people were beginning to drift home. I pointed out the row where my car stood.

"Where are you going to send your colt?" I asked.

"Where would you say?"

"I should think," I said . . . but I never finished my answer.

A car coming towards us between two rows of parked cars suddenly emitted two headlight beams, blinding us; and at the same moment accelerated fiercely, swerving straight towards Malcolm.

I leaped, flung myself at my father, my flying weight knocking him down. I fell on top of him, knowing that the speeding bulk of the car had caught me, but not sure to what extent. There was just a bang, and lights curving like arcs, and a fast crunch into darkness.

We were on the ground then between two parked cars, our bodies heavy with shock, in a sort of inertia.

After a moment, Malcolm struggled to free himself from under me, and I rolled awkwardly onto my knees. Malcolm pushed himself up until he was sitting with his back against a car's wheel, looking shaken.

"That car," he said, between deep breaths, "was aiming to kill me."

I nodded speechlessly. My trousers were torn, thigh grazed and bleeding.

"You always had . . . quick reactions," he said. "So now you know why I want you beside me . . . all the time."

IT WAS THE SECOND TIME someone had tried to kill him, he said.

I was driving towards Cambridge, anxiously searching in the rearview mirrors for satanically-minded followers but so far, thankfully, without success. My right leg was stiffening but I was in truth fairly used to that level of buffet through having ridden in three or four hundred jump races, incurring consequent collisions with the ground.

"When was the first time?" I asked.

"Last Friday."

It was currently Tuesday evening. "What happened?" I said.

He took a while over answering. When he did there was sadness in his voice. "One moment I was walking the dogs . . . well, I think I was, but that's it, I don't really remember." He paused. "I think I had a bang on the head . . . Anyway, the last thing I remember is calling the dogs and opening the kitchen door. I meant to take them through the garden to that field with the stream and the willows. Anyway, I woke up in Moira's car in the garage, and it's damn lucky I woke up at all . . . the engine was running . . ." He stopped for a few moments. "I was in the back seat, sort of tumbled over. I got up and practically fell through between the front seats to reach the key in the ignition, and when the engine stopped I just lay there. I felt better after a while. I stumbled out of the car and was sick."

"Did you tell the police?"

"Sure, I told them." His voice sounded weary at the recollection. "It was the same lot who came after Moira's death. They made a lot of notes and took samples—I ask you—of my vomit, and dusted over Moira's car for fingerprints. I think they thought I'd been going to commit suicide and thought better of it . . . or else that I'd staged it in the hope people would believe I couldn't have killed Moira if someone was trying to kill me . . ." He shook his head. "I'm sorry I told them at all, and that's why we're not reporting tonight's attempt either."

He had been adamant, in the car park, that we shouldn't.

"What about the bump on your head?" I asked.

"I had a swelling above my ear. Very tender, but not very big. The word I heard the police use about that was 'inconclusive'."

I drove carefully towards Cambridge, appalled and angry, thinking over what he'd told me.

"Who," I said eventually, "knew you were going to Newmarket Sales?"

"Who?" He sounded surprised at the question, and then understood it. "I've no idea. I didn't know myself until yesterday."

"Well, what have you been doing since the police left you last Friday night?"

"Thinking." And the thoughts, it was clear, had been saddening.

"Mm," I said. "About whether Moira was killed to stop her taking half your possessions?"

He said unwillingly, "Yes."

"And the people who had an interest in stopping her were your likely heirs. Your children. Also perhaps their husbands and wives, also perhaps even the witches."

"I don't want to believe it," he said.

The truth was that, apart from poor Robin, I didn't know my half-brothers and half-sisters well enough to have any certainty about any of them. I was usually on speaking terms with them all, but didn't seek them out. There had been too many rows. Under Coochie's reign the whole family had been banned from sleeping in the house, with the result that a storm of collective resentment had been directed at me, whom she had kept and treated as her own.

"Apart from thinking," I said, "what else have you been doing since Friday night?"

"When the police had gone, I telephoned the hire firm I use now and told them to send a car to fetch me. I could feel my heart banging away at a terrible rate. It was awful. I packed some things . . ."

As the ouskirts of Cambridge came up, he began to give me directions to the hotel where he said he'd spent the previous four nights.

"Does anyone know where you're staying?" I asked.

Malcolm knew Cambridge well, had been at university there, and it must have seemed to him a safe city to bolt to, but it was also the first place I would have gone looking for him.

"No," he said in answer to my question.

"All the same," I said, pulling up outside the hotel, "go and pack and check out of here, and we'll go somewhere else."

"It's not necessary," he protested.

"You appointed me as minder, so I'm minding," I said.

I asked the doorman of the hotel where I should park and turned, at his suggestion, through an arch into the hotel's inner courtyard. From there, through a back door and old-fashioned hallways, Malcolm and I went up one flight of red-carpeted stairs and down a lengthy winding corridor.

He brought his room key out of his pocket and, with it raised, said abruptly, "I suppose you didn't tell anyone I would be at the sales?"

"No, I didn't."

"But you knew." He paused. "Only you knew."

He was staring at me with the blue eyes and I saw all the question marks rioting through his mind. I was both astounded by his fear and considered it warranted.

"You said you trusted me," I said.

"I haven't seen you for three years . . . and I broke your nose . . ."

I took the key out of his hand and unlocked the door. I supposed I might have been suspicious of me if I'd been attacked twice in five days, considering I came into the high-probability category of son. I switched on the light and went forward into the suite, which was free from lurking murderers, that time at least.

Malcolm followed, only tentatively reassured, closing the door behind him. I drew the curtains and briefly surveyed the spacious but old-fashioned accommodation. "Did you bring any Scotch?" I asked. In the old days, he'd never travelled without it.

He waved a hand towards a chest of drawers where I found a bottle nestling among a large number of socks. I fetched a glass from the bathroom and poured him enough to tranquillise an elephant.

"Sit down and drink this."

He sat down, and tried not to let the glass clatter against his teeth from the shaking of his hand.

I said quietly, "If I wanted you dead, I'd have let that car hit you tonight."

He seemed to notice for the first time the physical consequences of our escape. "Is your leg all right?"

"Leg is. But can I borrow a pair of your trousers?"

He pointed to a cupboard where I found a second suit almost identical to the one he was wearing. He silently watched me change and made no objection when I telephoned down to reception and asked them to get the bill ready for his departure.

"Shall I pack for you?" I asked.

He nodded, and watched while I fetched his suitcase, opened it on one of the beds and began collecting his belongings. The things he'd brought spoke eloquently of his state of mind when he'd packed them: about ten pairs of socks but no underwear, a dozen shirts, two towelling bathrobes, no extra shoes. I closed the case.

"You could have decided not to go through with it tonight . . . at the last moment . . ."

"It wasn't like that," I protested. Saving him had been utterly instinctive—without calculation or counting of risks.

He said almost beseechingly, "It wasn't you, was it, who had Moira . . . Or me, in the garage . . . ? Say it wasn't you."

I didn't know how to convince him. He'd known me better, lived with me longer, than any of his other children, and if his trust was this fragile then there wasn't much future between us.

"I didn't have Moira killed," I said. "If you believe it of me, you could believe it of yourself." I paused. "I don't want you dead, I want you alive. I could never do you harm."

It struck me that he really needed to hear me say I loved him, so despite the conditioned inhibitions of my upbringing, I said, feeling that desperate situations needed desperate remedies, "You're a great father . . . and . . . er . . . I love you."

He blinked. Such a declaration pierced him, one could see. I'd probably overdone it, but his distrust had been a wound for me too.

I said much more lightly, "I swear on the Coochie Pembroke Memorial Challenge Trophy that I would never touch a hair on your head . . . nor Moira's either, though I did indeed loathe her." I lifted the suitcase off the bed. "Do I go on with you or not?" I asked.

He was looking at me searchingly, as if I were a stranger, which I suppose in some ways I was. He had never before, I guessed, had to think of me not as a son, but as a man who had led a life separate from his.

"Trust your instincts," I said.

Some of the tension at last slackened in his muscles. His instinct had been to trust me, an instinct strong enough to carry him to the telephone after three silent years. He finished the Scotch and stood up, taking a deep breath as if making resolves. "Come with me, then," he said.

I nodded.

He went over to the chest of drawers and from the bottom drawer produced a briefcase. I might have guessed it would be there somewhere: even in the direst panic, he wouldn't have left behind the lists of his gold shares or his currency exchange calculator. On impulse I went over to the telephone again and asked reception to call a minicab to take us to London.

"But your car's here," Malcolm said.

"Mm. I think I'll leave it here, for now. If no one knew you were going to Newmarket Sales, then it's probable you were followed there, from here. If you think about it, the car that tried to kill you was waiting in the sales car park, but you didn't have a car. You went there by taxi. Whoever drove at you must have seen you and me together, known who I was, and guessed you might leave with me, so although I didn't see anyone following us tonight from Newmarket, whoever-it-was probably knew we would come here, to this hotel, so they might be hanging about in the courtyard where we parked, where it's nice and dark."

"My God!"

"It's possible," I said. "So we'll leave through the front with the doorman in attendance, don't you think?"

"If you say so," he said weakly.

"From now on, we take every exaggerated precaution we can think of."

We set off without incident from the hotel, bill paid, luggage loaded in the minicab, doorman tipped.

"Why did you go to the sales at all?" I asked Malcolm, as the minicab headed towards the M11. "I mean, why Newmarket? Why the sales?"

Malcolm frowned. "Because of Ebury's, I suppose."

"The jewellers?"

"Yes. I knew they were going to have a showroom there this week. So then yesterday when I was wondering what would fetch you, I remembered the sales were close to Cambridge, and I decided on it not long before I rang you."

I pondered a bit. "How would you set about finding where someone was, if you wanted to, so to speak?"

To my surprise he had a ready answer. "Get the fellow I had for tailing Moira."

"Tailing?"

"My lawyer said to do it. It might save me some money, he said, if Moira was having a bit on the side. But she wasn't." He glanced at me. "What do you have in mind?"

"Well . . . I just wondered if he could check where everyone in the family was last Friday and tonight."

"Everyone!" Malcolm exclaimed. "It would take weeks."

"It would put your mind at rest."

He shook his head gloomily. "You forget about assassins."

"Assassins aren't so frightfully easy to find. How would you set about it, for instance, if you wanted someone killed? Put an ad in *The Times*?"

He didn't seem to see it as a problem, but he agreed that "the fellow who tailed Moira" should be offered the job of checking the family.

"What happened between you and Moira?" I said.

"She wanted Coochie's jewellery and I wouldn't give it to her. She kept on and on about it. Annoyed me, do you see? And then . . . well . . ." he shrugged. "She caught me out."

"With another woman?" I said without surprise.

He nodded, unashamed. He'd never been monogamous and couldn't understand why it should be expected. The terrible rows in my childhood had all been centred on his affairs: while he'd been married to Vivien and then to Joyce, he had maintained Alicia as his mistress. Alicia bore him a child while he was married to Joyce, and also one subsequently, when he'd made a fairly honest woman of her, at her insistence.

We discussed which hotel we should stay at that night, as neither of us felt like returning home. Home, currently, to me, was a flat in Epsom, not far from the stable I'd been working for. Home for Malcolm was still the big house in Berkshire where I'd been brought up.

Malcolm favoured our staying at the Dorchester, but I persuaded him he was too well known there, and we settled on the Savoy.

"A suite," Malcolm said at the reception desk. "Two bedrooms, two bathrooms and a sitting room, and send up some Bollinger right away."

I didn't feel like drinking champagne, but Malcolm did. He also ordered scrambled eggs and smoked salmon for us both from room service, with a bottle of Hine Antique brandy and a box of Havana cigars for comforts.

We ate the food and drank the brandy, still not totally in accord with each other. The three years' division had been, it seemed, a chasm not as easy to cross as I'd thought.

"Any day now," Malcolm said, carefully dislodging ash from his cigar, "we're going abroad."

"Anything you say. Only I'm supposed to ride at Sandown on Friday."

"I've never understood why you like it. All those cold wet days. All those falls."

"You get your rush from gold," I said.

"Danger?" His eyebrows rose. "Quiet, well-behaved, cautious Ian? Life is a bore without risk, is that it?"

"It's not so extraordinary," I said.

I'd always ridden as an amateur, unpaid, because something finally held me back from the total dedication needed for turning professional. Race riding was my deepest pleasure, but not my entire life. I'd never developed the competitive drive necessary for climbing the pro ladder. I was happy with the rides I got, with the camaraderie of the changing room, with the wide skies and the horses themselves and, one had to admit it, with the risks.

"Staying near me," Malcolm said, "as you've already found out, isn't enormously safe."

"That's why I'm staying," I said.

He laughed. "I thought I knew you. Seems I don't."

NEXT MORNING HE WAS UP before me, sitting on a sofa in one of his bathrobes and reading the *Sporting Life* when I ambled out in the underpants and shirt I'd slept in.

"I've ordered breakfast," he said. "And I'm in the paper—how about that?"

I looked. His name was near the end of the lists of yesterday's sales. *Lot 79, ch. colt, 2,070,000 gns. Malcolm Pembroke.*

He put down the paper. "Now, what do we do today?"

"We summon your private eye, we fix a trainer for the colt, I fetch our passports and some clothes, and you stay here."

Slightly to my surprise, he raised no arguments except to tell me not to be away too long.

"Trouble is," he said, "I don't have the private eye's phone number. Not with me. Joyce knows it, of course."

"How does my mother know it?"

"She used him," he said airily, "to follow me and Alicia."

There was nothing, I supposed, which should ever surprise me about my parents.

"When the lawyer fellow said to have Moira tailed, I got the private eye's name from Joyce. After all, he'd done a good job on me and Alicia all those years ago. So get through to Joyce, Ian, and ask for the number."

Bemused, I did as he said.

"Darling," my mother shrieked down the line, "do you know what your father's done?"

"No . . . what?"

"He's given a *fortune*, darling, to some wretched little film company to make some absolutely *ghastly* film about tadpoles or something. Some fool of a man telephoned to find out where your father was, because it seems he promised them even *more* money . . . I ask you!"

"Well," I said, "it's his money."

"Darling, don't be so *naive*. Someone's going to inherit it, and if only you'd swallow all that bloody pride, it would be *you*. If you go on with this bloody quarrel, he'll leave it all to Alicia's beastly children. So make it up with Malcolm *at once*, darling. Get him to see sense."

"Calm down," I said, "I have made it up with him."

"Thank God! At *last!*" my mother shrieked. "Then, darling, what are you waiting for? Get on to him straight away and stop him spending your inheritance."

Chapter Two

Malcolm's Victorian house was known as "Quantum" because of the Latin inscripton carved into the lintel over the front door: *Quantum in me fuit*—roughly, "I did the best I could".

I went there remembering the comfortable casualness that Coochie had imposed on it, not expecting that things would be different: I should have known better, as each wife in turn, Coochie included, had done her best to eradicate all signs of her predecessor.

I let myself in through the kitchen door with Malcolm's keys and thought wildly for a moment that I'd come to the wrong place. Coochie's pinewood and red-tiled homeliness had been swept away in favour of yellow walls, glittering white appliances and shelves crowded with scarlet geraniums cascading from white pots.

Faintly stunned, I looked back through time to the era before Coochie, to Alicia's fluffy occupancy, with broderie-anglaise frills on shimmering white curtains, and pale-blue worktops; and back further still to the starker olive-and-milk-coffee angularities chosen by Joyce. I remembered the day the workmen had torn out my mother's kitchen, and how I'd gone howling to Malcolm: he packed me off to Joyce immediately for a month, and when I returned I found the white frills installed.

I wondered what the kitchen had looked like in Vivien's time, when Malcolm had brought her there as his first bride. Vivien had been dispossessed and resentful by the time I was born, and I'd seldom seen her smiling. She seemed to me the least positive of the five wives and the least intelligent but, from her photographs, she seemed to have been in her youth the most beautiful. The dark sweep of her eyebrows and the high cheekbones remained, but the thick black hair had thinned now in greying, and entrenched bitterness had soured the once sweet mouth.

Vivien disliked, and was plaintively critical of, almost everybody. She had indoctrinated her three offspring with her own dissatisfactions to the point where they were nastily disparaging of Malcolm behind his back, though not to his face, hypocrites that they were.

Malcolm had steadfastly maintained them through young adulthood and then cast them loose, each with a trust fund that would prevent them from starving. He had treated all six of his surviving children in the same way; only his seventh child, Robin, would be looked after for ever. Whatever became of us in the future, he said, was in our own hands.

With the family in mind, I went into Malcolm's office. It was comfortable and cluttered, filled with his strong personality: the walls covered with dozens of framed photographs, the deep cupboards bulging with files, the bookshelves crammed, nothing very tidy.

His passport, he'd said, was in the second drawer of his desk, down on the right-hand side, and so it was, among a clutter of bygone travel arrangements. Malcolm's filing system was such that no one but he had the slightest idea where any paper or information could be found. His method, he'd told me, was always to put everything where he would first think of looking for it, and I'd seen such sense in that that I had copied him ever since.

Carrying the passport, I went upstairs to pack some more clothes for Malcolm in a suitcase, and felt an irresistible curiosity to see the room which had been mine. It was without soul: barren. The single bed showed a bare mattress. There was no dust, no smell of neglect, but the message was clear: the son who had slept there no longer existed. Shivering slightly, I closed the door.

I went down the stairs, and in the hall came face to face with a smallish man carrying a shotgun, the business end pointing my way. I stopped abruptly, as one would.

"Put your hands up," he said hoarsely.

I set the suitcase on the floor and did as he said. He wore earth-stained trousers and had mud on his hands. "Are you the gardener?" I asked.

"What if I am? What are you doing here?"

"Collecting clothes for . . .er . . . Mr. Pembroke. I'm his son."

"I don't know you. I'm getting the police." His voice was belligerent but quavery, the shotgun none too steady in his hands. He was then faced with the problem of how to telephone while aiming my way.

Seeing his hesitation, I said, "I can prove I'm Mr. Pembroke's son, and I'll open the suitcase to show you I'm not stealing anything. Would that help?"

After a pause, he nodded. "You stay over there, though."

I very slowly and carefully opened the suitcase, removed the contents, and laid them out on the hall floor. After that, I equally slowly took my wallet out of my pocket and laid it too on the floor. Then I retreated backwards.

The elderly gardener came suspiciously forward and inspected the show, dropping his eyes only for split seconds, raising them quickly, giving me no chance to jump him.

"That's his passport," he said accusingly.

"He asked me to fetch it." I paused. "I really am his son. You must be new here. I haven't seen you before."

"Two years," he said defensively. "I've worked here two years." He seemed to come quite suddenly to a decision to believe me, and almost apologetically lowered the gun. He gestured to Malcolm's things. "You better pack them again."

I began to do so under his still watchful eye.

"It was brave of you to come in here," I said.

He braced his shoulders in an old automatic movement. "I was in the

Arthur
Bellbrook

army once. Tell you the truth, I was coming in to phone the police, then you started down the stairs."

"And . . . the gun?"

"Brought it with me just in case. I go after rabbits . . . I keep the gun handy."

I nodded. "Has my father paid you for the week?" I said.

His eyes at once brightened hopefully. "He paid me last Friday, same as usual. Then Saturday morning he phoned my house to tell me to come round here to see to the dogs. Take them home with me, same as I always do when he's away. So I did."

I pulled out my chequebook and wrote him a cheque for the amount he specified. Arthur Bellbrook, he said his name was. I asked him if there was anyone else who needed wages.

He shook his head. "The cleaner left when Mrs. Pembroke was murdered. Said she didn't fancy the place any more."

"Where exactly was Mrs. Pembroke . . . er . . . murdered?"

"I'll show you if you like," he said, storing the cheque away in a pocket. "Outside, in the greenhouse."

He took me, however, not as I'd imagined to the rickety old familiar greenhouse in the kitchen garden, but to a white octagonal wrought-iron construction like a fancy birdcage on a secluded patch of lawn.

"Well, well," I said.

Arthur Bellbrook uttered, "Huh," as expressing his disapproval, and opened the metal-and-glass door. "The only thing as will survive in this place is geraniums. Mrs. Pembroke's passion, geraniums."

"Is this where . . . ?" I began.

"Yes," he said. "Poor lady. There's no one ought to die like that, however difficult they could be."

"No," I agreed. A thought struck me. "It was you who found her, wasn't it?"

"Yes. I was out for a stroll about seven o'clock, and I thought I would just see what state she'd left the place in. She played at gardening. Never cleaned the tools, things like that." He looked at the boarded floor as if still seeing her there. "She was lying face down, and I turned her over. She was dead all right. She had little pink dots in her skin; you get those from asphyxiation. They found potting compost in her lungs, poor lady."

26

"Thank you for showing me," I said.

He nodded and we both went out, shutting the door behind us.

"I don't think Mr. Pembroke liked this place much," he said unexpectedly. "Last spring, when she chose it, he said she could have it only if he couldn't see it from the house. Otherwise he wouldn't pay the bill. You see, they were all lovey-dovey when I first came here, but then I reckon her little ways got to him."

"What little ways?" I asked casually.

He glanced at me sideways with reawakening suspicions. "I thought you were his son. You must have known her."

"I didn't come here. I didn't like her."

He seemed to find that easily believable. "She could be as sweet as sugar . . . " He paused, remembering. "I don't know what you'd call it, really, what she was. But for instance last year, as well as the vegetables for the house, I grew a special little patch separately, to enter in the local show. Just runner beans, carrots and onions, for one of the produce classes. Well, Mrs. Pembroke happened to spot them a day or two before I was ready to harvest. 'What huge vegetables,' she says, and I tell her I'm going to exhibit them. And she looks at me sweet as syrup and says, 'Oh no, Arthur. Mr. Pembroke and I will have some of these for dinner tomorrow and I'll freeze the rest. If you want to grow vegetables to show, you must do it in your own garden in your own time.' And blow me, when I came to work the next morning, the whole little patch had been picked over, beans, carrots, onions, the lot. She'd taken them."

"Charming," I said.

He shrugged. "That was her. Mean, but within her rights."

Walking slowly, we arrived back at the kitchen door.

"I grew up here," I said, feeling nostalgia.

He gave me a stare. "Are you the one who built the secret room?"

Startled, I said, "It's not really a room. Just a sort of triangular-shaped space."

"I could use it," he said obstinately, "for an apple store."

I shook my head. "How do you know about it?"

He pursed his lips and looked knowing. "I could see the kitchen garden wall looked far too thick down at the bottom corner and I asked old Fred about it, who used to be gardener here before he retired. He said Mr. Pembroke's son once built a sort of shed there. He said he thought it had been bricked up years ago."

"I did brick it up soon after I built it, to stop my half-brother going in there and leaving dead rats for me to find," I said.

"Oh." He looked disappointed.

"You've been very helpful," I said. "I'll tell my father."

His lined face showed satisfaction. "You tell him I'll keep the dogs and everything in good nick until he comes back."

"He'll be grateful."

I picked up the suitcase from inside the kitchen door, shook the grubby hand of Arthur Bellbrook, and (in the car I had hired that morning in London) drove away towards Epsom.

Collecting my own things from my flat took half the time. Unlike Malcolm, I liked things bare and orderly.

I changed from Malcolm's trousers into some of my own, packed a suitcase and picked up my passport.

The telephone answering machine's button glowed red, announcing messages taken. I rewound the tape and listened to the disembodied voices while I picked out of the fridge anything that would go furry before my return. Something, since I'd left the day before, had galvanised the family into activity, like stirring an anthill with a stick.

A girlish voice came first, breathless, anxious. "Ian, this is Serena. Mummy wants to know where Daddy is. She knows you and he aren't speaking, but she insisted I ask you. So if you know, give me a ring back, OK?"

Serena, my half-sister, daughter of Alicia. Serena, seven years my junior, lay in my distant memory chiefly as a small fair-haired charmer who'd followed me about like a shadow. She liked best to sit on Malcolm's lap, his arms protectively around her.

Alicia, in sweeping out of the house when Serena was six, taking with her not only Serena but her son, Gervase, had left me alone in the suddenly quiet house, alone in the frilly kitchen, alone and untormented in the garden. There had been a time then when I would positively have welcomed back Gervase, despite his dead rats and other rotten tricks. Grown up, Gervase still displayed the insignia of a natural bully: mean tightening of the mouth, jabbing forefinger, cold patronising stare down the nose, visible enjoyment of others' discomfiture.

Serena, now tall and slim, taught aerobics for a living, bought clothes by the cartload, and spoke to me only when she wanted something done. "Mummy wants to know where Daddy is . . ." The childish terms sat oddly in the ear, somehow, coming from someone now twenty-six; and she alone of all his children had resisted calling Malcolm, Malcolm.

The next caller was Gervase himself. He started crossly, "I don't like these message contraptions. This is your brother Gervase, as no doubt you realise, and it is imperative we find Malcolm at once. He has gone completely off his rocker. I suppose you do know he has given half a million to a busload of retarded children? I got a call from some gushing female who said, 'Oh Mr. Pembroke, however can we thank you?' When I asked her what for, she said wasn't I the Mr. Pembroke who had solved all their problems, Mr. Malcolm Pembroke? Are you listening, Ian? He's irresponsible. If you ask me, it's the beginning of senility. You must find him, and tell us where he's got to, because he hasn't answered his telephone since last Friday. I expect to hear from you without delay."

His voice stopped abruptly, and I pictured him as he was now, an overweight thirty-five-year-old stockbroker, pompous beyond his years. In a world increasingly awash with illegitimate children, he increasingly resented his own illegitimacy and denigrated the father who had always accepted Gervase publicly as his son, and given him his surname by legal adoption. But Gervase had never outgrown his bitterness. It remained with him, festering, colouring his whole personality. To my mind, he would spend his last moments worrying that the word "illegitimate" would appear on his death certificate.

After Gervase on my answering machine came my half-brother Thomas, the third of Malcolm's children, born to his first wife, Vivien. Thomas, rising forty, prematurely bald, pale, sporting a gingerish moustache, had married a woman who acidly belittled him every time she opened her mouth. ("Of course, Thomas is absolutely useless when it comes to . . ." [practically anything] and "Dear Thomas is one of life's failures, aren't you, darling?") Thomas bore it all with hardly a wince, though after years of it, I observed, he had come to believe in and to act out Berenice's opinion of him.

"Ian," Thomas said in a depressed voice, "this is Thomas. I've been trying to reach you since yesterday lunchtime. Berenice is concerned about Malcolm. She keeps on and on about the amounts he's throwing away, and to be honest the only thing which has pacified her for a long time now is the thought of my eventual share of Malcolm's money, and if he goes on spending at this rate, well, my life is going to be pretty intolerable, and I wouldn't be telling you this if you weren't my brother and the best of the bunch, which I suppose I've never said until now. Can you do anything to reason with Malcolm, as you're the only one he's likely to listen to, even though you haven't been talking for ages, which is unbelievable considering how you used to be with each other, and I blame that money-grubbing Moira, I really do, though Berenice used to think that anyone coming between you and Malcolm could only be to my benefit, because Malcolm might cut you out of his will. Anyway, it really would save my sanity, Ian, if you could make Malcolm see that we all need that money."

The depth of the plea and the thought of the nonstop barrage of Berenice's disgruntlement made me feel more brotherly towards Thomas than ever before.

True, I still thought he should tell his wife to swallow her bile, but I understood vaguely why he didn't simply ditch her: he couldn't face doing what Malcolm had done, forsaking wife and children when the going got rough. It was from fear of making the same calamitous mistake that I had married no one at all.

Thomas's was the last message on the tape. I took it out of the machine and put it in my pocket, inserting a fresh tape for future messages. I also packed a small cassette player in my suitcase.

I put my suitcase in the car, along with my racing saddle, helmet, whip and boots, and drove back to the Savoy, where I was relieved to find Malcolm, unattacked and unharmed.

He was sitting deep in an armchair, dressed again as for the City, drinking champagne and smoking an oversize cigar. Opposite him, perched on the front edge of an identical armchair, sat a thin man of Malcolm's age but with none of his presence.

"Norman West," Malcolm said to me, waving the cigar vaguely at his visitor; and to the visitor he said, "My son, Ian."

Norman West rose to his feet and shook my hand briefly. I had never so far as I knew met a private detective before, and it wouldn't have been the occupation I would have fitted to this damp-handed, nervous, threadbare individual. He had streaky grey hair overdue for a wash, dark-circled brown eyes, and a day's growth of beard. His grey suit looked old and uncared for and he looked as much at home in the Savoy as a punk rocker in the Vatican.

"I came straight here," he explained, "from an all-night observation job, as Mr. Pembroke was insistent that it was urgent."

His accent was the standard English of bygone radio announcers, slightly plummy. I gestured to him to sit down again.

"Mr. West had just arrived when you came," Malcolm said. "Perhaps you'd better explain to him what we want."

I sat on the sofa and said to Norman West that we wanted him to find out where every single member of our extended family had been on the previous Friday from, say, four o'clock in the afternoon onwards, and also on Tuesday, yesterday, all day.

Norman West looked from one to the other of us in obvious dismay. He said unhappily, "I'm afraid there may be a conflict of interest." He cleared his throat. "Last Saturday morning I was hired by one of your family to find *you*, Mr. Pembroke. Now you want me to check up on them. I don't think I should, in all conscience, accept your proposition."

"Which member of my family?" Malcolm demanded.

Norman West drummed his fingers on his knee, but decided after inner debate to answer. "Mrs. Pembroke," he said.

Chapter Three

"Which one?" I asked. "There are seven of them."

The detective looked uncomfortable. "I only spoke to her on the telephone. I assumed it was the Mrs. Malcolm Pembroke for whom I worked once before, long ago."

"Did you find Mr. Pembroke," I asked, "when you were looking for him?"

West nodded. "In Cambridge. Not too difficult."

"And you reported back to Mrs. Pembroke?"

"I really don't think I should be discussing this any further."

"At least tell us how you got back in touch with Mrs. Pembroke."

"I didn't," he said. "She rang me two or three times a day, asking for progress reports. Finally, on Monday evening, I had news for her."

"I want you to find out which Mrs. Pembroke wanted to know where I was," Malcolm said.

Norman West regretfully shook his unkempt head. "I'm afraid . . . a client's trust . . ." he murmured.

"A client's trust, poppycock!" Malcolm exploded. "Someone who knew where to find me damn near killed me."

Our detective looked shocked, but rallied quickly. "I found you, sir, by asking Mrs. Pembroke for a list of places you felt at home in, as in my experience missing people often go to those places, and she gave me a list of five such possibilities, of which Cambridge was number three. I telephoned to the large hotels in Cambridge asking for you, and from the third I got a positive response. If it was as easy as that for me to find you, it was equally easy for anyone else. And, sir, if I may say so, you made things easy by registering under your own name. People who want to stay lost shouldn't do that."

"How is Mrs. Pembroke paying you?" I asked.

"She said she would send a cheque."

"When it comes," I said, "you'll know which Mrs. Pembroke."

"So I will."

"I don't see why you should worry about a conflict of interests," I said. "After all, you've already worked for various Pembrokes. You worked for my mother, Joyce Pembroke, to catch my father with the lady who gave her grounds for divorce. You worked for my father, to try to catch his fifth wife having a similar fling. You worked for the unspecified Mrs. Pembroke to trace my father's whereabouts. And now he wants you to find out where all his family were last Friday and yesterday, so as to be sure it was none of his close relatives who tried to kill him."

Norman West looked at his short, grimy nails. "Isn't this a police job?"

"Certainly," I said. "My father called them in last Friday, and he'll tell you all about it. And you have to bear in mind that they're also enquiring into the murder of Moira Pembroke."

Malcolm told West about his abortive walk with the dogs and his brush with carbon monoxide, and then described the near miss at Newmarket.

Norman West listened attentively and at the end said, "The car at Newmarket could have been accidental. Driver not paying enough attention. Seeing you both at the last minute, swerving desperately."

Malcolm looked at me. "Did it seem like that to you?"

"No."

"Why not?" West asked.

"The rate of acceleration, I suppose. Headlights on full beam," I said.

"A sloppy driver? Had a few drinks?"

"Maybe." I shook my head. "The real problem is that if the car *had* hit us—or Malcolm—there might have been witnesses. The driver might have been stopped before he could leave the sales area. The car number might have been taken."

West smiled sorrowfully. "It's been done successfully before now, in broad daylight in a crowded street. All the same, hit-and-run in a public place has its risks. If it was tried here, the putative gain must have outweighed the risk, or, er . . ."

"In other words," Malcolm interrupted, "they'll try again."

West looked infinitely weary. "I'll take your job," he said. "I'll need a list of the people you want checked. Names and addresses and daily routines."

I found a piece of Savoy writing paper on which to draw up the list.

"OK," I said, "first of all there's Vivien, my father's first wife. Mrs. Vivien Pembroke." After Vivien's name I wrote the names of her children: Donald; Lucy; Thomas.

"Thomas," I said, "is married to Berenice." I added her name beside his. "He is easy to deal with, she is not. Lucy married a man called Edwin Bugg. She didn't like that surname and persuaded him to change it to hers, so she is consequently herself a Mrs. Pembroke. Lucy is a poet. She makes a big production of unworldliness which Edwin, I think, has grown to find tiresome."

"Huh," Malcolm said. "Edwin's an out-and-out materialist, always tapping me for a loan."

"Short of money, are they?" West asked.

"Edwin Bugg," Malcolm said, "married Lucy because he thought she was an heiress, and they've scraped along ever since on the small income she gets from a trust fund I set up for her. Edwin's never done a stroke of work in his parasitic life and I can't stand the fellow."

"They have one teenage schoolboy son," I said.

West looked at the list and said to Malcolm, "What about Donald, your eldest?"

"Donald married a replica of his mother, beautiful and brainless. A girl called Helen. They live an utterly boring, virtuous life in Henley-on-Thames and are still cooing like newlyweds although Donald must be nearly forty-five."

"Children?" Norman West asked.

"Three," I said.

"Well," said West, taking the list himself and adding to it, "this is what

Alicia

Joyce

Vivien

we have so far. Wife number one: Vivien Pembroke. Her children: Donald (44), wife Helen, three offspring. Lucy, husband Edwin (né Bugg), school-age son. Thomas, wife Berenice . . . ?"

"Two young daughters."

"Two young daughters," he repeated, writing.

"My grandchildren," Malcolm protested, "are all too young to have murdered anybody."

"Psychopaths start in the nursery," West said, and he sighed, half disillusionment, half weariness. "Wife number two?" he asked, and answered his own question, "Mrs. Joyce Pembroke."

"Right," I said. "I'm her son. And I'm not married."

West methodically wrote me down.

"Last Friday evening," I said, "I was at work in a racing stable at five o'clock with about thirty people as witnesses, and last night I was certainly not driving the car that nearly ran us over."

West said stolidly, "I'll write you down as being cleared of primary involvement. That's all I can do with any of your family, Mr. Pembroke." He finished the sentence looking at Malcolm, who said, "Hired assassin," between his teeth, and West nodded. "If any of them hired a good professional, I doubt if I'll discover it."

"I thought good assassins used rifles," I said.

"Some do. Most don't. They pick their own way. Some use knives. Some garrotte." West looked at the list. "After Mrs. Joyce?"

Malcolm said sourly, "The lady you so artfully photographed me with at the instigation of, as you call her, Mrs. Joyce."

The West eyebrows slowly rose. "Miss Alicia Sandways? Well, so we have wife number three, with, if I remember, a little boy?"

Malcolm said, "I formally adopted Gervase when I married his mother, and changed his surname to Pembroke. Then we had little Serena." His face softened. "It was for her I put up with Alicia's tantrums the last few years we were together. I gave Alicia a generous divorce settlement, but she was very bitter. I wanted to keep little Serena . . . and Alicia screamed that she supposed I didn't want Gervase because he was illegitimate. She fought in the courts for Serena, and she won. Serena did suggest coming back to look after me after Coochie's death, but it wasn't necessary because Moira was there. When Moira was killed, she offered again. It was kind of Serena. She's a nice girl, but Alicia tries to set her against me."

West, in a pause that might or might not have been sympathetic, wrote after Alicia's name: Gervase, illegitimate, adopted. Serena, legitimate.

"Gervase has a wife called Ursula," I said. "They have two little girls. Serena, is unmarried."

West wrote that down, too. "Right," he said. "Wife number four?"

There was a small silence. Then I said, "Coochie. She's dead. She had twin sons. One was killed with her in a car crash, the other is brain-damaged and lives in a nursing home."

"Oh." The sound carried definite sympathy. "And wife number five, Mrs. Moira Pembroke, did she perhaps have any children from a previous marriage?"

"No," Malcolm said. "No previous marriage, no children."

"Right." West counted up his list. "That's three ex-wives still living. Er . . . by the way, did any of them remarry?"

I answered with a faint smile, "They would lose their alimony if they did. None of them has seen any financial sense in remarrying."

"They all should have done," Malcolm grumbled. "They wouldn't be so warped."

West said merely, "Right. So, er, discounting the invalid son and Mr. Ian here, there are twelve adults to be checked. Can I tell them all why I'm making these enquiries?" he asked.

"Yes, you damned well can," Malcolm said positively. "If it's one of them, and I hope to God it isn't, it might put the wind up them and frighten them off. Just don't tell them where to find me."

"I'll need all their addresses," West said.

Malcolm waved a hand. "Ian can tell you. He can write them down."

Obediently I opened my suitcase, took out my address book and wrote the whole lot, with telephone numbers. Then I got out a packet of photographs I'd picked up from my flat and showed them to West. I liked taking portraits, and taking a camera along had given me something positive to do whenever the family met.

"Would these help you?" I asked. "If they would, I'll lend them to you."

West looked through them and said he would like to borrow them. He put both photographs and lists away and said, "Right. I'll start first thing in the morning."

It would have been churlish to expect him to start that afternoon, but I can't say I liked the delay. I took him to the hotel lobby and saw him safely into a taxi.

Returning to the suite, I found Malcolm ordering vodka and beluga caviar from room service with the abandon to which I was becoming accustomed. That done, he smoothed out the *Sporting Life* and pointed to one section of it. "It says the Arc de Triomphe race is due to be run this Sunday in Paris. Let's go."

"All right," I said.

Malcolm laughed. "We may as well have some fun. There's a list here of the runners."

I looked where he pointed. It was a bookmaker's advertisement showing the antepost prices on offer.

"What are the chances," Malcolm said, "of my buying one of these horses?"

"Er," I said, "today, do you mean?"

"Of course. No good buying one *after* the race, is there? You buy me a good horse in this race on Sunday and we'll go and yell it home, boy, at the top of our lungs."

It took all afternoon and early evening to get even a tinge of interest from anyone. I telephoned to the trainers of the English—or Irish—runners, asking if they thought their owners might sell. I promised each trainer that he would go on training the horse, and that my father would send him also the two-million-guinea colt he'd bought yesterday.

Finally, at seven forty-five, a trainer from Newmarket rang back to say his owner would sell a half share if his price was met. I relayed the news and the price to Malcolm.

"What do you think?" he said.

"Um . . . the horse is quite good, the price is on the high side, the trainer's in the top league."

"OK," Malcolm said. "Deal."

"My father accepts," I said to the trainer. "And, er, the colt is still in the sales stables. Can you fetch it tomorrow?"

Indeed he could. He would complete the paperwork immediately if Malcolm could transfer the money directly to his bloodstock account, bank and account number supplied. Malcolm waved a hand and said, "No problem. He'll have it by tomorrow afternoon."

"Well," I said, breathing out as I put the receiver down, "you now own half of Blue Clancy."

"Let's drink to it," Malcolm said. "Order some Bollinger."

I ordered it from room service, and while we waited for it to arrive I told him about my encounter with Arthur Bellbrook. I told him wryly about Moira and the prize vegetables, of which he knew nothing.

"Silly bitch," he said. "Arthur lives in a terrace house with a pocket-handkerchief garden facing north. You couldn't grow prize stuff there."

"He seemed pretty philosophical," I said, "and, incidentally, pretty bright. He'd spotted that the kitchen garden wall is thicker than it should be at the corner. He'd asked old Fred, and heard about the room I built there. He wanted to know if he could use it as an apple store."

Malcolm practically ejected from his armchair, alarm widening his eyes, his voice hoarse. "My God, you didn't say yes, did you?"

"No, I didn't," I said slowly. "I told him it was empty and was bricked up twenty years ago." I paused. "What have you put in there?"

Malcolm subsided into his chair, not altogether relieved of anxiety. "Never you mind," he said.

"You forget that I could go and look."

"I don't forget it."

He stared at me. When I'd designed and built the pivoting brick door all those summers ago, he'd come down the garden day after day to watch, and had smiled at the secret. The resulting wall looked solid, but at one point there was a thick vertical steel rod within it, stretching from a concrete underground foundation up into the beam supporting the roof. Before I'd put the new roof on, I'd patiently drilled round holes in bricks and slid them onto the rod, and mortared the door in neat courses, so that the edges of it dovetailed into the fixed sections next to it.

To open the door, one had first to remove the wedge-like wooden sill which gave extra support to the bottom panel of the door when it was closed, and then to activate the spring latch on the inner side by poking a thin wire through a tiny hole in the mortar at what had been my thirteen-year-old waist height. Gervase had never found the door, and nor had anyone else, and as the years passed grass and nettles had grown long in front of the wall. Only Malcolm knew how to get in—and Malcolm had used the knowledge.

"What's in there?" I repeated.

"Actually," he said, calmly now, "quite a lot of gold."

Chapter Four

"Some people buy and sell gold without ever seeing it," he said. "But I like possessing the actual stuff. There's no fun in paper transactions. Gold is beautiful and I like to feel it."

"You're storing it in the wall . . . waiting for the price to rise?"

"You know me, don't you?" he smiled. "Buy low, bide your time, sell high. The price of gold swings like a pendulum. When gold prices rise, gold shares often rise by two or three times as much. I sell the gold first and the shares a couple of months later."

He did truly trust me, I thought. If he'd doubted me still, he wouldn't have told me there was gold behind the brick door. I stopped worrying about him buying the colt and the half share in Blue Clancy. I stopped worrying about practically everything except how to keep him alive.

I'd talked to someone once whose father had died when she was barely twenty. She regretted that she hadn't ever known him adult to adult, and wished she could meet him again, just to talk. Watching Malcolm, it struck me that in a way I'd been given her wish: that the three years' silence had been a sort of death, and that I could talk to him now adult to adult, and know him as a man, not just as a father.

We spent a peaceful evening together in the suite, talking about what we'd each done during the hiatus, and it was difficult to imagine that outside, somewhere, a predator might be searching for its prey.

At one point I said, "You gave Joyce's telephone number on purpose to the film man, didn't you? And Gervase's number to the retarded-children lady? You wanted me with you to see you buy the colt. You made sure that the family knew all about your outlays, didn't you?"

"Huh," he said briefly, which, after a moment, I took as an admission. One misdirected telephone call had been fairly possible: two stretched credibility too far. "How the hell do you know all this?" he asked.

I smiled and fetched the cassette player, and reran for him the message tape from my answering machine. He listened grimly, but with an undercurrent of amusement, to Serena, Gervase and Thomas. He said wryly, "I suppose they're what I made them."

"No," I said. "Personality is mysterious. It's born in you, not made."

"But it can be brainwashed."

"Yes, OK," I said. "But you didn't do it."

"Vivien and Alicia did . . . because of me."

Joyce, I thought, had at least played fair and had never tried to set me against Malcolm. She had agreed, in the divorce settlement made when I was six, that he should have custody of me: she wasn't basically maternal, and infrequent visits from her growing son were all she required. When I decided to make my life in racing she had been astonished at my choice, but had soon come round to checking the racing pages during the steeplechase season to see if I was listed as riding.

"What did you tell Thomas and Berenice?" I asked Malcolm.

With satisfaction he said, "I absent-mindedly gave their telephone number to a wine merchant who was to let me know the total I owed him for fifty or so cases of nineteen seventy-nine Pol Roger."

"And, er, roughly how much would that cost?"

"The 1979, the Winston Churchill vintage, is quite exceptional. Roughly twenty-five thousand pounds."

Poor Thomas, I thought.

"I also made sure that Alicia knew I'd given about a quarter of a million pounds to fund scholarships at the school Serena went to. I suppose she's furious I gave it to the school and not to Serena herself."

"Well, why did you?"

He looked surprised. "You know my views. You must all carve your own way. To make you all rich too young would rob you of incentive."

I certainly did know his views, but I wasn't sure I always agreed with them. I would have bags of incentive to make a success of being a racehorse trainer if he lent, or gave, me enough to start, but I also knew that if he did, he'd have to do as much for the others (being ordinarily a fair man), and he didn't believe in it, as he said.

"Why did you want them all to know how much you've been spending?"

"I suppose I thought if they believed I was getting rid of most of it there would be less point in killing me . . . do you see?"

I stared at him. "You must be crazy," I said. "It sounds to me like an invitation to be murdered without delay."

"Ah well, that too has occurred to me of late." He smiled vividly. "But I have you with me now, to prevent that."

I pondered. "What else have you spent a bundle on?"

He drank some champagne and frowned, and I guessed that he was trying to decide whether or not to tell me. Finally he sighed and said, "This is for your ears only. I didn't do it for the same reason, and I did it earlier. The nursing home where Robin is, needed repairs. So I paid for them. They needed a new roof. New wiring. That sort of thing. They asked my advice about fund-raising and I told them not to bother." He shifted comfortably in his armchair. "Robin's settled there. Calm. Any change upsets him, as you know. If the place closed, I'd have to find somewhere else for him, and he's lost enough . . ." His voice tapered off. He had delighted in Robin and Peter when they were small, playing with them like a young father. Good memories: worth a new roof.

"I know you still go to visit him," he said. "The nurses tell me. You will look after him, when I've gone?"

"Yes," I said.

He nodded, taking it for granted. "I appointed you his trustee when I set up the fund for him, do you remember? I've not altered it."

I was glad that he hadn't. At least, somewhere, obscurely, things had remained the same between us.

"Why don't we go and see him tomorrow?" he said.

"All right," I agreed: so we went in the hired car in the morning, stopping in the local town to buy presents of chocolate and simple toys designed for three-year-olds, and I added a packet of balloons to the pile while Malcolm paid.

"Does he like balloons?" he asked, his eyebrows rising.

"He gets frustrated sometimes. I blow the balloons up, and he bursts them."

Malcolm looked surprised and in some way disturbed. "I didn't know he could feel frustration."

"It seems like that. As if sometimes he half remembers us . . . but can't quite."

"Poor boy."

WE DROVE SOBERLY up the drive of the splendid-looking Georgian house which lay mellow and symmetrical in the autumn sunshine. Inside, its near fifty rooms had been adapted into a highly comfortable hospital for chronic, mostly old, mostly rich, patients. Dreadfully depressing, I found it, but for Robin it was the perfect haven.

He had a large room on the ground floor with French windows opening onto a garden. He looked at us blankly, as usual. He seldom spoke, though he did retain the ability to make words: it was just that he seemed to have few thoughts to utter. Brain damage of that magnitude, we'd been told, resulted in behaviour that was individual to each victim.

We gave him some pieces of chocolate which he ate, and unwrapped the toys which he fingered but didn't play with. He looked at the balloon packet without emotion. It wasn't a frustration day: on those, he looked at the packet and made blowing noises with his mouth.

Robin

We sat with him for quite a while, talking, telling him who we were while he wandered round the room. He looked at our faces from time to time, and touched my nose once with his finger as if exploring that I was really there, but there was no connection with our minds. He appeared healthy, good-looking, a fine boy: heartbreaking, as always.

We left, as I always left, in sadness, silence and regret.

"So bloody unfair," Malcolm said, halfway back to London. "He ought to be laughing, talking, roaring through life."

"Yes."

"I can't bear to see him, and I can't bear not to."

On FRIDAY, despite my pleas for sanity, Malcolm insisted on accompanying me to Sandown Park races.

"You'll be safer here," I protested, "in the hotel."

"I shan't *feel* safer."

I saw that the deep apprehension which he tried to suppress most of the time would erupt into nervous anxiety if I left him alone, and that he might do something much sillier than going to the races.

Accordingly I drove him south of London and took him through the jockeys' entrance gate to the weighing-room area, where he made his afternoon a lot safer by meeting one of his cronies and being instantly invited to lunch in the holy of holies.

I was due to ride in the second race, a steeplechase for amateurs. I looked around for the owner of the horse I was about to partner, and found my path blocked by a substantial, overweight lady in a wide brown cape. Of all the members of the family, she was the last I would have expected to see on a racecourse.

"Ian," she said accusingly, as if I'd been pretending to be someone else, "where have you been? Why don't you answer your telephone?"

Lucy, my elder half-sister. Lucy, the poet.

Lucy's husband Edwin was, as always, to be found at her side, rather as if he had no separate life. The leech, Malcolm had called him unkindly in the past. From a Bugg to a leech.

She was forty-two, my sister, with thick straight brown hair uncompromisingly cut, large brown eyes, her mother's high cheekbones and her father's strong nose.

"Edwin is concerned," she said, "that Malcolm is losing his senses."

For Edwin, read Lucy, I thought. She had a trick of ascribing her own thoughts to her husband. Edwin stared at me uneasily. He was a good-looking man in many ways, but mean-spirited, which if one were tolerant one would excuse because of the perpetual knife-edge state of his and Lucy's finances. I wasn't certain whether he had actually failed to achieve employment, or whether Lucy had in some way stopped him from trying.

"It isn't fair of him," Edwin said, meaning Malcolm. "He's throwing his money away in this profligate way as if his heirs had no rights at all."

"I'm sure he won't let you starve," I said.

"That's not the point. Do you know that he's given an *immense* amount of money to Lucy's old college to establish postgraduate scholarships for poets?" Edwin asked with thin fury.

"The Lucy Pembroke Scholarships," I said slowly. And there would be the Serena Pembroke Scholarships, of course. And also the Coochie Pembroke Memorial Challenge Trophy.

"Joyce said you would be here today, on this spot and at this time, if I wanted to reach you," Lucy said. "You've got to stop Malcolm. You're the only one who can, and Joyce says you're probably the only one who won't try . . . You *must* try, Ian, if not for yourself, then for the rest of the family."

"For you?" I asked.

"Well . . ." She couldn't openly abandon her principles, but they were bending, it seemed. "For the others," she said stalwartly.

I looked at her with new affection. "You're a hypocrite, my dear sister," I said.

In retaliation, she said sharply, "Vivien thinks you're trying to cut the rest of us out and ingratiate yourself again with Malcolm."

"I expect she would," I said. "I expect Alicia will think it also, when Vivien has fed it to her."

"You really are a bastard."

"No," I said, my lips twitching, "that's Gervase."

"*Ian!*"

I laughed. "I'll tell Malcolm you're concerned. I promise I will. Now I've got to change my clothes and ride in a race. Are you staying?"

"You're not taking it seriously," Lucy said.

I looked straight in her eyes. "Believe me," I said, "I take it very seriously indeed. No one had a right to murder Moira to stop her taking half Malcolm's money. No one has a right to murder Malcolm to stop him spending it. He is fair. He will leave us all provided for, when the time comes, which I hope may be twenty years from now. Malcolm is teasing you all and I think it's dangerous, but he is dismayed by everyone's greed, and he's determined to teach us all a lesson. So you tell them, Lucy, tell everyone, the more we protest, the more he will spend."

She looked back silently. Eventually she said, "I am ashamed of myself." She patted my arm. "We may as well see you race, while we're here. Go and get changed."

It was a more sisterly gesture and tone than I was used to, and I reflected with a shade of guilt that I'd paid scant attention to her own career for a couple of years.

"How is the poetry going?" I asked. "What are you working on?"

The question caught her unprepared. Her face went momentarily blank and then filled with what seemed to be an odd mixture of sadness and panic.

"Nothing, just now," she said, "nothing for quite a while." I nodded almost apologetically as if I had intruded, and went into the weighing room reflecting that poets mostly did their best work when young. Lucy wasn't writing; had maybe stopped altogether. And perhaps the frugality she had for so long embraced had begun to seem less worthy and less worth it, if she were losing the inner comfort of creative inspiration.

With such thoughts, I took off my ordinary clothes and put on white breeches and a scarlet jersey with blue stripes on the sleeves, and experienced the usual battened-down excitement which made me breathe deeply and feel intensely happy. I rode in about fifty races a year, if I was lucky . . . and I would have to get another job fairly soon, I reflected, if I were to ride exercise regularly and stay fit enough to do any good.

Going outside, I talked for a while to the trainer and owner of the horse I was to ride, a husband-and-wife team. The husband, George, was now a public trainer on a fairly grand scale, but the wife, Jo, still preferred to run her own horses in amateur races.

"Young Higgins is jumping out of his skin," she said as I approached.

Young Higgins was the name of that day's horse. We all interpreted "jumping out of his skin" as meaning fit, sound and pricking his ears with enthusiasm, and at the age of thirteen one couldn't ask for more.

"We'll see you in the parade ring, then, Ian, before the race," George said, and Jo added, "Give the old boy a good time."

I nodded, smiling. Giving all of us a good time was the point of the proceedings. Young Higgins was definitely included.

The minute George and Jo turned away to go off towards the grandstands, someone tapped me on the shoulder. I turned round and to my total astonishment found myself face to face with Lucy's older brother, Malcolm's first child, my half-brother Donald.

"Good heavens," I said, "you've never been to the races in your life."

"I haven't come for the races," he said crossly, "I've come to see you about Malcolm's taking leave of his senses."

"Did Joyce send you?" I said.

"What if she did? We are all concerned."

"Did she tell the whole family?" I asked blankly.

"How do I know? She phoned us. I dare say she phoned everyone she could get hold of. You know what she's like. She's your mother, after all."

He couldn't keep out of his voice the old resentment. My mother had supplanted his, he was saying, and any indiscretion my mother ever committed was in some way my fault. Donald was, in the family's opinion, the brother nearest in looks to myself, and I wasn't sure I liked it. Irrefutably, he was the same height and had blue eyes and middling brown curly hair. I didn't wear a bushy moustache though, and I just hoped I didn't walk with a self-important strut.

Donald's life had been so disrupted when Malcolm had ousted Vivien, Donald always told us, that he had never been able to decide properly on a career. He had only been nine at the time, a bit early for life decisions. In any event, as an adult he had drifted from job to job, coming to harbour at length as secretary of a prestigious golf club near Henley-on-Thames, a post which had proved ultimately satisfactory in social standing, which was very important to his self-esteem.

"Everyone insists you stop Malcolm squandering the family money," he said, predictably.

"It's *his* money, not the family's," I said.

"What?" Donald found the idea ridiculous. "You've got to explain that he owes it to us to keep the family fortune intact until we inherit it. You want to be well off one day just the same as the rest of us, it's only natural."

I was saved from both soul-searching and untrue disclaimers by the arrival of Helen, Donald's wife, who had been buying a racecard.

Beautiful and brainless, Malcolm had said of her, and perhaps he was right. Tall and thin, she moved with natural style.

"Do tell us where to watch the races from," she said.

"We're not here for that," Donald said.

"No, dear, we're here because we need money now that the boys have started at Eton."

"Do be quiet, dear," said Donald sharply.

"Eton costs a bomb," I said mildly, knowing that Donald's income would hardly stretch to one son there, let alone two. Donald had twin boys, which seemed to run in the family.

"Of course it does," Helen said, "but Donald sets such store by it. 'My sons are at Eton,' that sort of thing."

"Helen, dear, do be quiet." Donald's embarrassment showed.

"We thought Donald might have inherited before the boys reached thirteen," she said intensely. "As he hasn't, we're borrowing every penny we can to pay the fees. But we've borrowed against Donald's expectations . . . so you see it's essential that there really is plenty to inherit."

I opened my mouth to answer her but no sound came out. I felt as if I'd been thrust into a farce over which I had no control.

Walking purposefully to join us came Serena.

"Where's Daddy?" she asked.

Malcolm's little Serena, now taller than he, was dressed in royal blue with white frills at neck and wrists, a white woollen hat with a pompom covering her cap of fair hair. She looked a leggy sixteen, not ten years older. In her high-pitched, girlish voice she said to me coldly, "We want him to settle very substantial sums on us all right now. Then he can go to blazes with the rest."

I blinked. "Who are you quoting?" I asked.

"Myself," she said loftily, and then more convincingly added, "Mummy too. And Gervase."

It had Gervase's thuggish style stamped all over it.

Donald and Helen looked distinctly interested in the proposal.

I doubted very much that Malcolm would agree, but said only, "I'll pass on your message next time he gets in touch with me."

"But Joyce is sure you know where he is," Donald objected.

"Not exactly," I said. "Do you know that Lucy and Edwin are here too?"

They were diverted, looking over their shoulders to see if they could spot them in the growing crowds. Donald hooked his arms through those of Helen and Serena and made an announcement. "We three are going to have a drink and a sandwich." He whirled the girls away from me and marched them off.

In due course I went out to partner Young Higgins in the second race.

I put Malcolm out of my mind, and also murder. It wasn't difficult. The sky was a clear blue, the air crisp with the coming of autumn. The track lay waiting, green and springy, with the wide fences beckoning to be flown. Simple things; and out there one came starkly face to face with oneself, which I mostly found more exhilarating than frightening.

I fastened the strap of my helmet and rode Young Higgins out onto the track. Perhaps if I'd been a professional and had ridden up to ten times as often I would have lost the swelling joy that that moment always gave me.

Young Higgins was living up to his name, bouncing on his toes and tossing his head in high spirits. We lined up with the six other runners, all of whose riders I knew from past occasions. Amateurs come in all guises: there was an aunt and a grandfather riding that afternoon, besides a journalist, an earl's son, a lieutenant-colonel, a showjumper and myself. From the stands, only a keen eye could have told one from the other without the guidance of our colours, and that was what amateur racing was all about: the equality, the levelling anonymity of the starting gate.

The tapes went up and we set off with three miles to go, almost two whole circuits, twenty-two jumps and an uphill run to the winning post.

The aunt's horse, too strong for her, took hold of the proceedings and opened up an emphatic lead, and for about a mile after that there were no dramatic excitements.

"Give me room, blast you," shouted the lieutenant-colonel on one side of me.

"Nice day," said the earl's son chattily on the other.

The showjumper liked to set his horse carefully before jumps, as in the showring, and wasn't, in consequence, someone to follow into a fence.

The journalist was the best jockey in the race, a professional in all but status, and the grandfather was the worst but full of reckless courage. More or less in a bunch, the whole lot of us came round the bottom bend and tackled the last three jumps of the first circuit. The aunt was still in front, then came the lieutenant-colonel, myself and the earl's son in a row, with the showjumper and the grandfather just behind. I couldn't see the journalist: somewhere in the rear, no doubt, biding his wily time.

The lieutenant-colonel's mount made a proper hash of the last of the three fences, jogging both of his rider's feet out of the irons and tipping him into the air somewhere in the region of the horse's mane. I saw the lieutenant-colonel fighting without success to pull himself back into the saddle. I put out an arm, grasped his jersey and yanked him backwards, shifting his disastrous centre of gravity into a more manageable place and leaving him slowing in my wake, trying to put his feet back into his flying stirrups, which is never easy at thirty miles an hour.

After crossing the water jump for the second time, the showjumper made a spurt to the front and then slowed almost to a standstill on landing over the next fence; the aunt crashed into the back of him with some singularly un-aunt-like language.

"Lovely lady," said the earl's son appreciatively, as we passed the debacle. We jumped the last of the seven far-side fences together and in front, and put all our energies into staying there round the long last bend and over the three last fences.

Approaching the pond fence, I could sense the earl's son's horse beginning to tire. I could see that precious winning post far ahead, and for at least a few moments I thought I might win. But then the lieutenant-colonel reappeared at my elbow, and between the last two fences, as I'd feared he would, the journalist materialised from the outback and made it look easy, and Young Higgins tired into Middle-Aged Higgins on the hill. He and I finished third, which wasn't too bad, with the earl's son fourth. "A nice afternoon out," he said happily as we trotted back together, and I looked at the light in his eyes and saw it was the same for him as for me, a high that one couldn't put into words, an adventure of body and spirit that made of dismounting and walking on the ground a literal coming down to earth.

Jo was pleased enough, patting Young Higgins hard. "Ran a great race, didn't you, old boy?"

"You'd have been second if you'd let the lieutenant-colonel fall off," said George.

"Yeah, well," I said, unbuckling the girths, "there were a lot of hooves down there."

"Don't forget to weigh in." (George said it every time.)

When I left the weighing room and had changed into street clothes, I found that not only were all the same family members still on the racecourse, but that they had coalesced into an angry swarm and had been joined by one of the queen bees herself, my mother Joyce.

Joyce, in fur and a green hat, was a rinsed blonde with greenish eyes behind contact lenses which seldom missed a trick.

"Darling," she said, the syllables sizzling with displeasure, "did you or did you not send that weasel Norman West sniffing round to check up on my whereabouts last Friday?"

"Well," I said, half smiling, "I wouldn't have put it as crudely, but I suppose so, yes."

The battery of eyes from the others was as friendly as napalm.

"Why?" Joyce snapped.

"Malcolm was very nearly killed," I said flatly. "He and I asked Norman West to make sure that none of you could have done it."

Joyce demanded to be told what had happened to Malcolm, and I told her. She and all the others listened with open mouths and every evidence of shock, and if there was knowledge, not ignorance, behind any of their horrified eyes, I couldn't discern it.

"Poor Daddy!" Serena exclaimed. "How *beastly*."

"A matter for the police," Donald said forcefully.

"I agree," I said. "I'm surprised they haven't been to see all of you already, as they did when Moira died."

Edwin said, with a shake of the head, "How near, how near," and then, hearing the regret in his voice as clearly as I did, added hurriedly, "What a blessing he woke up."

"Malcolm wants to make sure that none of the family was at Quantum last Friday afternoon. If you cooperate with Norman West when he gets to you, you'll set Malcolm's mind at rest."

"And what if we can't prove where we were?" Helen asked.

"Or even remember?" Lucy said.

"Malcolm will have to live with it," Joyce said crisply.

"Living with it would present him with less of a problem," I said drily. "It's dying he wants to avoid."

They stared at me in silence. The reality of Moira's murder had been to them, I guessed, as to me, a slow-burning fuse, with seemingly no bad consequences at first, but with accelerating worries as time passed. The fuse would heat soon into active suspicions, I saw, which might tear apart for ever the fragile family fabric.

Would I mind? I thought. The answer, surprisingly enough, was yes, I would mind. Imperfect, quarrelsome, ramshackle as it was, the family was my origins and framework.

"Buy me a drink, darling," Joyce commanded. "We're in deep trouble."

She began to move off, but the others showed no sign of following. I looked at the five faces all expressing varying degrees of anxiety.

"I'll tell Malcolm your fears," I said. "And your needs."

"Oh yes, please do," Helen said intensely.

"Do come on, darling," Joyce said peremptorily over her shoulder. "Which way is the bar?"

I steered Joyce into the busy members' bar. I bought her a vodka and tonic with a plain ginger ale for myself, and we found seats at a table in a far corner.

Joyce quickly launched into her inquisition. "Where is your father?" she said.

46

"When did you last see your father?" I amended.

"What on earth are you talking about?"

"Oh, you know—that picture."

"Stop playing games. Where is Malcolm?"

"I don't know," I said. "Why do you want to find him?"

"*Why?*" She was astonished. She dug into her capacious handbag and brought out a newspaper clipping, which she thrust towards me. "Read that."

It said: *Second-string British contender is Blue Clancy, second in last year's Derby and winner this year of Royal Ascot's King Edward VII Stakes. Owner Ramsey Osborn yesterday sold a half share in his four-year-old colt to arbitrageur Malcolm Pembroke, who launched into bloodstock only this week with a two-million-guineas yearling at the Newmarket Sales.*

Ouch, I thought. "Malcolm bought half of Blue Clancy. Why shouldn't he?" I said.

"Sometimes, Ian," my mother said forcefully, "you are so stupid I could hit you." She paused for breath. "And what exactly is an arbitrageur, anyway?"

"A guy who makes money by buying low and selling high."

"Oh. Gold."

"And foreign currencies. And shares. And maybe racehorses."

She was unmollified. "You know perfectly well he's just throwing his money away to spite everybody."

"He didn't like Moira being killed. He didn't like being attacked himself. I shouldn't think he'll stop spending until he knows whether we have or haven't a murderer in the family, and even then . . ." I smiled. "He's getting a taste for it."

Joyce finished her vodka and tonic and looked at me bleakly. "Do you really think one of the family is capable of murder?"

"I don't know."

"But *who?*"

"That's the question."

"It isn't possible," she insisted. "Moira was murdered by an intruder."

"Another drink?" I suggested.

"Yes. Gervase is drinking, did you know?"

"He always drinks."

"Ursula telephoned me to ask for advice."

"Did she really?" I was surprised. "Why didn't she ask Alicia?"

"Ursula detests her mother-in-law," Joyce said. "We have that in common. Ursula and I have become quite good friends."

Amazing, I thought, and stood up to fetch the refills.

Joyce's eyes suddenly widened in disbelief, looking beyond me.

"I knew you were lying," she said bitterly. "There's Malcolm."

Chapter Five

I turned, not knowing whether to be frightened or merely irritated.

Malcolm hadn't seen Joyce, and he wasn't looking for her or for me but solely for a drink. I made my way to the bar to meet him and took him by the arm. "Why aren't you upstairs?" I said.

"I was outstaying my welcome, old chap. It was getting very awkward. They were waiting for me to leave."

"Joyce," I said grimly, "is sitting over there in the corner."

"Joyce!" He turned round and spotted her as she looked balefully in our direction. "Damn it."

"Prowling around outside we also have Donald and Helen, Lucy and Edwin, and Serena."

He looked apprehensive, as well he might. "Will Joyce tell them all that I'm here?"

"We'll see if we can stop her. What do you want to drink? Scotch?"

He nodded and I squeezed through the throng by the bar and eventually got served. He helped me carry the glasses back to the table, and sat where I'd been sitting, facing Joyce. I fetched another chair from nearby and joined my ever-nonloving parents.

"Before you start shouting at each other," I said, "can we just take two things for granted? Joyce wants Malcolm to stop scattering largesse, Malcolm wants to go on living. Both ends are more likely to be achieved if we discover who murdered Moira, in case it is Moira's murderer who wishes also to kill Malcolm." I paused. "OK for logic?"

They both looked at me with the sort of surprise parents reserve for unexpected utterances from their young.

"The police haven't found Moira's murderer, so we have now got to try to do it ourselves, which is why we engaged Norman West." I looked directly at Joyce. "Stop fussing over what Malcolm is spending and start thinking of ways to save his life, if only so that he can make more money, which he can do, but only if he's alive."

"Ian!" She was shocked.

"You roused the whole family this morning on the telephone, telling them where to find me, and now five of them that we know of are here. Much though we hate the idea, Moira's murderer may be here."

"No, no," Joyce exclaimed.

"Yes," I said. "Malcolm's primary defence against being murdered is people not knowing where to find him. Well, you, my darling mother, brought the whole pack here to the races, so now you'd better help Malcolm to leave before they catch him."

"I didn't know he'd be here," she protested.

"No, but he is. It's time to be practical."

"Do you have any ideas?" Malcolm asked me hopefully.

"Yes, I do. But we have to have Joyce's help, plus her promise of silence."

My mother was looking less than her normal commanding self and gave assurances almost meekly.

"This is not a private bar," I said, "and if any of the family have bought club passes, they may turn up here at any moment, so we'd better lose no time. I'll be back in a few minutes. Whatever happens, stay right here. If the family find you, still stay here. OK?"

They both nodded, and I left them looking warily at each other in the first tête-à-tête they'd shared for many a long year.

I went in search of the catering director and found him by sending urgent messages via the manager of the members' bar.

"Ian," he said, coming to the bar from the back, where the bottles were, "what's the trouble?"

My father, I told him, badly needed an immediate, inconspicuous exit from the racecourse and wanted to know if a case of vintage Bollinger would ease his passage.

"Not skipping his bookie, I hope?" the caterer said laconically.

"No, he wants to elope with my mother, his ex-wife, from under the eyes of his family."

The caterer, amused, agreed that Bollinger might be nice. He also laughed at my plan and told me he would see it went well.

I went back through the bar to collect Malcolm and to ask Joyce to drive her car to where the caterers parked their vans. She picked up her handbag with alacrity to go and do so.

"If you see the others, say you're going home."

"I wasn't born yesterday, darling," she replied with reviving sarcasm.

At the back of the bar, the catering director was watching the chef remove his white coat and tall hat.

"A case of vintage Bollinger for the caterer, a handout for the chef," I murmured in Malcolm's ear. "Get Joyce to drop you at a railway station, and I'll see you in the Savoy. Don't move until I get there."

Malcolm, looking slightly dazed, put on the chef's coat and hat and pulled out his wallet. The chef looked delighted with the result. Malcolm and the catering director left through the bar's rear door. I waited quite a long anxious time but eventually the catering director returned, carrying the white disguise, which he restored to its owner.

"Your father got off safely," he assured me. I asked where he would like the fizz sent and he took out a business card, writing his private address on the back. He shook my hand and went away, and with a couple of deep breaths I left the members' bar and walked back to the weighing room to pick up my gear. George and Jo were there when I came out carrying saddle, helmet, whip and holdall.

"We've decided to run Young Higgins again two weeks tomorrow at Kempton," Jo said. "You'll be free for that, won't you?"

"Yes, indeed."

"And Park Railings, don't forget, at Cheltenham next Thursday."

"Any time, any place," I said, and they laughed.

I saw none of the family on my way to the exit gate. With a sigh of relief, I stowed my gear in the boot of the car and set off towards London. As I drove, I thought about cars. I had arranged on the telephone two days earlier that the hotel in Cambridge would allow my own car to remain in their car park for a daily fee until I collected it, but I couldn't leave it there for ever. In the morning, I decided, I would go by train to Cambridge, fetch my car, drive it to my flat in Epsom, and then go back to London by train. I pulled into a petrol station and called Malcolm. He would scarcely have reached the Savoy, I thought, but it was worth a try; and in fact he picked up the telephone saying he had that minute walked into the suite.

"I'm glad you're back safely," I said.

"Your mother is a cat," he said. "She called me a raddled old roué done up like a fifth-rate pastry cook. What do you want after caviar, if I order dinner?"

"Chef's special."

"God rot you, you're as bad as your mother."

I FERRIED THE CARS in the morning. As I was leaving the Savoy, Malcolm was full of rampaging indignation over the non-availability of first-class seats on any flight going to Paris the following day for the Arc de Triomphe. I left him frowning but returned to find peace. He had chartered a private jet.

He told me that snippet later, because he was currently engaged with Norman West, who had called to give a progress report.

"Tell my son what you've just said," Malcolm commanded. "Give him the bad news."

West gave me a small apologetic smile and then looked down at the notepad on his knee. "Mrs. Vivien Pembroke can't remember what she did on the Friday," he said. "And she spent Tuesday alone at home sorting through piles of old magazines."

"What's bad news about that?" I asked.

"Don't be obtuse," Malcolm said impatiently. "She hasn't an alibi. None of the whole damn bunch has an alibi."

"I also called on Mrs. Berenice Pembroke." West sighed expressively. "She was completely uncooperative."

Malcolm chuckled sourly. "Tongue like a rhinoceros-hide whip."

"Was Thomas there, when you called?" I asked.

"No, sir, he wasn't. Mrs. Pembroke said he was at work. I later telephoned his office, and a young lady there said that Mr. Pembroke left the firm several weeks ago."

"Well!" I said, stumped. "I didn't know."

Thomas, I thought, had worked for the same firm of biscuit makers from the day he'd finished a course in book-keeping and accountancy. His promotions within the firm had been minor, and at forty he could see, I supposed, that he would never be boardroom material. How bleak, I thought, to have to face his mid-life limitations with Berenice cramming them down his throat at every turn. Poor old Thomas.

"Mrs. Joyce Pembroke," West said, "is the only one who is definite about her movements. On each relevant day, she was playing bridge. She didn't like me snooping, as she called it, and she wouldn't say who she was playing bridge with as she didn't want those people bothered."

"You can leave Mrs. Joyce Pembroke out," I said.

"Huh?" Malcolm said.

"You know perfectly well," I told him, "that Joyce wouldn't kill you. If you'd had any doubts, you wouldn't have gone off in a car with her yesterday."

"All right, all right," he said, grumbling. "Cross Joyce off." I nodded to West, and he put a line through Joyce.

"Yesterday, I called on Mrs. Alicia Pembroke and then later on Mrs. Ursula Pembroke." West's face showed no joy over the encounters. "Mrs. Alicia Pembroke told me to mind my own business, and Mrs. Ursula Pembroke had been crying and wouldn't speak to me." He lifted his hands in a gesture of helplessness.

"Did you get any impression," I asked, "that the police had been there before you, asking the same questions?"

"None at all."

"I told you," Malcolm said. "They didn't believe I was attacked. They thought I'd just staged the whole thing."

"Do you happen to have their telephone number with you?"

"Yes, I do," he said, bringing a diary out of an inner pocket and flicking over the pages.

I dialled the number and asked for the superintendent. His voice came on the line, plain and impersonal. "Can I help you, sir?"

"About the attempted murder of Mr. Malcolm Pembroke—"

"Who are you, sir?"

"His son, Ian Pembroke."

"Do you wish to give information, sir?" the voice said.

"I want to find out how the investigation is going."

"I can tell you, sir, the investigations into the alleged attack are being conducted with thoroughness."

"*Alleged?*" I said.

"That's right, sir. We can find no evidence at all that there was another party involved. There was no evidence of Mr. Pembroke being dragged from the garden to the garage, no marks on the path, no scrapes on the heels of Mr. Pembroke's shoes, which we examined at the time. There were no fingerprints except his own on the door handles of the car. He showed no signs of carbon monoxide poisoning."

"He was nearly killed," I said blankly.

"Yes, sir, well, I'm sorry, sir, but that's how the case stands."

"Thank you for talking to me," I said.

"Right, sir. Goodbye."

"*Now* what's the matter?" Malcolm asked, watching my face. I repeated what I'd just heard.

"Impossible!" Malcolm said explosively.

"No. Clever. Which door did you go out of, with the dogs?" I asked.

"The kitchen door, like I always do."

"But you can't remember actually going out. You remember that you meant to, isn't that what you told me?"

He frowned. "I suppose it is."

"So what if you never made it to the garden, but were knocked out by the kitchen door? And what if you weren't dragged from there into the garage, but carried?"

His mouth opened. "But I'm . . ."

"You're not too heavy," I said. "I could carry you easily in a fireman's lift."

"And the fingerprints?" Norman West asked.

"In a fireman's lift," I said, "you sling the person you want to carry over your left shoulder, don't you, with his head hanging down your back. Then you grasp his knees with your left arm, and hold his right wrist in your own right hand."

They both nodded.

"So if you're holding someone's wrist, you can put his hand easily onto any surface you like, including car door handles . . . particularly," I said, thinking, "if you've opened the doors first with gloves on, so that your victim's prints will be on top of any smudges you have made."

"You should have been an assassin," Malcolm said. "You'd have been good at it."

"So now you have Malcolm slumped in the back seat, half lying, like you said. So next you switch on the engine with the keys you found in Malcolm's pocket, and leave the doors open so that all the nice fumes pour into the car quickly. And there you have," I said, "a suicide."

We contemplated the scenario.

"If it happened like that," West said, "as indeed it could have done, whoever attacked you had to know that you would go out of the kitchen door at around that time."

Malcolm said bleakly, "If I'm at home, I always go for a walk with the

52

dogs about then. Take them out, bring them back, give them their dinners, pour myself a drink. Routine."

There was a short silence, then West said, "Do you want me to continue with your family, sir, considering how little progress I've been able to make with them?"

"Yes," Malcolm said heavily, "carry on."

"Before you go," I said, "I thought you might like to know that I asked the telephonist of the Cambridge hotel if anyone besides yourself had asked if a Mr. Pembroke was staying there last weekend. She said they'd definitely had at least three calls asking for Mr. Pembroke, two men and a woman, and she remembered because she thought it odd that no one wanted to talk to him, or would leave a message; they only wanted to know if he was there."

"*Three!*" Malcolm exclaimed.

"One would be Mr. West," I pointed out. To West I said, "In view of that, could you tell us who asked you to find my father?"

West hesitated. "I don't positively know which Mrs. Pembroke it was. And, er . . . even if I became sure during these investigations, well, I don't think I could. I did warn you about a conflict of interests."

"So you did. Hasn't she paid you yet, then?"

"No, sir, not yet."

He rose to his feet, and said he would be in touch. When he'd gone, Malcolm sighed heavily. "What did you think of Mr. West?"

"He's past it, and no match for the female Pembrokes."

Malcolm smiled with irony. "Few are," he said.

WE FLEW TO PARIS in the morning in the utmost luxury, and were met by a chauffeured limousine which took its place with regal slowness in the solid traffic jam moving as one entity towards Longchamp.

The French racecourse, aflutter with flags, seemed to be swallowing *tout le monde* with insatiable appetite, until no one could walk in a straight line through the public areas, where the crowds were heavy with guttural vowels and garlic.

The co-owner of Blue Clancy, Mr. Ramsey Osborn, turned out to be a very large, sixtyish American, alight with *joie de vivre*, who towered over Malcolm and took to him at once. Malcolm seemed to see the same immediate signals. They were cronies within two minutes.

I left them sitting down to lunch together and, confident enough that no assassin would penetrate past the eagle-eyed doorkeepers of the upper citadel of the French Jockey Club, went down myself to ground level, happier to be with the action.

I had been racing in France a good deal, having for some years been assistant to a trainer who sent horses across the Channel as insouciantly as to York. I loved the noise, the smell, the movement, the quick angers, the gesticulation, the extravagance of French racing. I wandered around, watching the first race from the trainers' stand, tearing up my losing *pari-mutuel* ticket, wandering some more, and feeling finally, without any horse to saddle, purposeless.

I returned to Malcolm's eyrie and found him blossoming in his new role as racehorse owner. He was referring to *Le Prix de l'Arc de Triomphe* familiarly as "the Arc" as if it hadn't swum into his consciousness a bare half-week earlier, and discussing Blue Clancy's future with Osborn as if he knew what he was talking about.

"We're thinking of the Breeders' Cup," he said to me, and I interpreted the glint in his eyes as a frantic question as well as an instant decision.

"If he runs well today," Osborn put in, qualifying it.

"It's a long way to California," I said, agreeing with him. "To the world championships, one might say."

Malcolm was grateful for the information but far from dismayed by it. Pretty well the opposite. I saw that we would be going to California.

Lunch seemed to be continuing all afternoon, in the way French lunches do, with tidy circles of Chateaubriand appearing, followed by fresh little cheeses rolled in chopped nuts, and tiny strawberry tartlets.

Malcolm and Ramsey Osborn passed mellowly to cognac and cigars and watched the races on television. No one was in a hurry: the Arc was scheduled for five o'clock and digestion could proceed until four thirty.

In due course, the three of us went down to the saddling boxes and met both Blue Clancy and his trainer. Blue Clancy looked aristocratic, his trainer more so. The horse was restless, his nostrils quivering. We watched the saddling ritual and the final touches: flick of oil to shine the hooves, sponging of nose and mouth to clean and gloss, tweaking of forelock and tack to achieve perfection. We followed him into the parade ring and were joined by his English jockey, who was wearing Ramsey's yellow and crimson colours and looking unexcited.

Malcolm was taking with alacrity to his first taste of big-time ownership. The electricity was fairly sparking. He caught my eye, saw what I was thinking, and laughed. "I used to think you a fool to choose racing," he said. "Couldn't understand what you saw in it."

"It's better still when you ride."

"Yes, I saw that at Sandown. And about time, I suppose."

Ramsey and the trainer claimed his attention to discuss tactics with the jockey, and I thought of the summer holidays when we were children, when Gervase and I had learned to ride. Malcolm had paid the bills uncomplainingly, but had never come to watch us. Then Gervase had been whisked away by Alicia, and in the lonely vacuum afterwards I'd ridden almost every morning, laying down a skill without thinking about it seriously, not realising that this holiday pastime would beckon me for life.

Blue Clancy went out to the parade and the rest of us moved to the owners' and trainers' stand, which was buzzing with tension.

"What chance has he got?" Malcolm demanded of me. "Seriously." His eyes searched my face as if for truth.

"He's got a good chance of being placed. Anything can happen. He could win."

Malcolm nodded, not knowing whether or not to believe me, but wanting to. Well and truly hooked, I thought, and felt fond of him.

I thought in my heart of hearts that the horse would finish sixth or seventh, not disgraced but not in the money. I'd backed him on the *parimutuel* but only out of loyalty: I'd backed the French horse Meilleurs Voeux out of conviction.

Blue Clancy moved well going down to the start. This is always the best time for owners, while the heart beats with expectation and while the excuses, explanations, disappointments are still ten minutes away. Malcolm lifted binoculars to his eyes with trembling hands.

The horses were fed into the stalls to everyone's satisfaction. The gates crashed open, the thundering rainbow poured out, and twenty-six of Europe's best thoroughbreds were straining to be the fastest, strongest, bravest over one and a half miles of grass.

I could see Ramsey Osborn's colours on the rails halfway back in the field, Blue Clancy moving easily, as were all the others at that point. In the Arc, the essentials are simple: to be in the first ten coming round the last long right-hand bend, not to swing too wide into the straight and, according to the horse's stamina, pile on the pressure and head for home. Sometimes in a slow-starting Arc, one jockey will slip the field on the bend and hang on to his lead; in others there is war throughout, to a whisker verdict. Blue Clancy's Arc seemed to be run at give-no-quarter speed, and he came into the finishing straight in a bunch of flying horses, lying sixth.

Malcolm shouted, "Come on," explosively, as if air had backed up in his lungs from not breathing. He was totally involved.

Blue Clancy was doing his bit, going faster, fourth . . .

The trainer, more restrained than the owners, was now saying, "Come on, come *on*" under his breath, but two of the horses already in front suddenly came on faster than Blue Clancy and drew away from the field. Hope died in the trainer with a sigh and a sag of the shoulders.

The finish the crowd watched was a humdinger which only a photograph could decide. The finish Malcolm, Ramsey, the trainer and I watched was two lengths further back, where Blue Clancy and his jockey were fighting to the very end, flashing across the line absolutely level with their nearest rival.

"On the nod," the trainer said.

Malcolm was high with excitement, his eyes blazing. "Were we third? Say we were third!"

"I think so," the trainer said. "There'll be a photograph."

We hurried down from the stand to the unsaddling enclosure, Malcolm still short of breath and slightly dazed. "What does 'on the nod' mean?" he asked me.

"A galloping horse pokes his head out forwards with each stride in a sort of rhythm, forward, back, forward, back. If two horses are close and one horse's nose is forward when it passes the finishing line, and the other horse's happens to be back . . . well, that's on the nod."

"Just luck, you mean?"

"Luck."

"My God!" he said. "I never thought I'd feel like that. I never thought I'd *care*. I only did it for a jaunt."

He looked almost with wonderment at my face, as if I'd been before him into a far country and he'd now discovered the mystery for himself.

Ramsey Osborn beamed with pleasure when an announcement confirmed Blue Clancy's third place, saying he was sure glad the half-share sale had turned out fine. There were congratulations all round.

"Let's go for it," Ramsey said. "The Breeders' Cup. All the way."

"We'll have to see how he is after today," the trainer said warningly. "He had a hard race."

"He'll be all right," Ramsey said with hearty confidence. "Did you see the distance? Two lengths behind the winner. That's world class."

The trainer didn't argue. The favourite, undeniably world class, had finished second. The French favourite (and mine), Meilleurs Voeux, had finished fifth, which made Blue Clancy better than I'd thought. Maybe he wouldn't be disgraced in the Breeders' Cup, if we went.

The afternoon trickled away with champagne, and Malcolm, almost as tired as his horse, sank euphorically into the limousine going back to the airport and closed his eyes in the jet.

"My first-ever runner," he said sleepily. "Third in the Arc. Not bad, eh?"

"Not bad."

"I'm going to call the yearling Chrysos."

"Why Chrysos?" I said.

He smiled without opening his eyes. "It's Greek for gold."

MALCOLM WAS FEELING caged in the Savoy.

On Sunday night, when we returned from Paris, he'd hardly had the energy to undress. By Monday morning, he was pacing the carpet with revitalised energy.

"I'm going back to Quantum," he said. "I miss the dogs."

I said with foreboding, "It would take the family half a day at most to find out you were there."

"I can't hide for ever. You can come and stay close to me there."

"Don't go," I said. "You're safe here."

"Keep me safe at Quantum."

He was adamant, and began packing, and short of roping him to the bedstead, I couldn't stop him.

I drove us down to Berkshire, stopping at Arthur Bellbrook's house in the village to collect the dogs. The two full-grown Dobermans greeted Malcolm like puppies, prancing around him as he fondled them. Real love on both sides, I saw. Uncomplicated by greed, envy or rejection.

I thought of the afternoon he'd let them out of the kitchen and then been hit on the head. The dogs must have seen or sensed someone there. They should have warned Malcolm.

"Do those two dogs bark when strangers call?" I asked.

"Yes, of course." Malcolm straightened, still smiling, letting the lithe bodies press against his knees. "Why?"

"Did they bark a week last Friday?"

The smile died out of his face. "No. I don't think so. I don't remember. No . . . not especially."

"How many of the family do they know well?" I said.

"Everyone's been to the house several times since Moira died. All except you."

Every possibility led back to the certainty we couldn't accept.

When we reached the house I made Malcolm wait outside with the dogs while I went in to reconnoitre, but no one had been there laying booby traps, no one was hiding behind doors with raised blunt instruments.

I fetched him, and we unpacked. We both took if for granted I would sleep in my old room, and I made up the bed. There was champagne in the cellar and a freezer full of post-Moira TV dinners. We weren't going to starve, I thought, inspecting them, though we might get indigestion.

Malcolm spent the afternoon in his office opening letters and talking to his stockbroker on the telephone, and at the routine time proposed to give the dogs their pre-dinner walk.

"I'll come with you," I said.

He nodded without comment, and in the crisp early October air we set off down the garden, into the field, and across to the willow-lined stream he had been aiming for ten days earlier.

"Last Monday," Malcolm said casually, watching the dogs sniff for water rats round the tree roots, "I made a new will. I thought I might as well. The old one left a lot to Moira. And then, after that Friday . . . well, I wanted to put things in order, just in case."

"What did you do with it?" I asked.

He seemed amused. "The natural question is surely, 'What's in it? What have you left to *me?*'"

"Mm," I said drily. "I'm not asking that. My question is more practical."

"I left it with the solicitor in Cambridge."

"Who's the solicitor?"

"I saw his name on a brass plate outside his office and went in on impulse. I've got his card somewhere. We discussed what I wanted, he had it typed, and I signed it in front of witnesses in his office and left it there for safekeeping."

"For a brilliant man," I said, "you're as thick as two planks."

Chapter Six

Malcolm said explosively, "You're bloody rude," and then, after a pause, "In what way am I thick? A new will was essential."

"Suppose you died without telling me or anyone else you'd made it, or where it could be found?"

"Oh." He was dismayed, then frightened. "The solicitor would have produced it."

"If he heard you were dead, if he were conscientious, and if he knew who to get in touch with. If he were lazy, he might not bother, he's under no obligation."

"You seem to know an awful lot about it."

"Joyce worked for years for the Citizens Advice Bureau, do you remember? I used to hear lurid tales of family squabbles because no one knew where to find the will."

We reached the far boundary of the field and turned back.

"What should I do then?" he asked.

"Send it to the probate office at Somerset House."

"How do you mean?"

"Joyce told me about it. You put your will in a special envelope they'll send you if you apply for it, then you send it to the central probate office. They register your will there and keep it safe. When anyone dies and a solicitor applies for probate, the central probate office routinely checks its files. If it has ever registered a will for that person, that's the will that will be proved."

He thought it over. "Do you mean, if I registered a will with the probate office, and then changed my mind and wrote a new one, it wouldn't be any good?"

"You'd have to retrieve the old will and reregister the new one. Otherwise the old will would be adhered to."

"Good God! I didn't know any of this."

"Joyce says not enough people do know."

"I kept a copy of my new will," Malcolm said. "I'll show it to you when we go in."

I didn't argue. He whistled to the dogs who left the stream reluctantly, and we made our way back.

"Just wait out here while I check the house," I said.

He was astonished. "We've only been out for half an hour. And we locked the doors."

"You regularly go out for half an hour at this time. And how many of the family still have keys to the house?"

He was silent.

"Stay here, then?" I asked, and he nodded sadly.

The kitchen door was still locked. I let myself in and went all through the house again, but it was quiet and undisturbed.

I called Malcolm and he came into the kitchen and began getting the food for the dogs.

"Are you going through this checking rigmarole every single time we leave the house?" he said, sounding as if he didn't like it.

"Yes, until we get the locks changed."

He didn't like that either, but expressed his disapproval only in a rather too vigorous scraping of dog food out of a tin. He put the filled bowls on the floor and said it was time for a noggin. I bolted the kitchen door and followed him through to the office, where he poured Scotch into two glasses. He then took some sheets of paper from his briefcase. "Here's my will," he said, and passed the papers over.

He had made the will, I reflected, before he had telephoned me to put an end to our quarrel, and I expected not to figure in it, but I'd done him an injustice. Sipping the whisky, I read through all the lawyerly gobbledegook and came finally to the plain language.

"To each of my three divorced wives Vivien, Joyce and Alicia I bequeath the sum of five hundred thousand pounds.

"My son Robin being provided for I direct that the residue of my estate shall be divided equally among my children Donald, Lucy, Thomas, Gervase, Ian and Serena."

A long clause followed with provisions for "if any of my children shall predecease me", leaving "his or her share" to the grandchildren.

Finally came two short sentences:

"I bequeath to my son Ian the piece of thin wire to be found on my desk. He knows what to do with it."

Surprised, I looked up and saw the smile in Malcolm's eyes. I laughed. "I didn't expect to be in your will at all."

"Well . . ." He shrugged. "I'd never have left you out. I've regretted for a long while . . . hitting you . . . everything."

"Guess I deserved it."

"Yes, at the time."

I turned back to the beginning of the document and reread one of the preliminary paragraphs. In it, he had named me as his sole executor, when I was only his fifth child. "Why me?" I said.

"The lawyer said to name someone I trusted." He smiled lopsidedly.

He stretched out an arm and picked up from his desk a leather pot holding pens. From it, he pulled a wire about ten inches long.

"If this one should get lost," he said, "just find another." He put the wire back in the pot and the pot back on the desk.

"By the time you pop off," I said, "the price of gold might have risen out of sight and all I'd find in the wall would be spiders."

"Yes, too bad."

I felt more at one with him then than at any time since he'd telephoned, and perhaps he with me. I hoped it would be a very long time before I would have to execute his will.

WE SPENT THE NEXT two days uneventfully at Quantum, being careful. I spent a short part of Wednesday wandering around Moira's greenhouse, thinking about her death. I wondered whether she had been alarmed to see her killer approach. Probably not. Quite likely she had herself arranged the meeting, stating time and place. Malcolm had once mentioned that she didn't like casual callers.

Malcolm spent the day reading the *Financial Times* and making phone calls: yen, it appeared from snatches overhead, were behaving gruesomely.

Although making calls out, neither of us was keen to answer incoming calls since the morning when Malcolm had been drenched by a shower of recriminations from Vivien, all on the subject of meanness. He had listened with wry pain and given me a résumé afterwards.

"One of the cats in the village told her we were here, so now the whole family will know," he said gloomily. "She says Donald is bankrupt, Lucy is starving and Thomas has got the sack and can't deal with unemployment. Is it all true? It can't be. She says I should give them twenty thousand pounds each immediately."

I explained about Donald's school-fees crisis, Lucy's crumbling certainties, Thomas with Berenice chipping away at his foundations. He said their troubles lay in their own characters, which was true enough. He said if he gave those three a handout, he would have to do it for us all. The answer was no.

He telephoned back to Vivien and to her fury told her so. I could hear her voice calling him wicked, mean, vindictive, petty, tyrannical and evil. He took offence and finally slammed down the receiver. All Vivien had achieved, I thought, was to make him dig his toes in further.

On the dogs' walk that afternoon, I reminded him that I was due to ride at Cheltenham the following day, and asked if he had any cronies in that direction with whom he could spend the time.

"I'd like to see you ride again," he said.

He constantly surprised me.

"What if the family come too?"

"I'll dress up as another chef." I didn't know if it was wise, but I persuaded myself he would come to no harm on a racecourse. When we got there I introduced him to George and Jo, who congratulated him on Blue Clancy and took him off to lunch.

I looked round apprehensively all afternoon for brothers, sisters, mother and stepmothers, but saw none.

Park Railings gave me a splendid ride and finished fourth. George and Jo were pleased enough, and Malcolm was thoughtful.

"I didn't realise you went so fast," he said, on the way home. "Such speed over those jumps."

"About thirty miles an hour."

We drove towards Berkshire and came to a hostelry he liked where we stopped for late-afternoon noggins (Arthur Bellbrook was taking the dogs home with him for the night) and waited lazily until dinner.

We talked about racing, or rather Malcolm asked questions and I answered them. His interest seemed inexhaustible.

We ate without hurrying, lingering over coffee, and went home, pulling up yawning outside the garage, sleepy from fresh air and French wine.

"I'll check the house," I said without enthusiasm. "Honk the horn if you see something you don't like."

I left him in the car, let myself into the kitchen and switched on the lights. I opened the door to the hall and put on the lights there too.

I stopped there briefly, looking round. Everything looked quiet and peaceful, but my skin began to crawl, just the same.

The door to the office and the door to the sitting room were not as I had left them. The door to the office was more than half open, the door to the sitting room all but closed; neither standing at the precise narrow angle at which I'd set them every time we'd been out.

I hadn't until then thought of myself as a coward, but I felt dead afraid of going further into the house. It was so full of dark corners.

With an effort, I took a few steps into the hall, listening. The heavy front door, locked and bolted like a fortress, had not been touched. I went over to the office, reached in with an arm, switched on the light and pushed the half-open door wider.

Everything was as Malcolm had left it in the morning. The windows shone blackly, like threats. Taking a deep breath, I repeated the procedure with the sitting room, the dining room and the downstairs cloakroom, and then with trepidation went down the passage beside the stairs to the big room that had been our playroom when we were children.

There was no one there. It wasn't really a relief, because I would have to go on looking. I checked the storeroom, where there were stacks of garden furniture, and also the door at the end of the passage, which led out into the garden: securely bolted on the inside. I went back to the hall and stood at the bottom of the stairs.

It was stupid to be so afraid, I thought. It was home, the house I'd been brought up in. One couldn't be frightened by home. One was.

I swallowed. I went up the stairs. There was no one in my bedroom. No one in five other bedrooms, no one in the bathrooms, no one in Malcolm's own suite. I hadn't looked under the beds. I switched off all the upstairs lights and went cravenly back to the hall.

Everything was still quiet, mocking me. I was a fool, I thought.

I went back to Malcolm, slid in beside him, behind the steering wheel.

"Someone may be here." I explained about the doors.

"You're imagining things."

"No. Someone has used their key."

We hadn't yet been able to have the locks changed, although the carpenter was due to bring replacements the following morning.

"I'm getting cold," Malcom said. "Let's go in, for God's sake."

"No . . . we're not sleeping here."

"What? You can't mean it."

"I'll lock the house, and we'll go and get a room somewhere."

"At this time of night?"

"Yes." I made to get out of the car and he put a hand on my arm to catch my attention. "Ian, all this is crazy."

"It would be crazier still to be murdered in our beds."

"But just because two doors . . ."

"Yes. Because."

He seemed to catch some of my uneasiness. When I was heading again for the kitchen he called after me, "Bring my briefcase from the office, will you?"

I fetched his briefcase without incident and set the office door at its usual precise angle. I did the same to the sitting room door. Perhaps they would tell us in the morning, I thought, whether or not we had had a visitor who had hidden from my approach. I left the house dark and locked and put the briefcase on the car's back seat.

On the basis that it would be easiest to find a room in London, particularly at midnight, for people without luggage, I drove up the M4 and on Malcolm's instructions pulled up at the Ritz.

"Our name is Watson," I said impulsively, suddenly remembering Norman West's advice and picking out of the air the first name I could think of. "We will pay with traveller's cheques."

Malcolm opened his mouth and closed it again. One could write whatever name one wanted on traveller's cheques.

The Ritz batted no eyelids, offered a double suite and promised razors, toothbrushes and a bottle of Scotch.

Malcolm, who held that sleeping pills came a poor second to Scotch, put his nightcap theory to the test and was soon softly snoring. I quietly closed the door between our two rooms and climbed between my own sheets, but for a long time I lay awake. I was ashamed of my fear in the house. I had risked my neck without a qualm over big fences that afternoon: I'd been petrified in the house that someone would jump out on me. The two faces of courage, I thought morosely: turn one face to the wall.

WE WENT BACK to Berkshire in the morning and couldn't reach Quantum by car because the whole village, it seemed, was out and blocking the road.

"What on earth's going on?" Malcolm said.

In the end I had to stop the car, and we finished the last bit of the journey on foot. We had to push through the crowds and were unpopular until people recognised Malcolm and made way for him. Finally we reached the entrance to the drive . . . and there, literally, rocked to a stop.

To start with, there was a rope stretched across it, barring our way, with a policeman guarding it. In front of the house, there were ambulances, police cars, fire engines, swarms of people in uniform.

Malcolm swayed with shock, and I felt unreal, disconnected from my feet. Our eyes told us: our brains couldn't believe.

There was an immense jagged hole in the centre of Quantum.

Chapter Seven

Our appearance on the scene was a welcome shock to the assembled forces. They had been searching for our remains in the rubble.

They told us that the explosion had happened at four thirty in the morning, the reverberation of it waking half the village. Several people had called the police, but no one knew where the explosion had occurred. The police drove round the neighbourhood until daylight, and it was only then that anyone saw what had happened to Quantum.

The front wall of the hall, the antique front door with it, had been blown out flat onto the drive, and the centre part of the upper storey had collapsed into the hall.

"I'm afraid it's worse at the back," a policeman said phlegmatically. "Perhaps you'd come round here, sir."

Malcolm nodded mechanically and we followed the policeman round to the left, between the kitchen and garage, through to the garden and along past the dining room wall. The shock when we rounded the corner onto the terrace was, for all the warning, horrific and sickening.

Where the sitting room had been, there was a mountain of jumbled dusty bricks, plaster, beams and smashed furniture spilling outwards onto the grass. Malcolm's suite, which had been above the sitting room, had vanished into the chaos. The roof, which looked almost intact from the front, had at the rear been stripped of tiles, the old sturdy rafters standing out against the sky like picked ribs.

My own bedroom had been on one side of Malcolm's. All that remained of it were some shattered spikes of floorboards and a strip of plaster cornice.

Malcolm began to shake. I took off my jacket and put it round his shoulders. He looked suddenly frail.

I retrieved a wooden armchair from the debris, and carried it over to him. He sank into it without seeming to notice it.

There were firemen and other people tugging at movable parts of the ruins. Several of them came over to Malcolm, offering sympathy, but mostly wanting information, such as were we certain there had been no one else in the house? As certain as we could be. Had we been storing any gas in the house? Bottled gas? Butane? Propane? No. We'd had no gas of any sort. Had we been storing any explosive substances whatsoever? No.

Time seemed disjointed.

Women from the village, as in all disasters, had brought hot tea for the men working. They gave some to Malcolm and me, and found a blanket for Malcolm so that I could have my jacket back in the chilly air.

A police car approached, its siren wailing ever louder as it made slow progress up the drive. Presently a senior-looking man, not in uniform, came round to the back of the house and took charge. First, he stopped all work on the rubble. Then he talked to the chief fireman. Finally he came over to Malcolm and me.

Burly and black-moustached, he said, as to an old acquaintance, "Mr. Pembroke."

Malcolm similarly said, "Superintendent Yale," and everyone could hear the shake he couldn't keep out of his voice.

"And you, sir?" the superintendent asked me.

"Ian Pembroke."

He pursed his mouth below the moustache, considering me. "Where were you last night, sir?"

"With my father in London," I said. "We've just . . . returned."

He said noncommittally, "We will have to call in explosive experts, as the damage here, on preliminary inspection and in the absence of any

gas, seems to have been caused by some sort of an explosive device."

If he'd expected any reaction from Malcolm or me, he got none, as both of us had come to the same conclusion the moment we'd walked up the drive. If the house had merely been burning, Malcolm would have been dashing about, saving what he could, dismayed but full of vigour. It was the implications behind a bomb which had knocked him into shivering lassitude: the realisation that if he'd slept in his own bed, he wouldn't have risen to bath or read the *Sporting Life*.

And nor, for that matter, would I.

"It's clearly impossible to talk here," the superintendent said. "So I suggest you come to the police station."

"What about the house?" I said. "It's open to the four winds."

"We will keep a patrol here. If you'll give the instructions, we'll suggest someone to board up the windows, and we'll contact a construction firm with a tarpaulin large enough for the roof."

"Send me the bill," Malcolm said limply.

We made our way out into the front drive. The rope across the gateway had been overwhelmed and the front garden was full of people, a constable trying vainly to hold them back.

A bunch in front of the rest started running in our direction as soon as we appeared, and with a feeling of unreality I saw that they were Gervase, Alicia, Berenice, Vivien, Donald, Helen . . .

"Malcolm," Gervase said loudly, coming to a halt in front of us, so that we too had to stop, "you're alive!"

A tiny flicker of humour appeared in Malcolm's eyes at this most obvious of statements, but he had no chance of answering as the others set up a clamour of questions.

Vivien said, "I heard from the village that Quantum had blown up and you were both dead." Her strained voice held a complaint about having been given erroneous news.

"So did I," Alicia said. "Three people telephoned . . . so I came at once, after I'd told Gervase and the others, of course." She looked deeply shocked, but then they all did, mirroring no doubt what they could see on my own face but also suffering from the double upset of misinformation.

More figures pushed through the crowd. Lucy, Edwin and Serena, running, stumbling, looking from the wounded house to me and Malcolm.

Lucy was crying, "You're alive! Vivien said you were dead."

"I was told they were dead," Vivien said defensively.

Serena was swaying, pale as pale. Gervase put an arm round her and hugged her. "It's all right, girl, they're not dead after all." He squeezed her affectionately.

"I don't feel well," she said faintly. "What happened?"

"Too soon to say for certain," Gervase said. "But I'd say one can't rule out a bomb."

They repudiated the word, shaking their heads, covering their ears. Bombs were for wars, for cold-hearted terrorists . . . for other people. Bombs weren't for a family house outside a Berkshire village, lived in by an ordinary family.

Except that we weren't an ordinary family. Ordinary families didn't have fifth wives murdered while planting geraniums. I looked at the familiar faces and couldn't see on any of them either malice or dismay that Malcolm had escaped. They were all beginning to recover from the shock and to realise how much damage had been done to the house.

Gervase grew angry. "Whoever did this shall pay for it!" He sounded pompous more than effective.

"Where's Thomas?" I asked.

Berenice shrugged waspishly. "Dear Thomas went out early on one of his useless job-hunting missions. I've no idea where he was going. Vivien telephoned after he'd left."

Gervase said masterfully, "You'd better come home with me, I think, Malcolm. Ursula will look after you."

None of the others liked that. They all instantly made counter-proposals. Malcolm looked as if he didn't know whether to laugh or scream. "I'll go wherever I want to," he said flatly, "and with Ian."

"It isn't fair," Serena said plaintively. "Ian gets everything, always. I think it's beastly."

The superintendent, who had been listening attentively, said at this point that plans to take Malcolm home would have to be shelved for a few hours.

Gervase raised his eyebrows. "Malcolm's done nothing wrong."

"I want to talk to the superintendent myself," Malcolm said. "I want him to find out who tried to destroy my house."

"Surely, it was an accident," Serena said, very upset.

Gervase still had his arm round her. "Face facts, girl." He hesitated, looking at me. "Vivien and Alicia told everyone you were both living here again . . . so how come you escaped being hurt?"

"We went to London for a night out and stayed there," I said.

"Very lucky," Donald said heartily, and Helen nodded a shade too enthusiastically and said, "Yes, yes."

Malcolm was growing tired of them. Not one had hugged him, kissed him, or made warm gestures over his survival. Lucy's tears, if they were genuine, had come nearest. The family obviously could have accommodated his death easily, murmuring regrets at his graveside, but looking forward to a safely affluent future. Malcolm dead would free them.

"Let's go," he said to the superintendent. "I'm cold."

The superintendent, Malcolm and I began to move towards the gate, but we had gone only halfway when Joyce pushed through the crowd and ran forward, fearfully distraught. She stopped when she saw us. Her face went white and she swayed as Serena had done, and I sprinted three or four long strides and caught her before she fell.

"It's all right," I said, holding her. "We're alive."

"Oh, I thought . . . Donald said . . . I've been crying all the way here, I couldn't see the road . . ." She put her face against my jacket and cried again with a few deep gulps, then pushed herself off determinedly and began searching her tailored pockets for a handkerchief. She blew her nose. "Well, darlings," she said, "as you're alive, what the hell's been going on?"

She looked behind Malcolm and me and her eyes widened.

"The whole bloody tribe come to the wake?" To Malcolm she said, "You've the luck of the devil, you old bugger."

Malcolm grinned at her, a distinct sign of revival.

The three ex-wives eyed each other warily. Any mushy idea that the near death of the man they'd all married might have brought them to sisterly sympathy was a total nonstarter.

"I want to see just how bad the damage is to the house." Joyce looked at me. "Come along, darling, you can show me."

"Run along, Mummy's boy," Gervase said spitefully.

I felt rebellious, tried to smother it, and sought for a different solution.

"You can all come," I said to them. "Come and see what really happened here."

The extent and violence of the damage at the rear of the house silenced even Gervase. All of the mouths gaped: in all eyes, horrified awe.

The press photographers moved in closer and took haphazard pictures of us, and journalists approached with insistent questions. Malcolm gathered his blanket round him, retreating into it like a Red Indian.

Alicia was doing her fluttery feminine act for the reporters, laying out charm thickly and eclipsing Serena's little-girl ploy. Nearly sixty, her hair was gathered youthfully high on the crown of her head in a ribbon bow, and I thought that it must be hard for Serena to have a mother who refused to mature, who for years had blocked her daughter's natural road to adulthood. Girls needed a motherly mother, I'd been told, and Serena didn't have one.

Edwin was having a hard time putting on a show of rejoicing over Malcolm's deliverance. "It's all very well for you," he said to me bitterly. "Malcolm despises me—and I don't see why I should care too much for him. Of course, I wouldn't wish him dead . . ."

"Of course not," I murmured.

Berenice said to me angrily, "It's all your fault Thomas is out of work."

I blinked. "How do you make that out?"

"He's been so worried about Malcolm's behaviour that he couldn't concentrate and made mistakes. He says you could get Malcolm to help us, but of course I tell him you won't, why should you, you're Malcolm's pet." She fairly spat the last word. She was older than Thomas by four or five years and had married him when she was well over thirty. Ten years ago she had been a thin, attractive woman lit up by happiness. Thomas had been proud of himself. They had looked, if not an exciting couple, stable and full of promise.

Ten years and two daughters later, Berenice had put on weight and outward sophistication and lost whatever illusions she'd had about marriage. I'd long supposed it was basic disappointment which had made her so destructive of Thomas, but hadn't bothered to wonder about the cause of it. Time I did, I thought. Time I understood the whole lot of them, because perhaps in that way we might come to know who could and who couldn't murder.

I looked at the house and shivered. We had returned unexpectedly on Monday; today was Friday. The speed of planning and execution was alarming. Never again were we likely to be so lucky. I was filled with a sense of urgency and foreboding.

Malcolm's dogs came bounding across the grass towards him. He put a hand out of his blanket and patted them. After them came Arthur Bellbrook with a face of concern which lightened when he set eyes on Malcolm.

"Sir! You're alive! I went to Twyford to fetch some weedkiller. When I got back, they told me in the village . . . that you were both dead."

I explained about our going to London, and asked him what time he'd gone home the previous day.

"Same as always. About three forty." He was beginning to get his breath back, his eyes round with disbelief as he stared at the damage.

"Did you go in the house at any time during the day?" I asked.

He switched his gaze from the ruins to me and sounded aggrieved. "No, I didn't. You know I couldn't have. You've been locking the place like it's a fortress since you came back, and I didn't have a key."

I said placatingly, "It's just that we're anxious . . . someone got in, they must have."

"Not me." He was slightly mollified. "I was working in the kitchen garden all day and had the dogs with me. If anyone had tried to get in the house, they'd have barked for sure, but they didn't."

Malcolm said, "Arthur, could you keep the dogs with you for another day or two?"

"Yes, I will." He looked helplessly at the heap of rubble spilling out across the terrace and onto the lawn.

The family had by this time divided into two clumps, Vivien's and Alicia's, with Joyce and I hovering between them, belonging to neither. The superintendent went from group to group asking that everyone should adjourn to the police station. "As you are all here," he was saying, "we may as well take your statements to save you being bothered later."

"Good God," Gervase said, "you don't think any of us would have done this, do you?"

"That's what we have to find out."

The family, including Malcolm and myself, packed into the three police cars standing in the front drive, and Gervase and Serena set off on foot to go back to the transport they had come in.

Malcolm and I arrived first at the police station with Superintendent Yale, and he ushered us through to his office and sat us down.

He looked at us broodingly from behind a large desk and inspected his nails. Finally he said to Malcolm, "All right. You don't have to say it. I do not believe you would blow up your house just to make me believe that someone is trying to kill you. That being so, we must take the attack in the garage more seriously."

"I would be dead twice over," Malcolm said, "if it weren't for Ian." He told Yale about the car roaring straight at us at Newmarket.

"Why didn't you report this, sir?" Yale said, frowning.

"Why do you think?"

Yale ran a finger and thumb down his large black moustache and didn't answer.

Malcolm nodded. "I was tired of being disbelieved."

"And . . . er . . . last night?" Yale asked.

Malcolm told him about our return from Cheltenham, and about Quantum's inner doors. "I wanted to sleep in my own bed. I was tired. Ian absolutely wouldn't have it, and drove us to London."

Yale looked at me steadily. "Did you have a premonition?"

"No, I don't think so. I was just . . . frightened," I said.

Yale said, "What of?"

"Not of bombs," I said. "I never considered that. Frightened there was someone in the house. I couldn't have slept there, that's all." I paused. "I saw the way the car drove at my father at Newmarket—and I believed him, of course, about being attacked and gassed in the garage. I believe he is in extreme danger. So, we've been moving around, letting no one know where to find us, until this week."

"My fault," Malcolm said gloomily. "I insisted on coming back here. Ian didn't want to."

Yale thought for a while and then said, "When you were in the house looking round, did you see anything except for the doors?"

"No, nothing."

Yale sighed. "The time-frame we're looking at," he said, "is between about three forty p.m., when the gardener went home, and ten thirty p.m., when you returned from Cheltenham." He pursed his lips. "If you hadn't stayed out to dinner, what time would you have been home?"

"About six thirty," I said.

"We had a drink at the racecourse after the last race," Malcolm said. "I had Scotch, Ian had some sort of fizzy gut-rot." He was enjoying having Yale believe him at last, and seemed to be feeling expansive.

Yale looked at me neutrally. He was difficult to read, I thought, chiefly because he didn't want to be read. He must have been forty or forty-five, and he looked as if he habitually had too little exercise and too many sandwiches. Perhaps now he'd dropped his over-smart suspicions of Malcolm, he could actually solve his case.

A policewoman came in and said, looking harassed, that she didn't know where to put the rest of the Pembroke family.

Yale thought briefly and told her to show them all to the interview rooms and have officers take their statements.

Immediately the door had closed behind the policewoman I said, "While they're in the interview rooms, I'm taking my father out of here."

"What about the house?" Malcolm began.

"I'll see to the house later. You're leaving here now, this minute. If Superintendent Yale will get a police car to take you to the railway station, I'll stay here."

"Certainly," Yale said.

I said, "Go to London. Go to where we were last night. Use the same name. Don't telephone anyone. Don't for God's sake let anyone know where you are."

Malcolm stood up. "All right."

"Where will you be?" Yale asked him.

"Don't answer," I said brusquely.

Malcolm looked at me, then at the superintendent. "Ian will know where I am. If he doesn't want to tell you, he won't."

Superintendent Yale followed us out of his office and detailed a driver to take Malcolm to the station.

"Don't go shopping, I'll buy us some things later. Do be sensible, I beg you," I said to him.

"I promise," he said; but promises with Malcolm weren't necessarily binding. He went out with the driver.

Yale gave me a short list of reputable building contractors and the use of his telephone. I chose one of the firms at random and explained what was needed, and Yale took the receiver himself and insisted that they were to do minimum weatherproofing only, and were to move none of the rubble until the police gave clearance.

"When the driver returns from taking your father," he said to me, hanging up, "he can ferry you back to your car."

"Thank you."

"I'm trusting you, you know, to maintain communications between me and your father."

"I'll telephone here every morning, if you like."

"I'd much rather know where he is."

I shook my head. "The fewer people know, the safer."

He couldn't accuse me of taking unreasonable precautions.

Chapter Eight

By the time I caught up with him later, in London, Malcolm had achieved a double suite at the Ritz with views of Green Park. He had lunched on Strasbourg pâté and Dover sole, and had reached the lower half of a bottle of Krug.

"Were you followed here?" he asked.

"I was not."

He was doing his best to pretend he had regained total command of himself, yet I guessed the train journey had been an anxious ordeal. How could anyone be the target of deadly unrelenting virulence and not in the end break down? I'd got to invent something better for him, I thought, than cooping him up in millionaire cells. Make him safe, give him back his lightheartedness, set him free.

"Um," I said, "I hope your passport's still in your briefcase."

"Yes, it is." He had taken it in his briefcase to Paris.

"Good."

An unfortunate thought struck him. "Where's yours?"

"In the rubble. Don't worry, I'll get a replacement. Do you have a visa for America?"

"Yes."

"How about if you go to America tomorrow?" I said.

"*Tomorrow?* How can I?"

"I'll take you safely to Heathrow and see you off."

"Dammit, that's not what I meant."

"No," I said. "Well . . . the Breeders' Cup races three weeks tomorrow at Santa Anita. Why don't we phone Ramsey Osborn? Why don't we phone Blue Clancy's trainer? Why don't you fly to Los Angeles tomorrow and have a fine old time at the races for three weeks? You can stay where the Breeders' Cup organisers do, at the Beverly Wilshire Hotel. Forget Quantum. Forget the bloody family. They won't know where you are and they'll never find you. I'll join you as soon as I can and I'll go on minding your back—if you want me to."

He listened apathetically at first, but by the end he was smiling. I'd proposed the sort of impulsive behaviour that greatly appealed to him.

"A damn sight better than rotting at the Ritz," he announced

"Great," I said. "Get out your diary for the telephone numbers."

It was soon settled. Blue Clancy would go over for the Breeders' Cup. Ramsey Osborn, booming away in Stamford, Connecticut, said why didn't Malcolm stop off at some good friends of his in Lexington on the way and feast his eyes on some *real* bloodstock? Ramsey would call them and fix it. Stay by the phone, you guys, he said. He would call back.

He called back within twenty minutes. "All set," he said. "They're expecting you tomorrow, and I'm flying down Sunday. They're real sweet guys, you'll love them. Dave and Sally Cander. Dogwood Drift Farm." He read out the telephone number. "You got that?"

Malcolm had got it.

Ramsey asked where Malcolm was planning to stay for the Breeders' Cup. "Beverly Wilshire? Couldn't be better. I'll make reservations right away." We had made his day, he said, and to have a good one.

The sitting room seemed smaller and quieter when he'd gone off the line, but Malcolm was revitalised. We went at once by taxi to his bank for traveller's cheques and then to Simpson's for replacement clothes and suitcases to pack them in. Malcolm paid for all of mine with his credit card, which was a relief. He'd thought of my other finances himself already and that evening gave me a bumper cheque.

"Your fare to California and so on. Pay Arthur Bellbrook. Pay Norman West. Pay the contractors for weatherproofing Quantum. Pay for the hired car. Pay your own expenses."

We dined in good spirits, the dreadful morning at least overlaid. He raised his glass: "To Blue Clancy" and "To racing" and "To life".

"To life," I said.

I DROVE HIM to Heathrow in the morning and saw him on his way to Lexington. He gave me a long blue look before he departed. "Don't think I don't know what I owe you," he said.

"You owe me nothing."

"Bloody Moira," he said unexpectedly, and waved as he went.

Feeling good about him, I telephoned from the airport to Superintendent Yale but got one of his assistants: his chief was out at Quantum and had left a message that if I phoned I was to be asked if I could join him. Yes, I could, and I arrived in the village about forty minutes later.

I stopped in front of the house and Superintendent Yale appeared from the direction of the kitchen, having been alerted by the constable at the gate, I surmised.

"How is Mr. Pembroke?" he asked, shaking hands.

"Shaken," I said.

He nodded understandingly. He was wearing an overcoat and looked cold in the face, as if he'd been out of doors for some time. We went round to the back garden.

The back of the house looked sad and blind, with light brown plywood hammered over all the windows and the bare roof rafters covered with a black tarpaulin. The devastated centre was still open to the elements, and several men in hard hats were working there, slowly picking up pieces from the huge jumble and throwing them into a rubbish skip.

"We've got a surprise for you," Yale said. He waved to a man in beige overalls with a blue hard hat, who came over and asked me my name.

"Ian Pembroke," I said obligingly.

He unzipped the front of his overalls, put a hand inside and drew out a battered navy-blue object which he held out to me with a small satisfied smile. "You may need this," he said.

Never a truer word. It was my passport. I was delighted.

I zipped it into my new Barbour and thought gratefully that I wouldn't have to trail around getting a new one.

"Now, we need your help," he said. He was a lean, highly professional sort of man, giving an impression of army. He said his name was Smith. He was an explosives expert.

"When you first came here yesterday morning," he said, "did you smell anything?"

I thought back. "Brick dust," I said. "The wind was stirring it up."

"Do you know what cordite smells like?" he asked.

"Cordite? Like after a gun's been fired, do you mean? No, I didn't smell that."

"Cordite was used very commonly as a general explosive," he said, "before Nobel invented dynamite. It's a sort of high-grade gunpowder, and it's still used in some quarries. It explodes like a gas. It doesn't punch small holes through walls like a battering-ram. It's more like an expanding balloon that knocks them flat."

I looked at the house.

"Yes, like that," Smith said. "But its strong smell lingers."

"Well . . . we didn't get here until ten, and the explosion was at four thirty in the morning, and it was windy. I should think any smell had blown away."

Smith shrugged. "We'll do microscopic tests. But it looks to me as if cordite is a strong possibility."

"Can anyone buy cordite?" I asked vaguely.

"No, they definitely can't," Smith said with decision. "Twenty years or so ago, maybe, but not now. Since terrorism became a part of life, most sorts of explosives are highly regulated. There are a few explosive substances on the open market, but detonators to set them off are not."

"What does cordite look like?"

"Loose grains, like gunpowder. You have to compress it. Confine it. Then you need heat to start off the chemical reaction, which proceeds at such a rate that the ingredients appear to explode."

I became aware of the audience beyond the rope in the garden. Arthur

Bellbrook was there again, talking away. He must enjoy being a celebrity, I thought. The dogs on their leads waited patiently.

A stray piece of memory connected Arthur to the smell of cordite, and I couldn't think why that should be until I remembered him carrying his shotgun into the house on the day he'd thought I was a burglar.

I cast the stray thought out but it sauntered back, telling me it was nothing to do with Arthur and shotguns. What then? I frowned, trying to remember. The smell of cordite on a misty morning, and the gardener . . . not Arthur, but old Fred before him . . . telling us children to go right back out of the field, he didn't want our heads blown off.

I walked across to where Smith in his hard blue hat bent to his task and said, without preamble, "Does cordite have another name?"

He straightened, with a piece of brick and plaster in his hand. "It's commonly called 'black powder'," he said. "Why?"

"Well, we had some here once. But long ago, when we were children. Twenty years ago at least, probably more. But I suppose . . . some of the family could have remembered . . . as I just have."

Yale, who had followed me, to listen, said, "Remembered what?"

"There used to be four or five great old willow trees down by the stream, across the field." I pointed. "They were at the end of their lives. Old Fred, who was the gardener here before Arthur, told my father they weren't safe and they'd have to come down, so he got some foresters to fell them. It was dreadful seeing them come down . . ."

"Go on," Yale said impatiently. "What's all this about trees?"

"The stumps," I said. "The tree men sawed the trees off close to the ground but left the stumps, and no one could get them out. Fred didn't want to leave them there to rot, so he decided to blow them up . . . with black powder."

"Ah," said Yale.

Black powder had sounded, somehow, as if it ought to belong to pirates. We'd been most impressed. Fred had got his powder and he'd dug a hole down below the stubborn roots of the first stump, and filled it and set off one enormous explosion. It was just as well he'd cleared us out of the field because the blast had knocked Fred himself flat although he'd been a hundred feet away. Malcolm had come running in alarm to see what had happened, and forbade Fred to blow up the rest of the stumps.

As I told the gist of this to Yale and Smith, the second reel of film was already rolling in my mind. "Fred," I said, "carried the box of black powder back to the toolshed." I paused, then added, "Wouldn't any explosive be useless after all this time?"

"Dynamite wouldn't last much more than a year in a toolshed," Smith said. "One hot summer would ruin it. But black powder—cordite—is very stable, and twenty years is immaterial."

"What are we waiting for?" Yale said, and walked towards the toolshed which lay behind the garage. He called over a pair of young policemen and told them to take everything out of the shed and lay each object separately on the ground.

Arthur Bellbrook came hurrying across. "What's going on?" he said suspiciously.

"When did you last clean out the toolshed?" Yale asked.

Arthur was put out. "I've been meaning to," he said defensively. "That's Fred's old rubbish, all that at the back."

The superintendent nodded, and we all watched the outgoing procession of ancient, rusting, neglected tat. Eventually one of the policemen came out with a dirty wooden box. He put it on the ground beside the other things, and I said doubtfully, "I think that's it."

Smith squatted down beside it. The lid was nailed shut. With a chisel, he prised it open and peeled back the yellowish paper which was revealed. Inside, half filling the box, there was indeed black powder.

Smith smelled it and poked it around. "It's cordite, all right, and in good condition. But as it's here, it obviously hasn't been used."

"Well," I said weakly, "it was only an idea."

"Nothing wrong with the idea," Smith said. He looked round at the growing collection of discards. "Did you find any detonators?"

He had everyone open every single packet and tin: a lot of rusty staples and nails saw daylight, but nothing he could identify as a substance likely to set off an explosion.

"Inconclusive," he said, shrugging, and returned to his rubble.

I tried to apologise for all the waste of time, but the superintendent stopped me. "When you saw the tree stump blown up, which of your brothers and sisters were there?"

I sighed, but it had to be faced. "Gervase and I were always together at that time, but some of the older ones were there too. They used to come for weekends still, after they were grown up. And I know Lucy was there, because she wrote a poem about roots shrieking blindly to the sky. She's a poet," I added lamely.

"All right, then. She was there. Who else?"

"Someone was carrying Serena on his shoulders when we had to leave the field for the explosion. I think it must have been Thomas. He used to make her laugh."

"How old were you all at that time?" Young asked.

I thought back. Alicia had swept out not very long after. "Perhaps I was thirteen. Gervase two years older, Lucy would have been . . . um . . . twenty-two, about, and Thomas nineteen. Serena must have been six, at that rate, and Donald . . . he would have been twenty-four."

Yale thoughtfully wrote in his notebook.

"But what does it matter, if the cordite is still here?" I said. I looked at the shattered house and said forlornly, "None of them could have done it."

Yale put his notebook away. "You may be right," he said.

Smith again came over to join us. "You've given me an idea," he said to me. "You and your tree roots. Can you draw me a plan of where the rooms were, exactly, especially those upstairs?"

I said I thought so, and the three of us went into the garage out of the wind, where I laid a piece of paper on the bonnet of Moira's car and did my best.

"The sitting room stretched about thirty feet. Above that"—I sketched—"there was my room, about eight feet wide, twelve deep. Malcolm's bedroom came next, I suppose about fifteen feet wide and much deeper than mine, then his bathroom and dressing room at the back of it." I drew it for them. "Malcolm's whole suite would have been about twenty-two feet wide by about eighteen feet deep."

Smith studied the drawing. "Your room and the suite together were more or less identical with the sitting room, then?"

"Yes, I should think so."

He borrowed my pen, did some calculations and frowned. "Where exactly was your father's bed?"

"The bed was against the wall between his room and the landing."

"And your bed?"

"Against the wall between my room and Malcolm's."

Smith considered the plan for some time and then said, "I think the charge here was placed centrally. Did your father by any chance have a chest or anything, at the foot of his bed?"

"Yes, he did," I said, surprised. "A long box with a padded top."

"Then I'd think that would be where the explosion occurred." Smith borrowed the pen again for more calculations and looked undecided.

"What's the matter?" I asked.

"Mm . . . well, because of your tree roots, I was thinking of an explosive that farmers use sometimes which is safer than cordite. You can buy the ingredients anywhere and mix it yourself." He smiled slightly. "But it's not easy to get the detonators to set it off."

"What is it?" I asked.

"Fertiliser and diesel oil."

"What?" I sounded disappointed and Smith's smile expanded.

"Ammonium nitrate," he said. "You can buy it in fine granules from seed merchants and garden centres, places like that. Mix it with fuel oil. Dead simple. As far as I remember, it would be sixteen parts fertiliser to one part oil. The only problem is"—he scratched his nose—"I think you'd need a good deal of it to do the sort of damage we have here. I seem to remember it'd be volume in cubic metres over three, answer in kilos."

"What volume?" I asked.

"The volume of the space you want cleared by the explosion. Say you want the effective destruction of twenty-seven cubic metres, OK? Volume of your bedroom, near enough. Divide by three, equals nine. Nine kilos of explosive needed."

"But you don't think this bomb went off in my bedroom," I said.

"No, I don't. Nine kilos of ammonium nitrate in your bedroom would have made a nasty hole all around, but I wouldn't have thought it would bring half a house down. So if we locate the device in the foot-of-the bed box, we are looking at something in the region of . . ." He did some more calculations, ". . . say at least seventy-five cubic metres for your father's bedroom . . . that's twenty-five kilos of explosive."

"That's heavy," I said blankly.

"Yes. A large suitcaseful."

"What sets it off, then?" I asked.

"Ah." He hesitated, then shrugged. "Ammonium nitrate fuel oil— ANFO—won't explode on its own, it's very stable. So you stick into it a package of something that explodes fast: the detonator, in fact. Then you arrange to heat the detonating substance, either with a burning fuse, or by an electrical circuit which can be achieved by ordinary batteries. The heat sets off the detonator, the detonator detonates the ANFO. And bingo . . ."

"At four thirty in the morning," I said, "it would probably be a time bomb, wouldn't it?"

Mr. Smith nodded happily. "That's what we're looking for. We'll probably find the pieces. We usually do if we look hard enough. They don't vaporise in the explosion, they scatter."

I DROVE UNHURRIEDLY to Epsom, but as soon as I let myself into my flat, I knew I wouldn't stay there. It was too empty, too boring. There were a few letters, a few messages on the answering machine, but nothing of great interest.

I had enjoyed being with Malcolm more than I'd realised. I missed him already, and in the time I'd spent with him, I'd developed a taste for spontaneity which made sitting around in my flat impossible. I packed a pair of breeches and a sweater, added some limp old shirts to the new ones in the Simpson's suitcase, closed up the flat and went down to the car park. My own car stood there, but I took the hired one again, meaning to turn it in sometime and return for my own by train. I set off in the direction of Quantum, without really knowing where I was going.

I felt an awful aversion to the task of searching the psyches of the family, but I ended up in a place from where visiting them all would be easy, taking by impulse the turning to the village of Cookham and booking a room there in an old inn.

I phoned Norman West. He said apologetically that he'd got no further with solving the Pembroke case, and thought there was nothing else he could do. Should he send his final report and account to Mr. Pembroke at the Savoy, or at Quantum House?

"Neither," I said. "We'd like you to carry on working." And I told him what had happened to Quantum and very nearly to ourselves.

"Dear me," he said.

"So would you mind traipsing round again to ask what everyone was doing the day before yesterday between three p.m. and midnight?"

He was silent for an appreciable interval. Then he said, "I don't know that it would be useful, you know. Surely, this time the police will make exhaustive enquiries? I think I must leave it to them."

I heard him sigh and could feel his disinclination.

"Look," I said, "could you just meet me somewhere?"

"I don't mind doing that," he said. "When?"

"Tomorrow?"

Tomorrow he was free in the evening. He knew the pub I was staying in, he would meet me in the bar at seven.

I thanked him for that anyway, and next telephoned two stables up on the downs to ask the trainers if I could ride exercise on their horses for several mornings, if it would be useful to them. The first said no, the second said yes. Start Monday. Could I be there by seven fifteen?

"Yes," I said appreciatively.

"Stay to breakfast."

Sanity lay in racing stables, I thought, thanking him. Their brand of insanity was my sort of health. I couldn't stay away for long.

I spent the evening in the bar in the pub, and dawdled Sunday away pleasurably enough, until Norman West appeared at seven.

He accepted a double Scotch with water, opened the large envelope he was carrying and pulled out some papers and my photographs, which he laid on the table between us. "You can have all my notes. You'll find there's a definite pattern about the movements of your family, and at the same time an absence of pattern. The murder of Mrs. Moira and the gassing of Mr. Pembroke both took place at about five in the evening, and at five almost all your family are habitually on the move. It's easy to lose an hour or so without anyone noticing, around that time. That's why it's been almost hopeless establishing alibis."

"I understand," I said thoughtfully.

"Newmarket was a bit different," he said, "because it meant someone being away for a whole day, assuming that Mr. Pembroke was followed from his hotel when he left at lunchtime for Newmarket." He sipped his whisky. "I thought it would be simple in those circumstances to discover which family member had been away all of that Tuesday, but in fact it wasn't, as you'll read. Now, if the explosive device was planted in

Quantum House between four and six, we're back to the . . . er . . ."

"Five o'clock shadow," I said.

He looked mildly shocked. It wasn't a laughing matter. "I've no doubt the same pattern will be found," he said.

"Couldn't you please tell me," I said, "which Mrs. Pembroke got you to find Malcolm? Whose name was on the cheque?"

He considered, staring at his drink as if to find wisdom in the depths. "I didn't get paid," he said. "I'm not sure, but I think it was the voice of Mrs. Alicia Pembroke." He shook his head. "I asked her if it was her, when I interviewed her. She said it wasn't, but I think she was lying. But two other people found out on their own account, don't forget, by doing exactly as I did, telephoning around. I hope Mr. Pembroke can't be found as easily at this moment."

"I don't think so," I said.

He nodded approvingly, and produced a smaller envelope from an inner pocket, which contained his account. I wrote him his cheque and he took it, rose wearily to his feet and shook my hand. I thanked him and he went greyly away, leaving me on my own with his notes. I began reading. Serena came first.

Miss Serena Pembroke (26), unmarried, lives at 14 Mossborough Court, Bracknell, a block of flats just off the Easthampstead Road. Miss S. has lived there three months. She works at Deanna's Dance and Aerobics Studio, High Street, Bracknell, teaching aerobics, and works mornings Monday to Friday 8.00 to 1.30 p.m. She and another girl work in rotation, half-hour on, half off. Most days, Miss S. takes the first half of each hour. Evening classes, Monday to Friday, 7.00-8.30 p.m. only. Miss S. does these alone.

Miss S. has bad menstrual cramps every month. Can't dance or exercise, and always takes two days off. The Tuesday of Newmarket Sales was one of these days. Miss S. called in Monday morning in pain, didn't work. She returned Wednesday.

Miss· S. leads sober, hard-working, regulated life. She likes shopping and on the Friday of the attack on Mr. Pembroke she says she bought food and a frilly white blouse at Marks and Spencer, she thinks. (Not sure of the day.)

Miss S. says Mr. Ian must have killed Mrs. Moira because she took away his inheritance, and he hated her. She says Mr. Ian must have tried to kill Mr. Pembroke for the money. The police are fools not to arrest him, she says. In my opinion, Miss S. wants the killer to be Mr. Ian because it would serve him right for being Daddy's pet. (Muddled thinking!)

I shuffled Serena to the bottom of the pack and came to the notes on Gervase and Ursula. Gervase first:

Mr. Gervase Pembroke (35) lives with Mrs. Ursula at 14 Grant St., Maidenhead, a detached house with a quarter-acre garden in good residential neighbourhood. They have been married for 11 years and have 2 daughters (8 and 6), both attending private school.

Mr. G. is a stockbroker who commutes to the City firm of Wells, Gibson & Cathcart. He has flexible working hours; he's his own boss to a great extent. He used to work harder than he does now and has become erratic of late, according to receptionist. I gathered Mr. G. sometimes returns from lunch the worse for drink, and sometimes doesn't return at all.

I interviewed Mr. G. at his place of work. I said as a preliminary that I understood he was the illegitimate son of Mrs. Alicia Pembroke, and the interview ended immediately. He physically hustled me out (bruise on left arm). I managed to say that if he could produce office records for the Tuesday in question, he would be in the clear. He said to consult his secretary, which I did. Mr. G. went into office that morning, she confirmed, and dictated two letters. Mr. G. told her he was going to see a new client, and left at 10.30 a.m. He didn't return to the office that day. He left the office the previous Friday (secretary's notes) at midday, didn't return.

Mr. G. has a strong, masterful manner, but must have insecurities (illegitimacy??) to make him drink and treat people badly. (My opinion.) No sign of financial straits. Jealous of Mr. Ian. Difficult personality. A bully.

I paperclipped Gervase together with a sigh. Norman West had a way of getting to the heart of things pretty smartly. What had he made of Ursula? I wondered.

Mrs. Ursula Pembroke (35), wife of Mr. Gervase, lives with him at 14 Grant St., Maidenhead. She looks after children and household.

Daughters' school is at the other end of Maidenhead. Mrs. U. shares the school run with a family nearby; Mrs. U's mornings are Tuesday and Thursday; afternoons Mon., Wed. and Fri.

On the Friday of the attack on Mr. Pembroke, the daughters were invited to tea by the other school run family. Mrs. U. left the daughters there after school (4 p.m.). Picked them up about 6.30.

On the following Tuesday, Mrs. U. spent the day in London. She had dinner in a steakhouse and went into a church to pray.

Mrs. U. nervous and evasive about trip to London. Possible (my opinion) that she goes to London to meet someone, doesn't want her husband to know. Who? Lover? Not possible, she hasn't that inner excitement. Priest? Doctor? Some sort of solace, I would say.

Mrs. U. unhappy woman but wouldn't unbutton. Loyal. Any wife of Mr. G. liable to be unhappy (my opinion).

Mrs. U. wishes Mr. Pembroke would give all the family a lot of money now so that they would stop griping about it. She sees nothing wrong in Mr. Ian, but her husband won't let her talk to him. She won't go against her husband. She has no money of her own, I'd say. She's in a trap. (Can't support children herself, couldn't leave without them.)

Poor Mrs. U. Poor Ursula. Could she have blown up Quantum? Perhaps, if she'd wanted to. She sounded desperate enough for anything, but if she had any sense her desperation should drive her to beg from Malcolm, not to kill him.

I clipped Ursula behind Gervase: for ever in his shadow.

I put Gervase and Ursula back in the envelope but had no mental stamina left for the next section on Thomas and Berenice. I ate some pub steak instead, and decided I would see the family in the age-reversed order Norman West had handed me, taking the easy ones first. Where was the bravado that had led me to tell Malcolm at Cambridge that I would stay with him just because it was dangerous?

Somewhere under the rubble of Quantum.

Serena

IN THE MORNING, I rode out on the windy downs, grateful for the simplicity of horses and for the physical pleasure of using one's muscles in the way they were trained for. Vigour seemed to flow in my arms and legs.

I thanked my host sincerely after breakfast and drove towards Quantum, thinking of the telephone call I'd made to Malcolm the evening before. He had arrived safely, he said, and Dave and Sally Cander were true-blue cronies. Ramsey Osborn had flown down. He'd seen some good horses and had some good ideas for spending money (wicked chuckle). How were things in England?

I said things were the same as when he left except that the house was wrapped up in tarpaulins. The state of the house troubled him for roughly ten seconds, and after that he said he and Ramsey might leave Lexington on Tuesday or Wednesday.

"Wherever you go," I said, "will you please give the Canders a telephone number where I can reach you?"

"I promise," he said blithely. "Hurry up and come over. I've got used to you being with me. Keep looking round for you. Must be senile."

"Yes, you sound it."

He laughed. "It's a different world here, and I like it."

He said goodbye and rang off, and I wondered how many horses he would have bought by the time I reached him.

Back at the pub in Cookham I changed out of riding clothes and dutifully telephoned Superintendent Yale. He had nothing to tell me, nor I to tell him: the call was short.

With a heavy lack of enthusiasm I returned to the car and drove to Bracknell. I parked and walked through the High Street to "Deanna's Dance and Aerobics Studio" where I asked the receptionist for Serena, explaining I was her brother.

"Back there," she said. "She's taking a class at the moment."

The studio ran deeply back to end in a wall of windows overlooking a small strip of garden. The floor was of polished wood, sprung somehow so that it almost bounced underfoot. The walls were white except for the long left-hand one, which was entirely of looking glass. The air vibrated with the pulse of music, inviting rhythmic response.

Serena herself danced with her back to the mirror. Facing her, in three spread-out rows, was a collection of female clients, bouncing in unison.

"Great, ladies, that's great," Serena said eventually, switching off the music machine. She gave me an unfriendly glance but turned with radiance back to the customers. "Take a rest, ladies."

The bodies filed, panting, through a door marked "Changing rooms".

Serena said, "What do you want?"

"To talk."

She looked coldly discouraging. She wore a sleeveless black body stocking with white jogging shoes and white legwarmers.

"I'll give you five minutes," she said. She stood with her hands on her skinny black hips and waited.

"Malcolm wants me to find out who bombed Quantum," I said.

She glowered at me. "Well, I didn't."

"Do you remember the day old Fred blew up the tree stumps?"

"No," she said. She hadn't tried to remember.

"Thomas gave you a ride on his shoulders out of the field, and the blast of the explosion knocked old Fred over."

"I don't know what you're talking about."

"Why are you so hostile?"

"I'm not. Where's Daddy?"

"With friends," I said. "It saddens him that you're hostile."

She said bitterly, "That's a laugh. He's rejected all of us except you."

83

"He hasn't rejected you," I said.

"He kicked us all out. I loved him when I was little." Tears appeared suddenly in her eyes and she shook them angrily away. "He couldn't wait to get rid of me."

"He tried to keep you, but Alicia wouldn't have it. She fought him in the courts for custody, and won."

"He didn't want me," she said fiercely. "He only said so to spite Mummy, to make her suffer. I know all about it."

"Alicia told you?"

"Of course she did. Daddy couldn't wait to get rid of us, to . . . to . . . throw everything about us out of the house, to blot us out."

She was deeply passionate, with the old feelings still smouldering after twenty years. I remembered how upset I'd been when Alicia tore out my own mother's kitchen, how I'd felt betrayed and dispossessed. I had been six, as Serena had been, and I still remembered it clearly.

"Give him a chance," I suggested.

"I did give him a chance. I offered to help him after Moira died, and he still didn't want me. And look at the way he's behaving. Throwing money away. If he thinks I care about his stupid scholarships, he's a fool. He can keep his damned money. I can manage without it."

She looked hard-eyed and stubborn. The old man in all of us, I thought.

"You've had your five minutes," she said. She sidestepped me and ran weightlessly out of the studio. It was pointless to pursue her. With leaden spirits I went back to the car and drove to Maidenhead to call on Ursula, knowing Gervase would be at work.

"Oh!" she said faintly when she opened the door to me.

"Where would you like to go for lunch?" I asked, at my most charming.

"Oh." She was irresolute.

"Come on," I said persuasively. "The car's warm."

She left the door, returning minutes later wearing coat and gloves.

"Gervase won't like this," she said.

We got into the car and I drove out of the town towards the village of Bray, and twice more on the way she said, "Gervase won't like this." We stopped at a small restaurant and she chose moussaka, several times looking over her shoulder as if her husband might materialise.

I ordered a carafe of red wine. Not for her, she protested, but when it came she drank it almost absent-mindedly. She had removed the coat and gloves to reveal a well-worn grey skirt topped by a blue sweater. She wore a string of pearls. Her dark hair was held back at one side by a tortoiseshell slide, and there was no lipstick on her pale mouth. The sort of appearance, I supposed, that Gervase demanded.

When the moussaka came I asked, "How do you get on with Alicia?"

She spoke as if picking her way through a minefield. "My mother-in-law," she said intensely, "has caused more trouble than anyone since Eve. She is ruining our marriage, I suppose you know that?"

I murmured an assent.

"I'd known Gervase for only four months when we got married. I didn't realise . . . She's twisted him from birth, hasn't she? With her awful lies and spite. She sets him against you all the time. Gervase says terrible things about you sometimes . . . I mean, violent . . . I hate it. I try to tell him not to, but he doesn't listen to me, he listens to her. She tells him over and over that Malcolm threw them out and never loved them. She's wicked. And look what she's done to Serena. She wants her to be a little girl, not to grow up. It's driving me insane, you know, her drip, drip, drip. She's the worst enemy you'll ever have."

"She wasn't always like that," I said, as she paused. "When she lived at Quantum, she treated me the same as Gervase."

"Then it must have started when Malcolm kept you there on your own, and as she's got older it's got worse. She hated Coochie, you know, and Coochie was nice, wasn't she? But Coochie banned all the family from staying in the house except you, and I think that's when Alicia turned against you. Or let it all out. I bet it was there inside all the time. Like Gervase keeps things in and lets them out violently . . . so does Serena . . . they're all like that."

She stopped abruptly, the raw truth quivering in her voice.

I said, "Is it Alicia that's causing Gervase to drink?"

"Oh!" Ursula gulped, the flow of anger ending, the misery flooding back. "It's just . . . everything. I can see he's unhappy, but he won't let me help him, he won't talk to me, he just talks to *her*, and she makes it worse. Please take me home."

I paid the bill, and we set off on the short road back to Maidenhead.

"I shouldn't have told you all this," Ursula said, when I stopped at her door. "Gervase won't like it."

"Gervase won't know what you've said."

"Thank you for the lunch. Did your mother tell you we've had lunch a few times in London, she and I? She gives me good advice."

I nodded. "Joyce told me you were friends."

"She's awfully catty about Alicia. It cheers me up no end." She gave me a wan smile and got out of the car. I drove away, and covered the few miles to Cookham in a few minutes.

I thought it might be interesting to see what Norman West had made of Alicia, and I searched through the notes until I came to her. West had written:

Mrs. Alicia Pembroke (59) lives at 25 Lions Court, London Road, Windsor, a block of flats. She maintains she can't remember what she was doing on the Friday or the Tuesday: she was pottering about, she says. "One day is much like another." I think she's being obstructive.

Mrs. A. is antagonistic to me personally because of my following her in Mrs. Joyce's divorce case, although in the end she benefited.

I asked her if she had ever hired me to work for her. She said no. (?) Mrs. A. is very bitter on subject of Mr. Pembroke spending money. Mr. Ian's name brought angry looks. Mrs. A. turned me out.

Short and unsweet, I thought.

I couldn't face going to see Alicia at that moment. Anyway, I didn't think her efficient enough to construct a bomb: a good enough reason for avoiding something I wanted to do as much as jump into a crocodile-infested swamp.

I didn't want to talk to Gervase either, but that couldn't be so easily avoided. I drove back to Grant Street in the early evening and parked along the road from No. 14, waiting for the master to return. Soon Gervase's Rover turned into his short driveway. Five minutes later, I walked along the road and rang the bell.

The door was opened by one of the children, who called over her shoulder, "It's Ian."

Gervase, still in his City suit, came immediately into the hall from his sitting room, looking inhospitable and carrying a cut-glass tumbler half filled with what I expected was Scotch.

"You'd better come in, I suppose." He was grudging, but pointed me to the room he'd left. "Do you want a drink?"

"Yes, please."

He poured from the Scotch bottle into a duplicate tumbler, and handed me the glass, gesturing to a jug of water which stood on a silver tray. I diluted my drink, sipped it, and said, "Thanks."

There was no sign of Ursula, but I could hear the two girls' voices in the kitchen and supposed she was with them. They would tell her I had come, and she would be worrying about our lunch.

"Malcolm wants me to find out who's trying to kill him," I began.

"It isn't me," he said belligerently.

"Do you remember old Fred blowing up the tree roots? When the blast blew him flat?"

He stared. "Yes, I do," he said slowly, "but that's years ago. It can't have anything to do with the house."

"Why not?" I asked. "That bang made a big impression on us. Memories last more or less for ever, they just need digging up. The explosives expert working at Quantum asked if I knew what cordite was, and I remembered old Fred."

Gervase did his own digging. "Black powder . . . in a box."

"Yes, it's still there in the toolshed. Still viable, but it hadn't been used on the house. They're working now on its being a homemade explosive called ANFO. Do you know what ANFO is?" I asked

He said no uncertainly, and I thought he wasn't being truthful. Perhaps he felt that knowing could be considered guilty.

"Malcolm's made a new will," I said.

"And left the lot to you, I suppose," he sneered bitterly.

"No," I said. "If he dies from normal causes, we will inherit equally." I paused, and added an invention. "If someone murders him, it all goes to charities."

Ursula

Gervase

He drank. "Where is Malcolm now?"

"Staying with friends."

We were still standing in the centre of the room, as the offer of a drink hadn't extended to a chair also. I looked at Gervase. He was heavyset and, I thought, getting heavier. He was the tallest and biggest of all Malcolm's children and easily the most forceful. He looked a strong, successful man, and he was cracking up for lack of a piece of paper that no one gave a damn about except himself.

Perhaps, I thought, there was something of that obsessiveness in us all. In some it was healthy, in others destructive.

Gervase said, "Will Malcolm advance us anything before he dies?"

His voice was, as usual, loud and domineering, but I looked at him speculatively over my glass. There had been an odd undertone of desperation.

"I did ask him to. He said he would think about it."

"Bloody old fool," Gervase said violently. "He's playing bloody games with us. Buying bloody *horses*. I could strangle him." He stopped as if shocked at what he'd more or less shouted with conviction. "Figure of speech," he said, hard-eyed.

"I'll try again," I said, ignoring it, "but Vivien tried, and rubbed him up the wrong way so that he stuck his toes in. Malcolm's obstinate, the way we all are, and the more anyone tries to push him, the harder he'll resist."

"It's you that got him to buy horses. He wouldn't have thought of it on his own." He was glaring at me.

"He can afford it," I said. "I think he's very rich."

"Think!" Gervase grew even angrier. "How do you know he isn't flinging away every penny? He's *got* to be stopped!"

"When Malcolm fled to Cambridge, did Alicia tell you where he was?"

"I don't know what you're talking about."

"Did you telephone to Malcolm's hotel in Cambridge?"

He hardly listened. He embarked on a tirade. "I'm fed up with your sneers and your airs and graces. You think you're better than me, you always have, and you're *not*. You've always weaselled into Malcolm's good books and set him against us and he's blind about you. Go on, get out of here." He stepped forward threateningly, one hand in a fist.

"Alicia tells you I sneer at you," I said, "but I don't. She tells you lies, you believe them. I've never set Malcolm against you. You hit me now, and I might think of it. If you want me to try to get him to cough up, you'll put that fist down."

After a long staring pause, he turned his back on me.

"Gervase," I said dispassionately, "try a psychiatrist."

"Mind your own bloody business."

I put my glass down. "Goodbye," I said.

He still showed me his back, and was silent. I shrugged and went out into the hall. Ursula and the two girls stood in the kitchen doorway looking anxious. I smiled at them and said to Ursula, "I'll be back," meaning that anything I could do to help her or Gervase, I would do.

Back at Cookham I telephoned the Canders in Lexington. I talked to Sally Cander. Malcolm had gone to Stamford, Connecticut with Ramsey, she said. She thought they were fixing some kind of deal. Yes, of course she had Ramsey's phone number, he was an old friend. She read it out to me. I thanked her and she said to have a nice day.

Ramsey and Malcolm were out. The woman who answered said would I like to leave a message. I asked her tell Mr. Pembroke that his son Ian had phoned, but that there was no special news.

I went to bed and in the morning rode out on the downs, and afterwards, from the house of the trainer whose horses I was riding, got through to Superintendent Yale's police station. He came on the line.

"Where are you?"

"At the moment, in a racing stable near Lambourn."

"And your father?"

"I don't know."

He grunted disbelievingly. "When can you meet me at Quantum?"

I looked at my watch. "In riding clothes," I said, "in forty-five minutes. If you want me to change, add on an hour."

"Come as you are," he said. "Mr. Smith says there's something to see."

Chapter Nine

At Quantum, the heap of rubble had been reduced to merely a mess.

I walked round to the back of the house and found Superintendent Yale standing beside a trestle table that had been erected on the lawn, with Smith standing close beside him. Their heads were bent in conference. I walked over to the two experts and said good morning.

"Good morning," they said, looking up.

Smith picked up an object from the table, holding it out to me. "We've found this," he said. "What do you think?"

I took the thing from him. It had been a coil of thin, white, plastic-coated wire, but the coils had been stretched so that the wire was straighter, though still curled. It was about eighteen inches long. About an inch of bare wire stuck out of the plastic at each end. Onto the plastic, near one end, someone had bonded a hand from a clock. The hand pointed to the bare wire, so that the wire was an extension of the hand.

I looked at it with despair, though not with shock. When I didn't ask what it was, Yale said with awakening suspicion, "Does your silence mean that you know what it is?"

I looked up at the two men. They hadn't expected me to know, were surprised by my reaction, even astonished.

"Yes," I said wearily. "Did you find any other bits?"

Smith pointed to a spot on the table. There were some pieces of metal and a grey plastic disc with a small hole in the centre.

"Was this a clock?" I said dubiously.

"A battery-driven clock," Smith said. "There's the coil from the electric motor." The coil was tiny, about a centimetre in diameter.

"How did you find it in all this rubbish?" I asked.

"We found various remains of the padded box which used to stand at the foot of Mr. Pembroke's bed. These small pieces became embedded in the lid when the box blew apart. The wire with the clock's hand on it, and this"—he picked up the flat plastic disc—"were in the same area." He turned the plastic disc over to reveal a clock face on the other side. "There should also be at least one other piece of wire somewhere, and some of the clock case and a battery or two, but we haven't found those yet. This was not actually an alarm clock, I don't think."

"No, it won't have been an alarm clock," I said.

The superintendent could contain himself no longer. "Will you please explain your familiarity with this device," he said formidably.

"It was a toy, for switching things on. Torch bulbs, mostly. It was incredibly simple."

"Explain," Yale commanded.

"You get an old or cheap clock," I said. "You fix a length of wire to one of the hands, like this, so that a bare bit of wire sticks out and makes the hand much longer."

"The hands are still on the clock, I take it?"

"Oh yes. All you need is for the bare wire to reach out beyond the edge of the clock face. Then you have a long bit of wire coming out from the centre, at the front, and you fasten the free end of that to a battery. One of those nine-volt batteries with things like press-studs at the end."

Yale sighed. "Go on."

"You need two more lengths of wire. One goes from the battery to whatever you want to activate. In our case, usually a torch bulb screwed into a metal holder. Then a third wire links the metal holder to the clock. We'd fix this wire with glue to the clock case itself, not to the hands, in such a way that the bare end of wire was pointing out forwards, towards you if you were facing the clock. Then you wind up the clock and set the hand with the wire where you want it, and just wait. The wired hand travels round towards the jutting-out wire and eventually hits against it at right angles. The circuit is thus complete from the clock wires to the battery to the light and back to the clock, so the light goes on. The clock hand keeps on trying to go round and the jutting wire keeps stopping it, so the light stays on. Well . . ." I finished lamely, "that's what happened when we made them."

"Them?" Yale said with comprehension.

"They were easy to make. I don't know how many we had, but quite a few. There might be one still in the playroom," I said.

Yale looked at me balefully. "How many of your family made these devices?" he asked.

"Everyone."

"And why," he said, "haven't you mentioned this before?"

I sighed. "Because," I said, "I didn't want you to find this. I wanted you to find something sophisticated, that no one in the family could have thought up."

Yale turned to Smith. "Did this toy really set off the bomb?"

Smith nodded. "It sounds just right. If you wire in a detonator instead of a torch bulb . . . it wouldn't need more current than that."

Not surprisingly, they decided to take a look in the playroom. We picked our way cautiously across the ankle-twisting rubble.

I hadn't been in the room at all since the twins had gone, and their playthings had overlaid those outgrown and abandoned by their elder brothers and sisters so that most of what I was looking at was unfamiliar. It took several minutes to locate the box I wanted. I opened it and found the old treasures undisturbed, looking more battered than I'd expected. I lifted out a couple of engines, a signal box and a brown plastic railway station. I suppose to any adult his childhood's rediscovered toys look smaller, deader, less appealing than he remembers.

I took everything out of the box, but there were no clocks.

"Sorry," I said. "They could be in anything. If they're here."

Smith began looking into any box whose contents weren't easily identifiable by the picture on top. I packed the trains back into oblivion with regret.

"Well, just look here," Smith said suddenly. "Gold mine."

He had produced from a jumble of Lego constructions a bright new-looking clock with a Mickey Mouse face. Mickey's hands in fat white gloves were the hands of the clock. To the minute hand was fixed a coil of white, plastic-covered wire. A second white coil was stuck to the scarlet clock casing, its bare end jutting out over noon. When Smith held it up, the white coils stretched down like curling streamers.

"I've never seen that one before," I said.

Smith picked away among the Lego. He rattled around and finally triumphantly produced a red and white Lego tower with a bulb holder lodged inside near the top.

"A lighthouse, wouldn't you say?" he asked, standing it upright.

"Someone must have made this for your twin brothers," Yale said. "Are you sure you never saw it?"

I shook my head. "I didn't live here then, only visited."

"I'll find out who made it," Yale said. "Can you find a box to put it in?"

Smith found him an empty Lego box and into it they packed the bright costar of an act that had brought half the house down. They took the lighthouse too.

As we walked back in the general direction of the trestle table, the superintendent asked me if I now knew who had bombed the house.

"No," I said, "I don't. Do you?"

He wouldn't say he didn't, but he didn't. He picked up the Lego box and marched off. I went on a quick hike round the garden to make sure all was well with the gold, and came upon Arthur Bellbrook digging potatoes within six feet of it. My heart jumped a bit. His was undisturbed.

We exchanged good mornings. He asked what he should do with the potatoes and I told him to take them home. He nodded his thanks. He would dig everything over, he said, ready for winter.

I left him bending again to his task, not sure whether he was a guardian of the gold or a threat to it. Malcolm had a nerve, I thought, hiding his stockpile in that place and seeing Arthur work so close to it day after day.

I drove to the pub in Cookham, took a bath, put on trousers, shirt and jersey and, accompanied by Norman West's notes, went down to the bar for a drink before lunch. I read:

Mr. Thomas Pembroke (39) lives with his wife Berenice at 6 Arden Haciendas, Sonning. Two daughters (9 and 7) at school.

Mr. T. used to work as quantity surveyor for Reading firm of biscuit makers, Shuttleworth Digby Ltd. He got sacked for wrong estimates several weeks ago. I was told unofficially at the firm that he'd cost them thousands by ordering six times the glacé cherries needed for a run of "dotted pinks". (Had to laugh!)

Mr. T. didn't tell his wife he'd lost his job, but went off as if to work every day. (Common reaction.) On Newmarket Sales Tuesday, he was "walking about", same as the previous Friday. Pressed, he says he probably went to the public library in Reading. He did that most days. He read the job pages in newspapers, but apparently did little to find work.

Mr. T. on brink of nervous breakdown (my opinion). I interviewed him in coffee shop. His hands trembled half the time.

Mr. T's opinion of Mr. Ian is very muddled (like the rest of him). Mr. Ian is "best of bunch, really", but also Mr. T. says Mr. Ian is Mr. Pembroke's favourite and it isn't fair.

With a sigh, I put Thomas back and started to read about Berenice:

Mrs. Berenice Pembroke (44 according to Mrs. Joyce), wife of Mr. Thomas, lives at 6 Arden Haciendas. Housewife.

Mrs. B. very hard to interview. First visit, nothing. Second visit, a little, not much. She couldn't produce alibi for either day. I asked about children and school journeys. Mrs. B. doesn't drive them, they go by bus. Mrs. B's mother lives on the bus route, and most afternoons the girls get off and go to their grandmother's for tea.

Interviewed Mrs. B's mother. Not helpful. Agreed girls go there most days. Sometimes (if cold, wet or dark) she drives them home at about 7 pm. Other days, they finish journey by bus. I asked why they go there for tea so often and stay so late. Told to mind my own business. Mrs. B. gave no opinion of Mr. Ian when asked, but looked as if she could spit. Says Mr. Pembroke is wicked. Mrs. B. slammed her front door (she hadn't asked me in!).

I put Berenice, too, back in the packet, and cheered myself up just a fraction with a slice of pork pie and a game of darts.

FROM THE OUTSIDE, Arden Haciendas were dreadful: tiny houses of dark brown-red brick set at odd angles to each other, with dark-framed windows at odd heights. Nevertheless, Arden Haciendas, as Joyce had informed me a year earlier when Thomas had moved there, were socially the "in" thing, as they had won a prize for the architect.

God help architecture, I thought, ringing the bell of No. 6. I hadn't been to Thomas's house before.

Berenice opened the door and, with ill grace, let me in.

Inside, the Haciendas were open-plan, with rooms at odd angles to each other. The front door led into an angled offshoot of the main room, which had no ceiling, but soared to the rafters. Windows one couldn't see out of let daylight in at random points in the walls. Horrible, I thought, but that was only, as Mr. West would say, my opinion.

Thomas rose to his feet from a heavily stuffed armchair. "Come in, old chap," he said.

Thomas was looking haggard and I was shocked. I hadn't seen him, I realised, for quite a long time. I thought of him as he had been at eighteen or nineteen, laughing and good-humoured, coming for week-ends and making Serena giggle. Now, he looked middle-aged, the head balder, the ginger moustache less well tended, the desperation all-pervading. Norman West's assessment of early breakdown seemed conservative. It looked to me as if it had already happened.

Gervase, he said, had rung to tell him about Malcolm's will and about Malcolm's wish that I should try to find out who wanted to kill him. Thomas couldn't help, he said. I reminded him of the day old Fred blew up the tree stump. Gervase had mentioned that too, he said. He remembered it clearly. He had carried Serena on his shoulders.

"And do you remember the timeswitches we used to make, with wire on the clocks' hands?"

He stared, his eyes gaunt. After a long pause, he said, "Yes."

"Did you make any more of them?"

Berenice interrupted. "Dear Thomas couldn't make a timeswitch to save his life, could you, darling?" Her voice was pitying, sneering, unkind. Thomas sent her a haunted look but no protest.

"In the rubble at Quantum, they've found a clock hand stuck onto some white plastic-covered wire. So," I said, "someone who knew how to make these timeswitches blew up Quantum."

"Oh, my God," Thomas said miserably.

"What of it?" Berenice said. "I can't see Thomas doing it. Not enough nerve, have you, darling?"

Thomas said to me, "Have a drink?"

Berenice looked disconcerted. Asking me to have a drink had been, for Thomas, an act of rebellion. I accepted with thanks, although it was barely five thirty and to my mind too early.

Thomas squeaked across the woodblock floor to the kitchen, which was divided from the main room only by a waist-high counter, and began opening cupboards. He produced three tumblers and then sought in the fridge interminably for mixers. Berenice watched him, her face screwed into an expression of long-suffering impatience. "Dear Thomas couldn't find a book in a library."

Thomas gave her a look of black enmity which she either didn't see or

93

chose to ignore. He opened another cupboard, and another, and finally found a bottle of Gordon's gin. He came round into the main room and poured from the bottle into three glasses, topping up with tonic.

He handed me a glass and held out the second to Berenice.

"I don't want any," she said.

Thomas's hand was trembling. He made an awkward motion as if to raise the glass to his own lips, then put it down with a bang on the counter, and accidentally knocked the gin bottle over. It fell to the floor, smashing into green shiny pieces, the liquid spreading in a pool.

Thomas bent down to pick up the bits. Berenice didn't help.

"Thomas can't get anything right, can you, darling?" The acid sarcasm in her voice had gone beyond scathing to unbearable.

Thomas straightened, with a face filled with passionate hatred, the worm turning at last, and by the neck he held the top part of the green bottle, the broken edges jagged as teeth. Berenice, cushioned in complacency, wasn't even looking at him and did not understand her danger. Malcolm said I had fast reactions . . . I dropped my own drink, grasped Berenice by both arms and swung her violently round and out of the slicing track of the razor-sharp weapon. She was furiously indignant, sprawling across the floor where I'd almost thrown her, still unaware of what had been happening.

Thomas dropped the fearsome bottle and stumbled off blindly towards his front door. I took two strides and caught him by the arm.

"Let me go . . ." He struggled, and I held on. "Let me go . . . I can't do anything . . . she's right."

"She's bloody wrong." I was stronger than he. I practically dragged him across the room and flung him into one of the armchairs.

"I've cut you," he said.

"Yes, well, never mind. You both listen to me. You're over the edge. You're going to have to face some straight facts."

Berenice had finally realised how close she'd come to needing stitches. She looked at my left shoulder where jersey and shirt had been ripped away and a couple of cuts were bleeding. She turned to Thomas with a bitterly accusing face and opened her mouth.

"Shut up," I said roughly. "If you're going to complain that he could have cut you, yes he could, he was trying to. Sit down and *shut up*."

She sat down weakly, her hair awry, eyes shocked.

"You goaded him too far. Don't you understand what you've been doing to him? Putting him down, picking him to pieces every time you open your mouth? You have now completely succeeded. He can't function any more."

I turned to Thomas. "And it's not all her fault. You've let her do it. You should have stopped her years ago. You've been loyal to her beyond reason and she's driven you to want to kill her."

94

Thomas put a hand over his eyes. "I didn't mean it," he mumbled. He put his head in his hands.

I went over to him. "Come on. There's still life ahead."

Without looking up, he said in a dull sort of agony, "It's too late."

Then the front door opened with a bang to let in the two girls.

"Hello," they said noisily, bringing in swirls of outside air. "Granny turned us out early. What's going on? What's all this glass on the floor? What's all that blood on your arm?"

Thomas

Berenice

"A bottle got broken," I said, "and I fell on it."

The younger one looked at the bowed head of her father, and in a voice that was a devastating mimicry of her mother's, vibrating with contempt, she said, "I'll bet it was Dear Thomas who broke it."

Berenice heard for herself what she'd been doing to her husband. Heard what she was implanting in her own children. The revelation seemed to overwhelm her, and she sought for excuses.

"I wanted a son," she said flatly. "Thomas got a vasectomy. He said two children were enough, we couldn't afford any more. It wasn't fair. Malcolm should have given us more money. *I always wanted a son.*"

Dear God, I thought: flat simple words at the absolute heart of things, the disappointment that she had allowed to poison their lives. Just like Gervase, I thought. So much unhappiness from wanting the unobtainable, so much self-damage. There was nothing to say. It was too late.

I went across to Thomas and touched him on the shoulder. He stood up. He didn't look at his family, or at me. I put my hand lightly under his elbow and steered him to the front door, and in unbroken silence we left the wasteland of his marriage.

I TOOK THOMAS to Lucy's house. It seemed to me, as I drove away from the pretentious Haciendas, that Lucy's particular brand of peace might be just what Thomas needed.

Lucy was in, to my relief, and opened the front door of the farm cottage where she and Edwin led the simple life near Marlow.

She stared at us. At my red arm. At Thomas's hanging head.

"Sister, dear," I said cheerfully, "two brothers needing succour come knocking at the gate. Any chance of hot sweet tea?"

Lucy

Edwin

Lucy glanced swiftly at my face, then took Thomas by the arm and led him into her book-filled sitting room. The cottage consisted of two downstairs rooms which had been partly knocked into one. The stairs, which were hidden behind a latched door, led up to three rooms where one had to inch round the beds, bending one's head so as not to knock it on the eaves. Laura Ashley wallpaper everywhere covered uneven old plaster, and rag rugs provided warmth underfoot. Lucy's home was unselfconscious, not folksy. Lucy herself, large in dark trousers and thick hand-knitted sweater, sat Thomas in an armchair and in a very short time thrust a mug of hot liquid into his unwilling hand.

"Drink it, Thomas," I said. "How about some gin in it?" I asked Lucy.

"It's in. Do you want some yourself?" she asked.

"Just with milk." I followed her into the kitchen.

"What's all this about?" she said.

"The last straw," I said, "has just broken Thomas. He's left Berenice. If someone doesn't treat him kindly, he'll end up in the nuthouse or the suicide statistics and I am not, repeat not, joking. He's in need of a bed."

"All right, he can stay here," she said.

She went back to the sitting room, and I followed. Edwin had appeared now, and had taken the second armchair. Lucy lowered her bulk onto a leather stool beside Thomas, which left no other seats. Resignedly I sat on the floor and rested my back against a wall.

"As I'm here," I said, "I may as well ask the questions I was going to come and ask tomorrow. It's about the timing device that set off the bomb at Quantum."

Thomas stirred. "I made it, you know. The Mickey Mouse clock."

It was the first time he'd spoken since we'd left his house. Lucy looked as if she thought him delirious.

"Do you remember those clocks?" I asked her.

"Of course I do. Thomas made one for our son. Did the Mickey Mouse clock explode. . . ?"

"No," I said. "The one actually used had a grey plastic dial with white numbers. The Mickey Mouse clock was intact, in the playroom."

Thomas said dully, "I haven't made one for years."

96

"When did you make the Mickey Mouse for Robin and Peter?"

"I didn't make it for them. I made it a long time ago for Serena. She must have given it to them."

"You were a nice boy, Thomas," Lucy said. "Funny and kind."

Edwin said restlessly, "I would have thought any timing device would have been blown to unrecognisable fragments by such a big bomb."

"It seems they often find pieces," I said.

"It serves Malcolm right the house was blown up," Edwin said with barely suppressed violence. "Flinging money about on scholarships. Keeping us poor. I suppose *you're* all right, aren't you?" There was a sneer there for me, openly. "He's never been fair to Lucy."

"Is that the authentic voice of Vivien?" I asked.

"It's the truth!"

"No," I said. "It's what you have been told over and over again, but it's not the truth. Most people believe a lie if they're told it often enough."

Lucy looked at me intently. "You care about this, don't you?"

"About being cast perpetually as the family villain? Yes, I dare say I do. But I was thinking also of Thomas. He's been told ad infinitum that he's useless, and now he believes it. I'm going now, Lucy." I stood up. "You tell Thomas that he's a worthwhile person, and maybe he'll begin to believe that instead."

"Yes," she said quietly, "I will."

I DROVE BACK to Reading, stopping at the hospital to have my shoulder and upper arm cleaned and stitched. There were three cuts, it seemed, variously deep, but with stitches they would heal quickly. The staff advised painkillers pro tem. I thanked them and eventually drove to Cookham feeling tired, but chiefly hungry, and having remedied both conditions satisfactorily, set off again next morning to ride.

Restored yet again in spirit by the dose of fresh air, I took a lazy day off from the emotional battering of the family and went to London to get my American visa. I bought a new sweater and had my hair cut and then went unhurriedly back to Cookham and in the evening bent again to Norman West's notes. Of Edwin, he had said:

Mr. Edwin Pembroke (53), né Bugg, lives with his wife Lucy in No. 3 Wrothsay Farm Cottages, near Marlow. One son (15) attends state school.

Mr. E. does the housework (not much) and shopping. He spends hours reading in public library (librarians agree). Goes to pub, spends more hours over one beer (barman indignant). Takes laundry to launderette. Listens to radio. Spends hours doing crossword puzzles.

Mr. E. good-looking man, complete drone (my opinion). Idle life suits him. Mr. E. has sharp sarcastic manner on occasions. Detests Mr. Ian, curses Mr. Pembroke but at same time wants money from him(!). Definitely thinks of Mr. Pembroke's money too much, broods on it, talked about it all the time.

Of Lucy, among other things, he had written:

Mrs. L. spends large parts of the day unaware of what's going on around her (my opinion). I had to repeat several questions. She listens to things going on in her own head (can't put it very well). Has no alibis for Friday or Tuesday. Can't remember where she was. (I believe it.) Goes for rambling walks. Mrs. L. very troubled over something, but wouldn't say what.

So much for Lucy and Edwin, I thought. What about Donald and Helen?

Mr. Donald Pembroke (44), eldest of Mr. Pembroke's offspring, lives at Marblehill House, detached chalet-style house which goes with his job, Secretary, Marblehill Golf Club, near Henley-on-Thames.

Mr. D. oversees and runs the whole place, is said to be good at it, members like him. Mr. D. likes his work. His social standing extremely important to him (my opinion). Keeps up appearances.

As to the Friday and Tuesday in question: no alibis ascertainable. Is always "round the place", never anywhere at set hours except first thing in the mornings (9 a.m.) to see to post with office staff. Has Mondays off, works Saturdays and Sundays.

Walks to work (barely 100 yds). Usually returns home at 7 p.m. (much earlier in winter), sometimes stays until bar closes.

Mr. D. has daughter at art school, high fees. Also twin sons who have started this term at Eton (how does he afford it?).

Mr. D. thinks it's very bad news Mr. Ian is back in Mr. Pembroke's favour. Certain to mean less inheritance for him (Mr. D.). Thinks Mr. Pembroke's recent expenditure unreasonable, "insane"(!). Says he's senile.

Mr. D. gave me rapid answers; busy. Says his financial affairs were none of my business, edgy on subject. Is he in debt? (My opinion, considering his expenses, probably.) Champagne lifestyle.

And Helen?

Mrs. Helen Pembroke (43), wife of Mr. D. Very good-looking lady. Very worried, wouldn't say what about.

Mrs. H. works at home painting views of Henley by hand onto plates, jugs, boxes; all china. Very quick, very good (to my eyes), nice pictures. Reasonably paid, she says. (What's reasonable?)

Mrs. H. works alone nearly every day, no alibis for Friday

or for Tuesday. Sometimes she drives into Henley to shop.

Mrs. H. ultraloyal to Mr. D. Says it's ridiculous to suppose Mr. D. would attack his father. Out of the question. (My opinion, she wasn't too sure.) They need more cash badly.

ON THURSDAY MORNING, I called in on a public library and looked up "explosives" in encyclopedias. Ammonium nitrate was there, also the proportion of fertiliser to diesel oil needed, also the formula for relating volume to kilos. The knowledge was freely available.

After lunch I went to the Marblehill Golf Club and found Donald in the clubroom. "Go over to the house," he said when he saw me. "I can't talk here." I did what I was told, like a good little brother.

Helen was resigned rather than annoyed to see me. "Gervase said you would come, and we had the police here yesterday. Not that we could tell them anything, or you either."

She was wearing a painter's smock over jeans and looked as though dressed by Dior. She took me into the sitting room and pointed to a chair, and with unconscious grace sat herself half on a polished table.

Donald came bustling in, telling me he could give me ten minutes.

"What did the police ask you?" I said.

"About Fred blowing up the tree stump. I said yes, of course we'd been there. Helen and I weren't married then. It was the first time she'd met Malcolm, she was staying the weekend."

"And the timeswitch clocks, do you remember those?" I asked.

"Naturally," Donald said.

Helen added, "Thomas made two for our boys for their birthday once, when they could just tell the time."

"Where's Malcolm?" Donald asked brusquely.

"I don't know."

"You're lying," he said, but for once I wasn't. Malcolm and Ramsey Osborn had left the Osborn residence, according to the female voice on the line the evening before, and had given her no number at which they could be reached. I could try again tomorrow, she said. Mr. Osborn should have let her know by then; he usually did.

"Did either of you," I asked, "trace Malcolm to Cambridge the weekend he was put in the car?"

I hadn't expected any answer but negative, but the question came at them unexpectedly and Helen practically jumped.

"Did you?" I said to her.

"No, of course not," Donald said quickly.

"The hotel at Cambridge said three people—two men and a woman—had asked if Malcolm was staying there," I said. "One was Norman West, who were the others? I'm not saying you went to Newmarket Sales, just did one of you trace Malcolm?"

Helen

Donald

They looked at me glumly. Then Helen said, "I suppose so."

"Why?" I asked.

Donald cleared his throat. "I needed his signature on a guarantee for a temporary bank loan."

"Go on, what guarantee?"

"We had to have the money in a hurry," Helen said. "The bank manager told Donald we could borrow it if Malcolm would guarantee it. Then we couldn't get hold of Malcolm. We had to think where he might be, and he's always going to Cambridge. Donald and I just talked about it, guessing, wondering . . . And then, well, while Donald was over at the club house I picked up the AA book and tried two hotels in Cambridge, and he was there, at the second. When Donald came home I told him and the extraordinary thing was, he'd had the same idea and got the same result." She paused. "We were pretty desperate, you see."

"Don't say that," Donald said. "Desperate gives the wrong picture."

"What did you need the money for?" I asked.

They looked at each other, foreheads wrinkled in worry. Finally, reluctantly, but as if coming to a decision, Donald said, "We had some interest to pay unexpectedly. I had negotiated three months' deferment of interest on a loan, or at least I thought I had, and then I got a threatening demand. I had to pay at once or they'd start proceedings." The desperation he said wasn't there definitely had been; it still echoed in his voice. "I couldn't have it getting around the golf club, could I?" he demanded. "No one in the family could lend me a large sum in a hurry. Our ordinary bank overdraft is always at maximum. The finance company was inflexible. I knew Malcolm wouldn't *give* me the money, he has those stupid warped views, but I did think he might guarantee . . . just for a short while . . ."

"But when you'd found him, you didn't get in touch with him?"

"No," Donald said. "I didn't relish telling Malcolm our troubles and Helen thought of a different way out."

I looked at her enquiringly. "Popped my baubles," she said with a brave attempt at lightness. "All my lovely rocks."

"Pawned them?" I said.

"We'll get them back," she said valiantly.

"What day did you pop them?"

"Wednesday. Donald took the money in cash to the finance company, and that gives us a three-months' breather."

Wednesday, I thought. The day after someone had failed to kill Malcolm at Newmarket. I left Donald and Helen among their antique furniture and behind their shaky facade.

Next morning, after a rejuvenating ride, I went along to Quantum to see how things were developing. Not fast, was the answer. The place was abandoned except for a solitary policeman sitting in a police car outside what had been the front door.

The policeman picked up his car radio and spoke into it to the effect that Mr. Ian Pembroke had turned up. A request came back, which he relayed to me: would Mr. Pembroke please drop in at the police station when he left? Mr. Pembroke would. I walked back to my car.

SUPERINTENDENT YALE shook my hand. Enquiries into who planted the bomb were proceeding, he said. "We interviewed the former gardener, Fred Perkins. We asked him about the tree stump and what he used to blow it up. Besides cordite, that is. What sort of a fuse."

I was interested. "What did he say? Does he remember?"

"He said he'd got the black powder and some detonators and some fuse cord from a quarryman friend of his. The black powder was in the box which we saw, the detonators were in a separate tin with the cord and the instructions."

"The instructions!" I repeated incredulously.

"Yes." He sighed. "We asked him what he'd done with the other detonators. He says Mr. Pembroke took them away from him that morning, when he came running out of the house. We need to ask Mr. Pembroke what he did with them, so . . . er . . . where is he?"

"I really don't know," I said slowly, "and that's the truth. I can find him, but it'll take a day or two." I thought for a moment, then said, "But would detonators still detonate after twenty years?"

"Mr. Smith thinks it possible, perhaps likely."

"What does a detonator look like?" I asked.

He hesitated, but said, "Mr. Smith said we might be looking for a small aluminium tube about the thickness of a pencil or slightly less, about six centimetres long. He says the tube contains fulminate of mercury, and the word 'fulminate' means to flash like lightning."

I reflected. "Did Mr. Smith find out exactly what the Quantum bomb was made of?"

"Yes. ANFO, as he thought. He said the whole thing was amateur in the extreme."

"Amateurs," I said drily, "run faster than anyone else."

As an amateur, I went to Kempton Park the next day and on Young Higgins I beat the hell out of a lot of professionals.

I didn't know what possessed me. It seemed that I was riding on a different plane. Young Higgins appeared inspired, and against more formidable opponents than at Sandown produced a totally different race.

I'd ridden against an all-professional field of top jockeys a few times before, and it was usually a humbling experience. I had the basic skills and a good deal of touch; I could get horses settled and balanced; I liked speed, I liked the stretch of one's spirit: but there was always a point, against top professionals, at which that wasn't enough. George and Jo were unfussed. "We didn't want to change you for a professional," they said in explanation. "It wouldn't have been fair." Maybe not fair, but prudent, I thought.

Perhaps because of the insights and realities I'd faced in a traumatic week, perhaps because of Young Higgins himself, I rode with a new sharp perception of what was needed for winning, and the horse and I came home in front by four lengths to a fairly stunned silence from the people on the stands who'd backed everything else on the card but us.

George and Jo were ecstatic. Young Higgins tossed his head at the modest plaudits. A newspaperman labelled the result a fluke.

I'd cracked it, I thought. That had been real professional riding. Satisfactory. But I was already thirty-three. I'd discovered far too late the difference between enjoyment and fire. I'd needed to know it at nineteen or twenty. I'd idled it away.

"This is no time," Jo said, laughing, "to look sad."

Chapter Ten

I flew to New York two days later, still not knowing where to find Malcolm. The voice at Stamford, Connecticut, still helpful but uninformed, had thought, the previous evening, that the gentlemen might have gone back to Kentucky: they'd been talking of buying a horse that they'd seen there a week earlier; she would tell them where I was.

Superintendent Yale didn't know I'd left England, nor did any of the family. I sighed with deep relief on the aeroplane and thought about the visits I'd made the day before to Alicia and Vivien. Neither had wanted to see me and both had been abrasive.

Alicia's flat outside Windsor was spacious and overlooked the Thames. She had let me in reluctantly. She was looking youthfully pretty in a white wool dress. Her hair was pulled high in a velvet bow on the crown of her head, and her neat figure spoke of luck or dieting.

"You might have said you were coming," she complained. "Gervase said you would, some time. I told him to tell you not to."

"It seemed best to see everyone," I said neutrally.

"Then hurry up," she said. "I'm going out to lunch."

"Did Gervase tell you about Malcolm's new will?"

"He did, and I don't believe a word of it. You've always been Malcolm's wretched little pet. He should have sent you back to Joyce when I left. I told him to. But would he listen? No, he wouldn't."

"That was twenty years ago," I protested.

"And nothing's changed. He's utterly selfish."

I asked her if she remembered the tree stump. "Of course. I was furious with Malcolm for letting Fred do anything so ridiculous."

And did she remember the switches? How could she forget them, she said, they'd been all over the house. Those clocks had all been a pest.

"You were good to me in those old days," I said.

She stared. There was almost a softening round her eyes, but it was transitory. "I had to be," she said acidly, "Malcolm insisted."

I asked her if she had engaged Norman West to find Malcolm in Cambridge. She looked at me with wide empty eyes and said blandly, "No, I didn't. Why would I want to? I didn't care where he was."

"Almost everyone wanted to find him, to stop him spending his money."

"He's insane," she said. "Paranoid." She turned away from me restlessly. "It's high time you went."

I thought so too.

If my visit to Alicia had been unfruitful, my call on Vivien was even more so. Norman West's notes had been minimal: name, address, no alibis. She wouldn't answer any of my questions or discuss any possibilities. She said several times that Malcolm was a fiend who was determined to destroy his children, and that I was the devil incarnate helping him. She hoped we would both rot in hell.

Meanwhile, I said, had she employed Norman West to find Malcolm in Cambridge? Certainly not. She wanted nothing to do with that terrible little man.

"It can't be much fun," I said, "living with so much hatred."

She was affronted. "What do you mean?"

"No peace. All anger. Very exhausting. Bad for your health."

"Go away," she said, and I obliged her.

I SPENT FOUR NIGHTS in New York before I found Malcolm; or before he found me, to be more precise. In daily consultations the Stamford voice assured me that I wasn't forgotten, that the message would one day get through. I had a vision of native bearers beating through jungles, but it wasn't like that, it transpired. Malcolm and Ramsey had simply been moving from horse farm to horse farm through deepest Kentucky, and it was from there he finally phoned at eight in the morning.

"What are you doing in New York?" he demanded.

"Looking at skyscrapers," I said.

"I thought we were meeting in California."

"Well, we are," I said. "When? I need to talk to you."

"Did you find something out?" His voice suddenly changed gear, as if he'd remembered almost with shock the world of terrors he'd left behind.

"A few things."

"Tell me."

"Not on the telephone. I'll meet you at the Beverly Wilshire, tomorrow."

He was quiet for a few moments, then he said, "I'll be there."

I arranged my air ticket and spent the rest of the day as I'd spent all the others in New York, wandering around, filling eyes and ears with the city, thinking painful thoughts and coming to dreadful conclusions.

MALCOLM KEPT HIS WORD and, to my relief, came without Ramsey. He was crackling with energy, the eyes intensely blue. He and Ramsey had bought four more horses in partnership, he said in the first three minutes. Like a forest fire out of control, I thought.

The Beverly Wilshire gave us a suite with brilliant red flocked wallpaper in the sitting room and vivid pink and orange flowers on a turquoise background in the bedrooms.

We dined downstairs in a bar.

"Tell me about the horses," I said; and heard about them through the smoked salmon, the salad, the veal and the coffee.

"Don't worry," he said, near the beginning, "they're not all as expensive as Blue Clancy and Chrysos. We got all four for under a million dollars, total, and they're two-year-olds ready to run. Good breeding; the best. One's by Alidar, even."

I listened, amused and impressed. He knew the breeding of all his purchases back three generations, and phrases like "won a stakes race" and "his dam's already produced Group One winners" came off his tongue as if he'd been saying them all his life.

"Do you mind if I ask you something?" I said eventually.

"I won't know until you ask."

"No . . . um . . . just how rich *are* you?"

"Hm." He thought. "I can't tell you to the nearest million. It changes every day. But at a rough estimate, I should say about a hundred million pounds. It would grow now of its own accord at the rate of five million a year if I never lifted a finger again."

"Did you think any more of letting the family have some of the lucre before you . . . er . . . pop off?"

"You know my views on that."

"Yes, I do."

"And you don't approve."

"I don't disapprove in theory. The trust funds were generous when they were set up. But your children aren't perfect and some of them have got into a mess. If someone were bleeding, would you buy them a bandage?"

He sat back in his chair and stared moodily at his coffee.

"Have they sent you here to plead for them?" he asked.

"No. I'll tell you what's been happening. You can do what you like."

"Fair enough," he said, "but not tonight."

"All right." I paused. "I won a race at Kempton, did you know?"

"Did you really?" He was instantly asking for every detail. He didn't want to hear about his squabbling family with its latent murderer. He was tired of being vilified while at the same time badgered to be bountiful. He felt safe in California although he had, I'd been interested to discover, signed us into the hotel as Watson and Watson.

"Well, you never know, do you?" he'd said. "It may say in the British papers that Blue Clancy's coming over, and Ramsey says this hotel is the centre for the Breeders' Cup organisers. By Wednesday, he says, this place will be teeming with the international racing crowd. So where, if someone wanted to find me, do you think they'd look first?"

THE WATSONS, FATHER AND SON, breakfasted the following morning by the pool, watching the oranges ripen amid dark green leaves. I gradually told Malcolm what was happening in the family, never pressing, never too much at one time, stopping at once if he started showing impatience.

I asked him casually if he remembered Fred and the tree roots.

"Of course I do," he said at once. "He could have killed himself." He frowned. "What's that got to do with the bomb at Quantum?"

"Superintendent Yale thinks it may have given someone the idea."

He considered it. "I suppose it might."

"The police asked old Fred what he'd used to set off the cordite, and Fred said he had some detonators, but after that first bang, you came out and took them away."

"Good Lord, I'd forgotten that. Yes, so I did."

"The superintendent wonders if you remember what happened to the detonators after you'd taken them away."

He stared. "It's twenty years ago, must be," he protested.

"Do you remember what they looked like?" I asked.

"Well, yes, I suppose so." He frowned, thinking, pouring out more coffee. "There was a row of them in a tin, laid out carefully in cotton wool. Small tubes, about two and a half inches long."

"You did realise they were dangerous, didn't you?"

"I probably did, but all those years ago ordinary people didn't know much about bombs, I mean, not terrorist bombs. We'd been bombed from the air, but that was different." He buttered a piece of croissant, added marmalade and ate it.

"If you imagine yourself going into the house with this tin of detonators, where would you be likely to put it? You'd put it where you would think of looking for it first, wouldn't you?"

"Yes," he nodded, "always my system." A faraway unfocused look appeared in his eyes, then he suddenly sat bolt upright.

"I know where they are! I saw the tin not so very long ago, when I was looking for something else. I didn't pay much attention. It's a sort of sweet tin, not very big, with a picture on top."

"Where was it?"

"In the office. On top of some of the books in the breakfront bookcase. Bottom row, more or less out of sight when the door's closed. On top of the Dickens." His face suddenly split into a huge grin. "I remember I put it there because the picture on the tin was 'The Old Curiosity Shop'."

I rubbed my hand over my face, trying not to laugh. Superintendent Yale was going to love it.

"They're safe enough there," Malcolm said reasonably, "behind glass. I mean, no one can pick them up accidentally, can they?"

FROM THAT QUIET SUNDAY morning until Wednesday, Malcolm and I led the same remote existence, being driven round Los Angeles and Hollywood and Beverly Hills in a stretch limousine Malcolm seemed to have hired by the yard, neck-twisting like tourists, dining in restaurants like Le Chardonnay, going out to Santa Anita racetrack in the afternoon.

Malcolm looked out of the long car's window as we were driven up through the hills of Bel Air on the way to the racetrack. He liked it immediately and so did I; it would have been difficult not to. Royal palms near the entrance stretched a hundred feet upwards, all bare trunks except for the crowning tufts, green fronds against the blue sky. The buildings were towered and turreted, sea-green in colour, with a metal tracery of stylised palm leaves along the balconies and golden shutters over rear-facing windows. It looked more like a château than a racecourse, at first sight.

Ramsey Osborn had given Malcolm fistfuls of introductions and, as always, he was welcomed as a kindred spirit upstairs in the club. He was at home from the first minute, as if he'd been born there. I envied him his ease and didn't know how to acquire it. Maybe time would do it. Maybe millions. Maybe a sense of achievement.

While he talked easily to almost-strangers (soon to be cronies) about the mixing of European and American bloodlines in thoroughbreds, I thought of the phone call I'd made at dawn on Monday morning to Superintendent Yale. Because of the eight-hour time difference, it was already afternoon with him.

"Where are you?" he asked with unstifled annoyance.

"Around," I said. His voice sounded as clear to me as if he were in the next room, and presumably mine to him, as he didn't at all guess I wasn't in England.

I told him where Malcolm had stored the detonators. "On top of *The Old Curiosity Shop*, as appropriate."

There was a shattered silence. "I don't believe it," he said. "Are you saying that anyone who borrowed a book from that bookcase could have seen the detonators?"

"Yes, I suppose so, if they've been there for twenty years."

"It is incredible that when someone thought of making a bomb, the detonators were to hand," Yale complained.

"Other way round, wouldn't you think?" I said. "The availability of the detonators suggested the bomb."

"The pool of common knowledge in your family is infuriating," he said. "No one can be proved to have special access to explosives. No one has a reliable alibi. Everyone can make a timing device and nearly all of you have a motive."

"Irritating," I agreed.

"That's the wrong word," he said sourly, and hung up.

Malcolm said, on one of our car journeys, after I'd been telling him about Berenice, "Vivien, you know, had this thing about sons."

"But she had a boy first. She had two."

"Yes, but before Donald was born, she said she wouldn't look at the baby if it was a girl. I couldn't understand it. Vivien's self-esteem utterly depended on having a boy. She was obsessed with it. You'd have thought she'd come from some tribe where it really mattered."

"It did matter," I said. "And it matters to Berenice. All obsessions matter, because of their results."

"Vivien never loved Lucy, you know," he said thoughtfully. "She shoved her away from her. I always thought that was why Lucy got fat and retreated into poetic fantasies."

"Berenice shoves off her daughters onto her mother as much as she can."

"Do you think Berenice murdered Moira?" he said doubtfully.

"I think she thinks that having more money would make her happier, which it probably would. If you were going to think of any . . . er . . . distribution, I'd give it to the wives as well as the husbands. Separately, I mean. So they had an independence."

"Why?" he said.

"Gervase might value Ursula more if she didn't need him financially."

"Ursula's a mouse."

"She's desperate."

"They're all desperate," he said with irritation. "It's all their own faults.

107

The fault, dear Brutus, is not in our stars but in ourselves, that we are underlings."

"I dare say," I said.

"The bell captain at the hotel gave me a tip for the fourth race."

Back to horses.

Another day, on another journey, Malcolm said, "What did Serena say, when you saw her?"

"She said you could stuff your money, or words to that effect. She also said that Alicia told her you'd only tried to get custody of her so as to be cruel to Alicia."

"Alicia's a real bitch."

Further down the road we were talking about the timeswitch clocks, which had been an unwelcome piece of news to him also.

"Thomas was best at making them, wasn't he?" Malcolm said. "He could do them in a jiffy. Serena brought one over for Robin and Peter which Thomas had made for her years ago."

I nodded. "A Mickey Mouse clock. It's still there in the playroom. I saw it."

"Serena made them a lighthouse of Lego to go with it, I remember."

On another day, I asked why Gervase minded being illegitimate to the brink of a breakdown.

"I don't know," Malcolm said. "Gervase always thinks people are sneering, even now. Someone rubbed his nose in it when he was young, you know. Told him he was rubbish. Boys can be so cruel. Gervase got aggressive to compensate, I suppose, and Ursula's no help."

He paused and looked at me speculatively. "Why don't you get married?" he asked.

I was flippant. "Haven't met the one and only. Don't want five."

"Don't you trust yourself?" he said.

That was sharp, I thought. That was unfair. It was because of him that I didn't trust myself: because in inconstancy, I felt I was very much his son. His imprint, for better or worse, was on us all.

ON WEDNESDAY, the Beverly Wilshire came alive as Ramsey had prophesied and Ramsey himself blew in with gusto and plans. We would go to parties. We would go round the horse barns. We would go to a Hollywood Gala Ball.

The Breeders' Cup organisers opened their reception room where everyone concerned with the races could have breakfast and cocktails (together if they liked) and talk about horses with the people they'd met at Epsom and Longchamp. Big bucks, big business, big fun.

Malcolm adored it. So did I. Life in high gear. Early on Friday, we went out to the racecourse to see Blue Clancy breeze round the track in his last warm-up before the big one. He looked fine, worked well, threw

Malcolm and Ramsey into back-slapping ecstasies. "Wait until to-morrow," the trainer said cautiously. "We're taking on the best in the world, don't forget. The hot money is for a California-bred horse."

"What's hot money?" Malcolm demanded.

"The bets made by people in the know. The people who have inside information."

Who cared? Malcolm said. He couldn't remember ever having more fun in his life: and I thought his euphoria was at least partly due to his three close approaches to losing it.

Along with a thousand others, we went to the ball, though in the stretch limo, not a pumpkin, and Malcolm danced with several ladies he'd known well for two days. He spent his time laughing. It was infectious. Everyone round him lit up like nightlights, banishing gloom.

We slept, we ate breakfast, we went to the races. There were seven Breeders' Cup races; various distances, variously aged horses. The first five each offered a total purse (for first, second, third and so on) of one million dollars. Blue Clancy's race, the one-and-a-half-mile Turf, had a purse of two million, and the climactic event, the Breeders' Cup Classic, promised three. The owner of the winner of Blue Clancy's race would be personally richer by six hundred and twenty-nine thousand dollars, enough to keep him in Bollinger for weeks.

We cheered home the first five winners. We went down to the saddling stalls and saw Blue Clancy prepared. We went up to the stands and bit our nails.

Five of the seven races were run on the dirt track, two on grass, of which this was the second; and most of the European horses were running on grass, the green stuff of home. Blue Clancy was taking on the Epsom Derby winner, the Arc de Triomphe winner and the winner of the Italian Derby. On paper, he looked to have an outside chance of coming fourth. In Malcolm's and Ramsey's eyes, he was a shoo-in. (Malcolm had learned the local jargon. It meant a sure-fire winner.)

Blue Clancy broke cleanly from the gate away on the far side of the course and his English jockey held him handily in sixth place. Ramsey and Malcolm were looking through binoculars and muttering encourage-ments. Blue Clancy, not hearing them, swung into the long left-hand bottom bend lying sixth as they turned for home. Malcolm's muttering grew louder. "Come on, come on."

There was no clear leader. Three horses raced together in front, followed by a pair together, then Blue Clancy. Too much to do, I thought: and the colt immediately proved me wrong. His jockey swung him wide of the others to allow him a clear run and gave him unmistakable signals that now was the time that mattered, now, this half-minute.

Blue Clancy accelerated. Malcolm was shouting, Ramsey was speech-

less. Blue Clancy in third place, all the crowds roaring. Blue Clancy still faster, second now. Malcolm silent, mouth open, eyes staring. The incredible was happening, awesome, breathtaking . . . and Blue Clancy had definitely, indubitably, won.

Malcolm's eyes were like sapphires lit from inside. He still couldn't speak. Ramsey grabbed him by the arm and pulled him, and the two of them ran, almost dancing, making their way down to greet their champion's return. I followed close on their heels, marvelling. Some owners were always lucky, some owners always weren't; it was an inexplicable fact of racing life. Malcolm's luck was stupendous. It always had been, in everything except wives. Blue Clancy was his latest gold.

I wondered ironically what the family would say. The fortune he'd flung away on horses had already come back: Blue Clancy was worth at least double what he'd been before the Arc.

Chrysos, I daydreamed, would win the Derby. The tadpole film (about sharks actually, Malcolm had told me) would win at Cannes. The Pol Roger would appreciate. Everyone would see the point of not murdering the golden goose. (Wrong sex, never mind. It was a light-headed day.) We could return home to welcomes and safety.

110

Only it wasn't like that. We would return home to an unassessable danger, and it was essential to be aware of it, and to plan.

I had searched for the solution that would cause us least grief. There was no truly easy way out. No overlooking or dodging what had been done to Moira. But if someone could plead guilty, and plead diminished responsibility owing to stress, there might be a quiet trial and a lifetime for us of visiting some sort of hospital instead of a prison. Either way, there were tears in our future.

On top of that I had to be right, and I had to convince Malcolm beyond any doubt that I was. Had to convince all the family, and the police, without any mistake. Had to find a way of doing it that was peaceful and simple, for all our sakes.

Sobered by what lay ahead, I nevertheless went to a post-race party in fine spirits. At the end of the evening, Malcolm and Ramsey slapped each other on the back, shook hands and promised like blood brothers to meet regularly on every major racecourse in the world. From cronies they had become comfortable friends, neither feeling at an advantage over the other.

When Ramsey had departed in the morning and left us alone, Malcolm looked at me as if coming down to earth for the first time since he'd left

England. With a touch of despondency, he asked for how long he was to be exiled for safety's sake.

"But you've enjoyed it," I said.

"God, yes." The remembrance flashed in his eyes. "But it's not real life. We have to go back. I know I've avoided talking about it, it's all so dreadful. I know you've been thinking about it all this time. I could see it in your face."

"I've come to know them all so much better," I said, "my brothers and sisters. I didn't care for them all that much, you know, before Moira died. We've met from time to time, but I'd forgotten to a great extent what we had been like as children."

I paused for a bit, but he didn't comment. "Since the bomb went off at Quantum," I said, "a great deal of the past has come back. And I've seen, you know, how the present has grown out of that past. How people easily believe lies, old and new. How destructive it is to yearn for the unobtainable, to be unsatisfied by anything else. How obsessions don't go away, they get worse."

He was silent for a while, then said, "Bleak." Then he sighed and said, "How much do they need, then? How much should I give them? I don't believe in it, but I see it's necessary. If the money wasn't there, they'd have sorted themselves out better. Is that what you're saying?"

"Yes, partly." It hadn't been, entirely, but as it had produced the reaction I'd wanted but hadn't expected, I kept quiet.

"All right, then," he said. "Draw up a list of who's to get what."

"All equal," I said.

He began to protest, but sighed instead. "What about you, then? I thought you wanted half a million to set up as a trainer."

"I've changed my mind. There's something else I want to do first."

"What's that?"

I hesitated. I'd barely admitted it to myself, had certainly told no one else. "Be a jockey. Turn professional."

"Good Lord," he said, astonished, "haven't you left it too late?"

"Maybe. We'll see. I'll have three or four years, perhaps. Better than not trying."

"You amaze me." He reflected. "Come to think of it, you've constantly amazed me ever since you came to Newmarket Sales. It seems I hardly knew you before."

"That's how I feel about you," I said, "and about all of the family."

WE SET OFF HOMEWARDS four days later, Malcolm studying gold prices and sleeping intermittently on the plane.

I thought meantime about invitations. About invitations like meat over bear-pits. The right invitation would bring the right visitor. The problem was how to make the invitation believable.

Part of the trouble was time. Would a trap work after all these weeks? Only one thing to do: try it and see.

I would need someone to deliver the invitation. Couldn't do it myself.

I knew the perfect person.

MALCOLM AND I went back to the Ritz as Mr. and Mr. Watson and he promised with the utmost sincerity that he wouldn't telephone anyone, not even his London broker. On Friday I went shopping in the afternoon and then confounded him at the brandy-and-cigar stage late that evening by getting through to Joyce.

"But you said . . ." he hissed as he heard her voice jump as usual out of the receiver.

"Listen," I hissed back. "Hello, Joyce."

"Darling! Where are you? Where's your father?"

"In Australia," I lied.

"*What?*" she yelled.

"Looking at gold mines," I said.

It made sense to her, as it would make sense to them all.

"He went to California, I saw it in the paper," she said. "Blue Clancy won a race."

"He went on to Australia afterwards."

"Darling, where are *you* now?"

"It doesn't matter where I am," I said. "To make it safe for Malcolm to come home, will you help me find out who killed Moira?"

"But darling, the police have been trying for weeks . . . and anyway, Gervase says it has to be Arthur Bellbrook."

"It's not Arthur Bellbrook," I said.

"Why not?" She sounded argumentative, still wanting it to be Arthur, wanting it to be the intruder from outside.

I said, "Arthur wouldn't have made a timing device exactly like we made as children, and he didn't have a motive."

"You've got an answer for everything," she complained.

I had myself for a while wished it to be Arthur. After all, there had been the affair of the prize vegetables, and he'd been in the army and might know about explosives. But he stood to lose rather than gain from Malcolm's death, and it was beyond believing that he would trace Malcolm to Cambridge, follow him to Newmarket Sales and try to run him down. That was the work of obsession.

Besides, whoever had tried to run Malcolm down at Newmarket had guessed he would leave the sales with me and would come to the car park, and at that point Arthur didn't know me. Hadn't met me until he came into the house with his shotgun, thinking I was a burglar.

Joyce said, "Darling, how do you expect to succeed where the police have failed?"

"The police can't do what we can do."

"What do you mean? What can we do?"

I told her. Malcolm's mouth opened and there was a long silence from Joyce.

"Let me get this straight," she said eventually. "You want me to telephone everyone in the family . . ."

"*Everyone*," I said emphatically. "If a husband answers, tell him, then ask to speak to the wife, and tell her too. And vice versa."

"Yes," she said. "I'm to say you're both in Australia. Right?"

"Yes."

"I'm to gush. Dreadful word, where *did* you learn it? I'm to let all this slip out as if it were of absolutely no importance. Darling, you can't mean I have to ring up *Alicia?*"

"Especially Alicia. And . . . er . . . do you know if the police are still guarding Quantum?"

"They told Donald that if he wanted constant guards, he'd have to get his own now. No one in the family wants to spend the money, so the police just have it on occasional surveillance."

"And has anything else happened in the family since we've been away?"

"No, nothing new. Thomas left Berenice, did you know that?"

"Yes . . . Is he still with Lucy?"

"Yes, darling, I think so. Do you want me to tell him too?"

"You might as well."

"I'm to phone them and gossip a bit, and then I'm to say that I don't really care who killed Moira, but I don't think the police were thorough. Is that right? They never thought of looking for her notepad, the one she used to keep in the kitchen. When anyone telephoned when she was in the kitchen, which was a lot of the time, she doodled their name with stars and things round it, and wrote notes like 'Donald, Sunday, noon' when people were coming to visit. I'm to say I've just remembered it, and I wonder if it's still there. I'm thinking of telling the police about it after the weekend. Is that right?"

"That's right," I said.

"And I'm to say, what if she wrote down the name of her murderer?"

"Yes," I said.

"But why, darling? Why do you think the killer telephoned?"

"Because Malcolm told me she didn't like people just dropping in," I said. "She preferred people to telephone first. And because Moira's greenhouse can't be seen from the drive. If anyone had come to see Moira unannounced that evening, they'd have found the house empty. If they'd telephoned first, she'd have said to come round to the greenhouse, that's where she'd be."

"I suppose that's logical, darling. The police always did say she knew her killer. All right then, darling. You want me to start those phone calls tomorrow but definitely not before ten o'clock, and to go on until I've reached everyone?"

"Just keep plugging along."

"What if they're out, or away?"

"Same thing. If nothing happens and we get no results, I'll phone you on Monday evening."

"Was that old bugger in good nick when you last saw him?"

"In excellent nick," I said.

"Can't help being fond of him, darling, but don't bloody tell him I said so. If there's one thing I regret in my life it's getting that frightful man West to catch him with Alicia. If I'd had any bloody *sense*, darling, I'd have turned a blind eye and let him have his bit on the side. But there it is, I was too young to know any better."

She said goodbye cheerfully, promising to do all the phone calls in the morning, and I put the receiver down slowly.

"Did you hear any of that last bit?" I asked Malcolm.

"Not a lot. Something about if she'd had any sense, she wouldn't have done something or other."

"Wouldn't have divorced you," I said.

He stared incredulously. "She insisted on it."

"Twenty-seven years later, she's changed her mind."

He laughed. "Poor old Joyce." He spent no more thought on it. "Moira didn't doodle on notepads that I know of."

"I dare say not. But if you were a murderer, would you count on it?"

He imagined it briefly. "I'd be very worried to hear from Joyce. I would think long and hard about going to Quantum to search for the notepad before she told the police."

"And would you go?"

"Yes. If it turned out to be a silly trap of Joyce's, I could say I'd just come to see how the house was doing." He looked at me questioningly. "Are we both going down there?"

"Yes, but not until morning. I'm jet-lagged. Don't know about you, I need a good sleep."

He nodded. "Same for me. And that shopping you were doing?" He eyed the several Fortnum and Mason carrier bags with tall parcels inside. "Essential supplies?"

"Everything I could think of. We'll go down by train and . . ."

He waved his cigar in a negative gesture. "Car and chauffeur." He fished out his diary with the phone numbers.

ACCORDINGLY, WE WENT DOWN in the morning in great comfort and approached Quantum circumspectly from the far side, not past the eyes of the village. The chauffeur goggled a bit at the sight of the house, with

115

its missing centre section and boarded-up windows and large new sign saying: "Keep out. Building unsafe".

"Reconstructions," Malcolm said.

The chauffeur nodded and left, and we carried the Fortnum and Mason bags across the windy central expanse and down the passage towards the playroom.

Black plastic sheeting still covered all the exposed floor space, and the boarded-up doors and the barred stairs looked desolate. Far above, over the roof, a second black plastic sheet flapped like a sail between the rafters.

Sad, sad house. Malcolm hadn't seen it like that, and was deeply depressed. He looked at the very solid job the police had made of hammering the plywood to the door frame of the playroom and asked me politely how I proposed to get in.

I produced a few tools from one of the bags. "There are other shops in Piccadilly," I said. "Boy scouts come prepared." I'd brought a hammer and chisel and a saw, and before Malcolm's astonished gaze proceeded to cut a head-high, body-wide, hole through the plywood.

"You didn't think of all this since yesterday, did you?" he asked.

"No. On the plane. There were a lot of hours then."

I freed the cut-out section and put it to one side, and we went into the playroom.

It was by that time nine thirty. If Joyce by any chance phoned the right person first, the earliest we could have a visitor was about half past ten. After that, anything was possible. Or nothing.

Malcolm had wanted to know what we would do if someone came.

"All the family have keys to the outside kitchen door," I said. "We never had the locks changed, remember? Our visitor will go into the kitchen that way and we will go round and . . . er . . ."

"Lock him in," Malcolm said.

I produced from the bags two stick-on mirrors, each about eight inches by ten.

"I thought you'd brought champagne," Malcolm grumbled. "Not saws and bloody looking glasses."

"The champagne's there. No ice."

"It's cold enough without any bloody ice." He wandered aimlessly round the playroom, finally slumping into an armchair. We had both worn the warmest clothes we possessed, but the raw November air felt as if it would be a match for the Simpson's vicuna overcoat and my new Barbour.

I stuck one of the mirrors onto the cut-out piece of plywood, and the other onto the wall which faced the playroom door, at the same height, not exactly opposite the door but a little further along the hall.

"What are you doing?" Malcolm asked.

"Just making it possible for us to see anyone coming up the drive without showing outselves. Would you mind sitting in the other chair, and telling me when the mirrors are at the right angle?"

He rose and sat in the other chair as I'd asked, and I moved the plywood along and angled it slightly until he said, "Stop. That's it. I can see a good patch of drive."

By eleven, Malcolm was bored. By twelve, we were into Bollinger in disposable glasses (disgusting, Malcolm said) and at twelve thirty we ate biscuits and pâté.

No one came. It seemed to get colder. Malcolm said it had been a rotten idea in the first place.

He said, "This person we're waiting for, you know who it is, don't you?"

"Well . . . I think so."

"How sure are you, expressed as a percentage?"

"Um . . . ninety-five."

"That's not enough."

"No, that's why we're here."

Time crept on. By two thirty, to stoke our internal fires, we were eating rich dark fruit cake and drinking claret. (Heresy, Malcolm said. We should have had the claret with the pâté and the champagne with the cake. As at weddings? I asked. God damn you, he said.)

I didn't feel much like laughing. It was a vigil to which there could be no good end. Malcolm knew as well as I did that he might be going to learn something he fervently didn't want to know. He didn't, deep down, want anyone to come.

"Joyce may have forgotten the phone calls," Malcolm said.

"She wouldn't forget."

A light-coloured car rolled up the drive, suddenly there.

No attempt at concealment. No creeping about, looking suspicious. All confidence. Not a thought given to entrapment.

I sat still, breathing deeply.

She stood up out of the car. She went round to the passenger side, opened the door and lifted out a brown cardboard box which she held as one holds groceries. I'd expected her to go straight round to the kitchen door, but she didn't do that, she walked a few steps into the central chasm, looking up and around her as if with awe.

Malcolm noticed my extreme concentration, rose to his feet and put himself between me and the mirrors so that he could see what I was looking at. I thought he would be stunned and miserably silent, but he was not in the least.

"Oh, no," he said with annoyance. "What's *she* doing here?"

Before I could stop him, he shot straight out of the playroom and said, "Serena, do go away, you're spoiling the whole thing."

I was on his heels, furious with him. Serena whirled round when she heard his voice. She saw him appear in the passage. I glimpsed her face, wide-eyed and scared. She took a step backwards, tripped on a fold of the black plastic floor covering and let go of the box. She tried to catch it . . . touched it . . . knocked it forward.

I saw the panic on her face. I had an instantaneous understanding of what she'd brought.

I yanked Malcolm back with an arm round his neck, twisting and flinging us both to find shelter behind the wall of the staircase.

We were both still falling when the world blew apart.

Chapter Eleven

I lay short of the playroom door trying to breathe. My lungs felt collapsed. My head rang from the appalling noise, and the smell of the explosive remained as a taste, as if my mouth were full of it.

The house was still standing. We weren't under tons of new rubble. The tough old load-bearing walls that had survived the first bomb had survived the second.

My chest gave a heave and breath came back. I moved, struggled to get up, tried things out. I felt bruised and unwell, but there were no broken bones; no blood. I rolled to my knees and went on them to Malcolm. He was alive, he was breathing.

I got slowly, weakly, to my feet, and walked shakily into the wide centre space. At the point where the bomb had exploded, the black floor covering had been ripped right away, and the rest was doubled over and convoluted in large torn pieces. Serena—the things that had been Serena—lay among and half under the black folds of plastic: things in emerald and frilly white clothes, pale-blue legwarmers, scarlet splashes . . .

I went round covering what I could with the black folds, hiding the harrowing truth from anyone coming there unprepared. I felt ill. I was trembling uncontrollably.

Malcolm groaned in the passage. I went back to him fast. He was trying to sit up. There was already a swelling on his forehead.

"God," he said in anguish. "Serena . . . oh dear God."

I helped him to his groggy feet and took him out into the garden through the side door, and round to the front of the house. I eased him into the passenger seat of Serena's car.

Malcolm put his head in his hands and wept for his daughter. I stood with my arms on the top of the car and my head on them, and felt wretched and sick. I'd hardly begun to wonder what to do next when a police car came into the drive and rolled tentatively towards us.

"Someone in the village reported another explosion . . ." The policeman looked from us to the house questioningly.

"Don't go in there," I said. "Get word to the superintendent. Another bomb has gone off here, and this time someone's been killed."

DREADFUL DAYS FOLLOWED, full of questions, formalities, explanations, regrets. Malcolm and I went back to the Ritz, where he grieved for the lost child who had tried so hard to kill him.

"But you said . . . she didn't care about my money. *Why* . . . why did she do it all?"

"To put it at its simplest," I said, "I think she wanted to live at Quantum with you. That's what she'd longed for since she was six, when Alicia took her away. She wanted to have back what had been wrenched away from her. I saw her cry about it, not long ago. It was still sharp and real to her."

He was listening with wide eyes, as if seeing familiar country haunted by devils.

"Alicia was no help to her," I said. "She filled her with stories of how you'd rejected her, and she actively discouraged her from maturing, because of her own little-girl act."

"Poor Serena." He looked tormented. "But Moira. . . ?"

"I think Serena made herself believe that if she got rid of Moira, you would go back to Quantum and she would live there with you and look after you, and her dream would come true."

"It doesn't make sense . . ."

"Murder has nothing to do with sense. It has to do with obsession. With compulsion, irresistible impulse. An act beyond reason. After Moira was out of the way, Serena offered to live with you at Quantum and look after you, but you wouldn't have it."

He shook his head helplessly. "She kept on about it. Asked me several times. Came to Quantum to beg me. I got tired of it and said 'No' pretty definitely. I told her not to keep bothering me . . ." He looked shattered. "She began to hate me then, do you think?"

I nodded unhappily. "I think she finally believed she would never have what she craved for. You could have given it to her, and you wouldn't. The rejection was ultimate. She told me she'd given you a chance, but you'd turned her down."

He put a hand over his eyes.

"So she set out to kill you, and finally to kill the house as well . . . to destroy what she couldn't have."

I still wondered, as I'd wondered in New York, whether it was because I, Ian, had gone back to live at Quantum with Malcolm that she'd come to that great violent protest. The bomb had been meant as much for me as for Malcolm, I thought.

119

"Do you remember that morning when she found we weren't dead?" I asked. "She practically fainted. Everyone supposed it was from relief, but I'll bet it wasn't. She'd tried three times to kill you and you were still alive."

"She must have been . . . well . . . insane."

Obsessed, insane. Sometimes there wasn't much difference.

"You knew it was Serena who would come."

"If anyone did."

"How did you know?"

"I saw everyone, as you know. I saw what's wrong with their lives. Saw their desperations. Donald and Helen are desperate for money, but they were coping the best way they could, pawning her jewellery. They thought you might help them by guaranteeing a loan. That's a long way from wanting to kill you."

Malcolm nodded.

"Lucy," I said, "may have lost her inspiration but not her marbles. Edwin is petulant but not a planner, not dynamic. Thomas . . ." I paused. "Thomas was absolutely desperate, but for peace in his house, not for the money itself."

"Go on," Malcolm said.

"Berenice is obsessed with herself and her desires, but her grudge is against Thomas. Money would make her quieter, but it's not money she really wants, it's a son."

"And Gervase?"

"He's destroying himself. It takes all his energies. He hasn't enough left to go round killing people for money. He's lost his nerve. He drinks. You have to be courageous and sober to mess with explosives. Ursula's desperation takes her to churches and to lunches with Joyce."

He grunted in his throat, not quite a chuckle.

"It couldn't have been Alicia or Vivien, they're not strong enough to carry you. And I couldn't imagine them constructing a bomb."

"So did you come to Serena just by elimination?" he asked.

"No," I said slowly. "To begin with, when Moira died, I thought, like everyone else did, that she was killed to stop her taking half your money. I thought the attacks on you were for money, too. It was the obvious thing. And then, when I'd seen them all, when I understood all their turmoils, I began to wonder whether the money really mattered at all . . . And when I was in New York, I was thinking of them all again but taking the money out . . . and with Serena everything fitted."

"It wouldn't have convinced the police," he said.

"Nor you either," I agreed. "You had to see for yourself."

We fell silent, thinking of what in fact he had seen, his daughter come to blast out the kitchen rather than search it for a notepad.

"But didn't you have any proof?" he said eventually.

"Not really. Except that I think it was Serena who got Norman West to find you in Cambridge, not Alicia, as West himself thought."

He stared. "Why do you think that?"

"Do you remember the tape from my telephone answering machine? Do you remember Serena's voice? 'Mummy wants to know where Daddy is.' Alicia told me positively that she herself hadn't wanted to know where you were. It was *Serena* who wanted to know, because she'd lost us after failing to run you over."

"I suppose Serena did sound like Alicia on the telephone. I sometimes thought it was Alicia, when she phoned. Breathless and girlish. You know. Norman West just got it wrong."

"She did call herself Mrs. Pembroke," I pointed out. "Just to confuse matters."

He was quiet for a while. "Although it was terrible yesterday, it was the best thing, really. We'll grieve and get over this. She couldn't have borne to be locked up, could she, not with all that energy . . ."

ON THAT SUNDAY MORNING also, we began telephoning to the family to tell them what had happened. We left a lot of stunned silences behind us. A lot of unstoppable tears. They all asked where we were: Joyce had told them we were in Australia. In London, we said, but didn't add where. Malcolm said he couldn't face having them all descend on him before he was ready. By the end I was dropping with fatigue and Malcolm had finished off half a bottle of Scotch. Long before bedtime, we were asleep.

WE WENT TO SEE Superintendent Yale on Monday. He shook hands. He offered sympathy. He asked if we knew why Serena had gone to Quantum with a second bomb, if we knew why she should have killed Moira and tried to kill Malcolm. We told him my theories.

"There will be an inquest," he said. "The coroner's verdict will be death by misadventure, I've no doubt." He paused. "Yesterday, we went to Miss Pembroke's flat and conducted a search. We found a few items of interest."

He reached into a carton which stood on his desk, and brought out a pile of twenty or thirty exercise books with spiral bindings and blue covers and after that a tin large enough to contain a pound of sweets, with a picture on top.

"The Old Curiosity Shop," Malcolm said sadly.

"Are there any detonators in it?" I asked.

"No, just cotton wool. Mr. Smith wonders if she used more than one detonator for each bomb, just to make sure. He says amateurs are mad enough to try anything."

I picked up one of the notebooks and opened it. In Serena's looping handwriting, I read: Daddy and I had such fun in the garden this

121

morning. We were teaching the dogs to fetch sticks. We picked a lot of beautiful daffodils and when we went indoors I put them all in vases in all the rooms. In the afternoon, we went down to the stream and picked some watercress for tea. Daddy took his socks off and rolled up his trousers and the boys—*no the boys weren't there I won't have them in my stories* . . .

I flicked through the pages. The whole book was full. Speechlessly I handed it to Malcolm.

"All the notebooks are like that," Yale said. "She's been writing them for years, I would say. Compulsive writing, I believe it's called."

Malcolm, plainly moved, flicking over pages, said, "She says I bought her a pretty red dress . . . a white sweater . . . a bright yellow leotard—I hardly know what a leotard is. Poor girl. Poor girl."

"She bought them all herself," I said. "Three or four times a week, sometimes."

Yale tilted the stack of notebooks up, brought out the bottom one and handed it to me. "This is the latest. It changes at the end."

I turned to the last entries in the book and with sorrow read: *I don't want Daddy any more. I think perhaps I will kill him. It isn't so difficult. I've done it before.*

There was a space on the page after that, and then, lower down:
Ian is at Quantum with Daddy. I can't bear it.

After a space, she had written my name again in capitals—IAN—and surrounded it with a circle of lines radiating outwards: an explosion with my name in the centre.

That was the end. The rest of the notebook was empty.

Malcolm sighed deeply. "Can I have them?" he said to Yale. "You don't need them, do you? There won't be a trial."

Yale saw no reason to retain them. He pushed the pile of books towards Malcolm and put the sweet tin on top.

"And the lighthouse and clock," I said, "could we have those?"

He produced the Lego box from a cupboard, wrote a list of what we were taking on an official-looking receipt and got Malcolm to sign it.

We took the sad trophies back to the Ritz, and that afternoon Malcolm wrote and posted cheques that would solve every financial problem in the Pembrokes' repertoire.

"What about the witches?" he said. "If Helen and that dreadful Edwin, and Berenice and Ursula are all having their own share, what about those other three?"

"Up to you," I said. "They're your wives."

"*Ex*-wives." He shrugged, and wrote cheques for them also. "Easy come, easy go," he said. "Bloody Alicia doesn't deserve it."

He wrote a final cheque and gave it to me. I felt awkward taking it.

"You should have double," he said.

ON TUESDAY, because I wished it, we went to see Robin. On the way we stopped to buy toys and chocolate and a packet of balloons.

I took with us the Lego lighthouse and the Mickey Mouse clock, over which Malcolm shook his head. "He won't be able to make them work, you know."

"He might remember them. They used to be his and Peter's, after all. Serena gave them the clock and made them the lighthouse."

Robin looked at us searchingly, trying to remember us and never quite getting there.

We gave him the new toys which he looked at, and after a while I opened the Lego box and brought out the old ones.

He looked at them for only a moment and then went on a long wander round and round the room. Then he came to me, pointed at the packet of balloons and made a puffing noise.

"Good Lord," Malcolm said.

I opened the packet and blew up several balloons, tying knots in the necks, as I always did. Robin went on making puffing noises until I'd blown up every balloon in the packet. His face looked agitated.

When they were all scattered round the room, bobbing about in stray air currents, shiny and festive, he went round bursting them with furious vigour, letting out the anger he couldn't express.

After this ritual, he went over to the table, picked up the lighthouse, pulled it roughly apart into four or five pieces. Then he picked up the clock and with violence yanked the wires off, including the Mickey Mouse hands.

Malcolm was aghast. Robin's rage shouted out of his mute body.

He took the clock in his hand and walked round the room smashing it against the wall at each step. Step, *smash*, step, *smash*, step, *smash*.

"Stop him," Malcolm said in distress.

"No . . . he's talking," I said. "He's telling us . . ."

Robin started shouting, roaring without words, his voice rough from disuse and hoarse with the change taking place, from boy into man. The sound seemed to excite him until his body was reverberating, pouring out sound, the dam of silence swept away. "Aaah . . . aaah . . . aaah . . ." and then real words, "No . . . No . . .No . . . Serena . . . No . . . Serena . . . No . . . Serena . . . No . . ." He shouted to the skies, to the fates, to the wicked unfairness of the fog in his brain. Shouted in fury and frenzy, on and on until he became mindless, without meaning, just words.

I stepped close beside him in the end and yelled in his ear, "Serena's dead."

He stopped shouting immediately. "Serena's dead," I repeated. "Like the clock. Smashed. Finished. Dead."

He looked at me vaguely, his mouth open, no sound coming out, the sudden silence as unnerving as the shouting had been.

"He doesn't understand," Malcolm said; and Robin went away and sat in a corner with his arms round his knees and began rocking.

"The nurses think he understands quite a lot," I said. "Whether he understands that Serena is dead, I don't know. But at least we've tried to tell him." Robin went on rocking as if we weren't there.

"What does it matter?" Malcolm said helplessly.

"It matters because if he does understand, it may give him rest. I brought the lighthouse and the clock because I wondered if Robin remembered anything at all. I thought it worth trying . . . didn't expect quite these results . . . but I think he smashed the clock Serena gave him because it reminded him of her, because she gave it to him and Peter shortly before the car crash. Somewhere in that woolly head, things sometimes connect."

Malcolm nodded, puzzled and instinctively alarmed.

"One could almost think it was that afternoon," I said, "seeing the twins happy at Quantum where she hungered to be, seeing you there with them, loving them; perhaps it was that afternoon which finally tipped her over into the insanity of trying to make her fantasy come true. It didn't come true . . . you met Moira . . . but I'm certain she tried."

Malcolm was staring, saying, "No! Don't say it! *Don't!*"

I said it anyway. "I think Robin saw the hit-and-run driver who forced their car off the road. In whatever mangled dreamlike way, he knows who it was. No, Serena, no, Serena, no . . . You heard him. I've thought ever since New York that it could have happened that way. Serena's obsession was full-blown a long time ago, long before she got rid of Moira. I think she killed Peter . . . and Coochie."

Epilogue

We all went back to Quantum a year later for the Grand Reopening Ceremony, the house bedecked with garlands and champagne corks popping.

After much soul-searching, Malcolm had decided to rebuild. Without Quantum as its centre, the family would have fallen apart, and he didn't want that to happen.

The rancour level lessened dramatically after the arrival of the cheques and the production of his will for inspection, and I was suddenly not everyone's villain, though still and for ever Alicia's. Malcolm, having deleted Serena by codicil, sent his will to the central probate office for registration and let everyone know it.

Malcolm still felt that he had pampered and corrupted his children, but he had to admit they were happier because of it. Everyone's life had settled into a new pattern.

Malcolm had been to the Arc again, and round the world with Ramsey Osborn. Chrysos had won the Futurity at Doncaster and was tipped for next year's Derby. Blue Clancy had gone to stud, syndicated for millions.

I had turned professional and ended my first racing season with a respectable score, and at the start of my second had become the chief retained jockey for my stable. I would be a trainer in the end, I supposed. Meantime I felt alive and fulfilled as never before.

Lucy and Edwin were still in the cottage. Lucy, coming to terms with not writing more poetry herself, had started on a scholarly commentary on the life and work of T. S. Eliot. Edwin was still doing the shopping.

Donald and Helen, whose problems had all been financial, wandered round the garden like lovers.

Gervase and Ursula were contented. I had been to see them soon after Serena's death. The change in Ursula, who let me in, was like unwrapping a brown paper parcel and finding Christmas inside. The old skirt, pullover and pearls had vanished. She wore narrow scarlet trousers, a huge white sweater and a baroque gold chain. She smiled at me like a shy conspirator and came with me into the sitting room. Gervase, if not overpoweringly friendly, seemed ready for a truce.

"I told Gervase," Ursula said sweetly, "that now that I can afford to leave him and take the girls with me, I'm staying because I want to, not because I have to. I'm staying as long as he gets help with this ridiculous fixation about his birth. Who *cares* that Malcolm wasn't married to Alicia at the time? I certainly don't. No one does."

Gervase, who in the past would have shouted her down, listened almost with gratitude. The bear that had run itself into a thicket was being led out by compassionate hands.

Thomas and Berenice had been seeing a marriage guidance counsellor. In Berenice, the fire had gone out: in Thomas, it had been faintly rekindled. No longer needing a job, he was learning to play golf.

Alicia came looking girlish, trilling away in a voice like an echo of Serena's, and everyone made polite remarks to her with gritted teeth.

Vivien complained that Malcolm had redone the house too much in Coochie's taste. Joyce made diplomatic friends with the married couple he had engaged to look after him.

All of the grandchildren were there, re-exploring the place: children's voices again in the garden. Robin, far away, had fallen silent once more and had never since that violent day wanted me to blow up balloons.

Malcolm and I walked out through the new sitting room windows and from the lawn looked up at the house. It felt whole again, not just physically, but at peace.

"I don't feel Serena's here, do you?" Malcolm said.

"No, she isn't."

"I was afraid she might be. I'm glad she's not." We went further down the lawn. "I sold the gold."

I glanced at him quizzically.

"The price rose sharply this year, as I thought it would. I took the profit. There's nothing in the wall now except spiders and dust."

"Never mind."

"I'm leaving the clause in the will though." The family had been curious about his leaving me the piece of wire, and he'd refused to explain. "I'll buy more gold, and sell it. Buy and sell. Forwards and backwards. One of these days . . ." his blue eyes gleamed " . . . you may win on the nod."

DICK FRANCIS

From being a champion jockey, Dick Francis has become one of the world's bestselling thriller writers. But how does writing thrillers compare with winning races? "Once I led an easy life," Dick Francis answers. "Went to work at noon and left at four. Spent about twenty minutes a day in gainful employment, the rest in gossip. Basic routine for a steeplechase jockey. Then, thirty years ago, a pen was pushed into my surprised hand, almost by accident. That pen persists there today, a tyrant forcing me to work ninety-hour weeks.

"I still think winning a race was terrific, but maybe in the next one I went end over end and all the satisfaction was gone. Writing gives me much more long-lasting satisfaction."

Even though Dick Francis finds writing hard work, he does enjoy it enormously and usually writes a book a year. *Hot Money* is his twenty-sixth novel. He got the idea for Malcolm Pembroke, a character who is always wheeling and dealing, from a number of parties he has attended near his home in Florida. Many of the guests are gold traders and financial speculators who "live in a fascinating world of their own", and he simply amalgamated them into one colourful personality. He also had help in his research on home-made explosives from his son, who is a physics teacher.

Dick Francis became a professional jockey after World War II and his career was meteoric. He became champion jockey at thirty-three, and retired three years later after suffering numerous injuries. Many people remember his famous Grand National ride on the Queen Mother's horse, Devon Loch, when the horse fell for no apparent reason close to the winning post.

But Dick Francis knows that the pen is mightier than the saddle. "Lots and lots more people know me now as a writer than ever did as a jockey. If I hadn't written my books, then someone might say, 'Dick Francis? Oh, he's the chap who didn't win the Grand National'. But I think, that if someone mentioned my name now, they'd say, 'Ah yes, that's the fellow who writes books.'"

Memoirs of an Invisible Man

A CONDENSATION OF THE BOOK BY

H. F. Saint

ILLUSTRATED BY ROBERT HUNT

They're after him. Invading his privacy.
Watching his friends. Laying traps in
doorways. Throwing nets over entire city
streets. Why? Most people would say that
Nick Halloway is an ordinary man . . . except
for one thing: a freak accident has left him
totally invisible. And now the American
government wants to catch him: he'd make an
unbeatable superspy, or at least an interesting
guinea pig . . .

But Nick prefers to control his own life.
And in a wild chase full of twists and
surprises he must not only stay one step
ahead of his pursuers, but learn to survive—
invisibly—as well.

Chapter 1

If only you could see me now. You can't and couldn't, but I'm here. And although the explanation is banal, the effect is altogether magical. If you were to walk into this room now, you would find it quite empty—an empty chair before a desk empty save for a pad of unlined paper. But above the paper you would see the pen, unheld, dancing over the surface, forming these words, pausing now and then in midair, reflectively. You would be entranced, or terrified.

Unfortunately, *I* am holding the pen, and if you were quick enough and I were not, you could get a perfectly solid grip on me and satisfy yourself by sense of touch that an unseeable but otherwise unexceptional human being was in the room. Or you could pick up a chair and beat me senseless with it. I am sorry to say this would not be an unusual course of action under the circumstances, for my condition, although perfectly anonymous, is undeniably bizarre. It provokes curiosity, and curiosity, I find, is a fairly vicious instinct. This is a trying existence. It is generally best to keep on the move.

For the first thirty-four years of my life I was exactly like everyone else, and while those years seemed compelling enough to me at the time, you would presumably not be reading a narrative entitled *Memoirs of a Securities Analyst*. Then, right in the middle of my rather ordinary way through life, a minor but altogether extraordinary scientific mishap rendered a small spherical chunk of New Jersey utterly invisible. As chance would have it, I was at the critical moment included in that spherical chunk.

131

The fateful morning began with Anne Epstein and myself on a train from New York to Princeton. Looking back on it, that morning did have an appropriately ominous quality, with dark storm clouds and bright April sunshine in continual and dramatic alternation, but at the time I noticed mainly the sunshine. I had drunk too much and slept too little the night before, so that it all had a euphoric dreamlike vividness, and although I knew that this feeling would soon mature into a piercing headache, at that moment I felt nothing but delight in the brilliant spring morning and the sight of Anne's smooth white skin.

What was she talking about? I remember that she had the *New York Times* open on her lap—she worked for the *Times*—and she was explaining something of great interest and importance to her that had to do with an attempt to redraw local election districts somewhere in the Midwest. To me, no human activity is so reliably boring and shabby as politics, but I furrowed my brow to indicate concentration. When Anne talked about politics, it only made her more exquisite. Her shoulder-length brown hair and her crisp clothing always seemed to fall casually but perfectly into place: she looked more like a television newscaster than a newspaper reporter. And even if I could not quite manage to maintain my interest in what she was saying, my heart and mind were absolutely flooded with interest in Anne herself.

Less than two weeks before, I had found myself seated next to her at dinner. We had been introduced once or twice before over the past couple of years, but she still found it necessary to ask me what I did, and I remember answering her question straightforwardly. Anne startled me with a conflagration of interest. It was probably because she had just recently been assigned to the business section at the *Times*. Confronted with a source of useful information, she had begun to ask questions about business and economics.

For the next week I devoted myself to getting her to lunch with me, to drinks, to dinner, wherever I could get her. She was agonisingly elusive, somehow never able or willing to be free for more than a few hours. But when she was there, she always gave me her full attention. She loved to interrogate me, and the longer my answers were, the better she seemed to like them. Now she twisted in her seat, her mouth set in an exquisitely prim expression. "About last night," she said. "It's not right."

Last night which, despite several hours' sleep, had not so much ended as spilled over into the morning, had been the first—and, as it would turn out, the last—night we spent together.

"What's not right?" I asked.

"It's not fair to Peter."

Peter was her fiancé, or friend, or whatever—his role seemed to shift continually. "To be perfectly honest," I said, "I haven't had a chance yet to work fairness to Peter into my moral calculations."

This remark seemed to anger her. She stiffened. "Well, I have, and if you were capable of taking me or anyone else seriously—"

"You're absolutely right," I interrupted. "I don't know why I say these things. Shyness, probably. It's to conceal the feelings and passions swelling up uncontrollably in the old breast. And moral scruples too. All hiding beneath the amiable exterior of a clown." I gave her what I thought was a winning smile.

"The exterior," she said a little nastily, "is entirely that of a banker. Which is what you are."

"Not really," I protested.

"Securities analyst. Whatever. The point is that you wear those nerdy pinstriped suits and old-fashioned shoes, and you're always acting so earnest and pretending to strangers that you don't ever quite know what's going on."

"These clothes are considered rather glamorous in some sets. No one but you has ever taken exception."

"You should widen your circle of acquaintances. Anyway, you look like a banker."

"Well, you, on the other hand, look unspeakably beautiful."

She turned away disdainfully, but no one has ever minded such a compliment. Her eyes became more amiable, and she said, "Tell me about today."

"Yes, today," I said cheerfully, misunderstanding her question. "I thought today we might rent a car in Princeton, put in a quick token appearance at MicroMagnetics, and then drive up to Basking Ridge. Some friends of mine have gone off to Europe for the year and left me the use of a beautiful place there. And even if . . ."

"I'm looking forward to this MicroMagnetics thing. It should be more interesting than the usual."

MicroMagnetics, Inc., as far as I had been able to determine in my rather perfunctory investigations, was a small corporation outside Princeton that performed research on the magnetic containment of nuclear fusion. Its principal asset consisted in the services of its founder and president, one Professor Bernard Wachs, whose imposing reputation for original work in particle physics had enabled him to obtain millions of dollars in government grants. The only apparent activity of MicroMagnetics to date had been the spending of this money in rather short order and, from my point of view, its first real contribution to humanity was to provide me with an occasion to entice Anne out into the countryside.

The week before, MicroMagnetics, Inc. had distributed, to a largely indifferent world, press releases proclaiming the invention of the "EMF", a new type of magnetic field that was to normal everyday magnetic fields as the laser was to normal everyday light waves. The press release described it as "a major discovery" and "a watershed". Now, many if not

133

all scientists think of their work in these terms, and I was entirely unmoved. But there was to be a press conference and a demonstration of some sort, so I convinced Anne that it was a story she really had to cover, and told my office I would be out of town the entire day.

It occurs to me that I should explain what I do. Or did. A securities analyst looks at a business and what it owns and does, and what the competition does, and at any peculiarities of the stocks or bonds that the business sells to raise money. From all this he tries to determine at what price people ought to buy or sell those stocks or bonds. I won't impose upon you further by explaining the different types of jobs a securities analyst can do, but I should explain that my particular job was slightly above average in glamour, had relatively reasonable hours, and required no selling. As long as I satisfied my partners, I remained virtually independent, and as much as twenty per cent of the time I enjoyed my work—which is a good average for any type of work I have ever heard of.

As it happened, I had a particular responsibility in my firm for covering the energy industry. Every few weeks someone would announce a scheme to float icebergs to Kansas with dirigibles or use sunlight to make water run uphill. As the whole thing was so fashionable, I would get a lot of phone calls soliciting my expert opinion. And there was always the remote but tantalising hope that one of these things would take off, in which case you might do very well for yourself.

Certainly I entertained no particular hopes for MicroMagnetics that day. My hopes revolved around getting Anne off as quickly as possible to Basking Ridge.

"What," I asked, genuinely puzzled, "makes you think MicroMagnetics will be so interesting?"

"It has a political dimension, for once."

"You mean as an alternative source of energy?"

"It's not alternative energy at all," she said with irritation. "It's nuclear."

Nuclear—as opposed to alternative—was bad. I knew that much about politics. "Actually, I don't think it is nuclear in the sense you mean: it wouldn't have anything to do with nuclear *fission* anyway. All the research these people have done is related to magnetic containment of *fusion*, which has none of the nasty properties your environmental friends object to."

"It's all nuclear," she said very definitely. "It is a crime against the earth and against future generations. If we had a government concerned with meeting the real needs of the people, we would be generating power directly from sunlight instead of poisoning ourselves. The technology exists today."

Her eyes narrowed, and her exquisite mouth set firmly, conveying moral rectitude. I seemed to have annoyed her.

134

"Yes, I see the force of what you say," I responded agreeably, since, except for whatever immediate fun you may get out of it, it is always a waste of time to argue with anyone about politics.

We were interrupted when the door at the end of the car opened with a crash, flooding us with the metallic noise of wheels and rails. The guard entered and proclaimed loudly, "Princeton Junction!"

Chapter 2

We stood on the platform and watched the train pull away.

The sky was completely dark now; it seemed about to rain. I announced to Anne that I was going to find a taxi, and she informed me that she had arranged to have us met by a representative of Students for a Fair World.

"Why Students for a Fair World? Princeton Yellow Cabs has better drivers," I protested.

"Shut up," she said affably. "This is probably him now."

Indeed, a young member of the revolutionary vanguard had appeared further down the platform. He was really quite striking—handsome with the small, fine features of a model, longish blond hair swept straight back, and dressed entirely in overlaundered, faded denim. He was observing us uncertainly.

"Yes, indeed," I said. "From the autumn line of revolutionaries by Ralph Lauren."

"How about letting me do my job?" Anne said to me, and then strode down the platform with a greeting smile. My heart full of sullenness, I followed as slowly as I could manage. If nearly grown men want to put on costumes and play cowboys and Indians or make-believe revolution, it is fine with me, but I didn't want them intruding on my morning. As I came up to them Anne was thanking him for meeting us.

"Not at all," he said. "If you hadn't called and told us this was taking place, we'd have missed it completely. This is just the kind of opportunity we're always looking for. Nuclear poisoning of the environ- ment—" He stopped as I joined them.

"Nick Halloway, Robert Carillon," Anne said rather quickly.

"Are you with the *Times* too, Nick?" He was staring at me, as if I were an unusual and somewhat suspect form of life.

"Gosh, no." I spoke with the most boyishly ingenuous air I could contrive. "Unfortunately. I mean, I wish I were. Actually, I'm with Shipway and Whitman. Great firm. Nice people." I grinned a large, friendly, foolish grin.

As I spoke, Carillon's eyes travelled up and down my grey pinstripe suit and came to rest on my shoes, which seemed to be particularly troubling to him. They were very good English shoes, made to fit my particular feet, and as things would turn out, it was lucky that I wore them that day.

"You're here, I take it, to see whether someone can make a profit on some new variety of nuclear energy," he said softly.

"That's it," I answered. "Always looking for the highest rate of return, wherever it may be." We were hitting it off splendidly.

Anne moved to take control. "How far is MicroMagnetics?"

Carillon seemed to welcome the interruption. It was ten minutes to MicroMagnetics. I considered taking a taxi on my own but decided that would seem childishly petulant. As the hero of the revolution hurried off up the platform to get the car, Anne shared with me her view of my behaviour.

"For heaven's sake, can't you be civil?"

"I thought I was being civil. Although I'm not sure why we're wasting time talking to this guy. Whatever possessed you to call these people and put them up to harassing MicroMagnetics?"

This question subdued her instantly. "I didn't put anyone up to anything. I was aware of the active concern of Students for a Fair World with certain issues, and it was part of my job to find out whether they were planning any action in response to a highly publicised event organised by the nuclear industry. And I wish you wouldn't mention this to anyone else. Especially at the *Times*."

"Anne, my love, this is not a highly publicised event. We shall probably be the only people who bother to come. But I absolutely adore you, and I won't tell a soul."

I smiled my most engaging smile, and we agreed on a truce. I would be civil to everyone I encountered. Anne would try to acquire in the shortest possible time whatever information she felt she needed, and we would not linger unnecessarily in the vicinity.

As we spoke, we could see Carillon at the end of the platform, where a road ended in a small circle. There was a dirty grey van parked there and behind it two saloon cars full of people. Revolutionaries travel in bands, never alone. Chairman Carillon stood by the van and watched the cars drive away, and then waved to us to come over. The whole thing made me a little uneasy somehow. My instincts were good. I should have paid attention to them.

The van had only two seats, and I ended up in the back on the floor. The body of the van was filled with cardboard boxes and what appeared to be building supplies and tools. I could see several coils of electrical wire and at least two large dry cells. I clambered awkwardly through the mess and found some cushions to sit on. There seemed to be an odd chemical smell in the van.

I could hear Anne and Carillon in the front, having an impenetrable discussion about the interrelations of various left-wing political groups. Then with an unpleasant shock I realised that the smell all round me was of gunpowder. I was evidently about to take part in a bombing. My hands trembled as I pulled open the top of one of the boxes and peered inside.

Carillon heard me. "Everything all right back there?" he asked.

"Quite a lot of equipment you've got here," I ventured, as conversationally as possible. "Looks like you're getting a head start on Independence Day this year."

There was a pause. Then he replied, "You might put it that way. As a matter of fact, we are going to have a little explosion today."

Anne seemed excited by this news. She had her pen and her little journalist's notebook poised for the details.

"That's the way to do it," I said. "Show them you mean business. Poof. No more MicroMagnetics. That'll make those jokers think twice about what line of work they get into next. Opens up my day too. No point my checking out MicroMagnetics now. In fact you might just drop me off—"

"We'll just be blowing up that guinea pig in the cage back there with you. We're creating a small simulation of a nuclear explosion, to make vivid the unacceptable horror of nuclear war."

I couldn't see a cage anywhere, but I felt a great sense of relief upon discovering that no major destruction was being undertaken. However, Anne, who, as far as I could tell, had just been contemplating the bombing of the entire plant of MicroMagnetics with enthusiasm, was suddenly aghast. "You're murdering an animal?"

"Exactly!" Carillon said, with triumph in his voice. "That's exactly the way everyone reacts. People are more upset about one small laboratory animal dying painlessly before their eyes than by all humanity being steadily poisoned with radioactivity."

There was a pause in the conversation, and then Anne, after a sharp glance in my direction, turned back and uneasily resumed her interview of Carillon.

I located the cage on the other side of the van. It was not much larger than the animal inside. I opened the hinged door and dumped the guinea pig out onto the floor. It lay where it landed, a fat, passive creature. I crawled back to my cushions, feeling suddenly a bit queasy from the motion of the van. I wished I were not down on the floor and that I had drunk less the night before.

When the van at last came to a halt, I hurriedly pushed open the rear doors and stumbled to my feet with as much dignity as I could manage. No sign of the guinea pig, but I left the doors open to give him as much of a chance as possible. At least his destiny was in his own hands now.

Anne and Carillon were standing by the front of the van, still in conversation. When I went round to them, Anne looked up at me and said, "I'm not quite finished, Nick."

"There's no hurry. I'll be over in front of the building. Bob," I continued, holding out my hand to Carillon, "I want to wish you every success today and in all your future endeavours."

He nodded curtly, ignoring my hand, and turned back to Anne.

I followed a footpath out of the parking lot through a break in a hedge, and found myself on the edge of a large lawn with enormous trees. To one side, a drive lined with oaks ran from the edge of the parking lot out to the road a hundred yards away. Beyond the lawn in every direction were fields bordered by trees. It was a beautiful place. The incongruous thing was that in the middle of it all was a brand-new long white rectangular building of the type that you would expect to find on an industrial estate. A paved walk led from the parking lot to the main entrance, where there were two steps up to a threshold flanked by two massive white wooden columns that supported a sort of colonial-style porch roof.

Off to one side there was a small concrete structure, into which ran enough power lines to supply a small city. They must be doing something here that required a lot of electricity. I took several deep breaths and decided that I felt better, although two little points of pain were beginning to define themselves as a headache. Perhaps someone inside would have some aspirin.

Although it was still early, a few people had already arrived and were straggling unenthusiastically into the building. The revolutionaries were hauling their cartons out onto the lawn and setting up their own little scientific demonstration right in front of the entrance. No one seemed in the least interested in them. Some of Carillon's people were crouched in front of the open door to the little concrete hut.

Carillon and Anne appeared through the hedge and joined the group on the lawn. I watched as Anne wished them all well, then turned and walked over to join me.

"Thanks for waiting." She seemed to be in a benign mood again. "The guinea pig is gone. Did you let it out?"

"Why would I try to stem the irresistible tide of revolution?"

"Well, you were the chief suspect. Anyway, it's gone."

"Pity. What will they do?"

"Search for a stand-in. They'd probably welcome the opportunity to use you. Shouldn't we go in? It's starting to rain."

"By all means. Tell me, do you have any idea what Carillon's people are doing in that electrical shed or whatever it is?"

"I think," said Anne, without bothering to look, "they're going to shut off power to the building as part of their demonstration."

"You mean they're going to just shut off all power to a laboratory with who knows what kind of equipment running in it? Don't you think that's a bit irresponsible?"

138

"As usual you're more concerned with private property than with people," Anne said good-naturedly.

"This particular private property is about to contain people. Us, to be precise. Look, Anne, why don't we just cut short our stay here? We can hire a car in Princeton and drive—"

"Nick, I'm absolutely going to stay through the press conference and the demonstration. And then we both have appointments with Professor Wachs afterwards. After that, I should really get back to New York for—"

"I'll tell you what. We'll go in and see Wachs together now. Then we won't have to hang around afterwards."

"The press conference is going to begin in twenty minutes. We'll never get at him before—"

"I'll get at him." I took her decisively by the arm and started across the lawn towards the building, to find Wachs. At that moment I believed I was going to get my way and have the day I wanted, and a final wave of euphoria swept over me. "We'll be gone by noon," I said. I would be gone by noon all right.

We strode through the entrance and found ourselves standing in a small reception room with a couch and a table. Behind a large desk sat a woman in her forties whose natural expression of truculent dissatisfaction had been highlighted by the careful application of great quantities of make-up. She took a brief disapproving look at Anne and then fixed her gaze on me.

"Take one press kit and go through the door to your left, then down the corridor to the conference room at the end. We'll be beginning in a few minutes." Her voice had no warmth in it.

"Thank you. That's extremely kind." I picked up a press kit. It was a glossy red folder that contained copies of a useless press release, an uninformative fact sheet, and a curriculum vitae of Bernard Wachs, Ph.D. "I wonder if you could let Dr. Wachs know that Mr. Halloway of Shipway and Whitman and Miss Epstein from the *Times* are here."

Her brow furrowed momentarily. "I believe we already have you down for an appointment at two o'clock."

"Actually," I said, "I was hoping we could get a few words privately with Professor Wachs now, before the press conference. I think it's possible that he would want to see us."

"He's far too busy now," she said severely.

"Do you think he might still be in his office?" I asked.

Her eyes darted momentarily to a closed door in the wall to my right.

"You'll both have to go to the conference room with everyone else. The door to your left."

"Yes, of course." I carefully put the press folder back on top of the pile on her desk. "The door to my left, you said?" I pointed firmly to the door on my right.

"No . . . yes . . . no!"

I walked distractedly over to the door on my right and pushed it open. Anne followed.

"You can't go in there!"

We found ourselves looking into an enormous carpeted corner office. The furnishings were undistinguished, but through the many windows there were wonderfully pleasant views of the lawn, the trees and the fields beyond. In the centre of the room was a large desk, in front of which stood a short, plump, rodent-like man. He seemed startled to see us in the doorway.

"You wouldn't be Dr. Wachs, would you?" I asked.

"Yes, yes, I am. How do you do?" He spoke with extraordinary rapidity, shifting his weight constantly from one foot to the other.

"Professor Wachs," called out the receptionist ominously, "these people—"

"I'm Nick Halloway, with Shipway and Whitman, the investment firm. And this is Anne Epstein from the *Times*."

"The *Times*? Come in, come in. I think you're going to be very excited by the work we're doing here." He gazed intently at Anne.

"Professor Wachs," insisted the receptionist, glowering in the doorway behind us, "it's very late—"

"Amazing facility you have here," I said to Wachs as I shut the door behind me, in the face of the receptionist. "I know you're terribly busy today, but I just wondered if we could get some information before you are completely tied up with this press conference."

"I wonder," Anne interrupted, to my irritation, "if you could tell us how you feel about the conflicting needs of society for expanded energy sources and for protection of the environment, as they bear on the issue of nuclear power."

Before Wachs could figure that out, I intervened. "Specifically, we were wondering why in your press release there was no real mention of magnetic containment. So much of the work you're known for has, of course, been related to the problem of containment."

"Yes, yes. You're right. This has nothing to do with containment . . ." He glanced nervously out of the window. "There seem to be some people out front constructing something."

"That's precisely what we want to discuss," Anne began.

"Those are students, demonstrators," I interrupted. "They seem to have some objection to whatever it is you're doing here. Which raises the question of just what you *are*—"

"Oh, students," he said, as if that would be a satisfactory explanation for anything whatever. "They don't like it when you take government grants. Protest all the time."

"They plan to shut off power to the building," I went on.

"Shut off power? That's our biggest single problem: the incredible quantities of electricity this work requires. The potential is unbelievable. It's all a question of capital."

I wasn't quite sure whether the potential he was talking about was electrical, scientific or financial.

The intercom on his desk buzzed. He picked up the phone.

"Yes, yes. I know." He looked up at us as he replaced the receiver. "We have to be getting down to the conference room."

He led us out through a door into an interior corridor.

"Now, we really don't have any time to look at this," he continued excitedly, "but I just want to show you the laboratory. Unfortunately, in the format of a press conference I can't really explain in a meaningful way what we're doing here."

We stopped halfway down the corridor, in front of a heavy metal door, and he pulled out a large key ring.

"I shouldn't, strictly speaking, be making a public announcement at this point. But"—and his eyes darted about—"we need funding. That's the key." He had paused thoughtfully with his hand on the door.

"We're all extremely interested in what you're accomplishing here," I said. "I don't think most people appreciate the significance of what you're trying to do." I wondered whether I would ever find out, even in general terms, what in fact he was trying to do.

He pushed open the heavy door, and we stepped into the laboratory. It was a large warehouselike area, with an appearance of thorough chaos. There were tables everywhere. Tables with desktop computers; tables with machine tools, with circuit boards, with plumbing. The centre of the room was filled with a massive metal ring ten feet across. Through it and round it were coiled further tubes and wires, which finally spilled out into the rest of the room, connecting to a dozen inexplicable projects on various tables.

Wachs led us over to a computer display filled with a grid of continually changing numbers.

"I don't know if it's obvious to you what's going on here," said Wachs jubilantly, "but at this moment a magnetic field is being generated—an enhanced magnetic field. EMF, we call it."

"Wait a minute," said Anne. There was a glint in her eye. "Do you mean to say that you're generating atomic energy right here in this room—fission or fusion, or whatever you call it?"

"Well, I wouldn't characterise it as fission or fusion."

"But whatever it is is actually going on right there?" She pointed sternly at the intestinal mass of tubes and wires. "Could you tell me what safeguards you have against radiation leakage or a nuclear mishap?"

"There's no more radiation here than you would encounter around an average radio transmitter," he reassured her. "What it's doing is generating electricity directly. No one will believe this. It's actually driving itself now." He was almost dancing up and down with excitement. "The only exogenous energy is what powers the control system. Except for that, it could run itself, virtually for ever."

Right there, I should have paid more attention. I knew that someone was about to shut off power to the building. And this man was telling me that he had some loopy process roaring away, which sustained itself but whose control system used outside power. Easy to see these things with hindsight. I couldn't know what the consequences would be. Too late now. But I am sorry. For Wachs as much as for myself. Although, really, the man was a lunatic.

"Dr. Wachs!" The receptionist had tracked us down.

"Yes, yes," he replied. "We should get in there right away."

He scurried out of the laboratory with me, Anne and the receptionist chasing behind. We entered a long, narrow room at the end of the building, filled with rows of folding chairs. At the back a slide projector had been set up.

There were roughly two dozen people in the room. A few of them might have been journalists. More likely they were friends or colleagues of Wachs's. Nevertheless, Wachs began by introducing himself and assuring us that he was not going to subject a non-academic audience to a technical account of his work.

With no warning the lights went out, and we found ourselves in total darkness. For an instant I thought that the Students for a Fair World had already struck, but from the startled silence emerged the excited voice of Wachs: "It is often with astonishment that we discover how differently men at other times have viewed magnetism. In the sixth century BC the Greek philosopher Thales observed the extraordinary ability of lodestone to attract other pieces of lodestone, as well as iron." A picture of a large stone appeared at the front of the room.

I was going to have difficulty sitting through much of this. My hangover was rapidly being intensified to an insupportable level. After fifteen minutes we had only reached the eighteenth century. If I could slip out of the room for a while, I might find a lavatory, or go outside and clear my head. I clambered from my seat and felt my way out.

I hurried down the corridor towards the front entrance. There was no one in the reception room now. I pushed open the door and stepped out onto the porch. There was a steady, uninviting drizzle. The students, undeterred by the weather, were right there erecting some part of their fair world.

A wave of nausea flooded over me. Really what I wanted was a lavatory. I tried the door to Wachs's office. Locked. The next door, however, opened into an enormous bathroom, which had, in addition to all the usual plumbing, an open shower stall and a sauna. There was a stack of freshly laundered towels and along one wall a row of hooks from which hung track suits and other random pieces of clothing. The employees of MicroMagnetics must use this as a sort of locker room.

I leaned my head into the washbasin and turned on the cold water, trying to clear my mind. But my headache was, if anything, worse. I located a bottle of aspirin in a medicine cabinet over the washbasin, and took three. I noticed that there seemed to be a high-pitched whining sound, but I could not decide whether there was really such a sound or whether it was a sort of overtone incorporated in the pain of my headache.

Somewhere within the building an electric bell went off. It was the kind of harsh, overwhelming bell that announces the end of class at school, and for an instant I thought inanely that Wachs's lecture must have ended. No, it was some sort of alarm bell. Above the sound of the bell there was still that painful throbbing whine. Someone ran by in the corridor, shouting something.

All the commotion would have something to do with the Students for a Fair World. Probably they had shut off power to the building. No, the lights were still on. Or perhaps they had simply set off a fire alarm. That would make sense. What they wanted was to get everyone outside so they would have an audience for their demonstration. As I thought about it, I was more and more disinclined to give them that satisfaction. I could hear a lot of shouting and slamming of doors; people were trooping down the corridor. If I stayed out of sight, I might spend the entire time comfortably inside while everyone else was herded out into the cold drizzle.

I pulled open a door that led directly into Wachs's office. The light suddenly went out and the alarm bell stopped. Evidently the Students for a Fair World had managed after all to cut off power to the building. With the alarm bell extinguished, I noticed more clearly that unpleasant piercing, whining sound. Some piece of equipment must still be operating.

I went over to the window to see what was going on. The people who had been driven out of the building milled forlornly about on the lawn. A steady drizzle descended on them all.

A few yards from the building the demonstrators had laid out a metal table top, which was apparently to be the site of this mock explosion. In the middle of it there was some sort of pipe and tin can device, nearly two feet high. Electric wires ran from it for approximately ten yards, to a spot on the lawn where most of the demonstrators had clustered round an assortment of cartons and random equipment.

Two of the students were attempting to stuff a cat into the cage that had been in the van. The cat seemed entirely disinclined to function as a guinea pig—it writhed, clawed and snarled—but eventually they had it

143

rammed more or less inside, with the cage door shut. Then they placed the cage on top of the device on the metal table.

Carillon now stepped out from the group of revolutionaries and raised a megaphone to his lips. "We live in a world in which people are valued less than profits and property," he intoned. "We are all guinea pigs!"

At this point Wachs appeared, charging across the lawn straight for Carillon, as fast as his plump legs would carry him. Carillon, noting in time the approach of the capitalist oppressor, shouted, "*Zero!*"

The people on the lawn instinctively stepped back from the anticipated blast. The igniting switch was thrown, and the sound of a large bomb resounded through the trees.

But the startling thing was that the complicated device surmounted by the caged cat remained absolutely as it had been. Instead, one of the cartons next to the detonator exploded dramatically. A splendid column of black smoke rose straight up almost eight feet into the air and began to spread out in the familiar mushroom form.

Wachs, who had stopped in his tracks for the duration of the explosion, shrieked something at Carillon and raced over to the device. He seized the cage containing the cat and slammed it angrily against the bomb mechanism. The cage flew open, and the cat burst from it, setting off in a frantic run towards the building. Carillon, outraged by this destructive attack on his unused bomb, charged over and began shouting at Wachs. Everyone on the lawn watched them in fascinated silence.

That horrible whining noise, which had begun to subside, suddenly swelled to a new level of intensity. Wachs looked up at the building, and an expression of horror filled his face. It may be that in that instant he became the one person who understood what was about to happen.

The quality of the light shifted, illuminating everything on the lawn in an unearthly, brilliant glow. Carillon's and Wachs's faces suddenly contorted into final, unspeakable agony, and as if in echo, expressions of horror appeared on the faces of Anne and all the others watching in safety in the background. Then I saw—it was the last thing I saw or remember—the flesh of Wachs and Carillon bubble brilliantly into electric flame.

Chapter 3

The morning arrived as usual. Unpleasant. Brutal sun. Must have left the curtains open. There was the sound of sirens outside. Whole body ached. Not even in my bed. I was lying on the carpet, and I realised with distaste that I had slept in my clothes. I must have passed out on the floor. Have to stop drinking so much. Not a siren, a cat howling somewhere. What had I done the night before?

Suddenly my mind filled with the final, pulsing vision of Wachs and Carillon transfigured horribly into flame.

I was wide awake now. I cannot possibly communicate the incomprehensible horror of that moment. I could make no sense of what I saw. I was lying on my belly on some sort of ledge, looking more than thirty feet straight down into a large, empty pit. But when I turned my head, I couldn't see anything supporting me at all. This heightened my terror to the point of panic. I had somehow to keep control of myself, think out exactly what my situation was, what I should do.

First of all, I had to keep absolutely as still as possible to keep from slipping off and plummeting to the bottom. The cavity over which I was somehow suspended seemed to be a perfectly smooth round basin, nearly a hundred feet across and, at the deepest point in the centre, about forty feet in depth. In a circular band ten feet wide, all round the rim of the pit, the earth had been burned and all vegetation incinerated. But immediately beyond this charred perimeter the grass grew green and trees bloomed, untouched by whatever had happened. I was suspended at a level slightly higher than that of the surrounding lawn and roughly halfway between the rim and the centre of the pit.

Barely holding down my nausea and terror, I tried to put everything together. I knew roughly where I was. This had been the site of MicroMagnetics, Inc. Where the building had stood, there was now nothing but a vast hole in the ground. I concluded that there had been an explosion that had left an enormous crater. The blast had evidently incinerated everything for another ten feet round the crater. As for me, I had somehow been thrown free and had landed on something. What?

It didn't quite make sense. Everything within the spherical range of the blast seemed to have been absolutely obliterated: there was not even the slightest trace of the building or its contents. But hadn't I been in the building? And what had I landed on, and how could I get down?

Everything seemed eerily still and deserted. There was only the unearthly, incessant wailing of a cat somewhere. I tried to tuck my head down to get a look at my body and whatever it was perched on. But no matter how far down I forced my head, I couldn't seem to get a view of myself—or anything else. Strange, because I could feel something like a carpeted floor against my face. Very cautiously I slid my hands under my chest, raised my upper body, and slid my knees forward until I was on all fours. I tilted my head down to see what I was kneeling on. I saw nothing whatever except the opposite side of the crater, and this incomprehensible visual result produced a dizzying wave of nausea: I felt that I was tumbling forwards, in a somersault through space. I think I must have shrieked and thrown my arms out in an instinctive attempt to grab hold of something. This left me grotesquely sprawled, but I still had the tactile sensation of lying on a carpeted floor. Less carefully now, but with even greater terror, I pushed myself up again onto all fours and then to a kneeling position.

With as much calm as I could muster, I shifted my gaze in a gradual arc from the crater rim in front of me down to my legs. Again my gaze encountered nothing but the crater far below. No legs! I shrieked again. It came to me instantly that both my legs must have been blown off. I must be dying. "Help here! Help!"

On the other hand it also came to me that I was kneeling, or anyway it felt as if I was kneeling. I shut my eyes, to gather my wits. This produced no change whatever. I could still see everything with perfect clarity, no matter how tightly I squeezed my eyelids shut. People are forever having arms and legs blown off in sensational accidents, but I couldn't recall a case of eyelids being blown off. Keeping my left hand on the ground for balance, I brought my right hand tentatively up to my face. With my fingertips I felt the area round the eyes. Definitely an eyelid. I could feel it move. I could feel the eyelashes.

But I couldn't see my fingers. Or my hand. Trembling, I reached down and felt my missing legs. They were intact and in the appropriate place. I straightened up so that my weight was on my knees, and ran my hands over my body. It was all there—clothed. Still, no matter how I turned my head or focused my eyes, I could plainly see that I was no longer material at all. Finally, in a flash of dreadful insight I arrived at an explanation that covered all the facts. Evidently I was dead.

But the headache, nausea and plain terror I felt were inconsistent with the basic idea of paradise. You couldn't have headaches in heaven. And anyway, I was still at MicroMagnetics. The former site of MicroMagnetics. I was right where my life had been brought to an end. It must be, I reasoned, that I was a ghost.

My mood picked up a bit. The ghost hypothesis gave me a frame of reference. There was even the possibility—I hardly dared formulate it in my mind—of some sort of immortality in my present form.

I explored the floor round me with my hands and began to inch forwards, on all fours. Nothing to look at but the dizzying sight of the crater's surface far below. Bracing myself with my hands, I slowly raised myself to a standing position. Then I slid my feet forward over the carpet in cautious shuffling steps, groping in front of myself with extended arms. The feeling was indescribably eerie. My left hand encountered a desk. I ran my fingers over its surface: it was covered with papers and books, all intact but invisible. I was in Wachs's office.

Now, for all I know, people may become ghosts, or angels. But I knew there could not be an afterlife for desks or broadloom. Some altogether extraordinary catastrophe had transformed me and my immediate surroundings, leaving us absolutely invisible but otherwise unimproved.

However fantastic this conclusion might seem in the abstract, I saw at

146

once that it was the least fantastic explanation of my situation that fitted all the facts. Keeping my left hand on the desk, I inched my way round it, located the chair with my right hand and sat down. It was a leather swivel chair, and from it I could take a long, careful, rational look at my surroundings—insofar as they were visible. The sun was up well over the horizon now. How long had I been unconscious? Probably since the day before.

It was a beautiful, bright, cloudless morning, and I could see everything with extraordinary clarity. What I had perceived as a crater was not a crater at all: it was evidently a spherical area in which everything had been rendered invisible, but remained perfectly solid. The sphere included all of the MicroMagnetics building, together with a good deal of shrubbery, lawn and earth around it. Plus that still howling cat, which must have remained in the building, like me.

I experimented with the objects on the desk before me. I flipped through the pages of a book. I rapped a pen sharply on the desk top and listened to the clear tapping sound. I found a stapler and stapled together some papers. It all worked perfectly. I cannot tell you how uncanny it felt touching, holding, manipulating those objects without being able to see them.

My head ached excruciatingly, and I felt again a mounting nausea. Weren't headache and nausea symptoms of radiation poisoning? I must almost certainly be dying. I hoped that when they rescued me, they would be able to see me somehow. How otherwise would they be able to give me medical help? I ran my hands over my body, trying to detect any injury. Nothing. Even my clothing seemed to be absolutely intact. I loosened my tie. Then, with both hands resting on the desk top for balance, I carefully raised myself to my feet and saw to my complete astonishment that I was not alone after all.

As I stood upright and looked back towards the other end of the building, my line of vision extended over the screen of shrubbery and across the parking lot to a large field, which had been incongruously bisected by a chain-link fence at least ten feet high, with strands of barbed wire coiled along its top. I was certain it had not been there the day before. Protruding above the shrubbery were the roofs of two grey vans and a black car in the parking lot. Everything else had apparently been cleared away, and the entire area on my side of the fence was deserted and motionless. However, the far side of the fence swarmed with people wearing military or police uniforms. There was every imaginable sort of vehicle: jeeps, trucks, tractors, vans, cars, all in drab colours which proclaimed them to be government property.

They had for some reason built an entirely new access road from the field directly to the far side of the parking lot. At the point where the road intersected the fence there was a large gate, also made of chain link.

As I watched, men were hanging opaque green fabric over the inside of the fence, so that my view of the field full of people and equipment was rapidly being closed off. I turned slowly, and with a vague apprehension saw that the entire area round me was encircled with the same metal fencing shrouded with fabric.

The sight of all those people bustling about on the other side of the fence filled me with longing for other human beings. "Help!" I cried. My voice was thin with fear. "Over here! Help!"

Of course they couldn't hear me. I was a hundred yards away; my shout was feeble; if they heard anything, it would be the howling of that cat. With a terrified start I remembered that I was inside a closed building. They would never know I was here. Radiation. They must be sealing off the area because of radiation. For months. Years.

I would have to get to them for help. If I could manage it. I was shaking all over and probably too weak with radiation poisoning to walk that far. Be calm. I must try.

I ran my hands along the edge of the desk to determine the axis of the building and then set out across the void. I held my hands out in front of me like someone walking through a dark house. It came as a startling relief when my invisible hands encountered the invisible wall. With more confidence now, I felt my way along the wall until I came to the bathroom door.

Searching with my right hand, I located the doorknob, twisted it, and swung the door open. Keeping hold of the doorknob, I took several steps into the room and groped with my outstretched left hand until I located the washbasin. The cat—I was certain now that it was in the reception room next door—intensified its howling. Remembering the bottle of aspirin from the day before, I found the door of the medicine cabinet, swung it open and began poking my right hand along the shelves. I encountered many small objects, some identifiable (shaving brush, tube of toothpaste, toothbrush) and some not. A number of them were sent clattering noisily into the washbasin. But I found the aspirin bottle. Or at least, I hoped it was the aspirin bottle. It had the right shape, but even assuming it was aspirin, would it be of any help in my oddly altered circumstances? Worth a try. I had a very bad headache. I tilted some tablets into my left palm, carefully counted off three with my right forefinger and pushed them into my mouth.

I turned on the cold water and, bending over and pressing my mouth to the tap, washed down the pills. I went on drinking greedily. The water was wonderful. I was, I realised, horribly thirsty. I splashed water on my face, and then drank again for a long time. I definitely felt better.

I would go now and get help. As I turned, I saw the black car moving slowly out of the parking lot and down the access road, away from me. The fencing was now completely covered, and when the gate swung shut behind the car, everything outside the fencing was screened from view. Except for the two vans, there was no indication of humanity anywhere. I was overcome with desolation.

Then, mysteriously, first one van and then the other began to move behind the shrubbery, turning out of the parking lot and proceeding slowly across the lawn, parallel to the front of the building. The first was the size of a normal delivery van. The second was more than twice as large, and an elaborate antenna protruded from an opening in its roof. The smaller van halted almost exactly opposite me and thirty yards back from the rim. The second van halted behind it. The effect was somehow sinister, and I stood there motionless, watching with uneasy fascination.

The front door of the smaller van opened. A muscular black-skinned man with an expressionless face climbed out of the driver's seat and walked with an erect military gait back to the other van. His garish red Hawaiian shirt only heightened the impression that he customarily wore uniform. A large, fat man climbed out of the bigger van and began to talk to him. The second man, too, although he wore elaborately tooled leather boots and a fancy western shirt, contrived to look like a soldier or a policeman. As he talked, he repeatedly broke into hearty laughter, but his small squinting eyes remained wary.

After several minutes a third man appeared from round the other side of the big van. He was older than the others, in his mid-forties, and wore a dark grey business suit that hung loosely over his frame. His hair was cropped extremely short, almost shaved, and the flesh which, despite his athletic bearing, was unwholesomely pallid, creased into folds, making his head appear repellently naked. He walked with a precise, almost rigid gait to a door in the middle of the big van and stopped. The door abruptly swung open, revealing a short Hispanic man who spoke several words and then disappeared back inside.

The man in the business suit walked over to the black man and the cowboy and muttered several sentences to which they listened attentively. He seemed to be in command: the moment he finished speaking, the other two walked briskly to the back of the smaller van. He remained where he was, his eyes moving carefully over the whole site.

The black man and the cowboy had pulled open the back door of the smaller van and were helping a man encased in a bulky white suit to climb laboriously out. It was the sort of suit that astronauts wear. Or, it struck me unpleasantly, the sort of suit that you see on the evening news when a damaged nuclear reactor is being inspected. It was just as I had feared: there was radioactivity. I was dying. I sat down on the floor feebly to await my rescue.

In one hand my prospective rescuer held a sort of long metal wand that was connected by a cable to the midriff of his suit. It must be a Geiger counter. The other three men were each putting on the sort of earphone and microphone device that television newsmen and football coaches wear. Then the man in the business suit nodded, and the astronaut proceeded ponderously across the lawn, directly towards me, sweeping his Geiger counter back and forth across his path.

The astronaut reached the edge of the crater. He stopped and turned to face the three men on the lawn behind, and nodded awkwardly, like a robot. Then he turned back to face the crater and swung the detector slowly out over the edge. I was so intent on witnessing the imminent extraordinary moment of discovery that I nearly forgot my own situation.

I now knew that everything was invisible to them too.

The man lowered the detector carefully until the end of it hit the invisible surface of the ground. He pushed on it a little. He tapped all round in a little circle. He pushed again, leaning his weight onto it. Then, like a boy testing thin ice, he tentatively swung one foot out over the edge and lowered it onto the invisible surface. He pushed down several times, as if expecting to plunge through, and then he carefully brought the second foot down. To give the ice a final test, he made a sort of awkward jumping movement, which, because of the suit, did not come to much. He looked truly amazing standing there in midair.

The man in the business suit had begun to speak into his microphone. The astronaut made a clumsy nodding movement and took several more steps towards the centre of the crater, waving the detector before him until it abruptly banged up against the invisible front wall of the building. He slid the detector over the surface as high as he could reach and as far out to each side. Then he laid the detector on the invisible ground. He pushed against the wall and began exploring it with his massively gloved hands. Soon he seemed to have located something: he delineated its rectangular contour by moving his hand around it several times. It was obviously a window.

I could see that the three men on the lawn were having an animated discussion. They had unfurled a large roll of papers. They would point at the papers, then look up and point towards my rescuer and then point at the papers again. Building plans. Then, presumably in response to some command, the astronaut picked up his detector and began to move back in my direction, keeping his left hand in contact with the wall. Only a few more steps would put him at the entrance to the building, but at the excruciatingly slow rate at which he was progressing, I felt myself becoming frantic with impatience. I stood up and set out to meet him.

I had my hands out in front of me, but my foot caught on something and I went lurching forward onto the bathroom tiles. I felt a stupefying impact through my entire body. Staying on all fours, I crawled pathetically into Wachs's office and along the wall to the door into the reception room.

150

Still kneeling, I reached up and found the doorknob. I turned it and pulled, then pushed. Nothing. The door was locked.

The man in the protective suit had located the two steps up to the threshold, and I could see his face now through the tinted face mask. He laid down his Geiger counter again and began moving his hands over the door. His right hand found the doorknob. He was having trouble turning it with his bulky gloves. The cat was howling insupportably now—it must have been watching the man as well. Abruptly the man's hand swung forward several inches. He had the door open! Suddenly I could hear him quite clearly.

"A cat! I swear it's a cat! Can you hear it? It's an invisible cat! There's nothing else it could be!" He paused, evidently listening to whatever they were saying to him through his earphones. "No, sir," he said. "This cat is going absolutely nowhere."

I was looking straight at the man. I cannot say why I did not call out to him at that moment. But I didn't. Perhaps the knowledge that people were at hand reassured me enough so that I felt I could do without them a little longer. Then, too, I wanted to see what the explorer would do with the cat. And perhaps I was feeling the first pathetic childish pleasure in my invisibility. I was right there, but they couldn't see me. Why give up the secret just yet?

The man had retrieved the detector and, pushing it through the crack in the door, was twisting it around inside the reception room. For some reason this made the cat abruptly cease howling. I heard the evil hissing sound that cats make when they are angry.

"There's no reading . . . This whole place is as clean as my elbow. I ought to take this suit off . . . Yes, sir."

My heart leaped. He seemed to be saying that there was no radioactivity. I almost spoke to him.

He withdrew the detector and laid it aside. He had one hand on the doorknob and one hand down at the threshold in what must have been the opening between the door and the frame.

"Come on, kitty, kitty, kitty," he chanted. The cat was emitting a steady hiss. "Kitty, kitty, kitty." Suddenly, the hand that had been holding the doorknob shot out and down, and the man lunged forward. He held his two hands in front of him, the palms facing each other and separated by the thickness of a compressed cat. There was a nasty snarl.

"Got it! I got it! *Easy*, kitty. Easy! Hold it!" The man clutched his hands violently to his chest in an apparent attempt to pin the struggling cat. He straightened himself with a jerk. He swung his right hand suddenly down onto his stomach, where it seemed to writhe for a moment. "Hold it, you little s.o.b.!" Then his left hand slapped down to his thigh. He was trying to lift his right leg. Then he swung his entire body violently round to the left and collided with the door, collapsing in an ungainly heap.

"Damn! Oh, that hurts. The thing is gone . . . Through the door. Sorry." He slowly picked himself up. "No, sir. You're right. There's no way I can be absolutely sure the cat is out of the building, sir . . . Yes, sir. I am closing it up, sir. I'm coming right away, sir."

It took me a moment to comprehend that he was about to leave the building, and when I did, I was instantly overcome with unreasoning panic again. "*Wait!*" I shrieked. "Help!" I banged on the door with my fists.

The man in white was absolutely motionless. I watched his eyes staring through the tinted visor, past me, through me . . . He very carefully shut the door behind him; then he shouted out in my direction, "Where are you, buddy? I can't hear you very well."

"Over here," I shouted back. "On the other side of this door." I banged again with both fists. "The door is locked!"

Without moving, and still staring warily, he began to speak very softly—but not to me. "Can you guys hold it for a minute? There's a live *human being* in here! Incredible! No, I can't see him! Can you?" This last was uttered with sarcasm, tinged with fear. "He seems to be in another room. Says he's locked in. This is crazy."

The astronaut had his back to me now and was facing the three men on the lawn, who were in animated discussion. Abruptly they stopped and looked over in our direction. The astronaut turned back towards me and shouted, "Can you see me, buddy?"

Good question. They had no way of knowing the laws of this little invisible universe; perhaps the invisible man saw all the invisible objects perfectly, just as before. Perhaps the invisible wall was opaque to him, as a wall should be. Or perhaps not. Or for that matter, perhaps invisible men are blind.

"No," I answered. "I'm in here." I suppose the escape of the cat was on my mind. Soon, of course, I would have to explain my situation to them accurately, but they didn't need that information now. We would all be cautious.

There was another pause. The men on the lawn were talking to my rescuer in white. Then he shouted to me again.

"Listen, buddy, I've got to leave for a minute and get help. I'll be right back. You hang on, buddy."

For some reason he slowly backed out of the building, as if I were an animal that might attack him. He walked back onto the visible rim of the crater, where he stopped and remained standing.

For nearly ten minutes none of us moved. Why were they standing immobile, when their only thought should have been to rescue me? I was afraid and angry. But I waited passively.

Then, in the background, I saw the fence gate swing open. An ambulance with a flashing light on its roof drove through and moved slowly towards the parking lot. Of course! They had only been waiting for proper medical support.

The black man walked up to the ambulance and two men in white medical uniforms climbed out. It looked as if they might be arguing. The black man was shaking his head. One of the men went back into the ambulance and returned carrying an empty stretcher. The black man took it from his hands and leaned it against the side of the big communications van. Everyone was once again inexplicably immobile.

Then the gate swung open again, and a black saloon car pulled through and drove directly up to the other vehicles. The driver climbed out of the car, went round and opened the boot. He pulled out two large green canvas sacks. At a sign from the black man he dumped these on the lawn next to the car and returned to the driver's seat. The two medical men, with apparent reluctance, climbed into the car. Why were *they* leaving? The car turned and drove off towards the gate.

The moment the gate was closed, the men on the lawn all turned towards the crater. The man in the space suit immediately began to make his way back to the building. The other men were pulling at the sacks. Out of one of them they produced another space suit, which the black man began to put on, somewhat uncertainly. Meanwhile, the man in the western shirt was opening the other sack. From it he pulled out and carefully unfolded what appeared to be a large net.

A *net?*

The original astronaut had made his way back into the next room again. He was shouting at me. "I'm back, buddy. Can you hear me? We've got medical help here. We'll have you out real quick now. You OK?"

"I'm great." I was feeling my way along the front wall of the building, where I remembered that there were two, perhaps three, windows. I reached the first of them and lifted. It slid open. I straddled the sill, and then, twisting round, I carefully lowered myself out through the window until my feet settled on the soft invisible lawn below.

Chapter 4

I walked over to the edge of the crater and stepped onto the visible rim. The charred surface was black and hard, and I thought I could see it smudge slightly under my steps. It was immediately easier to walk: I could now at least see the ground beneath my feet. As I continued out onto the soft green lawn I could see the grass crush each time I placed a foot down, and spring up again as I raised it.

I had not really made any reasoned decision to escape rescue; I was simply acting on instinct—out of anger, and fear. It was the net mainly. I felt that for the time being I should stay clear of these people, see what they wanted.

I took a wide circle round the man in the business suit and his cowboy companion and stepped up carefully behind them. I suddenly became quite conscious of my own breathing; it seemed extraordinary that they did not notice it.

They had the roll of building plans open at the floor plan of the ground floor, and I set about systematically memorising it. The man in the western shirt was maintaining a continuous conversation with the two men in space suits: "All right, Tyler, you're in front of the entrance now. Remember, you've got two steps up and you're on a little landing in front of the door." He had the southern accent and gregarious manner one associates with commercial airline pilots.

The other man, although plainly in charge, rarely spoke, and when he did it was to issue a brief command in a quiet, emotionless tone. Although his features were perfectly regular, there was something reptilian about the creasing, hairless flesh of his face and head. I disliked him from the first.

I could see in his left cheek an almost imperceptible twitching movement; he was probably angry, I thought. Removing his headset with deliberate precision, he spoke to the man in the western shirt in a soft but unpleasantly intense tone.

"Clellan, you know Morrissey and Tyler better than I do. I want you to impress upon them the critical importance of locating the man in the building. It is of very great importance to me; it is of very great importance to the government of the United States. I am relying upon you, Clellan." He walked over to the communications van, which he entered through the side door.

"You men hear what the colonel says?" Clellan said into his headset. "We're not screwing this one up . . . Is he still not answering? Well, keep talking to him. He has to be in there. Listen, he might have passed out. Tyler, when you get the door open, you wait this side of it until Morrissey finds the guy. Even if he's not moving, you get that net over him right away, hear?"

By this time they were in the reception room, and Tyler was bent over the door to Wachs's office, evidently searching for an invisible keyhole in the invisible door. A difficult task, particularly with those enormous gloves.

"You've got to try both keys," Clellan said. "You got it? OK, ease that door open real slow."

They were taking no chances of my slipping away like the cat. When Morrissey was inside, Tyler pulled the door shut, keeping hold of the invisible doorknob. With his detector Morrissey was poking gingerly at the floor all round the door.

"Come on, Morrissey, he has to be in there somewhere," Clellan was saying. "And be careful. Don't step on the poor guy. Any contamination? Nothing? The room is clean? All right, Tyler, you better get in there too. Go in easy and lock the door behind you."

This took Tyler several minutes. Morrissey was meanwhile moving through the room, waving his detector back and forth, colliding awkwardly with the furniture.

Clellan was growing unhappier by the minute. When Morrissey had completed his search of the room, he and Tyler turned and looked at Clellan expectantly.

"Damn!" barked Clellan.

"Disappointing," said the colonel, who had returned from the van, and stood beside him again.

The colonel and Clellan looked at each other, and then each of them shut off his headset.

Clellan spoke first. "We've only got Morrissey's word that there was ever anyone in there, sir. It's pretty unlikely, when you think about it."

The colonel was silent for a moment. "That's a possibility," he said. "But I am inclined to accept Morrissey's report. I would, by the way, like to see everything we have on Morrissey and Tyler. And on the man in the communications van—Gomez, isn't it?" He became silent again, narrowing his eyes, and then continued. "There certainly seems to have been a cat. And a human being is logically no more unlikely than a cat. In any case, Clellan, we lose nothing by assuming that there *is* a man in there. And if there is, the potential benefits are incalculable. We can hardly begin to conceive of the scientific and medical uses of a totally invisible, complete living human body. Even the most obvious experiments would yield information never before obtainable."

The conversation had taken a turn that held my interest totally, and I remained standing there with them, absolutely still, trying to hold my breath during the pauses.

"He'd make a heck of a field agent," offered Clellan. "He could go *anywhere! Anywhere!* You could have any information in the world!"

"At this point," said the colonel very quietly, "our only concern is to locate the man as quickly as possible."

"Would we really have to turn him over to the scientists?"

"Probably. But we might be able to keep control of him ultimately. The question is whether we can keep this whole thing secret. So far no one really knows there is anything more here than a hole in the ground."

"You mean we might get him back when the scientists were done?" asked Clellan hopefully. "Not that there would be much left after they were through with him," he added.

I was by now thoroughly terrified at the prospect of finding myself in the care of these people. I tried to imagine some of the very useful experiments that might be performed on "a totally invisible, complete living human body". Several came to mind, such as brightly coloured fluids being forced through vital organs, but nothing I wanted to make a firm commitment to right then.

I had to get away.

"Have those men work their way through the rest of the building as fast as they can," the colonel said suddenly. "We want to find that man and then make a complete inventory of whatever it is we have here."

Clellan turned his headset back on and began giving instructions to Morrissey and Tyler. The colonel turned abruptly and walked directly towards me. I jumped awkwardly out of his way, stumbled, and fell to the ground, crushing and denting the grass. My heart pounded with terror, but he strode past me to the large van. As I got carefully to my feet he re-emerged, holding a telephone set. As he spoke, he looked at the fence.

"That's exactly right. I want the guards at ten-yard intervals around the entire perimeter. Immediately. You can start on the alarms and the rest of it once they're deployed . . . That's right. Tell them that there may be contaminated animals here. If they see *any* movement whatever in the fence, they are to fire, even though they can't see what is causing it . . . The gate is not to be opened under any circumstances except on my orders."

The colonel looked up at Clellan.

"Clellan, who has a list of the people in the building yesterday?"

"Simmons has one."

The colonel spoke into the phone again. "You can get the list of known names from Simmons, down here. Start with the demonstrators and find out if anyone is missing besides Carillon. We know that someone remained inside the building, and we have to determine as soon as possible who it was . . . No, no description. Probably an adult male, but we don't have adequate confirmation of that."

I set out towards the gate, hoping that I would see some way to slip through it. When that proved hopeless, I made my way along the fence. As I watched my footprints appear magically on the lawn, like the diagram of a dance step, I began to understand my situation with a new clarity. If you have ever as a child had daydreams of invisibility, you will surely have imagined it as a state of extraordinary, almost limitless freedom. You never left a trace. You could go anywhere, take anything. You could listen to forbidden conversations, find out anything. No one could stop you, because no one knew you were there. No one could set rules or limits for you.

Well, surveying the visible record of my foxtrot across the lawn, I could already see some limits. And I had just spent nearly half an hour with two other human beings, finding it necessary the entire time to take excruciating care not to sneeze or sniff or collide with them. Rather than a magical state of extraordinary freedom, invisibility would be a series of tedious practical problems. Like life under any other sort of conditions, come to think of it. Still, if I hoped to maintain my freedom, I could never make a noise, I could never carry or wear anything in the presence of other people.

Except that I could, of course, carry the things I already had on my person—because they were invisible too. And anything else I might salvage from the building. That was it. The remains of the MicroMagnetics building were the only store of invisible objects in existence. Anything I might ever in my life want to use without betraying myself would have to come from there. And almost surely I would have to get it right now. I turned back across the lawn towards the building. It was, as they say, a once-in-a-lifetime offer.

As I approached the building's entrance I noted with relief that neither grass stains nor ashes from the charred rim were adhering to the soles of my shoes. Tyler and Morrissey, in contrast, had left smudges at the entrance so that I could now see where the steps and the threshold were.

The two of them were in the reception room again. Morrissey had a large red felt-tipped marking pen with which he was trying to make a line on the wall. The pen left only intermittent streaks glistening mysteriously in the air where the wall was, and when he swept his hand back over the streaks, all the ink came off on his glove. Tyler was down on his hands and knees trying the same procedure on the carpet, with much the same results. I wondered what in the world they could be trying to accomplish.

I stepped into the room with them. Careful to feel my way to avoid any collisions with walls or furniture, I found the door to Wachs's office, opened it, stepped through, and carefully closed it again behind me. When the latch snapped into place, Tyler looked up suddenly, then went back to his attempt at defacing the invisible carpet. I waited a moment and then groped my way to the bathroom.

I found the medicine cabinet and felt along each shelf, pulling out objects and dumping them into my pockets. The aspirin bottle, various toilet articles, a small metal box of bandages, toothbrushes, soap. My pockets became so heavy that I was afraid of tearing what was to be my only real suit for the rest of my life. With some difficulty I unfastened the shower curtain from its hooks and laid it out flat on the floor. Onto it I threw all the towels I could find and then the track suits hanging on hooks by the sauna. Then I emptied my pockets onto the heap. From a shelf above the hooks I got a woollen scarf and a metal box, which I opened to see if it was worth taking. Gauze, cotton wool, adhesive tape—a

157

first-aid kit. Onto the heap. I remembered having seen running shoes, and I searched the floor until I found them.

In the janitor's closet adjoining the bathroom I found two shirts, a pair of trousers and another, larger, metal box. It took me a little while to figure out how to open it. A toolbox! I was elated by this discovery. I pulled out a bucket, rags, a wooden broom handle. I could think of no particular use for these things, but I had no time to try to reason it out. I took everything portable that might conceivably be useful as a weapon or a tool—or that struck my terrified fancy.

In the back of the closet I found a stepladder about five feet high. Not nearly enough for the fence. I decided to leave it where it was. I carried everything else back into the bathroom and heaped it on top of the shower curtain. The toolbox, which was too heavy, and the broomstick, which was too long, I laid down on the floor next to the other things. I had to keep everything together. When you cannot see things, it can take for ever to find them.

Tyler and Morrissey had now given up on their marking pens and were working with a large roll of cable. They laid it out on the reception-room floor, along the junctures with the walls. When they came to a door, they would cut the cable with an enormous pair of wire cutters, to leave an interruption. They were methodically superimposing a visible floor plan on the invisible building. It struck me that Wachs's office would surely be next, and I wanted to go through it before they did.

I got hold of all four corners of the shower curtain and dragged the bundle back into the middle of Wachs's office. I explored the desk top, coming up with a letter opener, a ruler, a stapler. In the drawers I found paperclips, rubber bands, scissors, a Swiss army knife, Scotch tape. And, at the back of the right-hand bottom drawer, a gun.

This discovery was exciting. I felt more powerful, and I found myself glancing over at Clellan and the colonel, standing out on the lawn. It was a very small pistol. It took me several minutes to get the magazine open. I emptied it, counting six bullets, and then carefully refilled the magazine and slipped the gun into my jacket pocket.

My heap of objects had become very large. Tyler and Morrissey might walk in at any moment and literally stumble onto it. I had to get everything out of the building. I located a window and slid up the lower sash. The noise seemed to be cataclysmic, and I looked back to see whether Morrissey and Tyler had heard. They seemed quite caught up in their work.

Returning to my pile of invisible objects, I knelt down and gathered the four corners of the shower curtain into one hand. Then I dragged it over to the window. I could hear things dropping out of the bundle as I went. I hoisted the bundle up over the windowsill and lowered it to the ground below. Then I went down on my hands and knees to search the

floor for whatever I had dropped in transit. As I knelt on the floor Tyler and Morrissey pushed open the door and joined me in the office.

They went straight to work. Unfortunately, they started along the wall that separated the office from the bathroom. The broomstick and the toolbox were still on the bathroom floor, and I definitely did not want to risk their getting possession of that toolbox.

I got to my feet and walked ever so slowly, one step at a time, right between them to the bathroom door. It was not open wide enough for me to slip through, and when I gently pushed it, there was an awful creaking noise. Tyler stiffened. I heard him speak into his microphone in a low monotone.

"He's in here with us now . . . Yes, sir. Absolutely certain."

Morrissey had stopped moving too. Entering the bathroom, I bent down and patted the floor carefully. I located both the toolbox and the broomstick and then slowly lifted them. All three of us remained still for several long minutes. Then I began moving. As I stepped onto the carpeted floor alongside Morrissey I heard him say, "He's right here. I can feel him moving."

He lunged right at me. I shoved the end of the broomstick as hard as I could into his belly. He doubled up and collapsed onto the floor with a gurgling moan. Tyler looked about helplessly, and seeing nothing much to pursue, bent over Morrissey.

I continued straight on into the reception room, out of the front door, and round the corner of the building until I stepped into my pile of things. I tied the corners of the bundle into a knot, slipped the broomstick through the knot, and levered it—somewhat painfully—over my shoulder. Then, picking up the toolbox with my other hand, I set out across the lawn. I deposited everything at the base of an enormous copper beech tree nearby, where low, spreading branches made it impossible for anyone to walk past without crouching.

I walked back and continued foraging through the offices, adding booty to my hoard under the tree. Morrissey and Tyler were moving along very quickly now, and the building was taking form all round us like some enormous model constructed of pipe cleaners. I decided to follow them, staying a room or two behind, to take advantage of their wire outlines.

By early afternoon Tyler and Morrissey had outlined all the rooms in the front half of the building with wire, and I had looted them. As I was returning from the tree, where I had deposited my last load, I saw Morrissey unlocking the door to the laboratory. Curious, I slipped back into the building, walked carefully down the corridor, and stood almost next to him, waiting for him to admit me.

He bent down to pick up the radiation detector. As he straightened up he turned back and looked straight through me. It disconcerted me for an instant. I turned too and saw that he was looking at Tyler, who was coming down the corridor to join us.

Morrissey did not wait for him. Holding the detector in his right hand, he used his left hand to push open the door. I followed Morrissey straight in, ahead of Tyler. As Morrissey stepped past the door and let the hand that had pushed it open drop down to his side, something slammed violently against the entire length of my body. I stood there in a daze for many seconds before I comprehended that the heavy metal door had been pushed into me automatically by a closing spring. I reached up to feel my throbbing nose and cheek. Tender, but nothing broken.

Morrissey abruptly froze at the sound of the door hitting me. He whispered sharply into his radio. "He's right behind me. In the doorway!"

Tyler charged up the corridor and through the doorway, his arms extended to seize me. At the same instant Morrissey wheeled about, dropping his detector, and lunged at me. They both had their hands on me, and if they had not been wearing those suits and those clumsy gloves, they would have held me easily. In total panic I pulled loose from them, shoving and hitting them at random to get free. I staggered away from them along the wall inside the laboratory, my heart pounding. Tyler stepped to one side, and I heard the door swing shut next to him. He stood there, barring the exit.

"We got him," Tyler said into his headset. Then he looked at the middle of the room and spoke in a loud, self-conscious voice. "Listen, fella, we know you're there. We want to help you."

There was a pause. I said nothing.

"Listen, you got to let us know where you are."

There was another long pause. None of us had anything to say.

Tyler remained with his back pressed against the closed door, watching apprehensively for some sign of me. But Morrissey picked up his detector again and set out towards the centre of the room, waving the detector in front of him. He must be heading straight for Wachs's extraordinary device—whatever it was that had created this grotesque situation.

The way seemed to be clear, and he had become quite skilful at walking on the invisible surface, so that it was with considerable confidence that he stepped forward and plunged into the void. Or at least it must have felt like the void. In fact, he pitched abruptly into a nasty heap about ten feet below and then slid down and forward another five feet, as if he were on a playground slide. The detector, which he had lost hold of in the fall, slid down beside him.

For what may have been half a minute he lay there motionless, suspended a little less than halfway between where Tyler and I stood and the bottom of the apparent crater. He began speaking.

"Yeah, I'm all right. There's a hole here," he explained—rather superfluously, I thought. He tried to stand. "Ankle hurts!"

Favouring one foot, he began to step carefully forward towards us. After the first few steps he found himself on a steep incline. His feet slipped out from under him, and he slid back down on his face, feet first, to where he had started. He couldn't get out.

Apparently, the invisible sphere in which we found ourselves had a hollow core, perhaps thirty feet in diameter. Whatever piece of equipment had caused all this must have somehow disintegrated itself, leaving nothing but the cavity into which Morrissey had fallen.

I had lost interest in the laboratory. I wanted to get out.

Tyler was not moving from the door. Clellan, I saw with dismay, was walking across the lawn towards us. There was no time for deliberation. I reached into my pocket and fitted my hand round the gun.

"Tyler? Do you hear me?"

Tyler stiffened. "I hear you, fella. What can we do for you?"

"Tyler, I want you to move away from that door."

"I can't do that, fella. Listen, we—"

"Tyler, I have a gun in my hand. Now, I know you can't see it, so I'm going to fire it once, just so you can hear how it sounds." I fired it at the wall beside him. Tyler flinched instinctively at the noise. "Now, Tyler, if you don't move away from that door right now, I'm going to kill you."

At the report of my gun Morrissey had immediately begun to tear off his suit, and Clellan had started running into the building, a gun in his right hand. My choices were running out.

I tried to point the gun at Tyler's legs—it was difficult to be sure exactly where it was pointing—and pulled the trigger. An instant after the shot, blood began to ooze out of a little hole in Tyler's suit at about the level of his waist. Horrible. I had wanted to shoot him in the thigh. The other horrible thing was that he remained standing against the door, staring blankly ahead.

"Move!" I shouted.

Clellan was into the corridor. I found myself lowering the gun and pulling the trigger again. This time Tyler let out a little shriek and hunched forward, clutching at his left knee. I dropped the gun back into my pocket and stepped quickly up to him. Before he could straighten up again, I slipped behind him so that my back was against the door, and pushed him as hard as I could. He pitched forwards onto his face. I lifted his lower legs, shoving him headfirst into the cavity.

I turned to face Clellan just as he reached the entrance to the laboratory. I pulled the door open just as he reached out with his left hand to feel whether it was closed. Finding no door, he stepped uncertainly forward past it.

I had slid my left leg in front of him, and letting the door go, I clamped

162

my right hand hard into the back of his neck and shoved him forward so that he tripped over my leg and plunged into the cavity with the others. When he reached the bottom, he capsized Morrissey and slammed into Tyler, and the three of them tumbled into a heap.

As I turned to leave the building, I was shaking with horror and relief. I had never shot anyone before, never harmed anyone physically. No time to think about that now. I looked across the lawn and saw the colonel staring towards me. I would, I decided, have to speak to him. He was the one person who could arrange to let me through the gate.

WHEN I CAME UP to him, the colonel was talking by radio to the men in the building. I looked back and saw that they had formed themselves into a human ladder in midair, Clellan standing on Tyler's shoulders and Morrissey on Clellan's. There was a little pool of blood floating between Tyler's feet.

"Have you got it?" the colonel was saying. "Good." Morrissey had managed to struggle out of the pit, and Tyler had slumped back down to the bottom of the cavity, where Clellan was bending over him.

"All right," the colonel continued. "Get Tyler into the ambulance and out to the gate as fast as you can and come straight back. And Morrissey, when you're taking Tyler out through the gate, be careful. Make sure this person doesn't leave the area." The colonel unhooked his headset and pushed it into his side jacket pocket.

I hesitated. This seemed like a good moment to speak. I knew I should get on with it—the longer I delayed, the worse my chances became. But even under the best of circumstances it is awkward striking up a conversation with a stranger, and the circumstances here were grotesquely poor in every respect.

"Hello," I ventured.

He gave a start, more of a massive twitch.

"How are you?" He spoke slowly. Then he offered his hand.

"How are you?" I returned. There could be no question of letting him take my hand.

"Very well, thank you. My name is David Jenkins." When I did not respond, he went on, "Is there anything you need? We're here to help you."

His soft, insinuating voice was composed now. He withdrew his hand slowly, his eyes carefully searching all round for some visible sign of me. The grass was thoroughly trampled where we stood, but I nevertheless kept myself absolutely still. I was five feet away from him.

"There's nothing, really. I just wanted to talk to you, to try to work something out. By the way, I'm sorry for shooting Tyler. I didn't—"

"It was our fault as much as yours. I'm afraid we've handled the situation badly. I just want you to understand that we're going to do

163

everything for you that's humanly possible." He formed his features into what was surely meant to be a warm and reassuring smile.

"I appreciate that very much," I said in a firmer tone, "but I've already decided I don't want any help. All I want—"

"By the way, I don't know your name. What *is* your name?"

Caught off guard by the question, I felt trapped into answering and said the first thing that came to mind. "You can call me Harvey."

"Well, Harvey, I know that the last twenty-four hours must have been incredibly painful and disorientating for you, and I sense you are in some way apprehensive about us. It might be useful if I told you who we are and what our responsibilities here are. We're concerned with coordinating the collection, analysis and synthesis of information for the government. We know, of course, that you probably came here to participate in a political demonstration. But we're here to help you, and we don't care what your political beliefs are. The people who go into government service have every sort of political belief you can imagine, but there's one thing they all have in common: a commitment to serve something beyond their own personal interests."

"Just so," I said agreeably, although uppermost in my mind at the moment was my own personal interest in getting past the fence.

"Harvey, however horrible this may be for you, it puts you in a position to make an extraordinary scientific contribution to humanity, and frankly, I admire—"

"Well, of course there is science and so forth. But it seems to me that you and I should be figuring out how we could most usefully work together. I should be working with you as some sort of intelligence agent, don't you think?"

His brow furrowed and his lips pursed, but he said nothing.

"The more I think about it, the more obvious the whole thing becomes," I went on. "You've maintained extraordinary secrecy here, given the spectacular nature of what's taken place. No one but your men here knows I exist. Of course, I would have to rely totally on you for guidance. Without you I probably couldn't even survive. But with your direction we could be virtually omniscient."

His eyes narrowed, and he spoke softly and with a new intensity. "Harvey, I think you are right. And I think we're going to work well together. Now, the first step," he said briskly, as if he were casually mentioning an incidental detail, "is to get you properly looked at."

"David, I think that would be a terrible mistake. If we're going to work together, my whole value lies in no one's knowing about me. If you start calling in doctors and scientists, we'll lose control of the situation. It seems to me that what we have to do now is to arrange for me to slip out through the fence on my own. I'm ready to put myself in your hands: you can work out the details of how I get out unnoticed. But when you make

164

it possible for me to get out, that will be a kind of seal on our bargain, a show of good faith. Which we'll need if we're to work together."

"Harvey, I think you can understand that you can't just walk away from here unsupervised."

"I really don't see why not. It seems like a perfectly reasonable and natural thing to do. Furthermore, it's something I'm legally entitled to do. Wouldn't you say?"

"Well, not necessarily, Harvey." His tone became even more carefully patient and reasonable as the words became more threatening. "You have to understand that, entirely aside from the issue of national security, there has been extensive property damage. And at least two people lost their lives yesterday. Another man has been shot today, and we don't know yet how serious his condition is. At the very least, both local and federal authorities would be under a clear obligation to detain and question you. I think you can appreciate that, Harvey."

At the mention of my shooting Tyler I turned to see what was happening to him. All three men were out of the pit now. Clellan and Morrissey had loaded Tyler onto a stretcher and were carrying him across the lawn towards the medical van.

"Are you still there?" the colonel asked.

"I'm here. But I'm leaving now, with or without your help."

"Well, Harvey, I can't stop you," he said very patiently. "But I'm horrified at the thought of your trying to get past that fence. You couldn't possibly succeed; it would be tragic. Anyway, what would you do if you did get past the fence? Where would you go? How could you hope to survive on your own in this condition?"

"If I encounter any insoluble problem, I'll be back in touch with you."

"Harvey, even if you somehow did manage to get past the fence, we would of course come after you."

"How could you hope to track me down once I was out of here? I'm standing right in front of you talking to you, and yet even now you wouldn't be able to get hold of me."

"Well, Harvey, we do have some experience in locating people. And in this case we would be in a position to devote very substantial resources to the task."

"No amount would be enough. And anyway, who would believe in my existence? What sensible person would provide money for a search for an invisible man?"

"Harvey," he said softly, "if I walked the right three people from Washington through this building tomorrow, I could have enough funds to locate a hundred of you."

What he said seemed credible. It reminded me that I was in increasing danger. I had a great deal to do and I was wasting my time.

"Look here, David. Everything you say makes sense, and I suppose I'll have to do things your way. But I'd just like to take an hour or two by myself to think things through first. It's been a difficult day for me. You'll be around, I suppose?"

"I'll be right here when you want me, Harvey. You take your time and arrive at your decision freely."

As he spoke, I took one careful step backwards. It seemed to me that he was looking straight at where I had placed my foot. I brought back the other foot beside it. As I turned to walk away he was still studying the ground before him.

I would have to confront the problem of the fence now. I had no idea of what to do, where to begin. The whole enterprise seemed quite impossible. The area was sealed off and guarded more thoroughly and ruthlessly than a prison camp.

I walked back to the building and went straight to the janitor's closet for the stepladder. I hooked it over my shoulder and walked out to the gate. I set it up to one side of the gate itself and climbed the steps carefully. In order to see over the top of the fence, I had to climb right up onto the top of the ladder, so that I had nothing to brace myself against. More for balance than support I held a strand of the barbed wire between my thumb and index finger, being careful not to move it and attract the attention of the men below.

Directly behind the gate an area ten feet wide had been covered with wet sand, and there were men raking it smooth. Each tine of each rake left a perfectly clear fine line. Each step left a beautiful footprint. Along the fence, each on his little platform, stood one guard after another, holding an automatic weapon. Very unpromising. Sickening.

I could not see very far because of the way the perimeter curved, but in both directions the ground had been cleared in a ten-foot band along the fence, and sand was being spread. Not far off, I could hear chain saws. Closing in. My sense of balance seemed to evaporate, and I felt myself teetering. Slowly, unsteadily, I climbed down to the ground. The relief was wonderful.

I folded the ladder and started along the fence. They had been very thorough in screening the view, and nowhere could I find so much as a crack to peer through. About fifty yards along from the gate I could hear that I was opposite the chain saws and mowers. I risked mounting the ladder once more to survey their progress. It would not take them long. The fence ran for most of its length through fields, so that there was very little for them to cut. They would be slowed down, however, on the east side, where the fence bordered a wood. It was there that I would have my best chance.

I finally found what I wanted—a maple tree still standing close to the fence on the other side. I made one more brief, precarious ascent of the ladder to get a full view of the area. I didn't like my prospects particularly, but I decided it was worth a shot, as the unfortunate expression goes. I placed the stepladder directly in front of the nearest fence post so that I would be able to find it again.

I returned to the building, where Clellan, Morrissey and the colonel—without any protective clothing now—each sat in a different room, diligently writing at invisible desks—a troupe of levitating pantomimists representing office workers in an imaginary building. They were cataloguing all the objects in all the rooms. They had made my task as easy as it could be, under the circumstances. Each chair, table and desk had been marked off by a loop of wire round the bottom of each leg. With the help of those outlines I could immediately locate and carry out everything I wanted without stumbling into walls and furniture.

I found three small tables, all the same height. In the reception room I found a coffee table six feet long. I slid the pieces of wire off the ends of the legs, leaving the outlines on the floor as neatly as possible. Then I lowered each table out of the nearest window and carried it to the fence where I had left the stepladder.

From the conference room I carried off two wooden folding chairs. Finally, I returned to Wachs's office, where I pulled back the carpeting and with my penknife carved off several large pieces of the rubber underlay. Exactly what I needed. On my way back with the matting I stopped at the beech tree and searched through my sacks until I located a ball of twine.

I assembled the furniture about a foot away from the fence, experimenting with different arrangements until I had a sort of stairway composed of chairs and tables, interleaved with the rubber underlay to keep it all from slipping. I then tied everything together as best I could without being able to see the twine or the furniture or even my own fingers. I hoped it would prevent the whole lot from sliding disastrously apart. I climbed to the top to test the security of the structure. The surface of the table top was less than six feet above the ground but, standing on it, I felt as if it were sixty.

I climbed down and brought the stepladder over. The whole thing seemed implausible, but I wasn't going to think about it. I got up onto the first table, lifted up the stepladder and centred it on the surface of the highest table. I got out the twine and lashed the ladder to the table. My stairway had reached its full height. I was relieved to find the top of the ladder was several inches higher than the barbed wire coiled along the top of the fence.

I clambered down and dragged the coffee table over. Holding onto it, I climbed up until I was on the top table again. I hauled the coffee table up carefully and balanced it next to the stepladder. The next few minutes were hateful. I had to climb up to the second step of the ladder, slowly lift the coffee table to chest height, twist it round over the fence, and try to hook it over the branch of the maple tree on the other side. Unsure of whether the table would be long enough to reach the branch, I lowered it slowly. Held out at that angle, the weight became almost insupportable. I felt the far end come to rest on the branch. I pushed it further, so that one leg was hooked through a fork in the branch. With relief I lowered the near end slowly onto the ladder top. The table was barely long enough, and I was afraid that when the branch was weighed down it might pull the table off the ladder. I lashed the two together with twine, then set about making a final test of the structure.

Very carefully I climbed up onto the unseeable tabletop and inched my way on all fours out to the middle of it. It was not a pleasant vantage point. I was looking straight down on a barbed-wire fence and in either direction at a man with a gun whose job it was to shoot me if I made a mistake.

I was tempted to keep going. Not carrying anything, I would make no noise. I would be gone. I could see the men with their chain saws now only fifty yards away. They would not be long. And this was a tree they would certainly be cutting down. But I would need my equipment and supplies. Without them, I was finished anyway.

Returning over my bridge I had to crawl backwards, feet first, so that I could get back onto the stepladder. When I was on the ground again I made three or four trips back to the beech tree, hauling back seven sacks full of random objects and heaping them together under my pyramid. I took the smallest sack and, mounting the ladder, lifted it up onto the coffee table. I climbed up after it, pushed it across ahead of me to the other side, and then climbed down through the tree to the ground. I carried the sack about twenty yards back into the woods and left it on the ground next to a particularly misshapen pine tree which I was confident I would recognise.

I repeated the entire trip seven times, until I had everything safe in a large heap in the woods. I was sweating and trembling with the tension, but elated. I was nearly done here.

I climbed back over the fence and hurried to the building. I had one important task left. The colonel and his men were as I had left them, miraculously sitting in midair, working at invisible desks. The colonel was right, I thought. The spectacle before me would convince anyone that vast amounts of money should be budgeted, vast numbers of people assigned, to the study of these extraordinary phenomena. And even to the capture of the invisible man.

I went into Wachs's office first and closed the doors. I grabbed all the loose sheets of paper I could find, crumpled them, and tossed them under the desk. I took a cigarette lighter that I had found on Wachs's desk from my pocket and lit the pile until I felt the heat of the invisible flame spreading through the paper.

I hurried out of Wachs's office and ran past the laboratory to an office at the other end of the building. This time I dragged the desk over against the wall before setting the fire, to make sure it would spread to the building. I was making a lot of noise, and all three men were looking in my direction now. On my way out I set another fire in the reception room. I left the building with as much paper as I could carry.

When I got back to the fence, I spent another five or ten minutes crumpling paper and filling my structure with it. I mounted my exit stair for the last time and I set it alight. I climbed up and over to the tree, then crawled back out onto the table, cut loose the twine that tied it to the stepladder, and pulled it over into the tree. I could feel the heat from my burning tower of ladder and tables.

I took a last look at the building. The three men were running through the building now, and you could see from the way they moved that they were in a state of near panic, although, floating in thin air, their gestures seemed ridiculous. I went to my hoard and set about moving it in stages until I had everything neatly stored ten feet in from the road on the other side of the wood.

Suddenly there was a deep, resonating boom behind the fence, as if something had exploded, and the sky above MicroMagnetics seemed to shudder. I saw a patch of flame high up where fire had spread into the visible trees beyond the building. I hoped it would continue to spread and obliterate any sign of my escape.

Standing there alone in the woods, my heart pounding and my body shaking from fear and exhaustion, MicroMagnetics and all the extraordinary things I had seen—and not seen—already seemed remote and unreal, a receding dream. There was, nevertheless, the preposterous, terrifying, inescapable fact that I was invisible.

Chapter 5

For perhaps half an hour I sat trembling beside my invisible possessions and rested. I was on the edge of a wooded road. I felt, I suppose, like any escaped prisoner: elated at having scaled the prison walls but terrified by the lack of refuge in the world beyond them. It seemed safer, therefore, to sit and contemplate what I had escaped from rather than what I had escaped to.

I had certainly precipitated a great deal of activity. I could hear siren after siren howl up to the other side of the enclosed area. I hoped the fire would utterly consume the building and every invisible object in it—everything that could make my existence credible. Who would believe Colonel Jenkins now, without that building?

It was important to keep moving. What I needed urgently was a car that I could load up with my possessions and drive away. I knew that there must be an extraordinary number of vehicles at the MicroMagnetics site, many of them probably unattended.

I set out, walking back towards the entrance to MicroMagnetics, keeping on the left edge of the road in order to see any vehicle coming towards me. No one was going to swerve to avoid me. A red pick-up truck passed me from behind, and I was relieved to see that the road had not been closed off to civilian traffic.

A minute later I came round a bend and saw that ahead of me, on the left, another road ran at a right angle into the road I was on. Just beyond the intersection a roadblock had been created out of state police cars and large yellow plastic barrels. A gap had been left just large enough for a car to pass through, and in front of it stood a state trooper.

Somewhere on the other side of the roadblock there would be vehicles, some perhaps with ignition keys left in them. Whether that would be of any use to me would depend on whether there was some way to get round or through the roadblock.

I walked across the intersection and took a position just to one side of the point at which vehicles would have to stop. I waited to see what happened when a vehicle left the area.

It was ten minutes before an old pick-up truck came rattling up from the direction of MicroMagnetics. No one seemed much interested. It slowed down as it passed between the barrels, and the driver shouted out, "Reilly! Kevin Reilly!" The trooper glanced casually at the passenger window of the cab as he made his waving motion. The pick-up, without ever coming to a full stop, continued on over the crossroads and sped off down the road.

Definitely worth a try. I set off for the MicroMagnetics site. There were open fields on both sides of the road now. The tree-lined drive leading into MicroMagnetics was cut off by the fence and completely deserted, since the colonel's men had constructed their new access road further on, but strewn about the field on my left, immediately opposite the old drive, were roughly two dozen cars, completely unattended.

When I recognised the grey van, I felt a wave of something resembling vertigo. Carillon's van. Less than thirty-six hours ago I had arrived in it looking pretty much like anyone else. Now I looked like no one at all. Thirty-six hours. It seemed like the proverbial eternity.

I walked into the field to look at the cars. There was quite a varied selection to choose from, but it was Carillon's van that I wanted. For one thing it was more than big enough to hold my entire hoard. Also Jenkins would assume that one of Carillon's friends had made off with it, and it would confirm his assumption that I was a Student for a Fair World. They might never get around to checking on Nicholas Halloway.

There was one other thing about the van. I had a clear picture in my mind of Carillon standing in the parking lot yesterday morning and casually tossing the keys in through the open back doors. I took a long, careful look round. It was almost dark now, and as far as I could tell there was no one anywhere near. I took hold of the side door handle and pulled at it. The door slid open with a violent grinding noise, while in the same instant the interior roof light automatically illuminated the van like a signal lantern in the dark field. I lunged at the light and switched it off, my heart racing. I stumbled out and stood waiting to see whether anyone would come. In the distance there was noise and activity, but there was not a sound in the field around me. I climbed back in and searched the grimy metal floor until I found the keys.

I climbed into the driver's seat and wound down the window at my side. I sat there for several moments, collecting my wits and my nerve. I started the engine and moved slowly out onto the road, with the headlights still off. I wanted them to have as little warning as possible of my arrival.

When the cluster of cars and policemen came into view, I switched my headlights on and accelerated, driving through them at an aggressive pace and halting abruptly as far forward in the roadblock opening as I plausibly could.

"Reilly," I shouted out of the window. A policeman—not the one who had been there before—walked slowly forward towards my window. He held a large flashlight in one hand. In another moment he would surely be gazing in amazement at the empty driver's seat.

"Thank you!" I shouted amiably through the window, as if the hoped-for permission had actually been granted, and pulled away at a confident but not excessive speed. I had a glimpse of the policeman's face registering both surprise and indecision. He might decide to do nothing or he might radio to another police car. I had to keep moving.

In the illumination of my headlights I picked out the place where my things were, on the left side of the road. I pulled over. With the motor running and the headlights on so that I could see my footing, I charged over to my cache. I hauled the seven sacks into the van. Then the toolbox, the coffee table, the broomstick. I groped around on the ground for anything that might have slipped out of the sacks.

At that moment the headlights of a patrol car appeared in the distance. I lunged into the van and pulled away, crossing obliquely to the right side of the road. They were still more than fifty yards away. It should look to them as if I had been driving towards them the whole time.

I accelerated steadily. Looking into my headlights, they would not be able to see the empty driver's seat, and by the time we passed each other, I was going at forty miles per hour. I was terrified, but I resisted the temptation to accelerate over fifty. I kept watching the rearview mirror. No headlights appeared.

After five minutes I gradually began to calm down. I wound up my side window. In the dark no one was going to notice that my van had no visible driver. I could probably drive wherever I liked, except that eventually I would run out of gas or the sun would come up. The petrol tank was three-quarters full. Where was I going?

I slowed down. I had to think things through. I had a van full of irreplaceable objects. Ideally, I would like to take them home. The trouble was that I lived on the other side of the Hudson River, and to cross the Hudson River you have to be prepared to drive up to a well-lit tollbooth and hand the toll collector two dollars. I had in my pocket about a hundred and fifty dollars' worth of invisible bills. I had to find a temporary storage place for my things on this side of the Hudson.

I could see now where I had to go. It occurred to me, however, that I had no idea where I was. I began at each intersection to choose the most important-looking road. Like someone lost in the wilderness, who will always follow running water downstream: sooner or later one will encounter civilisation or the sea. I was rewarded eventually with a sign for Route 202 and made the turn marked "202 North".

In less than forty-five minutes I had found Richard and Emily's house in Basking Ridge. I switched off my headlights and drove up onto the lawn and round behind the house, so that even if someone should come up the drive, they would not see the van.

I found a torch in the van and set out to reconnoitre the grounds. There was the house itself, a small barn, and a pump house. I settled on the barn. It was unlocked and empty, both indications that no one would have any interest in it. Lying on the sawdust floor were some old, weathered pieces of timber. I used a ladder to lift several pieces of the timber up and across the rafters so that they made a sort of platform well out of reach. In twenty minutes I had stored all my invisible things securely in the rafters and smoothed the sawdust floor again. I assumed that I would be back in a few days to retrieve everything. But barring some extraordinary piece of bad luck, everything should be safe there indefinitely. When they were in the United States, Richard and Emily came down here for weekends, but most of the time the house stood empty.

I headed back out of the drive, not turning on the lights again until I was a quarter of a mile down the road.

AS I GOT CLOSER to New York I began to feel, for the first time, almost secure. I had successfully escaped. In another hour or two I would be safely back home in my apartment.

I drove into the city of Newark, New Jersey, a short train ride from New York. The bright lights made me anxious, but the streets were nearly empty.

I pulled up alongside a fire hydrant and switched off the ignition, leaving the key in it. Then I slid out onto the street. It seemed unlikely that Carillon's van would ever be located. An abandoned car in the city streets is like a bleeding animal in shark-infested waters. The predators strike instantly and strip it clean to the skeleton.

I walked to the station, dreading the next hour of dodging through crowds on public transport, but it was almost midnight and I had no difficulty avoiding collisions with the few other passengers boarding the train. Once I was sure they were all settled, I even allowed myself the luxury of a seat.

At Pennsylvania Station in Manhattan, I waited until all the other passengers had left the train and then hiked up the empty stairways. When I emerged into the main hall, it seemed to me as if I were returning to New York after an absence of years. I felt a relief verging on joy at being back, but at the same time I felt utterly remote from the human beings scattered through the cavernous room, none of whom could be aware of my existence. They were no longer people I might speak to or know: they were only objects whose unpredictable movements across my path constituted a mild danger against which I had to maintain my guard.

I made my way down to the subway, climbed over a turnstile, and boarded an empty coach on a northbound train. After a few transfers, dodging passengers as they came past, I reached Eighty-sixth Street on the East Side. When everyone else had left the platform, I plodded up the two flights of stairs to the street. I was very tired. When I reached my building, I found that I was trembling from nerves and exhaustion.

My apartment occupied the entire top floor of a brownstone house between Fifth and Madison Avenues. The three flights of stairs were sometimes demoralising, but because of the way the lower floors of the building had been extended into the back garden, my apartment had been left with a large terrace facing south and I was afforded a pleasant illusion of being surrounded by vegetation and sunlight. You entered the building through two windowed doors, between which there was a tiny vestibule containing the mailboxes, the doorbells, and an intercom.

I looked around to make sure no one was in the street, pushed open the outer door just far enough to get through, and slipped into the vestibule. I pulled out my keys and, out of habit, set about opening my mailbox, a difficult task now that the key was invisible. I slipped the mail into my side pocket. It took me another few minutes to single out my house key and then get the inner vestibule door open. I began the long trudge up the stairs.

I was most of the way up the first flight when I glanced down and saw the bizarre spectacle I was creating. The mail in my pocket was clearly visible to anyone who looked out from one of the other apartments, and it would seem to be bobbing inexplicably through the air, up the stairway. I bent over and held it in my hand next to the skirting board, where it would be less noticeable, and in this awkward position climbed up the remaining stairs.

The stairway ended on a small landing in front of my door. I got out my keys again. My body ached to be safely inside. The door swung open. I stepped in, switched on the lights, pulled the keys out of the lock, and pushed the door shut behind me. *Home free.*

I nearly swooned from elation and relief. Nothing could happen to me now. They couldn't get to me here. I stumbled deliriously into the kitchen, dropping the mail onto the kitchen table and tossing my keys on top, just as always.

The air was still and stuffy. Careful. Before I opened the kitchen window, I would have to switch out the lights. Otherwise some peeping neighbour would see the window sash rising mysteriously of its own accord. New Yorkers, who live over, under, and all around each other, take extraordinary pains to avoid any intimacy with their neighbours, but they are always watching, peering, spying.

I turned off the lights again and systematically drew each curtain. Then, when I opened some windows and got the lights on again, I found myself hurrying towards the refrigerator. As I pulled open the door I remembered half consciously that I had not drunk anything since morning or eaten anything for almost two days. Beer. I pulled out a bottle and with trembling hands twisted off the cap. It was wonderfully cold going down. Sit down. Home now. Safe. I felt euphoria spreading through my body.

Soon I was back at the refrigerator looking to see what there was to eat. A half-full container of loo shu pork. I got some chopsticks from the drawer and frantically pulled off the top. I shovelled the food in, swallowing it almost unchewed. When the box was empty, I found a quart of coffee ice cream and began greedily spooning it into myself. I noticed that I seemed to have spilled some food down my front. Better stop and clean my shirt, I thought. Important to keep it invisible.

But when I looked down at myself, I saw that I had not spilled anything at all. What I had done was to pour into my invisible oesophagus a hideously visible brown-and-yellow mixture. The sludgy concoction was piling up in my stomach, of whose exact location I had never, until this moment, really been quite sure.

I was becoming a sack of garbage. I suppose, on reflection, that is what I had always been, but nature had not formerly imposed this aspect of the human condition quite so vividly upon me. The nasty facts had been discreetly enveloped in opaque flesh. Now I was to be a transparent sack of garbage. I cannot begin to tell you how distasteful it was.

It was also disheartening. Frightening. I had thus far assumed—even almost grown used to the idea—that if I could not look like everyone else, at least I would be entirely invisible. All my hopes of avoiding capture had been built on that assumption. Now it appeared that not only would I not be safely invisible after all, but I would be manifested in the visible world exclusively as a gastrointestinal tract. Ludicrous.

A more hopeful thought came to me. Perhaps, as I ate and drank and breathed, my body would gradually reconstitute itself out of normal, visible particles of matter. Perhaps I should be eating as much as I could force down. Speed up the process. In a few weeks I might look like a human being again.

An unrealistic thought, I decided, and my mood plummeted precipitously. The most likely thing was that I would be neither visible nor invisible but rather a blotchy translucent sack of filth. Invisibility, which a few minutes before had seemed a horrible fate, now seemed infinitely desirable. Damn.

Chapter 6

The morning sun was flooding in through the uncurtained window and soaking into my body. It felt wonderful. Although I seemed to have passed out with all my clothes on. Hadn't even got under the covers. I could feel the rough bedspread against my cheek and see the empty bed, still made up.

Empty! The bed was empty!

Invisible! I was invisible! My mind exploded into total, terrible wakefulness, and I knew exactly where and what I was.

Horrified, I looked down at my digestive system. I was utterly invisible again. Somehow, during the night, the food I had eaten had been converted by my body to its own peculiar chemical or physical state. Or structure. Or whatever I was. My condition was preposterous. I had to fight down the panic, figure out what to do next. Calmly.

First of all, I took off my sweaty clothes. I hung up my suit and pushed the rest into an empty laundry bag. I emptied a dressing-table drawer and neatly laid out the invisible contents of my pockets in it. I found the keys on top of the mail in the kitchen and carried them back to the drawer. Everything in order.

I went into the bathroom. As I began to brush my teeth before the mirror, I was startled to see the toothpaste suddenly whipped into a fierce, foaming, Cheshire-cat grin. Rinse thoroughly. The smile became an outline formed by traces of toothpaste trapped in the crevice between gum and cheek. A regular walk in the fun house, my daily life. I got an electric razor from the cabinet and attacked the two-day beard, stopping frequently to check my progress by running my hand over my skin. Not much point in shaving at all, really, but I kept at it anyway.

As I stood in the shower soaping myself under the hot water I suddenly saw the form of my body outlined by the streams of lather, and I began rubbing the soap over myself furiously. Pointless. I got out of the shower and dried myself. The last traces of the Cheshire cat grin were nearly gone.

It felt good to be clean again, and it would have been nice to put on some fresh clothes. But fresh clothes would look odd walking through the apartment. I dumped my invisible clothing into the bathtub, turned on the cold water, and poured in some liquid soap.

I walked into the kitchen, sat down at the table and began automatically going through my mail. *Newsweek*. Save the Whales. Catalogues. If I was ever going to buy anything again, it would be through the mail. Or by telephone. I set the catalogues aside to save. Bills from New York Telephone, American Express. Any point in paying these? I was outside the whole economic system now. No, I absolutely had to pay them. That was my only hope. I would go on meeting my obligations, treating the outside world as if I were still there as usual. I opened the bills and took them to the desk in the bedroom, where I made out the cheques and sealed them in the return envelopes. How would I mail them? I left the envelopes in a pile on the desk. I was going to have a lot of problems. A lot of uninteresting everyday things would prove insolubly difficult.

I walked disconsolately back into the kitchen. I had to eat. Some bacon and eggs would do nicely. But if I ate now, I reasoned unhappily, I would be an unsightly sack of half-digested food for the rest of the day. For how long actually? I should try to find out how long the body takes to digest food. Colonel Jenkins would be systematically tracking down everyone who had been at MicroMagnetics, and I knew that above all I could not afford to be full of food just when some government inspector arrived to interview me. Perhaps they would call before coming? Should I be answering the phone? They would probably try to reach me at my office first. What would they be told there? I ought to talk to someone. Get a handhold on the human world.

I dialled my office number.

"Mr. Halloway's office," my secretary answered. I felt so comforted by the sound of her voice I thought I would weep.

"Good morning, Cathy."

"Hi! Where are you?"

"I'm home in bed. I'm not feeling very well. Do you have me down for anything today?"

"No, nothing today."

"Can you give me my messages for the last two days?"

"Sure, just a second. Mr. Peters, of Badlands Energy, returning your call. A Lester Thurson, of Spintex."

"No one else called? No one called and didn't leave a name?"

"That's everything I've got. I told them you were out of town. That's what you wanted, right?"

"That's perfect. Listen, I'm feeling a little off, today. I don't think I'll be in."

"I'm sorry to hear it. Is it serious?"

"No, no. It's nothing. Just not quite myself. Listen—"

"Have you been to the doctor?" Cathy was someone for whom visits to doctors were an important feature of daily life.

"No, I haven't. I don't think a doctor would be . . . Actually, that's an idea. I might go out and see a doctor at some point."

"Shall I say you're off sick?"

"No, no. Say I was in earlier and had to go out again. Say I'll be in and out all day. Hard to catch. Just take messages, and I'll get back to whoever it is."

"OK."

"Listen, Cathy. I hate to ask, really, but could you possibly bring some things to my apartment so I can work at home?"

"No problem. What do you want?"

"Just dump all my mail and messages into a folder. Do I have anything important in the next few days?"

"Wait a second . . . You have the monthly review on Thursday."

That would be the first real problem. The one meeting I really had to attend. "I'll be fine by then. Look, is there any money in petty cash—or do you have a couple of hundred dollars in your bank account? I'm completely out of cash and I haven't got any food in the house. I'll give you a cheque when you come by." As I talked, I became aware of how odd the telephone receiver seemed, floating magically over my chair.

"No problem. I can cash a cheque on the way. How many dollars do you want?"

"Two hundred would be fine—or make it two fifty, if you can."

"Do you want me to pick up some food or anything?"

"No, no. Actually, if you could bring a *Wall Street Journal* and the *Times*, that would be great. And when you go, remember to tell whoever's taking calls that I've just gone out. Nothing about being sick."

"Fine. I should be there in under an hour."

"Thanks very much, Cathy." I hung up the phone, took a sheet of paper and a pen from my desk drawer, and began to write, watching with amazement as the pen danced over the paper: *Cathy, Had to run out to the doctor. Apartment keys enclosed. There is a cheque for $250 on the coffee table. Dump the mail and the cash anywhere in the apartment. Talk to you this afternoon. Thanks, Nick. P.S. Please leave both keys locked in the apartment.*

I FOLDED THE NOTE round my spare keys and slipped everything into an envelope, on which I wrote *Cathy Addonizio.* Walking out onto the landing, I became conscious of the envelope bobbing and swooping through the air. There was no point in taking risks. The secret of survival, not to speak of success, is to take the risks you have to take but never the ones you don't. I held the envelope out over the railing and let it drop. Weighted by the keys inside, it plummeted three storeys straight down and landed with a plop on the ground-floor hall carpet.

I walked down to the entrance, pausing to listen for any sound behind my landlord's door. Nothing. Pushing the entrance door open, I slid the envelope along the floor and quickly picked it up and wedged it partway into my mailbox, with the name showing.

On regaining the safety of my apartment, I was startled to find that my heart was racing. After what I had been through the day before, this simple task should have seemed inconsequential. But the unrelenting fear of making some small error that would lead to discovery was grinding me down. One mistake and I would be noticed, and once noticed, I would be done for.

I placed a two-hundred-and-fifty-dollar cheque to Cathy Addonizio and my paid bills on the coffee table in the living room. Nothing to do now but wait.

It occurred to me that all the doors between rooms ought to be open, just in case Cathy inadvertently walked towards me and backed me out of the room. And what if she heard me moving? Breathing? It would be like sensing the presence of another person in the dark. It suddenly seemed to me that by having Cathy come here I had arranged my own destruction.

I finally heard Cathy's tread on the stair, followed by the sound of the key sliding into the lock. The door swung open and she stepped into my apartment. I was standing by the door to the kitchen so that I could observe her and at the same time be ready to escape. She walked over to the coffee table and laid out on it the large manila envelope and the two newspapers that she carried under her arm. Then she opened her handbag and took out a letter-size envelope—that would be the money—which she set on top of the pile, along with my spare keys. She picked up my cheque and the envelopes underneath it, inspecting each of them and then placing them in her handbag. Perfect. Now she would be leaving, latching the door behind her.

But for some reason she set down her handbag and double-bolted the door. She took a long, appraising look round and then ambled into the bedroom. I followed her, standing in the doorway. What could she be doing?

The first thing she did was to open the closet door and peer inside. Then she examined the top of my dressing table, studying a photograph

179

of me with some friends. What was she looking for? She pulled open one of the top drawers and glanced inside. The drawer below contained my invisible objects. Almost absent-mindedly, she pushed the top drawer shut and turned away.

I grasped, at last, what was happening. She was simply curious. She was a snoop. I was at the same time relieved and outraged. She was plainly without the slightest scruple or concern for the rules with which civilised people try to protect their own and each other's privacy. I was surprised, because I had known her for several years and had always held a very different opinion of her. I followed her to the couch, where she picked up her bag, and then to the front door. She stepped out into the corridor and pulled the door shut, pushing on it to make sure it had latched properly. From one of the front windows I watched her come out of the entrance and walk towards Madison.

When she had disappeared round the corner, I hurried into the kitchen. I drank a glass of cold water and watched it gallop unpleasantly down into my stomach. The trouble with water was that it did nothing whatever for hunger, no matter how much of it you consumed. And I was now extremely hungry.

I went back to my desk and looked up the number of the supermarket round the corner of Madison Avenue. A voice with the accent and the flat, indifferent rudeness of New York answered.

"FoodRite."

"Hello. I'd like to make an order for delivery."

"Name?"

"Halloway. I'd—"

"Address?"

"Twenty-four East Eighty-ninth. I—"

"Whaddyawant?"

"Let's see . . . I'd like some of those little bouillon cubes."

"Beef, chicken, or vegetable?"

"Which is clearest?"

"Clearest?"

"Yes, clearest. Which one is more transparent?"

"I don't know anything about transparent. Maybe the chicken. They're all the same."

"Give me one pack of each. Then, a case each of club soda and tonic. And some limes. And lemons. What about gelatine?"

"What about it? You want it, we got it."

"It's quite clear, isn't it?"

"What's this clear thing? We have gelatine if you want it. What do you want to do with it, anyway?" he added suspiciously.

"I'm looking for clear foods. No colour, and easy to digest. It's my doctor: he's told me to eat only clear foods."

180

"Look. Why don't you come in to the store? We got a whole section of health foods. No artificial insecticides or preservatives. I'm not saying you don't pay for it, but you know what you're getting. Granola. Unpasteurised milk. It's up to you."

"Send me a packet of the gelatine. What about those transparent Chinese noodles? Do you carry those?"

"Sure. One package of shining noodles. What kind of doctor you seeing anyway? Chiropractor, right?"

"Sort of. If you can think of any other clear foods . . . or even just foods that are especially easy to digest . . . preferably white, I suppose, if they aren't clear."

"Look, I don't digest food; I just sell it. You ought to come in to the store, figure out what you want. I can see you got problems, but we only got three phones here, and a lot of people want to call in orders."

"Of course. You're absolutely right. I hate to waste your time. Why don't you send me a pound of some very clear type of fish, and a small sack of potatoes."

"That it?"

"Yes. Let me try that for now, and—"

"Someone be in all afternoon?"

"Yes. How much—"

"You'll get a bill with the delivery." Click.

I called the pharmacy. The druggist, a much more amiable man, seemed mystified when I questioned him about the transparency of various vitamin pills, but he promised to do his best.

Ten minutes later the delivery boy from the pharmacy rang up on the intercom. I buzzed him in and unlocked my front door, leaving it slightly ajar. I turned on the shower and then stood waiting in the bathroom doorway. When the doorbell rang, I shouted across the room, "Come on in!" The delivery boy pushed the door open with a paper bag in his hands.

"I'm in the shower," I shouted. "Just leave it on the coffee table. There's a cheque there. The two dollars are for you."

He set the bag on the table and pocketed the two dollar bills and my cheque. "Thank you!" he shouted. At the same time he picked up from the coffee table an antique silver box and inspected it with interest.

"Thank you!" I shouted back. "Goodbye!"

He put the box down, walked back towards the entrance, and stopped to examine a cluster of photographs on the wall. "Goodbye!" he shouted back, and let himself out.

A pudgy boy arrived later with the groceries.

"You can just leave everything in the kitchen," I shouted from the bathroom. "The money's on the coffee table. Keep two dollars out of the change for yourself."

He deposited the sack of groceries in the kitchen. He touched nothing except the money I had left out for him, but he glanced furtively about the living room and scanned the mail that Cathy had brought and that I had left half opened on the table. I wondered if I behaved in the same sneaky, prying way when I was alone in new surroundings. Before letting himself out, he too studied the photographs.

As soon as I had the door locked again I turned off the shower and went into the kitchen and unpacked the groceries. I opened up the bouillon. The pathetic sight of the little cubes in their foil wrappers made my mouth water. I was starving. I heated up some water. I decided to try the beef—it sounded somehow more substantial. Under the circumstances it tasted exquisite.

I watched the dishwater-coloured liquid collect in my stomach. I could see that, although it was going to take longer than water, it was already starting to fade. I made up a serving of the chicken bouillon. It too was delicious beyond imagining.

If I could live on bouillon, I would never be visible for more than fifteen or twenty minutes at a time. I opened the vitamins and swallowed two of them, watching as the translucent amber capsules descended jerkily down to my stomach and sat there dissolving. Eventually a hole was eaten through one of them, and the contents gushed slowly out in a spreading stain. It was really quite fascinating. Too bad, in a way, that no one else would enjoy the spectacle.

I eagerly examined the gelatine. I was not quite sure what gelatine was, and the labels gave me very little help, but there seemed to be protein in it, and research indicated that seven out of ten women reported an improvement in their fingernails. I made up another cup of bouillon and poured a packet of gelatine into it. It didn't taste so good, but perhaps I was just beginning to get tired of bouillon.

I went back to my desk and called the office again.

Cathy answered. "Mr. Halloway's office."

"Hi, Cathy. Thanks for dropping off all the stuff."

"You're welcome. How are you? What did the doctor say?"

"Just a virus. Sorry I wasn't here. Have there been any calls for me?"

"A David Leary from the US Industrial Research Safety Commission."

That would be it. A pulse of fear ran through me. "What did he say?"

"He wants to arrange an appointment for some time this afternoon. I said you were extremely busy and you would be in and out of the office this afternoon and out of town most of next week. He said it was very important, and he gave me a number. Five-nine-four three-one-two-oh."

"If Leary calls again, tell him I'll be calling him."

"All right."

"Thanks again for bringing by all that stuff, Cathy. I appreciate it."

"You're welcome. I hope you're feeling better."

Well, they were after me. Of course, there had not for a moment been any doubt that they would be. The telephone call from Leary, whoever he was, should really have been reassuring: it meant that they did not yet know just whom they were after. Nicholas Halloway was still just one name on a long list. All the same, it was as if someone had fired a shot right through my wall.

I could put off calling back Leary until Monday morning. There would be nothing out of the ordinary about that: it was Friday afternoon. No, better fix a definite appointment right now. I couldn't risk having these people arrive unannounced at my office. Or at the apartment. And anyway, the more responsive I was in my dealings with them, the less interested they should be. But I dreaded making the call.

First I sat there with pencil and paper, writing out a detailed account of what I was supposed to have been doing for the last two days. I couldn't afford to have myself talking to anyone or doing anything that could be conclusively refuted by a simple telephone call.

The papers! There might be something I ought to know before talking to Leary. I went into the other room and searched through the *Wall Street Journal*, but there was no mention of MicroMagnetics. Deep in the nether regions of the *Times* was an article entitled "Laboratory May Have Violated Building Code", by Anne Epstein.

> The Mercer County district attorney, who is investigating a fatal fire in a Lamberton, New Jersey, research laboratory yesterday, suggested today that the laboratory may have violated local building and fire ordinances . . . Two deaths . . . A local official speculated that demonstrators might have damaged electrical lines . . . officials insisted that no radioactive material was located. Meanwhile, in an action considered unusual for an accident of this type, authorities have closed off . . .

No information whatever. Zero.

I dialled Leary's number, trying to compose myself.

"Five-nine-four three-one-two-oh," answered a female voice.

"Hello, I'd like to speak to Mr. Leary, please."

There was an immediate warbling sound on the line and then a male voice saying, "Leary."

"Hello. This is Nicholas Halloway, returning your call." I thought I sounded all right. Calm, civil, indifferent.

"Thank you for calling back, Mr. Halloway. I'm calling from the regional office of the US Industrial Research Safety Commission in connection with an investigation into the accident on Wednesday, April third, at the MicroMagnetics research facility in Lamberton, New Jersey. I would like to confirm that you were at the MicroMagnetics facility on that date." He spoke in a mechanical monotone, almost as if he were reading a prepared speech.

"Yes," I said. "Terrible thing. Horrible. Although, actually, I'm afraid I can't really be of much help to you. I wasn't feeling well, and I didn't actually see the explosion or whatever it was."

"We need a signed statement from everyone present at the time of the incident. We don't want to trouble you any more than necessary, Mr. Halloway. If you're going to be in your office, I'd like to stop by right now and get this out of the way."

"That would be fine except that I'm just on my way out. Could we do this over the telephone?"

"Mr. Halloway, we don't want to inconvenience you, but I'm going to need to talk with you in person. I'm only a few minutes away, Mr. Halloway, if—"

"Really?" I said. "Where are you? Perhaps I could stop by your office at some point."

"That's not necessary, Mr. Halloway. I could meet with you later this afternoon, or this evening as soon as you're free. Or I can come to your residence over the weekend."

"That's extraordinarily kind. Unfortunately, I'm getting out of the city for the weekend. But just let me look at my schedule here. Tell me— when do you absolutely have to have this wound up?"

"No later than Wednesday morning. I—"

"Let me see . . . Two o'clock Tuesday afternoon in my office?"

"Two o'clock Tuesday. Thank you, Mr. Halloway. I'll see you then."

No, you won't. You won't see me ever. Nor will anyone else.

I felt in a way relieved. I knew I was safe until Tuesday. I went into the kitchen and mixed myself a gin and tonic to celebrate.

IT WAS GETTING COOLER, and I went through the apartment pulling all the shades and curtains and then put on my bathrobe. It was a full-length robe and it made me feel more substantial. A human shape. I put my hands in the pockets so I wouldn't have to see the empty sleeve openings. As long as you don't look in a mirror, you never notice that you are headless.

While I prepared some fish and noodles, I switched on the television and found a basketball game. The food was unspeakably good, even if it did make a rather slimy mess in my stomach. Pale and glistening, like a massive slug. After dinner I dialled Anne at home. She picked up on the first ring.

"Hello."

"Hi, Anne. How are you?"

"Oh, it's *you*. I'm glad you called, Nick. I've been working on this Students for a Fair World story, MicroMagnetics. Do you realise that they've closed off the entire area? You can't get near the place. It's a massive cover-up."

"That's great, Anne. I—"

"Do you have any idea how incredible this story really is? This is the most serious disaster in the history of nuclear power."

"It is?"

"Two people dead. *Two fatalities!* That's why they have this total news blackout. This is a fantastic story. It's the most important thing that's ever happened to me."

"That's great. Actually, I wanted to talk to you about something related to the . . . accident."

"That reminds me. I have to talk to you. You were one of the last people to speak to Carillon. I want everything you can remember about his state of mind, about the political statement he hoped to make. Anything he said. It could be very—"

"Anne, I know the story is uppermost in your mind right now, but . . . I wanted to ask you about something else."

"What is it, Nick?" It was hard to tell whether it was concern or impatience in her voice.

"I don't know exactly where to begin. I want to ask you something straight out. Suppose I were to ask you, right now, if you were willing to drop everything and go off with me somewhere? For good. Just the two of us. Tonight."

"Is something the matter, Nick?"

"No, no. Listen, Anne, something that happened the other day . . . Seeing those two people die there, or whatever. Anyway, it's forced me to try to figure out exactly where I'm going from here in my life. And it's important to me to know exactly where you stand."

"Nick, could we talk about this some time next week? I have to get back down to Princeton tonight. I'm so tied up with this story, I really can't think about anything else right now. Have you talked to your therapist about these things?"

"I don't have a therapist."

"Well, you should, you know. There are some things a person can't handle alone. Nick, could you describe to me exactly what you saw at the moment the fire broke out? This is really important."

"I wasn't looking at that precise moment. Anne, I think you're right; maybe we should talk next week. I could collect my thoughts and give you any useful information then."

"That would be good. I'm sort of in a hurry now anyway. Good night, Nick. Take care."

When I hung up the telephone, I noticed that the television was still on. Basketball game. Hard to focus on it. Ridiculous to start putting all your hope in other people. What had I ever done for Anne that she should suddenly reorganise her life round me? When your need is great, you start assuming other people have to help you. This isn't really the sort of situation in which you can confide in other people: *This is Nick— Nick Halloway, remember? I'm calling because a little something has come up and I wonder if I could ask a small favour. I've just become totally invisible, and also I'm being sought by the authorities in connection with some felonies and I was wondering if you could put me up for a few years until I die or get caught or something . . .*

Chapter 7

I woke early again on Saturday and lay there for a long time staring at the wall and brooding miserably. Finally I trudged into the kitchen, where I heated up a large pan of water and dumped in a dozen of the bouillon cubes. Why fool around with a cup at a time? I drank a good quart of the stuff there in front of the stove. How long could a human being subsist on bouillon?

I found an unopened loaf of week-old white bread. I tore off a little piece and began devouring it greedily. I glanced down to watch its progress in my digestive tract. It seemed to go pretty quickly—much faster than the fish the night before. I really ought to be timing this. I got out a stopwatch and gobbled up another slice of bread.

Soon I was standing in front of the full-length mirror with pencil and paper, timing the digestion of everything I could find in my kitchen. From bread I moved on to strawberry jam and honey, then sugar, salt and flour. I cooked and ate a potato, an onion, several frozen string beans and a dozen peas. I would chew a bit of each new food thoroughly and then wait until it was well down the pipeline and had begun to break up and dissipate before I started on the next food. I worked my way gradually through everything edible in the apartment.

By midday I saw that I would have to do something to broaden the scope of my scientific investigations. I put in another call to FoodRite.

"I remember you," said the same voice. "Clear food, right?"

"Yes, that's right, except that actually I feel I'm ready now to try—"

"I've been thinking about your problem, and I got some ideas for you," he persevered. "You ever try winter melon?"

"I don't know that I have. Send one along by all means. I'd also like one of every other kind of melon. Of fruit actually. And one of each kind of fresh vegetable."

"*Every* kind of fruit and vegetable? What about clear foods? What about your health?"

"I'm feeling quite a lot better, thanks."

"Do you know how many kinds of fruit we have here?" He sounded upset. "You know someone has to bag and weigh each piece of fruit in this order? Have you talked to your doctor about this?"

"I'm changing doctors, actually. The last one seemed rather rigid. If you could also throw in some fish—"

"What does that mean, anyway: one of each fruit? You want one grape? One pea?"

"Well, you choose the portions. I appreciate it. I'll rely absolutely on your judgment."

I began to experience considerable amazement and interest at the sight of my own interior. I was able, that day, to arrive at the fundamental precepts that would govern my diet. First and foremost, total abstinence from fibre is critical to my survival. Seeds and kernels of every kind are also to be avoided at all costs, as are the skins of fruits. An undigested seed can linger in the lower intestine for days, making for an extremely unsightly appearance. Leafy vegetables require extreme caution. Sugar and starches, on the other hand, are the foundation of my diet. It is extraordinary how quickly the body breaks them down. Most of my protein comes from fish. I try to avoid colouring and dyes.

Another important rule for life that I have learned is to chew my food carefully. The use of dental floss after every meal is another imperative for me, as is cleaning carefully under the fingernails. Of course, in my case, little signs of bad grooming will not so much detract from my appearance as constitute it in its entirety. Fortunately, my invisible body and invisible clothing do not form what engineers refer to as a good mechanical bond with visible substances, which means that dirt and dust do not adhere to me very well.

I discovered another interesting thing that day. At some point in the early afternoon, as I stood in my darkened apartment with the curtains drawn, I had the idea of opening the door to the terrace and inspecting the digestion process in the sunlight: the sludge was suddenly dissipating much faster. I tried several more swallows, alternating between darkness and sunlight, and determined that the light did indeed speed up whatever it was that was taking place in my stomach.

It was late afternoon before I realised I was glutting myself to the point of nausea. Time to rest from my labours. I switched on the television and found a movie. Pleasant being safe at home. No point in thinking about Leary. Lots of time still. When the movie ended, I felt a bit of panic and immediately searched out another. It would be hard to say how many of them I watched before I finally staggered into my bed.

I was woken by the sound of the Sunday *Times* being dropped at my door. I went out and retrieved it. Only another two and a half days of safety, and then I would have to be prepared for the worst at all times.

I put on some Haydn and went through the paper, never quite finishing or taking in anything. About the recent events at MicroMagnetics there was no real information whatever. Which was both a relief and a disappointment. I could see that beyond my drawn curtains it was a beautiful day, and I knew that I would have felt better if I could have gone outside, but there would be thousands of people in the streets and the park today. In the afternoon I turned on the television. It was irritating, but I kept it on until some time in the middle of the evening, when I stumbled dully into bed.

On Monday morning I woke at dawn. I was becoming increasingly frightened as my appointment with Leary grew nearer. He had clearly been told he had to meet everyone in person. From the moment when I cancelled this first appointment tomorrow, I would have to assume that they might arrive at any time.

I called up Cathy. "I'm working at home all day today," I told her. "And it turns out that I have to be out of town all the rest of the week. Tell anyone who calls that I'm in Los Angeles."

"OK. And what about the monthly review on Thursday?"

"I'll call Roger and talk to him about it."

I hung up and thought for several minutes, then called my boss, Roger Whitman. I told him also that I would be working at home that day. "I'm a little behind," I told him, "and I can get more done here, where I'm not constantly interrupted by the telephone."

"Oh, Nick, it's good that you called. I have an idea I wanted to throw out for you before Thursday."

"Before you get into that, Roger, there's something I wanted to discuss. Do you have a few minutes now?"

"Sure. Shoot."

"Well, Roger, some things have come up kind of suddenly. Actually, the fact is, I've been thinking through my whole situation, and I've come to the conclusion that I have to make a major change. I've decided to resign. Effective immediately."

"Resign? What do you mean, Nick?"

"I'm leaving. Pursuing other interests, as they say."

"Nick, do you mind telling me where you re going? What are they offering you? We've known each other a long time, Nick. I just don't understand why you wouldn't have come in and discussed a thing like this with me first." He seemed genuinely hurt.

"Roger, I'm not going anywhere else. In fact, I'd rather not resign at all. I'd rather request a leave of absence, if that's all right?"

"Well, I suppose . . . Sure. Why not? Nick, do you mind my asking why you're suddenly doing this?"

"Roger, I'm honestly not sure how I ought to answer your question. It's—there've been some fundamental changes in my life."

"How do you mean, Nick? Maybe this is something we can work out."

"Roger, it's nothing that . . . Hell! Look, Roger, I'll tell you what it is

188

I've suddenly broken through to a new spiritual dimension. I find myself unexpectedly on another plane of awareness, and I need to withdraw from material concerns for a time and reconsider my place in the celestial scheme."

"Nick, I had no idea you felt like that."

"I didn't, Roger. This is all quite sudden. I had this experience the other day, a sort of epiphany. Slammed me right onto another spiritual plane, if you follow me."

"Look, Nick, take all the time you need. Get things squared away."

"I knew you'd understand, Roger. I always thought you had a spiritual dimension that people overlooked. In fact, sometime I'd like to discuss your own karma with you."

"Good of you to think of it, Nick. Listen, I have to run."

"A lot of people never stop to think how fragile and fleeting the material world is—"

"But if there's ever anything I can do to help, you let me know."

"Roger, thanks again for your understanding. Goodbye."

So much for my job. So much for Roger.

In the corner of my bedroom there was a metal ladder running up the wall to a trap door, which was the only access to the roof. I climbed up the ladder and unlatched the door. If they came for me without warning, this could be my escape route. From the roof of my building I could climb over to either of the adjoining buildings and work my way round the block. From my terrace I could see several routes from roofs down into the interior gardens in the centre of the block.

Next, I collected absolutely everything that connected me with anyone else in the world: letters, diaries, old tax returns, appointment books. I emptied out my desk drawers, took the photographs off the walls, searched through the pockets of my clothing, and dumped everything in the kitchen. Then I began crumpling a handful at a time into the oven and setting it on fire. If they did come after me, they would probably be able to find out everything, but I was at least going to slow them down.

It was more difficult than you might think, burning the photographs, seeing the images of people I had known well, had strong feelings for, melt and disappear in the flame. They were, in fact, being obliterated from my life. It verges on the poignant, seeing your whole existence laid out like that. My past was irretrievably gone.

Onto the fire with all of it. I read and burned on into the evening. My last night of safety. I went to bed early, trying to ignore the unpleasant sight of the bedclothes suspended over the missing human form.

ON TUESDAY MORNING I woke early again, but this time I climbed out of bed immediately, moving steadily with grim, fearful efficiency. I washed myself carefully and put on all my invisible clothing. Then I pulled open

189

the dressing table drawer and carefully loaded all the invisible objects into my pockets. From now on these would remain on my person. I reinspected the gun. Three bullets.

At five past nine I called Leary.

"Hello, Mr. Leary. This is Nick Halloway." I paused to let him say hello in return, but he said nothing, so I continued. "We had an appointment scheduled for two this afternoon."

"Yes, that's right, Mr. Halloway."

"Well, I'm afraid I'm going to have to ask if we can reschedule. I'm terribly sorry about this, but something's just come up, and I'm on my way out to the airport right now. Tell me, are you free any time towards the end of the week?"

There was an unpleasant pause before he replied, "The best thing would be if I came straight over to your office now."

"Golly," I said, "I appreciate your offering to do that at such short notice, but that really isn't possible. I'm going out the door the minute I hang up. How is first thing Friday morning? Nine thirty?"

"Nine thirty Friday morning will be good." His tone had shifted somehow, and I found his compliance more ominous than his former dogged insistence. "Thank you, Mr. Halloway."

Fine. I had put him off for three more days. And yet I didn't have a good feeling about the call. It was his sudden willingness to wait until Friday.

I sat there in my invisible business suit and brooded uneasily about how an entirely invisible human being might quietly live his life unnoticed. Not a trivial question, I can tell you! As long as I had my apartment and my bank account, I could order up food and eat it in safety and sleep in peace. But if they drove me out, how was I to get along? Where was I to go? It sounds as if it ought to be easy, but when you think about it, the desirable nooks and crannies across the face of the earth are pretty well inhabited. Perhaps I should go to another city. Another country. Which?

I think I must have spent several hours sitting there thinking the same tedious thoughts over and over. I don't think I noticed the ringing of the doorbells right away. Rather, I became aware that they had been ringing, but I couldn't say for how long, or exactly where.

Someone was ringing at each apartment in the building. Then he should ring mine too. I braced myself for the sound, but it did not come. If someone were selling something or looking for someone to accept a delivery, he would not omit just one apartment. Carefully I slid one of the front windows up and leaned out. A stocky middle-aged man in a short raincoat was standing in the outer doorway talking to Eileen Coulson, my landlady. After a moment he disappeared into the building behind her.

I wondered if that was Leary. I had a moment of panic in which I thought that the two of them might be coming up to my apartment, but the Coulsons had no key for it. Leary or whoever he was would just be asking questions. And what could he learn from Eileen Coulson that would be of any use?

But Leary must have been learning something. It was half an hour before he reappeared on the pavement and headed east. They were evidently not coming for me yet. And in the back of my mind was the reassuring knowledge that, even if everything went badly, I had prepared my escape route over the roof.

Which is why I reacted so promptly when I heard the first footstep on the roof. It had been less than an hour since Leary or whoever he was had disappeared down the street, and it seemed inconceivable that they would already be here for me. But I knew instantly that I had to assume that the roof exit was gone.

I ran for the apartment door, stopping only long enough to look through the peephole. No one visible in the hall. I opened the door, peered round cautiously without seeing anyone, and started running as fast as I could down the stairs. I pulled up short at the end of the second-floor landing. At the foot of the next flight and heading straight for me were five men. Three of them were Clellan, Gomez and Morrissey. They were almost running up the stairs, and they filled the width of the stairway, leaving no room for me to pass. The only thing I could do was turn round and quietly head back up, staying ahead of them.

Clellan was saying, "Now, remember, when we go in, that door closes and stays closed until you hear me say loud and clear I'm about to open it. And if you should see it open without me saying I'm about to open it, you start to shoot, hear?"

I could hear people muttering assent as they puffed up the stairs behind me.

"Gomez will try to get him with the tranquilliser gun, but if he gets out of that apartment, you get him any way you can."

When I got to the third floor, I continued past my door to where the corridor dead-ended. The men behind me collected at the head of the stairs in front of the entrance to my apartment. There was no question of slipping past them. I climbed over the railing and hung out over the stairwell. Clinging to the balusters, I edged my way back towards the men at the head of the stairs. The whole railing was wobbling horribly from my weight, but they were too busy with the door to notice. One of them had crouched down and was doing something to the lock.

When I reached the point where the balustrade curved round and began its slope down to the second floor, I stepped across and climbed over the banisters onto the descending flight of stairs. I paused and looked back up at the five men by the door. The man working on the lock stood up and stepped back. Each of the men reached into his suit and pulled out a pistol, except for Gomez, who was already holding the odd-looking tranquilliser gun with a long, thick barrel. Then Clellan nodded, and the door swung violently open. Morrissey, Gomez and Clellan charged into the apartment—my apartment—and the door slammed shut again immediately behind them. The two men left outside stood watching, their pistols pointed at the door.

I could hear footsteps running through my apartment, and I could hear Clellan's voice. "Mr. Halloway, there are armed men all round you with orders to shoot at any noise or movement. *Please do not move.* We are here to help you."

Extraordinary the way these people were always trying to help me. All these guns for my protection. Holding onto the banisters, I started back down the stairs as fast as I could go without making any noise. As I came down the last flight I could see two men standing in the vestibule between the two doors to the street. And beyond them in the street stood other men holding walkie-talkies: one of them was Jenkins.

I walked carefully the rest of the way down, until I was standing just inside the glass vestibule door. On my right was the Coulsons' door. I began jabbing the Coulsons' doorbell furiously. The men in the vestibule heard it ringing in the background and looked up curiously. If they had known what they were looking for, they would have had me. One of the men turned and went out to speak with the men in the street.

I could hear footsteps approaching from within the Coulsons' apartment. Why couldn't the woman hurry! Eileen Coulson was behind the door now, speaking. "Is it all right to open up again now?"

I remembered in time that I must not let her recognise my voice. I held my arm up against my mouth and called out, "Yes, ma'am. We're all finished here. I'd just like to use your phone for a moment, if I may." *Please* open the blessed door.

There was a sort of commotion as one of the men out on the sidewalk suddenly pushed through the group and started running towards the door. It was Jenkins.

The door in front of me swung open two inches and stopped abruptly. She had it on a police chain! Her eyes moved around in the crack, peering everywhere in a futile effort to see me. "Are you quite sure it's all right to open up now?" she asked.

"Yes, ma'am," I said. Jenkins was in the vestibule and saw the Coulsons' open door. I could see the urgency and anger in his face. The narrow little slit eyes. He began shouting. "Shut that door! Get that door shut!"

I took two quick steps backwards and charged the Coulsons' door, slamming sideways into it with all the force I had. The door swung open, pulling the police chain out of the door frame and pushing the large body of Eileen Coulson back into the wall of her hall.

I charged down the hall and into the living room. Jenkins was right behind me. When he found himself in the middle of the unfamiliar large room, he slowed up momentarily and looked around. That gave me enough time to pull open the double glass doors in the far wall and get out into the garden. The garden—only a New Yorker would call it a garden—was a small, lifeless paved area with metal furniture, surrounded by high wooden fencing. I grabbed a chair, slammed it against the back fence, and, standing on the ground beside the chair, began pushing and shaking the fence as violently as I could.

Jenkins was right there. Assuming I was on the chair, climbing over the fence, he charged, groping for me with both hands above the chair. I hit him hard with a closed fist in the side of the neck. He doubled over onto the ground.

I hoisted myself over the fence into the facing garden. I looked around. Two windows and a door, all locked. I went over the next fence. It was not so high, but it swayed precariously under my weight as I twisted over the top of it, and for a moment I thought it was going to collapse altogether. I looked up at the roof above my apartment. Gomez, staring down at the fence that I had just nearly wrecked, was raising his tranquilliser gun to his shoulder.

I turned and nearly collided with a woman of about fifty in a bathrobe. She had just got up from a plastic garden chair and was striding towards me shrieking, "Stop it! Stop that right now!"

I realised that she thought someone was knocking her fence down from the other side. I stepped out of her way as she strode towards the fence and glared truculently at it.

There was a small, explosive thud from the direction of my roof and a gash appeared at the base of her neck. She collapsed at my feet.

I ran over and pulled open the glass door into her apartment. There was other gunfire now, and glass shattered round my ankles. I charged up a staircase to the ground floor, where there would be a door to the street. I found an entrance hall, where I pulled open first one and then another door and charged out onto a porch. In front of me was a short flight of brownstone steps leading down to the sidewalk. Clellan was coming up them, straight towards me. He had seen the house door mysteriously swinging open. As he came, he held his arms outstretched to either side so that I would not be able to pass him unnoticed.

The metal railings that ran down both sides of the steps were too narrow to balance on, but I clambered up onto one of them anyway and charged down it for all I was worth. I hit the pavement with a loud thud and tumbled in a heap at the kerb.

Clellan knew at once what had happened. Despite his deplorable taste in cowboy hats and brightly coloured shirts, he was not a stupid man. He spun round and charged back down the steps, looking desperately along the sidewalk for some movement or clue to my location. I scrambled to my feet, quickly retreated several steps down the street, and turned back to see what he would do. At the bottom of the steps Clellan began dancing around in little circles on the pavement, exploring with his feet for what he hoped would be my injured body.

He stopped abruptly. He saw it was too late: I had got clear. He waited for a minute, listening for some sign of me, and then he said quite softly, "You there, Halloway?"

I did not answer. Two more men had just rounded the corner from Madison Avenue and were walking fast towards Clellan. I turned and saw that there were more men coming from the other end of the block. A black car had turned into the block from Fifth Avenue and was rolling down the street towards us.

"Halloway, you have nowhere to go. Halloway? You're making a mistake," Clellan was saying. He was talking louder now. "We're just going to have to come and get you anyway. Halloway?"

You can try. But it won't be as easy as you think.

Clellan stood there looking blankly around, talking to the void. The two groups of men approaching stared at Clellan, baffled by his bizarre behaviour.

I walked out into the middle of the street and started up towards Fifth Avenue. Halfway up the block I had to step aside between two parked cars, to let the black one pass, and inside, gliding slowly by me, I saw the face of Colonel David Jenkins, staring out impassively from the left rear window.

Chapter 8

My heart was still pounding as I walked south along the edge of Central Park. Now that I was suddenly thrust out into the glare of the sunlight, everything seemed too bright and too large. I moved as if in a dream among people and objects that whirled past in dangerous, unpredictable paths. Approaching Eighty-fifth Street, I looked back just in time to stumble out of the way of a boy on a bicycle who came hurtling out of the park straight at me. Moments later a small, erratically-moving dog suddenly swept across the width of the pavement, threatening to snare me with the leash that connected it to its owner. This existence requires constant vigilance. I particularly have to watch people on roller skates, with Walkman earphones plugged into their heads, who glide obliquely across sidewalks and then abruptly wheel out in broad, swooping arcs or little toplike spins, with an arm or a leg extended to cut me down.

I figured out that I was safest walking along the kerb, between the parked cars and the trees, where there were fewer people and where I could always escape into the street or even up onto an automobile. I wondered what Jenkins would be doing now. Going through my apartment, dismantling my home. It came to me that I no longer had a home, that it was unlikely, furthermore, that I would ever have a home again. What would I do next? The important thing was to keep moving.

As I walked towards midtown it became perfectly obvious to me where I would go. I would go where people traditionally had gone when they found it inconvenient or impossible to go home: I would go to my club. Midtown Manhattan is full of men's clubs ideally appointed for someone in my situation: large kitchens and bars, lounges, libraries, billiard rooms, showers, pools and private bedrooms. The Academy Club, of which I was a member, is a handsome old six-storey building on Madison Avenue, with cavernous public rooms that have not been full for generations. In those rooms I would never be caught in a crowd.

You enter up a short flight of stairs sheltered by an awning. Just inside the entrance and to one side is a desk, behind which Bill sits watching the door. He prides himself on knowing every member on sight, and although half of them seem to live in Palm Beach or London, I have never seen him fail. I stood outside the closed entrance door until a member came up the stairs, pulled open the door, and strode through. I slipped in behind him, and managed to get through before the door sprang shut again. Bill looked up and said, "Good afternoon, Mr. Ellis." As I slunk by the desk I realised that I had taken pleasure in the courtesy of Bill's greeting all these years and that I felt cut off without it now.

I crossed the hall. On my right were passages to private dining rooms. On my left was a vast high-ceilinged lounge with high-backed leather chairs and long tables covered with periodicals. The marble floor was covered with enormous Oriental carpets, and lining the opposite wall were tall windows that looked down onto the street. The club was filling up. Tea had just been put out, and the beneficiaries of trust funds, who had spent their afternoon on the squash courts, were taking small, civilised bites from English muffins. The stockbrokers, lawyers and bankers would arrive later, sweeping in to wolf down entire muffins in a single bite on their way to the bar.

I continued up the staircase past the first floor, which housed the main dining room, the bar and the billiard room, and on to the second floor, which was taken up with card rooms, meeting rooms and the library, which consisted of a maze of small alcoves formed by well-stocked bookshelves. In the most remote corner I settled into a large leather armchair surrounded by rows of books. I would sit here and rest. In a few hours I would be able to look around and find something to eat. By nine the club would be almost deserted. It was so extraordinarily quiet. Far in the background—it seemed miles away—I could hear the ancient elevator moving occasionally . . .

When I woke, it was completely dark. It seemed to be the middle of the night. All the lights out. Utterly still now. The only sound I could hear was my own movement in the leather chair.

I got up and made my way haltingly out towards the middle of the library, guiding myself by running my hand along the row of books. When finally I reached the entrance to the library, I saw dim illumination coming from the main staircase that wound up through the centre of the building. I stopped to listen for any movement and heard nothing.

I followed the marble stairs down in search of the kitchens. As I entered the main dining room, enough light shone in from the street through the tall windows for me to make my way easily to the swinging doors through which I had so often watched waiters appear and disappear. Beyond the doors was a small hall and an open staircase, which I followed down into total darkness.

I groped about helplessly for several minutes in what seemed to be a maze of counters and shelves, until I found the handle of an old-fashioned refrigerator and pulled it open. The small light inside shone suddenly out through an enormous room, creating a patchwork of huge shadows, endless tables, and monstrous antique kitchen equipment. The refrigerator was filled with bottles of fruit juice, and I gulped down a quart of grapefruit juice and then, leaving the door open for illumination, set out to explore.

I went methodically through the kitchen trying every cupboard and door. All locked. I would need keys. On a counter I found a large metal bowl of sickeningly sweet fruit salad which someone had forgotten to put away, and I unhesitatingly shovelled some into myself.

Glancing down at my stomach—I was altogether unsightly now—I began to worry again about who else might be in the building. There would at the very least be someone at the door all night for the people who were staying in the guest rooms. I would have to avoid the ground floor, and the third floor where the guest rooms were, but I should be able to explore the rest of my new home in safety. I went back up the stairs, out through the dining room, and hurried up the broad marble staircase to the next floor. I turned down a dark corridor, which I thought should lead away from the library towards a vaguely remembered back staircase, but the corridor turned several times inexplicably, until I was completely disorientated. When I encountered a small marble staircase, I followed it up. It opened into a corridor on what must be the third floor.

I pulled open the first door I came to and stepped into total darkness on what felt like a tiled floor. I ran my hands over the wall, along the door frame, until I found a light switch and snapped it on. I was in a small white tiled room, which I recognised as the anteroom to the steam room. On the right was a door leading to the pool, ahead was the steam room, and to the left, a small room with massage tables and sunlamps.

I looked down at my viscera, an ugly swirl, and an idea came to me. I switched off the light and made my way to the massage room. There were two long rows of sunlamps suspended over a massage table. I switched them on and climbed up onto the table.

I felt the light only as a vaguely pleasant, penetrating warmth, but its effect on my appearance was dramatic and immediate. The swirl began to disappear at once, and within minutes there was nothing whatever. It was a wonderful discovery. I would be able to eat and restore my invisibility almost at will.

Slipping off my clothes and putting them in a neat pile on top of a locker, I walked back through the anteroom and into the windowless room containing the swimming pool. I flipped on a light switch next to the door, illuminating the quivering blue water. Kneeling down at the edge of the pool, I slipped quietly in and pushed off. It felt wonderful. I swam up to the other end and back, and felt a sort of power and pleasure in my own movement. As I propelled myself up and down the length of the pool I could see that I was creating a large amorphous cavity or bubble, which moved awkwardly across the surface of the water, expanding and contracting with my strokes in a rhythmatic sequence of convulsions. It was a bizarre effect. One that would certainly hold the attention of anyone who happened to come into the room. I climbed out. The water beaded instantly on my body and seemed to drain magically from the air, like a miniature rainfall cascading down onto the edge of the pool. Footprints appeared mysteriously on the tiles as I walked.

Switching off the lights as I went, I returned and put on my clothes again. Calm and refreshed, I stretched out on a leather couch in the main dressing room and drifted into sleep.

At around seven o'clock in the morning I was awakened by the sound of doors banging in distant parts of the building, followed by voices and the faint clanking and grinding of the elevator. I quickly set out to make a thorough inspection of the building.

By midday I had toured as much of it as I could get at. I had to be constantly watching for the club employees, who by now had spread out through the building. The members, on the other hand, did not create a problem for me until lunch time, when they began to trickle and then crowd in. Knowing that for the next two hours the club would be as full as it ever got, I retreated up to the roof, where I sat on the edge of the parapet watching the traffic and the pedestrians below.

At two in the afternoon when the club had largely emptied out again, I went back down to the ground floor. There, beyond Bill's desk, is a little maze of offices in which the manager, the switchboard operator and the clerical staff all work. I spent the entire afternoon there observing the procedures for the reservation and assignment of the guest rooms and trying to determine the schedule for making the rooms up.

At around four thirty, as the club was beginning to fill up again, I crept carefully through the open door of the manager's office. He was sitting at his desk copying numbers onto a spread-sheet. Despite my care, he heard me come in—as people so often do—and looked up, but seeing no one, he returned to his work. I sat down on the floor in the corner and waited. He toiled on for hours. I cannot tell you how agonisingly boring this sort of thing can be: sitting there without moving, or clearing my throat, and with nothing to do but watch the man twitch and scratch his nose. With increasing intensity, I prayed for him to get up and leave.

It was almost quarter to seven before he abruptly stood up, folding the papers on his desk and stuffing them into a briefcase, and scurried out. I sat there for several minutes before starting my search. It is extraordinary how often people will return to a place moments after leaving it, to retrieve something they have forgotten. You begin to notice these things when you spend your entire waking life sneaking about.

Finally I stood up and stretched. Sitting down in the swivel chair behind the desk, I began going through the drawers.

I found two cardboard paperclip boxes full of duplicate keys of every sort. I picked out a selection, which I hooked onto a keyring and slipped into my pocket. I went through the rest of the office, concentrating particularly on the personal files and a breakdown of club staffing by hour, day of the week, and season. The most important thing I learned was that for most of the night the only employees on duty were the night doorman and an elderly watchman.

Some time after nine, when I had not heard footsteps or voices for twenty minutes, I unlocked the office door and swung it slowly open, stepping out into the corridor and peering round the corner. The night doorman was sitting behind his desk, furtively reading something that he held under the counter.

I went back and tried the keys until I found one that locked the manager's office. Then, taking a roundabout route, I went up to the top of the building and began working my way down through it again, testing the keys against each locked door I encountered. By now I knew my way through the building reasonably well, but I had to spend half my time keeping track of the night watchman, who every hour made a cursory tour of the premises. By two in the morning I had identified a passkey which, except for the guest rooms and the manager's office, seemed to open everything in the building, including countless closets and storerooms containing goods of every imaginable kind. The whole place seemed designed to be almost self-sufficient, a little autonomous world like an old ocean liner.

Only two of the guest rooms were empty, but one of the keys opened both of them, and concluding that it would open the others as well, I hid it in the lining of a chair at the end of the corridor. The rest of the keys

198

did not seem to open anything. I returned them to the manager's desk and locked his office, hiding the key in a decrepit fire hose by an emergency exit.

Keeping the passkey with me, I went back to the kitchen. Able now to open all the cabinets and padlocked freezers, I assembled on a tray what seemed by then to be an exquisite, and also rapidly digestible, dinner of bread and cake and cheese and a bottle of chilled white wine. On the third floor I had a sort of picnic under the sunlamp. Then, after a brief dip in the pool, I went down and let myself into the less desirable of the two empty guest rooms, where I locked myself in and went to sleep between clean sheets again for the first time in two days.

OVER THE NEXT WEEKS I settled into a comfortable routine in the Academy Club. Each evening I prepared myself a large meal, which I ate under the sunlamp. Then I washed and shaved in the well-stocked lavatory next to the main dressing room. There were razors, scissors, combs, brushes, and every sort of soap and lotion. The shaving soap did not adhere well to my face, but—as much to show myself exactly where my face was as anything—I daubed on huge quantities of it, and, gazing intently into the mirror, carved the lather out of the air.

Every week or so I did my best to cut my hair round the edges. And every few days I washed my clothes. I kept track daily of the reservations for guest rooms, and if there were any empty, I locked myself safely into a room for the night. When the rooms were all full, I stretched out on a couch or on bundles of freshly laundered towels. During the day I would read in the library. Or I slipped up to the roof and slept under the sun.

I made a point of going outside every day, usually at noon, when the club filled up. I was determined to get some exercise, keep my mind clear. Not lose all perspective.

I usually walked up to Central Park. The space—compared to the city streets, at least—made it easy to move around, and imagining that I was quite safe, I began to take long walks there, sometimes not returning to the club until evening.

On an overcast afternoon during one of those expeditions, I found myself on a bench at the edge of the fields near Seventy-ninth Street. A small group of schoolboys approached, none of them more than fourteen years old. I immediately got up and walked out onto the grass. I always retreat from groups of people, especially children.

The sky had suddenly turned quite black, and I was thinking how unpleasant it would be if I were caught here in a shower, miles from the club. As I stood there deciding how best to make my way back, sheets of rain abruptly emptied out of the sky, and I was instantly soaked. Two of the boys had run for the cover of a tree. The others, like me, stood there helplessly as the rain cascaded down.

"Hey! Look at that! A waterspout!"

I turned to look.

"Look! It's moving."

It took a long instant for me to grasp the awful fact that they were talking about me. The rain was spattering off me and pouring down the surface of my body to create an eerie, but clearly visible form.

"Hey, it's alive! What is it?"

"Some kind of animal."

"Looks like a person."

I had to get away from here. I turned and hurried off across the grass in search of some sort of shelter.

"It's moving again!"

Suddenly I felt a sharp blow in the back. I wheeled about and saw the boys following me in a pack, twenty feet behind. As I turned to look at them they held back warily. "You see that? I hit it! I hit it!" They were throwing stones at me!

With fear welling up in me like nausea, I turned and ran. As soon as I started to move they were after me.

"It's getting away!"

"Get it!"

One of them had found a short but solid-looking dead branch, and he held it upraised, ready to swing at me.

"Look at its tracks! Get it!"

It was true. I was leaving tracks as I ran, huge gouges in the wet dirt, and I turned onto a paved footpath. Suddenly I was standing at the edge of Seventy-ninth Street looking straight down at the sunken road cutting across the park fifteen feet below. They were coming up behind me. I half jumped, half slid, over the edge and down the face of the wall onto the sidewalk below.

"It went over the edge!"

They were already clambering down the wall. I ran east. Up ahead I could see the underpass where the road runs under the park drive.

"It's going into the underpass! Cut it off!"

In the shelter of the underpass, I watched the rain drain off me. Two of the boys had already entered behind me and were peering round intently. The other boy, who was still carrying the stick, had clambered down and was approaching from the other direction. I was invisible again, but I was trapped.

"You see it?"

"It's in here. I *feel* it."

A massive, deep puddle had formed over a clogged drain and flooded most of the road surface. I could not walk through it without giving myself away, so I stood there trembling in the middle of the sidewalk.

"It's just used up," one of them said. "Like a little tornado."

"Might have gone down the drain," said someone else.

"Nothing's going down that drain, not even water," said the boy with the stick. "Maybe it lives in the water." He started to lay about him wildly, banging at the water and the wall of the underpass. I had very little room to manoeuvre on the sidewalk, and sooner or later he was going to catch me with one of his blows.

A westbound Mercedes loomed up out of the torrent and slowed to a crawl as it entered the puddle. The boy with the stick retreated back up onto the sidewalk to let it pass. As the rear end of the car moved alongside me, I stepped over onto the bumper and with a metallic thump I landed on the boot, gripping the rims of the window frame with my fingers. As the car heaved under my weight the driver looked back to see a boy frantically slamming a large stick against the rear end of his car.

"The car! It's on the car! Stop the car!"

The driver abruptly accelerated, and the car, with me clinging desperately to the window edges, lurched off, leaving the boys behind. When it stopped for a red light at the edge of the park, I dropped off the back and stumbled down into the subway. Feeling like a half-beaten rat, I stood trembling miserably at the foot of the stairs until the rain stopped and I could get back to the Academy Club.

ALTHOUGH I CONTINUED to force myself to go outside regularly, after that I could no longer leave the club without a feeling of dread. It was so much safer inside. As the weeks passed, I began to take my existence there for granted, losing sight of how thoroughly odd it was. I was provided with all the necessities of life, and many of the luxuries as well. I was eating only one meal a day, but I had an extraordinarily varied menu to choose from, and a wine cellar better than any I could ever have provided for myself; there were books and newspapers, the cool, pleasant water of the swimming pool and acres of leather-upholstered chairs and couches. And I moved through the building at will, with complete confidence.

As for Colonel Jenkins, I no longer gave him much thought. It did sometimes bother me that there were only two exits from the building, but I think I assumed that he had given up by now. In any case, there would be no reason for them to suppose that I was in the Academy Club. I felt quite pleased with my own cleverness in choosing the club as a refuge, and I think I believed then that I would spend the rest of my life there. Also in its favour was the proximity of friends and acquaintances. There was comfort in seeing familiar faces.

I remember one day in the entrance hall I found myself suddenly face to face with Peter Wenting. He was not a close friend, but we had gone to the same school. He was saying to another man, whom I knew but could not quite place (you start forgetting the names), "Nick Halloway? No, he wouldn't be interested. Anyway, he's apparently dropped out and joined the Moonies or Hare Krishnas or something."

There is always something compelling about an overheard conversation about oneself, even when the people mean nothing much to one and nothing much is said. It began to bother me that my friends were talking in the next room, and increasingly I would think that I had heard my name. But when I stole up to them, they would always be talking about something else. And it bothered me the way Bill looked straight through me as I came through the door. He had, I noticed, acquired a new assistant, who stood next to him learning the members' names. He would never learn my name.

Living like this, among all these people but cut off from them, you begin to grow paranoid. Can they hear the water running into the basin? Will they notice the food missing? And when you decide they *have* begun to notice, you no longer have confidence in your own judgment. The night watchman had begun to vary his routine. The maids had begun to come in to check guest rooms that had not been booked. And one night I heard the doorman ask the night watchman, "Is he up there?"

It might have meant anything. You have to try to keep your sense of perspective. But perhaps they *were* aware of me. I became more cautious in my daily routine. I always wore all my clothes and carried all my possessions with me, and when I went to bed at night, I wrapped everything up in a single tight bundle that I could pick up and carry off in one hand if anything threatening should happen. I wanted to be ready to walk out of the room, or out of the building, at any moment.

As the weeks went by and June approached, there were fewer and fewer people in the club. The dining room was not open at weekends now, which meant two full days without fresh food. Then for several days the front entrance was closed off entirely with big sheets of plywood while they performed repairs of some sort on the door. This left only the service entrance, which opened onto an alleyway along the back of the building. To get through it you first have to pass through a vestibule consisting of a short corridor with a locked door at either end. Running along one side of the corridor is a counter, behind which a porter sits on a stool. Once you are in that vestibule you cannot get out until the porter reaches under the counter and presses a buzzer unlocking the doors. Rather than risk being trapped there, I stayed inside for three days, feeling more like a prisoner each day.

When I came down one morning and found that the plywood had finally been removed from the front entrance, I felt considerable relief and, by this time, even eagerness to get outside again. They had done surprisingly extensive work. There was new carpeting throughout the entrance hall, and the old hinged door had been replaced by a revolving door. The revolving door was a new problem for me.

I walked through the entrance hall to the door, keeping on the marble floor along the wall so that my footsteps would not show up in the thick new carpeting. Bill had half an eye on the entrance, and I knew that as soon as anyone appeared, he would be all attention. His apprentice, on the other hand, was staring at the ceiling with evident boredom.

I waited for nearly a quarter of an hour before a member by the name of Oliver Haycroft appeared. He hesitated at the sight of the new revolving door, then stepped forward to push his way through it. I took one quick toe-step onto the carpet so that I was poised to enter the opening opposite Haycroft when the door was in the right position. I was dimly aware of a faint buzzer going off somewhere in the background. As Haycroft pushed the door and stepped into his quadrant, I took a symmetrical step into mine, at the same time glancing back at the desk, where I sensed some movement. Bill's assistant was suddenly reaching oddly under the desk with his gaze fixed intently on the door. Bill was staring at him in consternation.

All wrong.

As Haycroft pushed the door round I pulled back out of it and hopped off the carpet again. The door turned ninety degrees and, with a sharp clicking sound of metal, came to an abrupt halt. Haycroft was trapped, and so would I have been.

Bill looked agonised at the sight of Haycroft shouting and banging angrily on the walls of his glass cage. Suddenly, Morrissey was standing there, looking at the situation appraisingly and giving instructions to his assistant, who was inserting some sort of key first into the bottom and then into the top of the door on Haycroft's side. One of the glass panels swung free, and Haycroft stepped shakily out into the lobby.

"Hell of a door," Haycroft said in an angry bluster.

"Yes, sir," said Bill. He looked resentfully at his supposed assistant. "I'm sure it won't happen again."

"I certainly hope not. I don't know what was wrong with the old door." Haycroft turned and headed for the staircase.

"I followed orders exactly, but I don't get it," the assistant doorman was saying to Morrissey. "No one was near the carpet. The buzzer just went off by itself. I set the door anyway, like I was supposed to, but the guy was outside when it went off."

Morrissey, ignoring him, was talking into some sort of telephone. "We've got him . . . Yeah, in the main door."

Outside, a van was backing up to the sidewalk, and several people dressed as workmen were erecting a plywood enclosure round the entrance. I recognised Clellan among them. In a moment they would be opening up the other side of the door, expecting to find me inside, and I realised abruptly that if I were not out of the club by then, I might never get out.

I ran down the hall, avoiding the carpet, and then halfway up the stairs behind Haycroft. "Fire!" I called out as loudly and urgently as I could without Morrissey hearing. "Please proceed directly to the service entrance and leave the building as promptly as possible."

Haycroft stood there immobile, with a baffled look on his face.

"Let's go, Haycroft! There are people dying up there! *Run!*" At that, he thundered down the stairs past me.

I turned and followed him into the vestibule of the service entrance. The door swung shut behind me, leaving the two of us locked in the short corridor. Haycroft turned to the porter sitting behind the counter, who would have to buzz him out. It was not the usual porter. It was Gomez. He looked up at Haycroft and said, "This door is closed."

"Well, open it! I know it's closed. The place is on fire!"

"This door can't be opened now."

Haycroft was screaming now. "Get that door open!"

Gomez locked startled. Watching Haycroft intently, he picked up the housephone and dialled two digits.

I had my penknife out and was trying to extract the little blade.

"Hello. This is Gomez." I had the blade open and was sawing into the telephone wire where it ran up the wall at the end of the counter. "I have someone here who's says there's a fire in the . . . Hello? Hello!" Gomez was flipping the cradle bar up and down.

I swung myself over the counter and slid down the other side. I located the buzzer button under the counter and began poking until I got the knife blade under the wires that ran to the button. I prised them loose, ripped them free of the button, and pressed the bare ends together, feeling the electric shock run through my fingers. The moment the wires touched, the buzzer began to sound and Haycroft pushed his way through the door and was gone. I gave the wires a twist to hold them together and dived over the counter.

"Hey, hold it!" Gomez was shouting. There was an expression of incomprehension on his face as he stared at the door and listened to the buzzer. But when I thudded onto the floor and scrambled towards the exit, he understood perfectly what was happening. As I pushed the door open I heard a gun go off once, then twice more as I raced down the alley and out into the street.

Chapter 9

I was shaking with fear and panic as I walked down Park Avenue. Jenkins had never stopped searching for me, and I had never been safe at the Academy Club. Just as I had figured out that it was the best place for me to go to ground, he had figured it out too. What was worse, I could still not think of anything better than going to another club—which meant that they would be waiting for me to do just that. But what choice did I have? There were the hotels, but they would only be more dangerous than the clubs, brighter and more crowded. I could certainly not go back to my apartment.

I decided, almost at random, to try the Seaboard Club first. It was smaller than the Academy Club, but it had a good kitchen and some guest rooms. I had the idea that I would gradually establish the same sort of secure, regular routine there that I had enjoyed in the Academy Club.

I stayed two days, until, while waiting outside the manager's office for a chance to slip inside, I saw Tyler limping down the corridor towards me. I think I must have been relieved to see him alive, but all I felt was dread as I hurried out onto the street.

I kept moving from club to club, but everywhere I went new locks would appear on kitchen doors, new exit doors would be installed, and new security guards hired. I slept somewhere different almost every night now. I could not tell how well they were keeping track of me, but more and more I felt that they were right behind me, that people noticed at once that I was there.

I was out in the streets much more, as I scurried from one hiding place to another, and I was becoming much better at moving among other people. Scuttling through Manhattan, I could see all round me enormous buildings full of rooms and apartments into which people locked themselves, safe from the world. I needed help, but I did not dare confide in anyone. I had to trick someone into helping me, someone Jenkins could not connect to me, whom I had known only casually, or a long time ago.

I spent several hours in the Ivy Club studying directories of past students and telephone books until I had several promising names. My first call was to a Charles Randolph, whom I had encountered probably a dozen times in my life and spoken to for a total of maybe twenty minutes, probably about golf and interest rates. I rang the downtown law firm for which he worked, and a woman's voice answered.

It was the first time anyone had spoken to me in weeks.

I could hear the voice with extraordinary clarity, but I could somehow not focus on the meaning of the words. She was speaking again, saying, "Hello. Hello?" over and over.

"Hello," I said. "This is Nick Halloway. Could I speak to Mr. Randolph, please?"

The telephone was silent for a moment, and suddenly a male voice boomed out, "Nick Halloway! I'll be damned. How are you?"

"Hello, Charley."

"I'm really glad you called, Nick. I was just thinking about you the other day."

I was bewildered by his effusive response. I was calling him precisely because we did not know each other this well.

"I haven't seen you in months," he was saying.

"Actually, no one's seen much of me lately. I've been under a lot of pressure. Not much chance to get out—"

"Hey, that reminds me. While I think of it, we're having a bunch of people over for drinks on the twenty-seventh. Around six thirty. If you're still in the city, why don't you come by?"

"Thanks very much. I'll probably be out of town, but if I'm here, I'd love to. Listen, I'm calling to ask a favour, actually. I'm mainly out on the West Coast these days, and last month I sublet my apartment. As it turns out, I have to spend the next few months here in New York, and I'm calling you on the off chance that you might know of an empty apartment somewhere."

"Right offhand I don't. Why don't you give me a number where I can reach you, and I'll ask around."

"Actually, it's probably easier if I get back to you."

"By the way, what *are* you doing anyway? I've heard all sorts of things. First, people were saying you'd joined the Hare Krishnas, and then I got grilled by the FBI for your security check. The Hare Krishnas require a security clearance these days?"

"The FBI?"

"I guess it was the FBI. They must have interrogated me for over an hour. 'When did you last see him?' 'Who are his friends?' That was the big thing: the guy wrote down the name of every person I could think of who you might have ever said hello to. Incredible. Are you infiltrating the Hare Krishnas or something?"

"Charley, I have to run now, but—"

"I guess you can't talk about it. But I'll tell you, everyone is really curious about what you're doing. You've turned yourself into a celebrity. Come by on the twenty-seventh. There'll be a lot of people you—"

"Listen, Charley, thanks a lot. I'll be in touch with you."

I hung up and mentally crossed off the other names on my list. Jenkins was being more thorough than I had imagined. He had invaded my past life and cut me off from it completely. Stay calm and figure out what is going on.

I dialled my office—my former office—and asked for Cathy.

"Nick! Hi! How are you?" She seemed excited to hear from me. The sound of her voice, which had been so familiar to me in my former daily life, made the blood drain from my head.

"Hello . . . How is everything?"

She was telling me who she was working for now and what she was doing. I should sit down a moment and let my head clear. "Well, how is everything going?" Hadn't I just asked that?

"Are you all right?" she was asking. It frightened me into something approaching alertness.

"I'm fine. Just got in. Jet lag."

She was asking didn't I want the phone message she had told me about.

"Of course," I said, "almost forgot."

"Jenkins," she said. "David Jenkins." Everything seemed to be going black, and I felt as if I were spinning through a void. Cathy's voice was reciting numbers. Telephone numbers. "He said to give him a call when you get a chance."

There was a little box of notepaper. Pencil on a string.

"Cathy, could you give me that number again, please?" I wrote it down, the pencil trembling. I repeated it. "Cathy, did he tell you to let him know if I got in touch with you?"

"No, he said he would know when you had called."

"Did he? Cathy, it's good talking with you. I've got to run."

I was sweating. I took one more look at the number, crumpled it up, and ran out into the street.

TWO NIGHTS LATER I came down into the kitchen of the Arcadia Club at two a.m. and found, sitting out in plain view, a large slice of cake. It was of a sort that would be particularly appealing to me, white with vanilla icing, sweet and easy to digest. Next to it, sprawled inert on the marble table top, lay a large rat, its mouth slightly open, its legs twitching. Whether it was dying or only drugged, I cannot say.

I knew that I would never eat another bite of food in one of these clubs. I spent a sleepless night on a couch near the entrance, and as soon as the morning staff began to arrive, I fled.

I walked over to Central Park West, the avenue that borders the park on the West Side, and selected a payphone. It was on a corner, so that I could see anyone who came within a block of me. I lifted the receiver and laid it on top of the coin box, so that with my head tilted back I could both speak into it and hear it, without it dancing about ostentatiously in midair.

I dialled Jenkins's number, charging the call to my office credit card. There was only one ring, then Jenkins.

"Hello, Nick. Thank you for returning my call." I had not yet uttered a sound. This line was for me alone. He was absolutely matter-of-fact, and his voice had that smooth, exaggerated sincerity that had annoyed me so much at our first meeting.

"Hello . . . I'm sorry, is it *Colonel* or *Mister* Jenkins?"

"Please call me Dave. How are you, Nick?"

"I'm a little off today. I didn't sleep very well last night."

"I'm sorry to hear that, Nick. Is anything the matter?"

"I came into the Arcadia Club kitchen last night and found a large, ugly rat in very poor condition next to a piece of cake that looked as if it had been set out just for me."

"I see," he said slowly. "It must be horrible for you out there, Nick. I'm sorry. Is there anything we can do to help you?"

"Yes, there is one thing. You could leave me alone."

There was a brief pause. "Nick, I know you understand that that's impossible. We're going to find you. I think we'll be bringing you in very soon now, but even if we don't, ten years from now we'll be making the same effort as today to find you."

"Colonel, you and I both know that just isn't true. I can only guess at what it must be costing but I'm certain you can't go on like this. What do you tell people you're doing, anyway? Some congressman is going to find out one day that you're looking for little invisible people, and then you'll be working at the post office."

"Nick, for very good reasons this project is classified, and very few people will ever have any idea at all what it is we're doing. Also, I have— sitting here on my desk now, as it happens—a small plastic cigarette lighter, which we found on the lawn after the MicroMagnetics fire. It's absolutely invisible. I've shown it to only two people, but it made a dramatic impression on both of them. No other argument had to be made for the importance of what we're doing. It would hardly be necessary to mention you."

"I still don't see what makes you think you'll catch me."

"Nick, it's only a matter of time. What you're doing is just too difficult."

A beat-up van came to a stop and waited, double-parked, a block and a half north of me. "You have this number. Just remember, Nick, if you ever need—"

"Tell me, Jenkins, do you trace these calls?"

"Why do you . . . I see. Would it help, Nick, if I gave you my personal assurance that no one will come after you now while we're talking?"

"No."

A truck moved up Central Park West into the intersection and without any indication wheeled round into the side street next to me. The van was starting forward again. As I jumped clear of the phone there was a little crash within the booth, and a dent appeared on the face of the telephone.

I turned and saw that the side door of the van was open and a thick gun barrel—probably the same sort of gun I had seen Gomez with before— was pointed at me. I scrambled back from the telephone box towards a building. Cars were stopping everywhere on both sides of Central Park West, and there were people all over the street. The truck filled the narrow street, its side swinging down as if it were a troop carrier, disgorging men and equipment. It all happened so quickly. First the nearly empty streets and then suddenly dozens of men all round me.

They were unrolling what looked like some sort of fencing. Two men were fastening one end onto the wall of the building several feet away from me, while two more men unrolled it across the sidewalk and out between two cars into the street. Another section was being unrolled from round the corner. I was being enclosed, along with the phone box. It was all happening in a matter of seconds. Beyond the fencing I could see other men spreading out what appeared to be an enormous fishing net. Gomez was out of the van, still holding the gun, watching warily.

By the time I had collected my wits enough to start moving, the fencing had already been completely joined up, so that it ran from one side of the building out into the street, encircling several parked cars and most of the intersection, and then back into the building again, round the corner. No time to think what to do. I started running straight at Gomez. At the last moment he must have heard me, because he tried to raise the gun, as if to shield himself, but it was too late. I hit him as hard as I could with my closed fist, grabbed the gun and heaved it over the fence into the street.

Without pausing I jumped onto the bonnet of the parked car behind him, then up onto the roof. Each step caused a loud metallic boom and a sudden, violent deformation of the car's body. No one had told the men what they were after, so, of course, their attention was focused on Gomez, who seemed to have inexplicably hurled his gun over his head and then collapsed on the pavement. I climbed up onto the roof of the van.

I saw Clellan now, on the other side of the fence, running up Central Park West towards me. He was shouting at Morrissey, who was clambering out of the end of the van with his face turned up to me. I jumped off the edge of the van roof towards the fencing several feet away. I meant to land on it lightly with one foot and push myself up and on over it, so that I would come down into the street on the other side. But the wooden slats buckled under my weight, and I came crashing down onto the partly unfolded net lying in the street below.

Clellan was screaming, "Stretch out the net! *Pull*, damn it!" The men, with no idea what was going on, moved round the net and began to take hold of it uncertainly. As Clellan tugged violently at one edge and the others began dubiously to spread it out, I felt the net pulling taut under me. I climbed frantically to my feet and then tumbled over again as the net was yanked under me. I half stumbled, half rolled across the spreading net, until I felt myself pitch off the edge onto the asphalt.

I scrambled away between two parked cars and over the wall into the park. Climbing up onto an outcrop of rock that loomed above the wall, I sat down to catch my breath and observe the commotion in the street below. The net was already being packed away and the fences rolled up. Normal traffic was beginning to flow again up and down Central Park West.

As I sat there, a nondescript white car pulled up across the street and Jenkins climbed out of the back. He walked towards Clellan, who came up to meet him, speaking rapidly. Clellan's forefinger made little jabs in the air, sketching out the location of the fence, the nets, the men, and then, with an abrupt sweep, tracing out my escape. He gave a little shrug and pointed up at the rocks where I was sitting. Jenkins's gaze shifted slowly up the rock and settled there. It seemed to me that he was staring directly at me. His face was impassive. Expressionless as a reptile.

Chapter 10

I had not eaten or slept for over twenty-four hours, and for the hundredth time I looked across the park at the tantalising New York skyline, composed of thousands upon thousands of inaccessible rooms and apartments. The greatest concentration of hiding places in the world. People would be going off on summer holidays now, leaving more and more of them empty.

I walked east to Second Avenue and spent the rest of the morning inspecting buildings, until I had one picked out to assault. It was one of those massive white brick buildings that everyone in New York professes to hate but in which almost everyone not very rich or very poor has to live. The one I chose had a particularly lax doorman whose attention seemed mainly focused on a portable radio. He had the main entrance door propped open, which made things easier for both him and me.

To the left of the entrance there was a marble counter, and jumbled onto the shelves beneath it and the floor behind it were stacks of mail and uncollected deliveries. Out of sight under the far end of the counter there were keys hanging from two rows of hooks. Most of the keys had little tags with apartment numbers written on them. I spent half the afternoon crouched behind the counter, sorting through everything. From the postmarks and the way the mail was bundled together, I was able to identify several apartments that had been empty more than a week.

I settled on 3C. Mr. and Mrs. Matthew B. Logan. They had both been gone for nearly ten days, which meant that they were almost surely on vacation. Furthermore, there would be only three flights of stairs to hike up.

Although there was nothing more I could do until that night, I did not want to go outside and risk being unable to get back in through the door. I could not go another day without food. I dozed fitfully on a concrete landing on the fire stairs for the next nine hours.

211

When I re-emerged into the lobby, groggy and dizzy with hunger, it was after midnight and there was a different doorman. He sat motionless on a chair, between the inner and outer doors, looking perfectly catatonic but with his eyes open and with a good view of the lobby through which I would have to transport the keys.

I went back behind the marble counter and carefully extracted the keys to 3C. Getting down on all fours, I crawled out from behind the counter and rapidly slipped the keys under the edge of the carpet that ran the length of the lobby. I began to crawl along the carpet, sliding the keys ahead of me. If anyone had been looking, he would have seen an odd, jerky little ripple running very slowly down the border of the carpet.

Round the corner and out of sight I picked up the keys and plodded up the fire stairs to the third floor. The carpeting in the corridor was laid wall to wall, but I got down on all fours again and slid the keys along the edge. At the door of 3C I had to take my chances getting the door unlocked, but moments later I was stepping into the apartment, pulling the keys free, and pushing the door shut behind me.

Warmth spread through my body. I was safely locked inside this splendid little apartment, where no one would ever find me.

Switching on a light, I made my way into the kitchen and pulled open the refrigerator door. Strawberry jam, five cans of beer and a bottle of champagne. They had cleared out the refrigerator before leaving. No matter. I snatched a spoon from the drying rack and greedily cleaned out the jam jar. I uncorked the champagne and poured myself a large glass. To my new life.

I turned my attention to the cupboards and found cans of tuna fish and sardines, and boxes of spaghetti. I went to work on a sardine can, managing to twist the key just far enough with my trembling fingers so that I could get the contents with a fork and shovel them into myself. More champagne. To a long and happy life. Safe and sound.

I put water on the stove to cook some spaghetti and made a tour of the premises. Two bedrooms and a large living room with a dining alcove. Not enough cupboard space and the ceiling too low. But it seemed quite wonderful to me. Another glass of champagne. I hoped the Logans were enjoying a wonderful and lengthy holiday.

I stacked *The Marriage of Figaro* onto the turntable and loaded several bottles of wine into the refrigerator for the days ahead. Perhaps they were taking the entire summer off. As I ate my spaghetti I considered my good fortune. I should have figured this out long ago. At any given time there must be thousands of apartments sitting empty.

I slept in the Logans' vast bed till midday and then showered and shaved, feeling wonderfully refreshed.

On a cork bulletin board in the kitchen was a list of telephone numbers. I dialled the one described as "oficio de Sr. Logan" and was told that Mr. Logan was out of the country and would not be back in the office until a week from Monday.

For the next two days I imagined I was safe.

On the third morning I was woken by the repeated ringing of the doorbell. I sat straight up in bed. The bell had stopped ringing and the lock was turning. I looked down at my intestines and saw that they were clear.

"I know there's been someone in there for at least two nights now, and the Logans don't get back for another week."

Two people stood in the open doorway of the bedroom. One was a middle-aged woman in a linen suit, and the other was a large man in grey work clothes. Probably the superintendent.

"I could hear classical music in the middle of the night and see the light under the door. You see? The bed's not made."

I stared at them stupidly. Don't come any closer, please.

"They could of left it like that," said the man. They turned and went into the living room.

"I heard the shower running last night. It's right next to my bathroom. And look at all these dirty dishes. Look at all this fresh garbage." They were in the kitchen now.

I scrambled out of bed and grabbed the bundle of clothes that I always kept beside me when I slept. Still naked and carrying my clothes under my arm, I slipped out of the front door and down the fire stairs to the street. I had been stupid. Careless. In New York your neighbours may not know you, but they know when you are running the water or when you have a phone call. They are always peering out through their little peepholes and peering in through your windows. This would be far more difficult than I had thought. I had not solved anything yet.

OVER THE COURSE of the summer I learned a great deal about New York apartment buildings. I learned which had elevator men, which had fire stairs that exited out of sight of the lobby. I learned where the mail was sorted and by whom, and which buildings had inattentive doormen.

I understood that I was in just as much danger as ever, and that I would have to think out every step I took. I could not go into an apartment whose entrance was visible from a neighbour's peephole. (Every front door in New York has one of those unpleasant little spy-holes.) I was careful not to leave any sign of my presence. I crept about in the dark, always listening for the sound of movement in the next apartment or of someone at the entrance. I made a point of getting keys back down to where I found them as soon as I got an apartment open, because missing keys would be the plainest possible way for me to signal my presence.

But no matter how careful you are people notice that you have been there, and I made a point of never staying in any one place more than a night or two. I could not afford to sit still and let Jenkins close in on me. I was spending half my time now searching out empty apartments.

But I knew that in the end I could not stay ahead of Jenkins like this. He would figure it out, if he hadn't already. And when cold weather came, things would become more difficult. There would be fewer vacant apartments. Building doors would be kept closed. When it snowed, I would be trapped in whatever building I happened to be in. And once I stopped moving, he would have me.

I had to find somewhere secure, a place of my own where I could stay put and arrange a reasonable life for myself. I would have to create a new identity, with a bank account and credit cards. Then I should be able to provide myself with whatever I needed. But to open a bank account or get a credit card you need a credit rating, and to get that you need bank accounts and credit cards. You also need a little something to put into the bank account.

But that might not be true of a brokerage account. A stockbroker might be willing to open an account without meeting you or even having a very solid reference, if there were some promise of real commissions. And furthermore, you could open a brokerage account without putting any funds in it for a while. You could even get the broker to make a trade if you had him convinced that a cheque would arrive by the settlement date, five days later. It would require a broker who was ready to overlook a few of the niceties for the sake of some commissions, but all my past experience of brokers tended to make me confident that I would find my man.

What would not be so easy was finding a name with a matching Social Security number that I could use, and I would absolutely need that to open any sort of account. And worse yet, I would need an address and a phone number where I could receive phone calls and statements under that name.

As it turned out, I got the address almost right away. I had spent a tedious morning looking for apartments in a building on Fifth Avenue and managed to learn only that "the people in 7C are away". There was a set of keys right there in the lobby, and I had no better prospect at the moment, so that night I returned.

It was a large, comfortable apartment with splendid views out over the park, and it looked from the first as if no one was living there. I found the mail piled up on the table in the hall, which meant that the doorman was probably leaving it there each day, but I was disappointed to discover that it had been accumulating for only about a week. I slept in a maid's room that looked as if it had not been inhabited for years.

In the morning, as I was going through the hall, I was unpleasantly startled by the sound of a key turning in the front door. A woman in her sixties entered and immediately gathered up the mail from the table. I followed her into a little study off the living room. She sorted through the mail, putting the personal letters into a large manila envelope, already addressed to Mr. and Mrs. John R. Crosby, somewhere in Switzerland. Then she began opening the bills one at a time and paying them from a chequebook that she withdrew from a desk drawer.

I moved a step closer so that I could read the exact address on the manila envelope. The Crosbys seemed to live in their own villa somewhere in Vaud. It all looked very promising indeed. The woman worked for a little more than an hour and then abruptly stood up, putting the chequebook and paid bills in the drawer. Then she gathered up the manila envelope and left, locking the front door behind her.

I immediately pulled out the chequebook and began examining the register. The woman had been there every Tuesday as far back as it went. In a state of excitement I spent the next two days going through the apartment, finding out everything I could about the Crosbys. I identified a spare key to the entrance and hid it outside on the back stairs.

At nine thirty on the next Tuesday morning I was in another apartment, dialling the Crosbys' number.

"Crosby residence," she answered curtly.

"I'd like to speak to Mr. Crosby, please. This is Fred Fmmmmph," I mumbled indistinctly.

"The Crosbys are not in New York."

"Still off in Switzerland, are they? I was afraid of that. When do you expect them to be in New York?"

"I'm afraid I don't know," she said, as if not knowing gave her considerable pleasure. "If you would like to leave a message, I can forward it. If you could spell your name?"

"You must be Mrs. Dixon, aren't you?"

"I am," she said, as if it were an affront to be addressed by name.

"That's wonderful. John and Mary talk about you all the time. The thing is, a bunch of us from Marley School wanted to hold a dinner for John . . . kind of honour him for everything he's done for the school. We were hoping he might be in New York some time in the fall."

"I see. I'm sorry, Mr. . . . um . . . that is, I'm sorry, but I'm afraid they won't be here before Christmas."

"That would be perfect. Perfect. Better not even to mention that I called, Mrs. Dixon. So as not to spoil the surprise."

"Of course, Mr. . . . uh—"

"Pleasure finally to speak to you, Mrs. Dixon. Goodbye."

I LEARNED FROM A TELEPHONE call to the Social Security Administration that I would have to "come in in person" for an interview, bringing "an original birth certificate and two means of identification". The nearest office was on East Fifty-eighth Street. I went in—"in person"—although I had nothing to bring and knew I would do badly in an interview.

The office was a single large room with fifteen or twenty drab grey metal desks. The applicant handed in his completed application together with his birth certificate and "evidence of identity". The interviewer, having noted the documentation provided, simply signed and stamped the application. The application form then made its gradual way to one of two women seated in front of computer terminals, and the information was keyed in and transmitted directly to a central computer somewhere in Maryland.

At five minutes after five, when the room was entirely empty, I switched on one of the terminals and typed in the same password and information I had seen one of the women use that afternoon. I called up the format for entering a new name into the system and typed in "Jonathan B. Crosby". Different enough from John R. Crosby but not so different as to invite comment from the postman or building staff. I entered the Fifth Avenue address and gave myself a birth date that made me exactly twenty-one that day—old enough to allow me to establish accounts but young enough to make plausible my lack of a credit record.

Jonathan B. Crosby's Social Security number appeared on the screen, and I committed it to memory. Happy birthday, Jonathan.

I WENT ON MONDAY evenings to the Crosby apartment to pick out any mail addressed to Jonathan B. Crosby. At first there was only my Social Security card to watch for, but I hoped soon to be getting all sorts of statements from brokerage firms.

Before I got a brokerage account, I needed to find an investment that would appreciate a great deal in a short time—and with virtual certainty. Of course, a lot of people feel they need investment ideas like this, and they are consequently not easy to come by, but my condition did give me some advantages.

One place to look for such situations is in the 13D business, named after the form you must file with the Securities and Exchange Commission when you acquire more than five per cent of the stock of a public corporation. If you are in this business, you look around for a corporation which you think is undervalued by the stock market. You get together with some friends and start gradually buying up the stock—as discreetly as possible, since you don't want to do anything to drive up the price unnecessarily. Then you cross the five-per-cent mark and pretty soon you have to start telling everyone more or less what you are up to, and probably you make an offer to buy out other shareholders at some price well above the recent market price. You hope in all this either that you will be bought off or outbid, in which case you expect to make a vast and rather quick profit, or else that you will wind up controlling the corporation. But no matter what happens, the price of the stock will probably have shot up dramatically.

There are all sorts of people in New York who are involved in this kind of thing pretty much all the time, and I began to spend my days, and some of my evenings, in their offices. I would spend hours listening in on meetings and telephone conversations. When someone was out of his office, I would slip in and read through whatever was on his desk. After a while I had several particularly promising situations.

In the meantime, however, I was making no progress at all in finding a broker. The trouble was, I couldn't use anyone who knew me as Nicholas Halloway, but on the other hand, given my condition, it seemed to be impossible to meet new people. Then I remembered Charley Randolph's invitation to his cocktail party. It occurred to me that a party might be the answer. Eventually I would need not only a broker but an accountant, and what better place to search for them than at social gatherings where I could observe large numbers of new people half drunk and talking continuously.

I started to go to parties almost daily for the next several weeks. It was the perfect time of year for it. The people who are still in the city in July, especially if they are single, will often go out every night of the week, wandering from one gathering to another. I would spot little bands of them in the street or climbing out of taxis, and follow them to their celebrations. When I found one that looked promising, I might hang about for hours, drifting from conversation to conversation, sometimes sipping cautiously from an abandoned drink in a corner, using as a straw the plastic shaft of an otherwise useless invisible ball-point pen from which I had removed the ink cartridge. At these moments I think I sometimes lost sight of the fact that I was not really a guest at the party.

By the middle of July I had taken a careful look at several likely-looking brokers, finally settling on one Willis T. Winslow III. I had first spotted Willy, as he is known to his friends, aggressively telling another young man a story about an exciting computer disc-drive manufacturer selling at forty or fifty times earnings. I could see at once that he held promise. Although it was early in the evening, he had already drunk a great deal and showed no sign of easing off.

Over the next few days I found out where Willy lived, where he had gone to school, who his friends were. I attended more parties with him. I even went in one day and stood next to his desk for several hours, listening to him talk to his customers over the telephone.

In the third week of July, I saw my opportunity. One of the offices in which I had spent many tedious hours over the past month was that of Myron Stone, who was one of the most successful and feared of the corporate raiders. Over the course of seven months he had quietly accumulated—for various anonymous accounts—just under five per cent of the stock of Allied Resources Corporation, at prices ranging from nine dollars and fifty cents to eleven dollars a share. And then he had paused for several weeks to marshal his forces for the final onslaught.

When the markets opened on Monday of the third week in July, Stone moved in for the kill. He began buying Allied Resources shares again, quickly running over the five-per-cent limit. He would now have ten more days before he would have to file his 13D form with the Securities and Exchange Commission, and announce his intentions to an unsuspecting world. In those ten days, using brokers and accounts under various names that people could not connect to him, he would amass as much more of the stock as he could, before the public announcement drove the price up and before Allied Resources' management realised what was going on and tried to stop him.

The day after Stone crossed the five-per-cent mark. I was at the Crosby apartment, dialling Willis T. Winslow's number.

"Hello, Willy? This is Jonathan Crosby. We met last night."

"Oh, of course," he replied. "How are you?" Willy's memory of the night before, as of all nights before, would be sketchy at best.

"Fine, thanks," I said with as much boyishly ingenuous enthusiasm as I could generate. "I really enjoyed our discussion, and I want to go ahead and open the account with you."

"Oh, of course. Uh, just let me get some information here, Jonathan. Now, how exactly do you want your name to appear on the account?"

I spelled it out for him. Jonathan B. Crosby. I gave him the Fifth Avenue address, and I could tell he liked it. He asked for the business address. I told him I wasn't really doing anything right now; I was just here in New York staying with my uncle while I figured out what I wanted to do. Social Security number? I gave him my new number. Bank references?

"Gee, to tell the truth, I don't think I've ever had a bank account. Unless you count the trust fund. I mean, whenever I need money, I call Herr Wengler in Switzerland—he's someone who works for my father—and he handles it. I mean, I'm about to open a bank account here. I just haven't really got myself organised yet."

He asked what I meant to open the brokerage account with.

"Open it with?" I asked. "I was hoping I could open it with you. Over the phone. Actually, I hoped to buy a stock today."

"I mean what sort of money or securities did you mean to put in the account to start with?"

"Well, that was one of the things I wanted to ask you. I was thinking maybe just one or two hundred thousand dollars at first and then see how it goes. Do you think that would be enough?"

"Why, yes," he said quickly. He would be mentally computing his share of the commissions on $200,000 worth of trades. "Yes, that would be a prudent level to begin with. Tell me, Jonathan, how are you going to be making payment? You don't seem to—"

"Oh, right. It's good you mention that. I'm going to have it wired or transferred or something. I don't know exactly how it works, but I've already talked to Herr Wengler. I'm supposed to get an account number from you so he can take care of it."

"I'm going to get that for you right away, Jonathan." I could hear him punching keys on a terminal. "Now, what are your investment goals for this account?"

"I guess making a lot of money, mainly. My grandfather and my father both did that, and I think I'd like to accomplish the same sort of thing."

"Yes. Well, that's very good, Jonathan. But I meant more your particular strategy: preservation of capital or yield or long-term appreciation or what?"

"Trading, I think. I'd like to get in there and really get an active feel of the market. I think I'd want to trade as much as I could."

There was a pause. Willis T. Winslow III must be dizzy with greed thinking about the commissions. I went on.

"I mean that's why I was so interested last night in hearing your ideas. I'm sorry to be in such a hurry, but I want to buy this one stock right away that this friend of my father's told me about."

"Well, we really ought to have some funds in the account to—"

"Oh, gosh. I must have misunderstood what you said last night. I thought that just so the money was there within five days . . . That's really why I was in such a hurry to open the account."

"And I don't have your signed application."

"Golly," I said. "I'm creating problems for you, aren't I? I didn't realise. Actually, I have the name of someone who my father knows at Kidder, Peabody. I think it's Kidder, Peabody. Is that the name of a brokerage firm? Anyway, he could probably handle this for me now, and then in a few weeks when I have a bank account and everything, I could give you a call again. Would that be better for you?"

"Jonathan, what exactly did you want to buy today?" His voice was a good octave deeper.

"Well, I wanted to buy"—I wondered how far I dared push him—"two thousand shares of a stock called Allied Resources. This friend of my father's said I should do it right away."

I could hear him punching the keys in the background.

"That's going at eleven and a half," he was saying distractedly. He would be doing the multiplication. If he baulked, I would settle for one hundred shares. The critical point was to get somehow from zero assets to any assets at all.

"The thing is, you'd absolutely have to have the funds here within five business days."

"I think it only takes twenty-four hours to wire it. That's what Herr Wengler told me. Are you sure this isn't too much trouble? I just don't want to let this opportunity go by."

"As long as the funds are wired tomorrow. Jonathan, I'm looking at some information on this stock right now. Do you know why your father's friend recommended it? It's not something I follow myself, but I see it hasn't been much of a performer this year."

I told him that the recommendation came from a very good friend of my father's and I was pretty sure it was going to work out. He told me he was sending some papers up by messenger for me to sign. I said I would be out when they arrived but I would put them in the mail.

I waited in the Crosbys' apartment all day. Around three o'clock the doorman brought up the account application and left. I signed everything and took it out to the mail chute.

I turned the television on to the cable channel that runs the ticker tape and watched eagerly until the end of trading. Allied Resources had closed at 12¼, which was not a bad start. I had already more than covered the commissions on the turnaround.

I waited until Thursday afternoon before calling Willis again. I told him that I had spoken to Herr Wengler and that the money was being wired and should arrive some time in the next two business days.

"That's fine," Winslow said absently. He had not begun to be worried yet.

"I'm going away for the weekend and I won't be back till Monday. I'll call you then to make sure everything's arrived."

"OK. I see Allied Resources has moved up a little bit here. It's trading around twelve and a half. Your friend seems to have put you into a good situation. Who exactly did you say he was?"

"Uncle David? He's a friend of my father's. Some sort of banker. He's on a lot of boards of corporations or something. I have to hurry to get my ride out to Southampton. Have a nice weekend."

On Friday, Allied Resources closed at 13½. I had forgotten the elation that could come with a winning bet. I called Willis again on Monday afternoon.

"Hi, Willy. I was just calling to make sure you got back my application and everything."

"Oh, Jonathan. I'm glad you called. I've been trying to reach you. Your account application arrived today, but we haven't received any money yet."

"Gee, that's awful. I don't know what could have happened. Herr Wengler said it should be here by now."

"Well, Jonathan, if you could just give me the name of the bank, we'll try to track down the problem."

"Gosh, I'd have to ask Herr Wengler about that. I don't really know anything about it . . . Maybe I should have him call you? Do you think that's a good idea?"

"That might be the simplest way to get it straightened out. Now you're sure he had the funds transferred?"

"Oh yes. He was absolutely clear about it. He's awfully precise."

"Well, I'm glad to hear that, Jonathan, because I've kind of stuck my neck out personally on that Allied Resources transaction, and tomorrow's the settlement date."

"Gosh, I'll get right on the phone to Herr Wengler. I mean, he's always absolutely reliable. By the way, how is Allied Resources doing?"

"It was up two points from where you bought it."

"Gosh. That's great, anyway. But I'm really sorry about the money. I'll call Herr Wengler first thing in the morning."

"I'll be right here."

Still only two points. And with Stone gobbling up every share he could find. I hoped this was going to work out.

Tomorrow would be Tuesday. I slept at the Crosbys' apartment that night. At seven in the morning I got up and switched off every telephone bell in the apartment, in case Willis called while Mrs. Dixon was there. She arrived at nine and left a little before eleven. There were no calls.

I went to another apartment to make my telephone calls. I didn't like to use the Crosbys' phone too much: Mrs. Dixon looked like the sort of person who would immediately notice a few dollars in the extra local units on the monthly bill.

I wrapped the receiver in a facecloth and for good measure held it against a portable radio which I tuned to pure static. I dialled Willis's number.

"Hello, Mr. Vinsslow?" I said rapidly, as soon as he picked up the receiver. "Rudi Schlesselgemuenze here, from the Schildkreuzige Landsschleierschafts Bank."

"Hello, I'm sorry but I didn't quite—"

"I am calling about the transfer of two hundred tausend dollars US funds originated by us to an account in the name of Jonathan Crosby."

"Yes, that's right," said Winslow eagerly. "Could you give me your—"

"Also, I vould vant to confirm the account number if you don't mind." I read off the number he had given me in as fast a staccato as I could manage.

"Yes, that's . . . I mean, I think that's . . . Could you read that again?" I read it again, less distinctly and perhaps even faster.

"We seem to have a faint connection here—"

"Ve are seeking to trace the funds now. Ve believe them to be somvhere in New York since yesterday. Ve should have the entire matter resolved vithin a matter of hours—and in any case, as you are dealing with the Crosbys, I hardly think you need be concerned."

"Could you give me your name and number in case someone at my end has to get back in touch with you on this?" said Winslow.

"Of course," I said. "Talk to you soon. Goodbye." I hung up.

Allied Resources closed at 15⅛ that day, and I knew I had pulled the thing off. It was just a question of how much further I could take it. I called Winslow again the next day just before four, so that the market would be closed by the time our conversation was over. Meanwhile, people were buying and selling Allied Resources at 16, which took the real pressure off us all. I told him gosh, I was sorry about all this, but Herr Wengler was absolutely amazed that the money wasn't there: he thought it had all been straightened out. Willis T. Winslow III sounded unhappy.

"The trouble is, Jonathan, I got called in on this. I should have waited until there were funds actually in the account."

"Gee, I'm really sorry," I said. "I don't know what to do."

"Well, Jonathan, I think we're going to have to sell your shares of Allied. The market's just closed, but tomorrow morning . . . I don't want to get caught here."

"Gee, absolutely. I just hope I haven't made any trouble for you. I feel terrible about this. Maybe I should just have them send another two hundred thousand. What do you think?"

"That might be a very good idea, Jonathan. I'll be able to sort everything out on my end. This won't in any way impair our working relationship. These things happen."

When they finally sold my shares the next day, they got 17¼ for them. After commissions I would net about ten thousand dollars, which was an excellent return on an investment of zero, and more than enough to build on. Jonathan B. Crosby suddenly had a positive net worth. At that moment I was absolutely sure I had won. Soon I would be opening a bank account, buying an apartment. Let Jenkins try to find me then.

Chapter 11

For the rest of the summer I worked long days and stayed in evenings, changing apartments every day or two. I devoted all my time to searching for new opportunities in the stock market, and although the work was dull and a bit shabby—ranging as it did from eavesdropping to outright burglary—I worked far harder than I ever had in my days as a conventional securities analyst with a handsome salary. But of course, the potential reward was so much more compelling now: survival.

After giving Willy and his employers a couple of weeks to settle down and turn their thoughts to other matters, I called and delivered once again my apology for the two hundred thousand dollars that had still not arrived. It was not a problem, Willy assured me—although with a bit more reserve and wariness in his voice than formerly.

"By the way," I said, "I have a little bit of money in my account, don't I?"

"Yes. Let me see . . . Ten thousand four hundred seventy-six and some change. I'm just looking at an interesting situation—"

"Actually," I said, "I had some suggestions from a friend."

"The same friend who put you into Allied Resources?"

"This is a different friend, actually. I wonder if you could get me four hundred shares of Westland Industries. That's over the counter. Is that the right expression?"

"Yes, it is, Jonathan."

"This next one is on the New York Stock Exchange. It's called RGP. Are just those initials enough?"

"Yes, they are, Jonathan."

"If you could get me three hundred shares, that would be great. I'm sorry to make this so complicated."

"That's perfectly all right, Jonathan. That's what I'm here for."

By the last week in August my portfolio was worth over forty-nine thousand dollars. Then Labor Day weekend arrived and suddenly there seemed to be no more empty apartments anywhere. I would spend whole days now searching for them, and I found myself frequently forced to remain in the same apartment for several days, although I knew how dangerous that was.

One day I was sure I saw Tyler. A large black man walking with a limp up Third Avenue. I had no idea where he had come from or where he was going to. He walked half a block, climbed into a grey saloon car, and drove away.

A few days later I thought I saw Gomez. I began to see all of them all the time, until I was no longer sure if I had ever really seen any of them. Always, when I rushed after them, they would be gone before I could get to them. I was watching for them constantly now.

Then, late one morning, as I emerged from the fire stairs in a large white brick building on Second Avenue, I saw Clellan at the other end of the lobby, talking to the doorman. Trembling, I walked very slowly and carefully up to where they were standing.

Clellan was saying in his hearty, cowboyish way, "Now, you know and I know that in a building this size there's no way you can monitor one hundred per cent who comes in and out. Which is why this citywide task force has been set up."

The doorman spoke with an East European accent. "The people that come through here, I could tell you things, you wouldn't believe it. You know what I mean?"

As the doorman spoke, Clellan's face suddenly took on an intent

223

expression, and following his gaze, I saw that he was staring directly at my feet, or rather, at the two footprint-shaped depressions in the carpet beneath them. For a moment neither of us moved. Then, very carefully, I put my right foot quietly down on the marble floor beyond the edge of the carpet. Clellan and I both watched as the carpet pile gradually straightened itself in the footprint. His hands twitched at his sides, as if he were uncertain whether to lunge in my direction. I withdrew the left foot, and the other footprint began to disappear from view. Clellan's hands relaxed.

"Halloway?" he asked softly. I said nothing, made no movement. Clellan's gaze went back to the carpet. No sign left there. "You there, Halloway?"

The doorman had stopped talking. He was watching Clellan now with a look of mystification.

"Halloway?" Clellan repeated. "We want to help you."

Quietly, slowly, I backed out through the open front door. I waited there for Clellan. He came out several minutes later and walked purposefully down the street to the next block, where he climbed into a grey car parked in front of a fire hydrant. As he drove off he had a telephone receiver in his hand and was talking animatedly.

I COULD NOT GO ON helplessly watching these people close in on me. My mistake was that I was always running, always retreating. I had to find some way to seize the initiative, to strike directly at Jenkins. But where exactly was he? Somewhere these people would have some sort of headquarters. What I had to do was track Clellan or Gomez back to it. There I would find my opportunity to strike back.

Then I suddenly understood why they always arrived and departed in their grey automobiles. It was precisely so that I would not be able to follow them. Jenkins had, of course, already thought all this through. I would never be able to track Clellan or Gomez or Tyler or Morrissey. They knew what they were guarding against. But Jenkins would have to be using other people who had no idea that they were searching for an invisible man and who would have no reason to think anyone might be following them. I had to do something just interesting enough to draw one of those people, but not interesting enough to warrant sending Clellan or Gomez.

The next morning I called my old office and, disguising my voice, told the receptionist that I would like to speak to Mr. Halloway. She told me that I was no longer employed there.

"He's not?" I said. "I had no idea he'd changed jobs. Do you have any idea where he's working now?"

She said that she had no number or address to give out, but that if wanted to leave a message, she would see that I got it.

"Will you?" I said. "That would be very kind. You could just tell him that Howard Dickison called. I have some news that I thought might interest him." I gave her Dickison's number.

I had encountered Howard Dickison at a party in July and recognised him as someone I had once been introduced to. I chose him now for two reasons. First, I did not know him, so that Jenkins's investigators would not have talked to him. Second, he had no office—he was a writer—which meant that I would not have to stake out both an office and a home.

Dickison lived in a brownstone in the West Seventies, near Central Park, and I went there immediately upon making my call and camped out on the front porch. He emerged at a little after ten thirty and I followed him over to a coffee shop on Broadway, where he consumed a prodigious quantity of eggs and bacon. I stood outside in the street and watched him enviously. He was back home again, ready to start his day, a little before noon. Nothing else happened the rest of that day.

I was back at Dickison's the next morning. The man I was waiting for appeared at exactly nine thirty. He was middle-aged and stocky and wore an ill-fitting brown suit. He walked up to the door and rang. Dickison appeared at the door, wearing a purple robe and evidently still more asleep than awake. He seemed confused by the presence of the visitor, who began speaking in a slow, mechanical monotone.

"Good morning, Mr. Dickison. My name is Herbert Butler. I spoke to you yesterday. Thank you very much for talking with me. We're performing a routine investigation of Nicholas Halloway in connection with a security clearance, and I'd just like to ask you several questions about him, which should only take a few minutes."

An expression of comprehension began to take form on Dickison's face. "I tried to tell you yesterday, I don't know Halloway."

"You indicated yesterday that you had met him socially—"

"I said I might have met him. I thought I recognised the name, possibly. But I have absolutely no recollection of him."

"Well, I'd like to ask you a few questions about any time recently when you might have attempted to contact Mr. Halloway."

"I have never attempted to contact Halloway, whoever he is. Look, I'm going to get myself some coffee." Then, as a grudging afterthought, "You had coffee yet?"

Holding the door for Butler to follow, Dickison retreated inside. The door shut behind them, and I could no longer hear what they were saying. After an hour the two of them reappeared in the doorway, neither looking particularly pleased.

Butler trudged out onto the sidewalk and turned east, with me following a few steps behind. At Seventy-second Street he descended into the subway, and we boarded an uncrowded southbound train together. Butler got off at Chambers Street. He walked north for several blocks and then entered a large institutional building. I followed right behind him through the lobby. He boarded an elevator half full of people; it was inconceivable that I should risk following him in, but I craned my head in behind him as he entered, so that I could watch him push the button for his floor. Six.

I found a stairway and charged up the six flights. As I paused momentarily behind the metal fire door I realised that I was panting audibly. I slipped through the door and found myself in a narrow hall by the elevators, facing a doorway in front of which sat a uniformed guard. Struggling to hold down my convulsive breathing, I tiptoed past him into a vast warren of dreary little cubicles and offices.

I found Butler sitting in a windowless cubicle, jabbing steadily at an old mechanical typewriter. His door was open and I leaned in just far enough to make out the name of Dickison at the top of the page he was typing. After an hour he brought out his work and handed it to a secretary. "Send two copies up to Special Liaison in fourteen oh seven— take the case number from the first page—and don't file anything down here."

That was all I needed. I trekked up to the fourteenth floor.

Room 1407 was actually two rooms, one of them a real office with windows and the other an outer office for a secretary. I sat down on a wooden chair to wait for the report to arrive. In the inner office I could see a man of about forty-five reading typewritten reports one after the other.

Soon an old man in a grey jacket came through wheeling a large mail trolley. He pulled out a stack of envelopes and dumped them onto the secretary's desk. She opened most of the envelopes. It was there: two copies. When she carried the mail in to the man in the inner office, I was right behind her.

He read my report carefully from beginning to end. Then he picked up the phone and tapped out a number.

"Hello, can I speak to Mr. Clellan? . . . Hello, Bob? Jim O'Toole. You know the guy who tried to get in touch with Halloway? Dickison . . . Well, we sent a man over to talk to him, and he denies ever having tried to reach him. I don't know what the story is. Why don't you take a look at the report and see what you think . . . OK. It'll all be here at the mail room on the first floor for pick-up any time . . . Sure. So long."

He took one copy of the report out to his secretary. "Put this into a package for Global Devices—no address—and take it down to the mail room for pick-up."

I hurried back down the stairs to the first floor in time to see the secretary leave the package for Global Devices. Just inside the entrance to the mail room was a long, broad counter, behind which three people were sorting envelopes and packages. After half an hour a boy of eighteen with a canvas bag slung over his shoulder stepped up to the counter. "I'm from Speedwell Messenger Services. Pick-up for Global Devices."

A woman behind the counter handed him a clipboard and said, "Sign on the last line." She went back and got the package for him.

While he waited for the elevator I raced down the stairs to the lobby. We walked together out to his bicycle. Nothing could be more hopeless for me than a bicycle. He unchained it from a no-parking sign and climbed on.

I had no clear idea of how it would help me, but I reached out just as he shifted his second foot onto the pedal and pushed the bicycle onto its side. The rider, completely unprepared, hit the street hard. I jumped onto the spokes of the rear wheel, crushing them hopelessly out of shape. The boy twisted free and studied the damage to the bicycle, wheeling it carefully up onto the sidewalk. He leaned the bike against the building and walked a bit unsteadily to a pay telephone. He dialled a number then said, "Hello, this is Angel . . . No, I'm still downtown. Somebody trashed my bike while I was inside making my pick-up . . . They just trashed it. What you want me to do? . . . Global Devices, One thirty-five East Twenty-seventh Street . . . Sure, I know how to walk."

I was on my way, full of triumph. I had tracked them down while they thought they were tracking me down. I was not altogether easy about walking in on them, but I had seized the initiative. I hoped I would think of something to do with it.

Chapter 12

One thirty-five East Twenty-seventh Street was an old, slightly seedy twelve-storey office building. On the directory in the lobby the office number for Global Devices was listed as 723, which would mean a relatively easy climb for me.

How convenient it would be if, with an occasional visit to Jenkins's office, I could find out exactly what he knew and what his plans were. But as I mounted the marble stairs my confidence began to give way to apprehension and then to outright dread. I was taking an enormous risk. I could go anywhere in the world to escape these people, and yet I had chosen to come here.

When I reached the seventh floor, I found a door marked "723" and below that "Global Devices, Inc". I waited. Normally I am willing simply to push open a closed door and slip through, but here I could not take chances.

After about twenty minutes a young woman came down the corridor, carefully holding in both hands a brown paper bag from which coffee dribbled. Without letting go of the bag, she managed to get one hand onto the doorknob and push the door open with her shoulder. Staying close to her, I followed her in.

I was in a large office containing several shabby secondhand desks. A woman sat at one of them typing. There was a closed door in the left-hand wall which must lead to the other offices. I watched the first woman unpack five containers of coffee onto her desk. After putting one cup on her colleague's desk and leaving one on her own, she gathered up the remaining cups and headed for the door, which she managed to open with some difficulty. I slid through behind her.

I stood now in a short corridor lined with doors. The woman pushed the first one open. Gomez sat at a desk with his back to us, looking at a computer display. On the opposite wall was an enlarged photo of me in a bathing suit, holding a drink. The photograph was pinned to the wall with a metal dart skewering my stomach, and it had been spun forty-five degrees, so that it looked as if I were beginning a long fall. Gomez turned round in his seat and counted out change to pay for his coffee.

Next we delivered coffee to Clellan, who was full of good-old-boy chatter. "Thank you, Jeannie. That's very kind. Well, don't you look fine today?" She blushed and smiled.

Then, carrying the last cup of coffee, she knocked on the third door, and I heard the voice within, although I could not make out the words. She pushed open the door, and from my position in the corridor I saw Jenkins sitting at a desk writing. I felt like a bird gazing at a snake.

I was startled by the drabness of the office. The desk and chairs were the sort you would find piled three high in a used-furniture warehouse. There was nothing on the dirty walls, and there were two dented green filing cabinets. The only sign of status seemed to be the presence of two telephones. It struck me that one of them would be for the number Jenkins had given to me.

She put the coffee slowly down on the desk. Without looking up or pausing in his writing, he said, "Thank you, Jean."

"You're welcome, sir." She stepped briskly out of the room. I considered momentarily whether I should slip through before she shut it. Better not to risk it. One involuntary cough or sniff, and I was finished. I had to wait until I could go in alone.

She pulled Jenkins's door shut and walked back to the front door, shutting that door behind her as well. I was trapped in the little corridor, surrounded by six closed doors which I did not dare open. I sat in a corner and waited.

When, after two hours, the door at the end of the corridor opened and Morrissey entered, I was almost glad to see him. He paused, holding the door open, and looked back into the outer office. I quickly picked myself up off the floor and moved towards him, thinking I might escape. One of the women was speaking to him.

"The meeting tomorrow is changed to two in the afternoon because Colonel Jenkins has a meeting with someone from Washington first thing in the morning."

Someone from Washington. I should be there for that.

Morrissey pulled the door shut before I got to it, and I retreated again to let him pass down the corridor. He knocked at Clellan's office and went in, closing that door behind him as well.

At around five o'clock Morrissey came out and left. Then Gomez came out. I watched him lock his office behind him. A little later Clellan emerged. He locked his office. Outside I could hear the women packing up for the day. As Clellan passed into the outer office there were loud goodnights, and then everything was still.

It was another two hours of waiting until Jenkins emerged, carrying an old, inexpensive briefcase. He locked his office and the corridor door as well. Hopeless. I was locked up in this little passage for the night.

I waited what seemed like a very long while, and then stretched out on the carpeted floor where, for the next twelve hours, I tried to sleep.

JENKINS WAS THE FIRST to arrive in the morning. I was on my feet and wide awake before he was through the outer door. I felt myself trembling from hunger and from having lain half awake on that floor all night. And also from fear, I realised. But I would stay with it through the meeting with the person from Washington.

Jenkins walked down the corridor and unlocked his door, leaving it open behind him. I waited where I was, absolutely still.

An hour later a bell sounded in the outer office, and Jenkins re-emerged and walked out to the entrance. This was the moment. I crept into his office. I could hear fragments of two voices approaching. I looked rapidly round the room for the safest place. The corner away from the door. No one walks into a corner. I sat down with my back against the wall, trying to find a comfortable position. I would not be able to move, perhaps for hours.

Jenkins stopped at the door to let the visitor precede him. The man was in his fifties, immaculately groomed and wearing an expensive suit. His eyes skipped round the room as he settled himself in the scuffed wooden chair next to Jenkins's desk.

"Temporary quarters?" His lips twisted into an urbane smile.

Jenkins, who had opened his mouth as if to say no, paused abruptly. "Yes, I suppose so. We're always in temporary quarters, really."

The visitor smiled. "I wanted to meet alone with you because, as you are doubtless aware, there are so many rumours floating around about your operation, and before we find ourselves facing a full attack on the budgeting for this, I want to be clear in my own mind exactly what our goals and priorities are here." He paused and ran his index finger delicately along his lower lip. "The budget for your operation, in fact, seems likely to run over twelve million dollars."

"And you naturally need to assure yourself that these expenditures are justified," Jenkins said. "I assume you've talked to Ridgefield? I've tried to keep him fully informed—"

"I *have* talked to Ridgefield, of course, but . . . Let me be frank, umm—your name is David Jenkins just now, isn't it? Perhaps it would be best if I called you that. Let me be perfectly frank, Jenkins. Ridgefield doesn't want to talk to me about this. He doesn't want to be on record as having known what is going on here. He doesn't want the responsibility. Whatever you may have told Ridgefield, you should assume that I know nothing about all this. You should present me—strictly off the record, for the time being at least—with all the facts."

Jenkins walked over to the filing cabinet and withdrew a folder of large photographic prints. "This building housed, until last April, a small corporation called MicroMagnetics, Inc." Jenkins's visitor showed a polite interest in the photograph while Jenkins recited the curriculum vitae of Bernard Wachs, Ph.D. He listed the names of the people who had worked for MicroMagnetics and what they had done there.

Jenkins began to describe the press conference. He had a floor plan of the building and grounds. There was a picture of Carillon. I found myself getting to my feet so that I could see the photographs, and I realised that I was quite unsteady. I reminded myself that I had not eaten for thirty-six hours. And on seeing those pictures and hearing those events recounted in that insinuating monotone, I felt the blood draining from my head. I was startled by the realisation that it had all taken place only five months before. I had to keep hold of myself.

Jenkins walked across the room. He pulled open a closet door, revealing a metal safe the size of a small refrigerator. I knew that I must get over there no matter what. One, two, three careful steps. He was turning the knob round and round, clockwise. He stopped at fifteen. Remember fifteen. Back round to thirty-seven. Forward to eighteen. Back to five. Fifteen, thirty-seven, eighteen, five. Easy, but my mind threatened to go blank with panic at the possibility of forgetting.

Jenkins pulled open the door to the safe, carried over another little folder, and opened it to reveal a small pile of black and white photographs. The one on top showed a lawn with what appeared to be a large hole or crater.

"And this is how the site appeared shortly after the explosion."

The visitor flipped through the photographs of the site. He stopped at a picture of three men suspended in midair. Throughout the space in which they floated, there was a network of lines forming squares and rectangles, as if someone had tried to draw in the outline of a building.

"I can't quite make out what's going on in this one," said the visitor, turning the picture at an angle and furrowing his brow.

Jenkins tried to explain. He pulled out the floor plan, along with the photograph of the building before the accident, and pointed from one to the other. "This picture is taken at a slightly different angle, but this man is standing in the room next to this door, and the man crouching above him is in the room directly above."

Jenkins's visitor was looking at the pictures with total concentration now. "What you are asserting is that the entire building is still there, only invisible." The man licked his lips nervously and blinked. "Have you had these photographs authenticated?"

"Well, from our point of view there wouldn't really be any need. The person standing in this first room is me."

"I see." He went back through the photographs.

Jenkins walked over to the safe and carefully groped inside. He returned holding his hands out oddly before him, palms upward. He was carrying something, and there was a little clatter as he deposited it on the desk in front of his visitor. It was several objects, and as he arranged them his hands moved mysteriously over the surface of the desk as if he was performing some magical incantation.

Then he held an empty hand out to his visitor and said, "You might like to examine this."

The man looked at Jenkins with an expression of discomfort and perhaps annoyance. He moved his forefinger self-consciously towards Jenkins's hand. Just before it reached Jenkins's palm, he started, jerking back as if he had been stung. He reached out again and took whatever it was and began to manipulate it, a look of astonishment spreading over his face.

"It's—it's a cigarette lighter. It's quite unbelievable. And is the whole thing like this? The whole building?"

"It was. It's been burned down."

"*Burned down?* How could that have been permitted to happen?" His thumb was jerking up and down comically, and you could hear the scratch of the flint. He moved the fingers of his left hand in a little circle over the right hand. Suddenly he emitted a half-stifled shriek, and his hands flew violently apart. "I see it still works perfectly." He sucked momentarily at the fingers of his left hand. "How much survived this fire?"

"I'm afraid that what's here on this desk is all we have. You'll find, in addition to the lighter, a portion of a glass ashtray, a screwdriver, and a bullet."

The visitor carefully deposited the lighter on the desk and picked something up and held it in his hand, which was shaking. "This bullet has

been fired," he said, turning it over in his fingers. "Have you had anyone look at this . . . I mean, from a scientific point of view?"

"We've sent pieces of the ashtray to Riverhaven and to the radiation labs. They refer to it as superglass. For security reasons we haven't for the time being told them that we have any other substances with these properties."

"And have they come back with anything? Do they know how it's done?" The man's voice had a little quaver of nervous excitement to it. So would mine have, if I had tried to speak then. I was trembling as I waited for the reply.

Jenkins frowned. "The fact is, they have many different ideas about how it must have been done. Too many. You should look at the reports. I would say the answer to your question comes down to 'no'."

"It's really quite extraordinary," said the visitor. He had the lighter in his hand again and was tapping it against the top of the desk. "Incredible." Although he made a point of maintaining his detached manner, his speech was disjointed now.

Jenkins turned to a stack of papers in plastic bindings arranged neatly on one side of his desk. "It's all here in summary. I've had copies of these reports prepared for you. And that," he said with the air of someone summing things up, "is pretty much where we stand."

"So this is all there is?" said the other man quietly. He tapped the surface of the desk where the unseen objects lay. "A pity. Because you started with an entire building. And then, several months and many millions of dollars later, you have only this. A mysterious fire and everything else is gone. How, by the way, did this fire begin? And why do you have a bullet there? Your narrative raises many more questions than it answers. In any case, based on what you tell me, this seems like a problem for physicists, not one that requires a massive intelligence operation, surely? Was there something else in the building that you people have somehow lost track of? Or does someone else know about all this? What is the problem exactly?"

Jenkins was silent for a moment and then said, "To begin with, there was a cat in the building."

"A *cat?* And was it—was it like the cigarette lighter?"

"Yes. Unfortunately, it escaped."

"You mean it survived the explosion?"

"That's right. One of my men had it in his hands, briefly. It struggled free and ran off." Jenkins gazed at the bare wall. "We've seen no sign of it since the first day."

"Well, presumably, it's dead. Even if it did survive initially."

"We have reason to believe it may still be alive." Jenkins handed over a photograph of me. Taken a little over a year ago at a wedding. I remembered it. "This man is named Nicholas Halloway. The photograph

233

is no longer really relevant. He was inside the building, and we've lost track of him as well. Although not so irretrievably as the cat."

"You mean this man is also . . . like the cigarette lighter?"

"That's right."

The man stared blankly at the photograph. "Where is he now?"

"Right here in New York."

"And that's what this is really all about? A human being has become invisible. And you're trying to capture him?"

"Yes."

"I see." They both sat in silence. The visitor gazed at my photograph, turning it to different angles, and then spoke again. "I take it that he burned down the building. And that he is armed."

"That's right."

"He's hostile, then?"

Jenkins appeared to reflect on this question. "I would say rather that he is uncooperative. In burning down the building, and even in his physical attacks on us, his motivation has been escape. Almost exclusively, I would say."

"Why? Why is he running away from you?"

"He's afraid of what will happen to him. Once we get him, he doesn't think he'll have any control over the situation."

"He's quite right, isn't he? It won't be very nice for him at all, will it?"

Jenkins was silent for several seconds. "Perhaps not. But we have to catch him."

"Yes," said the visitor. "Of course. We absolutely have to." He looked down at my photograph again. "Who is he? What was he?"

Jenkins began to recount from memory my curriculum vitae, leafing, as he spoke, through page after page of mounted and labelled photographs. He had an extraordinary amount of information. My whole life was, as the expression goes, passing before my eyes. Pictures, dates, names. All irretrievable. No way back to any of that now. Better not to consider the violent mob of emotions it stirred up. I was, from beginning to end, transfixed.

When it was all over, the other man said, "You people have done an extraordinarily thorough job here."

"I think it would be fair to say that I know more about Halloway than I've ever known about another human being," said Jenkins, wrinkling his face pensively and nodding to himself. "It won't be long now. If we don't catch him soon, he'll give up. He'll let us close in. His situation is hopeless."

"Well, you're probably right," said the visitor. He paused reflectively. "What you're doing here is extremely important, and I want you to know that I'm going to do everything I can to back you up as far as budgeting goes. However, for the time being—until you've actually apprehended

234

Halloway—I think it would be better if we both took the position that we had never discussed this matter. I think you should go on reporting to Ridgefield. But I will take along this lighter. It might be of help if any questions are ever raised about all this." He found the lighter on the desk and slid it into the side pocket of his suit jacket.

Jenkins opened his mouth, as if to voice an objection. Then he said, "Of course. I can see that that would be sensible. Be careful, though: these things can get lost very easily."

"Yes, I imagine so. Well, thank you for your time."

Jenkins walked with him out to the elevator. I walked with them too, slipping through the doors right behind them, but once I was in the hall, I raced to the stairway and charged down to the lobby. When the elevator door opened, I stepped right up beside the visitor and walked out into the street with him.

I had to do something right away. There would be no second chance. He walked east, his right hand fingering the magic cigarette lighter in his pocket. I planted my right foot directly in front of his, so that with the next step it caught, pitching him face forwards into the street. His hands flew out in front of him as he went down.

I was right there beside him, reaching into his pocket, and before he had begun to collect himself I had slipped out the lighter and stepped quickly off to the side. People were helping him to his feet. He checked his pockets.

Suddenly he was shouting, "Hold it! Hold it! I've lost something . . . That's right, a contact lens." He was down on all fours, muttering anxiously, feeling the street with the palms of his hands.

Eventually the man stood up, tight-lipped, looked despairingly at the ground, and then walked over and climbed into his car.

I stood out in the street debating what I should do. If Jenkins's visitor told Jenkins about the cigarette lighter, Jenkins would understand at once everything that had happened. I would never be able to enter those offices again. Furthermore, they were all about to have a meeting, presumably to discuss what they would do next to capture me. But above all, I knew I had to go back and try to do something about the contents of Jenkins's safe.

Fifteen, thirty-seven, eighteen, five.

I climbed back up to the seventh floor and waited at the door. It was nearly an hour before Morrissey arrived and let me in. I followed him to a room with a conference table, where I stepped quietly into a corner.

Everyone was there except Jenkins. Tyler sat erect in his chair. Gomez was helping Clellan set up a wooden easel to which a stack of large drawings was clipped. The one on top was a map of Manhattan, marked with little red rectangles. Particular apartments they were watching?

"Clellan, I hear you talked to him," said Tyler softly.

"Yeah, I talked to him," said Clellan with a loud laugh. "Only he didn't talk to me. I was standing in this lobby"—he pointed to a building on the map—"and suddenly I'm looking down at two footprints in the carpet, and I'm thinking, Nicky boy, maybe it's time to take a big jump at you, when one, two, the footprints step away, and I'm talking to thin air. The doorman thought I was a real wacko. Wanted to have me taken away."

"If anyone finds out what we're doing, they'll think we're all wackos," said Morrissey unhappily.

Jenkins entered the room. They all seated themselves round the table, with Jenkins at one end.

"I've been talking to Washington," he began. "I had a meeting here this morning, and the pressure is mounting. The trouble is that virtually no one really knows what we are doing and what is at stake, and the few people who do will not acknowledge it. As you can imagine, it would be unpleasant to have to justify this operation in the face of a political attack or some sort of investigation, if we ultimately came up empty-handed."

The others were all absolutely still, their eyes fixed on Jenkins.

"In any case, I don't envisage our facing any such problem. We may take Halloway this week, or it may be next week, but it will be soon. He is completely alone. He's under enormous pressure day and night. He only has to be careless once, make one mistake. If we stay on top of him a little while longer, this will be over. Together we're going to succeed."

Having finished his exhortation, Jenkins looked at Clellan, who began to discuss our encounter in the apartment building. He went on to describe the odd telephone call made by a Howard Dickison to my office and the subsequent interview with Dickison.

"Do you have the write-up of that interview there?" interrupted Jenkins. "I haven't had a chance to go over it."

Clellan handed over the report, then began to describe a new plan Gomez had contrived to trap me.

Jenkins was reading the report. When he got to the end, he looked up and interrupted. "Excuse me, but do we have the tape of this phone call?"

"No," Clellan answered. "Just the transcript. But I can have the tape sent over if you like." He had an enquiring look on his face.

"Yes, I think you'd better do that." Jenkins laid both hands flat on the table and closed his eyes in thought. Gomez glanced at him uneasily. The eyes opened, and Jenkins asked Clellan, "How do they send over these reports?"

Clellan blinked uncomprehendingly. The room was silent.

Jenkins spoke again. "Do they mail them, or what?"

Tyler answered. "We arrange for a commercial messenger service to pick everything up and bring it over."

Jenkins nodded. He was pressing two fingertips hard against his forehead, so that the skin turned white under them. Then he suddenly took a long, careful look round the room, stood up, and walked over to the door. I edged carefully along the wall until I was nearly next to him. He turned so that his back was to the door and he was facing the others. He spoke rapidly but clearly.

"I want you to pay very careful attention to me. We've overlooked something important, and it is possible that it will have immediate consequences. By the way, are any of you carrying guns? Just out of curiosity, could you show them to me?"

Suddenly both Tyler and Morrissey, although they seemed a bit mystified, were holding guns in their hands.

"Good. Halloway may be right—"

I hit him as hard as I could just below the breastbone, then got one hand behind him and the other on the back of his neck and pitched him forward. He fell against the edge of the table. I pulled open the door and charged out into the corridor, and as I entered the front office the two women looked up, startled to see the door swing violently open on its own. Someone was behind me. I heard a gunshot. The women were both screaming. Another gunshot. I pulled open the door out to the public corridor. Morrissey and Tyler were in the front office with me now, both holding guns in their hands. When they saw the open door, they raced out through it into the hall.

I stepped aside to let them pass and moved quietly back across the room. A moment later Jenkins appeared, with Clellan and Gomez on either side, steadying him. He was holding what looked like a shirt crumpled up against his face. Blood was dripping from it.

"What happened?" one of the secretaries shrieked.

Jenkins removed the wad of fabric, and blood streamed down his face and dribbled over his shirt and necktie.

"You'll have to go to a doctor," Clellan said.

Morrissey and Tyler reappeared in the doorway, looking out of breath and unhappy. "We followed him into one of the stairways, but after that we lost him," said Morrissey.

"Any indication that you might have hit him?"

"Can't tell."

"All right," said Jenkins. "Come inside and keep that door shut. And get those guns out of sight. Tyler, I'd like you to come with me to the hospital. Someone in the building may have heard the shots and called the police. Clellan, you stay here and deal with them. Also, get all the locks changed today. And then start looking for new office space. I want to be out of here as soon as possible. In the meantime, someone should be guarding that door at all times. I want to be sure that he doesn't get back in."

237

"Who was it? What happened?" the secretary asked again.

Jenkins turned towards the woman. "What did you see?"

"Nothing! I saw the door fly open, and there was nobody there, and then you all came running out and shooting."

Jenkins turned to the other woman.

"I didn't see anyone!" she said. "Who were you shooting at?"

There was a long silence. The men looked at each other. Then Clellan spoke, a little tentatively. "He's very fast."

There was another little silence, and Gomez spoke. "*Fast?* Fast isn't hardly the word for him. Fast is not the half of it."

Clellan turned to the second woman. "You say you didn't get a real look at him? But would you say he was medium build, light brown hair?"

"I really didn't see him. I couldn't say for sure," she said uncertainly.

"Gomez," said Jenkins, "could you see that Jean and Carmen get home all right? As soon as possible. This has been very trying for them. Tyler, could you take these keys and lock up my office?"

I was right down the corridor ahead of Tyler and through the open door into Jenkins's office. Tyler pulled shut the door, fitted in the key, and turned the lock. It did not matter to me. There was a simple knob to unlock it from the inside. I waited several minutes, and then went to the safe. Fifteen, thirty-seven, eighteen, five. The door clicked open. I pulled out the photographs of the invisible building and ran my hands over the shelves of the safe until I found the invisible objects. I slipped the ashtray, the bullet and the screwdriver into my pocket.

I went over and crumpled up several sheets of paper on Jenkins's desk and, with my new pocket lighter, set them on fire. I added the photographs to the blaze. Then I pulled open the desk drawers and the drawers of the filing cabinets and emptied their contents onto the fire. Seeing that everything was well in hand, I unlocked the door and slipped into the corridor. The door into the front office was closed, so I went up to it and waited.

I could hear their voices on the other side. Clellan was talking on the telephone to a locksmith. Morrissey was saying that he was sure he smelled something burning. After a while Clellan said that he did too. In a moment the door swung open, and the two men charged through.

As soon as they had passed, I slipped into the outer office. I unlatched the outer door and opened it. I could hear Clellan and Morrissey behind me. "It must be in the colonel's office!"

I set fires in the two wastepaper baskets in the front office and dumped whatever papers I could find into them.

"He must still be—"

"The main door!"

They were running back down the corridor towards me. Best to run now. I scurried down the stairs, out through the lobby and into the street.

238

Chapter 13

I had done Jenkins as much harm as I could contrive in the limited time available to me, and I knew that I had made his situation far more precarious. But I saw that I had done almost nothing to slow him down. In fact, by destroying his invisible objects and making him more vulnerable, I had only put more pressure on myself.

My most urgent task was to get Jonathan Crosby solidly established in the world, and to do that I had to find some way to open a bank account. Without a bank reference I could not even get a credit card, much less enter into a real-estate transaction. I needed an accountant or lawyer who regularly handled other people's affairs and who already had the right relationship with a bank.

When I first came upon Bernie Schleifer, certified public accountant, at a party in late September, he was manically extolling to a fellow guest the merits of a particularly bizarre tax dodge. Bernie's attitude and ingenuity struck me immediately as just right for my needs, and I could see right off that he was not a stickler for rules. In fact he is about as easy-going, when it comes to rules, as you can be without winding up in prison. I called him on the telephone.

"Hello, Bernie? My name is Jonathan Crosby. You may not remember, but I met you at a party a couple of months ago. I was intrigued by a tax-avoidance opportunity you were describing that involved erecting windmills on historical buildings for some sort of double investment tax credit."

"Oh sure, Jonathan, I remember now. I'm glad you called! We're not doing that particular deal any more, but I have something—"

"Actually, Bernie, I'm not so much looking for tax avoidance. What I want is someone who can handle all my personal bookkeeping and records and do my taxes."

"OK, Jonathan, let's *do* it! When can we get together?"

"Actually, Bernie, we can probably handle everything over the phone right now. I've just moved to New York this year. I've been living with my family in Switzerland and different places—"

"Tell me, Jonathan, are you a US taxpayer?"

"Yes."

"Oh, I'm sorry to hear that, Jonathan." He said it as if I had told him I had leukaemia. "Still, we may be able to work around it. Can you send me copies of your returns for the last two years? That'll give me an overall picture."

"This will be my first return."

"Great! That'll give us a lot more flexibility. And you might be able to let the state returns slide for a while, as long—"

"Actually, Bernie, my family all live in Switzerland, and they have some fairly substantial assets outside the country. I'd rather not do anything that would get the IRS interested in me, especially not just to save a few dollars. I'd rather do everything according to the rules."

"I get you, Jonathan. On the stuff out front you want to pay every penny you owe. There are situations where that's a really smart strategy. Let me just make a note of that one."

"Bernie, do you mind my asking what your fees will be?"

"It's a hundred dollars an hour, which is pretty standard."

Having visited his office and seen Bernie's billing, I knew it was not standard for Bernie. At $100 an hour I would be his best client, but under the circumstances that would be an excellent thing for both of us.

"That sounds very reasonable, Bernie. You know, I'm kind of busy, and I think I'd like to have your office handle all my financial stuff for me. I'm going to have all my brokerage statements sent to your office, if that's all right?"

At a hundred dollars an hour it would presumably be all right. I gave him Willy Winslow's name and number and told him to expect a call. Then I called Willy and told him to call Bernie and to change the mailing address on my account.

I waited a few days and then called Bernie again.

"Jonathan, baby! I'm glad you called! I've been going over your account, and you know, you've been having a pretty good year."

"I've been quite lucky. Bernie, the reason I called is that it suddenly struck me that I don't have a bank account here in New York yet. You don't by any chance know a good bank I could use, do you?"

"We keep a lot of our client accounts at Mechanics Trust."

"Well, that would be great if you could arrange it all for me. I could have Willy send over a cheque for ten thousand dollars to open the account, if you think that would be enough?"

"More than enough, Jonathan. I'll set up everything, and then you can just stop by the bank and sign the signature cards."

"Gee, if there's anything to sign, why don't you just send it to me here at my uncle's apartment? You know, now that I think of it, I'd rather have you get all the bank statements and everything. And put your name on the account so your office could pay bills for me and so on. Would that be all right?"

"Jonathan, leave it to me. We'll take care of everything."

By the end of the week I had my bank account. In a few weeks I would receive my first credit card. Jonathan Crosby was nearly a person.

THEN, ONE EVENING in early October, as I was walking up Central Park West, I saw a girl I had known once. Ellen something. Almost the only thing I remembered about her was that she had been very attractive, and now I was abruptly seized with an awful longing for her. There was no point, because I could not talk to her or touch her, but I followed her anyway.

In the middle of a block she turned in to a building, and a doorman sent her to the ninth floor along with another couple whom she greeted effusively. I could see that it would be a party. While they took the elevator, I trudged up the stairs. It took me much longer, so that by the time I pushed through the door of the apartment, she was already long inside. Most of the guests were younger than I, and you could tell at once that they all knew each other well. The noise was overwhelming. People in these situations do not notice how excited they have become, or that they are shouting rather than speaking to each other. It was probably a good party, but really it had nothing to do with me, and I made my way to the front door.

But then I happened to see Alice. It is always difficult to say why, in these situations, you are suddenly struck by someone, but I started at once across the room towards her. She was tall, in her late twenties, with strawberry blonde hair, and she wore a silk dress that clung to her in a way that was almost painful for me. Standing in a semicircle round her were several men, and whenever she spoke to one of them, she would bestow on him a dazzling smile. Because it was the only way to get close to her, I walked round the wall of other admirers and stood behind her.

"It seems awfully rude of you, Donald," she said good-naturedly, "to say these things against my grandmother."

"I'm not saying anything whatever against your grandmother." The man who spoke was dressed in khaki trousers and a blazer. Despite his youth, he had a pedantic, professional manner. "I'm only saying that you can't go about asserting the existence of ghosts."

"But why not?" she asked ingenuously.

"Because there is no satisfactory procedure for verifying or refuting such an assertion."

"Well, you could talk to my grandmother. She's perfectly clear about what she saw." The smile seemed to have some mischief in it, but the eyes were wide open and bright blue with innocence. "And anyway, why shouldn't there be ghosts and all sorts of things? Just because you've never seen or touched one . . ."

Donald, knitting his brow with irritation, continued in the logical track of his argument. "Because I have never needed the notion of a ghost to explain any sense data I have experienced."

"What would you do if a ghost appeared to you now?" Alice continued. "I mean, with incontrovertible sense data and all that? Suppose it stepped up and gave you a good pinch so there wouldn't be any doubt?"

"Well," Donald replied, "I would be quite amazed. I would have to extend and reorder the categories and concepts with which I think—"

"My point of view is much more useful and flexible. If a ghost pinched me, I wouldn't have to be amazed at all."

I have never before or since pinched a woman's bottom, and I am not precisely sure what moved me to it on this occasion, but I reached out and took a fold of silk and flesh between my thumb and forefinger and held it for a long, delicious moment.

Alice stopped speaking, and her entire body stiffened. I released my fingers. Then, with an effort, she resumed.

"I wouldn't be amazed . . ." She was looking at Donald resentfully, as if he were guilty of employing an unfair tactic. She looked down at his hands, which, as he was standing directly opposite her, could not possibly be culpable. She turned uncertainly to the men on either side of her.

This is wrong from every point of view, I thought. I should not be doing this. But with my two hands I gripped her upper arms, pressing them against her sides. She turned about suddenly, and I withdrew my hands. No one there. Nothing. She turned back to face the others with a look of vaguely defiant puzzlement. I gently took hold of her arms again. She looked down at her right arm where my fingers had made little indentations in her flesh, and she turned quite pale. I leaned over and kissed her exquisite neck. She shivered.

"Are you all right, Alice?" one of the men was saying. "Do you want to sit down for a moment?"

"No. No. I have to go."

"Do you want me to get you into a cab? Or take you home?"

"No. I'm—I'm meeting someone now. I have to go."

She walked straight out of the apartment, as if in a trance. I stayed right with her, my hand on her arm. When the door closed behind us in the corridor, I turned her round so that she faced me, and kissed her. She was utterly limp in my arms. Then, tentatively, she raised her arms and felt with her hands to see whether there was indeed some more or less human form there. Finding one, she folded her arms round me uncertainly.

I kissed her forehead.

"I can't believe this is happening to me," she said.

I kissed her again, and suddenly she clutched me tight. I held her to me. I too could not believe this was happening to me.

Down the corridor I heard an elevator door slide open.

"We have to go," I said.

"Oh, my God!" she said, and I realised that this was the first time she had heard me speak. I put my arm round her and walked her towards the elevator. She kept looking at me—or through me.

"Don't speak to me in front of other people. You have to act as if I weren't there."

She nodded dumbly, and we got into the empty elevator together. Alice stared straight ahead in a daze. What did she imagine about the inexplicable presence standing at her side?

We walked through the lobby together and out into the street, both of us half delirious. I still had my arm round her, and I kept looking at her. She was extraordinarily beautiful. I turned and kissed her, there in the street. She must have looked odd with her head tilted back and sideways and her mouth strangely flattened, because there was suddenly a doorman beside us saying, "Are you all right, miss?" I took her by the arm and led her down the street.

"Do you live alone?" I asked.

She nodded and then said, "I can't believe this."

I kissed her again. "You should hail a cab," I said softly.

When the taxi stopped, out of habit I opened the door for her. Fortunately, the driver did not notice, and it seemed to add to the dreamlike quality of the whole episode for Alice.

When we pulled up in front of her high-rise apartment building, I pulled her out of the cab, so that she appeared to lurch impossibly across the sidewalk and through the lobby into the elevator. I was beyond caring what kind of impression we made. I did not for that matter care if this was the last night of my life. All I wanted was this woman, right away. Somehow we made it into her apartment.

She began to run her hands over my body to verify that it was all really true. She had her hands round my head and suddenly found my mouth and began kissing me frantically. What could she have thought? Mastered by the brute blood of the air. Or whatever. We went on and on until we lost track of everything.

IN THE MORNING I woke to the sound of Alice straightening up the apartment. It was the most miraculous awakening I had known since the morning I had discovered my invisibility. There before me I saw a beautiful woman, with whom I had made love just a few hours ago. As she moved round the room she kept looking over at me—or rather at the bedcovers where they moulded my body—with an anxious frown.

"Good morning," I said.

She started. "Good morning. I thought you might be awake. How did you sleep? I mean, *do* you sleep?"

"I slept very well, thank you. How did you sleep?"

"Very well. Thank you."

There was a long, uncomfortable pause, "My name is Alice Barlow," she ventured finally. "Maybe you already know that."

Without thinking, I started to tell her my name. "I'm Nick—just Nick, really. I only use the first name now." For some reason my name seemed to distress her.

"What's going to happen to me?" She seemed extraordinarily nervous. "I mean, it sounds ridiculous, but have I forfeited my soul or something?"

"Oh, no, no, no," I hastened to reassure her. "Certainly not."

A nervous smile flickered over her face. "Then you're not—the devil, or anything like that?"

"Good heavens, no. Not at all. I'm just like everybody else."

This concession evidently struck her as preposterous, because she laughed. "Are you? Just like everybody else?"

"Well, of course there are differences . . ."

"Are there really? You know I *thought* I noticed something." Still laughing, she sat down on the edge of the bed and put her hand on my knee.

"You know, I don't think you should be taking this so lightly," I said. "For all you know, I still might inflict some terrible curse or suck out all your blood."

"Or turn back into a frog," she suggested. She pulled the sheet up to my shoulders and smoothed it so that my body took form. Her expression grew suddenly serious again. "Who *are* you? . . . *What* are you? If you don't mind my putting it like that."

The inevitable question somehow caught me unprepared. I didn't dare tell her anything. The first rule of survival for me was never to tell anyone anything.

"I *am* actually just like anyone else. That is to say, I exist in a different material modality."

"You mean you were here before? I mean, inhabiting a material human body, or however it works?"

"Yes. I used to have the same sort of body as everyone else."

"And you've come back."

"It's more that I'm still here." By the skin of my teeth.

"Is there something you have to do here? I mean, before you can be released from the world?"

"Not that I know of. Just the ordinary things, I suppose, like everyone else." This discussion made me uncomfortable. "If I'm careful, I may manage, with luck, to grow old and die."

She sighed. "No one will ever believe this."

I was suddenly filled with dread. "Alice, you must absolutely never speak of me to anyone. It's very important."

"If you don't want me to say anything, I won't. But why not?"

"I . . . It's not something I can talk about."

She stood up and looked down where I lay, her eyebrows raised sceptically. "Will I see you again? I don't mean see you. I mean, will I hear from you, or do you just fade into the sunset—or wherever it is you fade to?"

I was floundering in panic. "I don't know. It's not entirely within my control . . . Of course, I hope so. I'll have to see." It was the sort of risk I must absolutely not take. I had to keep moving.

She laughed, and her laughter seemed to contain a note of mockery. "You know, you're right. You *are* like everybody else."

"You don't understand," I objected. "It's not at all that—"

"You needn't worry. You're not the sort of person a girl is going to pin all her hopes on. There's a kind of elusive quality to you, if you want to know. I was just curious."

She stood before a mirror, drawing a brush through her hair with long, fierce strokes. After an uncomfortable silence she glanced in my direction. "Maybe you're some kind of alien. You probably ought to go out and get to know some of the other folks in the brave new world."

"I find that lately I'm having a lot of trouble getting to know people."

"You seemed to be managing last night." The corners of her mouth turned up to form the beginnings of an ironic smile. The thing was—if only I could think clearly about it—that no matter what the risk, I was, beyond any question, going to come back here.

"I thought that I might come back here this evening, if you're free." Having said that, I found that I felt suddenly quite elated.

"I'll be home from work a little after six." She turned her full dazzling smile on me. She walked over and, after inadvertently flattening my nose in the search for my face, kissed me once on the lips. Then, as she drew back and turned to leave, she reached out and touched my chest.

"Amazing," she said with a little laugh.

As she went through the door I called after her, "Remember not to say anything about me."

I waited several minutes to be sure that she was gone before going into the kitchen. I could not risk letting her see my digestive tract in operation. I greedily devoured several slices of bread. I knew that I was taking an unconscionable risk remaining here at all, much less making myself visible, but I was finding it difficult in my present mood to worry about anything.

I went through the apartment, taking an almost physical pleasure in touching Alice's possessions. Clothes. Skis. Tennis racket. The walls of the bedroom were covered with unframed sketches and paintings, many of them signed with the initials A.B. I was startled by the almost photographic quality of her draughtsmanship.

Once my stomach was clear again, I went out and walked to midtown, in such an exultant mood that I wanted to stop the other people in the street and tell them what a pleasure it was to be among them on that beautiful autumn day. Mainly just to talk to someone I called up Willy and discussed my portfolio. Even he could not undermine my mood. On the contrary, he reminded me that I was growing more substantial by the day, with a net worth now of over eighty thousand dollars. I was barely able to restrain myself from making some trades. Never buy anything when you are in a good mood.

I was at the door to Alice's apartment before six. I could hear her already inside, unpacking groceries in the kitchen. When I knocked, she came and looked through the peephole. Seeing no one there, she opened the door and kissed me.

"You don't walk through walls?" Her voice echoed through the hall. I put a finger on her mouth.

"You have to be more discreet," I whispered. I pushed her back into the apartment and shut the door behind us. "Alice, no one must know anything about me."

"I'm sorry, I forgot." She ran her hands up through my hair and then down my body, as if to make sure that I was entirely there.

"I went and bought all sorts of food for dinner, but then I realised I don't even know if you eat."

I hesitated. "Yes, I eat. Not very much."

"Then why don't you open the wine while I get dinner ready."

As she prepared the meal she glanced over at the corkscrew wrenching itself violently into the cork.

"It's just incredible," she said excitedly.

I poured some wine into the glasses. Then, full of apprehension, I let her watch the first sip of white wine going down.

"Amazing!" she said. "It's absolutely magical." She seemed genuinely delighted by the sight.

And when later I ate my first bite of the pasta, she was unaccountably even more entranced. "Incredible! You can see everything! You know, you would be marvellous in an anatomy class."

"That is unfortunately true," I replied glumly.

"Would you mind eating a little more? Really, it's beautiful! You can see it disappearing before your eyes."

Alice watched with fascination as I absorbed one bit of the material world after another. Then, abruptly, she furrowed her brow. "Are you in touch with other ghosts?"

"I am definitely not in touch with other ghosts."

"Well, is ghost the right word for what you are? I mean, what are you exactly?"

I felt again the temptation to confide in her, to tell her everything. Too dangerous. I saw now that it had been wrong to come back at all. Tomorrow I would really have to leave for good. "Does it matter what I am? I could be anything. The Spirit of Christmas Past, a visitor from Venus. Or I might be like anyone else—a bookkeeper who happened to fall asleep under a defective sunlamp or who stumbled into the wrong vat on a tour of a chemical plant."

"Well, that wouldn't be very romantic at all. I think I definitely prefer you as a ghost. You said you had lived in the material world before in a normal human body. Isn't that—"

"Yes, probably it's best to think of me as a ghost."

Chapter 14

I had absolutely resolved to leave for good in the morning, but somehow I found myself staying with Alice again that night, and the next night as well, until eventually, without there ever having been any discussion of the matter, we both took for granted that I was living there.

Alice worked in the East Thirties as a commercial artist, and when the weather was good we would go out together in the morning, walking from her building on York Avenue down the East Side to her studio. She would bump into me as we walked, to confirm my presence, and she would frequently break into a smile.

"It's so amazing. I mean walking down the street with you like this without anyone knowing. No one would ever believe it."

"Just be sure you don't give anyone the chance."

I would usually spend those days in law offices or investment banks or corporate headquarters, pursuing my securities research, if it is fair to call it that. When it rained, I would stay at home, reading and listening to music—without ever having to worry about being heard by the neighbours.

This was the first time since I had been driven from my own apartment that I had been free from constant hunger. Together, Alice and I prepared elaborate dinners each night. I also had her buy the most powerful sunlamp she could find so that I could burn myself clear again whenever I needed to.

Those evenings we spent together in her apartment were the most pleasant I had known in my new life—or even in my old life—and it seemed to me that I had everything I could ever have wished for. It is impossible for me to explain how wonderful it was just to be able to talk to another human being again.

AT FIRST WE STAYED in every evening. But the telephone would often ring, and I would hear Alice saying, "No, I'm really sorry, but I can't . . . No, I'm seeing someone—sort of . . . It is serious . . . I'd love to have you meet him, but we just can't on the seventeenth . . . Why don't we give you a call? . . . Sure. Bye."

I decided that I had to do whatever I could to make our curious life together as normal as possible, and so at the end of October I made Alice accept an invitation to a Halloween costume ball. She chose to dress herself as a witch, with a black robe and cape, which only set off the wholesome radiance of her features, and a black conical hat, from under which masses of strawberry blonde hair spilled out incongruously. Bewitching.

Whereas I, showing a lack of judgment that still takes my breath away whenever I think of it, had Alice wrap yards of white gauze bandages round my head, leaving only two little slits for the eyes. She bought me a pair of mirror sunglasses, and I bent the metal frame back so that no one could see in from the sides. In some thrift shop Alice found an old suit that fitted passably, and she made a trip to Brooks Brothers for gloves, socks, shoes and a shirt and tie. When I had got everything on, I looked just like Claude Rains doing H. G. Wells. I might as well have worn a sign saying "The Invisible Man".

As Alice and I walked across the East Side, I was exhilarated by the experience of being seen once again by other people, and once again occupying a full human place in the world. The ball was a benefit for the New York Institute of the Arts, and many of the several hundred guests had created stunning costumes for themselves. As she led me across the room, introducing me to her friends, I could feel her quivering with delight at my side—delight, presumably, at the magnitude and audacity of our secret.

"This is my fiancé, Nick Cheshire."

"Nice to meet you, Nick. Congratulations. Wonderful girl, Alice. I was beginning to wonder why we never see her any more."

"Nick's living in San Francisco, so we hardly ever—"

"Tell me, Alice," said a girl dressed as some sort of fairy queen, "is he good-looking?" She reached up for my glasses.

"Good-looking isn't the word for it," said Alice as we spun out of the fairy queen's reach and off across the dance floor through crowds of pirates, angels, vampires and gangsters.

Alice slipped her hands inside my jacket and round my waist.

"I apologise for introducing you as my fiancé. It just seemed like the easiest way to put everyone off."

"I'm delighted at the honour. I'm sorry that out of costume I'm so hopelessly ineligible."

"You do seem to be a rather poor prospect in some ways. Out of curiosity, are you permitted to get married?"

"Permitted? As far as I know, I'm permitted to do whatever I please. But I'm not sure how it would be possible. There are usually other people around on those occasions, and they might find my appearance a bit wanting."

"Can ghosts father children?"

Into my mind came the image of a wan, infantile form, translucent, with all the colour bleached out, like a leaf left floating for a winter in a swimming pool.

248

"I have no idea. I don't see how—"

Alice laughed. "You know, you have a kind of will-o'-the-wispy quality. It's just as well there's no question of taking you seriously." A waltz started up, and suddenly taking the lead, she set us whirling across the floor at breakneck speed.

THE NIGHTS WERE painfully cold now, but after our splendid Halloween outing I was all the more determined that Alice and I should not stay holed up like fugitives in her apartment. We began attending movies, picking out seats off to one side, and eventually we even began to go to museums and to the theatre. I would try to choose unpopular times and events, but with Alice there, I found that I could go almost anywhere. It was odd when I considered that not many weeks before, my life had consisted mainly of cowering fearfully in corners. Although I felt more secure than ever, I still bundled up my clothes each night and kept them beside the bed, but I had long ago hidden my gun away in the boiler room of Alice's building.

Really, the main danger now seemed to be that Alice would inadvertently give me away. At my insistence, when we were in public places she would speak to me under her breath, almost without moving her lips, like a stage ventriloquist. She became quite good at it, but from time to time, as we were walking down the street surrounded by other people, she would suddenly turn and speak openly to me, as if we were completely alone.

"What difference does it make?" she asked. "People will think I'm talking to myself. New York is full of people talking to themselves. And why is it so important, anyway?"

"I can't explain it to you now."

"Well, if it really were so important, you *would* explain it to me." She had stopped on the sidewalk and was facing me. She really did look like a madwoman standing there muttering to herself. "Nick, what do you do all day?"

"What I do wouldn't interest you." These discussions were always torture, and this particular one was made worse by the fact that it was ten at night in the middle of November. "Alice, it's very cold just now, and if I don't keep moving, I'll freeze to death."

We walked on in silence for several blocks.

"Those are the only clothes you have, aren't they?" she asked.

"For the time being, yes."

"You're cold all the time, aren't you? I feel you shivering next to me. How are you going to get through the winter?"

"I was hoping you wouldn't throw me out till spring."

"I really ought to, you know."

She wrapped her arms round me as we walked, perhaps out of

249

affection, or perhaps to keep me warm. It looked quite odd, and when I saw a police car turn down the block, I had to tell her that she could not hold on to me like that.

IT OCCURRED TO ME one day, as I sat riffling through a desk in an empty law office, that I had almost entirely stopped thinking about my past life. There was a telephone in front of me on the desk. Large corporations are the best places for me to telephone from, because the call can be traced back only as far as the central exchange, and they can't tell anything more than that I am on one of half a dozen floors of some vast office building. Without anything particular in mind, and knowing that it was a mistake, I called my old office.

Cathy greeted me enthusiastically and asked the usual questions, hoping for some exciting piece of gossip, but it seemed to me that she was no longer really interested in talking to me.

"There haven't really been any calls for you for a long time. Just what's-his-name. Dave Jenkins. He said if you called in—can you hold on just a second? Someone's buzzing me."

I was left on hold. I should hang up.

"Isn't that an incredible coincidence? That was Dave Jenkins! He said to tell you it was extremely important and you had the number."

"Thanks, Cathy. I have to run now."

I should not call him. I had already needlessly let him know that I was still alive and still in New York. And yet I felt impelled to find out what he had to say to me.

I dialled the number, and it was answered on the first ring by the silky, earnest voice. "Hello, Nick. How are you?"

"Swell. I've missed you. You called?"

"Nick, that was an extremely foolish and unfortunate thing you did when you destroyed government property in my office."

"Gosh. I'm sorry if I showed poor judgment."

"Nick, by destroying that evidence you've placed all of us, and indeed an entire organisation, in grave political danger. We need you now to assure our own survival. If not alive, then dead."

"You mean you guys might get in trouble? Gosh, I never thought of that."

"Nick, you're going to have to surrender immediately. If you don't, we have no choice but to kill you."

"Gee, I'm glad I called. I have to run now. You know how it is when we let these telephone conversations drag on."

When I walked out of the building, Morrissey and Gomez were already climbing out of a grey car parked at the kerb. They looked grimmer, more desperate. After all, I had hurt them badly. In fact, I seemed to be winning. They were under attack from the people they

250

worked for, and at the same time their chances of catching me were decreasing all the time. How could they ever find me now? As long as Alice didn't give me away.

THE WINTER WAS A SUCCESS for Jonathan Crosby. In the middle of April I would have to give the government a large part of the money I had amassed, but I would still be left with almost eight hundred thousand dollars—ten times what I had in October and far more than I needed to establish a safe existence for Jonathan Crosby. I should never have let that amount accumulate in one place. It was living with Alice that had made me so confident and careless. I set my accountant, Bernie, to work on the next step.

"Bernie, I've decided I'd like to own my own home."

"That's smart. There are a lot of tax advantages to ownership."

"Bernie, do you have someone in your office who could go around with the brokers and see what's available? I'm kind of busy just now. Let me tell you exactly what I'm looking for . . ."

I had Bernie and his broker describe all sorts of properties to me over the telephone, and although I was never able to get inside any of them, I went and looked at several buildings from the outside and peered in through the windows. In the second week of April we signed a contract on a brownstone on East Ninety-second Street, and at the end of June we closed. Bernie produced a lawyer, and the two of them handled the entire transaction.

The top three floors of my building were broken up into apartments occupied by rent-controlled tenants, leaving me with a large apartment consisting of all of the first two floors, a small basement, and an entirely useless garden. I could come and go as I pleased and have whatever I wanted delivered without anyone knowing anything. Outside there were broad stone steps leading from the pavement up to the ground floor, which served as the entrance for my apartment as well as for those on the upper floors. However, underneath the steps and out of sight of the street was another door, which I made the main entrance to my apartment.

I had Bernie hire a contractor to redesign the apartment for my special needs, and each evening I would let myself in and inspect the work so that I could phone in my instructions the next morning. I had them cut through the wall behind the mailboxes so that I could remove my mail from inside my living room. I had special blinds installed and heavy curtains, and I put in a complete alarm system and bars on all the windows. Of course I knew that if Jenkins ever found this place, nothing would keep him out, but I could eliminate the risk of some random burglar making an extraordinary discovery. I had them redo the largest bedroom as a workroom fitted out with woodworking and metalworking tools and a full set of locksmith's equipment.

I had already spent many days in a locksmith's shop, watching the work and reading books and equipment catalogues. As soon as the work was finished in my apartment I inserted new cylinders in the locks, with tumblers that would open with the invisible keys to my old apartment and office. This was such a convenience that I mailed two cylinders to Alice and installed them in her locks as well.

For some reason this made her uneasy. She wondered why I had keys at all and where I had got the cylinders for them suddenly. Perhaps it all seemed too practical for a ghost. But then lately Alice often seemed uneasy.

"What are you doing these days, Nick? You seem preoccupied."

"Alice, I find it difficult almost to the point of impossibility to think about anything else but you."

"Oh, yes? Well, I'd like to ask you something. If you should have to leave for some reason, would you do me a favour and let me know first?"

Why was she asking this? "Solemn promise," I said. "But you know I wouldn't leave . . . unless it was absolutely necessary."

Very likely it already was absolutely necessary. Every day I stayed increased the risk. Sooner or later something would happen to give me away. Still, I could put off leaving a little longer. Until I had my new life completely set up. I would, I reflected cheerlessly, have the rest of my life to live alone.

I spent most of the summer furnishing the apartment. I opened accounts at department stores and had everything delivered: furniture, kitchen appliances, cooking utensils, books, records. At last I had a telephone under the name of Jonathan Crosby, and I could now have all my mail sent to me at the apartment. I even stocked the kitchen with all the staple foods. I could at any moment have begun to live there on my own. But each night I would go back to Alice's apartment.

"ALICE, WOULD YOU do me a favour? There's a shop in midtown that has a clown suit. I want you to buy it for me. For some reason they won't take telephone orders. I've picked out a mask to go with it and some puffy white gloves."

"Why? Do you have a date?"

"I don't have a date. Just an errand to run. I'd like you to rent me an estate car for twenty-four hours as well."

"You're awfully mysterious lately."

"That's just a ghost's job."

"Is it? I've been wondering what a ghost's job is."

On a Thursday afternoon in early August I drove the rented estate car down to Basking Ridge, where I had hidden my store of invisible objects. People were extravagantly friendly the entire way. Whenever I passed a car with children in it, I would wave inanely and blow kisses, and everyone would wave back. I had called Richard and Emily's house several times during the last few days, most recently ten minutes before from a gas station, to make sure no one was there. I was out of the car, into the barn and back again with all my invisible possessions in under fifteen minutes. Then I was in the car again, heading down the drive.

When I got to New York, it was already dusk. I parked the car several blocks from my house. I slid over to the passenger side, squeezed myself onto the floor and pulled off the clown suit, stuffing it under the seat for Alice to retrieve later. Invisible again, I set about unloading my invisible possessions through the back and carrying them, one load at a time, back to my brownstone.

I HAD ALREADY begun practising with my workshop equipment, using visible materials. I was an indifferent craftsman with wood and had never so much as drilled a hole in a piece of metal in my life. Furthermore, because I could not see where my hands were, I was constantly slicing and scraping my fingers on saw blades and files and chisels. When I began working with invisible materials, these problems became even worse.

To start with, I fabricated a set of simple lock-picking tools and went about experimenting with them until I was quite proficient at opening locked doors and filing cabinets.

I had an invisible telephone, and with part of one of the receivers and some of the electrical wire I had salvaged I set up a supplementary alarm system. It was far less elaborate than the commercial one, but then you could not see it, so no one would ever be able to connect it. No matter how carefully Jenkins entered the apartment, there were certain things I knew he would have to touch. Such as the pages of this manuscript, neatly stacked on a table in my study. He would see the first words, "If only you could see me now . . ." and understand at once that it contained everything he wanted to know. Once he touched it, he would trigger my alarm system, and I would know he had been there. I wired my alarm into an old doorbell in the frame of my entrance door. Each time I arrived at the door, I pressed the bell, and there would be a single, just audible, click, which told me that nothing had been disturbed. One day I might push the button and not hear the click, and I would know that Jenkins had been there. I would turn away from the door and never return again.

I still brooded about Jenkins. Although it was true that I could not go near him, I reasoned that it might be possible to outflank him once again by going after his superiors. Towards the end of August I decided to attempt a trip to Washington.

I had my invisible lock-picking tools and, even more important, I had Alice with me, which meant that I had a hotel room to retreat to whenever I needed to eat or sleep. Alice had a number of acerbic things to say about visiting Washington in August and about my failure to explain the purpose of the trip, but once we were there, she spent her days cheerfully in the National Gallery.

I spent my days finding out everything there was to know about David Jenkins. The locks I encountered everywhere presented no problem. I had been afraid at first that I might be walking into a trap, but it quickly became clear that Jenkins had failed to anticipate me. I found everything I was looking for, although it took me not several days, as I had expected, but almost two weeks, and I had to spend many nights locked in offices or archives.

I found out almost immediately that Jenkins had moved his operations to the fifth floor of a loft building on West Thirty-eighth Street and that he had lost my trail completely. I wondered how long he could go empty-handed before his funding would begin to dry up.

More difficult was the task of tracing Jenkins's career through a succession of name changes and assignments from one agency to another, so that no one file contained anything approaching a complete account. In the end, I think I may have been the only person who knew everything about him—almost as much as he knew about me.

But just what use it all might be to me was not clear. I might tell Anne Epstein at the *Times*, who could tell the public. But the fact was that Jenkins had not really done anything or even said anything, on the record, that he could not explain away with a minimum of awkwardness. There seemed to be nothing more I could do.

AS I SAW THE SUMMER drawing to a close I turned to the most important project of all, the fabrication of new clothes. All I had was an assortment of articles of invisible clothing, most of them too small for me, and a collection of window curtains and upholstery pulled off the Micro-Magnetics office furniture. I had assumed that sewing would be much easier than the metalworking I had been doing. It was in fact much more difficult.

I experimented for several days with visible needles and thread, at the same time reading various incomprehensible books on needlework and tailoring, but I could see that, at the rate I was learning to sew, I would never outfit myself in time. I finally turned to Alice for help.

"Alice, do you know how to sew?"

"Of course. But why? Are your clothes beginning to wear out?"

"They seem to be holding up surprisingly well, actually."

"And what about you? Are *you* wearing out?" she asked. "Or are you going to stay the same for hundreds of years?"

"Based on the aches and pains and the wobbliness in certain joints, I would say I was getting older in the usual way."

"I'll tell you why I ask. I'm wearing out, myself, and if you're not, I'm not sure I can count on holding your interest through the winter years."

I always hated conversations like this. "So far I see no sign whatever of any waning of my interest in you. And anyway, I hope, with luck, to die of old age at around the usual time. Anything else would be miraculous.

"Well, you're here now. Wouldn't you call that miraculous?"

"I suppose it is in a way, but I've grown so used to it. It's really no more miraculous than you being here. Actually," I added, kissing her forehead, "your being here is altogether miraculous."

"Speaking of things you've grown used to." She smiled, but her eyes did not take part in the smile, and I wondered if tears were forming in them. Alice had been increasingly moody lately.

"You know, *you've* grown used to *me*, haven't you?" I said. "And the thrill is gone even from the secret, isn't it?"

"Well, what's the point of a secret you can't tell anybody?"

"Do you sew?"

"I told you I did. What would you like me to sew?"

"I just want you to show me how."

"You have new clothes, don't you? After wearing the same things every day for almost a year, you suddenly have all sorts of new things. But of course you can't discuss that. Or where you keep your clothes, or what you're doing, or why you're away so much now. Why don't you just show me what you want me to sew?"

After several unsuccessful experiments Alice worked out a technique whereby she basted pieces of visible tissue paper onto the pieces of invisible fabric, using thread unravelled from one of the invisible drapes. Then, once she had sewn everything together, she removed the paper. Out of the various fragments of cloth I had salvaged, she stitched together a patchwork overcoat, lining it with pieces of material cut from a track suit, and with other bits of fabric she lengthened the trouser legs and sleeves of the invisible clothing that was too small for me. The garments she produced in this way felt quite odd, and no one piece of clothing, not even the coat, was in itself very warm, but by wearing several layers at once, I was going to be able to survive the winter in reasonable comfort.

ONE EVENING, when I had fallen asleep on the bed, I woke to find Alice smoothing the sheet over my face.

"I was just curious to see what you looked like," she said.

"I don't look like anything," I said with annoyance, pulling the sheet abruptly away. But I at once felt remorseful and drew the sheet over my face again. "All right, then. What do you think? A good face, or just as well that you can't see it?"

"A difficult decision," she said appraisingly. "But the sheet doesn't suit you at all. Too much like a death mask."

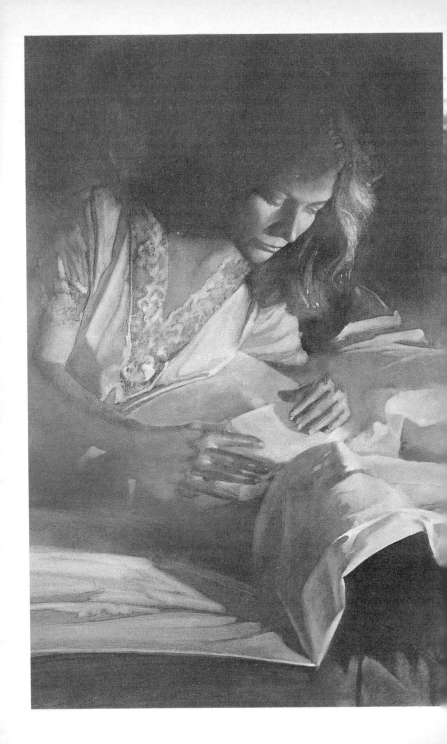

"Just the right effect for a ghost, I should have thought."

She pulled the sheet away and ran her hand over my face and down onto my chest. "Yes, that's definitely better."

"Alice, you haven't ever told anyone, have you? About living with a ghost?"

"Who do you imagine I would tell? I sit alone all day in my studio, and I spend the rest of the time with you. You're the only person I ever see. Or you would be, if I could see you."

"Well, who is James then?" The question escaped me before I was quite aware that I was asking it—it is never a good idea to ask that sort of question. "The one who keeps calling up and leaving messages on the answering machine."

There was a little pause.

"That would probably be Father James," she said, "calling about the exorcism. Did he leave an estimate?"

I did not reply, and there was another pause.

"Or then again it might just be James Larson," she resumed, "calling about the book jackets I'm doing for him . . . What's the matter? Don't you like exorcism jokes?"

"Not particularly."

"Sorry."

"The important thing is that you never tell anyone about me."

"Is that the important thing? It's good you tell me, so I don't lose sight of what's important and what isn't."

Alice seemed unhappy out of all proportion to whatever it was we had been talking about. But her moodiness was hardly surprising. It must be a rather odd and unsatisfactory life that she was leading with me, cut off from everyone she had known before.

"You know, Alice, you probably ought to get out and meet some nice, visible young men. You're going to waste your youth hanging out with wraiths."

Her eyes narrowed. "You think so? Maybe you should concentrate on your own affairs. Whatever they may be."

For everyone's sake, this was really the proper and decent moment to say goodbye to Alice. I had created another existence, another place in the world, completely private and impenetrable. I would be safe, and Alice would lead a real life.

But the trouble with this carefully reasoned conclusion was that it overlooked the only really important fact in the whole debate, which was that I loved Alice and I was going to go on living with her. If only I could have seen it then, I might have mentioned it to Alice. But I find that sometimes, in my concern with the solving of immediate problems, I miss altogether the heart of the matter, and I went on telling myself that I would only be staying with Alice a few more days.

257

Chapter 15

They came early one morning, just at dawn. A moment afterwards I realised that in my sleep I had heard the hissing sound made by whatever gas they were pumping in under the door and had been aware of Alice's climbing out of bed and walking towards the entrance to see what was happening. But the first thing I heard consciously was the awful gasping as Alice breathed in the fumes.

I remember stumbling out towards her and seeing her turn back from the door, her face convulsed. She took a step towards me and collapsed onto the floor. Locks were turning in the door.

I was wide awake now. From the instant I saw Alice, I held my breath. The front door had swung open and men in gas masks were pushing into the apartment. One of them held a short hose with a flat nozzle, connected to a large canister mounted on wheels. He was aiming it into the apartment, and the hiss of escaping gas was quite loud now. Somehow, I got a whiff: it was as if a bus had slammed into me. Two of the men were picking up Alice.

I was running across the living room and sliding open the glass door to the balcony. I remember leaning over the balcony railing, gasping for air and finding, miraculously, that I had in my hand the little bundle I had always kept by my bedside in readiness for this moment.

I leaned out and threw it onto the balcony below. The balconies were fenced round on all three sides with opaque glass panels mounted in a framework of steel rails. I climbed over and, holding onto one of the rails, lowered myself, so that I was dangling off the end. The view down was horrible: an endlessly repeating pattern of balconies, and then the pavement.

I kicked my feet about, trying to find the railing of the balcony below. Nothing. If only I could see my foot. I could see the railing right there, right beside the vertiginous view down to the pavement. Finally the toes of my right foot came to rest on the railing. I slid another fraction of an inch, until my left foot found the railing. I got the balls of my feet onto it and let them take some of my weight, then all of it. I was poised on the railing, steadied only by my tenuous hold on the balcony above. I took my hand off the railing and slid it under the bottom of the balcony above me. Trying to dig my fingertips into the concrete, I pulled myself forward until I had to let go of the post with my left hand too. I felt myself tilting forward, and came down on the balcony floor on all fours.

I heard footsteps above. "Anything out here?"

Looking up, I saw two gas-masked heads appear over the edge of the balcony and peer down. "The door was open when we came in. Better check the apartments above and below."

I was pulling on my clothes frantically. The moment the heads withdrew, I began lowering myself to the next balcony.

It was easier this time. For one thing I knew it was possible. For another I now had rubber-soled tennis shoes on my feet to help me get my footing. But by the time I had descended three more storeys, I was trembling with exhaustion and terror. I was not sure I could do this sixteen more times. I tried the door of the balcony I was on. It moved under my hand. I slid it open just a fraction of an inch and paused to look inside. A middle-aged woman stood in the kitchen in full sight of the balcony, brewing tea. I waited. Please hurry.

Finally, when she had filled her mug and walked out of the kitchen, across the living room and into the bedroom, I inched the door open and slipped through, latching it behind me.

I crossed to the entrance door, which emitted a piercing creak when I pulled it open. "Hello? Who's there?" I ran down the hall and onto the first fire stair. I thundered down it as fast as I could, five, six, seven storeys.

Somewhere below I heard a door open, and voices. I was still proceeding towards them frantically, two stairs at a time, but quietly now, so that I would not betray myself.

"How many of these stairs are there?"

"Just the two. You've got the main entrance on the avenue and the service entrance from the basement to the side street."

Two flights from the bottom I caught sight of part of Clellan's face below. I stopped altogether for a moment and then crept forward. Tyler was there too, and someone else.

"Why don't they lock?"

"They're fire exits."

"Well, get some armed men in from the street and put one on each of these doors right away. I want to see the other stairway."

I slipped out through the fire door and came down into the lobby right behind them. At the other end of the lobby I found Jenkins and Gomez. Gomez was letting people out through a revolving door, one at a time.

Jenkins was talking into a radio. "How many men have you got outside? . . . All right. Make sure they're ready to shoot at anything unusual . . . That's right, we got an armed fugitive."

Through the large windows of plate glass that ran from floor to ceiling I could see uniformed men wearing bulletproof vests and holding rifles. The situation was only going to get worse.

I walked up to a light upholstered armchair with wooden legs and shoved my hands into the crevices between the sidearms and the seat. Hunching forward with my head down, I heaved the chair up on my head and shoulders so that the four legs pointed ahead like the horns of a charging animal.

259

I heard a shout, then more shouting. I was running full tilt straight at the plate-glass window for an endless, excruciating moment, unable to see anything with the chair over my head.

When I hit, there seemed to be an explosion all round me. I felt something brushing against my legs, and there was a dense shower of broken glass. I heaved away the chair and immediately scrambled off to one side. I heard guns firing everywhere as I ran down the sidewalk and then scurried between parked cars into the middle of the street.

"Where is he?"

"I never saw him."

I stood in the middle of the street, panting. Morrissey was sweeping a metal cane back and forth over the sidewalk in front of the shattered window. Tyler was down on his knees feeling the pavement with his hands. He looked up as Clellan approached. "Blood, maybe."

"A lot?" asked Clellan. Hopefully, I suppose.

Tyler shook his head. "Not here, but that doesn't mean much. He must have been moving pretty fast."

"Look's like he's still moving," said Clellan morosely.

I was about to leave when I saw two men come out of the building carrying a stretcher. Someone must have been hit by the gunfire. But then I saw—they had left her face and bright hair uncovered. Alice! I was in a frenzy. Was she alive? This was all my fault. I discovered that I was running towards the stretcher, which for some reason they were holding in front of the open door of an ambulance.

Then I saw that Gomez was standing several paces away, his eyes moving warily. He was holding a gun. Further off and to the other side Jenkins stood watching, with his right hand in his pocket. The stretcher-bearers continued to stand motionless, as if exhibiting their load for public inspection. Suddenly I realised that they were waiting for me.

Alice stirred. I managed to make myself understand that there was nothing I could do. Jenkins made a sign, and suddenly the stretcher was in the ambulance, the door slammed shut, and the ambulance moved off. Gone. Jenkins walked over to where Tyler was still crouched over the pavement. I could not hear either of them, but I saw Tyler nod and point towards the place where I had crossed between two parked cars into the street.

It suddenly struck me that I must still be leaving a trail of blood, thick and sticky even though invisible. I moved my hands up my body. There was blood running down my legs and soaking through my torn trousers.

Run.

I raced down the avenue, and arrived at my apartment on Ninety-second Street several minutes later. I went down to my entrance and pushed the old buzzer button next to my door underneath. I heard with relief the little click. They had not found this place.

Inside I found everything undisturbed. I went into the bathroom and stripped off my clothes. I stood under the shower and then carefully dried myself all over. Then I explored every inch of my body with my fingertips.

Everything was all right until I got to my calves, but there my fingers encountered the moist, thick stickiness of open wounds. I ran the shower over them again and blotted them dry with the towel. I could feel the blood well up immediately and begin running down the outsides of my legs again. I could tell I had one bad horizontal gash on my left calf and two on the right.

I got gauze and adhesive tape out of the first-aid kit that I had carried away from MicroMagnetics. I bandaged both legs and rested for almost an hour, to make sure the wounds were closing. I put on fresh clothes and set out to use a payphone.

"Hello, Nick," answered Jenkins in his most unctuous, sincere voice. "How are you?"

"I'm fine. I mainly called to let you know that."

"That seems an imprudent thing for you to do. Unless you need help, or there is something you want to find out from me."

Jenkins was trying to provoke me into losing control. But I was already so angry that nothing he said could have affected me.

"Why did you take Alice, Jenkins?"

"We're going to talk to her."

"She doesn't know anything. You can let her go right now."

"Nick, I don't doubt you when you say she doesn't know anything. In fact, if you'd told her the truth about yourself, we might not have found you so quickly."

"How did you find me? Did Alice tell someone about me?"

"Take a look in any bookstore. You brought this on yourself. You have to learn to trust people, Nick. As for Alice, she'll be safe here with us until we have you."

"Jenkins, if I could trust you, I'd make the trade: me for Alice. But as you point out, I'm not good at trusting people. Just as you're not much good at inspiring trust."

I hung up. Had Alice given me away? I tried to make sense of what Jenkins had said about looking in a bookstore. I walked into the next one I came to, not much caring at this point if anyone noticed the door opening. I saw it almost right away. It was some sort of romance. *White Lies*, by D. P. Gengler. It must have been quite popular, because there were several stacks of copies. On the cover Alice had drawn herself swooning in the arms of an elegant but rather untrustworthy-looking man in a dinner jacket. It was an excellent likeness of me, one that Jenkins or any of his men would recognise immediately. On the back flap of the jacket were the words "Jacket illustration by Alice Barlow".

Jenkins was right: it was my own fault. But that was all beside the point now. I had to get Alice back. While doing as much damage to Jenkins as possible.

I walked several blocks further south and went into the offices of a large law firm to get a safe telephone. I found an empty conference room, closed the door, and dialled the *Times*.

"I'd like to speak to Michael Herbert, please." Michael Herbert was to me nothing but a name that I had seen in the *Times* and that I had heard Anne Epstein mention as if he were a friend.

There was ringing, and then a voice said, "Michael Herbert."

"I have some extremely confidential information for Anne Epstein, and I don't want this call to be routed to her extension." I was talking rapidly and softly. "Could you go to her desk and ask her to take this call on your extension? It's very important."

There was a pause, and then he said, "I'll see if she's there."

Several minutes later Anne's voice came on. "Hello, this is Anne Epstein. Who is this?"

"Hello, Anne. Do you recognise my voice?"

"I . . ."

"Don't repeat my name. This is Nick. You cannot tell *anyone* where you got the information I'm about to give you. It would be *extremely* dangerous for me. Do you understand?"

"Yes."

"What I'm about to tell you is going to seem utterly incredible and utterly silly. But it's deadly serious. A highly ranked intelligence officer, with extraordinary personal discretion over large amounts of secret budgetary funds, has become mentally deranged. He has gradually become convinced that we are threatened by invisible aliens from another world. To combat his own paranoid delusions, vast sums of money are being spent, valuable human resources are being diverted and illegal acts are being committed—burglary, arson, even abduction. Officials at the highest level of government, having initially failed to bring this thing under control, are being drawn into a massive cover-up. Anne, do you know where the Academy Club is?"

"Yes . . ."

"Get over there within the hour. Bring a photographer. This man— he's currently using the name David Jenkins—is about to cordon off the Academy Club and search it for imaginary enemies. I want you to be there to see this incident. All I can do over the phone now is sketch out the basic facts of this story, but I'll send you information on this man in the mail . . ."

By the time I had finished with Anne, she probably had a vision of herself as the next Woodward and Bernstein. I had to move quickly now. It was eleven, and I wanted everything to reach its peak during lunch hour, when the Academy Club would be at its fullest. From a telephone booth across the street from the club, I telephoned my old office and got Cathy on the line.

"Cathy, I can't talk now, but do you happen to remember the name of the doctor I saw two years ago? Eisenstein? Einstein? Something like that. I've lost my address book and I need the name . . . No, I'm fine. I'll call you back in five minutes."

I walked over to another payphone and called again several minutes later. "Essler. That's it. You don't happen to have his number there, do you? . . . Thanks. I'll have to stop in soon. Bye."

That should do it, right there. But to make sure, I walked in through the front entrance of the Academy Club. There was an electric eye across the front hall. I positioned myself directly in its path and stepped on the carpet. Jenkins had scattered things like this around the places where I had hidden myself last year. I had no idea if he was still bothering to watch for me in the clubs, but if he was, this should generate some excitement. Especially after the telephone calls to my office.

To be absolutely sure, I went upstairs to a telephone booth inside the club and called Dr. Essler.

"The doctor's not available now. Is it about an appointment?"

"Well, yes, but I have to speak to him."

"The first available appointment I have is in December."

"But it's urgent—"

"If you'll leave your name and a number where you can be reached, I'll try to have the doctor call you when he's free." She sounded unpromising. Try to get your children into medical school. No other service profession is in a position to treat people like this.

"I'm not anywhere I can be reached. I think I'd better hold."

"I'm sorry, sir, but you can't do that. The doctor may be . . ."

I left the phone off the hook and headed downstairs to slip out of the club again before Jenkins arrived. But halfway down the stairs I looked at the entrance and saw that the outside was already completely covered over with a tentlike structure, and there were several people gathered by the door, wearing gas masks.

Off the hall, I saw another man with a large canister on wheels, which was emitting a loud hiss. Just like the one in Alice's apartment.

Charging up the staircase, I came up short behind two members and three or four club employees looking distraught, clustered round men in gas masks. One mask was removed, revealing the face of a man I had never seen before.

"Everyone stay calm. We have a leak in a gas main. You'll all be evacuated as quickly as possible using the gas masks at our disposal. Nobody is in any danger if you follow directions."

This was not working out at all the way I had planned it. I had expected this to happen an hour later, when the club would be full. I had assumed that they would announce that a fugitive was in the club. I had pictured them leading out hundreds of indignant Academy Club members and then beginning a destructive search of the building. Anne would be there with photographers, and when the whole fiasco was well under way, she would go after Jenkins directly. Even if I were trapped in the building, he would have to give up and leave before they could find me.

But it was not like that. It was still only eleven thirty, and the club was nearly empty. The story about the leaking gas main seemed to satisfy everyone. People were straggling down the stairs to be evacuated and I could tell from the way they held towels and napkins over their faces that gas was already seeping up to this floor.

This was all a mistake. I ran through a doorway and found myself in one of the private dining rooms. There was a long table running down the length of the room and above it an enormous chandelier with elaborately curved arms branching out from a shaft that ran up into the ceiling. It was all I could think of. I climbed up onto the table and grabbed hold of one of the metal arms close to the shaft. It swayed a bit, and there was a cracking sound up at the juncture with the ceiling, but it held as I pulled myself up.

I managed to get first one leg, throbbing with pain, over a metal arm, and then the other. I twisted round until I was sitting with my chest and face right up against the central shaft. The whole thing was creaking. I unbuckled my belt and rebuckled it round the shaft so that I was held firmly against it. Then I unbuttoned the front of my shirt, slipped my arms out of the sleeves, and knotted them tightly around the chandelier post so that I was lashed in place.

I heard people moving in the corridor. I tried to relax my body so that when I went under, I would not suddenly slump and cause the chandelier to lurch. They were moving in with their canister, and I had just enough time before passing out to feel how painful and insecure my perch in the chandelier was.

THE FIRST THING I felt was the pain under my arm and across the side of my neck where I hung by my shirt from the chandelier. That brought me very quickly to a level of consciousness where I also felt the pain across my lower back where my belt cut into it, and a cramping discomfort in my thigh where it lay across a thin metal branch of the chandelier. My body had sagged down and now hung inertly from the chandelier like a sack of grain.

"Nothing."

Two men dressed in grey work clothes stood in the doorway.

"It sounded just like someone moaning."

"Let's take a look next door."

When they disappeared from the doorway, I tried to pull myself up so that I could untie the shirt and the belt. I felt groggy and miserable. When I had finally somehow freed myself and dragged my limbs off the chandelier arms, I lowered myself laboriously until my feet reached the table top.

I slid myself onto the floor and lay there in a heap. It must have been almost an hour before I stumbled downstairs and outside into the bright afternoon. The Academy Club was full of members again. In the street, people walked by without a glance. It was as if nothing had happened. But my body ached horribly. I should call someone. They have Alice. Better get it straight in my mind first, get home.

At the entrance to my building I pressed the button, on principle, but I didn't much care. I staggered in. If they knew about this place, let them come. I would be there, sleeping.

NEXT MORNING I had a *Times* delivered. I went through the whole thing, page by page, column by column. Nothing. Anne probably hadn't found Jenkins. I had to call.

I walked all the way down to midtown to get to a safe telephone system and called Michael Herbert. When I asked for Anne her voice came on right away, as if she had been waiting for the call.

"Hello," she said eagerly.

I asked her straight off, "Couldn't you find Jenkins?"

"Of course I found him. Your description was perfect. Everything was just the way you said, except for the gas leak. I wasn't expecting that. But we watched for almost half an hour. Jenkins was standing there the whole time, right in front of the building. Then when he was just about to go into the building, we went after him."

"Did you get a picture?"

"Great pictures. He blinked when Jimmy stepped up to him with the camera. I introduced myself, told him I was from the *Times*, and asked him if he was Colonel David Jenkins, alias Donald Haslow, alias—"

"What did he say?" I asked eagerly.

"Nothing. He stopped dead and just stood there."

"Didn't you ask him anything else?"

"Sure. All sorts of things. Why he was there, who he was representing, whether he had a search warrant for the Academy Club, whether the federal government officially believed that there was evidence of extraterrestrial life, all sorts of things."

"And what did he say?"

"Nothing. Basically, he just walked to his car, got in, and drove away. It was amazing. Within, I would say, ten minutes everyone was gone."

"And did they have a search warrant?"

"No. There was no search warrant. They're staying with the story of the gas leak. They're insisting Jenkins just happened to be driving by and stopped to take a look, like anyone else—"

"So there's no story?"

"Of course there's a story. It's a fantastic story. But you can't run something like this without checking the whole thing out. Did you send that stuff you were going to give me on Jenkins?"

"I'll put it in the mail for you," I said.

"Everything you gave me over the phone checks out perfectly. The entire editorial board and the legal department have been meeting on this practically around the clock since last night. Two people flew down to Washington this morning. It's wonderful! I'll be working on this full-time."

"When do you think there might be an article, Anne?"

"I don't know. A month, six months. There's an enormous amount of research to do on this. I want to give you a number where you can reach me any time you have information. This is a very patriotic and brave—"

"Good luck with this, Anne. I can't stay on this line too long."

"Wait—"

I tried to think it all through. I was not sure exactly where all this left Jenkins, but it could only be bad for him. I went to another office several blocks away and spent some time getting ready and going over exactly what I would say.

I dialled Jenkins's number, but it never rang: there was a click, and suddenly Jenkins was speaking to me. "Halloway!" His voice was as soft as ever, but it was distorted by anger.

"Good afternoon," I said.

"Halloway, you don't know what you're doing." His voice had a whining quality that seemed on the verge of turning into a snarl. "You're ruining the careers of dedicated, decent men."

"Jenkins, do you mind if I give this number to the *Times*? They've been having the devil of a time reaching you."

"We're going to have to kill you now. I wanted you alive, but now I have to settle for you dead, just to survive."

"I want you to let Alice go."

"She'll be with us until we have you." His voice took on a vindictive tone. "If she survives that long."

"Jenkins, a hundred people saw your men carry her off. The *Times* knows that you've ransacked the Academy Club without any warrant, but they don't yet know that you've abducted someone and are holding her hostage. But they *will* know, unless Alice is out within half an hour."

"Halloway, you can't get away with this. I have evidence of what you are. And I have tapes of these phone conversations."

"I never doubted it. I have some recordings too. I make them on tape cassettes I happened to carry away with me from MicroMagnetics.

Would you like me to play back the part of this conversation where you make the threats about Alice?"

There was a silence. I let him think for a while.

"Jenkins, if you don't let Alice go, you'll very shortly be in prison, or a lunatic asylum. Besides the things I know about from direct experience, I've found out where you were trained, where you've worked, every name you've ever used. I've also found out some interesting things about people you've worked with. I'm ready to give it all to the *Times* to use as they in their wisdom see fit."

"Halloway, if you destroy me, there will be someone else. People know about you by now. Sooner or later we'll get you."

"Do you have Alice at Thirty-eighth Street?"

Silence.

"I want you to tell her to walk straight up Fifth Avenue. And I don't want to see any of your people there. Do you understand?"

I waited, but he did not answer.

"Jenkins, I have to hang up. You have her out there within half an hour. I can't call back and discuss it."

I WAITED FOR HER on a bench outside Central Park from which I had a good view of both sides of the avenue. I had no idea whether they would let her go, but I certainly intended to keep turning the screws on Jenkins. When I had waited nervously for forty-five minutes without any sign of Alice, I found myself considering exactly what information I should turn over to Anne next. Certainly the location of Jenkins's office. Then I might start implicating other people above Jenkins. That ought to turn them against Jenkins and his project quickly enough.

Probably Jenkins was thinking through the same possibilities.

I saw her coming two blocks away, on the park side of the avenue, the same side I was on, and I rushed down to meet her. When I was within ten yards of her, I stopped by the park wall and waited for her to come up level with me. She looked dazed, as if she had not slept for a long time. When she was alongside me, I turned and started to walk parallel with her but several feet away.

"Nick?" she said, turning her head.

"Keep walking," I said softly. "And don't turn towards me."

Tears were running down her face.

"Alice, I'm sorry I got you into all this. What did they do to you?"

"Nothing." She was shaking her head. "They just asked a lot of questions. They said they were just trying to help you."

"What did you tell them?"

"Everything. I didn't realise it made any difference." She started sobbing out loud. "I'm so sorry, Nick."

"It doesn't matter. But don't turn towards me."

267

"They were all meeting when I left. Some people came this morning from Washington. Oh, Nick, it's my fault they found us, isn't it? It was that stupid book jacket. I should have told you about it."

"It doesn't make any difference."

"Why couldn't we have just gone off together?"

"That wouldn't have been much of a life for you."

"Idiot. That's my business."

We turned off Fifth Avenue and walked into the park. Alice told me about her interrogation. They had gone through the same questions over and over. Where had she met me? When? What did I do all day? Where did I go? What did I wear? They told her all about who I was and how I had become invisible.

"Then they tried to get me to help them catch you, and when I wouldn't, they began to threaten me. Oh, Nick, I told them everything before I ever realised."

"It doesn't matter. They didn't find out anything they didn't already know. No, that's not true. They did find out one thing. The most important thing. They found out about you."

Alice began to weep again. "That means we can't live together any more, doesn't it?"

We walked in silence for a while.

"There's one thing they didn't tell you about me. I kept meaning to tell you myself, but I never quite got to it."

"Of course not."

"I kept meaning to mention that I love you."

"A fat lot of good that does me if you're just going to sneak off without me."

"Alice, I'll do whatever you want, no matter how preposterous."

She wrapped her arms round me and kissed me, which made her look quite odd. We were standing in the middle of Central Park, and people were turning and staring, but it seemed like the wrong moment to say anything about it to Alice.

JENKINS HAD A DIFFICULT TIME for a while. He spent several months in Washington answering questions. He explained, not entirely to every-one's satisfaction, that his investigation was primarily scientific in nature. To talk of "invisible matter" was surely unwarranted. If he had ever used such an expression, it was only informally. There was, of course, the "superglass". Anyone who examined it would certainly understand why such an extraordinary effort had been made to reconstruct Professor Wachs's work and to investigate the circumstances surrounding the explosion of his laboratory.

But it was the fantastic rumours of "invisible men" that were particularly regrettable. It was true that there was at least one person still

268

at large who had been clearly identified as having been present at the site of the explosion, and who was known to have been responsible for acts of arson both then and subsequently, and an extensive effort had quite properly been made to apprehend him. It was also true that certain aspects of the whole incident would probably remain obscure, partly because of the difficulty of reconstructing events and partly because of considerations of security. There was the known involvement of certain left-wing radical groups, and conceivably of foreign powers.

Jenkins's subordinates were equally vague. It had been difficult to see much of anything at the MicroMagnetics site. A fuel tank had exploded and damage had been extensive. As to the scope of the subsequent investigation, it had really been in Colonel Jenkins's hands, and they did not have enough information to make any useful judgment. One thing everyone insisted upon was that no one had seen any invisible men.

Clellan was shortly thereafter assigned to the staff of a training camp in North Carolina. Morrissey was sent to a succession of exotic places to participate in the surveillance of drug traffickers linked to officials of foreign governments. Tyler lives in Virginia now and supervises the collection of obscure political information from obscure parts of the world. Only Gomez continued to work for Jenkins in New York.

As for Jenkins, in the end they decided that on the whole everyone had behaved appropriately and within the scope of his authority, and no useful purpose would be served by the broadening or prolongation of the investigation. Jenkins ended up in charge of monitoring the shipment of strategically sensitive technology through New York Harbor to hostile countries. I follow these things, and I note that people are pleased with the job he is doing. His budget has begun to increase dramatically, and he is beginning to devote more time to looking for me again. I cannot tell whether he has support in this from his superiors or not.

When Anne's article on the Academy Club incident finally ran, it lacked excitement. Anne and her employers soon saw that the story was going nowhere and, losing their initial enthusiasm, abandoned it. Anne has since been assigned to the Washington desk, which pleased her enormously.

I HAVE VERY LITTLE more to tell you, and very little time. I should have liked to be able to offer you, from my unique vantage point, some valuable insight into the human condition, or some intelligence of an invisible purpose in the world. If it is there, I have not found it yet. No doubt I am looking right at it and just can't see it. Like the pattern in the carpet. Like me, for that matter.

I know now, as I write these final words for you, that Jenkins is closing in again. I can tell that he is about to find Jonathan Crosby's apartment. But I don't care. I will be gone. And this time I will be much more difficult to find. Unlike the leopard, I am going into other spots.

The trouble is that Alice expects to come with me. I have tried to show her why that would not make sense for either of us. The risks would be awful. Of course, anything is possible, and I have given it some thought. Perhaps it could be done.

Perhaps one day as Alice is riding home on the subway she will step out, just as the doors close, onto the platform of a station where she has never got out before, and dart up the stairs into the street. She will climb into a waiting car and we will drive off over a bridge or through a tunnel for ever. The next day she will have brunette hair, cut short, and different clothing, and we will be in San Francisco or London or back in New York, with different names and ages and accents.

I have tried to explain to her why this is not a reasonable course of action. I have tried to give her a rational account of my whole situation—with what success, it is hard to say.

"Nick, explain to me once more your theory of what happened to your body." The expression on her face is one of smiling innocence or perhaps of mockery—I am never quite sure. "Tell me again what a quark is."

"It's perfectly simple, really. It's one of the basic building blocks of matter. What the whole world is composed of. Although really, I suppose, it's more a mathematical abstraction . . . in a manner of speaking."

"So that the world would be composed of mathematical abstractions? You know, I think I prefer my own manner of speaking. You're a ghost after all. You died in that accident, and you've been sent back to accomplish certain very important things."

"What sorts of things?"

"Doing the right thing by me, to begin with. I think I'd like a church wedding."

"I don't see how that's possible, practically. Or even theologically, given your theory that I'm a ghost."

"It's your job to figure it all out. You promised you'd do whatever I wanted."

Time is running out, and I can't stay here much longer. But it seems to me that in the end I'm going to try to do what Alice wants. I don't know. It is preposterous, but what's the point of it all otherwise? Anyway, as long as we keep moving, we should be all right.

H. F. SAINT

New York businessman Harry F. Saint was in his forties when he decided to give up his business as a developer of athletic clubs to pursue his lifelong dream of becoming a writer. It was a calculated risk for this father of four children, but his wife, Joanne, encouraged him to give it a try. Once embarked on his new career, Saint himself had some doubts. "In every other kind of work I've done, you get feedback every day," he says. "People either buy your product or they don't, the deal closes or it doesn't, you get the account or you don't. There are immediate results. But with a novel, you write for months, even  years, without having any idea whether it's going to work out."

For a first novel, *Memoirs of an Invisible Man* worked out very well indeed. Even before publication the book earned more than two million dollars from the sale of film, book club and paperback rights. As the author modestly puts it, "It's like winning a lottery."

In person, Mr. Saint displays a quiet humour. That humour has found its way into the book, along with a detailed knowledge of subjects ranging from the working of the digestive system to the financial intricacies of Wall Street. His familiarity with Manhattan comes from many years' residence there. Today he and his family live on the outskirts of the city in a spacious Victorian house overlooking the Hudson River.

With his success now firmly established, Harry Saint is hard at work on a second novel. Despite pleas from readers, it will not be a sequel to *Memoirs*. "I'm through with invisibility," he states flatly. All he will reveal about the new book is that the action will almost certainly take place in New York. "I like New York," he says. "It has more things happening in it than any other city in the world."

Seal Morning

A CONDENSATION OF THE BOOK BY

ROWENA FARRE

ILLUSTRATED BY TED LEWIN

A
CLASSIC
OF OUR
TIME

Lora, an orphaned seal, is an enthusiastic vocalist who also performs with abandon on the harmonica, xylophone and trumpet. She loves picnics, eagerly laying the places herself, and is always the first to collect the letters from the postman.

Lora is part of the appealing menagerie portrayed in this amusing and moving account of a young girl's seven years on an isolated Scottish croft, with only her Aunt Miriam for human company. As they learn how to exist in their harsh new environment, the young Rowena observes with perception and compassion an ever-growing family of pets, as well as the local wildlife and the croft's infrequent visitors.

Chapter One

The county of Sutherland is composed for the greater part of moor, bog and water. Trees are a rarity; birch and pine scatter the moors singly or in small groups. Outcrops of rock, often weathered to strange shapes, are strewn over the landscape. When a storm is approaching, or in the half-light, this boulder-strewn landscape is eerie and to some people even frightening.

After twenty years as a teacher in one of the Home Counties, my Aunt Miriam, with whom I lived, decided to give up her career and return to her native Scotland. Her original plan had been to buy a small house near Inverness, where she had lived as a girl, but on hearing of a croft for sale at a moderate price in a remote part of Sutherland her pioneering spirit got the better of her, and, against the advice of friends and relations, she bought the place.

The croft possessed no conveniences. Lighting was by paraffin lamps. Water had to be carried in buckets from a stream. There was no telephone. To get medical aid entailed a journey on foot or by trap to the nearest *clachan*, or village, some twelve miles away, to put through a call to a township, for no doctor or nurse lived in the clachan. A path, little better than a sheep track, wound from our door over the moors. It gradually merged into an unsurfaced road, and for the last six miles, before entering the clachan, there was actually a coating of tarmac on it. During winter, stretches of this road would be covered by deep snowdrifts, making travel along it impossible for weeks at a time.

Behind us we left a countryside of trim fields and tall elms under which drowsed placid cattle, and we installed ourselves in an area where to ignore the white heads of cotton grass which sway over the bogs, or to fail to take one's bearings in an oncoming mist, could mean death.

To the west of us was the Ben Armine range. To the east were the Knockfin heights. Large tracts of the Ben Armine country, and the country to the north, consist of deer forest. Up here this does not mean an area covered by trees, but uncultivated, usually hilly, country given over to deer and other game. Rivers and burns crisscross this countryside. To the north is a string of lochs, including the beautiful Loch a'Chlair and Baddanloch. A glance at a map of this area will show that the only names are those of loch, river and hill; it is devoid of the name of town or clachan.

The move to our new abode took three weeks. Every stick of furniture and piece of luggage, including an upright piano, had to be transported over the last six miles in a farm wagon. We also brought with us two grey squirrels and a weakly specimen of *Rattus norvegicus*, i.e. a common brown rat. He had been presented to Aunt Miriam by one of her former pupils before we left.

"I do hope you won't take his gift the wrong way, Miss Farre. He knows you are very fond of animals," the anxious father of the donor explained. Aunt accepted Rodney in the spirit in which he was given, and passed him on to me.

Of all the animals I have reared I can think of none which has given me more trouble than this ratling. His mouth being too tiny for the insertion of an old-fashioned pen filler, I had to administer milk at all hours of the day and night by means of a piece of screwed-up cotton wool. By the time we had settled into the croft his health, somewhat to my pride, was less precarious and he was becoming energetic and inquisitive. He was soon climbing the parlour curtains, and showed much interest in going over the contents of the sewing basket. Indeed, Rodney came near to being a full day's work.

Within a week of arriving at the croft we received a visit from our nearest neighbour—Mr. McNairn, a shepherd who lived seven miles away. He carried in his arms a pair of otter cubs as a present for Aunt. The news had already reached him that she was "fond of animals".

As well as the feeding of ourselves, which was a problem in these remote parts, we also had to satisfy the voracious appetites of the animals. It was almost frightening to watch the otter cubs race through their meal of homemade brown bread and milk laced with oil, and, having licked clean the plate, look round for more. Rodney, too, developed an alarming appetite, for so small a creature. His main dish was the same as the otters', without the oil, but fruit, vegetables, cakes, chocolates and biscuits went down equally well. Between meals, he would climb into the wastepaper basket and chew up old envelopes. Fortunately, as they grew older all our animals became largely self-supporting, the otters catching fish in the numerous streams and the nearby *lochan,* or small lake.

Our days began to run to a pattern of rising, tending the animals, breakfast, my lessons—I was ten when I went to live in the croft—carrying in the day's supply of water, cooking, walks over the magnificent countryside, during summer a trip to the clachan once a fortnight to collect provisions in the small pony trap we had bought, and in the evenings playing the piano and reading.

My aunt had saved enough from her teaching to bring in an income of some seventy-five pounds a year. Her talents were various, and throughout the seven years spent in Sutherland she earned approximately eight pounds per year by painting designs on wooden platters and fruit bowls. The undecorated platters and bowls were sent up regularly by a London store during the spring, summer and autumn and were returned by Aunt at intervals during these seasons, duly painted in bright colours.

When I first came to these wild parts there was one thing which impressed itself most forcibly on my consciousness, and which remains my most potent memory. That was the silence. It was a permanent, living silence. Thunder, driving rain and keening wind were sounds which seemed to emanate from it and fade back into it. Sometimes, particularly on a hot summer's day, it was unbroken by even a stirring of wind. At other moments, the sudden bark of a deer only emphasised its depth. It was a vast, unseen but ever-present reality.

The croft consisted of a kitchen-cum-parlour, a small bedroom apiece, and a tiny room which was used as a workroom, or a guestroom when we had visitors. All the rooms were on one floor. Outside, within a few yards of the croft, was a partitioned byre. One side was the pony's quarters and the other was used for storing drums of paraffin, bins of grain, tinned food, and the animals' biscuits and fodder. After a few months two goats were added to the livestock, and then we had fresh milk.

It had seemed likely that, with streams and the lochan so close, the otter cubs, on growing older, would quickly return to their natural life. We made it a rule not to keep an animal if it wished to leave us, unless it had been injured or was sick. Otters are great wanderers and travel for miles over the countryside, swimming and on foot. However, Hansel and Gretel, as I had named them, seldom wandered far from the croft that first summer, and returned each evening. At night they slept in a straw-lined box in the parlour.

The squirrels, Cuthbert and Sara, took quite a while to adapt to this strange wilderness. The wide open spaces filled them with alarm and set them bolting through the door and into their wicker cage on the slightest provocation. Gradually, they became bolder and took to climbing onto the thatched roof of the croft, which soon became their favourite playground. Here they were often joined by Rodney. Cuthbert developed an unfortunate habit of sitting on the chimney. We kept a fire in the range day and night, winter and summer. As he peered down the hole or warmed himself in the chill weather on the heated bricks, he would become drugged by the smoke, topple over, and come hurtling onto the range. Although he twice singed his coat badly and sustained minor shock, it took an even bitterer experience before he learned to avoid the chimney. This time he landed in a saucepan of porridge which, though hot, had luckily not come to the boil. He was a sorry mess when I plucked him out, and did not appreciate a bath and brisk rub-down. After that he left the chimney alone.

The first winter in our new home was exhausting. For days at a time we were unable to leave the croft because of the heavy falls of snow. The snow was succeeded by fierce winds and heavy downpours. The hours of daylight were brief. Often the darkness extended past noon and we were cooking lunch by lamplight. By half past four it was growing dark again.

THE FOLLOWING JUNE, I spent a holiday with friends on the isle of Lewis in the Outer Hebrides. The weather throughout my stay was very rough. Walking along the beach one morning, I saw a fisherman coming towards me carrying a young seal in his arms. He told me it had probably been washed off its rock during the night by the gale and separated from its mother. Many young seals are lost in this way. What was unusual was that it was a Common Seal, a species more often found on the east coast, the Hebrides being the breeding ground of the larger, less intelligent Atlantic Seal. Although my knowledge of seal upbringing was scant, I asked the fisherman if I might have it, and to my joy he placed the seal in my arms. A bottle was presented to me by a kindly woman and I was instructed how to fill it with warmed milk mixed with a little oil. Seals' milk is very rich, containing almost ten times more fat than cows' milk. Lora, as I had named her, took to the bottle without fuss and showed every prospect of thriving. She became very tame almost from the start, and enjoyed being handled and stroked.

A fortnight later I set off on the two days' journey home with Lora, a somewhat bulky parcel weighing over thirty-eight pounds, wrapped up in a tartan rug. Animal lover though I knew Aunt Miriam to be, I had decided to take my pet back unannounced, as a "surprise", trusting that Lora's affectionate nature would win Aunt over to the realisation that a home without a seal lacks a vital member of the family party.

Chapter Two

Seals have beautiful and expressive eyes. Even as a pup Lora learned to use hers with telling effect. A look from her was enough to send me running to fill her bottle or to pick her up. Aunt Miriam, too, having stated categorically on my arrival home that the pup must be taken back to the

sea as soon as she could fend for herself, was won over by Lora in a few days, and much to my relief the seal's departure was not mentioned again. But already we had left her return to her natural element too late anyway, for seals, when reared by hand, become devoted to their human owners. If taken out to sea in a boat and dropped over the side, a seal will follow the vessel or, if the owners manage to make a getaway unnoticed, the deserted creature, in spite of its slow gait, will often travel miles overland in an attempt to find its old home.

Bringing up a seal was no light task. Left on her own for a while, Lora would start the curious baaing sound that young seals make. If no one hastened to her, this would change to plaintive whining interspersed with angry barks until she was given attention. As a pup she had a bottle four times a day. My first mistake in seal upbringing was to allow her to have it on my lap. Even when fully grown, measuring some three and a half foot and tipping the scales at over three hundredweight, she would still try to scramble onto a stranger's lap. Once on my return from a walk I went into the parlour to find Lora entrenched on a breathless and terrified lady visitor.

"She started to bark each time I tried to make her get down and I wasn't sure if seals bit, so I didn't push her too hard," I was informed. I promptly ordered a reluctant Lora onto the floor.

Allowing her to sleep at the bottom of my bed was another mistake. A seal pup on one's feet is one thing, but a fully grown seal quite another. It took me several weeks to train her to lie on a low bamboo couch at nights and to refrain from surreptitiously trying to clamber back onto the bed.

When on dry land, seals move by pulling themselves along on their flippers. No sooner was she past infancy than Lora started to waddle after me round the croft and trail me over to the byre. If I set out on a walk, her wails of protest at being left behind would pursue me into the distance. I decided that I must train her to become more independent and capable of amusing herself. We kept a small rowing boat in a sheltered inlet of the lochan. One day I took her out in it and dropped her over the side. In a moment she was swimming vigorously, diving, twisting and circling the boat with incredible swiftness. From a slow-moving, awkward creature she had turned into one of the utmost grace and speed. Each day after that she spent many hours swimming with the otters in the lochan. Should we want her, a call from us would usually bring her to the shore.

Now that she had discovered her true element and was growing older, our food problem was eased considerably, for she hunted her own fish. But she was not averse to a raw carrot, porridge, and, as an occasional treat, a spoonful of oil from a sardine tin. At night she had a supper consisting of dog biscuits soaked in milk and oil.

Training animals who live in one's own home is somewhat like training children: each individual must learn to fit into the life of the household, scope must be given for particular talents to develop, and allowances made for varying degrees of intelligence. In the case of a highly intelligent animal like the Common Seal, elementary training is quick and easy. Lora soon learned that her mackintosh was kept on one of the dresser's lower shelves, and that when she came in from the lochan she must sit on it. When still a pup she would bark for one of us to lay it out for her. As she grew older she taught herself to pull it off the shelf and to spread it out fairly adequately on the floor. As seals have stiff, shiny hairs, most of the water pours off them, and the drying process is comparatively short.

Quick to learn, Lora's inquisitive nature got her into trouble more than once. Anything a little strange or new had to be investigated. Thus she would pull at the tablecloth and bring down a shower of cutlery and glasses. The squirrel's cage had eventually to be hung up out of her reach, for she was always pushing her nose through the small door, which was kept tied back, and the squirrels, until they had become used to her presence, would be driven into a frenzy of alarm. During a particularly good relay of an opera she knocked over the battery wireless set, and before Aunt Miriam could reach it a knob was almost torn from its socket. This meant five weeks for us without a radio. We tried to steer her avid curiosity into more fruitful channels.

I began teaching Lora to fetch and carry different objects and to take the mail from the postman. The post was delivered twice a week. There was a box set on a short pole about two miles along the track from us. Here we were supposed to collect it, but the postman, being a sociable soul, generally walked the odd two miles to the croft for a chat and a cup of tea. It was not long before Lora learned to know on which days he arrived and at approximately what time. When she caught sight of his figure coming up the hill, she would start towards him. On meeting, he would place the letters in her mouth and she would follow in his wake. There was one unfortunate occasion when, halfway to the croft, she decided to go for a swim in the lochan taking the mail with her. Needless to say, that bundle of letters was lost for ever.

What gave her especial delight was to be allowed to unpack the shopping basket when we returned from a trip to the clachan or township. Tins would be lifted out carefully and, if round, rolled across the floor; exciting looking packages would be shaken hard. The basket emptied at last, she would carry it to its place by the kitchen cupboard.

THE CROFT STOOD in a little oasis of emerald grass. This greenery extended for about five yards in front, before meeting with the heather. To the rear of the croft was a clearing of earth for the growing of a few vegetables, and this was ringed by the grass which acted as a slight barrier against the moorland. Stones seemed to grow like weeds in this tiny patch of ground, yet in the "garden" we started to grow quite a variety of vegetables: radishes, lettuce, spinach, cabbages and leeks.

A kind and valiant friend came to stay with us for a week bringing roots and herb cuttings, together with heavy flowerpots to plant them in. Unfortunately, there was no earth to spare from the garden so we had to dig for it on the moors: hard labour with a vengeance. The earth was put through a coarse sieve to get rid of the ubiquitous stones. The cuttings meanwhile were being kept alive in a bowl of water. When there was enough sieved earth, we potted them and trusted they would "take". Surprisingly, several did and we were able to vary our somewhat monotonous diet by adding herbs and herb sauces. In winter we ranged the pots along the sill. No matter what the weather, we could still pick parsley to make a savoury porridge, and a sprig of thyme or a leaf of lemon verbena for an oatmeal sweet.

During our first summer we collected large stones to make a wall round the garden to act as a windbreak and to keep out the rabbits. We piled up

the stones until the wall was about three feet in height and two feet thick.
Inside this we fixed wire netting, several feet away from the wall, as an
additional protection against the rabbits. We soon found that, apart from
their burrowing skill, the rabbits were expert climbers and leapers. One
morning I noticed one sitting on the wall. I watched it, in the hope of
discovering how it set about clearing the last fence. For a moment it
seemed to be measuring with its eye the distance between the wall and the
wire netting. Then, with a leap, it was across and had landed in the garden.
As the little sportsman took a preliminary nibble at a radish leaf I felt
almost willing to let him continue the feast. Then I remembered the many
days of hard labour I had spent digging up stones and sowing rows of

seeds. I summoned Aunt Miriam and we gave chase. Many minutes of running and jumping over the vegetables left us exhausted and angry but the rabbit, unconcerned, sat cleaning its face beside a cabbage.

"Fetch the landing net," said Aunt Miriam curtly.

This net was used to land fish, but it should land a rabbit as well. After more minutes of hectic running and jumping, the rabbit was cornered and bolted into the net. What now?

"I can't kill him," said Aunt promptly.

Certainly I could not. We rarely ate meat, and a rabbit hotpot would have been welcome. But not, I believe, a hotpot made from this rabbit. It seemed ridiculous to free him after all the trouble he had given us, and allow him the opportunity to make a return visit to the garden. But that is what we did, tipping him over the wall whence he disappeared into the heather.

Mr. McNairn called later on in the day, and we told him about the rabbit. "It's a dog you are wanting," he said. "Rabbits smell a dog same as mice smell a cat and keep away."

"No," said Aunt firmly, "we can't have any more animals!"

"There's no point in wearing yourselves out over a patch of garden unless you hae a dog to keep away the varmints. You can make him sleep over in the byre and never let him put a foot in the croft. He'll be nae trouble to ye."

In due course a yellow mongrel pup called Ben arrived. He stood low on the ground, had flop ears, and was barrel-chested. But in spite of a somewhat heavy and ungainly build he was fleet of foot. He would sit on the wall watching for a slight movement in the heather, at which he would spring off and investigate. He proved an excellent deterrent to the rabbits. After his arrival we began to have rabbit on the menu frequently, for whenever he caught one he would bring it back, dead but never badly mauled. Having no dog companion, he took up with the otters who were about the same size as himself. He would swim considerable distances after them in the lochan and when I threw the ball out to them from the house, he would try to reach it before they did.

After a week in the byre Ben managed to become a permanent member of the croft, sleeping at night on the matting in front of the range. During the evenings there would be quite a gathering in the parlour. The larger animals, Lora, Ben and the otters, would put up with the smaller fry with fairly good grace. But during the day, when out in the open, Rodney and the squirrels had to look sharp when the otters or Ben were around. The sight of a rat or squirrel streaking past the croft proved too big a temptation, and we were never able to train them not to chase these small creatures.

Soon after our arrival I began keeping a notebook in which I wrote down words which held a definite meaning for various members of our animal fraternity. I excluded only the goats and the pony. Under the heading "Rodney" I find six words: basket, out, raisins, nuts, roof and Rodney. When any of these words were spoken to him he would, if in the right mood, act in a definite manner. "Basket!" for instance, would send him, generally at a snail's pace, into his box filled with dry grass. "Nuts!", however, would send him running towards the left-hand side of the dresser in which was kept a tin of nuts. "Raisins!" would have him running eagerly over to the right-hand side in which was kept the tin of raisins. Although the words "nuts" and "raisins" sent the squirrels scampering to the dresser in anticipation, they were never able to distinguish, as could Rodney, between the two words. On either being spoken they would keep up a brisk scamper, back and forth in front of the dresser, squeaking excitedly, until duly rewarded. Lora, as was usual in little tests of this kind, came off best. The total number of words under her column is thirty-five. Here are a few of them: basket (her own bamboo couch); in; out; here; Lora; Aunt; Ben; Hansel; Gretel; Mr. Dobbie (the postman); boat; swim (this word had the same effect on her as "walk" has on most dogs and had to be used with discretion); ball; sing; mouth organ; trumpet; stick (a drumstick with which she used to play the xylophone); biscuits; plate (her own plate); mackintosh.

Among other things that Lora learned in her early days was never to leave the boat until told to, for there was a danger of its being overturned, unless Aunt Miriam or I was sitting in the right spot to counterbalance her dive. She also learned never to touch the boat while swimming under it. Before this lesson was firmly instilled, though, she had overturned the boat twice, on both occasions fortunately on a hot summer's day when I was wearing a bathing suit.

Sometimes Lora would surface holding a stone in her mouth. Gradually she learned that when I said "stone" and pointed with a finger down at the water she was expected to dive for one. Unlike Ben with the rabbits, Lora never brought back any fish she had caught. All her catches were gulped down on the spot or taken onto the shore and eaten there. Not once was I able to extract a fish from her in exchange for a biscuit.

Chapter Three

Since ancient times it has been known that seals are attracted by music, and this fact has been woven into many legends. And men have known of the Common Seal's ability to learn to play different instruments. I have an eighteenth century book in which there is an engraving of a Common Seal playing the bagpipes.

Whenever Aunt Miriam or I struck up on the piano, the other animals would take no notice. Not so Lora. She would wriggle over, lean against the piano or (more inconveniently) the player's legs, and listen with an expression of intense concentration and joy, her whole body swaying now and then to the music. When the music stopped she would sit quietly for several minutes, still under its spell. Her reactions to my singing, however, were humiliating.

A relation had sent me a mouth organ and a book of songs for a birthday present. I decided to do a little singing practice each day. After a preliminary scale or two, I started singing "Men of Harlech". To my annoyance, I heard a loud groan beside me. Looking down I saw Lora, and continued singing. Whereupon she broke into a roar. Seals have perhaps the largest vocal range among mammals. Their repertoire includes grunts, snorts, barks, peculiar mewing, hisses, and a wail which often rises from a deep bass to a treble. The roar turned to a hiss, and my reedy efforts were soon outclassed. Then I had the idea of letting her sing on her own to my mouth organ accompaniment. After that, when I played a simple tune at a fairly slow pace she made valiant efforts to follow the music in a tuneless wail. A sudden high or low note, or a piece played too quickly, plainly annoyed her, for she would start to grunt and beat about with her foreflippers—a habit of hers when angry. Within a week she was able to get through "Baa-baa Black Sheep" and "Danny Boy", and was beginning to learn "Where my Caravan has Rested".

She began to pester me for the mouth organ. I was playing it outside the croft one afternoon and, growing weary of the grunts and whines and a heavily whiskered nose pressed against my face every so often as she attempted to wrest it from me, I finally placed it in her mouth, and soon she considered it to be hers. Having gained possession of it, she found that it emitted no sound in spite of being gnawed with vigour. So she started tossing it up into the air and catching it as though it were a ball, and then rolling on it. All to no effect. Taking it in her mouth once again she gave a loud sigh of desperation. This produced a blast of noise from the mouth organ and galvanised Lora to fresh efforts. I set off for a walk. When I returned in about an hour there were most curious sounds coming from the rear of the croft. Lora had learned the blow-suck method and there she was, blowing and sucking feebly, in a state of almost complete exhaustion, for she had apparently been doing this ever since I had left her. From that day onwards the mouth organ was her favourite toy, replacing in her affections the rubber ball which she shared with the dog and the otters.

A young friend of mine, after visiting us, sent Lora a toy trumpet. She soon learned to render earsplitting blasts on this when it was held for her. Another admirer sent her a small xylophone, complete with beater. She would hold the beater in her front teeth and bang any note to which I pointed. Her self-imposed practising on these various instruments drove us almost to distraction at times. It became necessary to put them out of her reach and allow her to play them only for short periods in the evenings. An unfortunate result of the singing lessons I had given her was that now, whenever Aunt or I began to play the piano, Lora, if she was in the vicinity, would lift her head and wail. It is well-nigh impossible to struggle through a Brahms sonata with a seal singing at the top of its voice. So most of our playing had to be done when she was in the lochan.

Pessimistic friends and relations had all predicted that our stay at the croft would be short. "Mind you come and see us as soon as you get back to civilisation," was the tone of the letters we received. When a year had passed and we were in no hurry to return to civilisation, the tone of the letters changed, and many a harried, town-dwelling friend wrote saying she envied us the peace and quiet of our lives. Peace we had certainly found, but a musical seal, two boisterous otters and other fauna do not make for quiet.

BIRDS ARE COMPARATIVELY TAME up here, though not so numerous or varied in species as in the coastal areas. Among those which visited the vicinity of the croft were ring ousels, stonechats, blackbirds, thrushes, twites and meadow pipits. Close by the byre grew a rowan tree and two silver birches, and this tiny glade attracted a number of birds. A cuckoo was a regular visitor during the summer months. We missed its haunting, two-note song when it migrated. This bird grew so tame that it would perch on an outstretched arm and fly onto our shoulders.

A person who has the inborn quality of being able to attract wild creatures is a rarity, but Aunt Miriam was such a person. Her mother noticed when she was quite a small child that if she were left alone in the garden birds would hop round her and flit onto her shoulders. At the approach of anyone else they would fly off. Animals were drawn to her too. She never had any fear of them.

Although I did not possess this gift, I did discover a very useful means of holding the attention of wild seals. It also largely dispelled their fear of me. At my school down south I had made and learned to play a simple bamboo finger pipe. We had been at the croft well over a year before I bothered to unpack it. On hearing the sound of the pipe music Lora—who was sitting outside shaking a tin which a thoughtful guest had filled with pebbles for her—came in, dropped the tin on the floor, and sat herself in front of me. It appeared to me that she went into a light trance: her eyes had a faraway look and she seemed quite oblivious of everything except the music. And this was the way pipe music always affected her. Again, as with the piano, it made no impression on the other animals.

Whenever I took one of her instruments from her, Lora would whine and bark. Having seen the effect piping had on her I began to use subtler methods. While Lora was going over the national anthem for the umpteenth time on the xylophone, I would start playing the pipe. She would glance up, the beater would drop from her mouth, and in a moment she would be spellbound, sitting quietly with her eyes half closed. Still playing, I would sneak away her toy and place it on a shelf. On these occasions she never whined for its return.

ALTHOUGH VISITORS to the croft would tell us in their letters that they were looking forward immensely to the quiet of the wilderness, the rude shattering of this quiet by one of Lora's recitals did not appear to worry them in the least. On the contrary, guests enjoyed every minute of them and were as disappointed as she was when they were brought to an abrupt close by Aunt or myself. But a week of listening to Lora running through her repertoire was not the same thing as hearing it month after month and, eventually, year after year.

After a time we were forced to the rather humiliating conclusion that friends came on visits mainly to get acquainted with Lora; our company, peace and quiet, the beauties of the countryside, were little more than sidelights.

"Where is she?" a guest would ask, the moment he had dumped down his suitcase and gulped a cup of tea.

"Out in the lochan."

"Well ... can't she be got in?"

We would stroll down to the lochan, the guest carrying the trumpet in readiness, and we would stare across the sheet of water, devoid of any sign of animal life. I would call and presently we would see the small, dark speck of Lora's head coming towards us, with perhaps a smaller one nearby belonging to an otter. Soon she would be ashore and, the trumpet pressed against her mouth, giving a rendering of "Danny Boy". Her boisterous good nature and love of showing off before visitors made her ever ready to play.

A certain uncle of mine took a great fancy to her. At his home outside Aberdeen he used to hold monthly *ceilidhs* (musical evenings) at which local talent used to perform. Uncle Andrew became obsessed with the idea that Lora should be a guest at one of these ceilidhs. Shortly after he had visited us, he arrived one evening in his shooting brake to collect Lora and me. We set off early the following morning. I packed two suitcases, one containing my belongings, the other Lora's instruments and her mackintosh. Uncle informed me that he had laid in a large supply of fish, biscuits and oil. The lengthy journey was accomplished without a mishap. Lora took the bumps and jolts calmly and appeared to enjoy the ride.

On the evening of the ceilidh, I led her into the drawing room. A well-known singer of mouth music (unaccompanied singing) was coming, and had consented to start the evening with a song. A performer on the melodeon, a small reed organ similar to a harmonium, was to take the platform next, followed by Lora giving an exhibition of xylophone

playing. Lora, the most sociable and extrovert of creatures, greeted the guests warmly. I suggested to Uncle, as the first artist took her place at the far end of the room, that I should shut Lora in his study until it was her turn to perform. But he and several of the guests vetoed this suggestion at once. The singer smiled charmingly and managed to sing a few notes of an old Hebridean air before the inevitable happened: Lora raised her head and roared her way from a deep bass to a seal top C. The audience were hysterical with laughter. When a certain amount of calm had been restored, someone suggested that Lora be allowed to perform first; thus she would get her little act off her chest and be willing to listen to others. It was blatantly apparent that he had no knowledge of seals, but she was lifted bodily onto the top of the piano, and the xylophone was placed before her. She took the beater from me and started off with aplomb on

"Baa-baa Black Sheep". The audience strained forward. I caught murmurs of, "Yes, I recognised that bit."

Loud applause greeted the final slither of the beater along the length of the instrument, which denoted the end of "Danny Boy", and this was followed by vociferous calls for an encore.

"Carry on," said Uncle, beaming at me.

I announced "Where my Caravan has Rested". Lora got off to a speedy start, whacking notes left, right and centre: the caravan had apparently got loose from its moorings. There was a loud crash as the xylophone fell to the floor, pushed off by Lora's exuberant playing. The audience rose to its feet. After a short pause in which to recover their breath, people uttered exclamations of delight: "Marvellous, isn't she?"

"Yes, brilliant. I didn't happen to know the tune myself, but I'm sure she played it superbly. Encore!"

The turn ended somewhat more soberly with a rendering of the national anthem.

After supper, I made up my mind to take things in hand a little. While the rest were busy eating and talking, I managed to inveigle Lora into Uncle Andrew's study and close the door on her. The study unfortunately was not soundproof and when the music started, her piteous wails drew someone at once to let her out.

I made her sit by my side and told her severely to be quiet. The result was no less disastrous. Seals have free-flowing tear ducts, and the patch of skin immediately below the eyes is continually moist. Lora, overcome with frustration at not being allowed to take part, sat with tears pouring down her face. The sympathetic guests pleaded on her behalf and the evening finished with a singsong in which, I need hardly say, Lora outsang the rest of us. But I was assured by Uncle that the ceilidh had been a great success.

Chapter Four

The country up here is uncluttered by housing and lofty vegetation. At first one misses the woods and the green lushness of field and hedgerow, and one even longs at times for such homely sights as an errand boy swinging down a street on his bicycle or a display of wares in a grocer's shop. But very soon the wilderness begins to exert its fascination, and its grip on one tightens as the weeks go by. Roads may curl through the valleys and, in certain districts, telegraph poles stand like lopped trees against a horizon, but these man-made things only emphasise the vastness and wildness of the land.

The grass, short and tough, is of a greyish-green colour, almost a dull blue in certain lights, and it is interspersed with clumps of heather. Many of the summits of the high hills are devoid of vegetation. Some are covered with loose scree which makes walking difficult. The sounds are of water flowing down the hillsides, rain, wind, the cries of birds and animals. On a hot day when a fair distance from the croft I would sometimes hear the clink of the spade hitting a stone as Aunt Miriam dug in the garden, or her voice calling an animal. Except for a few such sounds, and the sight of the croft lying encircled by hills, there was nothing else to bring to mind humanity and its doings.

One learns to appreciate what, in less harsh places, one almost takes for granted. One's eyesight sharpens too. One's hearing becomes keener. And from this barren land one never ceases to pluck strangely rewarding experiences.

We had been at the croft two years and I believed that I knew the country within a mile's radius fairly well. As I was walking over the hills one day quite close to home I found myself going down an incline at the bottom of which was a thick tangle of birch scrub I could not remember having seen before. Pushing my way through the birches and undergrowth I faced a tiny lochan. Birds flew upwards or scuttled to hide in the reeds. Floating on the brown peat water were the white heads of water lilies. Since then I have seen great lakes covered with these flowers but none has given me more pleasure than this lochan—hardly bigger than a good-sized round table—hidden in a dip in the austere Sutherland hills.

Throughout the seven years we lived here the only people we saw were the friends who visited us, Mr. Dobbie the postman, Mr. McNairn and the Frasers, an old crofting couple who were our next nearest neighbours after him. They lived nine miles distant.

MUCH HAS YET to be learned about the movement of seals under the water and the length of time they can remain submerged. When Lora was in the lochan I began going out in the rowing boat, a stopwatch in my hand. The length of her dives varied from a few seconds to several minutes. The longest dive I timed lasted over sixteen minutes. She was then in her fourth year. Grey seals have been known to submerge for twenty-two minutes and the great elephant seal, whose domain is the southern seas, for thirty-five, but it seems possible that longer dives for all species have yet to be recorded. Since a seal's ears and nostrils are closed while under water, it is believed by some that seals find their food mainly by sight. I myself am a little doubtful of this.

We took Lora in a friend's car to the mouth of a tidal river. The estuary was not deep. The water was very muddy and discoloured. While we ate our sandwiches Lora went swimming and, after a dive lasting less than a minute, surfaced with a fish dangling from her mouth. During the course of the afternoon she caught several others. Perhaps seals use their whiskers to aid or replace eyesight on occasion. It was three years later that we motored again to within a mile of this spot. We sat on the beach while Lora swam in the sea. When the time came to go home she was not to be seen. Repeated calls brought no result. At the end of an hour of calling and scanning the ocean, all to no purpose, I remembered the estuary and suggested, without much hope, that we go and look for her there. It was always a worry when she disappeared as seals make an easy target for a man with a gun. There was no sign of her when we reached the river's mouth but I called her name and she soon appeared on the opposite side of the bank and swam across to us, having, no doubt, done a little fishing in the meantime. This incident is curious. During the previous visit she had swum only a few yards into the open sea and could not possibly have seen the beach we had just left, as it was round an escarpment of rock, yet some instinct had connected the two places and had taken her back to the fishing territory again.

There was a rock about twelve feet high which overhung the lochan where the water was deep. Lora used to enjoy diving off it. After a time, the otters came to enjoy this sport too, flinging their long, supple bodies from it in the most carefree manner and trying to push one another off in a general roughhouse. Both wild seals and otters enjoy playing games, and they have their own traditional ones. Otters in all parts of the world make mud chutes on riverbanks and slide down them, landing with a splash in the water. During winter they make snow chutes and, kicking off with their hind feet, their forepaws doubled under at their sides, they slide down as swiftly as a toboggan. This game Lora came to learn from the otters. Otters are swift and strong swimmers but they do not have the speed of a seal. When any water game was in progress Lora was an easy winner.

It was sad to watch the persevering Ben doing his best to keep pace with these three expert swimmers. They knew his limited capacities in the water: Lora or an otter with the ball in their mouth would glance behind to make sure Ben was following in the faint hope of seizing it. They would deliberately slow down and, when he was within a short distance of them, dive below the surface and reappear a little later in another spot. This always set Ben barking with exasperation.

Besides having a rowing boat, I later became the proud possessor of a collapsible canvas canoe with a double paddle. I could get up a good speed in this, but never became fast enough to beat Lora or the otters when starting even. Seals and otters are ever eager to take part in a game, so I devised a water race. They would remain on the shore or rock until I shouted the word "Go!" having in the interval given myself a generous start.

A series of splashes behind would assure me that my adversaries had dived from the rock and were after me. I would paddle furiously, but in spite of my initial advantage I seldom won. While a race was in progress there would be no sound except for the dip of the paddle in the water and an occasional bark from the rather highly strung Gretel. But no sooner had they clambered ashore at the far end of the lochan than they would start to bark excitedly.

When racing, Lora seldom raised her head as she did when swimming more leisurely. Her body, just breaking the surface of the water, was like a dark torpedo. The actual colour of a Common Seal's coat is a greenish amber, scattered liberally over the upper parts with brownish-black spots. Like all seals, she took pleasure in swimming on her back in leisure moments—as did the otters—sometimes holding the ball between her front, flipper-like, paws. Both she and the otters could reverse in the water as easily as a fish. Their bodies when swimming appeared to be boneless.

I was out on the lochan one day with a full boatload comprising Lora, the otters and Ben, when I received one of my periodic duckings. The cause of it was a deer. Ben started to yelp furiously and then dived over the side of the boat. I just caught sight of the deer's black nose, and its antlers parallel to the water, which was all that could be seen of it. The boat gave a tremendous lurch as Lora and the otters followed Ben's lead, and I found myself in the water. I managed to right the boat and collect the oars before clambering back into it. The noise and commotion were shocking. Scal and otters had caught up with the deer and were snapping and diving about it. I was afraid that it would use its antlers on them if they did not keep their distance, but it swam on relentlessly. When it sprang to the shore it gave itself a brief shake and then galloped away towards the hills. It was a magnificent stag with a full head of antlers. Ben next took up the chase. Having made land he scampered after it, in full cry like a trained deerhound. He did not return till late that evening, worn out with the chase and too weary to touch any food. After that day he frequently took himself off to the hills, sometimes from early morning till late evening, and was always so tired when he returned home that he would flop down and go straight to sleep.

LOOKING THROUGH THE NOTEBOOK I kept for that year I find two events I considered worthy to be underlined in red ink.

"July 20th—the arrival of Sith" (reads one of these entries). "The most delicate, beautiful creature I have ever seen. His coat is a dark red dotted with white spots. These will disappear as he grows older. Long, flexible ears edged with black hair. Have not measured him yet but should say he stands at about thirty-eight inches. Orphan. Brought over from the Reay Forest by a friend of a friend of Mr. McNairn's. Five weeks old. Spent most of the evening trying to think of a name which would convey delicacy and speed. Finally decided on Sith. (This is Gaelic for fairy.) Has the byre to himself at the moment as the goats and pony sleep out during summer."

This creature, whom on arrival I considered to be a veritable gift of the gods, was a roebuck calf. Nothing is more delightful than to watch one of these exquisitely formed little creatures as it leaps into the air and springs effortlessly onto any hillock lying in its path. But the temperaments of these creatures leave much to be desired, as I was later to discover.

Like all our animals, he was reared without ever being given a slap or touch of the stick; all training was done by voice and gesture. At first we were amused by his predilection for butting every living thing which came within its orbit, including ourselves. But as the sharp little horns started to grow we began to find his playfulness—as we had first termed his delight in butting—not quite so amusing. Vainly I would order him in severe tones to desist. It was useless.

Nor did he hesitate to use his excellent set of teeth to good purpose. He had no desire to nuzzle an outstretched hand. All he wanted, and quick, was that bit of carrot or apple. If the hand did not proffer the expected titbit then it received a hard bite. It was no use protesting inwardly, as I used to, that having gone to considerable trouble to rear him I was entitled to a little friendly affection. Sith, the fairy, did not turn out to be quite the gentle, affectionate creature I had believed him to be on our first acquaintance.

The other animals too, not without cause, found his presence irksome in the extreme. Most of them had their favourite resting places. Ben's was the wall round the garden. Here he would lie for hours, sleeping, watching all that was going on in the lochan below, now and then reversing his position so as to be able to see what was taking place around the croft. Sith found it easy enough while still a youngster to spring onto the wall. And though still a youngster it was apparent he possessed remarkable strength for his size. With a well aimed butt he sent Ben flying off the wall with a surprised yelp. It was not to be the only occasion that Ben was the victim of such an experience.

An atmosphere of apprehension prevailed when Sith was around. One day I discovered the gallant little Rodney being ruthlessly butted against an outer wall of the croft. Though firmly pinioned and with much of the air knocked out of him, he still managed to squeak with fury and struggled to free himself. The space between Sith's horns then was not so much more than two and a half inches, but, by great good fortune, with each butt the horns landed either side of Rodney. I shudder to think of his fate if it had been otherwise. No sooner had I released him than he went for Sith's hind legs, Sith meanwhile having turned his attention to me. A sharp bite from the incensed Rodney sent him flying along the track with a grace which always held me spellbound.

I am glad to say that Sith eventually took himself off. But we had not seen the last of him.

I awoke suddenly one night to find the light of a full moon streaming into the room. It was not the moon shining on my face which had awakened me but the sound of a lettuce being uprooted and munched. Hurriedly flinging off the covers, I crossed the room and looked out. A charming sight, to all but a crofter, met my gaze. The sky was a vivid, mysterious blue. Under the round white disc of the moon lay the darker blue hills and the black rocks. The water of the lochan shone black and silver. Nearby in the garden every plant was clearly silhouetted and touched with a film of blue. So was the sylphlike roebuck methodically wrenching up the lettuces. I climbed out of the window, not stopping to put on my slippers, and walked over the earth in my bare feet. Sith came high-stepping towards me and promptly landed a butt on my legs which were covered only by a flimsy cotton nightdress. My cry of anguish woke all the inhabitants of the croft. Sith made a leisurely getaway over the wall.

"Have you been sleepwalking?" Aunt Miriam asked, seeing me standing there in the middle of the vegetable patch.

"Sith!" I moaned, hobbling into the parlour.

A lamp was lit to throw more light on the scene. It was revealed that my left leg was streaming with blood from a gash just below the knee joint. The gash was not very wide but it was a good deep one. Aunt Miriam threaded a needle with white silk and dipped silk and needle into a pan of boiling water. Then she proceeded to sew me up. My moonlight encounter with my late pet had cost me three stitches. Found to be missing the following morning was one row of lettuce.

For those who are romantically minded, let me add that Sith returned once more to his old home, this time accompanied by a doe. The pair of them leapt onto the wall but were promptly seen off by Aunt before they did any damage.

The other event which I underlined in red concerned a song-thrush. This thrush, a cock, never left the vicinity of the croft for long. Whenever there was a spell of severe weather we would put out food for the birds each day and hang a large straw-filled box in the lee of the croft. The box was built of wood and the entrance was a round hole at one side. Breac (meaning speckled), as we called him, used to take advantage of these amenities. However, if a window of the croft was open, he would fly in and perch on a picture rail, out of reach of the animals. Should one of us call he would fly down onto a hand or shoulder. His singing was above thrush average. Almost every morning when the weather was mild he used to fly into Aunt's bedroom around six o'clock, perch on the bed rail and utter clear piping notes until Aunt roused herself and spoke a few words to him. Then he would hop about the room and take a drink from the enamel water can.

That March—a little later than thrushes further south—Breac and his mate started to build a nest in the rowan tree by the croft. Throughout the day he dutifully fed his mate as she sat on the eggs. He was far too busy now to come into the croft, though he would spend a minute on our shoulders if we were in the open. When the four young were hatched, the tempo of his working day increased. Like most birds during the nesting season, he lost weight and his appearance, previously sleek and trim, began to be bedraggled. Human beings are not the only ones who like to have their offspring admired. As we were having breakfast one morning there was a tap on the window and, looking towards it, we saw the whole thrush family lined up on the sill.

These youngsters became as tame as their parents and all attained maturity. A limit had to be drawn somewhere. When a fledgling hopped inside I would place it on a finger and put it out again. Aunt found the early morning situation rather more difficult to deal with, for now Breac and his whole family would arrive and line up on her bed rail, the fledglings cheeping loudly.

There was also a number of birds of prey dwelling in these parts, as a result of which the lives of Rodney and the squirrels were in constant danger. Their habit of sitting on the roof added to their peril, but there was nothing we could do to protect them short of shutting them up in cages, a penalty we had no intention of submitting them to. Better a short life and a gay one than a dreary life in a cage. As things turned out, Cuthbert's life was a short one. He was snatched off the roof one day in the claws of a peregrine falcon.

Chapter Five

Among the jobs we had to get through during the summer were digging, drying and stacking peat; scything grass for hay, and stooking it; and picking berries—for bottling, and jam- and wine-making. We dried herbs, mushrooms and edible fungi. Repairs to croft and byre were carried out. Every fortnight we made a trip to the township in the pony trap to collect supplies. A certain number of tins of food and fuel and items of clothing would be stored against the following winter. The garden became too small for our needs and so we made another one on a patch of ground near the lochan where the soil was richer, and with these two gardens our supply of fresh vegetables during the summer months was assured.

When living in remote parts it is necessary to know how to deal with minor accidents and illnesses, and to have a basic knowledge of diet so that one can plan well-balanced and healthy meals. Throughout our years at the croft we did not suffer a single illness and kept clear of even slight colds. Tinned and dehydrated foods were used only in an emergency during summer, and as a supplementary food during winter. Cakes and bread were made from brown flour. Besides our home-grown vegetables, we also made good use of wild greenstuffs.

Out on a walk we discovered a ruined *shieling*. In the old days people used to bring their cows and goats to the high hills during summer so that the animals could crop the rich grass, and up in these high pasturelands they lived in simple stone and thatched dwellings called shielings. Only one wall of this shieling was still standing. Almost equalling it in height was a profusion of nettles. They proved a welcome food supply, especially in spring when the young tops were very tender. I would walk up to the shieling wearing a pair of leather gloves and carrying a basket. Having filled the basket with nettles, I would strip the stems from the older leaves. They were cooked like spinach, then turned into a heated dish with dabs of butter added. The flavour was delicious. For a supper dish we used to top the nettles with a poached egg; for lunch we would grate a little cheese over them or, if we had been lucky with our tomatoes, souse them in tomato sauce.

We took it in turns to milk the goats. During the summer we rose early, at six or six thirty, and while one was setting the breakfast table the other would be on the milking stool.

When both goats were in milk there was plenty for our needs. The surplus milk was converted into cheese. When the milk had curdled, it was poured into a linen square which was strung up from a branch of the rowan. When the whey had dripped off, salt and pepper were added to the curds, and sometimes a few chopped herbs. The result was goat's-milk cottage cheese.

FIRST TO BE UP in the mornings were the otters, who would go down to the lochan for a swim. As they grew older we often did not see them again till the evening when they returned for their supper of bread-and-mash. Next to rise would be the squirrels.

After Cuthbert's sudden departure, Sara took to sleeping with Rodney in his box. There had always been considerable competition between Cuthbert and Rodney for her attention. As there was no female rat around, Rodney looked to Sara for companionship. This had not put him in favour with Cuthbert. Furious chitterings and squeaks used to come from the vicinity of the roof and then we would know that the two males were at it again. Sara would come pelting in at the door, chirruping with agitation, and climb hastily into her wicker basket, but before long the two rivals would be hurrying after her. It was no wonder that her temper sometimes became frayed. Tension relaxed after Cuthbert went. The basket was removed from the hook, and henceforth she and Rodney shared the box between them.

It amused me to watch Rodney sitting still for minutes at a time while Sara went over his coat. Rats, incidentally, are quite clean creatures. When living away from drains and refuse they are not dirty or verminous. Rodney spent a lot of time each day washing his face, nibbling his fur, going over his tail, whiskers and ears. To reach the various parts of his anatomy he would contort his body to a surprising degree. When it came

296

to cleaning the patch behind his ears he would lick a paw thoroughly, like a cat, and then sweep it behind and over the ear. After Sara had finished off his grooming to her satisfaction she would sit with her head cocked to one side and Rodney learned to know that this attitude of hers meant that she expected her coat to receive attention now. He would nibble away industriously at her thick fur, so long in comparison to his own.

WE TOOK CARE to note and remember the places where various berry bushes grew. One spring Aunt Miriam discovered two sloe bushes in a thicket at the side of a loch. We returned there in autumn to collect the berries. That and every following year we made several bottles of sloe wine.

We also found a wild raspberry patch and most seasons we picked about five pounds of berries for jam. The fruit was also eaten fresh and baked in tarts. We always tried to have some thirty pounds of jam bottled by early September. A pound jar between us lasted a week, and at that rate of consumption thirty pounds saw us through from mid-September to April. We never had visitors to stay during winter and so were able to reckon the quantities of food required then to a fairly narrow margin.

ONE PARTICULAR DAY in the high hills stands out in my memory. I had walked higher than was prudent when alone. But it was mid-June, the sky was a brilliant, translucent blue, larks sang into the breeze and the walking was good. A mountain hare gave me a sharp glance as I passed, then continued with its feeding. Now and then I heard the curious dry croak of a ptarmigan—a bird of the tops. I had left Strath na Seilga (valley of the River Seilga) and was climbing in the direction of Creag Mhor. The azure loch, Gorm Loch Mor, as it is called in Gaelic, lay to my right. Stopping a moment to survey the countryside below me, I saw to my annoyance that I was being followed by Ben. A dog is a troublesome companion when one is wanting to observe wildlife, for it chases and scares every creature away. I waited for him to catch up. Then I fixed round his neck a leather belt I had been wearing and we continued upwards.

Soon he started to strain hard on the improvised lead. I managed to pull him up just in time. Less than a foot from him I saw a nest of young ptarmigans. It was not a nest in the usual meaning of the word, for the birds lay in a shallow hollow in the ground. Their sandy and grey plumage made them almost indistinguishable from the surrounding earth and stones. Having dragged the excited Ben over to a rock and fastened him to a convenient projection, I returned to the birds. Disregarding Aunt's instructions on no account to touch nestlings, let alone remove one, I took out a handkerchief and, kneeling down, put a hand among the warm, apparently fearless brood of seven. Carefully I lifted one out and placed it on the handkerchief, tying the square of linen in such a way that only the

297

tiny head and tail were visible. Then I went back to the yapping Ben and started for home, the lead in one hand, the ptarmigan in the other.

The sky was no longer so blue, and thin, vaporous clouds were forming. Down a cleft of the *corrie*, or small steep hollow at the head of the valley, blew a long streamer of mist. The sight of it made me double my pace. Puffs of mist, less vaporous now, blew with increasing frequency into the corrie. I started to run because I realized I must reach the end of it quickly and get a good view of my bearings. I was about five miles from home, high up in the hills. But it is not mileage that makes for distance in these parts; it is the rough going, the variability of the weather conditions, and the danger of bogs and exposure. Besides a compass, we usually took with us when walking in the hills a jersey and windproof jacket each, in case the weather turned cold, and kept in reserve a sandwich and a bar of chocolate. All these things I had neglected to do.

I stood on the open hillside and noted the River Skinsdale far off in the valley below, the croft to the right, and a great boulder lying at the bottom of the hill which I would have to make sure of passing on my left, from there bearing steadily in a southerly direction, avoiding three large areas of bogland. There was no path to follow, the whole of the way. As I started down the hill, keeping my eyes on the boulder and trying at the same time to avoid rocks and loose scree, the mist swept over the brow of the hill and enveloped me, blotting out every landmark. These mountain mists are as white as cotton wool. If caught in one, the best plan is to take what shelter one can find, pull on sweater and windcheater, and stick it out. But I was clad in a cotton dress, and had eaten all the sandwiches. Stumbling down the hill, I managed by some miracle to reach my first objective, the boulder.

Putting the ptarmigan into a pocket, I started off due south. Ben walked slowly at my side. I kept a firm grip on the lead, and his company was now most welcome. I held out my free arm and was just able to see the tips of my fingers; beyond them all was covered as though by a white blanket. I began to feel very cold and tired. It was increasingly difficult to calculate how long I had been walking since the mist descended, and how far I had come. I started to run, and Ben dragged back on the lead. There was a squelch as I stepped up to my ankles in bog. During the ensuing seconds, after I had hastily stepped out again, I lost all sense of direction.

On walks with Ben I would often call "Home!" to him when the time came to go back, so that he would know I was returning. Now I spoke this word to him and trusted he would lead us to the croft. For what seemed ages he continued to sit without making a move.

"Home!" I repeated urgently.

At last he got up and with no sign of hurry began to walk forward; I followed, clinging to the lead as a drowning person might cling to a length of driftwood. We continued to walk at a slow pace. As the damp grasses flicked round my ankles I expected at any moment to sink into a morass. We reached firmer ground, where the grass grew shorter and more wiry, and I began to breathe more easily. Ben meandered round rocks, sometimes turning right, sometimes left, in a most haphazard manner.

Our walk through the mist began to have a dreamlike quality. The rear portion of Ben's anatomy was visible to me, while his forequarters and head faded into the mist. Then my left hand touched stone—a wall—and turning my head I could just see a faint light shining from behind a window. Still leading, Ben walked through the open door of the croft.

As I sat in the glow of the lamplight, clad in dressing gown and slippers and spooning up hot soup, I suddenly remembered the ptarmigan. I had taken off my dress and hung it in the cupboard, forgetful of the wee bird. He proved to be a hardy specimen and was still very much alive. Unwrapping him from the handkerchief I gave him a few drops of warm milk and put him into a cage. Owing to the circumstances of my homecoming, my crime in removing him from the nest was hardly commented upon by my aunt.

This young bird, which I named Jim, was successfully reared. Every three hours during the day he received a small quantity of heather shoots and chopped fresh berries. Ptarmigan are almost exclusively vegetarian. In the evenings he was let out of his cage and flew about the parlour. He developed into a fine bird with a bright red comb over his eyes. When he was about six weeks old he was released.

As I was somewhat superstitious by nature in those days, Ben's feat of homefinding in the mist began to appear to me in retrospect to be an act of almost occult significance. It was the only time he had followed me against orders, and it was the only occasion I had got truly lost. Whether he possessed psychic powers or not, he certainly possessed great intelligence and a better knowledge of the hills than we did. Of the dogs I have owned since, none has had such character, nor such tremendous energy.

WE MADE THE MOST of the long summer evenings, seldom going to bed much before half past eleven. It was about this time that Ben would start to get restless. If the doors and parlour windows were shut, he would spring onto the window ledge and stare out, now and then giving a whine of impatience. As soon as a window or door was opened he would be out and away. Sometimes he reappeared after we had finished breakfast, his coat darkened with sweat, and flopped down exhausted to sleep until midday. At other times he would return in the early hours before dawn. We decided he must have discovered a female several miles distant and that it was to her he went each night.

Then on a certain afternoon Mr. McNairn walked into the croft, his rifle slung over his shoulder. He said that a dog was chasing and mauling his sheep. He suspected the Frasers' mongrel collie, a ne'er-do-

well in his estimation. Heated words had been exchanged between him and Mrs. Fraser, she denying vehemently that her dog would so much as sniff at a sheep. He had left her with the warning that he was keeping his gun loaded and would shoot any dog he saw in the vicinity of his flocks.

Two days later as we were working in the croft garden I saw Mr. McNairn walking up the hill, his rifle slung over his shoulder as before. With sudden intuition Aunt glanced at Ben who was lying asleep on the wall, and said, "It's him." And I knew she was right. It seems incredible to me now that neither of us till that moment had harboured the slightest suspicion that it was Ben who was guilty of chasing sheep.

Mr. McNairn pointed a finger at him when he reached the croft, saying, "I found a sheep which had been run to its death yesterday, and early this morning I saw him through my field glasses, skivvering along Pollie Hill way."

Ben was taken inside and given an enema. The result, which contained traces of sheep's wool, proved his guilt. As with other dogs which become addicted to sheep chasing, Ben had clung to the animal's throat as it ran until the wretched creature had died through asphyxiation, exhaustion and terror. There can be no reprieve for a dog which chases sheep. Ben was led off straightaway by Mr. McNairn and shot, his body left unburied among the hills.

Chapter Six

Ben's unhappy ending filled us with gloom. To lower our spirits further, the weather broke the day after he had been shot, and for almost a week rain fell in a steady, grey downpour. The goats stamped morosely in the byre, vegetables floated in pools of water and much of the garden soil was washed away. Every time we left the croft we had to wear mackintoshes and gumboots. Then the rain suddenly stopped and the sky shone a clear blue, flecked with white clouds. We ceased talking about the advantages of civilisation in wet weather—visits to cinemas and cafés, friends in to tea—and cut slices of bread and cake, and prepared to spend a day in the open.

"Another hour in the croft and I would have had a nervous breakdown," said Aunt Miriam.

We walked until we came to a stretch of the Blackwater. The river flowed swiftly, the heavens reflected in its surface. We turned up a tributary where the waters were more sluggish. On the banks grew willow, birch, rowan and alder. As we were eating our lunch we heard the high whistling sound which otters make to call each other.

Presently a head appeared through the reeds, and the otter gave another whistle and came straight towards us. It was Hansel. Another moment passed and then Gretel appeared. They helped us finish lunch and followed us home. They were in their third year and wandering far from the croft. We knew that one day they would leave us for good.

MOST YEARS THE HAY was cut in July, and forked into conical stacks around pikes. A fortnight or so later the pikes would be lifted and the hay forked into the trap, the pony being led to the byre where the hay was unloaded.

Haymaking was not particularly onerous work. But digging peat was gruelling. Two large wicker panniers were fixed on either side of the pony. We walked over to the peat hags wearing gumboots and carrying spades. During my first years at the croft, while I was too small to dig, my job was to lift the damp clods into the panniers. The bricks of peat were laid out to dry and then stacked at the side of the byre. Peat digging, drying and stacking went on throughout the summer, a seemingly endless task.

In September we made a special trip to the township to send off Christmas presents to friends and relations, and to collect the presents we had ordered for one another by mail at the same time as Yuletide fare and decorations. Written on each package we sent off was the instruction that it was not to be opened till the twenty-fifth of December. It was, of course, often possible to make trips to the township during late autumn and winter, but we could never be sure exactly when. On getting back home we wrapped up our presents and put them away in the dresser with the boxes of dates, preserved fruits, chocolates, nuts and raisins.

SEVERAL OF THE FRIENDS who stayed with us during summer grew so enthusiastic about the life we were leading that they were all for throwing up their jobs, spending their savings on crofts, and living the simple life themselves. Aunt Miriam always begged them, before they bought a place, first to spend a *winter* in a croft.

Really, there are very few adults these days who possess the mental and emotional self-sufficiency necessary for leading a satisfactory existence in these remote parts. When the daylight lasts for only five or six hours, when the Never Silent—as the Norsemen called the wind—howls down the corries and the snow is lying so deep that even the deer are unable to reach the croft in search of food, then one learns what it means to be cut off from the outside world, and either one grows to appreciate spells of complete isolation, or else the isolation begins to sap one's confidence and to terrify.

From mid-September to April or May we were alone in the croft, and for weeks, sometimes months, we saw nobody except each other. Even the postman was rarely able to call in during winter for a chat.

As the hours of darkness lengthened, we seldom rose before nine and were in bed by nine thirty. Reading in bed was strictly forbidden because of using up too much paraffin. The only occasion I have ever known Aunt Miriam to smack an animal was when she discovered Hansel chewing up a precious packet of candles.

What remained of them was swept into a pan, melted down and reformed into rough oblongs. We never wasted a scrap of candle grease or a drop of paraffin. When there was a heavy deluge of rain during winter, the day was spent in semidarkness. We cooked and ate by lamplight, religiously turned out the flame when the meal was finished, and allowed ourselves a brief two hours of light again after supper before turning in to bed. Except for the briefest exits to answer the calls of nature, the animals lay for hours on couch, carpet, or in box, and were very little trouble. We cut their food down when they took next to no exercise.

Keeping goats and a pony meant that we always had to cross over to the byre twice a day in order to milk, feed and water them. Even this short journey of ten strides could be arduous. Several times I watched Aunt from a window going along the path on hands and knees because the force of the gale prevented her from standing upright. I too had to take my turn at milking when one of the fierce gales was blowing, and make my way across in this ignominious position. When a gale was blowing hard from the east it was often impossible to open the back door and we were compelled to use the front one only. A strong westerly gale meant using only the back one. After a heavy fall of snow during the night it would take us a hard morning's work to free the doors and dig a path from the croft to the byre. Our preliminary exit on these occasions had to be through a window because the weight of snow jammed the doors tight. Sometimes when it had been snowing for several days on end and the snow level reached eight or nine feet—up to the roof of the croft—we would dig in shifts from morning till late at night, working by lamplight, in order to keep the path clear and the windows free from the pressure of snow. I would stand on a box in the high narrow pathway we had cleared and stare over the snow wall across the white countryside, enjoying the sensation of being completely cut off from the rest of the world.

One of the most difficult lessons we had to learn was to be content to do very little, during winter especially, for quite long periods. From childhood it is dinned into us that we should be continuously busy—Satan finds work for idle hands, and so on. But it is fatal, living in these parts, if the mind and hands are continually seeking for something to occupy them. When the stockings have been darned, the animals fed, the hour not yet come to light the lamp to read, then surely one should be able to sit for a while without feeling restless or guilty. Yet modern upbringing has made the art of relaxing and emptying the mind of petty concerns a difficult feat. Nevertheless, we learned to accomplish it, to the dismay of energetic friends when they came to stay.

"Don't you get bored stiff when you are snowed in?" they would ask.

"Never," we would assure them truthfully.

"What do you *do* when you've finished the chores?"

"Nothing much."

At this, looks of deep suspicion would cross their faces. "I feel sure too long at this life wouldn't be good for one. Don't you reach a stage of not wanting to do anything?"

"Yes."

MOST ANIMALS ENJOY playing in the snow. If it was not too deep the otters would race out and roll over and over in it, then chase each other like dogs. As they had been reared in a croft from infancy I had to show them how to make a snow chute and slide down it. I chose a steep hill and beat a length of snow hard with a spade, making the first descent myself on a tin tray. Soon the otters were flying down the chute, forepaws tucked well in to their sides, back legs used for giving a brisk send-off and then kept out straight. No sooner had they reached the bottom than they hurried up to the top for another go. Lora barked furiously at seeing Hansel and Gretel descending in quick succession but was too nervous, for a long while, to attempt the descent herself. Presently she tried a short slither, but rapidly manoeuvred herself over to the side with her flippers, not caring for the sensation at all. I took an otter down with me on the tray. The other followed by itself close behind. Lora was left alone at the top, barking her annoyance. I called to her. With obvious trepidation she ventured once more onto the slide, moved her foreflippers and was off to a slow start. Her pace increased swiftly. Her run ended in a great uprush of snow and the length of the chute was extended by several yards. After that, she had no more fear of going down. The following morning she waddled straight up to the chute. But she was able to make only comparatively few runs, for it took her many minutes to reach the top again.

Not all the slides went smoothly. Once Hansel started off just in front of Lora. Owing to her greater weight, Lora soon overtook him and he was pushed forward at an increasing speed by her body. When the end of the chute was reached there was a piercing, bloodcurdling bark from Hansel as Lora swept right over him. Aunt and I, who were watching from the top, both automatically put a hand across our eyes. I fully expected to see a flattened, defunct Hansel when I looked again. But his body possessed the qualities of India rubber and when I did look in his direction he was giving himself a shake and then running up the hill for another slide.

Even when the ice on the lochan was several inches thick we never ventured out on it ourselves. But the first job Lora and the otters set themselves to do on these wintry mornings was to free their plungeholes of the ice which had formed over them during the night. The otters would dab at the ice with their forepaws and press down with their bodies, and Lora would press down with her nose and foreparts. Both seals and otters have a wonderfully acute sense of direction. One year there was a plungehole—too small for Lora to enter—underneath the rock from which they dived. It was fascinating to watch the otters dive off with hardly a moment's hesitation and go straight through the hole. Its circumference did not appear to be much larger than their bodies. After a swim under the ice-covered water they would reappear again up the hole, having found it, apparently, without any difficulty. An otter's sense of direction on land is as unerring as it is in water and they will return to old holts, as otters' lairs are called, after months and years.

Chapter Seven

Our third winter at the croft was the worst we ever experienced. One day towards the end of October the sky had that dark, steely look which betokens a cold spell. The goats and pony, which up till then had been staked out on the turf, were led into the byre. We filled up bins and scuttles with peat and coal and stacked more peat by the front and back doors. Buckets were filled with water from the stream, two for the croft and two for the byre. It got so cold during the night that we both had to get up to close our windows and put more blankets on the beds. Small gritty nodules of snow and ice rattled against the panes. For three days a blizzard raged. All that could be seen from the windows were the dark shapes of the hills and the byre and a white ground haze. The cold was so bitter that returning from the short journey to the byre our fingers were numb and rigid. To fetch more water from the stream was an agonising task, for the cold gale lashed stinging grains of icy snow against face and hands. It became so gloomy, sitting in the croft listening to the high-pitched whine of the gale and the incessant swish of the frozen nodules against the panes, that we kept the lamp burning all day.

On the fourth day the gale abated and large flakes of snow began to whirl down. The cold was still intense but we forced ourselves to start digging a path round the croft and over to the byre. Twenty minutes of digging was all that we could stand and then we came in and revived ourselves with cups of tea before recommencing shovelling. Snow reached the level of the eaves but we managed to keep pace with it. Three feet from the croft was an encircling wall of it, the top surface extending outwards across the countryside, the inner sloping away slightly from the croft and beaten hard with the flat of the spade to prevent toppling and crumbling. The path between croft and wall, which ran out to the byre, was the only stretch of ground on which we could walk. When the drifts were so high that it was impossible to fetch water from the stream, we scooped snow in buckets from the top of the wall and melted it down on the range.

Once or twice a day we cautiously raised the lid of our birdbox, which was placed in the lee of the croft, to make sure that none of the birds which had sought sanctuary in it was ailing. It was difficult to see them among the thick straw and extract the invalids without frightening the rest. The small china dish was refilled with grain and bits of fat and the lid closed again. In the lee of croft and byre, more birds would crouch in the snow under the shelter of the eaves. Each morning we found dead birds, and others which were very weak. Of those we were able to reach we put the ones suffering from exposure into a lidded basket. After one morning's collection, there were ten birds in Aunt Miriam's basket: a stonechat, a twite, three blackbirds, two thrushes, a snow bunting, a starling and a chaffinch.

First aid was administered on a table in Aunt's bedroom. The birds were placed round an oil lamp and the gentle heat gradually restored their circulation. The inert bodies would become warmer to the touch, a wing would move slightly, faint cheeps grow louder and break into twitters. Those which revived were put into cages, the smaller birds being kept separate from the larger. A few drops of warm milk were forcibly administered. Dishes of bread-and-milk and scraps of fat were put in each cage, then green felt was laid over the wire-meshed front to keep out light and induce the invalids to sleep.

I happened to go into the parlour while this operation was taking place to fetch another piece of felt. Whilst in there I distinctly heard two taps on the pane. So did the otters, for they woke up at once from their doze and stared fixedly at the window. The taps were repeated and I thought I saw something white move outside. The chances of its being a ghost did not strike me as beyond possibility. My legs suddenly felt very weak, yet I returned to Aunt's room and informed her that *something white* was tapping on the parlour window. Without any ado, she went and opened it. Flakes of snow blew into the parlour and with them fluttered a white ptarmigan. (The plumage of these birds changes to white during winter, with a few bars of black on tail and wings.) The bird flew to the dresser and after walking along the top rail flew down and alighted on Aunt's shoulder. He appeared to be quite at his ease.

"Could it be Jim?" said Aunt.

Sure enough, it was. When I brought out a tin of sultanas he flew over to me at once. He used to be given a sultana as a treat occasionally in the past. When the lid was removed he poked his neck into the tin and helped himself. Jim stayed with us three days, until the worst of the weather was over. Then we opened a window and he flew out. We never saw him again.

It is always a pleasure when one can watch and listen to former sufferers pecking up morsels of food from one's hand and singing and chirping gaily. Hearing birds indoors one realises the strength and carrying power of their voices. We were treated to brilliant displays of singing by thrushes and blackbirds, but these songsters are best enjoyed in the open, for their voices are too powerful indoors. As soon as there was a break in the weather those birds which had recovered sufficiently were let out. Many we never saw again but others revisited the croft, some almost daily.

We often got back to the croft after a walk to find, if a door or window had been left open, several of our late guests disporting themselves on picture frames and furniture. A healthy bird is as inquisitive and full of vitality as a healthy mammal, and it can be very destructive. We returned one day to discover artificial flowers in a bowl pecked to pieces and a china ornament knocked off the mantelpiece and broken. A starling was on the writing desk, extracting envelopes from a packet. It had upset the inkwell and from the desk a stream of ink descended onto the carpet. As it had walked over the white tablecloth, spread for tea, its ink-stained claws had made a delicate winding pattern which several washings failed to remove. But the disadvantages of birds entering the croft were compensated for by the charm of their company.

Deer often came down to the croft in severe weather in search of food, their lean flanks showing the effects of poor grazing. There was nothing we could do for them. The cold seemed to make them tamer; they would stand about watching us, their breath streaming white from their nostrils, and allow us to approach to within quite a short distance before moving slowly off. One day when I was sitting in the parlour I was frightened by a loud snort, followed by an antlered head appearing through the window. The stag regarded me calmly for a while, and then withdrew.

ON CHRISTMAS EVE we decorated the croft with greenery, clipped candles to a small artificial fir tree and hung coloured glass balls and lengths of tinsel on the branches. The tree was placed on top of the piano whose straight, varnished sides were beyond Sara's climbing powers. On our first Christmas at the croft we had unthinkingly placed a real fir, appropriately decorated, on a cane table. Hearing an ominous splintering of glass we rushed into the parlour to find a silver ball lying broken on the floor and the lighted tree rocking back and forth precariously as the two squirrels clung to its branches and busily gnawed off twigs.

After this we decided that there must be no more lighted candles on the tree. With an open range and oil lamps and no fire brigade handy, we had to be very careful about placing a guard in front of the range and keeping lamps and exposed flames out of reach of the animals.

Our Christmas lunch consisted most years of mushroom soup made from mushrooms we had picked and dried during autumn; tinned turkey, oats and bottled carrots; Christmas pudding and brandy butter, and then preserves, nuts and chocolates. We drank homemade sloe wine.

We put out an extra quantity of food for the birds on Christmas morning, looking on them as our guests, as no human friends were able to visit us. Each animal was given a treat in the way of food. A tin of sardines was opened for Lora and the otters. Rodney and Sara had nuts and raisins. We unwrapped presents received from friends months before as well as those sent especially for an animal. One year a package addressed to Lora was found to contain a drum, sent by a young cousin of mine.

"Oh, horror!" said Aunt Miriam. "Shall we give it to her?"

Much to our relief, Lora effectively rendered this gift useless by sitting on the vellum, which promptly tore.

Chapter Eight

On going to the stream one morning the next summer, bucket in hand, I saw to my surprise, behind a boulder, a white bell tent. A figure presently emerged clad in shorts, checked shirt and a turban; he politely took the bucket from me and filled it at the stream. As we walked back to the croft I learned that he and his brother—still asleep in the tent—were the sons of an Indian friend of my father's and were studying in England. They had found their way to us with the aid of map and compass and a sheaf of instructions. A letter announcing their arrival reached us two weeks later.

Ram and Narshidas had brought packets of photographs of their homeland in their mountainous rucksacks. My parents had spent the greater part of their lives in India and I had been born there, so it gave me great delight to look at the pictures, which included several of the beautiful Nilgiri Hill district where we had lived for several years.

Lora took a great fancy to Ram. She would sit by the tent in the early mornings waiting for him to emerge, whereupon she would drop a pebble or a bit of stick at his feet as an offering. Only a few visitors were treated to this sign of her affection.

Mr. McNairn called while our Indian guests were with us and we were astonished to hear him telling them that as a youth he had sailed to Ceylon and India in a trading vessel. He was equally surprised to learn that my earliest years had been spent in India. In spite of being neighbours we had been quite unaware until then of these facts about each other. With his white beard, brown, strangely unlined face, his slow, gentle way of speaking and his stately walk and gestures Mr. McNairn reminded me of a venerable wise man and I would never have suspected that his whole youth had been spent on the seas and travelling in the East. He was nearing forty when he returned to Scotland and took up shepherding.

When we first knew him he was in his mid-sixties. As he regarded one with blue, farseeing eyes, one got the feeling that he might have the gift of second sight. But Mr. McNairn, unlike many Highlanders, could not abide any "airy-fairy talk" as he called it.

It was Mr. Fraser who was the seer and spellbinder.

"Mr. Fraser!" I exclaimed in surprise when someone informed me that he was a wise man of renown, and that people came long distances to seek his advice or ask him to put a spell on a sick animal for its recovery.

Mr. Fraser was clean-shaven and his brown eyes were as fast-moving as a town-dweller's. If a conversation amused him he would laugh uproariously. If it bored him he did not trouble to hide the fact. Mr. Fraser accepted fairies and the efficacy of spells in the same way as others accept the power of electricity. He did not believe, so much as *know*.

Both his parents had come from the west and held reputations as healers and seers. As is the custom in northern Scotland and the Hebrides, occult information is passed down from father to daughter and mother to son. So he was instructed by his mother.

Though expert in the use of spells, Mr. Fraser kept a good stock of medicines—both for human and animal use—in a wooden box. "There's nothing like helping medicine along wie a spell or a spell wie a teaspoon o' medicine," was his advice.

"COULD I HAVE THE COMPANY of Lora a while, to help wie a spell?" Mr. Fraser asked me one day.

He had walked over to us with an old crofter whose new cow, bought only two weeks back with a little pile of money he and his wife had saved, was seriously ill. He had informed Mr. Fraser—to the latter's pleasure—that he was not going to have any vet tampering with her.

We went down to the lochan. Repeated calls did not bring Lora to the shore, so I returned to the croft for the trumpet. When I blew several strong blasts Hansel and Gretel arrived on the scene in answer to the summons, but as Mr. Fraser pointed out, otters did not have the mystic powers of seals. We stood about in the hope that Lora would appear. I felt very reluctant to let the old crofter go back without his cow having the benefit of her mystic power. In all, his walk to and from his home would total close on thirty miles. Then I saw Lora lying a few yards away between two rocks eyeing us placidly but making no attempt to come over. She wiped her nose with a flexible foreflipper and stood almost erect as she surveyed the countryside. At last she swam across the inlet.

Mr. Fraser asked the crofter and me to stand a short distance away. He opened a tin box in which were some herbs and what appeared to be a lump of clay. As he worked the herbs into the clay ball he held it under Lora's nose. Then he spoke to her earnestly for a minute and put the herbal ball back into the tin. Beckoning us over, he handed the tin to the crofter, telling him to feed the ball to the sick animal when he got home, and on the following morning to give it a pint of "straight medicine" made up according to his instructions. He informed us that it was Lora's breath that lent such a vital quality to the spell.

I am happy to report that the cow recovered and lived to a ripe old age. But as to whether its recovery was due to the spell or the straight medicine or to both—I cannot offer an opinion.

ONE SUMMER AUNT MIRIAM received a letter from a friend asking if we would put up a Canadian couple for a week. They were both of Scottish extraction and were anxious to spend some time in a remote part of their ancestral homeland. We awaited their arrival with trepidation, wondering whether two sophisticated visitors from Toronto would fit into croft life.

When the Dacys arrived, they assured us that they could quite easily squeeze into the minute spare bedroom and were looking forward to helping us about the croft. After supper we sat outside chatting. Soft air blew through the grasses and a line of stags moved slowly over the crest of a distant hill. All was peace and beauty. Our animals had taken themselves out of sight and were apparently occupied with their own doings. Saying that the spell of the highlands had already gripped them, our guests went off to bed.

Sometimes on summer evenings the approach of night was barely perceptible. The moon rose to replace the sun and with its coming a different spirit—mysterious and utterly calm—penetrated the hills, but the colouring of the night sky differed little from that of evening. So it was, on that particular night.

Aunt Miriam and I strolled about long after our guests had gone to bed. It must have been past twelve when we decided to retire. I had changed into a nightdress when the silence was pierced by a woman's scream. More high-pitched screams followed from the direction of the Dacys' bedroom and were interspersed with gruff, panic-stricken shouts. My first thought was that the Dacys must have knocked over their paraffin lamp and that the croft was now ablaze. Then came a scream so fraught with terror that I concluded some unimaginable horror must have crawled over the Dacys' windowsill and into their room. I waited until I heard Aunt running across the parlour before I followed in her wake.

Mrs. Dacy, wearing a chiffon nightdress, was crouched in the square window space, effectively blocking out the moonlight. A torch shone on the carpet where it had apparently been dropped. Mr. Dacy, clad in pyjamas, was standing on top of the chest of drawers. Both were speechless with terror when we entered at the double. Aunt picked up the torch and directed it about the room. The only object it revealed which could conceivably have caused the panic was Rodney, who was sitting on the bed lethargically cleaning his whiskers.

"Is that what's...?"

Mr. Dacy indicated by a brief gesture that it was.

Aunt Miriam turned her attention to Mrs. Dacy. "But, Mrs. Dacy—it's only a rat!"

"Did you say *only* a rat, Miss Farre?"

We were apt to forget that rats on the loose do not appeal to everyone. I picked up Rodney, who had curled up on the bed, and shut him in my room. When I returned the Dacys had descended from their perches and Mrs. Dacy was telling Aunt in a shaking voice how, having been sound asleep, she had woken with a start to feel something warm and furry brush past her face. Her husband, sleeping beside her, woke too, and then ...

"Don't try and say any more, dear. Sit down."

"You tell them, Elwin." Mrs. Dacy sank onto the bed.

"We both felt small paws and a tail move over our heads. And when I switched on my flashlight there was this rat sitting on the sheet just above us. We naturally dived beneath the bedclothes, but then ..." He also sat down beside his wife. "It came right in after us. I once met up with bugs in a log cabin but I've never been any place where there's been rats."

"Rodney's a tame rat," I ejaculated, not liking to hear him associated with bedbugs.

"Tame or not tame, I don't care for rats running about the house and under the covers," said Mr. Dacy firmly.

Aunt apologised. "It won't happen again, I promise."

"Well, I think, Miss Farre, that we will leave tomorrow," said Mrs. Dacy with finality, as Mr. Dacy tenderly laid a silk dressing gown over his wife's shoulders.

"Tea," murmured Aunt.

"You see," Aunt explained later, as, slippered and dressing-gowned, we sat drinking that Highland palliative for all ills, "it's seven miles to Mr. McNairn. He has to walk two miles to the Frasers' and Mr. Fraser then has an hour's walk to the man who owns the wagon to find out from him when he can come over with it to our croft. Things can't be arranged quickly up here, I'm afraid."

"Well, Elwin's a good walker. He'll be able to reach the man's croft by midday and get him to come back with the wagon—won't you, Elwin?"

I thought I detected a flicker of doubt in her husband's eyes but he replied promptly enough that he would.

The following morning, accompanied by me, he started off. After four miles of tramping over a seemingly endless switchback of hills we sat down on a boulder and took a rest. The weather broke over our heads, and as neither of us had brought a mackintosh we were drenched in less than a minute.

"Wouldn't there be a danger of stepping into a bog with the rain coming down like this? I can't see more than a yard ahead."

"Yes," I replied without hesitation.

"Could you keep that rat shut up if we stayed on?"

I assured him I could. We both turned and started to squelch back.

Rodney spent a somewhat confined week, but towards the end of it both the Dacys were able to insert crumbs through the wire mesh of his cage without flinching, and, moreover, were talking earnestly of returning in two years and renting a croft for the summer. It was with regret that we bade each other farewell.

Chapter Nine

Five years of croft life had wrought certain changes in us. We seldom glanced at the parlour clock unless to note whether it was time to listen to the news or to a particular radio programme. The weather and seasons regulated our working day, our rising and retiring. Living apart from a community and being as nearly self-contained as is possible in these islands, we often felt that we were in a domain inhabited, so far as humanity was concerned, solely by ourselves, Mr. Dobbie, Mr. McNairn and the Frasers. Events in Glasgow or London seemed as remote to us as happenings in Calcutta. I was perfectly content to go on living thus, and I found it more and more of an effort to take an interest in outside news. My only concern was that I should fail to pass an educational test—for which I journeyed occasionally to Edinburgh—and be compelled by the authorities to go to a boarding school. To avoid this, I worked diligently at my lessons and miraculously never failed a test. Every so often Aunt Miriam would suggest that I spend a week or so staying with young cousins and their families, but I would suggest that they visit us instead. This they were always eager to do.

During these five years the two gardens had improved considerably. Our animals had also done well, and like ourselves they had not suffered a single illness. Rodney, between his second and fifth year, filled out a lot. When a friend and her miniature dachshund came to stay there was little difference between its weight and size and that of Rodney, though the dog stood higher than he did. The first thing Rodney did on meeting this canine visitor was to give it a sharp nip in the leg. The dog, a most docile creature, thereafter bolted whenever Rodney approached him.

It surprised us that the otters had remained with us so long. They wandered off for days at a time but always returned sooner or later. One of their holts was under a rock near the lochan. Here they would retire for hours, coming up if I called them. In their fifth year they wandered off on one of their frequent excursions. When three weeks had gone by and they were still away I reconciled myself to the idea that they had most probably gone for good.

Then one night I woke to hear an animal outside the croft give several low whines as though it were in great pain. I heard Aunt Miriam go out, and full of foreboding I followed her. Gretel was lying on the step. In the light of the torch I saw that she was completely exhausted and that one of her forepaws was dreadfully torn, the lower part being almost severed from the upper. The paw was completely crushed. Aunt carried her into the parlour and a short inspection showed that it would be useless to try to heal her. Apart from her wounded leg, she was so emaciated that this alone would have made recovery doubtful. She was given an injection to end her life. Nine miles from us would have been the nearest distance in which she could have got caught in a trap. Somehow she had managed to free her paw from its grip, and had travelled those miles, or more, back to her old home. When she left us earlier, at five years and four months old, she weighed twenty-one pounds. After her death she was put on the scales and they registered nine and a half pounds.

The following morning Hansel appeared. He sniffed at the step where Gretel had lain the previous night. Then he went through all the rooms. Otters become very attached to one another and frequently mate for life. As if finally realising that to search any further was useless, he went out again. I made him up a plate of bread, milk and oil, which he ate. For the rest of the day he wandered in the vicinity of the croft. Then in the evening he departed, and that was the last we ever saw of him.

AFTER GRETEL'S DEATH I felt a sudden desire to get away from the croft for a while. With Aunt Miriam's permission, I started a trip which I had often contemplated. This would take me through that desolate stretch of country which continued almost unbroken from the door of our croft northward some thirty miles to the mouth of the Strathy. A good road crossed this country midway from Kinbrace to the Naver valley, north of which roadways and accommodation were virtually non-existent. I took enough food with me to last five days, by which time I reckoned to reach the coast. Food consisted of two loaves, fat, dehydrated potatoes, dried bananas, tea, and a tin of condensed milk. Berries and dandelion leaves I would gather en route to supply vitamin needs, and I hoped to be able to buy an occasional egg and glass of fresh milk from a crofter. My camping kit consisted of a light silk, waterproofed tent, sleeping-bag, saucepan, frying pan, Primus stove, matches, compass and map. I also took the bamboo pipe with which to amuse myself during the evenings.

The first part of my route took me along the River Skinsdale and up through the Borrobol Forest. From there I headed due north until I came to the road. I crossed it and entered the country which I had come to explore. That first night in new territory I spent encamped in a birch spinney close to Loch Leum a Chlamhain, with Ben Griam Beg rising behind me. This large hill is typical of many in Sutherland which rise to one thousand five hundred feet, and whose slopes are composed of grass and loose scree.

During the evening I cooked my main meal of the day, and as I was eating supper and idly watching a grouse in flight, I saw it suddenly snatched up in the talons of a golden eagle. I had twice before seen this great bird swoop on prey lying on the ground, but I had never before seen it catch prey in the air. At this campsite I also found a young water shrew under my sleeping-bag when I lifted it up on the following morning. The shrew hurried off lochwards, no doubt to search for grubs.

The country swept onwards, hill succeeding hill. Streams ran between clumps of dwarf willow, and under rocks which stood like prehistoric monsters on the skyline. On my third day's walk the land grew flatter and I was able to see far into the distance. From now on I increased my pace; a few dried bananas and half a loaf were all that was left of my food supply. For three days I had not seen a single person and had only once glimpsed far off the white walls of a lonely croft. On the fifth evening I pitched my tent near the region of Strathy Bay.

Here, surrounded by eggs, rashers of bacon, a can of milk, butter and a loaf of bread, all purchased from a crofter woman, I was just starting eagerly to prepare a really good supper when I saw a Common Seal resting on a rock a little way out to sea. I drew the bamboo pipe from my rucksack and piped a few notes. The seal raised its head and listened. With extreme caution, and still piping, I inched down the beach. I was able to reach the fringe of the sea without my quarry leaving its rock. Then I lost my balance and sat down with a splash in the foam, and the seal immediately plunged into the shallow water and made out to sea.

The next morning the seal was back, sunning itself on the rock. This time I was able to get to within about eight feet of it. I did not attempt to get any closer and started to back away again. Its eyes never left me until I was well up the beach, and then it relaxed and turned over on its side, enjoying the sunshine. When I left the beach it was lying on its back, its head hanging over the rock in an attitude of complete repose. Resting seals seem to favour this attitude. Lora often lay full-length on her back with her flippers hanging limp at her sides and her eyes closed.

Chapter Ten

One April when the snows had vanished from the hilltops, Aunt Miriam decided to go away for a spell to friends in Argyll. I drove her down to Lairg in the trap, returning home alone with the monthly provisions. It was the first time my aunt had been away from the croft during the six years we had lived there and with only the animals for company I soon discovered that, good companions though they were, I was not cut out for a hermit's existence for any lengthy period.

To while away the long evening hours Lora and I had several musical soirées. Though she was never a laggard about practising, I kept her so hard at it she occasionally flung down the beater or mouth organ in exasperation. By the time Aunt Miriam returned I wanted my pet to have learned three more tunes: "Roses of Picardy", "Drink to Me Only with Thine Eyes", and "A Nightingale Sang in Berkeley Square", the first two to be played respectively on the mouth organ and xylophone, the last to be rendered vocally. It was while Lora and I were in the middle of one of these soirées that I noticed far off along the valley the flicker of a small fire, against which a figure was now and then silhouetted.

Early the following morning an old tinker came to the door and asked if I could spare him milk and bread in return for a job of work. This old man and his wife, who were both in their eighties, told me that after many years of roaming the Scottish countryside they had at last bought a cottage on the shores of Wester Ross and settled down to a seminomadic existence. But in spring they would set out on the road again and not return until weeks or months later. Like most tinkers these days, they earned their living not by mending pots and pans, as did their ancestors, but by working in the fields doing casual labour.

They camped in the valley for a week, helping me with the gardens and the livestock in return for food and milk, before moving southward.

WHEN I WENT TO FETCH Aunt Miriam I knew at once by the expression on her face—not to mention the raucous meows coming from a basket—that she was returning home with more fauna.

315

"I've brought them for you," she asserted, but I was not taken in by this.

The increasing din coming from the basket made me wonder whether it contained miniature tigers. In fact I was not far wrong, for my aunt had been presented while on her visit with a pair of wildcat kittens.

I believe there is no recorded instance of one ever having been tamed, even when reared on the bottle. Secretly I think Aunt Miriam felt that, given the chance, she might succeed where others had failed. But from the moment the kits were let out of the basket they were handled with leather gloves, and gloves it remained during their entire sojourn with us. These small beasts, which had only known their mother for a very short period, never came to accept their human owners in the slightest degree.

The wildcat differs quite considerably in appearance from the domestic tabby: the length of leg is longer, the tail shorter, blunted at the end and black-tipped; the skull is broader. It is easily the fiercest of our larger mammals. The kits were put in a cage over in the byre and during the day this was carried out and faced with a wire run. At first they were fed from a bottle and were then put on raw rabbit and hares' meat. No amount of handling or soft words counteracted their inborn ferocity. On picking up a kit to give it the bottle, one invariably got a full set of claws in the glove. Later on, whenever a dish of meat was placed in the run we would be greeted with snarls and looks of glaring hatred.

The more highly developed mammals have a strong "play" tendency and the wildcat is no exception. So we started to play with the kits, hoping that by this means they might become a little tamer. They did respond to this treatment, though not to us. Should I drag a piece of paper attached to a string in front of them they would run after it, but if I then bent down to stroke them their claws would come out and they would snarl and hiss.

WHEN THE CATS were three months old a friend of mine came to stay, bringing with her a ginger tabby named Susie. This cat was the gentlest of creatures and had led a placid existence as the family pet.

The two wildcats were put in separate runs and, with the owner's permission, Susie was placed for a while each day with the male. At first for her own safety she was left there in a cage, round which the male prowled and sniffed, sometimes giving vent to long-drawn-out, eerie yowls. His attitude gradually changed to indifference; he would walk about the run without giving the cage a glance or would stretch himself full-length on top and lick his paws. Then one day when we went to collect the cage we found Susie purring happily inside and the male purring noisily on top. The following day Susie was put into the run without the protection of the cage while we stood outside, leather-gloved, ready to go to her rescue should she be attacked. After watching each other a moment, the two began to walk slowly round the run in follow-my-leader style, uttering meanwhile hideous yowls. Unable to stand the noise any longer, we left them in full chorus and retired to the croft, though we remained ready to hurry back should sounds of a fight break out. When we did return the two were asleep, side by side. From then on Susie spent the greater part of the day with the male, who became very attached to her, moping during the periods she was removed from the run.

Her mistress left, having temporarily bequeathed Susie to us in the cause of natural science. We kept careful watch over our temporary guest and months later we sent her owners a wire which caused considerable speculation at the local post offices. The wire ran as follows: *Have we your permission to mate Susie with wild male?* It was answered in the affirmative.

Shortly after mating had taken place, she was collected and driven back to her home. During the latter part of her stay with us her behaviour had deteriorated; she was given to sudden fits of temper. Once, stooping to pick her up, I received a scratch all down my forearm.

We heard in due course that she had given birth to three kittens. They had the wildcat markings of black and grey stripes with black-tipped tails, but their underparts and chests were a light ginger. As in all cases of crossbreeding between the wild and tame varieties, the dispositions of the kits were those of the wildcat and they proved to be as untameable as our purebreds had been. When able to fend for themselves they were let loose in barren country to live according to their true natures.

Susie, the once exemplary pet, never returned to her former good behaviour. The reports we had of her from time to time stated that she seemed continually restless and that strangers to the house had to be warned not to touch her lest they get scratched. Then she took to absenting herself for a day or two, and eventually she left the house one day and did not come back.

WHEN THE FEMALE WILDCAT, which had been put in a separate run on Susie's arrival, began to show signs of poor condition and moping I begged Aunt Miriam not to turn her loose—as we had previously agreed to do if these symptoms occurred—but to try and restore her to her former health and fiery spirits. And my aunt gave a reluctant consent.

The first thing we did was to try putting her back with the male, but he attacked her ruthlessly every time, so we gave up making the attempt.

One evening I heard piteous mewing coming from her box and on lifting up the top found her lying on her side with her eyes closed. She turned her head and opened her eyes, looking straight into mine, and I saw in them nothing but pain and misery; all the old fire had gone out of them. Filled with contrition, I picked up the box and placed it by the open door of the run so that she could walk out and gain her freedom. The male cat by then was also in poor health, though his condition was not so serious as the other's. I opened the door of his run too and walked away. I did not see him go, but the next morning his cage was empty.

I was looking from a croft window, however, when the female left, and I saw her walk with extreme slowness from the box, her thick untidy fur fluffed out from her thin body by the wind, her head held down. She walked forward for several yards and then sank exhausted among some tufts of grass. I continued to look out of the window at frequent intervals to see whether she had moved, until the small grey form was erased by the deeper grey of dusk. Next morning when I went to search for her she was lying dead in the same spot. This experience confirmed my feeling that *for no purpose whatsoever should a bird or animal be caged except for the briefest period.*

Chapter Eleven

Over to the northwest of the croft lay a series of hills, covered with grass and scree. Beyond them lay a somewhat higher hill, the lower slopes of which were covered with coarse grass, this in turn giving place to heather. The heather continued to grow abundantly down the far side of the hill, which led onto a brief moor. Here were pools of bright green grass, rushing burns, silver birches and quite an extensive pine wood. I was particularly fond of this stretch of countryside and hardly a week went by during the summer months when I did not visit it. In late summer, when the purple heather was in flower, the contrast between these few acres and those surrounding them was even more noticeable, for the hills below would be bleached to a dull russet and on hot days the loose scree would burn through one's shoe leather like glowing coals. Nor did the boulders on their slopes offer adequate shade from the sun's beams. But in the pine wood the branches flung out great patches of shade, splashed with brilliant sunspots. On warm days the pungent reek of pine resin from the wood could be smelt for miles.

THERE IS SOMETHING exhilarating in being out when a gale is sweeping over the hills. And so I set out for the pine wood one day during our last winter when the snow was lying only on the tops of the higher hills. Walking against the wind, I tucked my chin into my collar and attempted to gain headway. For several miles the only trees in view were a few scattered birches which bowed and rose at the touch of the wind. Except for the boulders, everything appeared to be in motion; clouds, birches, even the hills which rolled away to the far horizon.

Going down a declivity, sheltered from the wind, I unwittingly interrupted a curious little performance given by an ermine. The grass, because of the nearby burn and the sheltered position, had retained its spring greenness. Against this bright green carpet sported a cream-coloured ermine with the usual black tail-tip. It was leaping and prancing

318

with abandon. When ermines are at this game it generally means that they are trying to decoy prey, keeping a puzzled bird or beast watching in uneasy astonishment as they perform acrobatics, flicking their lithe bodies into the air, leaping all the while nearer and nearer until they suddenly make a dash and seize the unwise onlooker.

In this case there appeared to be no other creature about. Perhaps the noise of the wind had excited him. I only managed to witness seconds of his performance before he became aware of my presence and sped down a rabbit hole.

One mammal which changes the colour of its coat during winter is the blue or mountain hare. It is a charming sight to see a hare in its white winter coat when the snow is lying on the ground, snug in a snow hollow, fur fluffed out, ears laid back. If something catches its attention its black-tipped ears will prick forwards and it may stand on its hind legs to get a better view.

One winter day of brilliant sunshine, with the snow lying deep and in perfect condition, I came across a pack of hares, gathered within a short distance of the croft. There must have been over fifty of them, most of whose coats had turned fully white. From the nonchalant attention they gave me it soon appeared that I was presumed safe company. A few hopped out of my way as I approached, others sat almost motionless, their black-tipped ears pricked, several were chasing fellow hares, while yet another would make a quick spring, as though testing its paces, and come to a sudden halt. I stood and watched this gathering of the mountain clans for many minutes. Then a signal seemed to pass among them and they sped away across the snowfields, their immensely strong hind legs thudding out a tattoo on the crisp snow.

I DO NOT KNOW whether sounds are in fact more audible at night or whether they simply seem so because of the deeper stillness. But it was during the night that an owl's notes would strike clearly against the background of silence and dark; from far off the bark of a fox would echo along the corries and be greeted with an answering bark from the other side of our hill. An otter's whistle down by the lochan would make me wonder as I lay in bed whether Hansel had returned to his former haunts.

On still winter nights when the ground was covered in deep drifts of snow and the air was sharp with frost, the sounds would be intensified still further. During my years at the croft the high, fierce cries of the stoats hunting at night never ceased to strike me as being particularly sinister. The stoat often hunts in a family party consisting of mother and offspring, or larger mixed packs of families and lone stoats banded together. Small though these creatures are, I nevertheless hope that I do not meet up with one of these larger packs when out in the countryside. An indomitable courage and ruthless ferocity are the two main characteristics of stoats, and they have been known to attack a human when hunting together.

Well do I remember a cosy winter evening on which we first heard the cries of a pack of these little hunters. We were sitting before the fire drinking Lamb's Wool. This beverage is made by roasting a cooking apple and whipping up the pulp in a glass of hot milk until it is frothy. Sugar and a dash of beer or white wine is then added to taste.

"Whatever's that noise?" Aunt Miriam asked, putting down her glass and going over to the window.

Her ears were sharper than mine and for a while I could hear nothing. Then I thought I detected a faint yelping as from a pack of miniature hounds after its quarry. When the yelps sounded as though they were passing the croft we opened the door and looked out. In spite of there being only a sliver of moon the stars and snow filled the atmosphere with sufficient light to see distant ranges of hills. A white object sped by, followed by a moving mass of tiny darting creatures. They, too, were white, and it was only after some seconds that we recognised them as stoats in full cry. I could understand how superstitious crofters in the old days often believed a pack of yelping stoats on the warpath to be no creatures of flesh and blood but a pack of demon dogs out to catch the souls of men. Next morning we found in the snow their tracks and the tracks of a hare, stains of whose blood and scraps of fur we found, as mute evidence that the stoats had enjoyed a good night's hunting.

Another winter's night, we heard above the noise of a gale the unmistakable cry of a storm petrel blown far inland. The cry pierced the lashing wind at intervals and seemed to come from ground level. Thinking the bird had probably met with some harm Aunt Miriam put on a mackintosh and, torch in hand, went out to search for it. By good fortune, she discovered the petrel in the lee of the byre. One of its wings was slightly damaged and so we kept it four days until it was able to take to the air again.

A very eerie cry to listen to at nights is that of the wildcat. The long-drawn-out meows have often interrupted my dreams. I think there must have been a rock near us which was much favoured by a particular cat because for nights in succession its cries would come from the same direction, not far off. Once a faint answering cry made me sit up in bed to listen more intently. And I felt during the long pause which followed that my cat was listening too, every nerve in its body tensed. Then it set the air vibrating again, with a throaty meow which this time ended with a peculiar waver as though begging the distant feline to answer. It did. And so it continued back and forth until just after five thirty, the cries of my cat meanwhile growing gradually fainter as it hurried towards the other. When both cries were coming from a distance, and then had faded away altogether, the sound of them persisted in my mind for the remainder of the night.

Chapter Twelve

Before Aunt Miriam left for the croft, and during the earlier period of our residence there, she had been asked a series of alarming questions guaranteed to put a more nervous person off such a project altogether. "What would you do if ... ?" they invariably began. "If one of you happened to develop an acute appendicitis, or toothache, or chopped a finger off with the axe?" Or "If the roof fell in during a snowstorm?" "If you happened to be snowbound and ran out of paraffin, or flour ... " or some other vital necessity. Quite frankly, I don't know what I should have done if Aunt Miriam had developed appendicitis during a snowstorm.

During our first winter we did in fact run out of various commodities and items of food. But it was no great hardship to retire to bed earlier than usual because paraffin for the lamps was running low, or to exist for a while without sugar. It was during the last winter that we experienced a more severe crisis.

Every autumn among the food stored for winter use was a large supply of sacks of biscuits for our various domestic animals. Biscuits apart, each species of our domestic animals had its own special dietary extras. A seal should get large quantities of oil, therefore we had to order and cart home tins of edible oil for Lora. Nuts had to be got in for the squirrels, as well as raisins for an occasional fillip to their appetites. Tins of dried milk had to be laid in for the otters—we could spare them little goat's milk—and this was mixed with a teaspoonful of oil and a cup of water and poured over the biscuits. But the otters, fortunately, hunted for a goodly portion of their food, as did Lora, otherwise feeding them would have been prohibitive.

It was towards the end of the winter season with snow lying deep round the croft, making a journey to the township out of the question, that I went into the byre one morning to find the two goats looking comatose. I put their condition down to the weather and thought no more about it. The following morning their stomachs were distended and it took more than a few prods to get them to stand on their feet. Then I saw that the tarpaulin covering the stores at the far end of the byre had been pulled out of position and that tins and packets were scattered in chaotic disorder. Only three bags of biscuits remained intact. The goats had managed to chew through the cloth coverings of the others and devour the contents. They had also trampled cardboard boxes containing dried fruit, peas and lentils, stored for human consumption. What remained of these was scattered over the floor in confusion.

A paraffin stove was kept in the byre and on it I melted down a bucket of compressed snow for the goats' and pony's drinking water. Having given it to them, I went to tell Aunt of the disaster. On returning to the scene of the crime Aunt's first action was to seize the bucket and place it out of reach of the goats. One of them had already drunk its fill, the other fortunately was only approaching the bucket for a drink when we entered. We salvaged what we could from the damaged packages, took out the two remaining bags of biscuits and firmly roped down the tarpaulin round the re-stacked stores.

Although Rodney's and Sara's share of this food was meagre indeed compared to Lora's—one tiny helping soused with milk, in a saucer, for the two of them—we decided that they must forgo it until we had obtained more bagfuls, and take pot luck, every available biscuit being reserved for Lora.

Next morning we heard a loud bellow of pain coming from the byre. The goat which had drunk its fill after the night's orgy was now paying the penalty with severe pains, the water having swollen the biscuits and increased the strain on its already distended stomach. It was led from the byre and, taking a chance, Aunt Miriam poured a strong emetic down its throat. The goat was violently sick and some of the pressure on its stomach was thereby removed. Later on came a large dose of castor oil. Although its greed was the means of increasing our labours sevenfold during the following days, I could not help feeling as I led the now pitiful-looking creature back into the byre that it had fully atoned for its orgy. Both goats were henceforth chained to their stalls each evening.

Luckily we still had a good supply of flour for our own consumption and we used it to bake four batches of plain biscuits each day. These were mixed with the remainder of the others for Lora's feeds. At the end of twelve days—when we were able to make the journey to the township again—we both felt we never wanted to bake again.

DURING THE BISCUIT EMERGENCY, Rodney and Sara had been living on scraps from the table, together with an additional ration of raisins. This change in their diet was much appreciated and the eventual return to plain white dog biscuits soaked in milk was not welcomed. Both had been models of good behaviour whenever a meal was in progress, never pestering the diners for leftovers. Now, owing to the fact that I started handing them down bits from my plate, they grew worse than a pair of badly trained dogs. The saucer of biscuits was left untouched and they applied their wits to getting some more tasty morsel of food, such as they had been enjoying over the last twelve days.

To ascend a pair of outstretched stockinged legs is no great feat for either squirrel or rat and if a morsel was refused, nothing daunted they would proceed to climb up my legs, onto my lap and thence onto an arm, and from this vantage point descend—if I was not quick enough to stop them—onto the plate. Until they were broken of this unfortunate habit, I had to remember to keep my skirt tucked up and my legs tucked in. When no scraps were forthcoming and no route to the plate negotiable they protested loudly with high-pitched squeaks and chirrups.

When Aunt went to live at the croft she had no idea how long she would stay there; if the life suited her she intended to stay on indefinitely; if not, she would go elsewhere. After seven years, having found contentment and adapted herself admirably to the life, she had no thought of leaving. For myself, aged seventeen, much as I loved the life I was having to face the prospect of leaving it, and to decide—as the majority of young people born to crofter parents do—how I was going to make a living; for it is a sad fact that except in a minority of cases it is impossible to live solely by crofting. My father, who had been living in India throughout these years, had sent Aunt Miriam an allowance for my upkeep. When I reached the age of seventeen he thought I should begin to pay my own way. I asked Aunt to let me stay at the croft until the autumn of that year, at which season I promised to join the ranks of the wage-earners. To this she agreed and my problem was shelved for a few months longer.

DURING THE SEVEN YEARS she had been with us Lora had slept each night in my room. Even if she did absent herself for a day, she always returned home to sleep. No dog could have been more faithful or devoted to her human companions than she was.

In the water I had trained her to follow the boat at command, swim ahead or beside it, or dive underneath without touching it. She would also dive for objects which I threw into the shallower parts of the lochan and bring them up again. When we were going for a picnic on the other side of the lochan she enjoyed carrying the plastic teacloth over, swimming on ahead while we, and sometimes Rodney, followed behind in the rowing boat. Both of these two mammals were keen picnickers, and when the picnic basket was carried ashore from the boat they would nibble and mouth at its straps until the lid was raised. Then Lora would set to work and start the unpacking, first unrolling and spreading out the cloth, then dropping a plastic cup by each of us. The packets of sandwiches and slices of cake—which were always well wrapped, let me add for the benefit of the squeamish—were placed on the spots indicated. Meanwhile Rodney would be waiting anxiously for these proceedings to end. An occasional stern "Sit!" was necessary if he showed signs of moving in the direction of the food. Before we started eating, titbits were handed out in the shape of cake crumbs, and a tin of sardines emptied onto a plate.

One day, that last spring, I crossed the lochan in the rowing boat and as it slid under the high projecting rock which we called the animals' diving board, Lora, who must have been resting there, plunged in after the boat, sending up a cascade of water. As I rowed onwards, she followed in my wake, swimming in circles round the boat, sometimes on her back. After mooring the vessel I bade her goodbye and set off with my basket in search

323

of wild hyacinths. She was sitting in shallow water, peering over the side of the boat. Her ladder was not fixed to it so she was not able to get in. When I turned round she had started to swim back across the lochan.

That was the last I saw of her. She did not return home in the evening and though we searched and called her name for many hours during the days which followed we received no answering bark nor found any clue as to why or how she had disappeared. The Frasers and Mr. McNairn kept a lookout for her, with no result. Enquiries in the district proved equally fruitless; there had been no strangers or sportsmen about, so far as was known, and nobody reported a seal venturing down a river which might have conceivably attracted her away with it. And so we never solved the mystery of her disappearance. With her going I lost the closest and most intelligent animal friend I have ever had.

Chapter Thirteen

For ten days after her disappearance we kept to the vicinity of the croft in case someone should come with news of her, or in case she herself should suddenly turn up. Then, as supplies of paraffin and food were running very low, we harnessed the pony to the trap and set off for the township.

Throughout the early spring we had worked hard in the gardens. The young vegetables were coming along well and we felt assured of a plentiful supply in the near future. These vegetables constituted, together with milk and bread, the mainstay of our diet.

When we got back that evening the wall round the croft garden was

broken down, and we saw to our dismay that literally every vegetable had been trampled down or uprooted. The pieces of wire netting with which most had been covered over had also been torn up and kicked aside. From the hoofprints in the soil we realised that a herd of deer had raided the croft in our absence.

Aunt Miriam, who was seldom given to fits of depression, found it hard to keep cheerful after this setback. Lora's going had affected her as much as it had me, and with this last bit of bad fortune her spirits became temporarily low. I urged her to go away for a while, and she agreed to go to stay with friends in faraway Berkshire.

"Don't bother to do anything to the garden until I get back," she said before leaving. "Then we'll set to work together."

I took her at her word and spent most of the daylight hours making trips in the canoe up various rivers. During the evenings as I sat in the parlour, alone except for Rodney and Sara, and watched the moths fly in through the open window and flutter round the lamps, the feeling grew in me that the time was fast approaching when we would both leave the croft.

I received a letter from Aunt in which she said that she was enjoying her stay very much and that she and another guest, a Canadian, had been for some long walks together. Then came a further letter asking if I would mind her staying on another fortnight. When she returned I received a shock, for she informed me somewhat diffidently that she and this Canadian she had met had decided to get married.

"But Aunt, you can't do that!" I remember saying in astonishment, instead of offering her my best wishes. Somehow it never occurred to me in those days that anyone over the age of thirty-five could seriously contemplate getting married; such is adolescence.

It was arranged that the wedding would take place in three months, by which time my father would have returned from India.

So we started to pack. The trap and pony were sold. The Frasers and Mr. McNairn were given a goat apiece.

"Well, the morning of your life is over now," said Mr. Fraser as I bade him goodbye, adding, "You will be wandering far in the coming years."

His prediction proved correct, for in the years which followed I wandered extensively through Britain and later typed and dishwashed my way up to Greenland, where I spent some time studying a seal colony. On my return to London I felt a compelling urge to escape from crowds and traffic, and wander once more among the Sutherland hills, taking a look at my old home. It had been untenanted since we left it. Soon after her marriage my aunt had gone abroad, taking Rodney and Sara with her.

I set off for Sutherland with my camping kit, as I wished to camp several days among the hills. In my heart, I felt doubtful about the wisdom of such a trip. Since leaving I had heard that Mr. McNairn had died and the Frasers had moved to a distant clachan, so there would be nobody to visit.

As I climbed the last hill and looked in the direction where the croft had stood I found it hard to credit what my eyes saw. All that remained of our former home was now in ruins and overgrown with nettles. In the five years since we had left it, the roof had fallen in, the glass panes had slipped from the windows and the walls were crumbling. Using my rucksack as a buffer, I pushed my way through the nettles and gazed into the room which had once been the parlour. Nettles had even sprung up between the broken stones. At one side of the room, just as we had left it, was a wooden chair, covered with mildew. Next I peered into my old room. There, disintegrated almost past recognition, was Lora's bamboo couch, and protruding from under it was a rusty toy trumpet.

The byre was in the same ruined condition. I sat down on a heap of stones, wishing I had never come. Who would have guessed, I wondered, that the stones on which I was sitting had once enclosed a trim garden?

I decided to retrace my footsteps straight away. The sight of the croft had depressed me too much to think of camping close by. But as I turned to go my eyes were held by the rolling hills and the dark waters of the lochan; these were the same, unchanged from the day I had first seen them. Then a small incident occurred which raised my spirits further. A thrush flew from the rowan tree and alighted on my shoulder. It was not Breac or any bird which had been a constant visitor to the croft, but it might have been one of Breac's offspring, or perhaps a victim of a winter gale which we had tended for a few days. It sat on my shoulder while I surveyed the familiar landscape, and then as I turned to go it flew off and perched on the ruined building that had once been home.

ROWENA FARRE

"SEAL GIRL MYSTERY," "THE LADY VANISHES," and "OH! ROWENA— WHERE ARE YOU WANDERING?" shouted the newspaper headlines when Rowena Farre created a literary mystery by disappearing immediately after the publication of her bestselling book, *Seal Morning*.

Rowena Farre was born in India, the daughter of a brigadier. When she was seven, her parents sent her back to Britain to be educated, and put her in the charge of her Aunt Miriam. Together they made their home first in Buckinghamshire, then in Kent, before moving to the croft in Sutherland.

After Rowena Farre left the croft she trained as a typist, but she loved the outdoors too much to tolerate the confinement of an office. She preferred to earn her living during the summer months as a fruit-picker and farm worker, travelling extensively throughout Britain. During World War II, she served as a WAAF officer.

Although she had been writing for her own pleasure since early childhood, *Seal Morning* was Rowena Farre's first published work, with the exception of a short article in a county magazine. The book was an immediate success, but the author vanished, appearing a month later to explain that she had been travelling with gipsies, and had not heard of all the publicity. After the publication in 1962 of her second book, *A Time from the World*, her publishers lost touch with her again, this time for five years. Then a reporter discovered that Rowena Farre's name was really Daphne Lois Macready, and that she had returned to England secretly from travels in Australia and India, where she had undertaken an ascetic regime of meditation. Many of those experiences are described in her autobiography, published in 1969 and called *This Beckoning Land*.

In 1979 this attractive, reclusive woman died at the age of fifty-seven, but her humour and sensitivity continue to give pleasure to the readers of *Seal Morning* and her other books.

REDCOAT

A CONDENSATION OF THE BOOK BY
Bernard Cornwell

ILLUSTRATED BY NEVILLE DEAR

The British Redcoats march into Philadelphia,
victorious over George Washington's rebel
army. Union Jacks wave in the streets and cries
of "God Save the King" ring out. There are
parties and balls and entertainments. And in the
splendour of high society, Redcoat and rebel
appear to have called a truce . . .

But while Sir William Howe and his Redcoat
officers dance the nights away, the rebels are
making secret preparations for revenge. Some
plot behind closed doors. Others, like the
beautiful Martha Crowl, mingle with the British
in order to pass information to the rebel forces
gathering outside the city.

The time of reckoning is at hand—for the
lilting music of the dance is soon to be drowned
by the beat of the drum, and rebels and
Redcoats alike must pay the price . . .

Chapter One

The Bloodybacks stole through warm darkness to the killing.

A hidden moon offered a wan glow which silhouetted the jagged spikes of pine tops on the western horizon. The eastern sky was studded with stars. The paths beneath the trees were dark, utter dark: a blackness in which long files of men cursed softly. The sun would rise to bring the steamy, breath-stealing heat of the full day; yet even now, in the night's small hours, there was a close, stifling warmth that made the men sweat beneath their thick woollen coats. Red coats. The men were soldiers: six companies of Redcoats who followed their leaders through a wooded defile towards a tavern, a crossroads, and the enemy.

A stream made its homely sound to the south, the wind rattled pine branches, while the night hordes of insects drowned whatever noise the nailed boots made on the dry and fallen needles.

A whispered order was passed down the files of men. They stopped and crouched. Private Sam Gilpin's hands were slick with sweat. His body prickled with the heat. A horse whinnied.

It had to be an enemy's horse, for the Redcoats had come on foot. The sound told Sam that the enemy must be very close, and despite the cloying warmth he shivered suddenly.

His musket would not fire. None of the soldiers' muskets would fire, for they had been ordered to unscrew the dog-heads and take out their flints. A musket without a flint could not spark the powder, so it could not fire a bullet, but nor could a careless man stumble in the dark and fire a shot which would warn the enemy.

"Follow!" Again the order was a whisper. Sam's company was led off the path into the blackness beneath the trees. Each man tried to walk silently, yet twigs snapped, dry pine needles crunched together, and once a brassbound musket butt crashed loud against a tree trunk.

The sound made the men freeze, but no warning shout came from the enemy lines. The file moved again and Sam saw the smear of a red glow to his left.

"Down!"

Sam stopped, crouched. The redness was the remnant of a campfire. There were other dying fires visible through the trees. The glowing embers revealed the shapes of dark buildings—Paoli's Tavern. Again a horse whinnied, but Sam could see no movement round the fires.

"Bayonets! Bayonets!" The order was a hoarse whisper.

Sam tugged his bayonet free of its scabbard, slotted it over his musket's muzzle and twisted it into place. The grease that kept the bayonet free of rust was sticky in his palm. All round him he could hear the scrape and click of the seventeen-inch blades being fixed. It seemed impossible for the enemy not to hear, but still there was no shout or musket flash.

There was fear in Sam, but also exhilaration. He feared letting his comrades down, he feared Captain Kelly's disappointment or Sergeant Scammell's scorn, he feared his own fear, yet he also had the fire of a young man's pride inside him. They were the red-coated Bloodybacks, the kings of the castle, cocks of the dungheap, soldiers of the King, and in a moment they would be unleashed like rough-pelted hounds to tear and savage the King's enemies.

Footsteps sounded to his right and Sam saw the tall shape of Sergeant Scammell pacing along the company's front. "Go for their bellies or throats. Don't tickle the bastards, kill them! You hear me?" Scammell's voice was a mere whisper, but still fearsome. Few men in the company liked Scammell, but even those who hated him were glad of his presence this night, for, in the confusion of battle, the sergeant displayed a chilling efficiency. The embers of the enemy's campfire reflected dull red on the steel of Scammell's bayonet.

Sam's twin brother was nervous. "You'll stay close, Sam?" Nate asked.

"I'll stay close." Sam offered reassurance, just as he always offered reassurance to Nate. On nights like this, back home in England, the brothers had sometimes crouched in the squire's coverts where, while Sam eagerly anticipated the sport, Nate would inevitably fret about mantraps and gamekeepers. Sam had always led, and Nate followed, but this night their prey was more deadly than the squire's deer.

Sam watched the enemy's dying fires. Perhaps in England the hearth of his parents' cottage was similarly fading as it waited for the morning's rousing. Captain Kelly had told Sam that the sun rose later in England than it did here, but Sam did not understand the concept, and so he imagined that it was at this very moment that his mother's cockerels would be ruffling themselves to wake the world and his father's dogs would be twitching in their sleep beside the kitchen fire.

"I wish they'd start," Nate muttered beside him.

The night sky's edge was touched with a hint of grey to pale the brightness of the eastern stars. It was the false dawn. The land was still black. The enemy horse whinnied again, and Sam licked dry lips and flirted with the fear of what was about to erupt in the night. Captain Kelly, his sabre drawn, stood at the edge of the trees, staring at the enemy. Kelly was tall, quiet, and liked by the men. Before they marched, he had said this was the enemy's rearguard, left to harass the British advance, and the Redcoats were to destroy the rearguard, not with bullets but with the seventeen-inch blades.

The order, when it came, was soft. "Go, go, go!" Somehow Sam had expected the blare of trumpets, the unfurling of great silk colours, the panoply of pride to drive a soldier on to death.

"Move!" Scammell was hissing at the men. The officers were out of the trees now, walking in the moonlight that seeped between the rifted clouds. Sam followed. To his left, beyond the track, he could see the lines of soldiers coming like ghosts from the trees.

The ground was rough grassland, tussocky and uneven. The men advanced in three ranks which were made ragged by the dark and by their eagerness to close on the sleeping enemy. Except that they might not be sleeping: Sam, in the leading rank, watched for the dim glow of a linstock that could touch fire to a cannon's charged barrel.

A dog caught the scent of strangers and barked. One of the humped shapes by a fire stirred and sat up. The steel-tipped lines advanced, their boots noisy in the grass.

The dog's barking became frantic, and the sound stung the advancing officers to throw stealth to the wind. "Charge! Charge!" The second word was drawn out like a banshee's howl of death.

And the men, unleashed, cheered. Their nerves, made tight by apprehension, threw them forward. No enemy cannon crashed fire and death. No muskets blazed from the dark. The enemy sentries slept. The Redcoats had achieved surprise.

The first of the enemy died in their sleep.

Others woke to see the bright surprise of blades above them, or scrambled out of their blankets, but too late. The British were surging on through the waking encampment, and their sound was a surly growl of effort punctured by the butcher's chop of steel in flesh.

His spirit soaring with the joy of battle, Sam ran to the skirmish's front, careless of where his brother might be. He saw two of the enemy running to a stand of muskets and he caught one, tripped him, kicked the man in the jaw, then stabbed the second in the back. The man screamed, then fell, dying, screaming, but his voice was drowned by other screams and by the triumphant shouts of the Redcoats.

Muskets sparked to Sam's left.

"Incline left!" Captain Kelly's voice was calm. "Form! Company will advance at the double! Steady, lads!"

Perhaps half the company obeyed, the rest were too busy with death.

"Charge!" Sam saw the huddle of enemy break. One man, perhaps an enemy officer, since he carried a sword, screamed defiance and made a lone attack upon the Redcoats. His sword cracked against a parrying musket barrel, then Sergeant Scammell's blade grated on the enemy's ribs, the man gasped, and two more blades thrust him down to ragged ruin. The rest of the enemy ran, disappearing into the forest.

The killing seemed to end as swiftly as it had begun. A moment of triumph and savagery, then the shouts of officers and sergeants brought the killers to discipline. Grinning Redcoats, strangers, were round Sam now. The light companies of six different regiments had marched to this attack, and nearly all had wet bayonets. Pickets were set, and a handful of prisoners found at the tavern were prodded into the field. All in shirts and trousers only, they stared in horror at the bloody bodies that lay twisted in the pale grass. One man vomited. Another wept. Others faced their captivity with bitter, proud faces.

Nate found Sam. Nate's bayonet was unblemished. "Like pigsticking," he said in a kind of wonderment.

Sam was resharpening the tip of his blade with a stone. "I'm surprised you didn't run with the bastards."

"Not on my own, I wouldn't." Nate surreptitiously pulled his bayonet through a sticky patch of bloodied mud to make it look as though he had fought as hard as his comrades.

He watched for Sergeant Scammell as he made the deception, but Nate's persecutor was far off. "But I am going to run," Nate said obstinately.

Sam nodded towards the dead. "You'll end up like them."

"We'll all end up like them," Nate said, staring at his sticky bayonet, "unless we run."

The heat was rising. The corpses would stink if they were not buried soon, but first they must be plundered. The enemy dead were being stripped of clothes, searched for coins, and their teeth wrenched out to be sold to the men who made false teeth for the wealthy.

"They'll catch you if you run." Sam spoke with harsh affection to his twin brother, then pointed his cleaned and sharpened bayonet towards Nate. "If you're lucky they'll flog you, but they'll probably kill you."

He drained the last of the tepid water from his canteen and tried to count the dead, but gave up at a hundred. No Redcoats had died. The flies buzzed. The first staff officers were arriving on horseback to see the night's carnage, which had turned the field round the tavern into a shambles. The laughter of the newcomers was loud.

One of the officers came from the tavern with a trophy. It was an enemy flag, one of the new standards that had appeared on the battlefields this summer. Wheeling his horse, he rode with the banner towards his companions. He passed close to Sam and as he did so the sun struck the enemy flag and made it luminous. Sam, momentarily shadowed by the great flag, flinched from the glow of its thick red and white stripes that carried a circle of white stars on a blue upper quadrant. Sam blinked as if to rid his eyes of the banner's gaudy dazzle.

The Bloodybacks had come in the night and taken steel to the sleeping Yankees. Now Sam Gilpin, Redcoat, lay on the grass and slept.

IN THE SMALL HOURS of the morning of Friday, 19 September 1777, Jonathon Becket woke, startled, when lights flamed suddenly in the streets. Trumpets sounded, children cried, and shutters were thrown back as people leaned out to shout for news.

The news proclaimed that British horsemen had been glimpsed crossing the Schuylkill River at the Upper Ferry. The Redcoats were coming, and Philadelphia panicked. The truth, which was lost in the night's alarm, was that a rebel cavalry patrol had been searching the river's western bank and had been mistaken for the invading British.

The Patriots fled in the darkness. Men who were delegates to the rebel Congress hastily threw their papers and valuables into travelling cases. The Liberty Bell was already gone from the State House, and the papers of the State Library and the money from the Public Loan Office had been sent to hiding in the western valleys of Pennsylvania. And now the Patriots, the architects of revolution who had fashioned the Declaration of Independence, followed.

Coaches were harnessed and brought to house doors. Furniture was wrestled down street steps and laden onto wagons. Women cast anxious glances westwards, fearing to see the red coats come into the flamelight. Philadelphia had been appointed the home of the revolution, the capital of the new American nation, and its godly citizens feared that the coming of the enemy would be like the descent of the Philistines on the Children of Israel.

There was terror and haste, yet not every citizen feared the Redcoats. There were Loyalists in Philadelphia, Tories who were eager for the restoration of British rule. Abel Becket, whose warehouses dominated the city's wharves, was one such Loyalist. A tall man with cropped black hair that was usually disguised by a neatly curled white wig, he was thin, and the passage of fifty years had made his face haggard. Abel Becket was a merchant, and his guile and wealth had allowed him to survive the thin years of rebel rule in the city. He had traded with rebels, for there had been no other choice in the last three years, but the trading had given him no pleasure and little profit.

Now, as Abel Becket happily made preparations for the British arrival, Jonathon Becket, hastily dressed in black, limped down the staircase.

"Uncle!" Jonathon dragged his right foot, swollen and twisted, behind him. "What's happening, sir?"

"The British are crossing the Schuylkill. The rebel scum are running, and God alone knows what mischief they'll fetch on us in their panic."

"Who's at the warehouse?" Jonathon asked.

"I've sent for Woollard."

"I'll go, sir."

"It isn't safe."

For answer, Jonathon pulled back his coat to reveal a pistol's butt protruding from his belt. For a second Abel Becket was torn between concern for the safety of his nephew and for the fate of the expensive goods stacked in the warehouse. Cupidity won, and he dragged back the bolts of the front door. "Go carefully."

"I will, sir." Jonathon hobbled into an astonishing scene. Like a hive brutally kicked apart, Market Street was in chaos. A wagon was being whipped away from the opposite pavement, loaded as high as the hay barges that came down the Delaware in late spring: beds and tables, chairs and cases, all were lashed crazily high on the wagon's bed, but, as Jonathon watched, a spinet jerked loose from the hastily knotted ropes and shattered in a splintering discord on the hard-rutted mud. A carriage, its four horses being flogged to speed, bumped a wheel over the broken fragments of inlay and ivory. No one seemed to notice in their desperate hurry to escape.

Jonathon plunged eastwards through the crowds. He heard snatches of hectic conversation. British cavalry were said to be plundering the Northern Liberties, Hessians had started burning Southwark, while the Redcoats were drowning those citizens who attempted to escape across the Delaware River. Jonathon, his face showing the pain of walking, struggled through the chaos.

He had been crippled at birth twenty years ago when, to his mother's screams, he had been dragged into the candlelight with a twisted right leg that would never grow to full strength. His mother had died, but Jonathon, to his father's astonishment, had lived. There were times when people even forgot that Jonathon was crippled. If he could not run, then he could ride a horse as well as any man. He might limp when he walked, but he stood tall and had his family's thin and handsome looks.

Now, amidst the panic, Jonathon was jostled by the crowd, but he pressed doggedly onwards. As he neared the city's wharves, he found himself part of a flood of refugees who sought the Delaware's ferries, which could take them across to the New Jersey shore. Turning into an alley that cut down to the wharves, he saw that his uncle's warehouses were still padlocked and inviolate, but that the big flat-bottomed shallop which was tied to Abel Becket's quay was swarming with refugees who hampered the crew's efforts to set sail.

"Stop!" Jonathon had worked four years on the waterfront and had a voice that could carry to a ship in the river's centre.

A man who was wrestling with the complicated spring which held the shallop against the river's current recognised the limping figure in the flickering torchlight. "He's a Becket. Ignore the bastard."

"I said stop!" Jonathon dragged the pistol from his belt, pointed it into the sky, and pulled the trigger. The men on the boat, appalled by the sudden noise, stared at him. Jonathon spoke calmly. "That shallop is to carry gunpowder to General Washington's army. The powder's been paid for. If you want to take the boat, then you take the powder with it. If you don't take the powder, then the British will capture it and use it against you." He pushed the pistol back into his belt. "Besides, that boat's unballasted, so you'll all drown unless you put some weight into her."

Jonathon's last words, or perhaps his voice which was so calmly confident, persuaded the refugees. Jonathon kept his authority over the reluctant men by giving quick and confident orders. Planks were rigged from quay to shallop, then the vast barrels were rolled out of the warehouse, across the quay, and lowered with a slung whip into the hold. Each barrel held four hundred pounds of best gunpowder, all of it captured from a British merchantman taken the previous autumn by a privateer from Chesapeake Bay. Jonathon had bought the powder, then resold it at a fair profit to the rebel army. It was primarily to rescue the precious cargo and keep it from the British that Jonathon had come out into the hectic night.

As the barrels rumbled over the stones, a huge hulk of a man with shoulders humped like a plough-ox lumbered down the quay and demanded to know who had authorised the loading.

"I did."

Ezra Woollard's anger was checked as he saw his master's nephew limp into the light. He scowled. "Why give the bloody stuff away?"

"The Congress have paid for it, and the Congress shall have it." Jonathon was tall, but he seemed dwarfed by the massive Woollard, Abel Becket's wharfmaster and foreman. Like Woollard, Jonathon worked for Abel Becket, but in a few months he would enter into his inheritance and become a part owner of the Becket business. Until then Ezra Woollard treated Jonathon with a careful mixture of contempt and respect which made clear the foreman's resentment that, in time, this crippled young man would become his master.

"Or would you be sending the powder away," Woollard asked maliciously, "because your sympathies have been turned by a woman?"

Jonathon did not rise to the taunt. As he watched, the heavy shallop warped into the stream and, its sails unleashed, caught the dawn wind to carry its burden northwards.

Woollard was gone. Jonathon locked the warehouse, then turned his back on the water. The streets were quieter now. The Patriots had fled, and the Loyalists, sensing that the British army was not yet come, explored the dawn-lit city to see who had stayed and who had gone. The Tories had always outnumbered the Whigs in Philadelphia, and Jonathon realised that his city would welcome the British occupation.

He limped to the corner of Market Street and Fourth Street, where he climbed the steps of a tall stone house.

The shutters were open, indicating that the household was awake, so Jonathon hammered on the door. He yawned, then glanced westwards to where the city's streets faded into the countryside. No red coats moved there. The only sounds in the city now were the crowing of cocks and the lowing of cows waiting to be milked. There had been a time when dawn in Philadelphia had been a cheerful cacophony of church bells, but the rebels had taken all the bells to be melted down for cannons.

The door opened as he knocked on it again. "My God, you're early!" Martha Crowl grimaced at the bright sunlight. "Do come in, dear brother."

Jonathon stumped behind Martha to her upstairs parlour. "I half expected you to have left."

"And leave all these pretty things to be mauled by a Redcoat?" Martha gestured about her parlour which was, indeed, filled with pretty things. Martha's lawyer husband had bought paintings from Europe, and furniture from the finest cabinet makers in London. He had been a man of taste and refinement, and, Martha liked to say, a man considerate enough to die early so that she, at twenty-six, was already a widow of fortune. Crowl had also, in addition to his wealth, left Martha with a daughter, who was now six years old.

"Lydia didn't wake up," Martha said. "God knows why. Would you like some tea?"

"Please."

Martha crossed to the bell pull. She was as tall as her younger brother, and had the same narrow face, which some thought too bony to be accounted beautiful, but she compensated for that with a natural elegance. Her hair, like Jonathon's, was jet black, but this morning it was hidden beneath a mobcap. She turned back to her brother. "You look quite filthy."

"I've been loading eighty barrels of the finest cylinder charcoal powder, saving it from the British."

338

"Who never arrived," Martha said drily. "Perhaps they won't come at all now?"

"Not if General Washington can stop them."

"He didn't last week, did he?" The British, advancing cautiously from their ships in Chesapeake Bay, had been met by the rebel army at Brandywine Creek, where General Washington had been outflanked and defeated. It was the old story. Only at Trenton, during the previous winter, had Washington won a battle.

Though their uncle was a Tory and a Royalist, Martha and Jonathon had chosen the rebel allegiance. Now it seemed that their allegiance was to be tested because, for the first time since the fighting had begun, the British were coming to Philadelphia.

Martha surreptitiously watched Jonathon massage his right thigh. "Hurting?"

"I walked further than usual."

"Poor Jonathon." Only Martha could offer him pity, for, since his birth, she had been his closest companion. Marriage had taken her from his home, then their father had died and Jonathon had become a ward of their uncle, but the closeness of brother and sister had never faltered.

The tea came. Jonathon was sitting on the window seat, staring ruefully at the shingled and tiled rooftops. "I just can't bear to think of them coming here! Strutting up our streets! Flaunting themselves in our houses! Mocking our people!"

"If they come at all." Martha did not sound hopeful, but it was a time for Patriots to clutch at straws. "I heard they might go south, to Baltimore."

Jonathon seemed not to hear. "I can't stay and see them gloat. So I'm leaving."

Martha went very still. "Leaving?"

"I've been useful so far." Jonathon's words were suddenly febrile. "I'm a good trader! I've served the Congress well! I've supplied the army with hides, pig iron, flints and powder, but the British are coming! Now I will have to take British gold and sell to British traders, and I can't do it! I won't do it!"

"So what *will* you do?"

"I can ride!" Jonathon slapped his right leg. "And all a cavalryman needs to do is ride and fight. I'm going to volunteer."

"Oh, you can ride!" Martha said scathingly. "But suppose the horse gets shot? What will you do? Hop away from the enemy?"

Jonathon laughed. "If I have to, yes."

"Good God, Jonathon! You're a fool!" She stood up and walked away from him, then turned. "Or is this Caroline's doing?" Jonathon offered no answer and Martha, irritated by his calm, snapped at her brother, "You can't marry her!"

Jonathon smiled. "I haven't asked her to marry me."

Martha felt her irritation growing. "You know Ezra Woollard wanted to marry her?"

"And she said no."

"She's a tradesgirl! She sells me vegetables!"

"And I'm a tradesman," Jonathon laughed. "But the answer to your original question, dear sister, is that Caroline has tried to dissuade me from leaving the city. She thinks like you."

"That's something in her favour," Martha said acidly. "My God, haven't you done enough? I won't let you do it." She walked back to the window seat. "If you go away to fight, you'll lose your inheritance, and all our father's work will be for nothing! Ezra Woollard will take the business. Abel likes him! And Uncle Abel hasn't a son to leave anything to! Is that what you want?"

"I think I want what you want, liberty."

"God help us!" Martha stared into her brother's dark and amused eyes, then sat down beside him. "Suppose I offer you another and even better way of fighting against the British?"

"Tell me."

Martha sought the right words. "I'm staying in the city because it's my home, and it's Lydia's home, and I can't bear to think of us being harried about the countryside by a pack of Redcoats. So I'll endure them, but I'll fight them! I'll entertain them, Jonathon, I'll give them wine and music, and I'll listen to their jests, and all the time I'll be listening. You can do that! If you trade with the British you'll become intimate with them. They'll trust you. They'll tell you things. And you'll see things on the wharves! What troops arrive and how many. Those are the things we have to tell our army, and it's a far more useful task than pulling a trigger!"

"Maybe."

"Not maybe! Of course it is!" Martha sought for another reason to make Jonathon stay and, in her desperation, used an argument that would fly in the face of all she wanted for her brother. "And Caroline will stay. You'll be close to her! So will you wait? That's all I ask! Just wait!"

"So that you can dissuade me?"

"So that I can persuade you that by staying you can do more damage to the enemy than by going, that's why!"

"I'll wait," Jonathon said. "I wasn't planning to leave immediately, so you've time to harass me."

"It's not harassment." Martha closed her eyes. "I've lost my mother, father and husband. Am I now to lose you?"

"God's already played his joke on me," Jonathon said deprecatingly, "and I doubt he plans worse. I think," he added calmly, "that I'd like another cup of tea." Thus Philadelphia, fairest of cities on the American coast, waited for the beat of foreign drums. The Redcoats were coming.

Chapter Two

"'*Talion!*'" The sergeant major's voice could be heard three fields away. "'*Shun!*'"

Seven hundred boots thumped onto the dry pastureland. Ten companies were on parade, formed into three sides of a square. Sergeants, canes ready, prowled. The sun sparkled from belt buckles and musket fittings.

The sky was cloudless and an oppressive, humid heat itched beneath the men's thick red woollen coats. Sweat glistened on their faces.

Facing the paraded battalion, where the fourth side of the square should have been, was a tall tripod made of split rails. A soldier, stripped to his dirty breeches, was lashed by wrists and ankles to the newly split wood. No leather pad covered the man's kidneys, a sure sign that his officers wanted him to die.

Two men watched from a hundred yards away. They were not in the battalion on punishment parade, and thus were free to express opinions that could have doomed them to the same fate as the prisoner.

"What he did wrong," Private Nathaniel Gilpin said, "was getting caught."

"What he did wrong," Sam Gilpin corrected his twin brother, "was to run. Asking for trouble, running." The man was a deserter, recaptured. To desert the army was the unforgivable sin, and the sin most savagely punished.

Like the man pinioned to the tripod, Sam was stripped to the waist, but Sam faced no punishment. Instead, he rolled up his breeches, waded into the small stream and, whistling as he worked, began to scrub down Captain Kelly's mare, Cleo. The horse stood quietly. It was not Sam's job to look after her, but all the battalion officers knew that Sam Gilpin did a better job than their own servants and so were happy to pay him a shilling or so to groom and doctor their beasts. He had always been good with animals.

His brother Nate seemed obsessed by the flogging. The drums sounded across the field as the two soldiers with the whips whirled the lashes twice about their heads before bringing the thongs slashing down onto the victim's back. Nate flinched with each stroke. "Must bloody hurt."

"Of course it bloody hurts! It's meant to, isn't it?" Sam ignored the flogging. He was happy working with horses: a reminder of the world he had left behind when he took the red coat three years before. He was twenty years old now, tall, with a cheerful, lively face. His hair, naturally golden, was now whitened by flour paste and drawn back into a stiff queue. "Don't watch!" He was brushing the dust from the horse's flanks, seeing how the shine of the coat was growing back. He touched the long

341

scar on the mare's haunch. A rebel bullet had gouged her pelt at Brandywine Creek, but Sam had made a poultice of old bread and cobwebs which had worked its usual miracle. The wound was healing well. He stroked the mare's nose. "Tough old thing, aren't you, Cleo? Ain't a Yankee who can kill you, eh?"

"Poor bastard." Nate was watching the blood stream down the victim's white breeches. The man jerked and twisted in his bonds as the alternating lashes landed.

"Don't watch!" But just as Sam said it, the victim spat the leather wedge from his mouth and gave a wavering scream that pricked the mare's ears back and made Sam turn despite his distaste. "He shouldn't have run," he repeated.

"I'll do it properly," Nate grinned. He was darker than Sam, but they shared the same mischievous face. Tall, country-bred boys, they had been the recruiting sergeant's dream; only now Nate had a dream of his own. He wanted to desert. He wanted to run because he was certain that, somewhere beyond this humid coastal plain, there was an American paradise where crops grew without effort, where the apple trees were so heavy with fruit that boughs broke under the succulent weight, and where, most important of all, Nate could be alone with Maggie. There was no hunger in Nate's American paradise, no touching the forelock to the squire, and no red coats. No army.

"They'll catch you." Sam did not believe in Nate's paradise. "And they'll flog you till your ribs are bare. Don't be a bloody idiot, Nate." Sam's affection for his brother made his voice angry. He turned away and untangled the mare's mane. He remembered the pleasure he used to take in grooming the great plough-horses on high days back home.

Three heifers, thin and mournful, were driven to the stream's edge thirty yards away. Behind the animals and their butchers came a straggle of the battalion's wives and children. Muskets were cocked, aimed, and three shots sounded flat and harsh in the humid air. The three heifers shuddered and crumpled heavily onto the grass. The women, their own knives drawn, crept close like wild animals to snatch for flesh.

"Beef tonight." Nate forgot the flogging for a moment. "Be a change from bloody pork. Maggie's there. She's seen me."

"For God's sake, Nate, leave her alone!" Sam led the horse a few yards upstream, to take his brother away from the girl's gaze, but a fallen willow trunk barred escape in that direction. The flogging went on, mercifully silent again. The man had been sentenced to one thousand lashes of the six-thonged cat. A group of officers, their uniforms bright in the evening sunlight, checked their horses to watch the deserter's agony.

Sam heard a telltale splashing in the water just beyond the patient mare.

"Nate!" Maggie smiled in nervous greeting. Her skirts trailed in the water which, reflecting the late afternoon sun, made ripples of light on her thin, sun-browned face. Nate embraced her. The girl looked over Nate's shoulder at Sam. "Hello, Sam."

"Mrs. Scammell." Sam acknowledged her presence very formally.

"I got you this." Maggie had a bloody scrap of oxtail that she offered to Sam. It was Maggie who had put the idea of desertion into Nate's head, and Maggie who knew that Nate would not run without his brother. Maggie was forever trying to persuade Sam to join them, but Sam was not unhappy in the army. He had discovered he could fight as well as the next man, he liked the horses, and he reckoned he could avoid the punishments.

He refused the oxtail. "Give it to your husband, Maggie."

"I never church-married him!" She was suddenly vehement.

"Don't need to, do you?" Sam considered it his job to look after Nate. "Now go away, Maggie! You want to have Nate flogged? Look, girl!" Sam pointed to the tripod. "It ain't pretty, is it?"

But Maggie would not look at the blood-soaked man. She drew Nate into the shelter of the mare's flank where they were hidden from the battalion's bivouac in the meadow. Flies buzzed at Sam's sweat-soaked chest and face as the lovers twined sad arms and stared at him, as if capable strong Sam was the person who could answer their dreams and take them away from the army.

Sam could understand Nate's obsession. Most of the women who followed the battalion were drudges, but Maggie was somehow different. Her brown hair was greasy and lank, but it framed a wistful, appealing face that made men want to protect her. She looked, Sam thought, ever on the point of tears, but also as if a single kind touch or loving word would light up her face with happiness.

Which happiness Sam wished for Maggie, but in New York she had chosen Sergeant Scammell, and the sergeant was a jealous man. "Why don't you wait for him to die in battle?" Sam had asked her. "Then you could marry Nate legal!"

"I want to go home," Maggie would say.

Her home was in Connecticut. It was of Connecticut that Maggie spoke when she filled Nate's head with her dreams of paradise. Maggie had run from that paradise once and gone to New York, where she had become a shilling whore in the Holy Town where the brothels did their business. Now she had fallen for Nate and wanted to go home. "They'll give you fifty acres each," she pleaded. "Fifty acres, two sows and a hog. They promised it!"

"Promises are easy," Sam said. The rebels had indeed promised the land and the hogs to any man who ran from the British army, but Sam doubted if the land would be worth a thimble of spit, and reckoned the hogs would be fevered, if they existed at all. So Sam would not run with them. "But if you do run"—he leaned against the mare's flank—"then do it proper! You can't muck about in a red coat, Nate. One side or other will have you.

You need proper clothes, you need some money, you need to know where you're going. You have to have somewhere to hide the first two days, till the cavalry's gone. Have you thought of any of that? Have you?" Sam dipped his brush in the water to scrub at the mare's pelt.

"Oh, that's grand." And onto the trunk of the fallen tree stepped Sergeant Michael Scammell, his face shadowed by the peak of his silver-fronted tricorn hat. He was a big man, strong-chested and flat-bellied, a handsome man, too, with a kind of power in his face and voice that cowed other men. "Kiss the girls and make them cry, is that it, Nate?" The sergeant jumped into the stream and walked towards the lovers.

Maggie raised the oxtail in a pathetic attempt to placate him. "I got this for you."

"Shut your face!" Scammell whipped at the scrap of meat with his metal-topped cane, sending it spinning into the long grass beside the stream. He brought the cane whistling back, slicing it hard over his wife's cheek. "Now, piss off, Maggie! And wait for me. Move!"

Scammell watched her go, then turned back to face Nate. "You want to do something about that, Private Gilpin?" The cane flicked out again, scoring down Nate's jawbone. "If I smell you on her, Nate Gilpin, I'll cut your liver out and push it down your bloody throat. You understand me?"

"We was only talking."

"Only talking!" Scammell moved with a sudden vicious speed to hook Nate's ankles with his right boot and elbow him down into the stream. He put his cane beside Nate's face, turning it. "See that?" A body, soaked in blood and with tatters of skin hanging from its spine, was being carried away from the flogging tripod. The man had died beneath the lash. "You see what happens, Nate Gilpin, when you aggravate your betters?"

"Yes, Sergeant." Nate stared up into Scammell's tough, knowing eyes.

"I'll have you on a bloody tripod and I'll flog you myself," Scammell hissed, "if you so much as look at my bloody woman again. You hear me?"

"Yes, Sergeant."

"The girls like you, don't they? Handsome Nate!" Scammell's face suddenly twisted and he slashed with the cane again, opening cuts on Nate's cheek and forehead. Then he stepped back. "Get up and piss off."

Nate scrambled out of the stream and Sergeant Scammell watched him go, then sat on a branch of the fallen willow. He wiped a smear of blood from the cane's tip. "Are they planning to run, Sam?"

"Not if I can help it, Sarge."

"That's not what I bloody asked, is it?"

Sam looked at Scammell. Other men hated this tall, confident sergeant, but Sam was not so bothered. He recognised Scammell's virtues which, though harsh, kept the company safe in battle, and, by treating the big sergeant with a fearless honesty, Sam had found he was treated fairly in return. "They're not going to run, Sarge."

344

Sam had hated watching Scammell cut his brother's face, but to have offered brotherly assistance would have been to invite a flogging on a charge of striking a superior officer. The knack in the army was caution, and Sam reckoned he had that knack pretty well mastered.

Scammell opened his pouch and took out a tuft of red wool. "For you."

Sam took it. The tuft was about three inches long, tightly woven, and dyed a brilliant red. "What is it?"

"Put it on your hat. We're all going to wear them, Sam." Scammell laughed. "Remember the other night, when we struck those bloody Yankees? The bastards are whining now, aren't they? Saying we was unfair. We should have woken them up before we killed them. So the lily-white bastards have said they'll take revenge and we're going to show them who to aim for, Sam. Wear it to show them who did the damage. The bastards will think twice when they see the red hackle on our hats!"

"I reckon they will." Sam was oddly pleased, reckoning that the red badge was a mark of honour. "I'll sew it on tonight, Sarge."

Scammell still sat on the willow branch. "I watched you the other night, Sam. You were good."

"Yankees were asleep," Sam said in a modest disclaimer of the praise, yet the sergeant's approval was pleasing.

"You're a good lad, Sam, so don't spoil it." Scammell scooped a handful of water to his mouth, then stood up. "If Romeo and Juliet piss off, Sam, I might reckon it was your fault for not keeping an eye on your brother. You understand me?" He climbed onto the bank. "We're Bloodybacks, Sam, and we stay Bloodybacks till we're wounded, or dead. There's no way out, none." Scammell picked up the oxtail from the grass. "Tell your brother that." He nodded, then strode towards the turf bivouacs.

Sam brushed the mare's tail a last time, then flopped into the stream to cool himself. Fires sent the smell of cooking into the sky. He found himself looking forward to the coming meal, and to the small laughter of comrades. He knew Nate's foolishness could endanger that small happiness.

Because, for a Redcoat, there was no paradise: only the army, the smoke of battle, and the pride of a red hackle that proclaimed a man's expertise in the slaughter. Sam had taken the King's Shilling, and in return he had promised his life. Sam would be a Redcoat till death, and be bloody proud of it too.

THE RIDGES FADED into a far distance, until, at the western horizon, they melted into the shimmer of pale sky. In the valleys between the ridges there were farms, roads, even small towns, yet from this vantage point the landscape seemed virgin. "Like Britain," Sir William said, "when the Romans came."

"Not the happiest simile, perhaps?" Lord Robert Massedene ventured. "You remember they left, sir."

"So they did." Sir William spoke absently. To the southwest there was a smudge of smoke in the cloudless sky, but the smoke was too distant for any of the horsemen to tell what burned.

The little group of horsemen were on a bare hill. Below them, curling about the hill's base, an earthen road was stirred into a choking dust by marching men, as battalion after battalion followed their mounted officers towards the day's bivouac. Guns, their bright barrels dimmed by the dust, spewed up yet more dust that settled on the engineers' high wagons. The army's women and children staggered along the road's verges.

Major General Sir William Howe, Commander-in-Chief of His Majesty's Army in North America, was a burly man, heavy in his saddle, with a dark, coarse face which went ill with the gaudy lace and shining braid of his senior rank. The face suggested a man of little thought and choleric temper, but in truth he was a lazy, placid and most genial man, known as Goodnatured Billy to his friends and aides. He now turned and gazed eastwards at the gentle hills and deep woods that stretched to a far river plain made faint by the haze of heat.

"A remarkable landscape," he said happily. He supposed the bright gleam to be the Delaware River. "Shouldn't we be able to see Philadelphia from here?"

"The city's to the right, sir." Lord Robert Massedene, twenty-two and an aide to Sir William, was short and stocky, with a round boyish face that bore a cheerful and indomitable grin. He pointed to where, in the hazy distance, Philadelphia was hidden by a swell of wooded ground. Sir William stared into the shimmering landscape. "Music," he said suddenly. "Music! We must have music in the city. I want to see people happy. It must be aglow in dark times, a winter of joyfulness." Sir William was a distant cousin of the King, yet he hated the royal policy and had, when the rebellion began, sworn never to fight against the colonists he so admired. Impecunity had changed his mind, for he needed the commander-in-chief's salary to pay his many debts, yet he prized his appointment as Peace Commissioner even above that of commander-in-chief. He yearned for peace and believed the prize would come with Philadelphia. "We shall seduce them with success, and dazzle them with benignity."

Lord Robert smiled. "But there won't be any joy in the city, sir, till we've taken the river forts."

"We'll take them." Sir William dismissed the problem of clearing away the rebel forts that barred Philadelphia from the sea, and which would stop the British ships bringing supplies into the city. "The Rangers left this morning, John?"

"Yes, sir." The newcomer, Captain John Andre, aide-de-camp to

General Grey, confirmed that the Rangers had indeed ridden into the endlessly ridged landscape that shimmered in the heat.

"I suppose watching won't help." Sir William swung himself from his saddle, then groaned as a stab of pain pierced his spine. Sir William's father had suffered dreadfully from a painful back, and Sir William feared the same affliction, but this twinge happily passed swiftly. "You can eat with us, John?"

"That's why I hurried, sir. Your table puts General Grey's to shame."

"I'm serving mere commons today, John, but you're most welcome!" Sir William liked Andre, and would dearly have liked to make the young man into one of his own aides, but he dared not poach from one of his generals. That was irritating, for Sir William needed another aide now that the army was strung along the winding Pennsylvanian roads, rather than crammed into its New York garrison where messages could be quickly acknowledged.

The soldiers slogged along the road while, above them, servants fetched food and wine to the hilltop for Sir William and his military family. Besides John Andre there were Lord Robert, Major Zeigler, interpreter for Sir William's Hessian regiments, and his private secretary. Hamlet, Sir William's dog, was pampered by all of them, fed the choicest meat and tempted with water flavoured with wine. The horses cropped at the hill's thin grass and the servants waited out of earshot. It was a gentle scene, only lacking ladies to give it domestic charm, yet it was spoilt for Sir William by the worries that constantly made him search the western view.

Sir William's army, ever manoeuvring itself closer to Philadelphia, was fast exhausting its stocks of musket cartridges. It was not battle which had depleted the men's cartouches, but fear. Each night, marooned in the vastness of the American wilderness, the pickets became nervous. They fired at phantoms, and in minutes whole battalions were woken, seized their muskets and joined the fusillade. Orders and threats had failed to stem the waste.

It was a waste of fearful cost. Each paper-wrapped cartridge had to be brought from Britain to New York, and thence in smaller ships to Chesapeake Bay, from where it was dragged in wagons over the ragged roads. Cartridges were like gold, yet each night the infantry hammered the empty darkness as though they possessed an inexhaustible supply. Sir William's only hope now was the arrival of a convoy of wagons loaded with precious ammunition.

The convoy was late.

Somewhere in the dark trees, somewhere in the mysterious landscape, the convoy was lost. The Queen's Rangers, tough Loyalist horsemen who were born to this empty land, had gone to search for it.

Thomas Evans, Sir William's principal servant, climbed to the hilltop. "We ought to be going, Sir William."

"You're concerned for my safety, Tom?" Sir William twisted, causing another spasm of pain in his back, to look down the hill's eastern flank. The army's rearguard was marching past. The army was safe enough wherever it stood, but once it had vacated ground, the rebels mysteriously flowed back to occupy it. "You can clear the plates, Tom, but we're going to wait for a few moments before we leave." Sir William wanted to see the heavy wagons, swollen with cartridges beneath the roped tarpaulins, lumber into view. No officer knew better what disaster threatened if the wagons did not arrive.

He stared fixedly to where the road disappeared into the deep shadow of trees.

And where, quite suddenly, a green-coated horseman appeared. He was a Ranger! More green-coated horsemen appeared, all Americans who fought for their king, and behind them came the wagons which the Rangers had sought. Sir William's face cleared. "God's still an Englishman, eh?"

Then the elation drained from the watching horsemen. God might be an Englishman, but He had sent only three wagons. The tarpaulin of the third was scorched, while all three were guarded by Hessian troops who walked like men who had struggled through the valley of the shadow. This was not the convoy, but rather the remnants of the convoy.

A red-coated officer walked his grey horse with the Hessian infantry. He stared up the hill, saw the bright uniforms of the staff officers and, with a weariness that was visible from the summit, climbed into his saddle. He spurred his horse up the hill.

The approaching officer proved to be a lieutenant, his handsome face dirty with sweat and powder stains. When he took off his hat to salute Sir William he revealed fair hair matted to his skull. His red coat, which had the facings and turnbacks of an unfashionable infantry regiment, was stained with blood and scorched by fire.

"Lieutenant Vane, sir," he reported to Sir William.

Sir William's usual affability had faded at the sight of the shrunken convoy. "Are you here to tell me, Lieutenant Vane, that there are only three wagons?"

"Yes, sir."

Sir William rarely showed temper, but in the face of Vane's calm words that temper threatened. "What did you do with the rest?"

Vane stiffened. "I did nothing, sir. The convoy was not my responsibility. Fifty wagons left the Head of Elk, sir, but they were ambushed ten miles out. The rebels drew the escort to the north of the road, then sent horsemen from the south." Vane's voice was bitter. "They hamstrung the draught animals and burned the wagons, sir."

Sir William instinctively glanced towards the smudge of smoke on the horizon, assailed by thoughts of the crisis he had feared.

"There weren't many rebels, but one burning wagon set fire to another, and we could only save three."

"We?" Howe looked back to the lieutenant.

"My servant and I, sir." Vane gestured towards a Redcoat who waited at the foot of the slope. "We were returning to the army, sir, and were ordered to march with the escort."

"Then where's the escort commander?" Sir William asked.

"Major Woodward deemed it wiser to return to Chesapeake Bay, sir."

"He . . ." Sir William paused. "Go on, Vane."

Vane seemed embarrassed. "I believed the army's need to be extreme, sir, so thought it best to bring the three wagons. The Hessian company volunteered to make the journey with me." Vane straightened in his saddle. "I'd like to commend their bravery to you, sir."

A lieutenant had presumably defied a major, then brought his tiny force through the dark woods and past the small farmsteads where the men with their deadly rifles lived. Usually a full battalion was needed to escort any convoy through such terrain.

Now, with sweat running down his face and making rivulets through the dust and powder stains, Vane waited as though he expected a reprimand. "I'm sorry it was only three, sir."

"It would have been none without you!" Sir William said warmly.

"Vane." Lord Robert said the name musingly. "There are Vanes in Northamptonshire, are there not?"

"I wouldn't know. My family was in trade." Vane made the embarrassing admission with a touch of defiance.

"Was?" Sir William asked gently.

"My father died, sir. I used my inheritance to buy a commission."

It was evidently not a very successful investment, for Vane was already in his middle twenties, when a richer man might expect to be a captain at the very least. Clearly Vane could not afford to buy his next promotion, nor could an unconnected tradesman's son expect the patronage that a nobleman's relative might enjoy. Vane was an ordinary officer from an ordinary regiment facing the ordinary tedium of a soldier's career. Except that, in these last two days, Vane had proved himself as brave as any man in the army.

"How long have you been in America?" Sir William turned his horse and, to the aides' relief, at last led his party off the hilltop.

Vane followed Sir William. "Since December, sir."

Sir William beckoned Vane to ride on his right flank. "You were at Brandywine, then?"

"Indeed, sir." Vane's voice sounded warm at the memory of that recent battle in which the rebels had been pushed out of the path of the British advance.

Sir William smiled. "You enjoy soldiering?"

"Indeed, sir."

"I'm glad you chose it instead of trade, Lieutenant! 'Pon my word I'm glad! Three wagons are better than none, eh?" Sir William, reminded of his problems, fell silent until the horsemen reached the road and could spur after the three wagons. Vane's servant, carrying a musket, trudged in the dust. Sir William smiled at Vane. "Your man can meet you at headquarters? After supper?"

"Indeed, sir." Vane was too tired to show astonishment at being invited to eat with the commander-in-chief. He gave instructions to his servant, then caught up with Sir William, who was wondering aloud how he was to fight without ammunition. "I've threatened to flog any man who fires without orders," Sir William complained, "but it doesn't work! Flogging rarely does work." He turned in his saddle to Vane. "How would you stop the pickets blazing away my ammunition, Lieutenant?"

"I'd make the battalion officers pay for every wasted cartridge out of their own pockets, sir."

"Good God!" Sir William curbed his horse in his enthusiasm. "It's a splendid notion! Touch an officer's pocket and you harness his obedience, isn't that so, Robert?"

Lord Robert agreed it was so.

"My God, Vane! I have all these clever aides and not one of them thought of . . ." Sir William's voice faded away, then a broad smile came to his face as a notion which, in its own way, was as splendid as Lieutenant Vane's, came to him. "You deserve a reward, Vane. I have a mind to make you my aide-de-camp."

Vane was astonished into incoherence. He stared at Sir William and, at last, managed to stammer a response. "But you don't even know me, sir!"

"I know you're brave! I've discovered you're not without clever notions! What more do I need to know?" Sir William, seeing Vane's expression, was delighted. "It's not such a great thing, Vane. You're more likely to die in battle as an aide! Isn't that so, John?"

Andre smiled. "Welcome to the marble, Vane."

"The marble?" Vane looked dazedly at the elegant Andre.

"Your tomb in Westminster Abbey," Andre explained. "For now you are on the path to glory."

"If you accept," Lord Robert observed drily.

The words startled Vane into acceptance. "I do, sir," he said to Sir William, "and am honoured beyond any thanks I can give. I shall do my utmost to prove worthy, sir."

"I'm sure you will." Sir William was warmed by the man's response. "But you can't be a lieutenant, Vane! That won't do at all, oh no! My colonels don't take lieutenants nearly seriously enough. I'll gazette you captain this night."

"Sir." It was all Vane could say. Promotion, more pay, patronage: all

350

had come to him on a rutted road that had been kicked to dust by a passing army.

"And I can't go on calling you Vane, either. What did they christen you?"

"Christopher, sir."

"Christopher, eh? Do we call you that, or Kit?"

"Kit will do very well, sir."

"Or Kitten?" Lord Robert suggested mischievously.

Vane turned and stared into his lordship's eyes. For a second there was a chill in the hot day. "I'm never called that. By anyone."

Massedene saw how pale Vane's eyes were. "No offence, Captain Vane."

"Shall we go, gentlemen?" Sir William smiled at his young men. The commander-in-chief might be short of ammunition, but he had Philadelphia within his grasp, a new aide, and a belief that peace was but a few weeks away; and so Sir William, Goodnatured Billy, was a happy man.

Chapter Three

On the Sunday after the Patriots fled from Philadelphia, the British had still not come. It was reported that George Washington's army was still attempting to block the British advance on the city, though few Loyalists expected it to succeed.

Abel Becket, in his deepest convictions, was a fervent Loyalist. Liberty, to Abel Becket, was a word conjured by the lawyers to rouse the mob, and should the ignorant win and the King's writ be expelled from America, it would bring ruin to a seaboard. For how could thirteen colonies on the edge of the known world, hope to trade without the protection of a greater power?

And trade, Abel Becket believed, would bring America greater blessings than any slogan. Trade brought money, and so Abel prayed for the arrival of the British and the opening of the seaway. He had even gambled on British victory, for in his warehouse he had hoarded a stack of sawn black walnut, ready for the day when it could be sent to the London market for real coin, rather than the depreciated rebel paper dollars. Yet if the trade was to come to the city, then first the rebel forts on the Lower Delaware would have to be taken.

The next morning, standing on his wharf, Abel Becket watched two large shallops that, under grey sails, beat into the cold north wind. Both boats were crewed by armed men.

"Look at them!" Abel spat his derision into the breeze. The ships carried the new rebel flag of striped red and white. "It looks," he said scathingly, "like a clown's pantaloons unfurled."

The boats had come from the rebel forts.

Beside him, obsequious as ever in his master's company, Ezra Woollard chuckled.

Becket watched them go. "You say the rebels are obstructing the river?"

"They're sinking pontoons at Billings Island, sir."

"You've got details?"

"And maps." Woollard followed his master back into the warehouse, past the great baulks of walnut and the fragrant bales of linseed that would sail to Ireland. Yet nothing could sail before the British came and the forts were taken.

Ezra Woollard, in Abel Becket's private room, put his plans of the rebel defences on the table. "I was thinking," Woollard said, "that these should reach the British."

"Indeed." Abel Becket's agreement was whole-hearted.

"They're north of the city now. It won't be a difficult ride."

"I can spare you." Becket stood by his window, which looked down into Water Street.

Woollard smiled. "I was thinking, sir, that maybe I wouldn't be the best messenger. I'm no hand at dealing with gentlemen."

Woollard's humility came hard, for as a young man, not so long ago, he had prospered as an independent merchant in Philadelphia. He had made his fortune as a dealer in New Jersey tar, but his business had been broken by the British naval blockade, and he had only been saved from bankruptcy by Abel Becket. The older man had paid the debts of the ailing tar business and made Woollard into his foreman. It was a good bargain, for Woollard had the skill of a trader and the physical force of a man toughened by a hard trade.

"Are you suggesting," Abel Becket asked, "that I should ride to the British myself?"

"You'd be better at persuading them than myself, sir. But I was thinking of Master Jonathon."

"Ah." Becket went back to the table and sat down. He stared at the plans of the rebel defences. "I don't think he'd make a very willing messenger."

"I heard," Ezra Woollard said slyly, "that the Reverend MacTeague preached from Joshua twenty-four, verse fifteen, yesterday? 'Choose you this day whom ye will serve'. Master Jonathon must choose."

"Jonathon is my nephew." Abel Becket was dressed in his customary black, with an old-fashioned black Steinkirk about his neck, and the sombre clothes added an odd force to the warning note in his voice.

"It's not for me to interfere in family affairs," Woollard said, "but it seems to me, sir, that the British will be in a position to reward some families in this city, and to punish others. They'll bring trade, but they'll not give trade to merchants whose loyalty isn't absolute." He paused, as if to give his master a chance to protest, but Becket stayed silent.

"And they could hear, sir, how Master Jonathon hurried eighty barrels of fine powder out of the city the other night! They'll not like it!"

"It was paid for."

"With paper, not coin, which they'd have given us." Again Woollard paused, but again Becket stayed silent for the foreman knew that he was expressing the fears of his employer. "And, with respect, sir, his sister doesn't help. It just seemed to me, sir, and with the greatest of respect, that Master Jonathon should be made to display a proper loyalty."

Becket frowned. "I've no doubt that, in time, he'll do just that."

"Not if what I hear is true. He's sweet on Caroline Fisher."

Becket frowned. "Whom you once wanted to marry?"

"That was before I knew of her levelling views, sir. She's a rebel, and fervent! Now it's none of my business, sir, but it seems to me that if Master Jonathon can be forced into showing a proper loyalty, then Caroline Fisher will scorn him as quickly as she can."

Becket, troubled by the information, walked restlessly back to the window.

"Jonathon's young," he said, almost to himself, "and the young like to flirt with dangerous views. But he's good!" He turned back to Woollard. "He's as talented a trader as you or I, Woollard!"

"So we mustn't lose him, sir. We mustn't let the likes of Caroline Fisher and, begging your pardon, sir, Mrs. Crowl, turn his head to nonsense! Make him choose." Woollard gestured at the plans that lay on the table. "Send him to the British, sir, and no one will doubt his loyalties after that." He paused, and he saw the doubt on Abel Becket's face. He made his voice confiding, almost reassuring. "He's a good lad. He just needs his mind made up for him."

"Maybe." Becket still stared into the street. "Caroline Fisher?"

"A slut, sir, if you'll forgive the word. She needs a good whipping. I'd hate to see a girl like that taking all the profits from your hard work." Woollard shrugged. "Forgive me for saying too much, sir, but it's all in our interest if the British favour us. And if you want me to ride north with the papers I'll gladly do it."

"No." Becket, his mind evidently decided, turned back. "Leave them with me."

"Sir." Woollard bowed his head, then clattered down the stairs to the counting house where the empty desks showed how trade had suffered in these last years. Three clerks only worked where once a dozen had scratched at their ledgers. But Woollard's mind was not on clerks; instead he considered the fate of a business that he had a mind to own, to which end, and for the most justifiable of reasons, a cripple must be forced into a decision. Jonathon must choose.

OPPOSITE PHILADELPHIA, on the Delaware's eastern bank, was marshy land that rose to low sandy ridges that were thickly wooded. It was poor land, yet from it Caleb and Anna Fisher had made a farm.

It lay south of where the Cooper River joined the Delaware and its value had been enriched by its proximity to Philadelphia where, in the covered market, Caleb sold melons, cucumbers, pumpkins, squashes, mulberries, apples, cherries and chestnuts. His wife churned milk to butter, made cheese, and baked high-crusted pies that were carried across the river for sale. The reward for their work was a weatherboarded house of warm snugness. It was not a rich farmstead, but to the Fishers it was a palace.

"The Lord's been good to us," Anna liked to say, even though she had lost three children in infancy. Her only surviving son had grown up and married. Then he too had died, with almost all his family, in one of the dreadful fires that sometimes swept through the small wooden houses built on Philadelphia's margins. One baby had survived that fire: Caleb and Anna's grandchild, who had lived ever since on the farm and who had become dearer to her grandparents than any other person on earth.

Caroline was eighteen now, four years past marriageable age, yet her grandparents made no move to force her into wedlock. They had even supported her refusal to wed the rising Woollard when his business had looked set to make a fortune. Caroline had her own thoughts on marriage. It would come, but in her own time.

And there would be plenty of choice, for she was a girl who caught the eye of men. Her golden hair was lightened by the sun to a gleaming paleness that contrasted with her tanned skin from which a pair of blue eyes challenged the world. She could ride like a boy, milk a cow like a dairymaid, and handle a river shallop like a waterman.

It was the shallop that made Caroline noticed, for, as her grandfather grew older, it became her duty to take the farm's produce over to the city's quays. A bright-haired girl sailing a boat with such skill was bound to provoke attention but, like all the river sailors, she wore a knife at her belt to cut at tangled rigging, and there was something about her face that suggested the knife could be used for more than slashing ropes.

Not all the farm's produce went to the market. Caroline carried the choicer fruits and cheeses to her special customers, among whom was Martha Crowl, and it had been at the widow's house that Caroline had first met Jonathon. At first she had felt a pang of pity for the young man. He had limped beside her as she returned to the wharf and they had discovered that each was orphaned, and that each was a Patriot living in a Loyalist house.

Caroline's grandparents' loyalism was not like Abel Becket's, who held the creed as a matter of fervent belief. Anna Fisher remembered seeing the old King before she sailed to America. "A grand man, he was! A grand man!" She insisted that he had smiled at her, and that one smile had kept her loyal for nearly sixty years. Caleb believed a Christian should be ruled by a king, because, just as land needed water or a calf milk, it was natural. To him the rebellion was a fuss across the river, nothing more.

But Caroline had never seen a king, and she crossed the river to hear the city's debates, and the rebellion seemed a fine thing to her. Caroline, like Jonathon Becket, would be a rebel.

They had known each other for a year, and their meetings had always been in the city. Jonathon would waylay Caroline on the wharf and insist on carrying her baskets to market. Sometimes they spoke of the rebellion and Jonathon would list what supplies he had found for the rebel army that week, and how his sister made up the profit above the meagre payments the Congress would allow so that his uncle would be content to sell to the hated rebels. Always Caroline knew that this charming, eloquent and wealthy young man was trying to tell her that he was in love. Why else would he inflict the pain of the long walks on himself?

"He'll be rich," Anna Fisher sometimes teased Caroline.

Caroline had grimaced. "He'll have to live in the city, won't he?"

"If that's where the money goes, and it usually does."

Caroline could not imagine herself living in a city. Yet, if Jonathon had his way, and his way could be as forceful as it was amusing, she would live there. He had not offered marriage, but he would, and Caroline did not know how she would respond. She admitted to herself that she almost feared the moment when Jonathon would finally demand her response.

Then, in the last week of September 1777, on a Tuesday evening, Jonathon came to Caroline's house for the first time.

He arrived at sunset. At first, as Caroline watched the strange horseman come down the track from the plank bridge across the Cooper River, she did not recognise Jonathon, but then he lifted his hat and smiled. "Watching the sunset?" he asked, as he reined in beside her.

"I'm deciding what cattle we'll keep." Caroline nodded towards the cows that grazed on the marshland by the river's edge. "The wind's taking their milk early this year. There's a bad winter coming."

Caroline saw how, on horseback, Jonathon lost his crippled appearance. The right stirrup, to encompass his club foot, was made twice as large as a normal iron, but he sat straight and tall and she sensed how hard it must be for him to walk when he could ride so well. "You want the horse to drink?"

She ducked through the fence and led the mare round to the cattle trough by the milking barn. From here, when her face was hard by the warm flanks of the cows as she milked them, Caroline could see the glorious sight of the city across the river. In high summer, on still days, the spires and roofs were reflected as cleanly as if the steel-flat water was a mirror. In spring the tiles and shingles lost their starkness, as the poplars on the streets came into new leaf, while in winter the snow gave the city a shining glory. Now, in the turn of summer to autumn, there was a golden darkness to the city that was accentuated by the absence of masts from the quays.

"You've come a long way." She wiped the sweat from the mare's flanks.

Jonathon, secretly wishing she had shown more enthusiasm for his arrival, slid from the saddle. "I left the city at nine this morning, crossed at Davie Logan's, and here I am."

He had ridden miles to the north, crossed the Delaware, then ridden long miles back on the New Jersey bank. Caroline shook her head in amazement. "What's wrong with the usual ferry?"

"Everything. I didn't want to be seen. And I wanted to see you. Can we talk?"

Caroline took him to a small rise of pale grass on which they could sit. "You've run away?" she asked.

"I'm not sure if that's an exact description. Perhaps I've been driven away? I was asked to deliver these to the British." Jonathon fumbled in a pouch at his belt and produced folded papers. Then, as she looked through the sheets, the words poured out of him. He had not liked to refuse his uncle directly. Rather than provoke a terrible argument with him, he had decided to let Abel Becket believe he was riding in obedience to deliver the treacherous papers to the enemy.

"But you're not going to deliver them, are you?"

For answer Jonathon took the sheets from her and tore them into scraps. "I shall have to write to my uncle and tell him I disobeyed. I suppose that's a cowardly way of doing it, but it seemed for the best." He scattered the scraps into the wind.

Caroline watched them blow away. "What will your uncle do? Will you lose your inheritance?"

Jonathon smiled. "Does that matter? The time has come for Patriots to define their ideals."

To Jonathon this was not a war about a stamp tax, or about threepence on tea, but a war about God's own country where honest men could make a new heaven on an old earth. There would be no more Placemen from London, sent to live in the great houses and take their unearned salaries from honest folk. Instead there would be a good people on a good soil. America. What was an inheritance against that great ideal?

Caroline listened and, because she dealt in realities more than in ideas, she asked a flat question. "And what will you do if you lose your inheritance?"

"I'll farm," Jonathon teased her, and was rewarded by a shocked look of disbelief. He laughed. "I can become a lawyer, maybe a politician. But there is only one thing to do now, and that's to fight. Nothing else matters, so long as we're free, and so long as you're waiting for me when I come back from battle."

He spoke casually, but Caroline had known, as soon as she had recognised the strange horseman, that Jonathon had come to demand a decision of her. She was suddenly swept by a great pity for him. How could a cripple live in the harsh world of gunfire and sabre blades?

"You want me to wait?"

"It's more than I deserve," Jonathon said. He stared at Caroline. Her looks did not match the refined and elegant delicacy of the city, which so prized a fashionable paleness that the Fisher farm sold lemons, cucumbers and tomatoes to be made into poultices for blanching the skin. Caroline's was a wilder and rougher beauty which some men might have thought coarse, but which had enslaved him. "It's more than I deserve," he repeated, "but I even dare to want you to do more than wait for me."

Caroline knew what that further question was, and she did not want to face it now. She frowned. "You shouldn't be going at all. God gave you other skills. Can you sit in a saddle all day? Do you have the strength for that? Imagine galloping and turning, twisting and fighting!"

But Jonathon was stubborn. "I can do whatever I have a mind to do. God gave me that strength, and it will be enough."

"I pray so." Caroline stared towards the dark and intricate skyline of the city. "Have you got food for the journey? I'll make something." She took refuge in practicality. "And you can sleep here tonight. There's a bed that folds down in the kitchen for strangers."

Jonathon sensed her evasion and gently he took her hand. "I don't care where I sleep, but I do care that you'll wait for me."

Caroline knew she had deflected the greater question, and she could not deny him the answer to the lesser. She nodded. "I'll wait." And, as soon as the words were said, she saw that she had implied assent to both questions, for his happiness was as golden and huge as the sinking sun on the edge of the world. He held her suddenly, pressing his face to her hair. "I'll wait," she said again, but this time unprompted, a gift of her own wild and free will.

Jonathon felt as though he had leaped from darkness into light, and from confusion into the glorious promise of love. He was a Patriot, and he would fight for his country against the Bloodybacks and their Hessian mercenaries, and he would fight for this girl whose love he would earn and keep for ever.

Jonathon, forsaking trade, was a rebel at last.

Chapter Four

The company's evening parade was held on a patch of worn grassland close to the wood and turf bivouacs that were the men's homes. Sergeant Scammell harangued the light company. "Listen to your Uncle Scammell and don't you dare bleeding laugh or I'll skin your bloody arses." He paced menacingly down the front rank. "We are short of ammunition. Therefore you are only to fire your muskets if you get an order to fire your muskets. Not from a corporal, but from me. If any of you bastards fire without a bleeding order I'll have the skin off your backs!" Scammell's disgust at such an order was obvious, but the force with which he delivered it made the men nod nervously. "Night pickets! To me!"

The night pickets trailed disconsolately behind Sergeant Scammell to mount their guard where the cultivated fields gave way to the thick, dark woods. The men who remained in the bivouac crouched about their fires, drank their ration of rum, and glanced enviously towards a small house where refugees from the nearby village of Germantown had taken shelter. "There's women over there." Liam Shaughnessy, a thin man who had a bad cough, nudged Sam's arm. "You want me to hold one down for you, Sam?"

"It's all right, Liam, I can manage."

"Nate can manage, can't you?" Shaughnessy laughed, and the laugh turned into a grating cough. He spat into the fire, then grinned at Nate. "Scammy's on duty all bleeding night. You should tuck yourself in with Maggie."

"What would you know, Liam?" Nate hated to hear men talk so familiarly of Maggie.

Shaughnessy gave an evil grin. "He sold her to the colonel last night. Two shilling, Nate, that's what I heard."

Nate twisted towards Shaughnessy, but Sam pushed him back. "Shut up! Both of you!"

"I'll give the Irish bastard a kicking!" Nate pushed against his brother's restraining arm. Shaughnessy had pulled his bayonet scabbard round on its shoulder sling and grinned wickedly, as if inviting the attack.

"For God's sake, calm down!" Sam glared at his brother. "You cause enough trouble as it is."

Night was falling. All round Sam the presence of the army was betrayed by cooking fires that lay across the darkened folds of ground like a blanket of fallen stars. Rain began to fall, hissing on embers, a dog limped past Sam's fire, somewhere a child cried. The pickets were quiet at the encampment's dark edge.

"I'm going to run," Nate said stubbornly.

"You always talk about it," Liam sneered, "but you never will."

"I will." Nate still dreamed of Maggie's paradise beyond the horizon. "You'll be jealous. I'll be tucked up with a girl and you'll be sweating on a march somewhere."

"I'll be flogging you," Shaughnessy laughed.

Nate ignored the Irishman, turning instead to his brother. "Would you flog me if I ran, Sam?"

"I'd knock your bloody head off, you silly bastard," Sam said lightly.

"I mean it, Sam." Nate stared earnestly at his brother. "Would you?"

Sam rubbed his face. "I said how I'd look after you, brother, and so I will. You stay with me, and there'll be no call for a flogging." He looked at his twin and saw the unhappiness on his face. "For God's sake, Nate! There'll be girls in their hundreds in Philadelphia! Just waiting for us. Everyone says so. They want us to come!"

"It's Maggie," Nate said simply.

"Damn Maggie." Sam looked away to see an American youth, scarcely more than a boy, nervously exploring the battalion's bivouac. He wore ragged brown trousers and a cast-off torn coat, and had an odd, widebrimmed hat above his long hair. An old pistol was thrust into his rope belt. He gestured uncertainly towards the lights across the fields, as if to suggest that he was merely on his way to the village.

"You want something?" Sam spoke a little gruffly, but the boy looked relieved. "The guns," he said pathetically.

"You want to see the cannons?"

"Yes." The boy jerked his head at the small house. "I'm from there."

Sam pointed towards the village. "Guns are in the market place, lad. Ask nicely. You don't want your head blown away by a nervous sentry, do you now?"

The boy, who was merely curious about these strange red-coated creatures who had appeared during the day, seemed grateful for Sam's few words which, if not altogether friendly, were not downright hostile either. He grinned, then wandered uncertainly onwards, weaving a cautious path around the knots of resting men.

Sam lay back, careless of the rain.

Nate dropped his voice so that only Sam could hear him. "Maggie's got some civilian clothes, like you said. She's got some food, too, and some money. We're going to do it, Sam, we're really going to do it!" Nate suddenly twisted round to stare north. "What the hell's happening?" The muskets, which had been ordered to stay silent, were firing.

Sergeant Scammell's voice, far out on the edge of the encampment, shouted fiercely, but the muskets blazed again in a snapping crackle of volley fire.

Men stirred by the sudden shots rolled out of their shelters and grabbed their guns. More musket fire stabbed the darkness from the picket line. Someone whooped a howl of delight and the first shots from the camp itself crashed loud in the night. This was an antidote to boredom, an irresistible opportunity, and men stood in the firelight, pulled their triggers, then reloaded eagerly. The firing was infectious. The American boy, startled by the commotion, stood helplessly amidst the excited men.

"Stop firing! Stop firing!" An officer's voice shouted from behind Sam.

Slowly, fitfully, the firing died. Officers and sergeants, roused from sleep, gradually beat order into the men and drove them back towards their fires. Other officers galloped from the village, angrily demanding to know which pickets had fired and upon whose orders.

Corporal Dale's picket had fired, and done so without orders, and Sergeant Scammell, the guard sergeant, was rousted back to the lines where, in a voice loud enough to be heard in the next battalion, he swore it was the neighbouring troops who had first fired.

Lieutenant-Colonel Elliott, his face red from an evening's drinking, knew that the battalion officers were threatened with a fine for this night's work, that the guard sergeant would be reduced to the ranks, and the men flogged. He did not care about the flogging, but he cared about one of his best sergeants and about his own pocket. He drew Scammell to one side where the two men bent their heads together.

"He's getting a right roasting," Nate laughed.

Laughter died as Sergeant Scammell about-turned and marched with a grim face towards the company. "Get in your beds, you scum! And put those muskets in the stands!" His hard face sought a victim and settled on the young American boy who, bemused by all the firing and fuss, still grinned half-wittedly beside Sam's bivouac. "You! What are you doing here?" Scammell pointed his metal-topped cane at the farm boy.

The boy seemed incapable of speaking, so Sam spoke for him. "He wanted to see the artillery, Sergeant."

Scammell, amazingly, smiled. "The artillery! You want to see the cannons, is that it, lad?"

"Yes, sir." The boy nodded.

"You should have said! Come on then, lad. I'll show 'em you, and I'll give you a bite to eat. You're hungry, I dare say?"

"I am." The boy, perhaps fifteen or sixteen years old, lapsed into embarrassed smiles under the sergeant's unexpected friendliness.

"What's your name, lad?"

"James, sir."

"Well, come on, Jimmy-me-lad! Rare big guns, we've got."

Sam watched the sergeant lead the boy away and supposed that the hapless James would be blandished into joining one of the Loyalist regiments. And quite right too, in Sam's view, for why should the Americans not fight to put down their own troublemakers? He crawled into his bivouac, laid his head on his hat, and closed his eyes.

He woke in the cold, wet dawn as reveille sounded. Sergeant Derrick, a vast-bellied and affable man, was fully dressed, cheerful, and rousting through the shelters. "Let's be having you bastards! Up and shine! Sam! Nate! I want you two! Fetch some axes! Lively now!"

Derrick wanted timber cut. It seemed an unnecessary chore to Sam, for there were plenty of fence rails still to be stolen from the fields, but the brothers, axes over their shoulders, followed the sergeant towards the woods where the dawn made the shadows mysterious and grey.

"Start here, Sarge?" Sam gestured towards a birch tree that grew at the edge of the woods.

"Too wet." Sergeant Derrick stared round at the trees. "Over here, boys." He prowled the wood's margin, walking as carefully as a poacher. It seemed to Sam that the big sergeant was searching for something other than timber to be cut and, after just a few slow paces, Derrick found it. "My oh my! Look at that, lads!"

Sam edged past Nate to see.

A corpse lay in the long grass. It was a boy dressed in a torn coat and baggy trousers belted together with a length of frayed rope. A floppy, wide-brimmed hat lay a couple of feet from the dead boy's head, while next to his outstretched right hand, and fallen into the grass, was the old pistol. The boy's long hair was bright with dew, and in his skinny throat was a ragged-edged hole. It was the same boy who had edged so shyly towards Sam's fire the night before, the boy who had only wanted to stare at the soldiers' big guns. "A Yankee-Doodle-Dandy," Sergeant Derrick said softly, "with a bullet in his gullet."

In the dawn light Sam could see that the boy's pistol had no lock, and could never have been fired. The gun was nothing but a toy for a growing boy too interested in soldiers.

"That ain't a rebel," Nate said fiercely. "He was called James! He was with Scammell last night. He was talking to us! Just before the firing!"

Sergeant Derrick stood very close to Nate. "Listen. That is a rebel. He was shot last night after firing at our picket. That's what happened, Private Gilpin, and that way none of our lads fetch a skinning, none of our sergeants loses his stripes, and none of our Jack-puddings has to pay a fine. Do you understand?"

"But—"

Sergeant Derrick struck Nate's face a stinging blow. "You didn't hear me, son! It's a rebel. He was attacking us, so the bloody picket did the right thing. Or do you want a kicking? Is that it, Nate Gilpin? You want the sergeants to have a mill with you?"

Sam looked past Derrick. The boy looked oddly peaceful. His hands were curled into fists and his legs slightly drawn up. Sam supposed Scammell had stabbed the boy with a bayonet to make it look like a bullet hole. "He wasn't a rebel, Sarge." Sam's voice was tentative.

Derrick turned on Sam. "Of course he wasn't a bloody rebel! I know it, you know it, and Nate knows it, but the bloody army doesn't know it!"

The sergeant glared at the brothers, and Sam understood that, because Scammell had seen them talking with the boy after the firing, it was important that they keep their mouths shut. Sergeant Derrick, who was popular, had been deputed to square the Gilpin brothers. "The silly bastards say we're not supposed to fire," Derrick went on, "but they can't blame us if we were attacked, can they? So here's the enemy!"

"I talked to him," Nate said staunchly. "Sam did too, didn't you, Sam?"

Sam said nothing.

Nate pleaded with his brother. "Sam?"

Sam shrugged. "He could have been spying on us, couldn't he?" Sam knew instantly he had done wrong, that he was condoning murder, but he wore a red hackle now to show that he was one of the elite men who had taken their blades to the enemy at the tavern. Sam had earned Sergeant Scammell's praise, and Sam did not want to lose that approbation. And how could Sam and Nate, mere privates, take on the sergeants and officers who would insist that this pathetic corpse was a rebel soldier?

Sergeant Derrick grinned at Sam's answer, then went to the field's edge where he waved his arms and hollo'd towards the nearest pickets.

The battalion officers arrived, and after them came a staff officer mounted on a big black horse. The undergrowth was trampled around the boy's body as a ring of uniformed men stared in triumph at the puny corpse. Sergeant Scammell, chin shining from an early shave, proclaimed that the body was proof that the pickets had indeed been attacked, and therefore justified in returning fire.

"There you are!" Lieutenant-Colonel Elliott, vindicated, looked up at the staff officer.

"Damned lucky for you, Elliott!" The staff officer asked to see the boy's weapon and Sergeant Derrick picked the broken pistol out of the grass.

"It got damaged, sir," Derrick said confidingly.

For an instant, a suicidal instant, Sam had the urge to step forward and proclaim that the American boy had been with him when the shooting started, and his right foot actually moved involuntarily forward, but then he caught Scammell's gaze: the sergeant's eyes were as hard as stones and filled with a promise of dreadful violence. Sam froze.

The staff officer fingered the weapon's rusty hoops. He smiled. "Dangerous men, these Yankees." He threw the broken toy into the undergrowth. "One armed rebel," he said.

"Good shooting," Elliott beamed. "And alert pickets, wouldn't you say?"

"I'd say you're off the hook, Elliott. I'll tell the general." The staff officer wheeled his horse and spurred away.

There was a murmur of relieved laughter from the men, then Elliott nodded at Scammell. "Bury him before his mother finds him. And well done, Sergeant."

"Thank you, sir."

Later, after the boy had been tipped into a shallow grave at the wood's edge, Nate stared almost in horror at his twin brother. "You're a bastard, Sam. It was murder."

Sam was troubled. He knew murder had been done and that an innocent was dead, but this was the army and Nate's squeamishness would win no wars. Yet his brother was right, and Sam knew it, and he wondered why right and wrong became as blurred as the mist which still lingered on the pastures. "I'm sorry," he said finally, and with undisguised misery.

Nate put his arm on Sam's shoulder. For the first time ever it seemed as if Nate were the stronger of the two brothers. "You want to get out, Sam," Nate's voice was troubled, "before they change you."

"I'm not changing."

"You'll be like Scammy," Nate said. "You've got to get out, Sam, before they twist you. Come with Maggie and me."

But Sam did not respond, for there was nothing to be said and nothing to be done. Because he was a Redcoat.

THE BRITISH WERE COMING. It was certain now. George Washington's army, attempting to stay between the Redcoats and Philadelphia, had been outmanoeuvred, so nothing now stood between the city and the British. Indeed a message had already come, brought by the first Redcoat to appear in the streets, which requested the citizens of Philadelphia to stay within their doors while the troops arrived. The message had only increased alarm among the ladies of the city. If General Howe warned honest folk to stay indoors, then surely the danger must be dreadful?

But on the morning of the British arrival, the crowds, despite the request, gathered early, stretching from the Northern Liberties to the city's centre. The British, it was clear, would be welcomed to the rebel capital not by a handful of Loyalists but by crowds in their thousands.

New Jersey Loyalists crossed the river by ferry, and across their path went a shallop with a single girl at its helm. Caroline Fisher also went to Philadelphia, though not to cheer. A weak sunlight cast long shadows as she moored the shallop and climbed to the wharf. To avoid the crush she went south along the quays, then cut into the city along the narrow path by Dock Creek.

"Hey!" The voice came from behind her. Caroline ignored it.

"Caroline!" The call was followed by pounding footsteps that made her turn.

It was Ezra Woollard, breathing heavily. He offered her a quick smile. "Been a long time, girl."

Caroline's face showed disgust. "I hadn't been counting the days."

"You wouldn't, would you? Been too busy with Master Jonathon, haven't you?" Woollard laughed. "He came to see you last Sabbath, didn't he?"

"I don't have to tell you—"

"Come on, girl!" Woollard interrupted her, "I heard from Davie Logan! The cripple crossed the river twice, and where the hell else would he be going? So where's he gone now?"

Caroline was hatless and her hair was bright in the shadow of the warehouses that edged the creek. She glanced sideways, but Woollard's closeness had trapped her against a brick wall. She looked defiantly into his face. "He went to deliver your message to the British, Ezra. All your careful plans."

"Jonathon never bloody got to the British."

"Don't curse to me, Ezra."

"Don't you lecture me, girl!" Woollard was determined to discover what had happened to Jonathon. Five days had passed since the boy had ridden from the city, and in those five days there had been no news of him. Woollard was certain that, had Jonathon ridden to the British army as his uncle had ordered him, some news would have come by now. Woollard had followed Caroline to snatch this chance of discovering the truth. "He's gone to General Washington, hasn't he?" He let the question linger. "Tell me where he is."

Caroline twisted away from him, but Woollard plucked her back. This morning Abel Becket, with other prominent merchants, was waiting to surrender the State House to the British, and Woollard would have liked to take some firm news to his employer. He wanted to tell Abel Becket that Jonathon had forfeited his share of the business, so he pinned Caroline against the wall with his left hand, while his right threatened her face. Water lapped in the creek behind him, carrying its stinking load of ordure

364

between muddy margins that were littered with dead rats. "I want to know where he is, and you know. So you tell me, girl, or I'll have you in front of the magistrates this morning and we'll see how you like a taste of the Correction House."

"The Correction House!" Caroline was scornful.

She pushed against his left arm, then, in sudden submission, leaned on the wall and sighed. "Do you really think someone as badly crippled as Jonathon can fight?"

Woollard frowned. "So if he ain't with the rebels, girl, where is he?"

Caroline shrugged in resignation. "He went to Frankfort."

"Frankfort?" Woollard's surprise turned into a sudden gasp as a slice of pain shot through his left arm. He jerked back and Caroline slashed with her knife again, this time towards his eyes, and Ezra Woollard ducked and twisted away. Then Caroline, unable to resist the temptation, pushed him and watched as he teetered, arms flailing, and fell, bellowing, into the fetid mud of the creek. Water spewed up, Woollard's hat fell off, and the girl's mocking laughter echoed from the high dark walls.

Caroline did not wait. She crossed the drawbridge over Front Street and turned up past the City Tavern, bedecked with bunting. The crowds blocked her path, and now, far away, she could hear a sudden thumping, a rhythmic, pounding sound that punched at the sky. Thin over the thumping came the sound of instruments. It was a band playing "God Save the King".

Caroline tried to push between the people who stood thick on the pavements by Christ Church.

"Get back, girl," someone growled. Then the street erupted into a huge cheer and Caroline saw the first horsemen riding by. They were all Americans; Philadelphians who had ridden to guide the British home.

For the British had come at last. Bands played, officers' horses caracoled elegantly, while their riders doffed plumed hats towards the prettier women; one officer, more handsome than the rest, bowed towards a fair-haired beauty leaning from an upper window, and the crowd cheered. A general, looped with golden aiguillettes, rode amidst his aides—Lord Cornwallis, sent by Sir William Howe to take possession of the city. Caroline thought he rode like an insolent conqueror into an enemy capital.

An infantry company goose-stepped past. At their head a sergeant led a black bear on a silver chain. At times, prodded by its keeper, the bear reared hugely on its back paws and flailed the air. Behind him came soldiers helmeted in mitred shakos faced with brass, while their faces had huge, thick moustaches waxed into upturned tips. They had silver buttons on yellow waistcoats and silver cords hanging from their dark blue jackets. Meaty white-breeched thighs rose in the grotesque march before the gaitered boots slapped down into the mud.

"Hessians!" a voice near Caroline said, and Caroline thought with despair of the volunteers who made up General Washington's army. What chance did Jonathon have against these demonic automatons? For the letter Caroline carried confirmed that Jonathon had volunteered, and was now in the rebellion's service.

Behind the Hessians, mounted on mud-flecked horses, came a troop of the Queen's Rangers, American Loyalists all, dressed in their plain green hussar uniform with black plumes and cresset badges. Many had relatives in the crowd and they waved and blew kisses to the women.

A louder cheer greeted a group of British cavalry officers, and even Caroline reluctantly thought she had never seen anything so splendid as their fur-edged pelisses and froggings of brightest gold.

She edged away, but a rumbling sound made her turn back to watch again. The great guns were passing, deadly machines of brass and wood and iron, with vast wheels and carriages hung with dangling buckets and coiled chains. The mouths of the cannons were stained a deep, ragged black; evidence that these machines had fired and, Caroline presumed, killed. She felt a sudden despair for Jonathon. How could such a gentle boy live in a world where guns ruled? Yet she also felt a surge of pride in him, so much so that, to her surprise, the tears welled up in her eyes.

Then came the camp followers, women with insolent eyes stalking beside wagons heaped with grimy bundles; grinning filthy children; a woman with a baby at her bare breast, another woman, fat as a barrel of salt cod, waddling hugely down the centre of Second Street and, in mockery of the officers ahead, waving at the onlookers. She had a goat tied to her belt, while behind her a ragged flock of cattle, goats, sheep and razorbacked hogs was herded by urchins with long staves. It was a circus of beggars come to town, the effluent of the slums parading like conquerors.

It was only when the camp followers had gone that Caroline could cross the road and run down Market Street. She twisted into an alley, let herself into a back yard, and thence down a flight of stone steps to a basement kitchen where Jenny, Martha Crowl's black maid, looked surprised to see her. "It's not market day, Miss Caroline!"

Caroline opened her bag and brought out a crumpled and sealed letter. "That's for Mrs. Crowl, Jenny. It's important."

Jenny wiped her hands on her apron and took the letter. "You want to wait, Miss Fisher? There's tea in that pot."

Caroline waited as Jenny took the letter upstairs. To her surprise, the black woman returned to say that Mrs. Crowl would like to see Caroline in the parlour. "It's up the stairs and the first door you see," Jenny said. "She'll be glad of company on a day like this."

But when Caroline reached the beautifully furnished parlour, she found that the widow Crowl already had company, in the form of the Rev.

Donald MacTeague who, teacup in podgy hand, turned in some astonishment when Caroline arrived. Such girls, he thought, should not be invited into the parlours of society, but Martha Crowl had ever favoured flamboyant behaviour, and the Rev. MacTeague was too much of a gentleman to make any comment. He stood up, gently disposing of six-year-old Lydia, who had been trying to crawl onto his lap. "It's Miss Fisher, is it not?"

"Indeed, sir."

"I have enjoyed your grandmother's most excellent pies, indeed I have. You watched the arrival of the legions?"

"I did."

"Such a happy day! Such a happy day!" MacTeague sat down again, then tilted the teacup and smiled benevolently at the ragged girl. "I thought I would offer my protection to the widow Crowl." He bowed to Martha, who, in a wide-skirted dress of lilac silk, sat in the window with the unopened letter beside her. She looked calmly fashionable, dressed as if for a ball rather than in mourning for a city lost.

"The Reverend MacTeague," Martha said drily, "is concerned that I might be killed by the vengeful British. In which case he would lose my pew rent."

"You jest, dear lady!" MacTeague was pained. "I come as a Christian duty, nothing more!"

Lydia was standing by a window, and now turned excitedly to her mother. "Is that a lobster?"

"Yes, my dear. They're best boiled." Martha stared at a red-coated soldier who wandered down the far pavement.

MacTeague offered a pained smile, while Caroline, made nervous by the elegance of the room and the presence of the unctuous priest, hovered nervously by the door. Martha, with a peremptory gesture, indicated that she should sit on the sofa beside the hearth.

"So!" said MacTeague, looking at Caroline. "You ignored the warning to stay indoors, Miss Fisher?"

"Yes, sir. There weren't many of them," Caroline blurted out.

MacTeague smiled. "They haven't sent their full power, dear me, no! Most of the army remains at Germantown, I'm told. Mr. Washington is loitering to the north, so Sir William waits to do battle there. Our prayers will support him."

"Yours might," Martha said, "but not mine."

"Dear Mrs. Crowl," the priest murmured, then stood up. "We may disagree about earthly things, dear lady, but about the more important matters, I trust, never." He bowed to Martha, then, less formally, to Caroline. "If you need me, then summon me! Good day, ladies."

"He wants," Martha said when the priest was gone, "to ingratiate himself with our conquerors. I think MacTeague fancies himself as the first Bishop of Philadelphia." Martha spoke scornfully, then critically examined Caroline who, till now, she had only glimpsed delivering vegetables and fruit to the kitchen downstairs. Then she picked up the letter from Jonathon.

She seemed to take a long time reading her brother's words.

Caroline waited. Lydia, bored with watching the strangely dressed men in the streets, crossed the room and climbed onto the sofa.

Martha laid the letter down. "Did he write to you as well?"

"Yes, ma'am."

Martha sighed. "He shouldn't have volunteered."

"No."

"It isn't as if there aren't enough two-legged men in America to fight without Jonathon being sacrificed!" The words were said angrily, but, immediately they were spoken, Martha shook her head in rueful sadness. "However, I suppose I'm proud of him."

"I think you should be," Caroline said defiantly.

"Uncle Jonathon?" Lydia had heard the name and now sought news of her missing uncle.

"He's become a soldier, dear," Martha explained. The letter said that Jonathon had been appointed an aide-de-camp to a cavalry commander called Colonel Jackson Weller. He explained in the letter that the appointment was not due to any virtue inherent in himself, but rather because he had brought the rebel army a good horse, saddle and bridle. Martha tried to explain to Lydia what an aide-de-camp was, then, failing, ordered the child to go down to Jenny in the kitchen. "I have to talk to Miss Fisher, my dear."

After Lydia left, Martha picked up the letter once more. "Jonathon says he's going to marry you." Her voice was cold.

"Yes, ma'am."

"If he is," Martha said with a flash of annoyance, "then for the Lord's sake stop calling me ma'am. You make me sound ancient!"

"I'm sorry."

"Forgiven." Martha examined Caroline. "I must say my poor brother has an eye for a certain sort of beauty. Do you want to marry him?"

Caroline shrugged. "I said I'd wait for him."

"Which doesn't answer my question." Martha, in a susurration of silk, crossed the floor to stand close to the sofa. "Are you going to marry him?"

Caroline felt offended by the questioning and was driven to a sulky defensiveness. "I know his family doesn't wish for that."

Martha seemed amused. "Why on earth should you think that?"

Caroline gestured at her thick, heavy skirts and plucked at her blue ticken jacket. Compared with the luxury of the room and the lavishness of Martha's clothes, she felt poor and negligible, and her gestures spoke it all without needing words to point the contrast.

Martha turned away from the girl. "My husband's family disapproved of me, most strongly. I was not wealthy, though God knows I brought him a large enough portion. They wanted Thomas to marry some spineless child from Virginia who'd have brought him eight thousand acres of tobacco land. They were not happy with me. I was definitely shoddy goods."

"But your husband defied his parents?"

"Clearly he did." Martha shrugged. "I'm not sure he was very wise, for we were not well suited. But I married Thomas for his money. I wanted to be rich, you see. I never wanted to be thought shoddy again. Is that why you want to marry Jonathon?"

"He wants to marry me."

"And Jonathon has a way of getting what he wants. It's the leg. He uses it to blackmail the world." Martha laughed softly. "He'll be very uncomfortable as a soldier."

Caroline was nonplussed by the sudden change of subject. "I'm sure."

"He's rather like me in some ways, he likes his comfort. I can't see him giving up the city for a farmer's life, can you?"

"No."

"And you look, if you'll forgive me, unsuited to the city."

Caroline thought she would rather face Ezra Woollard in a stinking alley than this needling examination. She was blunt. "You're saying we shouldn't marry?"

"I would never be so impertinent!" Martha said, quite forgetting that she had told her brother exactly that.

She turned to stare down at a mounted British officer who was talking with a girl on the opposite pavement. "I don't oppose your marriage," she said in an oddly strained voice, "because if I did I might lose Jonathon. And I have yet another reason for desiring your friendship." Martha still stared down at the officer who flirted with the girl. "I imagine that it will be hard to send letters to men in General Washington's army now that the Reverend MacTeague's friends have arrived?"

It was another confusing tack in the conversation, but one Caroline felt able to cope with. "I should think so."

Martha turned. "But you live across the river, so you can do it safely?"

"So long as the British do not garrison Cooper's Point."

"Why should they?" Martha, with a trim Philadelphian's arrogance, implied that there was nothing worth capturing in New Jersey. "Can you send more than letters?"

Caroline frowned. "More?"

Martha explained. "I'm asking whether you could send information to General Washington's army. Information that I might hear and would wish to pass on."

For the first time since she had entered the room, Caroline smiled. "I'd be proud to do that."

"That's why I stayed in the city. I can do more for our cause by sending news out of the city than I ever could by fleeing from it. And you can help me."

"I'd like to," Caroline said.

"Then, dear Caroline, you must consider yourself a welcome guest in this house. You are, after all, my prospective sister-in-law." Martha held out both hands to Caroline, who, quite flummoxed, hesitantly crossed the room. Martha, to Caroline's astonishment, kissed her. "Don't make him unhappy." The words were whispered fiercely.

"I won't."

"And I won't be your enemy." Martha drew Caroline to the window. "For we have enemies enough in the city now, without quarrelling amongst ourselves." Martha stared down at the British officer and tears ran down her face.

"It's the shame of it," she explained, "the shame of it." Because Philadelphia, without a shot being fired in her defence, had fallen.

Chapter Five

Captain John Andre, an elegant and fastidious man, stood in the window of the farmhouse that had been sequestrated for Sir William Howe's Germantown headquarters. He was watching the red-coated infantry camped in the pastures nearby: men who, in their search for firewood, had wrought destruction on what had once been a lovely orchard.

He turned towards the tallboy where Sir William's decanters were kept. On his way he gave a glance of mock horror at Vane, writing at a table. "Do you have to work so hard, Kit? You make the rest of us seem positively idle."

Vane smiled, but said nothing. Even now, two weeks after his sudden promotion, he could be startled awake by the sheer pleasure of his new captaincy and, as recompense to his patron, no aide worked harder than Vane in these dull, cold dog days of early autumn.

The troops, like most of the aides, idled. Lord Cornwallis, the second-in-command, had been sent to occupy Philadelphia with a small force, while the main army camped around Germantown to guard the approaches to the city. It was believed that George Washington, smarting under the loss of the rebel capital, might attempt to re-capture the city.

Andre, having poured himself a glass of rum, looked over Vane's shoulder and showed immediate alarm because Vane was working through the commissary accounts, a record of all the headquarters' expenditures for horses, food, lodgings and necessaries. "For God's sake," Andre said, "don't be too efficient."

"Because Sir William's stealing money?" Vane smiled. "I suppose every general does. All I'm doing is hiding it more efficiently."

"Good God!" Andre stared with grudging admiration at Vane. "You are ambitious!"

"Is there anything wrong with that?"

"One should never admit it."

Vane shrugged. "My father lost most of his money before he died, my family is sliding into obscurity, so my only hope of advancement lies in working hard." He regretted the words as soon as they were spoken, feeling that they revealed his naked self to a man who might be a rival. In truth, Andre, a frequent visitor to Sir William's headquarters, was the friendliest of all the elegant young men who inhabited Vane's new world. It was Andre who now explained that Sir William needed the extra money for his expensive American mistress. "Lizzie will be here as soon as the city's safe, and then you'll hardly see Billy at all. He's besotted."

"Is she pretty?"

"More beautiful than an angel. Intelligent, too, which is a most unfair conjunction. Her husband's been fobbed off with a job in New York."

"Is Billy married?"

Andre wondered if he detected a prudish note in Vane's question. "Not so long as he's in America."

"Ah." Vane closed the account books as footsteps sounded outside. It was dusk, a time when the aides liked to gather in contemplation of supper. All except Vane were bored, fretted by the necessity to linger in the countryside while the urban delights of Philadelphia were so close. Lord Robert Massedene, heading straight for the decanters, offered Vane a glass of claret. "I went to see your new horse, Vane. Very impressive."

"He's fast." Vane's duties demanded two horses, and so he had borrowed money to buy a magnificent black stallion.

"I'm sure he's fast," Massedene allowed, "but a little young, perhaps? He ain't nagged properly, not for battle. One cannon shot, Vane, and that stallion will get the shivers. Cling to your old mare in battle, and find a good man to nag the stallion. Just a word of advice."

It was a word of advice that irritated Vane. He had no intention of riding the stallion in battle until it was properly trained, and he found Massedene's assumption of his ignorance patronising. He disliked Massedene. He resented that the younger man should have such an effortless career, fuelled by noble birth, while Vane, who perceived himself as an abler man, must struggle for advancement.

The dislike was accentuated by their opposing views on the rebellion. Massedene, like Andre, only wished to see the rebellion ended, and did not much care how that culmination was achieved, so long as there was peace. Vane, like the Hessian interpreter Zeigler, believed that republican sentiment in America could only be stamped out by a military victory.

It was an argument that continued at that night's supper table. Major Zeigler, coming late, reported to Sir William that a schoolmaster from one of the Pennsylvanian German settlements had come to the Hessian lines and reported that the rebel army was planning to attack the following morning. They would march through the night, the schoolmaster had said, and attack at dawn. Massedene airily dismissed the man's claim. "Washington won't dare attack us. One more licking and his men will desert in their thousands!"

"I think you're wrong." Vane rather surprised himself by offering the contradiction. "I believe Washington will attack. He has to win a victory to restore his men's morale."

John Andre trimmed a candle. "I too think Mr. Washington has to attack. He'll fight to draw the French into the war."

Sir William, presiding over his young men, smiled. "I don't deny that the French would like to embarrass us, John, but would King Louis encourage republicanism?"

"The mere threat of French intervention," Andre said, "might persuade London of the need to make peace."

"Or victory," Vane said.

"Just peace." Sir William smiled at Vane. "We can't win a military victory, Kit. Everyone recognises that. The army's only here to force the rebels to the negotiating table."

Vane looked in astonishment at Sir William. "We can't beat them, sir?"

"Don't sound so forlorn! Of course we can't! My dear Kit, we had to abandon Boston to find the forces to take Philadelphia. It takes five thousand men to garrison a city and another five thousand to scour the countryside about that city for food, so we only have sufficient men to hold three cities, perhaps four, in all this gaping wilderness. Then we have General Burgoyne's army in New England, and must garrison Canada and the Floridas. Dear me, no. It would take a hundred thousand men to defeat the rebellion, and who'll pay for that, eh? My dear Kit, I fear you'll have to accept the mathematical logic of war. Our army is too small to take a continent."

He ended the discussion by stating his firm belief that, if the rebel army were marching to the attack, the cavalry patrols would discover it. Also, Sir William had doubled the army's pickets and, thanks to the happy arrival of three new convoys of ammunition, those pickets could now blaze into the night with impunity. "So we shall ignore a schoolmaster's tittle-tattle," Sir William suggested, "and play a hand of whist instead."

More port was opened, the cards broken out, and the candles guttered down to smoking stumps before Vane stumbled up the stairs to the linen store that he shared with Major Zeigler as a bedroom. A stomachache woke Vane just before dawn and drove him into the garden where he squatted by a quince tree that was wreathed in a new and thickening fog. A

372

cook whistled in the kitchens, and from the side path came the homely clanging of water pails.

"Sir! Sir! Are you there, sir?" It was Vane's servant, Private Smithers.

He grinned down at his master. "Two eggs for breakfast, sir? Bought them off the gunners."

"Who stole them, you fool, but I thank you anyway." Christopher Vane was partial to eggs. "Fry them and I might be restored to life."

A rattle of musketry sounded from the north. Vane stood, buttoned his breeches, and groaned as a pang of agony lanced through his head.

Sir William's servant appeared in the garden with a full chamber pot. "Good morning, sir!" He tossed the pot's contents onto the lawn, then frowned as another fusillade muttered and crackled. "They're a bit frisky this morning."

"It's the fog. It unsettles people."

Vane bent to the pump and splashed his face with water. The musketry died, then splintered again, this time reaching a crescendo of noise that was sustained like thunder. Vane stood, water dripping from his face, and stared helplessly northwards into the fog.

"Kit! Kit!" Sir William's voice called from an upstairs window.

"Sir!" Vane ran into the house. "Smithers! Smithers! Leave the eggs. Saddle the mare!" He raced upstairs, buttoned his jacket and buckled on his sword. Otto Zeigler gaped from his tangled blankets on the floor. "What's happening?"

"Either the pickets have gone mad or it's an attack. My hat? Oh God! My hat!"

"Here." Zeigler had been using it as a pillow.

Vane threw himself through the door and collided with Sir William. A messenger, smeared with mud, had already found the general who, calm in the panicky atmosphere, checked Vane's haste with a raised hand. "Go to the Beggarstown outpost, Kit. Find out what's happening. I'll join you there."

"Yes, sir."

Smithers was tightening the girth of Vane's mare. "Orders, sir?"

"I'm going to Beggarstown. Bring me some food if you can."

Vane spurred northwards, heading up the main street in the ever-thickening fog, towards the incessant crackle of musket fire. It was around five in the morning. A dog raced out of the Meeting House yard and yapped at the grey's heels, then, sudden and heart-stopping, a musket ball whiplashed from the blind fog to crack past Vane's face. A wounded Redcoat crawled back down the road. The first signs of battle.

VANE GALLOPED PAST two more wounded men dragging themselves to safety, then dimly, to his right, he saw a company of Redcoats in front of a grove of trees. He swerved off the road, jumped a flooded ditch, and galloped to the company's rear. The men were in their ranks, as tightly locked together as the pieces of a child's jigsaw puzzle. "Fire!" their captain shouted, and a volley stabbed smoke and flame into the fog. The stench of burnt powder assailed Vane's nostrils. "What's happening?"

"Rebel skirmishers, sir!" a sergeant at the rear of the company answered. A captain was giving the firing orders. The men had scraps of red cloth in their hats as marks that this was one of the light companies that had taken part in the action at Paoli's Tavern two weeks before.

"What rebels? Where?" Vane's questions seemed suddenly superfluous, for a flicker of musket balls slashed into the ranks. A corporal screamed and went down.

"Close up! Close up!" The sergeant ignored Vane.

Another British company, beyond the road, was still in skirmish order, the men picking targets in the fog and firing from a kneeling position. Vane spurred his horse back to the road. His job as an aide-de-camp was to help his master comprehend the battle. Thus he went forward towards the enemy, ahead of the foremost British troops. He had no idea if he was supposed to go so far forward, but he was intent on doing all that Sir William had asked and more. Captain Vane, plucked from regimental obscurity, would prove himself to be the best aide that any general could wish for.

He walked the mare forward, foot by nervous foot. Vane could feel his horse quivering in apparent fear. Her ears were pricked, reacting to every hissing bullet in the grey, wet fog. Vane wondered if the horse caught her nervousness from him, but then decided that even to think of the question was proof that he was not afraid. Once more the odd, calm joy of battle, which he had first known at Brandywine, surprised and pleased him. But then a sudden swirl of wind lifted the fog and in the momentary gap he saw the brown, red-faced uniforms of the rebel army. The enemy troops were in open order, but Vane had an impression, nothing more, of a mass of men further back marching beneath a gaudy banner. There were flecks of white in their hats.

A bullet drove a splash of mud up beside Vane's horse, and another bullet hissed behind his head as he turned and galloped away. Rebel taunts followed him, but Vane had done his job and seen the enemy. He galloped past the British skirmishers and saw a knot of mounted men spurring up the road, part of Sir William's staff. "The general?" Vane shouted.

"Over there!" A dragoon major pointed towards the company Vane had first visited, and Vane swerved in that direction. Men were giving ground and taking cover in the trees.

"Form up! Form up!" Sir William was behind the retreating men. "It's only a scouting force. We don't run from scouts! Captain! Form your men, if you please, sir! Let me see firmness!"

Sir William saw Vane, waved, then suddenly a cannon ball fired from the rebel front smashed into the branches above the commander-in-chief's head. Twigs, leaves and scraps of wood showered down as Sir William's horse reared and twisted.

"Not a scouting party, sir! They're in force," Vane shouted to Sir William. "I saw them, sir. Coming straight down the road!"

"Back!" Sir William shouted at the men whom, a moment before, he had ordered to stand and fight. "Back! Inform your flanks, sir! Form on the Meeting House!"

"You must go, sir!" Vane tried to seize the bridle of the general's horse, but Sir William jerked away. He was staring into the dirty, grey half-light of the fog-shrouded dawn.

"My God, this is rich, Kit!" Sir William was oddly elated as he watched the first rebels appear in the fog. Their bayonets were the brightest thing in all the dawn, brighter even than the scraps of white paper they all wore in their hats. Sir William, who liked all things American, was predictably impressed by his enemy. "They come on damned well, Kit, damned well! Don't they look well?"

Vane finally seized the bridle and turned the general's horse by main force. "Back, sir, I do beg you!"

The British outpost line was in full retreat now. The wounded were being dragged towards Germantown, while the dead were left where they had fallen. On either side of the road, colours high, the rebels advanced with bared bayonets.

The general let himself be drawn back out of the enemy's sight. "I'll form Musgrave to hold those rogues up! You fall back with these fellows. Keep an eye on the flanks!" Sir William lightly punched Vane's upper arm and spurred away with his entourage, passing a single horseman who was riding towards the enemy.

"Breakfast, sir?" It was Private Peter Smithers, mounted on Vane's new horse, the young and expensive black stallion with its three white socks and bright white blaze. Smithers held out two slices of bread between which he had put the fried eggs. "Breakfa—" He could not finish the word because a rebel cannonball, fired blind into the fog, had taken off his head as neatly as if a headsman had swung an axe. The young stallion, frightened by the smell and by the crack of bullets, reared high with eyes white and teeth bared.

"God!" Vane stared aghast at his servant's headless trunk. He had the insane urge to dismount and comfort the dead man, then he looked up to see the stallion bolting into the fog bank. He turned to follow his terrified horse when a rebel shout of triumph made him turn the mare's head towards safety. Damn and damn and damn!

The enemy had come from the fog in the dawn, and between them and Philadelphia was nothing but a bewildered army which had been surprised. Mr. Washington had his battle.

375

SAM'S REVEILLE had been the blistering crack of gunfire in the dawn, followed by urgent shouts as sergeants ran through the bivouacs. No one knew what was happening, there was no time for breakfast, only a milling confusion as men struggled into their packs, boots and belts, then fell into rank. Some of the battalion's women came running with scraps of bread and flasks of rum for their men. Maggie came. She smiled shyly towards Nate, but did not approach him. Instead she held out a cloth-wrapped bundle that Sergeant Scammell snatched from her as he strode towards the company.

Nate leaned confidingly towards Sam. "We're running today," he whispered.

Sam looked at his brother in amazement. "It's a bloody battle. Don't be a fool."

"She's going to hide over by the woods. I'm going to join her. Easy in a battle, isn't it? No one knows what the hell's happening."

A staff officer mounted on a grey horse sped past, then a flurry of orders turned the battalion towards the north up a mud-slick road in the fog.

They wheeled right into a rough pasture where two light galloper guns were deployed. As the battalion was brought to a halt, and faced front, both guns fired. They kicked back with shocking force, digging their trails into the mud so that the wheels bucked off the ground as vast gouts of grey-white smoke thickened the fog. Then, though there was no indication of what effect the two cannonballs might have had, the crews limbered up the guns, whipped their horses, and slewed back towards the encampment.

Captain Kelly, mounted on his mare Cleo, rode to a point fifteen paces ahead of the company. "Load." His voice was quite soft. Sam took out one of the thick, paper-wrapped cartridges and bit the bullet off. He lifted the musket's frizzen and put a pinch of powder into the pan, closed the lid, then upended the musket onto its butt so that he could pour the rest of the powder down the barrel. He stuffed the crumpled paper after it, spat the bullet into the muzzle, then drew out the long, brass-tipped rammer and thrust it hard down the barrel to compact bullet, paper and powder in the breech. The rammer went back into its hoops. Scraps of powder, gritty and saline, were left on his lips.

"Stand easy!" Captain Kelly called. He brought out a watch, clicked the lid open, then yawned hugely.

Sam borrowed a stone from Liam Shaughnessy and obsessively sharpened the tip of his bayonet. He felt strangely confident. He believed he had earned the red hackle that he wore so proudly. Before, at the battles around New York and at Brandywine, he had been scared of the enemy, but now he felt that the enemy might be even more scared of him.

His spirit was fired, his musket loaded, and he was a Redcoat who could not be beaten. Sam was ready.

A HUGE CHEER SOUNDED to Jonathon's right. It was a regiment of Virginians, flayed to ardour by their colonel. They fought, the Virginian colonel said, for liberty, and to make widows weep in England. This day they were going to humble the damned English. "For what are you?" the colonel shouted.

"Americans! Americans!"

"So kill the bastards! Kill the bastards! Kill the bastards!" And the Virginians took up the cry like a great yell of defiance that challenged the clinging fog.

Jonathon was lost, confused, excited and terrified. None of his competence as a merchant could help him in this, his first battle. Colonel Jackson Weller, who had appointed Jonathon as his aide, spoke excitedly of the massive attack General Washington had planned this day. For the first time ever the Continental Army, reinforced with the States' Militia, outnumbered the enemy. The Patriots would advance in four great phalanxes to strike at the British line, and the British, Weller had said, would not know where the Americans came from. As soon as General Howe thought he had found the main attack, another would slice in from another road and, in just a few hours, the lobsters would be carved, cooked, and served as a delicacy for General Washington's delectation.

"We're going to win, Johnny!" Jack Weller had said, and Jonathon had agreed, but now, in the fog, he could not make head nor tail of what was happening.

"Remember all I told you, son?" Sergeant Spring walked his horse to stand beside Jonathon's, and leaned over to tap the drawn sabre in Jonathon's hand.

"I think so, Sergeant."

Spring was a fatherly man and an expert horseman who was also a Methodist preacher. He knew all about young men going fresh into battle. He leaned over and took Jonathon's sabre into his own hand. "Use the edge, son, not the point. Hack with it, don't spear with it, and let your horse do the work."

Jonathon was grateful for the reiterated lesson. "Yes, Sergeant."

"And keep your weight off your right stirrup. You don't want to tumble by leaning too far." This was the sole reference to Jonathon's twisted leg. "If you can't reach an enemy, then go for a closer man."

"I will."

Spring smiled and handed back the sabre. "And don't chop your horse's ears off, son."

"No, Sergeant." Jonathon was suddenly terrified he would do just that. He had been feeling strangely guilty about the mare, wondering if he would be accused of stealing it from his uncle, but Colonel Weller had said that horse-thieving was a small transgression in a man who fought to steal a whole country from the tyrant.

And this day, God willing, Jonathon would strike a blow against that tyrant, and his battle shout would be, not Liberty, but the name of the girl he loved. So now Jonathon rode for Caroline, and the memory of her had given him courage in the damp discomfort of a soldier's life.

It was a life in which Jonathon had never worked so hard, been so sore, slept so briefly, nor been so happy. His leg had seemed an obstacle to those who had given him advice in Philadelphia, but here, among the fighting men, it did not matter. If he was slow in reaching the horse lines he was mocked good-naturedly, but no one called him a cripple, or wondered why he had volunteered for the fight. He was accepted, and today he would reward his comrades' friendship by showing that a wealthy young city boy could fight as well as any man.

"Johnny! Johnny!" demanded Colonel Weller, galloping from the fog.

"Sir?"

"You know where Forrest's scoundrels are?"

"Yes, sir."

"That's more than most people do." Weller was scribbling with a lump of charcoal on a sheet of paper. "They're militia, so they probably can't read. Ignorant country bastards, they are, but don't tell them I said so." He kept on writing.

Jonathon waited. The colonel was a huge man, bigger even than Woollard, with a battered face and a grating voice. Gossip said that he had been a wastrel and a gambler before the rebellion had found a use for his restless energy.

Today Weller wore a brown leather jerkin with the red sash of his rank about his waist. His hard-planed face was shadowed by a brimmed hat that bore the scrap of white paper which, in the confusion of uniforms and homespun, was the Patriots' mark for the day. He finished scribbling and held the paper out to Jonathon. "If Forrest can't read, tell him to advance anyway. Straight up the gully, then slant towards the village. Tell him, then come back here. I want you by my side today. A good man beside me makes me feel better."

Jonathon, whose face had been drawn with worry all morning, suddenly laughed. "Yes, sir!"

He wheeled the roan mare and trotted to the west. Somewhere behind him a rebel band of flutes struck up the Jacobite "White Cockade" as a taunt to the enemy's Hanoverian monarch. Then, with a shout, and beneath their great flag, the Virginians went forward and Jonathon, riding in the fog, was determined that on this day of battle he would become a man worthy of the girl who waited for his return.

He would fight, he would conquer his fear, and he would strike a blow for the cause; not with the point, but with the edge. For this day, with God's blessing and in defence of a God-given liberty, Jonathon would become a soldier.

Chapter Six

Just as Sam thought that his battalion was doomed to wait for ever in the fog, Colonel Elliott turned in his saddle and signalled with his sword arm to Captain Kelly. The captain's sabre rasped out of its scabbard. "Light company! Skirmish order! One hundred paces only!"

Sam was in the light company: the skirmishers who had the honour of first meeting the enemy. Their job was to act as a screen for the remaining nine companies: a screen which tried to unsettle an advancing enemy with aimed musket fire. But, as Sam and Nate went forward together, no enemy was visible in the fog.

"Far enough!" Captain Kelly had ridden forward with the company.

Sam knelt. Ten paces either side of him were other men, while staggered back between the front men were their partners. Nate, Sam's partner, would advance after Sam had fired. Nate's loaded musket would offer protection as Sam reloaded. And so they would fire, turn and turn about. The other companies, waiting invisible in the fog behind, would stay in tightly locked ranks to pour out massed volleys of musket fire.

Nothing stirred the mist before the skirmish line.

Sam stared into the fog. He put the brass butt of his musket on the ground and leaned on its barrel like a shepherd resting on a crook.

"You all right, Sam?" Nate asked.

"You're still here, then?" Sam grinned at his brother.

"For the moment."

"Don't be a fool, Nate. I'll miss you."

"Come with me."

Then suddenly, brown-clothed men with white papers in their caps charged from their right flank. No one in the light company had heard them.

"Right flank, incline! Close!" Scammell's shout pumped warm panic into Sam's chest as he glimpsed the enemy coming so suddenly from the misted valley.

"Fire!" Sam twisted half right, pulled the trigger. The butt gave its mule-kick to his shoulder, and flaming scraps of powder burned his cheek.

"Close on me!" Scammell, as ever, was superbly calm in battle. The skirmishers had been surprised and outflanked, but Scammell was coping as though the attack were merely an inconvenience.

"Rejoin! Rejoin!" Captain Kelly galloped towards the danger, pointing back towards the main battalion that would greet this attack with a numbing volley. "Go! Go! Go!" His bugler, left alone in the mist, sounded the retreat.

A musket ball hit Cleo. The mare screamed, and the captain kicked his feet from the stirrups as the horse reared, twisted and fell.

Nate grabbed Sam and pulled him back. "Run, Sam!"

"Move!" Scammell, still calm in the panic, was shouting at the light company, but the shouts of the rebels were closer. They seemed to Sam to be screaming like fiends. He ran forward, but suddenly the fog ahead of him blazed with a flickering of myriad tongues of fire, and a musket volley crashed around his ears, like the beat of thunder in his skull.

"God!" Nate sheered away. There were American light troops between the skirmishers and the battalion now and Sam, suddenly confused, ran away from both, ran blindly in search of any shelter.

Another crashing volley behind, more flames, then Sam saw a rail fence and dived for its scanty cover.

More of the light company took refuge by the fence: Sergeant Derrick with a half dozen men. "Kelly's dead. They got him with bayonets," he said.

It had all happened so suddenly. Sam had imagined seeing the first figures in the fog, then fighting as he had been trained, before the bugle ordered him back to the waiting battalion which would blast the enemy away with its practised volleys. Instead, in a sudden paroxysm of violence, the Yankees had hooked in from the fog and now Sam was lost in a frightened huddle on a strange battlefield. Captain Kelly's horse, that Sam had tended so lovingly, was beating its hooves on the ground as it lay dying. Men, bleeding and dying, lay crying in the fog.

Sam spat a bullet into his musket and rammed the charge down the barrel. He could hear the volleys crashing between the two bodies of troops, and he could hear the screaming of wounded men and an American officer shouting that these men wore the red badges.

"Right mess, innit, Sam?" Sergeant Derrick said.

"What are we going to do?"

"Take those hackles off, that's what we do." Derrick pulled off his hat and ripped the red wool away. "All of you! I'm not going to be slaughtered for a scrap of bleeding wool! Get 'em off!"

The men obeyed. Sam ripped off the red wool, the sign of his pride, and hurled it into the pastureland.

"Behind! Behind!" Sergeant Derrick, voice rising in panic, twisted to face north.

Sam writhed round and saw more brown-clothed men in the fog. It was a new enemy skirmish line that advanced on the right flank of the first attack. He put the musket to his shoulder, then heard hooves to his right and saw the shapes of mounted men hammering in a sudden gallop.

"Run!" Sergeant Derrick bellowed in panic.

"Fire!" Sam shouted the word. "Fire, fire, fire!"

Perhaps six men instinctively obeyed Sam. They made a rough line, they shouldered their muskets, and they pulled their triggers. Smoke blossomed, and through its screen Sam saw a horseman throw up an arm, then fall sideways from the saddle. A trumpet was screaming in the morning, hooves were like drumbeats from hell, and the bright surprise of drawn sabres sliced into the Redcoats.

Sam seized Nate's arm and dragged him to the right. The horses crashed past. Sam stumbled, and the fall saved his life. A sabre hissed by his head, missing by a hand's-breadth.

"Nate!"

"I'm here!" Nate was flat on his face, cowering from the drumming hooves.

And now, to the north, the second battalion of rebel troops marched from the fog. Men ran from its ranks with bayonets raised.

"Don't!" Nate screamed, holding up a hand to ward off the blow.

"Get up!" the rebel snarled. The American had a thin, tanned face which seemed to Sam as hard as dried leather.

Sam and Nate stood up. Other survivors of the light company were also taken prisoner. All were stripped of weapons, ammunition, food.

"Move!" The leather-faced rebel jabbed his bayonet into Sam's ribs. "Move, you bastard!"

Sam stumbled over the pasture. He was shaking. Sergeant Derrick lay lifeless, his guts spilt blue on the field. Liam Shaughnessy was bleeding from the belly, dying. The smell of blood was thick as smoke.

"Sit, you bastards!"

There were ten prisoners from the light company. They sat. Then, out of the fog, shambling in a dispirited and defeated mass, more captured Redcoats were pushed towards Sam's group. Most of the battalion, behind its volleys, had fallen back before the rebel charge, but a good sixty prisoners had been taken.

A dozen Americans were ordered to stay with the prisoners. The guards were grinning and confident men who chewed tobacco as they ordered the Redcoats to collect the wounded and drag the dead into a heap.

A dismounted American officer prowled around the prisoners. He stopped by Sam and Nate. "You two! Come here."

The brothers, apparently chosen at random, were taken fifty yards up the road to where a young American, wearing riding boots and with an empty sabre scabbard at his hip, lay white-faced on the grass. His breath was coming in gasps. His right thigh was a mess of blood that had been staunched by a twist of rope tightened about his leg at the groin.

"Look after him," the American officer said. "If that leg starts to bleed again, tighten the rope. If he wants water, give it to him." The officer dropped a canteen onto the grass, then untethered a horse tied to the rail fence behind the wounded man. He swung himself into the saddle. "I'll be back. You keep him alive, you bastards, or I'll crucify you both! You hear me?"

"Yes, sir," Sam said. He turned to the American who, he saw, could be no older than himself. The wounded man had a thin, pale, handsome face and long black hair. He was trying to sit up and the pain was making him cry out.

"It's all right," Sam said. "It's all right. Calm now." Sam had always been a genius with sick horses, and now he found he had the same ability with this wounded lad who, eyes flickering, looked at first with alarm at his red-jacketed comforter, and then seemed to relax.

"Here," Sam said, "I'll pull you up. Slow now." He eased the American up and propped him against a fence post.

He wetted his right hand with water and rubbed it over the lad's face. It did not seem at all odd to be giving help to an enemy. "You're going to be good as new," Sam said. "It's only a bullet hole!"

The American gave a weak smile. "My first battle," he said. "My first battle." He had tears of pain on his cheeks.

"Come on now." Sam wiped the tears away. "You don't want to cry in front of an Englishman!"

"Lobsters," the lad said.

"Lobsters?"

"That's what they call you. We call you." The American's breathing was easier now, much easier. Sam saw how good his clothes were: he was wearing a coat of the finest wool weave, a linen shirt and a thick, leather sword belt.

"Are you an officer?"

"I don't think so." The American grinned weakly. "I was an aide. My name's Jonathon Becket."

"Like the archbishop, eh?" Sam said.

"He died," Jonathon said weakly.

"Don't be soppy," Sam said sternly. "I'm Sam, that's Nate. We're twins. I was born first, and I got all the brains." Sam was suddenly glad that this was not the horseman who had fallen to his panicked volley. Sam had seen that man lying dead, so Jonathon must have been hit by another bullet fired elsewhere in the misted confusion. "You ain't too bad," Sam said with rough comfort. "Leg's torn up a bit, but the bone's not broken. You're going to be all right." Sam was staring at Jonathon's wounded leg, and he saw beneath the blood that the leg was twisted and that its foot, encased in a grotesque boot, was clubbed. God help the rebels, Sam thought, if they were sending cripples to war. "I've seen worse wounds," he said to encourage the American.

"That was on horses, Sam," Nate said chidingly.

"I mended a horse once that speared itself on a fence post," Sam said, "and I had it trotting like a winner in a month! I'll have you on your feet, Yankee." He saw Jonathon shiver so he took off his thick red coat and draped it about his enemy's chest to keep him warm.

"My first battle," Jonathon said. He looked as if he were about to cry, not with pain, but with the shame of failing so signally in his very first battle.

"You'll have other battles," Sam said.

"Not if I lose the leg."

"What are you talking about?" Sam's scorn was both kindly and truthful. "I reckon you must be an officer if you're making a fuss about a little scratch like that!" Sam knew the wound was far worse than a scratch, but he also saw how his enemy was needing this comfort, and was, indeed, clinging to every word with a desperate hope.

Jonathon laughed. "It wasn't much of a leg to start with."

Sam smiled. "It was the one God gave you, Yankee, so you might as well hang on to it. You'll fight again, Johnny. I'll have you on your feet, I'll have you fighting, even if it is for the wrong bloody side. I promise it!"

Sam had made a promise, while about him, in the smoke-thickened fog, the rebel army marched on.

CAPTAIN CHRISTOPHER VANE had begun to believe that God intended great things for him; why else would Providence have let him survive the first hours of a battle in which he, Christopher Vane, had seen things that before this day had only dwelt in nightmare?

He had watched the advancing rebels savage the retreating light infantry. No prisoners had been taken as the attack flooded down Germantown's main street, for the memory of the night attack at Paoli's Tavern was still fresh. Men were chopped and stabbed and skewered with bayonets.

A musket ball had plucked at the skirts of Vane's coat, another had thumped on its hide-stiffened shoulder and ripped off an epaulette, while a third had drawn blood from the back of his hand. He stayed with the retreating light infantry, obeying Sir William's instructions. Twice he fended off bayonets with his sabre, and he had shot two men with his pistols. The world had become a small, stinging circle of fog in which men panted, screamed, shot, stabbed and died. Time was chaos, in which Vane was once again astonished by the exultation of battle.

"Move yourself, sir, move over!" a voice bellowed at Vane.

Vane turned in his saddle and was astonished to see a British battalion drawn in tight formation across the road with their three ranks of muskets aimed at his horse. He spurred to the battalion's flank, clearing it just as their first massive volley pulsed smoke and flame into the fog.

"Who are you?" he shouted at a lieutenant.

"Fortieth, sir!"

These, then, were the men Sir William had placed to check the rebel thrust, and Vane felt a fierce joy as the battalion went into the deadly rhythm of platoon fire. Each half company fired separately, immediately after the half company to its right, so that the muskets spat in unending

ripples of flame down the long front. The men worked with a soulless precision. They fired, reloaded, rammed, fired, reloaded, rammed, and the only untoward movements were the flickers as red-coated men fell backwards from the enemy's fire.

"Close up! Close up!" the sergeants shouted. The wounded were dragged back, and the men shuffled again into their locked formation without breaking the tempo of their work. The front rank knelt on their right knees, the centre rank stood behind with each man's left foot hard against the right foot of the kneeling man in front, while the rear rank locked their right boots against the centre rank's left feet.

The muskets pumped smoke to thicken the fog through which, their blood roused by imminent victory, the Americans charged. They paid for their temerity. This was not light infantry, scattered in a skirmish line, but a formed battalion that could hammer bullets in a rhythm of death.

"Close up! Close up!"

The battalion's colours of heavy, fringed silk jerked from bullet strikes. Sergeants armed with wide-bladed halberds guarded the precious flags. "Steady!" the colonel shouted. "Well done! Well done! Steady now, lads!" He pushed his horse between two files of men to stare into the smoke-fouled fog. "Cease fire! Cease fire! Load!"

The battalion went silent. Enemy fire still spat through the fog, but the platoon fire had repelled the first rebel attack.

The Americans had withdrawn into the smoke-pearled fog in order to regroup. Now, with a cheer, they made a fresh and spirited charge. Vane heard them before he saw them.

"Wait!" the colonel shouted. "Wait, my boys! Wait!"

The American cheer rose into a howl of blood-lust that rang until, just as it seemed to Vane that the colonel had left his volley too late, the sword flashed down and the command was shouted. "Fire!"

Seven hundred muskets flamed together in one terrible stinging volley that threw the attacking line into ruin. "Front rank, rise!" The colonel was standing in his stirrups now, sword raised. "Battalion will advance! On my word!" The sword pointed forward. "March!"

The shining halberds swung down and the Redcoats went forward, not in a loose running mass like the rebels, but with a silent and deadly efficiency. The surviving enemy did not wait to contest the charge, but edged warily backwards.

"Halt! Reload! Front rank, kneel! Wait for my word!" The colonel's sword went up. "Rear ranks only!" The blade seared down. "Fire!" Another heavy volley coughed and flamed, this one slashing into rebel ranks already disordered by the 40th's murderously disciplined fire. This was infantry work at its awesome best, but it was not enough. The colonel, the front quietened for a moment, trotted round to the right flank where he saw Vane.

"You're Kit Vane, aren't you?"

"Yes, sir."

Colonel Musgrave watched his two rear ranks finish their reloading. "Bastards are turning my left flank. Nothing I can do about it, so I'm going to earth." Musgrave gestured towards a substantial, brick-built house behind him. "Cram the lads in there and invite 'em to dig us out. Perhaps you'd tell Sir William?"

"Of course I will, sir."

Colonel Musgrave, his wig in place and his white stock impeccably tied, stared northwards. "I suspect this is their main lunge, Vane. I could have sworn I saw Fat George. He sits on a horse like a pregnant fishwife, but he's brave enough." Musgrave took out a snuffbox, opened the lid, and offered a pinch to Vane. "But after that little lesson I suspect they'll bring up their cannon, don't you? So I think the house is the best thing. Try and relieve us when you can."

"Of course, sir." Vane refused the snuff. "You think they've got behind us?"

"No doubt about it. You'll have an exciting ride, Vane. Death or glory, eh? Good luck." Musgrave laughed grimly, then cupped his hands. "Left flank, incline to the rear! Smartly now!" He shook his head proudly.

"They're good lads, Vane, the very best, but it's time I got them tucked up safe. You'll give my compliments to Sir William?"

"I will, sir."

"Tell him he owes me a pipe of port if the Fortieth live through today."

A HALF MILE BEHIND the house, the commander-in-chief waited in the centre of his main defensive line at the southern edge of Germantown.

John Andre, horse lathered, galloped in from the fog. "General Grey's compliments, sir, and Luken's Mill is still in our hands."

"Thank God."

"But he needs men, sir. The outposts were badly cut up. We put Elliott's battalion in support, but he lost a good few men."

"God help them," Howe said.

Slowly Sir William was piecing together a picture of his battlefield, and it was not pretty. American columns were advancing down at least three roads, and the fog made their progress almost impossible to measure. He might already be surrounded.

Yet, though Sir William had once sworn never to fight against the Americans, neither did he intend to lose to them. They might hold the initiative now, but Sir William was no mean commander. The flanks, he decided, must be staunch. The right flank, deeply wounded by the rebel attack, was demanding reinforcements, but Sir William now refused the request. This battle would be decided in the heart of the field, and Sir William would strengthen the centre of his line and hope that the rebel onslaught did not come before he could assemble the men who must first withstand the assault, then counterattack. He fretted for the arrival of men from the city's garrison. He twisted in the saddle to look for his servant. "Evans? Is Hamlet safe?"

Tom Evans, mounted on one of Sir William's spare horses, held up the general's dog. "Quite safe, sir."

"Good man. As long as he's safe we can't lose, eh?" Forced laughter sounded as Sir William turned back. In front of him a battery of artillery pointed down the wide, fog-shrouded main street, but the waiting barrels were still masked by red-coated infantry that sniped at enemy skirmishers flitting past like phantoms in the whiteness. Then between those enemy skirmishers, and riding like a man set to win a fortune on a steeplechase, came a red-jacketed officer.

Hat awry and one epaulette torn, Vane slowed his mare to a trot. He took off his hat to Sir William. "Good morning, sir! Musgrave's gone to ground in a large house, but he thinks this is their main lunge. He's fairly sure he saw Mr. Washington with them."

"Our intrepid George is never far from the main action, is he?" The scrap of information was useful to Sir William, for it confirmed his suspicion that the struggle in the village would decide the battle, but it was small comfort. He had nothing like enough men assembled yet to check a determined thrust.

"Did Musgrave hold them at all?"

"He gave them hell for a while, sir."

"Let's hope they need an hour to reform." It seemed a vain hope on which to pin victory, but it was the only hope Sir William had at that moment.

Vane was yearning for an acknowledgment of his achievement from Sir William. He thought that praise was coming when the commander-in-chief noticed Vane's bloodied uniform, but a spent musket ball fluttered between the two men and a yelp sounded from behind. Tom Evans had been struck by the ball. It had only bruised him, but the shock was sufficient to make him release Hamlet who, barking and brisk, scampered towards the enemy.

"Stop him!" Sir William shouted. "Stop him!"

There was a maelstrom of gunners and Redcoats diving at the dog, which barked, swerved, then ran free into the fog. It disappeared.

"I'm sorry, sir." Evans was massaging his bruised shoulder.

"God's teeth! You fool!" Sir William's temper was an awesome thing. The dog had been a gift from his Boston-born mistress, and the loss of it struck sore. It also tempted fate because of Sir William's jest that had tied the dog's safety to the battle's outcome. Soldiers are notoriously superstitious. The general brooded behind the guns while the aides waited further back.

"I've lost my spare horse," Vane said angrily as he and Andre dismounted by the gun limbers. "A hundred guineas gone in the fog!"

Andre could not help laughing. Britain was on the brink of losing a battle, perhaps losing thirteen colonies, and the general was making a fuss about a lost dog and Vane about a horse. Then Andre saw he had offended Vane and was immediately penitent. "I'm sorry, Kit, truly."

"Not as sorry as I am. And I didn't get breakfast!"

"We can remedy that, at least." The gunners had a mess of lentils and salt pork standing on a limber and, in return for Andre's silver, happily allowed the two officers to spoon their fill from the lukewarm pot. From somewhere behind came the sound of hooves and Vane and Andre turned to see a mud-spattered Massedene gallop from the mist.

Massedene spoke with Sir William, then trotted back to his fellow aides. He slid stiffly off his horse. "We're bringing every spare man from the city. God knows if they'll be in time. Is that food?" He turned to stare into the fog out of which came the sound of cannonade and musket fire. "My God, is it that bad?"

"I rather think Mr. Washington has wrong-footed us." Andre spoke quietly. "It's going to be mildly desperate, I think."

Massedene stared northwards. "How many of them?"

"God knows." Vane imitated Andre's insouciance. "They're as thick as penny whores round a barrack gate."

"I never lingered in such places," Massedene said carelessly, "but I'll take your word for it."

Vane, knowing he had been slighted, looked angrily away. The mist was clearing, and the rebels held the war's outcome in the palms of their powder-stained hands.

All that the despised George Washington needed to do was squeeze.

Chapter Seven

The horse, empty stirrups flapping, trotted jauntily out of the fog.

It was a young horse: a black stallion with a distinctive white blaze and three white socks. It saw the prisoners and swerved away with its handsome head tossing. One of the guards whooped and ran towards it. The beast avoided him easily. Other guards ran to help. Sam thought they were like children playing a boisterous game.

"They're Virginians," Jonathon said. He grinned as the stallion thudded northwards into the fog to escape the loud and clumsy pursuit. "I'm not. I'm from Philadelphia."

The guards, their prize lost, wandered back to the prisoners. Musket fire still sounded through the fog. The prisoners sat silent.

Sam turned as a new bout of firing erupted in the south, then another in the west. It was impossible to tell what was happening, but he had an idea that the fog was slowly clearing. He could just see the black stallion, head erect, perhaps seventy yards to the north. He guessed the animal was frightened, but then a thicker waft of fog hid the horse again.

"God!" A lance of pain streaked up into Jonathon's groin and belly. He shifted. Sam had bandaged his wound with a dead man's torn shirt, then released the tourniquet. "I'm going to lose the leg."

Sam scorned such pessimism. "No! You'll be dancing again!"

Jonathon tried to laugh and sobbed with pain instead. "Do I look like someone who ever danced?"

"So what's wrong with having a hobble?" Sam looked at the leather-clad clubfoot. "Must be bloody useful for kicking the lights out of people you don't like." Sam saw that the pain was still flickering, and, because he had nothing better to offer, he uncorked the canteen of water. "Pity it isn't good ale, eh? I miss the ale. Good, thick ale."

Jonathon wanted distraction from the pain. "Go on."

So Sam found himself talking about home. About Parson Harvey who shot rooks from the church tower with a blunderbuss, and about the sound of the hunting horn drifting over cold fields in winter, and about Plough Monday when there was a great feast up at the Hall.

"Did you have a school?" Jonathon asked.

"Parson's wife made us learn letters, but not much." Sam had learned the really useful things from his father: how to shoe a horse and how to stop an earth so a dog fox, coming home with a full belly on a January morning, would be up and about for the gentry to hunt. How to spot a steel trap, set to snatch a man's leg in a wood, and how to take a cock pheasant with a throwing stick. How to loop a pike, or lime a singing bird for the London market, and how to spot a good ratting terrier in a litter.

"And girls?" Jonathon asked.

Sam grinned. "We had girls. Summer nights! Back of the wheatfields." His homesickness made his voice plaintive.

"Why did you join the army?" Jonathon asked in some astonishment.

"My daft brother dared me to." Sam punched Nate's shoulder. He remembered how Nate had come running home with news of the bright gold the army was offering to recruits.

Nate and Sam had been seventeen then, and Sam was sure there would be more than gold, that he would strut through a market place with silver loops hanging from a braided jacket and a pretty girl on his arm. Such a future seemed better than the bawling, echoing stables where in winter the ice made a skin on the stones.

"This bloody fool dared me," Sam said wistfully to Jonathon. And so the twins had run to the town and taken the King's Shilling and discovered the promised bounty was spent on boots, brushes, stockings and flour for the hair. "It bloody hurt, that!" Sam laughed.

"What hurt?" Jonathon asked.

"Your hair, see?" Sam turned to show the American boy the thick pigtail that hung stiff behind his head. "You have to grow it first, then they pull it back. You can't close your eyes, it's so tight! Honest! Then they smear it with tallow, twist it round a leather pad, and fill it with flour. It's called a queue."

Their first lesson as soldiers had been how to stand straight and unmoving as the stiff leather collar abraded the skin under their chins into two bloody welts that slowly calloused into hard, white ridges. Then they had learned to march in the high-knee, boot-thumping step, how to fire their big, clumsy muskets, and how to stand in the battle line while death whipped at them.

They slept two in a bed, head to toe, and the barrack rats would chew their flour-stiffened queues at night. They ate the slops the King gave them. They were beaten, whipped, snarled at; and they knew it was for ever, for the only escape was through wounding or death. Sam had broken his mother's heart. If he had not been a fool, his mother said, he could have become the squire's chief coachman and worn a triple-caped coat. Instead he had thrown it all away for a dare. He shrugged now. "Why did you join?" he asked Jonathon.

"Because I want our side to win," Jonathon said. "Because tyrants in London will make us slaves."

"You're as daft as him!" Sam gestured at his brother. "No one's enslaving you! I've never heard such gammon! Slaves! You're the ones with slaves, not us. Us enslave you? You're daft as lights!"

"You should go and tell George Washington! He'd probably stop fighting." Nate grinned at his brother. "What do you know about it, Sam?"

"I'm English, and I'm bloody proud of it," Sam said belligerently.

"So'm I," muttered Nate, "but I'm still off." He looked towards the rebel guards.

"Don't," Sam said. "Please, Nate."

"Maggie, Sam, Maggie." Nate's answer was laconic. "I promised. She's waiting for me."

"You want to desert?" Jonathon had been listening to the conversation.

Nate grinned. "It is my ambition, my good Yankee, to find somewhere to live in America. My loyal brother here is nervous, but not me. Nathaniel Gilpin has had enough of King George's army, and if you ask me, Sam, we should both now resign our red coats and run like hell."

"You should. And you'll get liberty!" said Jonathon, with the true passion of a young revolutionary.

"I've got liberty!" Sam said, in blithe disregard of his predicament. "And he ain't interested in liberty. He's got a girl."

"A Yankee girl," Nate said to Jonathon with sudden enthusiasm. "She's waiting in a spinney over there. She's pretty as a picture!"

"So's mine," Jonathon said warmly. "She's called Caroline." There was a sudden burst of musket fire to the south, where the Virginian regiments had marched.

The black stallion had come closer again. Its nostrils were dilated and its eyes showed white. It had the stance of an animal ready to flee at the smallest provocation. "If you get me on that horse," Jonathon said to Nate, "I'll come with you. I promise I can get you past our lines. I can ride, even if I can't walk."

Nate looked at his brother. "You could catch it, Sam. Will you?"

"Just so you can run away?" Sam was scornful.

"It's my life, Sam!" Nate was suddenly angry. "We ain't tied by chains, you and I. You be a soldier, Sam! You be the best goddamned soldier you can ever be, but let me be what I want to be!" Nate's eyes were glistening. "Sam, please!"

"You're both mad," Sam said, but he stood up and, ignored by the guards, ducked through the fence rails.

He walked very slowly towards the handsome black horse. It was scared. Its muscles twitched beneath the glossy, mud-flecked skin.

"Easy, boy! Easy!" Sam stopped twenty paces from the stallion. It must have belonged to a British officer, for it had the royal cipher embroidered on the tail of its dark blue saddlecloth. "It's all right, boy, all right. Nothing to fret about. Only Sam coming for you." Sam talked the soothing nonsense as he walked closer and closer to the trembling, white-eyed stallion. Its ears pricked and its front right hoof pawed at the ground. "Haven't seen a horse like you for years! Good boy, now. Easy, easy, easy." Sam plucked a handful of grass and, still talking, held it out to the beast. He let the stallion smell him. "Good boy, now, good boy." The horse, still quivering, stepped towards Sam who, very gently, reached with his free hand for a ring of the bit. He took it, then let the horse take the grass. "Easy, boy, easy, easy."

He soothed the stallion, rubbing its flanks and letting the nervousness flow out of it. It had been lost in the fog, terrified by cannon and musket fire, and now it trembled as Sam rubbed it down. "All right, boy. Let's see how you go, shall we?" Sam took the saddlehorn in his left hand and pulled himself onto the stallion's back. The horse shivered, its ears pricked back again, but Sam knew how to soothe nervous animals. "Good boy, good boy. Easy now." He touched its flanks with his heels and the stallion, obedient to his touch, walked forwards.

The noise of battle seemed to be all round Sam now, but he was riding this magnificent horse and, for a few seconds, he forgot his predicament. There was a pure pleasure in being in the saddle.

"Sam!" Nate called. The rebel guards were watching Sam now and one of them put a musket to his shoulder, but the range was too great to try a shot. Sam kicked his heels back. He could ride back to his own lines. He could forget Nate's madness and go back where he belonged.

He turned the horse southwards, and there coming from the mist was a miracle: Redcoats.

Lines of Redcoats. Redcoats marching beneath their colours, to take victory where they had tasted defeat.

Sam stared.

Ahead of the advancing line were the skirmishers and Sam recognised Scammell at the fore. Sam grinned. The handful of prisoners had also seen their salvation. They stood and cheered, and their guards fled.

"Sam!" Nate's scream was despairing, frantic.

"You're too late!" Sam shouted. He stood in the stirrups and waved. A bagpipe skirled suddenly, fierce and blazoning, revealing a Highland regiment on the road's flank.

"Sam!" Nate was leaning on the fence, frantically gesturing for Sam to bring him the horse. "Sam!"

"We've won, Nate! We've won!" Sam's exhilaration soared. "We've bloody won!"

Sergeant Scammell was waving now, shouting incomprehensibly at Sam, and the sight of his hated enemy made Nate turn and run. He ran

392

northwards, running to the freedom that had haunted his dreams in the weeks since the army had come ashore in Chesapeake Bay. He took off his red coat as he ran and threw it down.

"Private Gilpin! Halt!" Scammell, leading the skirmishers, and far ahead of the battalion, shouted at Nate.

Nate floundered on.

Sergeant Scammell pulled back the cock of his musket. He put the brass butt to his shoulder and aimed.

"Put it down!" Jonathon Becket, lying by the roadside fifteen yards from Scammell, aimed his pistol.

But Sergeant Michael Scammell feared no wounded rebel. He fired.

Sam turned, shouting, screaming, but Nate was arching his back and in the very centre of his spine a great smear of red spread on his dirty grey shirt.

"Sam!" Nate was on his knees now, still trying to go forwards. "Sam?"

The range must have been thirty yards. A long shot for a musket. Fifteen yards was no great distance for a pistol, but Jonathon's shot, fired from an enfeebled hand, went yards wide. Sergeant Scammell walked up to the boy, and ground his boot's heel into Jonathon's wounded thigh. Jonathon screamed.

Nate twitched, face-down on the road. Blood soaked his shirt. His head turned towards his brother. "Sam? Sam?"

"Nate!"

Sam had kicked the horse onwards. He jumped the fence, reined in, and slid out of the saddle. Loyalist cavalry had appeared in the pasture beyond the fence, and some were on the road ahead, but Sam saw none of them. He only saw his brother.

"Sam." Nate was crying now. The sobs became great pangs of agony in which Sam could hear the word "Mother" again and again.

Sam lifted his brother, cradling him. "Nate?"

But Nate could not hear. Nate bent his back like a man broken on the wheel and his scream pierced through the fog in terrible agony before the blood, flooding up his windpipe, choked it off. Sam, holding his brother as though he could put his own life and strength into Nate's body, felt the terrible jerk as the scream ended, and there was silence.

"Nate?" Sam asked. "Nate?"

A shadow fell over Sam. Sergeant Scammell had seized the black horse's bridle and now, standing above Sam, he looked down on the dead boy. "He was running, Sam."

"You murdered him."

"He was running!" Scammell snapped the words. "Now get your red coat on before I say you were running, Sam Gilpin!"

Sam laid his brother in the mud. He stroked Nate's cheek once, then he stood up. "You murdered him."

Scammell stared coldly into Sam's eyes. "Be careful, Sam."

"Bastard."

Sam's world had changed. Everything had changed. "Bastard!" He hit Scammell one huge blow; a blow that snapped Scammell's face round and made the sergeant release the horse. Sam seized the reins, then blinded by tears, he pulled himself onto the stallion's back. He heard shouts. The field was a blur of red coats, of flags, of thinning smoke and tears. He saw his brother's dead face, and then he kicked his heels and the stallion took him away from the smoke and the red coats. Scammell shouted in rage behind, but Sam did not hear, for his brother, with all his dreams of paradise beyond the hills, was dead. And Sam, riding to nowhere, wept.

BANDS PLAYED. The fog was a cacophony of brass and drums, all punctuated by gunfire and the unending musket fire.

The sound jarred Sir William's ears as he waited for his doom to burst down the village's main street. Yet moment succeeded moment and no American columns appeared beneath their lifted banners.

"You don't think ..." Sir William heard himself beginning to express the hope of victory, for, in the chaos, drawn by Sir William's will, there was now the shape of a counterattack ready to advance. Sir William looked at his watch, and nodded. "Put the hounds to work."

The colours of three regiments were heaved into the sky. Officers calmed horses and sergeants filled their lungs. "By the right! Quick march!"

The attack, lurching and ponderous, advanced. Trumpets extolled them to victory, galloper guns protected their flanks, and the great fringed squares of silk led them towards the cauldron of noise where the rebel strength lay.

Washington had held victory in the palm of his hand, but let it go.

In the centre of the field, where the rebels could have broken Sir William's defences, Washington had turned aside to attack the house where Musgrave's 40th had gone to earth. Rebel cannonballs bounced from brick walls to be answered with jeers and musketry. The dead thickened in the garden and orchard, and the dead were all rebels.

Outside the village, where men marched to support the central fight, the fog brought fratricide. Two rebel regiments, each mistaking the other for the enemy, opened fire. Rebel slaughtered rebel, and on their flanks, like an avenging torrent, the red-coated counterattack drove home. The Americans gave ground, and the retreat turned into flight.

God wore a red coat that day.

The American centre had nearly snatched victory, but faltered. The right had struck a Hessian-defended ravine, and halted. The rebel left had driven deep into the British lines and captured the bivouac area, where the chance of plunder checked their advance as surely as any Redcoat volley. Their officers had tried to roust them onwards, and wondered when the promised support would come from the centre or the left. It did not come, and the Virginians were stranded.

Captain Christopher Vane rode towards that embattled flank. He met a brigade major who offered him a flask of brandy and gestured towards the sod bivouacs that studded the gardens and fields. "Full of Virginians," he said cheerfully. "They're trapped. We've sent two battalions to the north. Ten minutes, Kit, and they'll have to surrender." The major raised the brandy flask in a toast. "I give you joy of the day."

"Indeed!" Vane felt the exhilaration of victory as Redcoat volleys scoured the edge of the bivouacs. The Virginians who had fought so deeply into the British line were being crammed into a small tight scrap of hell where the bullets thudded and the smoke thickened. Around them, making a new fog with powdersmoke, the Redcoats and Hessians fired.

The rebel fight ended when from somewhere in the fog-shrouded horror a voice shouted for the Germans to hold their fire, and a white shirt, pathetically torn, waved from the rebel ranks.

"I think that'll serve!" the major said cheerfully. "You care to join me, Kit?"

They rode forward, swords sheathed, and from all around the bivouac other officers trotted towards the rebel regiment. The first Redcoats and Hessians were tearing at rebel coats and pouches, seeking coins or rum, food or keepsakes. Vane watched them, then saw the enemy officers walk out with their swords ready to be surrendered. Vane took pleasure in the sight, but knew, perhaps better than any man, that had it not been for Washington's blunders it could well have been the Redcoats who now offered their reversed blades to the victors.

That horrid thought made Vane twist his mare away. He rode through the sullen and defeated ranks and saw, to the north, other British battalions marching in pursuit of the enemy. A cheer sounded, drawing Vane's attention to where a group of British prisoners welcomed their liberators.

And Vane saw his stallion.

He saw the black horse with its white socks being ridden by a white-shirted man who jumped a rail fence then leaped from the saddle and clutched the body of a dead man. Another man, a Redcoat, took the horse's reins.

Christopher Vane stared, scarcely believing his good fortune. He shouted, but was too far away to be heard.

Then he saw the white-shirted man stand, turn, and hit the Redcoat. The Redcoat stumbled and the other man was climbing into the saddle and galloping northwards.

The exhausted mare would never catch the black stallion. Vane shouted uselessly, then saw deliverance. From the wooded valley at the far side of the road, pursuing the rebel guards who had tried to escape, burst the green uniforms of the Loyalist hussars. Six of the Loyalists had jumped the fence into the road to complete the encirclement of their victims and, in doing so, had headed off the stallion.

The boy who rode the black horse turned away as though he would set the stallion to jump the fence into the field. He rode, Vane noted, beautifully, but the stallion stumbled at the verge and gave time for Vane to leap the rail, turn, lean over and take the black horse's bridle.

The stallion, recognising its stable companion, whinnied and ducked its head. The horses nuzzled each other and Vane found himself staring into the battle-maddened eyes of a young, good-looking boy.

Vane fondled the stallion's ears. "My horse. I do thank you."

"Your horse?"

Vane could see that the boy's wits were gone to the wind.

"What's your name, soldier?"

"Me? Sam, sir. Sam Gilpin."

His eyes were puffy and the musket stains on his face streaked with tears.

"Gilpin! Off that bloody horse!" Sergeant Scammell, who had run after Sam, took his hat off to Vane, his only acknowledgment of the officer's presence. "Off, you bastard!" He seized Sam's leg, twisted and pulled, and the boy tumbled from the saddle. "Bastard!" Scammell kicked Sam as Captain Vane, still scarcely believing his good luck, pulled the horse away from the two men and led it towards a group of mounted officers.

Lieutenant-Colonel Elliott, introduced to Vane, offered a flask of rum and congratulations. News was exchanged, and relieved laughter sounded loud on the muddy road.

"You look as if you were in the thick of it." Elliott said.

Vane glanced at the dried blood on his breeches. "It was my servant, sir. Fellow had the ill manners to die all over me."

A scream came from the roadside and Vane turned to see an American prisoner being forced to his feet. The prisoner was a wounded cripple who could not stand, so a lieutenant ordered a stretcher to be made from two captured rebel muskets and two jackets.

Then a shout made Vane look to where the fair-haired boy who had been riding the stallion was backed against the fence by the furious sergeant.

Vane frowned. "That lad there, Sam Gilpin. Is he any good?"

"He works miracles with horses. God knows why he didn't join the cavalry."

"He seems to be in bad odour with his sergeant?"

Elliott smiled. "Scammell's not a man to cross, Vane."

Scammell was spitting words into Sam's face. "You hit me, Sam Gilpin! You hit me! I'm going to have you flogged till your ribs are polished!"

Sam stared back, murder in his face. "You shot him!"

"He was running and you didn't stop him!" Scammell struck Sam's face once, twice, a third time. "You bastard!"

"Enough!" The voice came from behind Scammell. It was the strange officer who had stopped Sam's panicked flight.

"Sir?" Scammell stood to attention.

Christopher Vane was not certain why, a moment before, he had asked Elliott's permission to intervene. Perhaps it was because he had seen Sam Gilpin's skill with the stallion, or perhaps it was the euphoria of victory. Whatever, Vane now held Sam's fate in his hand. "Were you running, Gilpin?"

"He killed my brother, sir."

"I didn't ask you that!" Vane made his voice sharp. "Were you running?"

"No, sir!" In truth, Sam did not know what he had been doing.

"He's bloody lying, sir!" Sergeant Scammell had been hit by Sam Gilpin and Sergeant Scammell was not a man to let such an insult pass. He feared that this officer's intervention might interfere with natural justice. "He's a bloody liar, sir, and he's going to the tripod."

Vane could not resist swatting the man down. "You can't flog my servant. At least not without my permission, Sergeant."

"Your servant, sir?" Sergeant Scammell put as much outrage as he dared into his voice.

Vane chose to take the question as an honourable salutation. "Thank you, Sergeant." He looked at Sam. "Can you cook, Sam Gilpin?"

Sam stared uncomprehendingly at the blood-spattered officer.

"Cook, sir? No, sir."

"But you can learn. And you can ride. Take it." He threw the stallion's reins to Sam. "And follow me."

Sam did not move, only stared.

"Well?" Vane was relishing the role of God. Just as Sir William had plucked him from the humdrum duties of a regimental officer, so Vane would now use his staff officer's patronage to rescue this private. "You'd rather be flogged?" Vane asked.

Sam broke free of the sergeant and, hurrying lest this quixotic officer change his mind, went and scooped up his red coat which had fallen from Jonathon's body, then swung himself into the saddle. He checked when he saw that two soldiers were stripping Nate naked ready for the common burial pit. All soldiers were stripped thus, but it was hard to watch. Sam would have liked to say a prayer, or even to have dug a separate grave, but there was no time, for his new master was impatient.

"Come on," Captain Vane said, "I'm devilish hungry."

Sergeant Scammell could do nothing: the British had a victory and Sam had been saved. But Sam was a twin no more, and everything, by the touch of fire and steel, was changed.

Chapter Eight

Mrs. Elizabeth Loring, glorious Lizzie Loring, stood beside Sir William Howe and smiled in gracious welcome at her lover's guests.

Mrs. Loring wore a polonaise of blue watered silk, cut very low, its skirt slashed over a petticoat of ivory brocade. Beneath her breasts hung strings of pearls, while on their upper slopes, bravely bared and powdered, lay two small beauty patches of black velvet. Her golden hair was piled in a baroque confection of curls and swags that sparkled with pearl tears hanging on silver hooks from bows of crimson silk. The elaborate coiffure soared to its peak a full fifteen inches above the top of her head.

Sir William himself was resplendent in a coat of brightest red, festooned with loops and chains and lace of gold. A white silk stock, fashionably plumped about a golden pin, bulged between his collar turnbacks, a gilt and enamel star blazed from a diagonal blue sash that lay across his comfortable belly. Wigged, fashionably red-heeled, and happy, he stood beside his paramour, the proudest man in Philadelphia.

Sir William was delighted with everything about this splendid evening. He had commandeered as his Philadelphia headquarters the most lavish of the great mercantile mansions in the city, and as the musicians struck up the popular tune of "Youth's the Season" he rocked up and down on his high red heels, replete with a warm and generous happiness. He had won a victory, Philadelphia was safe, his own wife was in England, and Lizzie's husband was in New York.

Champagne, which, because the rebel forts still barred the Lower Delaware, had been fetched overland from the victualling ships in Chesapeake Bay, was poured into fine crystal glasses that tinkled a ragged rhythm beneath the sweeter sound of violins, bass viols and flutes. Two hundred guests were present, perhaps more. They were there to celebrate the restoration of the monarchy to America's largest city. A great fire, banked within the marble fireplace, warmed the room so well that the glazed garden doors had been flung open and some of the guests had drifted onto the lantern-lit terrace. A chandelier, hung with crystal drops and blazing with three score of white expensive candles, shivered in the night breeze coming from the windows.

"Mr. and Mrs. Abel Becket!" A uniformed major-domo, magnificent by the double doors which led into the hall, announced the newcomers in a sonorous voice.

"Loyalist merchant," Sir William's private secretary whispered into his master's ear, "of importance."

"Upon my word, it's Mr. Becket! My pleasure, sir, my extreme pleasure!" Sir William, who had never met the man before, treated Abel Becket as though he was an old and valued friend. "And your dear wife."

Sir William bowed low over Hannah Becket's pudgy hand. "You will permit me to name Mrs. Elizabeth Loring to you?"

Lizzie offered her lace-gloved fingers to Mr. Becket, who seemed transfixed by the generous bosom that lay just beneath his gaze.

"You must call me Elizabeth."

"Indeed, ma'am." Abel Becket wondered that any man, least of all a commander-in-chief, could bring his mistress to meet respectable people.

"You must tell me"—Sir William was amused by the shocked reaction of his guest to Lizzie's splendours—"how we can best serve your trade, Mr. Becket? You merchants are our strength in the colonies."

"You can take the forts, Sir William." Abel Becket decided that bluntness was the best policy. "The river will freeze, sir, freeze! And if we don't have a chance to float our cargoes out we'll be ruined, and if the city isn't victualled you'll be ruined with us."

"I shall take the forts," Sir William said. "Indeed, that is my chief object in these coming weeks."

"Weeks!" Abel Becket, fearing that his purchase of black walnut might prove the ruin of his fortune, could not contain his indignation.

"Slow and steady, Mr. Becket!" Sir William beamed happily. "Now, let me worry about the fortresses while you partake of some champagne."

Abel Becket sheered away and took his wife to the safer haven of the Rev. MacTeague's company.

"What a dull man!" Lizzie said to Sir William. She had bright, large eyes that now left Abel Becket's retreating back and fixed themselves on a red-coated officer whose sword slings were of new silver chain, and who wore bright new aiguillettes to denote his status as an aide-de-camp. "Is that your new boy?"

"Indeed it is. Captain Vane!"

Vane crossed to Sir William, was introduced to Mrs. Loring, and bowed low. Lizzie left her gloved fingers in Vane's hand. "Sir William tells me you showed exemplary bravery at Germantown, Captain."

"He's very kind, ma'am." The praise was balm to his ears.

Lizzie put an arm into Vane's and led him across the room to a table heaped with food. She helped herself to an oyster. "The best in all the world," she sighed.

"Ma'am?"

"The oysters, Captain! You surely admit that America has the finest oysters?"

Vane, who was frequently irritated by the colonists' habit of claiming all things American to be finer, larger or more beautiful than anything else in existence elsewhere, could not bring himself to contradict this dazzling American beauty. "They're very fine, ma'am."

"Fine?" She laughed, slipped her arm into Vane's again, and led him onto the terrace where a few late fireflies glittered prettily in the dark shrubbery which hid the slave quarters and the stables. "No girl, Captain?"

"I'm the duty aide tonight."

"How seriously you do take your duty," Lizzie said.

She danced two steps in time to the music, then scooped up a glass of champagne from a passing orderly. "Do you think this is the beginning of peace, Captain?"

"Do you, ma'am?" Vane was guarded.

"Billy does. And he plans to stay in the colonies once the treaty's signed."

"Have the rebels accepted talks?"

"They will." Lizzie perched delicately on a stone balustrade and smoothed out her lustrous skirts. "As long as we treat them with dignity. I'm told, Captain, that you're one of those who believe the rebels must be punished for their temerity in defying King George?"

Vane wanted to say that his views were none of Mrs. Loring's business, but he knew this woman's power precluded such a challenge. "If we concede to the rebels at the negotiating table, ma'am, then we encourage other men to follow their example. The whole Empire will then seethe with hooligans! No, ma'am, rebels must be punished as a lesson to others."

Lizzie Loring pretended to consider his words. "But then, having whipped the children, how do you rule a nursery that is disaffected through hatred for you?"

"Let them hate us."

"So long as they fear you?" Lizzie smiled. "But I wanted to plead with you to support Sir William's ambitions, Captain. He wants to make peace without more killing, and I believe that wish deserves the support of his military family."

"Indeed, ma'am." Vane said it neutrally. He was not going to change his mind just because she bared half her breasts and smiled sweetly. Yet he knew it would be dangerous to make an enemy of a woman who had such influence. "I can assure you, ma'am, that no aide is as assiduous as I in the discharge of my duty. Will that satisfy you?"

Lizzie Loring appeared not to be listening to him, and Vane turned to see what had drawn her attention.

He looked, and the world stood still.

A woman, tall, slender and young, stood imperious and splendid in the doorway. She wore a simple dress of scarlet cotton. Her hair was witch black and curled softly about a narrow fine face that was given character by a touch of anger.

A lieutenant, whose task it was to usher guests about the mansion this evening, led her across the terrace to Sir William's duty aide. "Sir? May I name Mrs. Martha Crowl?" The lieutenant was nervous.

Vane bowed to her. "Captain Vane, ma'am. May I name Mrs. Elizabeth Loring?"

"Mrs. Crowl would urgently like to speak with the commander-in-chief," the lieutenant explained. "I told her Sir William was..."

"Sir William would be delighted to meet you," Lizzie interrupted, as she waved the lieutenant away. "He's been trapped with some tedious merchants. Shall we rescue him?"

A delegation of Philadelphia's merchants had cornered Sir William. They bored him, but Sir William knew he must show interest in their problems. "I do assure you," he said for the third or fourth time, "that the river forts will be taken. Upon my word, gentlemen, they will!"

Abel Becket demanded to know by what date the river would be free for traffic. "I have cargoes ready for Britain! Sawn walnut, Sir William, which is already late for the market."

"I'm sure, I'm sure." Sir William's backside was roasting because of its proximity to the antechamber fire. "But the river will be open in good time."

"Before the ice comes, I hope," Becket went on. "Or the French?"

The last remark piqued Sir William, who offered one of his rare frowns. Such talk was defeatist. "The French, Mr. Becket, do not want to be embroiled in a republican rebellion! France is a monarchy. Besides," he brightened, "the rebellion will soon be over. We have had the good fortune to smite Mr. Washington another blow. And very soon, gentlemen, we will hear of General Burgoyne's success. New England chopped away!"

Much to his relief, Sir William saw Lizzie discreetly beckon to him. "You must forgive me, gentlemen." He hummed and hawed as though matters of great military moment demanded his immediate attention.

And in a way, they did, for Martha Crowl, taken to the empty library of the house, confronted Sir William with a bitter accusation of callousness. Had Sir William, she demanded, visited the hospitals where the rebel wounded had been placed?

Sir William, who admired ladies of spirit, even when they interrupted his carousing, confessed that he had not.

But Martha Crowl had troubled herself to visit the hospitals, and now she told Sir William of the horrors in the overcrowded wards, and of the untended agony that the wounded suffered. Lizzie Loring, sitting at the room's edge, listened with Captain Vane.

"And my own brother," Martha said, "is dying in one such hospital."

There was silence in the library, except for the tinkling music that echoed down the corridor outside.

"I am so very sorry," Sir William said at last. He frowned, seeking more adequate words, but found none. "I am so very sorry."

"I have tried to have him moved," Martha said, "as I tried, Sir William, to take comfort to all the wounded. Both requests were denied me. Your doctors will not tend the American wounded until your own men are treated, nor will they allow our own doctors into the hospitals. It is not civilised, Sir William."

"No." Sir William was upset by Martha's news. "Might I ask, forgive me, but are you of the rebel persuasion, Mrs. Crowl?"

"I am a Patriot, sir, and proud of it."

"I am grateful for your honesty. Truly." Sir William paused again. "And do I presume, ma'am, that as you are here alone your husband is fighting for Mr. Washington?"

"My husband is dead, sir, but doubtless had he lived he would have fought in General Washington's ranks."

Sir William heard the stress on the word "general", and smiled. He looked at Christopher Vane. "Are you the duty man, Kit? Perhaps you'll notify the hospitals that any civilians wishing to tend the rebel wounded must be offered every facility?"

Vane nodded. "I'll have the order drafted tonight, sir."

Sir William turned back to Martha. "You say your brother is dying?"

"Unless his leg is removed, yes." Martha hesitated, but could not resist rubbing salt into Sir William's discomfort. "I should not even have known, Sir William, had I not insisted on searching the hospitals. And they would not permit me to remove Jonathon."

"It will be arranged immediately."

Vane looked at Martha. "Where is your brother, Mrs. Crowl?"

"In the State House, Captain."

"You wish him moved where?" Vane was pencilling notes in a small notebook.

"My house is the limestone building on the corner of Fourth and Market. Might I suggest you bring Jonathon through the back yard and down the steps to the kitchen? I shall have a surgeon waiting."

"My servant will bring him, ma'am. Your brother's name?"

"Jonathon Becket."

Sir William gave a start. "Not Abel Becket's son?"

"His nephew, Sir William, though Mr. Becket has disowned him." Hurt by Jonathon's rebellion, Abel Becket had indeed told Martha to tell him that he was a traitor and had forfeited his rights to his inheritance.

Martha had spoken with a biting scorn, but she softened her tone as she bowed her head towards the commander-in-chief. "I am grateful to you, Sir William."

The bow was returned. "I only regret the necessity that brought you to this house, ma'am."

"I am thankful I came." Martha seemed surprised at the ease of her victory, then became flustered when Vane offered her his arm.

"You said the matter was urgent, ma'am. Shall we therefore attempt to deal with it urgently?"

402

"Yes, Captain." Martha took the proffered arm and left the room.

Sir William blew out a long, appreciative breath. "I hope Vane knows what a chance he has! A beauty if ever, besides yourself, I saw one."

"Let us hope she teaches him some sense."

"You don't like Kit?" Sir William sounded surprised.

"He's an ambitious man, and a proud one. That's dangerous, William."

"But I'm a general and he's a captain, so I think we can sleep easy in our bed. Shall we return to our guests?" Sir William smiled his benevolent smile and went back to the dance.

THE DUTY OFFICER at the State House was an elderly and morose lieutenant whose breath stank of rum. He held Private Sam Gilpin's authorisation close to the guttering flame of a candle stub. "Sir William Howe? Sir William has to send you in the middle of the bloody night, does he?" The lieutenant gave the seal-embossed paper back to Sam, grudgingly acknowledging its authenticity. "You are here to find one bloody Yankee and take the bastard away, is that it?"

"Yes, sir."

"Good luck, son. They've been dropping off their perches like poxed sparrows, so the bastard's probably dead." The lieutenant yawned. "Take a lantern, don't set the bloody place on fire, and don't wake the bleeders up. They're trouble enough as it is."

Sam, thus admitted to the State House, helped himself to a lantern which he lit from the guardroom's candle. Life as an officer's servant, he was finding, was full of surprises. The captain had returned early from the general's reception, roused the sleeping Sam from the kitchen floor, and demanded that he immediately discover a wounded rebel soldier in the State House. "Twenty years old. Called Jonathon Becket. He must have been wounded very close to the place where you assaulted the sergeant." Captain Vane liked to remind Sam of that crime, thus ensuring Sam's wary gratitude.

"Go and find him. Someone must have a list of their bloody names. Wake them up, stir them up, use Sir William's authorisation. And hurry!"

"Jonathon Becket, sir? Like the archbishop?"

"Are we here to discuss history? For God's sake, wake up, Sam!"

"But I know him, sir! I looked after him!"

"God sent me a paragon!" Vane whirled on Sam with sudden good temper. "When God made you, Samuel Gilpin, he excelled his normally botched-up work. Up, thou scum, find him. There's a woman at stake. Put wings on thy feet. In brief, Sam, hurry!"

Thus Sam found himself in the State House. No register of the wounded had been made, so he would have to go through the makeshift wards one by one, but it was a not unwelcome task. In the last few days Sam had been plagued by his memories of the wounded American who had tried to help

403

Nate run. Jonathon in some curious way seemed now to be a link with Nate.

Sam started his search upstairs. The building stank of festering flesh, rotting wounds, vomit, dung and death. The real hospitals, such as they were, had been given to the British wounded, so these rebels, casualties of Germantown, were consigned to the State House where in agony they waited for death. Some slept, some were already dead, while others blinked towards Sam's sudden lantern flame and, desperate for help, reached pathetic hands towards the small light. "Friend?" a voice issued from the shadows. "Friend?" Sam stooped with the lantern, but the speaker was not Jonathon. The man's hand wavered towards Sam's sleeve. "Water? Please!"

Sam offered his canteen. The whole room, waking slowly, began a horrid and beseeching moan for help.

"Did you have to? Was this really necessary?" A petulant voice spoke from the doorway, and Sam turned to see a red-coated corporal blinking away sleep, looking at him.

"Corporal? I'm looking for a lad who was wounded at Germantown."

"He's probably dead. They die constantly, you know."

"This boy was crippled," Sam said. "He had a twisted leg and a clubfoot."

"Ah!" the corporal said. "The good-looking boy with the black hair? He was alive yesterday, I think." He beckoned Sam to follow him and, at the foot of the stairs, led Sam through a corridor fouled with excrement and into a handsomely panelled room. "These," he said, "are the fortunate ones. They're not so badly wounded, you see." He raised Sam's arm so that the lantern revealed more of the high-ceilinged chamber. "This is the very room where the rebels signed their Declaration of Independence." The corporal laughed.

"Their what?" Sam had never heard of any declaration.

"Never mind." The corporal looked at the wounded, who, seeing the lantern's glow, had begun their horrid moaning for help. "Not that it's done them much good, has it? Your fellow was over there, beneath the window."

It was hard to see how these lesser wounded were more fortunate than their comrades, unless it was that they would take longer to die. The room smelt putrid. It was a charnel house.

But, beneath the window, Sam saw the lad he had knelt beside at Germantown, and he saw, too, that Jonathon was now ill far beyond the single wound that Sam had tended. The lad's eyes were bright with fever, the thin body shaking in delirium, and Sam felt a welling of guilt and pity as he stepped across the crammed bodies to kneel beside the quivering American. "Jonathon?"

As Sam spoke the word, so Jonathon's eyes slowly focused on Sam's,

then a puzzled look spread across his face, and after the puzzlement came a look of such relief that help had come, that Sam knew he would cry for pity if he did not speak. "I'm getting you out, Johnny."

"You're taking him?" The corporal sounded shocked.

"Orders," Sam said, "from Sir William Howe." He had learned just what power he could wield with those magic words.

"Who's a fortunate Yankee, then?" the corporal asked of no one in particular. "Can you manage?"

"I can manage." Sam lifted Jonathon and, the filthy body light in his arms, carried him to the house in Market Street where, just as Captain Vane had foretold, a physician waited in the candlelit kitchen. With him was a tall, elegant lady and a black maid who cried out in shock as Sam carried the awful burden through the door.

Sam laid the body on the table, then returned to the back door, to be checked by the doctor's angry voice. "You did the damage! You can help repair it!"

"Me?"

"You're a Redcoat, aren't you? One of the fine men come to save us from ourselves?" The physician spat the words angrily. "Come here, and do something to help."

The physician was stripping the clothes from Jonathon, cutting through the rotting, fouled, pus-stiff layers of cloth with long shears. The tall handsome lady blanched, while the black maid helped with quick and efficient fingers.

As the doctor lifted the last layer of linen away, Sam stared with horror at the twisted and lumped flesh that was Jonathon's right foot.

"Don't gape!" the physician snapped. "It'll have to come off. Water, Jenny! Sheets." The physician was almost entirely bald, with a bad-tempered plump face. He opened a wooden carrying case lined with velvet, which held saws and knives and augers and forceps and wicked, small scalpels. He took out a bone saw, two knives and one of the scalpels, then stooped to Jonathon's shrivelled right thigh. "There's no skin to stitch over the stump. Have you got tar? No? Then red-hot pokers! You!"—this was to Sam—"come here!"

Sam went to the kitchen table where the doctor was looping a great leather strap round table and patient.

"Pull it tight," the doctor said. "I don't want him to move." Another strap went round Jonathon's waist and two more about his healthy left leg. "Pokers, Martha! Pokers!"

Martha thrust three pokers into the fire while Jenny worked the leather bellows. The physician peeled off his jacket and pulled on a bloodstained apron. "It's going to hurt him."

"Will brandy help?" Martha asked.

"I doubt if he can drink it," the physician said, "but it'll help me." He looked belligerently at Sam. "He's strapped down, but he's going to flap like a landed fish. You're to keep him still, you understand? Don't watch what I'm doing, just hold him tight!"

"Yes, sir."

"Martha! Get the brandy, and more light, more light!"

They waited. Jonathon moaned and turned his head from side to side. Then Martha came back to the kitchen with a couple of silver candelabra. She also carried a black bottle of brandy which the physician snatched. "Now, go to your brother's head, Martha. Hold his face, give him reassurance. He probably won't hear you, in fact he'll probably die, but we can try to undo what our royal masters have done. Jenny! Keep that fire hot!"

The physician had hooked a razor strop onto a meat hook and was now scraping a knife blade up and down the leather. "They will tell you," he said to the kitchen at large, "that it takes twenty minutes to slice off a leg. That is nonsense. I have done it in ninety seconds, and will do so now. Anything longer is too great a shock to the constitution. It is not pleasant for anyone, least of all the poor bloody patient, but if you want to give him even a quarter of a chance of survival, you will help me by not screaming, fainting or otherwise displaying feminine weaknesses. This also goes for our gallant British soldier. Hold tight and think of England, but do not let that thought make you vomit. Are the pokers red-hot?"

"Yes, sir." Jenny was clearly nervous of the physician.

He laid down the knife and poured himself a generous cupful of brandy. "God bless us all." He drained it. "If God is gracious, he'll stay unconscious. Hold him."

Sam laid his arms over Jonathon's midriff. Martha put her long, white fingers against her brother's cheeks, and the physician took the knife. "Courage all!" he said grimly, then plunged down with the bright feather-edged blade.

Jonathon uttered a scream and at the same moment his body went into a paroxysm of such vicious power that Sam had to fight it down with all his country-bred strength.

"Keep him still!" the physician shouted, as the gleaming blade cut round the thigh to spill a shock of pus and blood.

The knife was discarded and the bone saw snatched up. The doctor grunted, the saw teeth skidded, caught, then began their rasping noise. Jonathon, thankfully, had fainted. Sam was looking away from the operation, staring at the dark-eyed lady whose eyes, all unknowing, stared into his.

The physician gave one last heave with the saw, then with a second knife he slashed at the remaining flesh.

"Pokers! Quick, girl! Quick!"

Jenny handed the first poker to the physician, and Jonathon's body jerked again as the red-hot iron cauterised the flesh. "Next!" Another steaming hiss. "Next!" And Sam closed his eyes as if to blot out the awful sound and smell.

"Ninety-eight seconds!" The physician was sweating. "Bandages!" The bandages had been soaked in lead acetate to fight infection. "You!"—this was again to Sam—"Take the leg out and bury it."

Sam picked up the grotesquely twisted leg by the ankle, took it into the yard, dropped it onto a small patch of grass, then sat, miserable, against the wall.

A cry made him look up. A small child, nightrobed and frightened, had appeared in the doorway. She called for her mother, and Sam, fearful that the child would see the severed leg, ran to gather her into his arms.

"It's all right, it's all right."

The child had been woken by the awful scream. Sam explained, as gently as he could, that the awful noise had been the sound of someone who had been hurt, but was now being made better.

"Who?" The child was reassured by Sam's words.

"Someone called Jonathon."

"Uncle Jonathon?"

Sam heard the horror in the child's voice, and hastened to allay it. "He's going to get better! I promise!" Sam suddenly remembered the kick of the musket, the blossom of smoke, the exultation of an enemy down, and he thought how it all came to this: a soldier's reward of blood and saws and screaming in the night.

Perhaps Nate had been lucky. Suddenly Sam knew that his brother's death and Jonathon's survival were inextricably linked; he also knew that he must keep the promise he had just made to this child if his brother's soul was to find its paradise beyond the furthest stars. A rebel's life must be saved, and Sam had promised it. Sam, through Jonathon, would make amends.

Chapter Nine

In the belief that unalloyed pleasures could end a rebellion and seduce the affections of soured colonists, Sir William, aided by Lizzie Loring, determined to make the life of Philadelphia's society into a dazzle of ostentatious enchantment. Party succeeded party, dinners blended into candlelit suppers, while musicians, instead of inspiring the red ranks into the smoke of battle, whirled dancers round the city's polished floors. Philadelphia would see, and the rest of America would understand, that the British tyrants of rebel propaganda were, in truth, the bringers of joy and the only true hope for wealth and peace in the colonies.

Yet the war could not be entirely forgotten in the first weeks of the British occupation of Philadelphia. There was still the tiresome nuisance of the rebel forts on the lower river, and the city must be ringed with guardposts to protect its revellers from rebel raids. However, within that protective ring Sir William would have laughter, and his aides were ordered to become the ringmasters of enjoyment.

Captain Vane embraced the order with alacrity, for Captain Vane was in love.

On the night when Jonathon's leg was severed, Vane had waited for the widow's thanks which, when they came, were brief but gracious. In the days that followed Vane besieged the widow with flowers and gifts. He was in love, and he loved with all the passion of a young man who believed he had met, in one woman, the very pattern of his secret longings. He told Sam he was in love, for a man could not keep such secrets from his servant, and he shared the happy news with John Andre.

"You claim she's beautiful?" Andre teased Vane.

"As a dark angel."

Andre smiled. "So when am I to meet this paragon?"

"I shall bring her to Billy's bacchanalia."

"Then I shall try not to swoon at her appearance."

Billy's bacchanalia, the nickname for an open-air rout, was ostensibly a welcome to autumn, but really just an excuse to revel in the Neck—a lovely place of mature trees between the converging rivers, where lavish houses, built as summer retreats by wealthy Philadelphians, graced the banks. It was in the garden of one such house that Sir William had ordered a late dinner to be served so that the guests could eat and drink in the fading evening light. Musicians played within carefully fashioned bowers among the trees from which, like pale moons in the afternoon sun, Chinese lanterns waited for nightfall.

The day was cloudy, but dry. Lizzie Loring, magnificent in a dress of white satin slashed over a scarlet petticoat, strolled on Sir William's arm, and to the left and right officers and their ladies bowed and curtsied in welcome.

Martha arrived in a polonaise of midnight blue, with her dark hair piled almost as high as Lizzie Loring's. The two women had become friendly since their first meeting and Lizzie now drew her lover to Martha's side. Sir William bowed. "Your brother, dear Mrs. Crowl, how is he?"

"The physician wants to bleed him. I think it is an atrocious idea. The poor boy's lost enough blood as it is, so I shall tell the doctor to take his leeches away."

"But your brother is recovering?" Lizzie asked anxiously.

"He becomes no worse," Martha said. "Captain Vane's servant is being very kind to him, and that seems to help."

"He's a good fellow, Sam," Vane said. "And a genius with sick horses, Sir William."

"Doubtless your brother will soon be trotting," Sir William said genially, before inviting Vane and Martha to share his coach for a visit to the lower battery which guarded the confluence of the Delaware and the Schuylkill rivers. Other guests had gathered, to be offered wine and oysters. However, it was not the refreshments which drew the small crowd to the river's edge, rather the distant sight of white smoke puffing across the southern marshes. Each new puff, jetting on the horizon, was followed seconds later by the dull crump of a gun firing.

The river forts must be taken, and so Sir William had moved troops into the salt marsh south of the city. The river swirled and slid between the islands, running towards Delaware Bay, where Lord Howe, brother to Sir William and Admiral of the North American Fleet, waited with the ships that should soon unite Philadelphia once more with the open sea.

The British controlled the Delaware's northern bank, where, on the marshes of Province Island and Carpenters Island, the British engineers had made great rafts of tree trunks, from which their guns could fire south at Fort Mifflin, which stood on the aptly named Mud Island in the very centre of Delaware's wide stream. Beyond Mud Island and Bush Island, where the Americans had a barricaded battery, lay the nine-foot parapets of Fort Mercer, on the New Jersey shore. Forts Mifflin and Mercer, strongholds in a slough of wetness, were under siege not just by land, but by sea. British gunboats and frigates added the weight of their shot to the bombardment. Sir William would have liked more naval boats in the wide river, but the Americans had sunk vast obstacles downstream and it was painfully slow work to warp even a single warship through the current-ridden gap. This was war at a creeping pace: the dour work of engineers and gunners.

Martha, watching the distant gunsmoke from Sir William's open carriage, smiled at the commander-in-chief. "You'll have to explain what's happening, Sir William. It's an utter mystery otherwise."

"It's just slow, steady work, my dear. We shall reduce Fort Mifflin by gunfire, then we shall use its guns to fire on Fort Mercer."

"Which will surely take a long time?"

"I fear so, unless they surrender. I wish they would, for they've proved their bravery and can achieve nothing more."

Martha smiled an acknowledgment of Sir William's compliment to the rebel garrisons. "But in the meanwhile," she insisted, "we shall all starve?"

"I will not allow you to starve, Mrs. Crowl. No, we shall build a floating bridge across the Schuylkill." Sir William waved towards the swiftly flowing river. "And we shall bring food from Chesapeake Bay."

"It seems an extraordinary undertaking," Martha said archly, "just to win a victory over a few troublesome colonials!"

Sir William did not rise to the bait, and the party broke up when Martha declared she would walk back to where the dancing was to take place.

"I fear"—Martha put her arm into Vane's—"that our politics will never agree, Kit."

"We can try." Vane was so pleased that she had given him her arm that his thoughts were upon anything but politics. He gestured with his free hand at a grassy walk which went off at a tangent from the main path, wending its way into the shadow of trees that promised the chance of intimacy. "Shall we take that path?"

Martha, who knew well what he wanted, had no intention of granting it. Her friendship with Vane was useful, for he offered her protection against the venom of the Loyalists who resented her continued presence in the city. Martha was mindful, too, that an aide-de-camp to the commander-in-chief was a man who could well let slip details of British intentions that she could pass on to the rebels. However, she had no desire to pay for those details with intimacy, though, for the moment, she would not discourage Captain Vane from his infatuation. She ignored his invitation to take the shadowed path, declaring that she was impatient to meet his friends who waited where the musicians tuned their instruments for the dancing. Vane hid his disappointment but, consoled by her smile, he took Martha in his arms to join the dancers who scattered themselves in pretty array across the lawn, while the music drowned the distant gunfire which marked the flat land where men died.

Sir William Howe, who had gone to watch a cricket match before the setting sun ended play, returned in his carriage. He checked its progress to watch the dancers. "It's how I imagined it would be," he said to Lizzie.

Lizzie grimaced. "They say, my dear, that if you don't take the forts swiftly there will be hunger. And hungry people do not make good company."

"True." And Sir William's smile widened, for Sir William practised a deception on the rebels. He spoke openly in society about his slow but steady plans to take the forts, while in secret he was preparing a daring stroke which, he believed, could free the city and bring peace in its wake.

For in three days' time Sir William proposed to do precisely what the city's merchants urged on him. In three days' time Fort Mercer would be assaulted from the land. Three thousand Hessian troops would cross the Delaware by night. Because their preparation for the crossing could not be concealed, the story had been spread about that they were going to scour central New Jersey for food and forage. In truth they would turn south and, by dawn, be ready to rush an unprepared Fort Mercer. It was a bold plan, and if the rebels should get wind of it, it would fail.

Thus only a handful of men were privy to the secret. The Hessian commander, General Donop, knew; Lord Cornwallis had been told, and General Howe's own aides knew, for they must write the orders that would be distributed at the final moment. Admiral Howe knew, for the handful of boats he could warp past the obstructions would distract Fort Mercer's defenders with broadside fire as the land assault went in. But beyond those men, all of whom Sir William trusted absolutely, no other officers had been informed.

Now, as they watched the dancers shimmering on the wide lawn, Sir William told Lizzie Loring. He told her because he could not resist boasting to his lover of the clever deception he had devised. "If I build a floating bridge, you see, everyone will know that the siege will take a long time, so, even though the siege will be over in three days, I must still boast of my plans for the bridge." Sir William chuckled happily. "You understand?"

"Perfectly, my dear." Lizzie linked her arm into her lover's and leaned snugly against his stout body. "So you're attacking in three days?"

"In three days, though naturally I trust you to honour the confidentiality."

"Of course, though I shall be hard pressed not to boast of your cleverness."

Sir William enjoyed the praise. He rapped the carriage door as a signal for Tom Evans, his trusted manservant, to drive on. "The river will be opened to the sea, my love, and wealth will flood in." Peace would come with the ships. Peace and plenty, and all depended on the swift fall of two stubborn forts.

As the carriage turned about a stand of trees, Sir William saw the

411

sudden and glorious sight of the city illuminated by a wash of evening sunlight; the buildings seemed to glow with a golden light beneath a darker sky. "The New Jerusalem," Sir William said.

"Complete with Pharisees?" Lizzie asked.

But nothing could spoil Sir William's mood. He was experiencing a sudden upwelling of pure joy that he interpreted as a spiritual portent of victory. He stared at the city of brotherly love, and knew that, when the seaway was opened and trade began to thrive, he could make a glowing, just and happy peace in this well-named city.

"I really do believe that when the rebellion is ended, I shall live here." Sir William paused, smiled at Lizzie, and, ignoring the existence of his own wife and of Lizzie's husband, amended the happy hope. "*We* shall live here, my love."

And, in such happy expectations, Sir William took his paramour to the sunset party where lovers danced.

"EGGS?" SUGGESTED the commissary sergeant.

"Just two for myself," Sam said. "Captain Vane doesn't like eggs any more."

"You'll want eggs, Tom?"

Tom Evans confirmed that he would take eggs for Sir William, as well as buckwheat, cucumbers, oysters, clams, nutmeg, pulses and mutton. "He fancies a roasted saddle. He'll need two for tonight."

"Lucky Billy, lucky Lizzie." The sergeant pushed open a door to reveal a dozen bedraggled sheep penned in a small yard. "You want to kill a couple for me, Sam?"

Sam drew his bayonet and obliged, then received one leg of mutton for his own master. Food shortages might threaten if the forts were not taken, yet this warehouse was a cornucopia: there were barrels of salt pork and beef, casks of limes, hogsheads of spirits and sacks of rice; there were molasses, currants, cases of gin; baskets of salt, boxes of cheese and firkins of butter: all of it guarded by a commissary that was swiftly becoming one of the richest trading houses in the city. Gold changed hands here for food, and Captain Vane daily expected Sam to find delicacies to be bought with the goods Vane appropriated from the house where, with two other officers, he lodged and which was the property of an absent Patriot. "It isn't stealing, Sam," Vane had said, "but punishing a notorious rebel."

"How do you know he's notorious, sir?"

"You've never heard of Benjamin Franklin?"

"No, sir." Sam had looked at the portrait of the house's owner which hung above the mantel. "Funny-looking bastard, sir."

"That funny-looking bastard, Samuel, is trying to get the French to join the war against us. I hope a Parisian whore gives him a dose of the pox. Now, take that clock and don't accept any less than three pounds for it."

So Sam offered the clock to the commissary sergeant, who shook the gilded, marble-mounted timepiece to ensure its works did not rattle about in the case. "Two pound?"

"He wanted four, Sarge."

"He's pissing into the wind then, isn't he? Four pound for that rubbish? Two pound."

"Two ten?"

"Two five."

"Done."

Sam took the coins, less the price of the lamb, eggs and two bottles of claret. "Any Keyser's Pills, Sergeant?"

"Won't be any till the fleet gets through, Sam."

"Liquorice?"

The sergeant sucked a dubious breath. "Bloody scarce, Sam! It'll cost you five shilling!"

"Ah! Come on!"

"Five or nothing!"

Sam hesitated, then decided to tell Captain Vane that the clock had only fetched two pounds. "Bleeding robbery," Sam grumbled as he walked away from the warehouse with Tom Evans. "Five bob for a scrap of root!"

Tom Evans, as befitted the privileged intimate of a commander-in-chief, rarely spoke to any of the other officers' servants. However, he had a soft spot for Sam Gilpin, who was always respectful and helpful. "You know how to cook a leg of lamb, Sam?"

"Put it on the spit, light the fire and keep turning."

Evans flinched and gave Sam careful instructions on how to roast the lamb. "Eating it today, is he?"

Sam shook his head. "He's with Billy tonight."

"Getting ready for the battle, then."

"Battle?" Sam asked.

"Gawd, you must be bleeding simple, Sam Gilpin! They're attacking the bloody forts in two days."

The news did not entirely surprise Sam, who had noted how Captain Vane had been more than usually secretive in the last few days, writing for hours. "How did you find out, Mr. Evans?"

"Everyone knows!" Evans said scornfully, taking pleasure in displaying his knowledge, which he had garnered while driving Sir William's carriage the previous evening. "Everyone who's anyone, that is."

"I expect they forgot to tell me," Sam said lightly.

Sam rather liked working for Captain Vane. It was not an onerous job. The other officers' servants in the lodgings divided the work with Sam and, for the most part, he found himself looking after all the horses. He cooked occasionally, and otherwise his duties were chiefly the cleaning of

Vane's uniform which, because the captain was in love, had to be done with meticulous care.

Indeed it seemed to Sam that both he and Vane spent more time in Mrs. Crowl's house than in their own lodgings. The captain went through the front door to pursue his siege of the widow, while Sam went in by the servants' back yard to fulfil the promise he had made on the battlefield. Sam took Jonathon food from the commissary warehouse, and medicines, for Jonathon was slow to mend. Mrs. Crowl had asked for the liquorice and Keyser's Pills, which Sam had promised to deliver that evening.

Sam announced himself in Martha's kitchen with a mock fanfare. "Two tails of mutton, one box of candles, and the liquorice I promised." Sam flinched from the kitchen's steaming heat. "What on earth are you doing, Jenny?"

Jenny, aided by two kitchen maids, was heating water over the fire then pouring it into a vast, zinc-lined tub that stood on the kitchen flagstones. She ignored Sam's question. "Look at the state of you!"

"I slaughtered a couple of sheep." Sam was wearing his old battle-stained red coat and grey breeches. "Tail?"

"On the table," the black woman said cheerfully. "And wipe your feet before you come in here, Sam Gilpin. They're filthy!" Jenny poured a last great cauldronful into the steaming tub, then shooed the two maids out of the room. "Your boots are like the rest of you, filthy!"

"Filthy, foul, stinking, disgusting, disgraceful, rank, nasty!" Mrs. Crowl had come into the kitchen. "You hear me, Sam Gilpin? Nasty, horrid, awful, British. You. You're filthy! Get your clothes off."

"What?"

Martha smiled at him. "You're going to have a bath, Samuel."

"No, ma'am! Please, ma'am!" Sam backed round the kitchen.

Martha locked the back door. "I like you, Sam. You may be a British soldier, but you're actually, somehow, quite likable, but if you're visiting this house I want you clean. I want you to go on visiting, it's good for Jonathon. But you stink!"

"No worse than anyone else!"

Martha held out a wooden rolling pin. "Hit the British bastard, Jenny! Sam, dear Sam"—Martha was trying not to laugh—"when did you last take a bath?"

"Ain't never bathed. Not in hot water!" Sam shook his head. "It's bad for you, isn't it? Gives you the fever. Everyone knows that."

"Then I'll slaughter a Redcoat for America and throw you in!" Martha advanced menacingly on Sam. "I bath, Sam," she said, "once a week. All over, isn't that right, Jenny? And Jenny baths, Sam," Martha said invitingly. "You can't smell us a mile off, can you? Pigs don't flee from us in horror, strong men don't faint. Even Captain Vane baths! But you! You're foul! Now, get your clothes off!"

414

Sam drew himself up to his considerable height. "I am not, ma'am, going to undress in..."

"You pompous ass!" Martha said. "Jenny! Throw a bucket of water over him."

"No! Please, no!" Sam watched Jenny pick up a bucket. "All right. But I'll do it on my own!"

Martha nodded. "A proper reticence. Think of yourself as a horse, Sam. Give yourself a good hard scrub with a brush first. Then the soap. And don't forget your hair. Untangle that silly thing at the back and put it all under water! I want you clean, Sam."

"Yes, ma'am."

"We shall leave you in peace," Martha said, "but if you run away you'll never be allowed back. No more of Jenny's ale, no more sitting by the fire while every other Redcoat catches fever in the swamps."

"Yes, ma'am, very good, ma'am."

Sam waited for the women to leave, briefly considered flight up the kitchen steps to the back yard, then resigned himself to the dreadful ordeal. He slowly undressed before putting a tentative foot in the water.

It was hot; instinctively he pulled back.

"We're coming in!" Martha's voice called gaily.

"No!" But the door opened, and Sam's only escape was to plunge into the scalding tub. He bellowed in shock. Water splashed over the sides as Martha and Jenny marched into the kitchen.

"Wash him, Jenny!"

"No!" Sam clutched his updrawn knees.

Martha burst into laughter at the sight of Sam's outraged face. Jenny, also laughing, began scrubbing Sam's back. "Good God!" Martha said, "he's white!" Shuddering with pretended horror, she picked up his clothes and dumped them into a bucket of cold water. "Red coats," she said disdainfully, "are worn only by dancing masters."

"We taught your George Washington to dance, didn't we?" Sam said belligerently, then was forced to seize the stiff brush from Jenny before she plunged it embarrassingly deep. At least the soap and grime in the water were saving his modesty now. "It ain't fair," he said.

"Maltreated Sam." Martha smiled. "Nice Sam. What on earth are you doing in the army, Sam?"

"Fighting you lot."

Martha laughed. "Do you like it?"

Sam considered his answer. He had liked it well enough before Nate had died, and he supposed, now that the pain of his brother's death was receding, that he was liking it still. Better to be Captain Vane's servant than Sergeant Scammell's target. A week before, exercising the young stallion, Sam had met his old company returning from duty on the marshes. Maggie, they said, had fled into the wild unknown, and

Scammell blamed Sam for it. Sam had avoided the sergeant, but he knew that one day a confrontation must be endured.

"Ain't bad," Sam said, but without much conviction. "As long as you don't get shot."

"You can't always order that happy event, can you?" Martha unwrapped the liquorice root and dropped it into a pot. Suffused with hot water it was a valuable specific against fever. "Were there any Keyser's Pills?"

"No, ma'am. I was lucky to get the liquorice."

"Damn you British," Martha said mildly. "Jonathon will be dead before you get supplies into Philadelphia!"

"No, he won't." Sam surrendered the brush back to Jenny. "They're going to take the forts the day after tomorrow, so the river will be open before the week's end. I'll get you Keyser's Pills by next week, I promise."

Martha stared at Sam. "The day after tomorrow?" she asked innocently.

"Hessians are crossing the river."

"How do you know that, Sam?"

"Everyone knows!" Sam repeated Tom Evans's scornful answer.

"Do they indeed?" Martha walked behind Sam to start untangling the flour-matted queue of his hair. "But who told you, Sam?"

"Billy's servant."

"So it's only gossip?"

"No!" Sam said indignantly. "The captain's been scribbling for days now. Orders, I suppose. And all behind a locked door!"

"He never said anything to me," Martha said ruefully. "Nor did Sir William ..." Her voice tailed away as she perceived, with absolute conviction, how a great deception was being practised on the city.

Suspecting from Martha's silence that perhaps, contrary to Tom Evans's assertion, not everyone knew, Sam turned in alarm.

Martha divined his concern accurately. "Don't worry, Sam. I won't tell the captain you said anything. Not a word." And, to Sam's astonishment, the widow Crowl stooped and gave him a swift kiss on his newly cleaned forehead. He blushed, but Martha nodded to Jenny who, grinning, yanked Sam's feet upwards. At the same moment Martha thrust his head under the water. He bellowed, got a mouthful of soapy filth, then came up streaming and protesting. Jenny attacked his hair with a brush to drag out the thick detritus of powder, candle grease, sweat and grime.

Martha smiled. "Golden hair, who would have believed it?" She crossed the room and fetched a cotton sheet. She ordered Sam's clothes to be thoroughly scrubbed and Sam himself to stop being idiotic, to stand up, and to wrap himself in the sheet. "You haven't got anything Jenny and I haven't seen before. There's clothes on the dresser, Sam. They belonged to my late husband. They'll be a loose fit, but you can wear them till your

416

uniform's dry. And you'll take the liquorice up to Jonathon? I'd do it myself, but I have to write a letter."

Sam waited till Jenny's back was turned before he scrambled out of the tub and seized the cotton sheet. He went into the scullery to dress and came out grumbling. "I feel like a plucked chicken."

"No one ever died of being clean, Sam." Jenny elbowed him out of the way. "And you're a good-looking boy, you don't want to waste it! Now go and see Master Jonathon!"

Jonathon, lying in the wide bed, did not recognise Sam at first. "What have they done to you?"

"Primped me up like a filly going to market! How are you?"

Jonathon was pale, thin, and a sheen of sweat covered his face. The room stank because the cauterised stump still suppurated. Sam, walking round the bottom of the bed, suddenly stopped. He stared at himself in a tall looking glass built into the door of a linen press. "Bloody hellfire!" He was staring at a tall, well-built man with golden hair and a strong, cheerful face. He turned to admire his profile, then laughed. "If my mother could see me now!"

"She'll see you one day."

"Maybe." Sam suddenly thought of his poor mother's grief when, in a few weeks' time, she learned of one son dead. He plucked at his white shirt. "Not like a red coat, eh?"

"It's better . . ." Jonathon stopped, turning his head towards the sound of voices on the stairs.

Following Martha into the bedroom came a smiling golden-haired girl who held up a cardboard box. "Keyser's Pills! Grandfather found them!"

"Caroline!" Jonathon reached both hands towards her as she bent to kiss him.

And Sam, watching, understood why Nate had been willing to risk all for a girl.

This girl was far more beautiful than Maggie. This was a wild-looking golden girl with blue eyes and a determined set to her face, who at the moment showed only joy at being with Jonathon. "We found the pills in Grandmother's Bible-box," she said.

"Your pills and Sam's liquorice." Jonathon's excitement had put a wash of colour into his cheeks. "That's Sam."

"Don't be fooled by his clothes," Martha said drily. "He's really a tyrannical monster come to enslave us. This is Miss Caroline Fisher, Sam. She's going to marry Jonathon."

Caroline smiled at Sam. "You're the one who's been so kind to Jonathon. Thank you."

"I haven't done much." Sam was bashful. "I keep saying he'll be dancing in a month. Right down Market Street, ain't that so, Jonathon?"

"I never could dance," Jonathon said.

417

"You just hop to the music," Sam said, "and I'll carve you a wooden peg. There was a fellow in our village with a wooden leg. He used to dance up a storm!"

"Never!" Caroline said.

"We sawed an inch off his peg once." Sam grinned. "He thought he was drunk. Went lurching up the street like a cart with a broken axle!" He laughed, suddenly at his ease. "Had my ears boxed for that."

"Deservedly," Martha said. She had seen how the girl smiled at Sam's tale, and how Sam blushed for Caroline, and Martha, feeling suddenly much older and wiser than her twenty-six years, thought what mischief might be brewed here. A clean Sam, she thought, looked remarkably handsome in his borrowed clothes. "Perhaps you'll go and frighten Lydia with a bedtime story, Sam?"

"Yes, ma'am." Sam smiled a nervous farewell at Caroline, and obediently left the room.

"But don't leave the house." Martha followed him onto the landing. "Caroline shouldn't walk the streets alone. Can you see her to the quayside?"

"I'll be glad to, ma'am," Sam said.

So, two hours later, but now in a damp uniform and with his hair once more flour-whitened and tight about its leather pad, Sam walked beside Jonathon's girl. He carried a bundle: a gift of candles from Martha to Caroline's grandparents. A light rain fell, but Sam did not notice. They talked of Jonathon. "He'll never fight again, will he?" Caroline said.

"Not with a peg leg," Sam said. "But there's more to fighting than pulling triggers. There's more paperwork than you'd dream of! And he's a scholar, isn't he?"

"Yes." Caroline sounded wistful.

"Our lot are always scribbling," Sam said scornfully. "You can't put a shoe on a horse without a barrowload of paper. Waste of time."

Caroline walked in silence for a few paces. "Will Jonathon get better?"

"He'll get better." Sam said it with grim determination.

Caroline smiled at Sam. "He's lucky to have you."

Sam shrugged. "He was good to my brother, you see."

"Jonathon said your brother died."

"Yes." And oddly it was not hard to talk of Nate now, not with this girl. Sam found himself telling Caroline about Nate and Maggie, and how their dream had ended with a bullet in his brother's back.

"What happened to the girl?" Caroline asked.

"I heard she ran off. Best thing, really."

Caroline walked in silence for a few yards. From a dark narrow alley they came onto the wide flame-lit quays. Sentry posts, each with its own blazing fire, were set all along the wharves, part of the great ring which the British had set about Philadelphia.

Caroline led Sam north towards one of the artillery batteries where the gunners, recognising her, shouted a friendly greeting. She went down some dark steps and untied a boat.

"You sail that yourself?" Sam asked with some astonishment.

"All by my small self." She smiled up from the dark well of the dock. Behind her, reflecting the moonlight, the water rippled silver and black. She held out her hands for the bundle of candles. "You and I, Sam, we'll get Jonathon better?"

Sam handed her the package. "We will." He watched as she pulled a single dark sail up the mast. "How do you know where you're going?"

"There's a light over there. It's home."

"Get there safely, miss."

Caroline smiled her thanks, then thrust a single scull over the shallop's transom. Sam, stepping back, saw a white rectangle on the bottom step. He ran down, picked it up, and felt the blob of wax that sealed the letter. "Did you drop this?"

Caroline was fending the boat away from the quay. Her face, as she looked back, showed sudden alarm. "It fell out of the bundle," she said.

"Here!" Sam stretched so far across the widening gap that he almost fell into the water. Caroline reached towards him, their fingers clutched for safety, and Martha's letter nearly slipped into the river. Sam lurched upright, then safely handed the letter to Caroline.

"Thank you, Sam." Caroline's eyes seemed bright in the gloom. "Goodnight!" With easy skill she was twisting the single stern scull to drive the boat out of the wharf's shelter and into the wind. She waved when the boat heeled, then sat to the tiller.

Sam watched the dark shadow all across the river into the black shadows of the far bank. He felt something he could not describe, but knew it to be a part of happiness. He remembered that Jonathon was to marry Caroline but, whether he wished it or not, his head was filled with the surprise of her golden hair, the memory of her fingers strong on his, and of laughter so easily shared. And Sam's world, for the best of all reasons but without good hope, suddenly seemed brighter.

Chapter Ten

On the morning of the attack on the rebel forts, Sir William Howe awoke with a wondrous sense of well-being, quite belying his forty-eight years and in defiance of the port and fried oysters which he had taken at a late supper.

Abandoning Lizzie amongst a warm tangle of blankets, he went to his dressing room, where Tom Evans shaved him and remarked that it was a fine day. It was indeed, Sir William replied as he inhaled the mingled scents of shaving soap and brewing coffee. Lord Robert Massedene, the day's duty aide, fetched in the morning business.

"Last night, sir, there was a rumour that General Burgoyne had surrendered at Saratoga," he said.

Sir William's good humour could not be dented. "Rumour, Robert! There's always rumour!" He went to the table where coffee, sliced ham, bread and butter waited. He glanced at the reports. "Do I have to read them, Robert, or will you just tell me the news?"

"Donop marched on time, sir. Your brother's ships are coming up river. The sun has duly risen. God, the preachers assure us, is in his heaven."

"For which, amen." Sir William spread butter on bread and cocked a professional ear to the gentle thumps that shook the casements. "No great increase in cannon fire, Robert. You think Donop's late?"

"We shall know soon enough, sir," Massedene said comfortingly. "Captain Vane will be first with the news, I'm sure."

"How he does yearn for the smell of powder!" Sir William had been amused by Vane's earnest request that he be allowed to accompany the grenadiers in their assault on Fort Mifflin. "Is he so tired of life?"

"He is avid for reputation, sir. And victory."

"And for the widow, I think." Sir William chuckled.

"Doubtless, sir." Massedene spoke drily.

Sir William stared at his aide, then gave a slow smile. "You're jealous, Robert! The widow has conquered you as well!"

Massedene denied it, though without conviction. "It's Vane I find hard to stomach, sir. He has a tradesman's view of life. There's profit or loss, and nothing in between. But I don't deny his bravery, sir, and I trust he will bring us news of victory today."

"Oh, indeed!" And Sir William allowed himself a silent wish for the safety of his aide.

Who, crouching under a dyke to stay out of a chill wind, waited for the attack to start. He had been waiting since first light. He had waited as the handful of frigates and gunboats, their topsails washed pink by the rising sun, laboriously threaded their way upstream past the obstacles of the riverbed, and still he waited. "Donop's late!"

"Sir?" Sam shivered as he huddled at the base of the dyke, armed with musket and bayonet.

"Are you frightened, Sam?"

"No, sir. No more than another man, sir."

Vane smiled. "I've seen you frightened, Sam. It was that sergeant. The one who was hitting you when I so kindly rescued you."

"Anyone'd be scared of Scammy, sir. Right bastard, he is."

"Describe his bastardy, Samuel. Amuse me." Vane, bored, wanted to pass the time, and so it was that Sam found himself describing Sergeant Scammell. He astonished himself by hearing a grudging admiration in his voice as he depicted Scammell's bravery, but there was no admiration when he spoke of the night when Scammell had been on picket duty.

"He killed that lad, sir!"

"Truly?" Vane was intrigued by the story.

"But don't do nothing, sir! I shouldn't have told you!"

"I would not take from the army a man who sounds so valuable," Vane said. "We need ruthless men, Sam, if we're to put this rebellion down." He stood up and stared across the river.

At any moment he expected to hear the thump of the light galloper guns that had accompanied Donop's Hessians, but, as the morning ached slowly onwards, no firing came across the still grey sheet of water. Two frigates and three gunboats, with leadsmen chanting the fathoms, inched upstream. By noon the clouds threatened rain, but a wind had risen to ruffle the water and heel the warships over.

"This is insanity!" Captain Vane's temper was frayed by waiting. He even thought of returning to the city to see whether Sir William, for some strange reason, had called off the Hessian attack, but curiosity held him to the marsh dyke beyond which, heavy on the river bank, longboats waited to ferry the grenadiers to the shoals off Mud Island and the capture of Fort Mifflin. The men, bored by waiting, slept beneath the dyke or sharpened already-sharpened bayonets.

At dinner, taken at half past one with the grenadier companies, Vane snapped open the lid of his new watch that had once hung from a chain on Benjamin Franklin's belly. "It was supposed to be a surprise attack! They should have attacked at dawn."

A moustached major put pork in his mouth and chewed it slowly. "This is the army. When does anything happen on time?"

Sir William Howe, still in Philadelphia where he had been persuaded he must stay lest his absence alert the enemy, also fretted. But at three o'clock, when his dinner was still taking its stately course, a shout from the guards and a rattle of hooves proclaimed the coming of, if not news, at least excitement. Sir William threw down his napkin and, trailing half fed officers, went to the courtyard where a blindfolded man sat on a horse. The stranger was escorted by two dragoons and, miracle of miracles, had Sir William's missing dog, Hamlet, on a long leash tied to one of his stirrups.

"Hamlet!" Sir William ran forward to help, then snapped at one of the dragoons, "Release him, release him!"

"The rebel, sir?"

Sir William, a frantic dog now in his arms, noticed for the first time that the blindfolded man was, indeed, a rebel. The man had come, a lieutenant of dragoons said, under a flag of truce, and had been blindfolded so that he could not carry back details of the defences that barred the northern approaches to the city.

The man, released from his blindfold, bowed to Sir William.

"My name is Colonel Mitchell."

"Sir William Howe," Howe introduced himself.

Mitchell smiled. "Your dog, I guess? We found him with our army, sir, but his collar betrayed his true allegiance. He comes, sir, with General Washington's compliments, and upon the general's particular orders."

"That's kind of ..." Sir William paused, not wanting to dignify the rebel commander with his due rank, but gratitude made him gracious "... General Washington, and you will inform him, sir, that I am in his debt. There's no thanks I can render?" Sir William, truly delighted by Washington's gesture, stroked the small dog which, happily, seemed none the worse for its adventure. "No gift I can return, Colonel?"

Mitchell gave a crooked smile. "General Washington, sir, asks nothing of you, in the belief that he can take whatever he wants."

"Very good! Very good! Bravely said, sir!" Howe beamed at his officers, expecting to see them share his jollity, but, except for Massedene, they seemed unamused. "You will give the general my respects, sir, and my regrets that we should find ourselves enemies."

"At least," Mitchell seemed bemused by this affable reception, "we no longer need count General Burgoyne amongst our foes."

"The rumour has reached you too, has it?" Howe's delight at being reunited with his dog could not be spoilt. "I just hope Gentleman Johnny never finds the rascal who spreads such scandal about him!"

"More than a rumour, sir. He surrendered at Saratoga."

"Splendid! Splendid!" Sir William was quite undismayed. "My thanks again, sir, my sincerest thanks! I regret the need to blindfold you again, but you will understand?"

The rebel colonel left, and Sir William went back to dinner where he fed brawn to his prodigal pet, and fussed and combed the dog. He only ceased when, from the south and west, the guns rose to a thunder to tell the city that a battle was being waged.

The battle had flared suddenly. One moment the warships had coasted out of range, the next a crash of gunfire beyond Fort Mercer informed the waiting troops that at last, at long last, the Hessians were attacking. The warships went about, sails flapped, broadsides thundered. On the marshes every gun in every British battery opened fire. The grenadiers' officers, bawling orders, chivvied their men over the mud and into the waiting boats manned by seamen from the fleet. Sam, scrambling with the cheering grenadiers, followed Vane into the left flank boat. He could see smoke beyond the far fort now, but he was more worried about the closer Fort Mifflin, which was ringed by British guns. "They're not firing back, sir," he said hopefully.

"Perhaps they're holding their fire for us, Sam," Vane teased his servant cheerfully. Or perhaps the fort had been so battered by gunfire that its men just waited for a chance to surrender.

"Put your backs into it. Row!" The twelve launches crept across the shoal water. Gulls, startled by the cannon fire, wheeled overhead.

Then a different note intruded on the gunfire: a deeper sound betraying a larger gun, and Sam saw a spreading cloud of smoke come from the ramparts of Fort Mifflin. A frigate, sailing slowly past the water ramparts, seemed to shiver as the enemy ball struck home.

"That fort ain't a dead 'un," a lieutenant called from the bow.

"Will be soon!" Vane was exhilarated. The waiting was over, and he would charge with these splendid men into the churned wreckage of the gun-hammered fort.

"*Augusta*'s gone aground!" The bosun was pointing at the frigate which had taken the enemy's opening shot.

The words were no sooner said than the complete line of the water-facing ramparts of Fort Mifflin erupted in flame-jetted smoke as the American batteries poured their fire at the stranded frigate. A second frigate, bow guns cracking sharp, sailed to the rescue.

"I thought we was occupying a beaten fort!" Sam protested.

"The more enemy," Vane said loudly, "the more glory!"

Sam's boat grounded on a mud shoal and a sergeant's sharp voice ordered the men over the side. "Get your feet wet, you bastards!"

"Skirmish order!" a major in the next boat shouted. The other launches ran their keels onto the mud and the bright red coats of the grenadiers spilled into the shallow water. "Forward!"

"Into the breach, Sam," Vane laughed, and drew his sabre.

It seemed madness to Sam. They were a half-mile from the fort, and most of that half-mile was a stretch of waterlogged mud into which men sank up to their knees. There were small rippling creeks, the ribs of an abandoned boat, and always the sticky, sucking mud across which the chain of men was struggling towards the smoke-wreathed fort. The other battles, across and on the river, seemed extraneous, something happening in another place, nothing to do with Sam.

The grenadiers, at last reaching the more solid ground of Mud Island, crouched at a bank of sand. They were waiting now, Vane explained, for Fort Mercer to be captured and for its guns to be turned on Mifflin. The rebels in Mifflin were beginning a desultory musket fire, but the distance was too great for it to be effective. However, the distance was not so great that the rebels' insults, shouted from behind their parapets, could not be heard. "Ignore them!" The major strolled behind the crouching men. "We'll make them eat their words soon enough!"

They waited. The artillery duel filled the sky with a great rumbling, as if massive casks were being rolled on boards overhead. Sam, watching the fort over the dune's crest, saw wooden palings flung about like firewood. Yet above the fort, somehow unscathed, the rebel flag still snapped in the wind.

   As did the flag above Fort Mercer. That fort's guns, far from having been captured by the Hessians, were firing at the grounded frigate. A second naval boat, much smaller and further down river, was also aground and also under cannonade.

   "She's on fire, sir!" Sam was staring at the *Augusta*.

   For a second it seemed that every gun on the river stopped firing as, around the water arena, men stared at the stricken boat. A lance-blade of fire drove up from amidships and went on, spearing up, higher than the highest topmast. The lance of fire twisted, faded, then, just as it seemed the boat was safe, the whole frigate blasted itself apart in a great, gouting, flame-filled explosion. Debris, spat from the boiling fire-lit cloud, splashed into the water.

For a few numbing seconds it was oddly silent.

Then the shock of the explosion came with a deafening noise like an earthquake, and ash, driven by the flames and carried by the wind, sifted like black snow onto the water. Great ribs stood clear in the fire that raged in the open hull. The water, flooding back from the explosion's thrust, caused smoke, black as the clouds of hell, to boil up over the broken waves.

"Oh, God." Vane stared open-mouthed.

The second grounded boat was also aflame. Boats rowed its crew away from their doomed vessel.

Then, from the rebel fort, came a cheer: a triumphant and derisive cheer. One man stood on the nearest bastion and cupped his hands

425

towards the grenadiers. "You bastards! Do you like the American welcome?"

Vane, his mood plunging to despair, seized Sam's musket and fired at the taunting rebel.

"Missed!" The man laughed, jumped down, and a small cannon, loaded with canister, opened fire. The balls, whistling and snapping, flayed overhead.

"Back!" The grenadier major, knowing that everything had gone wrong this day, shouted at his men. "Back!"

Vane wanted to go on; he wanted to charge the impudent fort. Madness and revenge made him incoherent. He wanted to go forward, but he was given no choice. "Back!" The major shouted the order again, and back Vane went with the grenadiers. They floundered to the boats. Two men were dead, three injured. The second grounded warship, a sloop set afire by its own crew lest the enemy refloat her, exploded, but in the day's misery it went unnoticed.

Over Fort Mercer, as over Fort Mifflin, the rebels' striped flag still flew.

"Sir William will take it hard!" Vane himself seemed close to tears as they rode from the Schuylkill's Middle Ferry to the city. "It went wrong, Sam, dreadfully wrong! I hate to bear the news!"

But Sir William had already heard, and Sir William, in despair, sat by the fire with a sleeping Hamlet at his feet. He tried to smile as Vane, muddy and exhausted, came into the room. "I know what happened, Kit."

"I'm sorry, sir. The forts *will* fall." Vane found himself offering consolation.

"Oh, the forts will fall!" Sir William said. "But for what, Kit? We can't win here! We can't take every town and every village and every bridge and every damn farmhouse! And if we did, how would we govern them? They've tasted victory. They'll never let go now, never!"

"Victory, sir? It was only a repulsed attack!"

"No. Victory. At Saratoga." Sir William said the name bitterly. "Wherever in God's holy bloody hell Saratoga may be." He lifted a sheet of paper. "Brought by a cutter from New York, then overland."

Vane crossed the room and took the dispatch. He read it, and closed his eyes. "Oh, God." The shame of it was too much. "The whole army? Surrendered?"

"To rebels." Sir William, in a fit of anger, snatched the paper back and threw it on the fire. "I prayed it wasn't true. I prayed!" He looked suddenly much older than his forty-eight years. "I've done my best, Kit. I've tried to protect their women and their houses. I've offered them amnesty, redress of their grievances, peace! They talk of tyranny, and I have practised decency! Christian, gentlemanly, English decency!" He shuddered suddenly. "Perhaps I should give them what they want. Fire and sword and hate without end!"

Sir William was preaching Vane's gospel, but Vane could not take advantage of it. He felt too sorry for this kind and broken man. "But you won't, sir."

"No. And now the French will come in. It's all they needed." Sir William thumped the chair's arm. "Saratoga!"

God had doffed his red coat, and an army's hopes were ashes in a cold wind, drifting to an empty sea.

CAPTAIN VANE, walking through cold streets, went to change out of his muddy uniform before seeking the widow's solace, hoping that friendship would let her give sympathy, even love, on this sad night. He turned into the alley which led to his lodgings and had to step aside as a drunken John Andre staggered into the street. "Kit?"

"It's me, John. Are you all right?"

Andre considered the question. "I'm drunk, but I'm going to Mrs. Taylor's. Best thing to do, Kit, after a defeat. Get drunk and get a whore. Would you care to come?"

"I've given up whores, John."

"God Almighty!" Andre stared at Vane, then turned and shouted at the torchlit street. "He's in love! He's in love!"

"John!" Vane protested.

"It doesn't matter, Kit. I'm just drunk. Can you believe the news from Sara... Sara... wherever it is?" Andre found a flask of rum in his tail pocket. "Perhaps it isn't true." Andre sucked at the flask. "Have you asked for the widow's hand yet?"

"Not yet."

"Faint heart never won fair trollop. And if you don't, Kit, others will." Andre, with a great effort, staggered into the torchlight.

Vane ran after him. "What do you mean?"

Andre turned. "I mean, my dear friend, that your woman is giving a reception tonight. Were you invited?"

"A reception?"

"Music, wine, jollity. Our friend Massedene told me."

"God!" Vane ran, his feet lent speed by a flood of jealousy. At Martha's house he found the windows blazing with candlelight, and music spilling into the street to enrage a group of Loyalists who were only prevented from taking revenge for this unseemly celebration by the presence of four armed Redcoats who guarded the house front.

Vane pushed open the front door in time to hear a toast being announced. "To Saratoga!"

"To Saratoga!" Perhaps a dozen of the city's most strident Patriots were in the room. Every guest drank, except Robert Massedene, who, with quiet amusement, watched the proceedings. Three musicians, two violinists and a flautist, sat in the bay window. In front of them, proposing the toast, Martha was dressed in a flamboyant dress of scarlet silk looped with ribbons to match those in her hair. "Captain Vane! You still have the mud of the marshes on you!"

"Where I watched men die today, ma'am." The presence of Massedene enraged Vane almost as much as this flaunting of a rebel victory.

"Were they Redcoats who died?" an elderly man, a respected doctor in the city, enquired of Vane. "I am here because of a British defeat, so why should I cease my celebrations because of your news?"

"God damn you!"

"Enough!" Massedene crossed the room to Vane. "It really might be better if you left, Kit."

Mastering his rage, Vane looked at Martha. "Do you wish me to leave, ma'am?"

"I think you should have a glass of wine, Kit." She smiled at him and, with her natural and quiet grace, took his arm and led him into the small breakfast room which lay behind the parlour. "I would have invited you, but I only heard about Saratoga this afternoon."

The word was like a knife in Vane's pride. "You'd invite me to celebrate that?"

"Why ever not? I attend all the celebrations of British prowess, Kit. Would you deny me this one chance of enjoying a Patriot victory?"

Vane stared through the window. "You could hardly expect me to take pleasure in such a thing, though it seems Lord Robert Massedene has a more pliant allegiance."

"I think not. He informed me of the surrender with great regret, but he was also kind enough to offer his protection to me tonight. You were not available, otherwise, naturally, I should have asked you first. Would you have been as kind as he?"

Vane turned from the window and, with a great effort, said what was dearest to his heart. "I would be kind to you." He paused. The thought of losing her was unbearable. "I would be most kind to you, dear Martha." Vane thought of all the men to whom he had declared his passionate love of this woman, and he thought of the disgrace if he were to lose his status as her companion. "I would be more than kind. You know that."

It was Martha's turn to go to the window and stare into the night. "I never wanted the British to come to Philadelphia, Kit, and I wept on the day you arrived. I should perhaps have fled, but I wasn't brave enough." She turned to him. "And I hope, indeed I know, that one day you will leave. Till then I will not willingly make anything more than a friend of any man who wishes to see my nation defeated."

Vane listened with growing despair and now seized on one sentence. "We won't leave. The Redcoats won't leave!"

Martha shook her head. "You gave up Boston to take Philadelphia. What will you give up to take Charleston? Or to defend the West Indies if the French come into the war? And they will! Today's news will bring them over the Atlantic, because they want the sugar islands! One island is worth the trade of two of these colonies, and London would rather surrender Philadelphia a dozen times than yield Antigua. So you're already defeated, Kit, you've lost! Don't you understand that?"

Vane shook his head wearily. "We haven't lost. We won't lose!" It was a stubborn declaration of faith, something to cling to as he heard the greater hopes of love sliding away. "We may lose now because we're led by men who wish to be kind to the rebels, but that will change! We'll bring real soldiers here! Like me, ma'am. And we'll win!"

Martha shook her head sadly. "Dear Kit! You merely want to kill rebels now to salve your pride. You despise us, Kit, and you can't bear to be beaten by people you despise!"

"I do not despise you." Vane seemed to quiver with anger. However, to lose this woman would be to suffer a public rejection and so, in desperation, he checked his rage and sought her pity instead. "Martha, I love you."

Martha heard the agony, and knew what a hollow, hurt soul lurked in this man. He thought the world despised him for his birth, and he sought solace in the trappings of success. Vane, Martha knew, would always want a gaudier uniform than the next man, and a more beautiful woman than his rival. She made her voice gentle. "You do me honour, Kit, but I cannot return your love. However, I will be a friend, so long as you understand that we simply do not need you any more."

Vane, stung by her rejection, did not hear the kindness in her voice. "You were quick enough to seek our help when your brother needed rescue!"

"That's stupid, Kit, and you know it!" Martha's voice was sharp. "I asked for help because it was the British who put Jonathon into that hospital!"

"And who released him! And what gratitude did we have?"

"Dear God!" Martha closed her eyes in exasperation. "What pathetic hopes, Captain Vane, you had of that night!"

Vane saw now that all Martha had ever wanted was a red-coated sleeve to ward off enmity within a Loyalist city. He saw too that she pitied him, and that realisation sparked the anger he had tried to conceal. "Damn you, madam."

Martha opened the door which led to the servants' staircase. "It seems we are not to be friends, Captain. Goodnight. Please don't call again."

"God damn you!" Vane snatched up his cocked hat and slammed his way down the stairs and into the street.

A cold night wind came from the dark river. Clouds, edged with silver, sailed before the moon. Sentries' boots echoed from Chestnut Street and the glare of their torches flickered long shadows from the pavement stanchions. Vane walked blindly, not knowing where he walked. He had been rejected. He had been scorned and spurned and pitied, and the desire for revenge was pure and fierce.

A whore lurched out of a shop doorway. "Colonel? Colonel?" They called every officer Colonel. "Lonely?"

"Get out of my way!" Vane's rage exploded. He backhanded the woman, hurling her onto the wooden shutters of the store. Captain Christopher Vane, in this inchoate war that spluttered along the coastline, had found his enemy and she had slashed his pride, for which offence, Vane swore, he would one day see her grovel as he, this night, had pleaded for her kindness and been rejected.

Chapter Eleven

The Loyalists' belief in the invincibility of the King's army had been broken. Hunger added its misery, for cargo ships, still barred from the city by the rebel forts, languished in Delaware Bay while the convoys of army wagons, dragged from Chesapeake Bay across roads that had been turned into mud by the autumn rains, could not bring a tenth of the food the city needed. Indeed the wagons' priority was powder and shot for the siege guns, not food for hungry bellies, and so the city's larders emptied and prices doubled.

The Rev. MacTeague, invited to dine with Abel Becket and his wife some two weeks after the dreadful news of Saratoga, picked moodily at the salt pork. "I cannot conceive how these disasters could have happened, truly I cannot."

"The forts," said Abel Becket, "will fall!" If the forts could not be taken by sudden escalade, they must be starved and cannonaded into submission. For submit they must, or else a score of Philadelphia merchants, among them Becket himself, would be ruined. That prospect, which had been made more gloomy by the disaster at Saratoga, made Abel Becket a poor after-dinner companion when the two men retired to Becket's study.

MacTeague sipped his tea. "Your nephew's health is much improved."

Abel Becket jabbed at the fire which, made of green wood, burned badly. "Jonathon spurned me. His future is his own now."

"Lesserby disagrees."

The mention of his lawyer's name made Becket wary. "I cannot see why he should involve you."

"I am your pastor, as I was your brother's." The priest smiled with a false innocence. "Lesserby told me of your discussions with him, and I am now cast in the role of a humble messenger and charged to tell you that, under the terms of your dear brother's will, there is no legal certainty that Jonathon can be denied his portion of your business." MacTeague sipped tea again. "He will be twenty-one in April, I believe? And he will certainly live till April," MacTeague added.

"One prays so," Becket said automatically.

"Indeed, indeed." Distant gunfire from the continuing siege on the marshes sounded beyond the window, then there was silence again.

Abel Becket had presumed Jonathon's death. Now he heard of his nephew's survival and he understood precisely what that news implied. He turned to the priest. "Jonathon will be in his sister's power."

"Indubitably," MacTeague nodded. In April Becket would be forced to pay one quarter of his profits to the junior partner—if profits there were. "And the money," MacTeague said meaningfully, "will doubtless be put to work against our interests. You heard of your niece's indiscretions two weeks ago?"

"Indiscretions!" Becket exploded with anger. "A flaunting, MacTeague! Wantonness!" Martha's celebration had caused deep offence amongst Philadelphia's Tories. "She'll not take Jonathon's profits if I can help it!" Becket said.

"Lesserby says you cannot help it unless . . ."

Becket glanced sharply at the plump, shrewd priest. "Unless?"

MacTeague walked to the window. "Medical opinion is divided on the efficacy of bleeding, Becket. Some new opinion preaches against it. Your niece shares that modern opinion. She denies Jonathon the benefits of scarification and, though he is much mended, he is not yet fully recovered. Could that be because he lacks proper medical attention? I ask myself that question, indeed I do." He turned. "Allow me, very humbly, to remind you that you are Jonathon's legal guardian until April. If it is your opinion that he will only live if he is bled, bled he must be." The priest shrugged. "Though I doubt whether the procedure can be peacefully done in Mrs. Crowl's household."

Becket understood instantly. "I should bring him here?"

"Should a boy not convalesce in the happy surroundings of his own home? And if Jonathon were here, Becket, he could not sign away his interest in the business to his elder sister, could he?" MacTeague went back to his chair. "There is, however, one obstacle. He is, officially, a prisoner of the British, and they have signed him over to Mrs. Crowl's household. They could insist that he stay there."

"But she's a rebel!"

"A popular one!" MacTeague shook his head sadly. "Our city is now ruled by men who value entertainment and frippery above sobriety. In that society Mrs. Crowl is an ornament. That creature of Sir William's has become an intimate of Mrs. Crowl's!" For a fleeting second MacTeague was tempted by the thought that Saratoga might be a divine judgment on British immorality. "But I have a suggestion for you."

"Please," Becket invited.

"I am thinking of the proposed bridge at Middle Ferry. You are selling them the materials?"

"Not unless they increase the price they've offered." Becket was scornful of the proposed floating bridge which, after the failure of the assault on Fort Mercer, would have to be built on the banks of the Schuylkill. The bridge would undoubtedly quicken the trickle of wagon-borne supplies, but it would shift no heavy cargoes of black walnut.

"The British are suddenly impatient." MacTeague closed his eyes and steepled his fingers before his face. "They need nails, tar, cables, timber, and all before the river freezes. A gift would make them look gently upon the giver." The priest's eyes opened to stare at Becket.

"A gift?"

"You must think on the matter. I believe the officer at Sir William's headquarters who is most inimical to Mrs. Crowl is a Captain Christopher Vane." MacTeague chuckled. "I am sure that, in return for a gift of some worn-out timber and frayed rope, Captain Vane would be happy to arrange for a prisoner to come to your loyal house." MacTeague looked at the clock on the mantel and pretended surprise. "So late already! You must forgive me. Such a good dinner!"

MacTeague proved to be a happily accurate judge of the purchasing power of nails, elm, tar and cables, and so, at dawn two mornings later, Ezra Woollard went with two men to the back door of Martha's house, while Abel Becket, with four others, went to the front.

Becket hammered on the street door. Jenny, the black maid, answered it and was pushed aside by the surge of big men. She screamed. One of the menservants ran up from the basement to find himself staring down the brassbound muzzle of Abel Becket's horse pistol.

"Open the back door," Becket said.

The servant turned as Ezra Woollard's hammering echoed through the kitchens, then whirled back again as Jenny screamed at him to keep the door shut. Abel Becket slapped her. One of his men pushed her face against the wall. The manservant, appalled, fled to open the door.

"What in God's name are you doing?" Martha, dressed in a silk robe and with her hair in a mobcap, appeared at the head of the stairs. Lydia, in a flannel nightgown, clung to her mother's skirts.

"I've come for my nephew." Abel Becket faced his niece from the foot of the stairs.

"Don't be ridiculous. He isn't well enough to be moved. Nor does he wish to be moved."

There was another rush of feet as Ezra Woollard's men jostled up the stairs from the kitchens. The hall was suddenly filled with big men.

Abel Becket climbed the stairs towards his niece. "If you stop me taking Jonathon to where he can receive proper medical care, then I will have you in the courts! He is my ward, made so by an order of the judiciary!" He

432

stopped two steps beneath her. "The doctors advise he should be bled. Stand aside."

Martha did not move. "If you bleed him, you will kill him."

"Stand aside." Becket climbed the last two steps and Martha pushed him back. He gripped her arm to save his balance and for a second or two uncle and niece grappled at the stair top. Lydia screamed, then Ezra Woollard shouted at the hired men to help. They pounded up the stairs, and Martha was thrust aside by the rush. She heard above Lydia's terrified weeping her brother groan with pain as the bedclothes were snatched away from him. "Let him alone!" she shouted as her brother's limp, blanket-covered body was carried onto the top landing. Then new voices sounded in the hall and a red-coated officer came running up the stairs. Jenny, keeping her wits about her, had summoned one of the British patrols that were charged with keeping the peace.

A nervous young lieutenant appeared at the stairhead. He frowned to see Martha in such obvious disarray, but he was clearly too young and confused to know what he should do.

"These men have broken into my house," Martha shouted at the lieutenant. "They're kidnapping my brother and you will please stop them!"

"Get out of my way!" Above them, Abel Becket pushed through the men, making a path for the one who carried Jonathon. He checked when he saw the scarlet uniform. "Who are you?"

"Lieutenant Jarvis, sir. Of the seventh."

Becket took a paper from his pocket which he held towards Jarvis.

"This is a warrant, Lieutenant, duly signed at your headquarters, giving Jonathon Becket into my care." He thrust the warrant into the lieutenant's hands.

Jarvis read it. His sympathies were with Martha, for she was a woman, and beautiful, but the paper bore a seal he recognised. "The lad's in pain, sir." He hesitated. "It might be better to give him a few more days? Doesn't do to shift the wounded about, sir, not if it can be helped."

"It might be better," a new and languid voice spoke from the hallway, "if you were to obey your commander-in-chief's warrant, Lieutenant."

The voice was mocking, casual and triumphant. Captain Christopher Vane climbed the stairs. He took off his cocked hat. "Good morning, Mrs. Crowl. Can't you keep that wretched child quiet?"

Martha snatched the warrant from Jarvis's hand. " 'Signed on behalf of the Commander-in-Chief by Captain Vane.' " She read the words scornfully. "What were you paid, Captain?"

"You're being offensive, ma'am. Your brother requires skilled medical attention which he will now receive. You men! Make way!" This was to Jarvis's soldiers in the hall. "Mr. Becket!" Vane pretended to notice Becket for the first time. "Good morning, sir!"

433

Jarvis, outranked, could only watch as the moaning Jonathon was carried down to the hall. The men followed. A table had been broken in the hallway and two of the delicate banister supports had been snapped. Vane flicked at the broken wood. "This is not chargeable to the army's account. You resisted a lawful order, ma'am."

Martha was still hugging Lydia close. "I would not take your money if you offered it on bended knee. You've killed that boy!"

Captain Vane stood in the patch of morning sunlight that came through the open street door. His smile was mocking, almost pitying. "I can always arrange for your brother to be fetched back here, ma'am."

Martha shuddered. "Were my uncle's thirty silver shillings not enough for you, Captain? Get out!"

But Vane wanted to enjoy the full measure of his victory. "I was thinking of quartering myself here, ma'am. You have an empty room now, do you not? Don't you think we could be happy here?"

"In a house where you once grovelled for my affections?" Martha laughed at him. "If you dare come to this house again, Captain Vane, I will burn it down around you. Now leave!" She plucked a vase from a table on the landing and hurled it down the stairs.

Vane stepped nonchalantly aside, watched the vase shatter into fragments, then went to the door. A Patriot had been humbled, and Captain Vane had gained a small, but not yet full, measure of his revenge.

Vane went next to the stables, constructed out of a sequestrated Lutheran church, where Sam spent most of his time, and told Sam that he was never again to visit Mrs. Crowl's house.

Sam, astonished by the abrupt order, said nothing.

The next day, perhaps because Vane needed his servant's loyalty at a time when he felt the rest of the city was mocking his failure, he offered a lame explanation to Sam. "The physicians insisted that Jonathon was to be moved, Sam. And the lawyers! It's no good fighting lawyers."

"Of course, sir." Sam knew as well as Vane why Jonathon had been moved: not because of doctors and lawyers, but because the widow had thrown Vane out of her house, and Sam had no intention of letting a lovers' tiff prevent his visits to the widow's house. His freedom as an officer's servant gave him ample opportunity to visit the warm kitchen where Jenny offered a teasing welcome and where, more importantly, Sam could pretend that his meetings with Caroline were accidental.

The kitchen's warmth became especially welcome as the days became colder. Since the repulse of the attack on the river forts, the river fighting had become grimmer. A floating bridge, made with Becket's timber, was thrown across the Schuylkill at Middle Ferry, and wagons carried new supplies, new ammunition and new men down to the marshes. Heavy guns, slung off warships, were taken to the siege, and mortars bedded on the dykes to arc shells into the defences.

The marsh reeked of powdersmoke. Men died in waist-deep water. Then yet more guns had to be dragged through the ever colder October days. No one in the city could remember an October so cold.

Food grew scarcer. Firewood too was scarce. Each succeeding day brought colder winds and smaller fires. Sir William's revels might distract the wealthy, but the mass of people, like the common soldiers, suffered. The month's ending was marked by gales that shrieked over the marshes and tore shingles from the city roofs. November brought calm, but with the calm came frosts that made the brittle grass of the wetlands into an expanse of shining white spikes. Men shivered, and wondered if the river was swirling more slowly, ready to lock the city up in ice and bring starvation.

As the nights grew colder, Vane would send Sam to the city's most fashionable brothel on William's Alley with orders to bring back a girl. "You know the sort I like, Sam. No insipid blondes."

On one such night, Sam, in his hooded watchcoat and thick gloves, knocked on the door of the discreetly shuttered house, and shivered as the maid let him into the elegantly furnished hallway. "Cold as bloody Muscovy out there." Sam rolled his torch on the outer steps to extinguish the flames.

"Who is it?" A voice spoke from the parlour.

"Captain Vane's man," the maid replied, and the parlour door immediately opened.

A short, cheerful and motherly woman stood there. "Sam! How very chilled you look. Come inside. Thank you, Marie!" Mrs. Taylor had developed an affection for the ever-willing Sam, who had dosed and steamed the strangles out of one of her carriage horses. "How is the captain?" she now asked.

"He's bad-tempered, ma'am. He hates the cold." Sam smiled his thanks as she invited him to sit down. "He'd like Belinda, if that's possible?"

"Dear me, no! Belinda is at General Grey's." Mrs. Taylor happily boasted of the high company her girls kept. "I shall ruminate." She picked up her black-bound ledger, then looked up as a peal of laughter sounded from an upstairs room. "Lord Robert Massedene," she explained. "Such an amusing young man."

"And a gentleman," Sam said warmly. Sam had heard through the servants' gossip that his lordship had striven to have the wounded Jonathon returned to his sister. It had been to no avail. So Jonathon had been abandoned to his uncle's care, and Sam could no longer visit him. "I tried to see Jonathon," Sam told Mrs. Taylor, who provided a sympathetic ear, "but they told me to go away. Mr. Becket wouldn't even let Caroline see him!" Sam sounded outraged.

"Well, he wouldn't, dear, would he?" Mrs. Taylor said reasonably. "I mean, she's hardly a fit bride for a Becket! He's an educated young man."

"She can read." Sam was defensive.

"I can read, dear, but I doubt that makes me suitable either!" Mrs. Taylor sighed. "Not that there'll be any marriage, Sam, with anyone! I hear the young man's dying."

"Dying?"

"It isn't the leg, dear," Mrs. Taylor said, "but the quinsy."

Sam stared at the kindly woman. "You're sure?"

Mrs. Taylor gave a coquettish shrug. "I shouldn't say, really, but you're a discreet young man. His priest visits us, dear. Not for that, of course! But to offer spiritual comfort to the girls. He likes to talk."

"The quinsy? I can cure that!" Sam said robustly.

"If you're allowed to try," Mrs. Taylor said dubiously, before looking down at the pages of her book again. "I've got a new girl with, well, darkish hair? Sacharissa?"

"That ain't her name!" Sam was amused by the wondrous names Mrs. Taylor invented for her employees.

"It is the name of a poetic heroine. I am astonished to find you so ignorant, Sam Gilpin. Sacharissa's foible is that she is unwilling to leave the house, but can I assure her that she'll be safe with you?"

"She'll be safe," Sam said.

"And she can't lie idle here, can she? Very well, Samuel. What has Captain Vane sent tonight? Another of Mr. Franklin's possessions?"

"Yes, ma'am." From the watchcoat's deep pocket Sam drew out a tube made of morocco leather, from which he extracted an ivory spyglass edged with brass filigree work. "He thinks it's worth three nights, ma'am."

"I think it is, yes." Mrs Taylor wrote the details in her ledger. "I shall keep it for Mr. Franklin." Mrs Taylor was collecting the more valuable possessions of the Patriots, which she declared she would one day return to them. She stood up. "Help yourself to tea while I prepare Sacharissa for her outing."

Sam waited.

"You'll be quite safe, girl, don't be fretful." Mrs. Taylor's voice sounded in the doorway. Sam turned, and found himself staring into a pair of wistful brown eyes.

"Good God! Maggie!" Sam said.

"Sacharissa, dear," said Mrs. Taylor.

"Sam?" Maggie was dressed in a fine woollen cloak and wore her hair piled high on her head. She was clean, pretty, and oddly changed. Sam thought she would not be out of place at any of the fashionable receptions which he was sometimes forced to attend as an orderly.

"Where's Nate?" Maggie asked eagerly, and then, as if sensing the news from Sam's face, she crumpled onto the sofa and began to cry.

"The brickdust!" Mrs. Taylor yelped in alarm and plucked a handkerchief from her sleeve. She dabbed at the girl's eyes. The shortages in the

436

city had driven most women to the use of powdered brick instead of rouge, and before Mrs. Taylor could prevent it tears had streaked the carefully applied dust.

"What happened?" Maggie wailed.

Sam knew no gentle way to break the news. "He's dead, love." He felt tears in his own eyes. "Scammy shot him in the back."

Now there was fear in Maggie's eyes. "I can't go!" she sobbed. "He might see me!"

"You'll be all right." From the watchcoat's second pocket Sam drew out a small pistol. "See, Maggie?"

"Sacharissa!" Mrs. Taylor insisted.

"But Scammy knows I'm here!" Maggie cried.

"He doesn't, dear." Mrs. Taylor shrugged at Sam, then persuaded and bullied the girl into gloves, hat and shawl. "Do your face when you get there, dear. You'll be safe!"

Sam took the girl's arm and helped her into the alley. She made Sam tell her more about Nate's death.

"I waited for Nate," she said forlornly. "Two days, I did. Then I walked up by the river. I got to Frankfort, but it wasn't any good. You can't make money as a maid." She sniffed. "Mrs. Taylor's nice."

"I like her," Sam said warmly.

"I get three guineas a night now!" Maggie said with obvious pride. "I'm saving up, see? I might get on a ship!"

"Back to Connecticut?"

"To London!" It seemed Maggie had a new dream now: no longer the promised fifty acres with its three hogs, but the brighter dream of a bigger city. "Or perhaps I'll meet an officer, Sam, someone who likes me. But not if Scammy finds me."

"He won't," Sam said. They were walking in the centre of Fourth Street; it was safer to stay in the centre of the street than to risk the pavements which were so close to the dark alley entrances. The flames of Sam's torch lit the spreading rime of frost on the hard mud.

Maggie shivered. "What's this captain like?"

"He's all right. He ain't rough, dear, I promise."

She smiled up at Sam. "You got a girl?"

Sam paused for a second, thinking of Caroline's bright hair, then shook his head. "No."

Maggie held his arm close. "If you want, you know..." She stopped suddenly, scared by an infantry patrol that walked along Arch Street in search of men breaking the curfew. Their hooded watchcoats made them look like ghostly monks. The last man in the patrol stopped to look at Maggie as Sam hurried her past. The man went on watching until Sam plucked her into the shadows of Cherry Alley.

"He recognised me!" Maggie said.

"He just fancied you!" Sam pushed open the back door of Vane's lodgings and helped Maggie off with her cloak. "It's upstairs, love."

"It always is." She dabbed hopelessly at her face.

When the couple had been served with wine and picked oysters, Sam went back to the kitchen where wax, tallow and lampblack boiled in a pot to make boot blacking. Sam wished that Maggie had not returned. He suddenly perceived the war as a maelstrom that sucked innocent people in to their destruction; it had killed Nate, reduced Maggie to this pathetic Sacharissa, and now threatened Jonathon with the hard racking death of quinsy.

But that, at least, was something Sam could try to cure. Not with bleeding, but by an older method, and he would have to find the ingredients to make the ancient magic work. To which end Sam spent the next week searching for the ingredients he needed and, as he did, so the fighting on the river came to its inevitable end.

More of the obstacles that had prevented Lord Howe's ships from sailing up the river in force were dragged away, and the battle fleet made a stately progress towards the stubborn forts. The *Fury* and *Roebuck*, *Somerset* and *Liverpool*, *Pearl*, *Isis* and *Vigilant* opened their gunports and fired across the stark blackened ribs of the *Augusta*. The answering fire from the American forts died slowly.

A dozen prisoners were taken to the 1st Grenadiers' headquarters behind the Pest House Battery, and there Major Zeigler spoke with the captured rebels. He wanted to know the fate of the Hessian General Donop, who had been wounded and captured during the failed assault on Fort Mercer.

After the interrogation, Zeigler sought out Sir William. General Donop, the Hessian reported, had died three days after his capture. "A bad death, Sir William, painful."

"I'm sorry, Otto."

The Hessian shrugged. "War is cruel, *ja*? To us and the rebellers. But they were warned we were going to attack."

Sir William, standing by a window of his headquarters, turned to stare at his interpreter. "They were warned?"

"*Ja.* The previous day. A rebeller lieutenant told me so."

Sir William frowned. Only a handful of his men had been privy to the secret attack, but Sir William remembered with a sinking feeling that he had also told Mrs. Loring. "It won't happen again, Otto."

"You knew about it, sir?" Zeigler was puzzled by his master's calm reaction to the news of treachery.

"Otto, look!" Abandoning the grim news of betrayal, Sir William pointed through the window to where, above the roofs of the city, the first tall masts of approaching warships could be seen. The seaway was open, and the merchants' fortunes would be rescued.

THE CUP WAS JUST over five inches high and had been lovingly polished to a glowing sheen. "It's ivy root," Sam explained. "I carved it, but Miss Caroline polished it." He smiled at Caroline as he spoke, and she smiled back.

Sam, with Caroline's help, planned a miracle, to save Jonathon's life.

"It's beautiful," said Martha.

"It'll do," Sam said modestly. He sat at Mrs. Crowl's kitchen table with Caroline opposite him and cups of tea between them. Any crudely hacked-out receptacle would have satisfied the magical formula, but Sam and Caroline would not be content with anything but the very best.

The cup, Martha thought, was a reflection of what they meant to each other, but were too stubborn to admit. She thrust the thought away. "So we have the cup," Martha said, "and now we just need to fill it."

"Lord Cathcart has a mare in foal. I reckon she's near term."

"And she'll suffice?"

"She'll suffice," Sam tried out the word, "as long as I get to her first. I'm spending my nights there, but if the captain wants me home, then . . ." He shrugged.

"Let's hope he doesn't." Martha listened to the rain. It had fallen ever since the forts had been taken.

"And if it is tonight, I still think I should—" Sam, stubbornly reverting to a well-worn argument, was cut off by Caroline.

"*I'm* going into the house, Sam!" Caroline stared defiantly at the Redcoat. "What would Jonathon think if I didn't try?"

The magic required a cup, a potion, and that either Sam or Caroline should insinuate their way into Abel Becket's house. Caroline was insistent that she would deliver the elixir.

"I should come with you, then," Sam said.

"And who looks after the front of the house?" Caroline demanded.

Sam nodded reluctantly. "I suppose it's the best way."

Martha smiled at their agreement. "The most convenient night is a Thursday, because Mr. Becket's always at a lodge meeting."

Sam shrugged. "It depends on the mare, ma'am. We might have to go any time."

Martha looked at the girl. "Don't get caught by Mr. Becket."

"Thump the bastard," Sam said, then immediately blushed for using the word. "Forgive me, ma'am."

"I wouldn't mind thumping him," Martha said, "or your precious captain."

The clock in the hall struck four and Sam grimaced. "I have to go, ma'am. He wants me macaronied."

"Macaronied?" Martha asked.

"All prinked up, ma'am. I have to serve at a supper party." He plunged into the seething rain.

AT THREE IN THE MORNING Sam helped a drunken but happy Captain Vane to bed. Then he changed into his old uniform, pulled on his watchcoat, and went out into the night.

The rain spat now, driven by a swirling wind that gusted about the street corners and flattened the flames of Sam's torch. He turned into an alley, then pushed through a gate and saw a slit of lantern light above a stable door. Instantly Sam feared he was too late, but Lord Cathcart's groom, waiting beside the mare's stall, shook his head. "You almost missed it, Sam. It's coming any time now." The groom shivered. "It's too cold a night to be born."

Sam ducked under the chain. The mare was trembling with fright, but Sam gentled her. The wind howled. The other horses stirred uneasily in their stalls.

The foal came a half hour later, slithering in blood onto the straw, then struggling to stand on its skinny legs. Sam crouched under the mare's belly where he held a wooden canteen to the swollen dugs. The mare snapped once, but Sam soothed her, then used his fingers to draw the mother's first milk into the canteen. When the small barrel was full, he put the half-cleaned foal to suckle.

Sam paid the groom, then carried the canteen into the grey wet dawn. He had carved the cup, and now he had the beestings: the first milk of a mother. Served in a virgin cup of ivy, no medicine was stronger, and no medicine had ever been prepared with so much love. Now all that was needed was for the magic to be smuggled to Jonathon in the big, servant-guarded house; into which, this coming night, with Sam's help and some small luck, Caroline must go.

Chapter Twelve

Caroline waited in the shadows of an alleyway behind Abel Becket's house, and through chattering teeth counted aloud to three hundred.

An infantry patrol, miserable in the rain, slouched past the alley's far end and Caroline shrank back under an archway. "Two hundred and three," she whispered, "two hundred and four."

The sound of music came thin above the hissing rain from the British commander-in-chief's headquarters, only a short distance away. Caroline could not remember a time when so much music had been played in the city: the city was drenched with music, drunkenness and gambling. Caroline's grandfather, reading his morning scripture across the river, had said that gambling was the devil's work. Caroline now wondered what Caleb Fisher would make of his granddaughter's nocturnal prowling. "Two hundred and sixty, two hundred and sixty-one."

A late carriage splashed past the alley, its lanterns showing mud-

440

spattered horses and dripping trace chains. "Two hundred and ninety-nine," Caroline counted, "three hundred." She readied herself, hoping that Sam had counted at the same speed as she had.

Sam was in another alley; one that debouched into Market Street almost directly opposite the front of Abel Becket's big house. It was almost ten o'clock. Sam, for once, carried no lit torch as a protection, but the pitch-soaked lanterns outside Sir William's house flickered on the rain-battered street. He counted to three hundred, took a deep breath, and stepped out of the alley.

Sam's first stone smashed a pane of glass in a window of Abel Becket's parlour. The second clattered uselessly on the limestone wall between the windows, the third shattered the fanlight above the front door, just as the door was snatched open by a servant.

Sam's job had been to draw the household away from the rear of the big house. Now, he fled in the darkness to wait for Caroline.

Sam's evening had begun at Martha's house where he had given Caroline the beestings, then taken her to the alley behind Abel Becket's stable yard. She wore a heavy haversack at her belt. Sam had thought to bring an old horse blanket which he had thrown across the shards of glass cemented into the wall's top. Now, hearing the crash of breaking windows, Caroline jumped to hook an arm over the thickly folded wool. Glass spiked through the layers of cloth and tore her flesh. She hissed with the pain, but tried to ignore it as she scrabbled for purchase on the wet bricks and pulled herself up. Blood trickled warm on her forearm.

She perched for a moment, then jumped down into the space behind the stables. The bitch chained outside Abel Becket's feedstore snarled at the black shadow that suddenly materialised in its territory. Caroline fumbled in the haversack and threw the dog a quarter-leg of mutton that Sam had stolen for just this purpose.

Caroline paused for a moment, letting her eyes adjust to the darkness in the yard, then ran to the smokehouse and pulled herself onto its sloping roof. Her boots slipped once as she explored the sash window above it. It was locked, as Martha had warned her it would be. Caroline slipped a knife blade between the two sashes and tugged at the metal latch. For a second she felt despair, then the latch yielded and she pushed the window up. A canvas curtain inside billowed fiercely, then subsided as Caroline, safe inside, pulled the window shut. She stood still and listened.

Voices shouted from the front of the house, but there was no sound close to her. In the darkness, she climbed the uncarpeted steps of the servants' staircase, sidled into the corridor and opened Jonathon's door. As she stepped into the room, she knew she smelt imminent death.

The last time she had seen Jonathon he had been mending fast. Now his skin was a sickly yellow-white in the light of the single shielded candle that burned on a dresser beside the bed.

"Jonathon?" Caroline whispered the name as she unslung the rain-soaked haversack and put it on the bed. "Jonathon?" She could see scars of clotted blood on Jonathon's arm; square after square of scabs that made a strangely regular pattern. She put her hand on his forehead and was astonished by the heat she felt. "Jonathon?"

His eyes flickered open, closed, then opened again. He stared at her. "Dreaming." His voice, thanks to the quinsy, was like a rasp on stone.

"You're not dreaming, Jonathon. I'm here!" And now Caroline was crying because the look on his face was so astonished and so pleased that she felt as if her heart was being torn in two. She held him, and her cheek felt the fierce, fever-burning heat of his face. He was saying her name over and over again, sobbing in disbelief and joy.

Caroline gently pulled herself away. "You have to sit up."

Jonathon frowned. "I can't."

"Of course you can." She put her arm under him and lifted him. "What are they doing to you?"

"That thing." Jonathon feebly indicated a strange device that stood beside a Bible on a chest beneath the window. Caroline ignored it for a moment, propping Jonathon on the bolster and pillows instead. She saw how the bedsheets and blankets were stained from the daily bloodletting and she felt a surge of fury that he should have been reduced to this pathetic weakness by the doctors. Yet not so weak that he could not suddenly laugh. "You came!"

"Of course I came. I tried before, but your uncle's servants wouldn't let me in." Caroline was talking just above a whisper as she unbuckled the knapsack and took out the wrapped cup and the canteen.

"I—" but whatever Jonathon wanted to say was drowned by an awful, racking cough. He fought for breath, his thin chest heaving beneath the red flannel that had been wrapped round his ribs. "I'm dying."

"You're *not* dying," Caroline said stoutly. "You're going back to the army!" She was pouring the first of the beestings into the cup.

"And you?" Jonathon asked.

Caroline knew what he wanted. "I'll come with you. But only if you drink this! Head up now!"

Jonathon obeyed. Caroline very carefully supported his head and held the cup to his lips. It was like tending a child.

Jonathon drained the cup. It took a long time, for his throat was swollen with the disease. He grimaced, then watched as Caroline poured more of the creamy yellow liquid into the cup. "What is it?"

"Sam's magic," Caroline said. "Mare's beestings. More now!" She held the cup to Jonathon's lips again, then wiped the trickles from the heated skin. "Last bit!" She poured the dregs from the canteen into the cup and made Jonathon finish them. "That wasn't bad, was it?"

Jonathon, exhausted, shivered as Caroline helped him down into the bed again. He held her hand, gripping it as though he would never let go.

She leaned over and picked up the odd metal device. "What is it?"

"A scarificator. A bleeding-machine." The device resembled an oversize nutmeg grater, three inches square, with a handle protruding from one face, while the opposite face was pierced with holes like a colander. There was a trigger on the handle, and a small lever which Caroline, taking her right hand from Jonathon's fevered grip, pulled back exactly as if she were cocking a musket.

"Hold it away from your other hand." Jonathon's voice was weak, but his breathing was easier.

Caroline obeyed and with some trepidation pulled the trigger. The implement jumped like a snapping mousetrap in her hand as a dozen symmetrically arranged blades, each wickedly sharp and shaped like a gouge, sprang through the holes. Each small blade was stained with dark clotted blood and Caroline understood now the regular patterns of scars on Jonathon's arm. The machine was a device for bleeding patients, drawing the blood in one quick and multiple sting of pain.

"It's the very latest thing from London," Jonathon said.

"They're barbarians. They're not going to use it on you again." Caroline pushed the scarificator into the pocket of her skirt.

"They'll be angry if it's lost," Jonathon said. He lay exhausted, his hand seeking hers again. "Do you think I'll ever leave?"

"You'll leave," Caroline said, and she began to tell him of the preparations she had made. Sam would help them find horses so that they could ride north to join Washington's army. She made her words sound hopeful.

"My uncle won't let me go."

"He won't know. If I can get in here, then I can get you out. And you'll get better, Jonathon. Sam says everyone gets better after beestings."

Caroline stayed with Jonathon till he slept. Once there were footsteps outside the door, but no one came in. She waited till the clock in the hall struck half past eleven. Then, very gently, she kissed his hot forehead, and left him the ivy cup as a reminder of the stolen visit.

Candlelight flickered from the open stairwell as Caroline slipped down to the window, eased it up, and climbed out into the rain. Fearing the broken glass on the wall, she went to the carriage entry and unbolted the small door that was let into one of the big gates. She pulled it open and stepped into the darkness of the alley.

"Caroline!" The voice was Sam's, strangled and desperate. "*Run!*"

Shadows moved, and darkness overwhelmed her.

HAVING THROWN THE STONES, Sam had run north, crossed Market Street, then slipped into the alley that ran behind the Becket house. He could just see the dim shape of the horse blanket on the wall's coping to tell him that Caroline was still inside. Shivering in the cold rain, he backed into an archway to wait for her.

The movement was sudden beside him and Sam, expecting a blow, twisted hard away, bounced off the gatepost and came back fighting. A musket butt slammed into his belly, and a second man jabbed another into his head, knocking his hat off.

Sam slipped, fell, and a boot thudded into his thigh. He pushed up, and again a musket butt swung at him. This time the dark night exploded scarlet and white. A knee was pushed into his belly and a bayonet was cold at his throat.

"One word, Sam, and you're dead." It was Sergeant Scammell's voice. "Who's the whore, Sam? The one who went over the wall? Robbing the gentry, are you?"

"She ain't a whore. She lives here."

"Don't muck around with me, Sam!" Scammell hissed the words. Sam's head was in the mud, held there by the bayonet. "I don't care about your whore," Scammell said. "Only about mine. You was seen in the street with Maggie a couple of weeks back. I've been keeping an eye on you ever since, Sam." Scammell chuckled. "She works for a Mrs. Taylor, don't she?"

"Dunno, Sarge."

"You know, Sam! And I know. Three guineas! I want that money, Sam, and you're going to get it for me, because she's mine, boy." Scammell's voice hissed above Sam in the darkness. "She's mine! She was nothing when I met her, nothing. A bull whore that I made into a guinea girl."

Sam's head, though still hurting like the devil, was clearing. He could see the dark shapes of the two men above him, but his right boot had found a purchase on a sprung plank of the door beside him. He braced himself, ready to heave, but he knew he had to keep Scammell talking until some chance, however slim, occurred. "If you know where she is," Sam tried feebly, "then why don't you get her?"

"Cos the old cow that runs her won't let anyone in, will she? Officers' territory, that, but your Jack-pudding sends you to fetch his doxies, don't he? So this is what you're going to do for me, Sam Gilpin. You're going to Mrs. Taylor's and tell her that your Jack-pudding wants Maggie now. Then you'll bring her to me instead of him. You understand?"

"She mayn't want to come, Sarge." Sam shifted slowly. In one of the deep watchcoat pockets he had a small pistol that he usually carried about the city.

"She'll come," Scammell said, "cos you'll make her come, boy. Else, Sam, I'll take your whore instead of Maggie."

Sam heaved, but Scammell, ready for it, slapped a handful of gritty mud into Sam's face. Sam choked, gagged and spat, but the bayonet pressed and threatened and he lay still, listening.

He heard the window go up. He braced himself, but Scammell's fingers

444

groped for his eyes and pressed and Sam knew he was beaten. He lay still. A dog whined and its chain rattled on cobbles.

He could just see the top of the wall where the blanket lay folded, and he watched it; then the bolts on the gate squealed and grated.

"George!" Scammell hissed the word, and Sam knew instantly who the other man was: George Cullen, who boasted of having killed three women before joining the army to escape from the justices. Cullen, who delighted in pain.

The gate opened. Sam spat the mud from his mouth, twisted his head away from the pressing fingers, and heaved with his right leg. "Caroline! Run!"

The bayonet sliced up Sam's jawbone as Scammell was jerked forwards. Caroline screamed, then the scream was abruptly cut off as Cullen wrapped her in a greatcoat and forced her down into the mud.

Sam clawed with his left hand for the sergeant's face, but his right was plunging into the pocket and scrabbling for the pistol. The sergeant chopped down with his left fist, then laid the seventeen-inch blade across Sam's throat. "If you don't stay still, I'll take your whore now, in front of you! Is that what you want?"

Sam went still, but the pistol was in his hand now. The weapon was tangled in the cloth, but very slowly Sam eased the flint back as he tried to twist the short barrel towards Scammell.

Caroline was squirming and kicking, but Cullen contemptuously picked her up and slammed her against the wall. She gasped with pain, then gave up the struggle. Cullen laughed. His right hand was pinning her throat against the wall. With his left he lifted her skirts.

"Very nice," Scammell said. "Very nice. So listen, Sam. You go for Maggie, and you bring her back to me. If you don't, Sam, then you won't see this doxy again."

Caroline suddenly twisted. Cullen grunted as he slapped her head against the wall, then pushed his left hand back beneath her coat. "Little bitch was going for this." He tossed her knife onto the ground.

"You've got an hour, Sam." Scammell eased the bayonet away from Sam's throat. "Are you going to do it?"

Sam pulled the trigger.

He did not dare leave Caroline with these men, even for a minute, let alone an hour. He had to fight now, and he prayed that the cloth of the pocket would not trap the flint's fall, and that the rain had not soaked through to turn the powder in the pistol's pan to grey sludge.

The pistol fired.

The report was muffled by the cloth. The bullet, driven up through the layers of thick wool, seared across Scammell's inner thigh like a red-hot whip. The sergeant jerked back. Sam heaved up and tore the pistol free of his smouldering pocket. The bayonet slashed at him, missed, and Sam hit

Scammell in the face with the pistol and was suddenly free. He threw himself to his left and scrabbled for one of the two muskets.

Then Cullen yelped as pain stabbed through his leg. Caroline, in the flurry, had thrust the scarificator against Cullen's thigh and pulled the trigger. She dragged the blades down, gouging bloody grooves of torn flesh that made Cullen instinctively snatch at the pain's source. As his hand left her throat, Caroline twisted away. "Run, Sam!"

Sam hammered the musket's butt at Cullen's head as Caroline tore herself free, then abandoned the weapon and ran with her. He took her hand and pulled her along. He turned left at the alley's end, and they sprinted up Fourth Street. A dog barked. A patrolman, seeing the dark running figures, shouted.

Sam turned at the corner of Arch Street. Scammell and Cullen were on the pavement, both men limping, but the sight of the patrol drove them back into the doorway.

"Come on!" Caroline tugged his hand. The rain was on her face, the Redcoats were chasing them and she was laughing.

"Here!" Sam had seen a half-open gate. They fell through it into a pitch-black alley with a timber roof. Sam pushed the gate shut and crouched, listening.

A voice, speaking close behind them, made Sam gasp and turn. "Who are you?" It was a man's voice.

Sam bunched himself to fight this new threat, but Caroline said, "We're running from the lobsters."

"I know all about running away," said the strange man. He sounded elderly. "I'm just locking up, children. You will find the gate easy to climb when the soldiers are gone. God bless you." The man shuffled past them, the gate closed, and Sam heard a key grate in a padlock. The footsteps of the patrol were loud beyond the arch, and Sam heard the old man bid the soldiers a courteous good evening. No, he had not been troubled by any hooligans.

"Where are we?" Sam whispered to Caroline.

"It's the city synagogue," she whispered back. She laid a finger on his lips. The rain drummed on the boards above them and dripped through the gaps in the crude roof.

Sam sat with his back against the synagogue wall. Caroline sat beside him. She was shivering, so he took off his heavy watchcoat and draped it about her shoulders so that, encircled by the coat and his arm, she had to lean against him and he could smell her wet hair and feel the warmth of her face close to his cheek. He put his other arm round her and she buried her face in the cloth of his red uniform. It all seemed so natural. Sam hugged her tight and close, warming her, while beyond the gate the footsteps faded away.

"We shouldn't," Caroline murmured into his coat.

"No." Though Sam did not move.

Caroline pulled away, forcing Sam to release one arm. She sniffed as though close to tears. "Jonathon's terrible, Sam. They're murdering him!"

"He'll get better now." Sam spoke with absolute confidence.

Caroline smiled. "Do you ever give up, Sam?"

"Never." There was a glimmer of light from carriage lamps as a coach splashed past the synagogue. "If you do, the Green Man will get you."

"The Green Man?"

"A sprite." Sam's voice was soft in the darkness. "He has a devil's soul and a green skin. He lives in the woods, see, and he eats you if you get frightened. You can hear him sometimes. He has feet like great tree boles moving in the leaves, and a voice like a gale."

Caroline listened to the conviction in his voice.

"My grandad saw him once up in the top woods. A girt thing he was." Sam's voice took on the burr of his native village as if, for a moment, he thought he was back there. "A great thing shifting among the dark, but if you don't fear him, he won't trouble you."

"Do you miss England, Sam?"

He smiled. "Not now."

"No?" She sounded disbelieving and Sam, although he knew he should not, answered Caroline by gathering her into his arms again and Caroline, though she knew she should not, let herself be drawn into that safe encircling embrace.

"I promised Jonathon," Caroline's voice was very small, "that you'd help find us horses when we go."

"I'll do that."

She paused, then shrugged in Sam's arms. "He shouldn't go back to the army, not with one leg, but he insists. Martha says he should study law. She says it doesn't matter if a lawyer's only got one leg." She stirred and her face looked palely up at Sam. "But lawyers live in the city, don't they?"

Sam supposed she was right. "I couldn't live in the city," he said. "I'm glad to have seen one, but I couldn't live in it. Like being in prison."

"Yes."

There was silence again between them. Caroline still shivered and Sam held her very close and gently stroked her hair, but with a touch so light that Caroline could almost persuade herself that it was unintentional.

"Will you stay a soldier, Sam?"

"I don't have a lot of choice, do I?"

"But with those two men?" Caroline shuddered.

"They ain't all like that. Most of them are decent sorts of fellows. Weavers."

"Weavers?"

"No work back home, you see, so they join the army." Sam grinned. "We have enough weavers to put a blanket over Philadelphia."

"But do you really want to stay a soldier, Sam?"

Sam hesitated. "Not like I used to, perhaps."

"What do you want?"

Sam hesitated again. What he wanted was what he had now—this girl in his arms—but that was something that could not be said because of a lad who lay in sweating sickness. Sam shrugged. "A piece of land wouldn't be a bad thing, and a few mares to breed from." He paused for a second. "I sometimes dream about that."

"You can have it here, Sam!"

"Three hogs and fifty acres?"

Caroline frowned, not understanding. "Fifty acres?"

"That's what the rebels offer, but they don't give it you. Leastways, I hear they don't."

Caroline kept silent. She wanted him to say what it was that he desired, and she wanted him to say it without invitation. She wanted that gift on this cold night, and Sam, pensive beside her, offered it. "What I want I can't have."

Caroline's voice was very quiet. "So you do give up sometimes? The Green Man will get you, Sam, and gobble you up."

"Will he?" And Sam, because he could not help it, and because he wanted to, kissed her.

He kissed her wet cheek, then put an arm round her shoulders and drew her face to his as though he would warm her and comfort her and hold her against the dark for ever. Caroline sighed and stayed. The dirt on Sam's face was harsh on her skin, but she felt comforted.

He held her close, but had nothing to say, for he knew, and she knew, that there was nothing to say. Instead, they must keep their promises to Jonathon, and the kiss was just a moment stolen from what might have been, but could never be.

THE DEAD SEASON CAME. Winds brought sleet from an aching sky above a frozen land. The river was grey as Welsh slate, promising ice in the long dark silences of the American winter. Philadelphia's straight streets, bereft of their trees, were bleached to a stark paleness in which the red-coated soldiers, shrunken by the wind, moved slow and shivering. The wind cut at faces, made skin raw, and chilled fingers blue.

Winter threatened to end all navigation between Philadelphia and the sea. Lord Howe took the fleet north to the deeper anchorage of Rhode Island, leaving only a handful of small warships to fend off the rebel gunboats that still sometimes snapped at the shrunken seagoing trade.

The city's mood grew bleaker as its population rose sharply. Not only was the army in residence, but refugees from the ravaged hinterland came in search of shelter and food. There was scarce enough of either.

Only the wealthy did not suffer. The shops, replenished by the ships which had sailed upriver after the capture of the forts, offered luxuries to the affluent. Watch-chains, court plasters, hair powder, wigs, silk stockings and pomatum were all plentiful; so too were wine, brandy, gin and rum. Yet cheese, flour, meal, rice and meat were already as scarce as in the weeks before the river forts fell. Prices rose, beggars multiplied, and the lowering sky threatened the snow that would make misery worse.

It was the dead season: a time when the weak things of the earth died, but Jonathon mended.

Caroline knew, because one of the kitchen maids in Becket's house now smuggled letters between her and Jonathon.

"It was Sam's beestings," Caroline said.

"I rather think it was." Martha heard the pride in the young girl's voice. "So! Jonathon will be on a wooden leg by spring." She said it cheerfully to see how Caroline responded.

The response was not enthusiastic. Caroline punched at the small logs in the kitchen grate with a poker. "He wants to go to Trenton. He says he'll clerk for the army. He knows he can't fight."

"And you'll go with him?"

Caroline nodded. "I promised. And I can make him very happy."

"Yes, you can." Martha walked to the small window that looked into her courtyard. Sleet tapped on the pane. "How's Sam? I haven't seen him for many a long day."

"Sam's busy. He's doctoring horses and saving money."

Martha heard the warmth in Caroline's voice. She turned. "Do you see him often?"

"Sometimes." Caroline was evasive.

Martha went back to the fire and stretched out thin hands to the flames. "Would you like some advice?" She did not wait for an answer. "It might be best if you stayed on the other side of the river. I'll tell Sam you can't come to the city till the danger of ice is past."

Caroline did not reply, but just stared into the small flames.

"Or I could say you were frightened of those men who attacked you?" Martha suggested. "But whatever I say, my dear, it will save you a deal of confusion."

Caroline frowned. "I'm not confused." She stopped, remembering the night beside the synagogue. She shook her head. "Sam's a Redcoat."

"Sam's a Redcoat of whom you're very fond, and I can't say I blame you. But you've a promise to keep, so stay on the other side of the river." Martha's voice was firm. "You don't scratch at a half-healed wound. Let it alone."

Caroline looked at the older woman. "And your messages?"

Martha shrugged. "There'll be no fighting till spring, but if I've something of importance to send, I'll have a servant deliver it to you."

Caroline looked into the fire again. "I'll tell Sam. And I can't see

Jonathon now anyway"—her voice was wistful—"so it's all for the best."

"Yes. It is."

Caroline left, and that night the first heavy snow came. It snowed all night and all next day. Heavy, soft flakes whirled around rooflines and heaped in alleyways. For a few days at least, spirits rose. In the twelve days of Christmas there were snowball fights on the Centre Commons, while horse-drawn sleighs on their steel-lined runners appeared in the streets. There were sledge races on the Neck, and by New Year the river was hard frozen, so skates could hiss and scrape on the gleaming ice.

Each day Sam watched for the ice to melt, but instead it seemed to thicken. January turned to February in the hardest winter in living memory. The snow turned to slush, then was freshened by new falls. Food supplies shrank and men died of scurvy. Forage parties trudged out into blizzards to search the nearer farms for hidden supplies, and sometimes, in the short cold days, musket fire echoed over the pitiless land to tell of a brutal skirmish between Redcoats and rebels.

Such rebels were on patrol, for General Washington had pulled the Continental Army back to winter quarters at a place called Valley Forge. Lizzie Loring thought it sounded like a very cosy place. "All those blacksmiths' fires in a valley? I imagine they're very snug."

"I seem to recall we burned down the forges last summer," said Sir William, "and their deserters tell us it's the most hideous place."

Lizzie stood at the bedroom window. Icicles hung from the eaves beneath a grey sky in which the sun, low over the State House roof, was paled to a sickly yellow disc. "Is that what you'll say when you desert us?" She turned. "Will you say how hideous America is?"

Sir William, his hopes of an early peace now gone, had offered his resignation to the government in London. Touched now by her unhappiness, he could offer small consolation. "Perhaps they won't accept my resignation."

"But if they do?"

"You can come to England."

"I can't imagine Lady Howe appreciating such a thing."

"No." Sir William, wearing a skullcap and heavy robe, stroked his dog which lay curled at his feet by the fire. "But if there's peace, my dear, I'll stay."

"Will there be peace?"

"If the French don't come, yes."

"And if the French do come?"

Sir William thought, as he stirred the negus which warmed on a trivet by the flames. "It will be a different war, my love. A war about sugar and islands and fleets. It will be an old-fashioned European war, and all because of threepence on tea." He said the last words bitterly.

"And you'll leave, and you'll tell them in England that America was never worth fighting for, and that it's a hideous place with dull people and ranting preachers and a foul climate."

"No," Sir William said, "I won't." He crossed to her, and gathered her into his arms. "I shall say it was the place where I knew the greatest happiness of my life. And lost it."

It was winter, and the land was shrouded with white, waiting for spring.

Chapter Thirteen

The building was cavernous, dark and echoing. It reeked of paint, but on this night in early April 1778, that thick stench was mingled with the odours of powder and perfume. Silks and calico rustled in the darkness. A woman giggled and was immediately hushed.

Only four lights, each an oil lamp placed within a reflecting hood, burned in the building's gaping interior. The small flames cast a flickering glow into a painted scene that depicted green hills, deep woods, and a stream flowing towards a stone-built village with a spired church. The painting hung like a vast curtain across the stage of Philadelphia's theatre, reviving sweet memories of the English countryside for the officers who stood in the pit's darkness.

Somewhere deep in the theatre a hidden drum began a slow beat.

A trumpet, much closer at hand, seared an abrupt fanfare that made the crowd shiver with delicious alarm. More than two hundred people were standing in the darkness to watch the lit stage.

The fanfare ceased. The drummer gave a final flourish. A pause, just long enough for the spectators' apprehension to increase, then a voice sounded from the apparently empty stage.

> "Once more ambitious of theatric glory,
> Howe's strolling player appears before ye!"

On the word "appears", the four lights at the front of the stage were abruptly doused and other lamps, placed behind the painted scene, were unhooded. The English landscape, painted on a great sheet of gauze, disappeared to be replaced by a black-cloaked man, Captain John Andre, who bowed to his audience. At the same instant two doors, one on either side of the stage, were thrown back and lines of uniformed men marched in carrying tall candelabra to light the theatre's interior.

Andre held up a hand for silence. He smiled. "My Lords, Ladies, Gallants, Friends! The Society of Gentlemen of the Army and Navy, which I have the humble honour to represent this night, welcomes you to the playhouse!"

More applause. The candelabra were being placed on linen-covered tables that were heaped with food and wine.

"A playhouse where we, this winter, have been delighted to offer you the rarest gems of the dramatic art! *The Constant Couple!*" There were mocking cheers at the mention of the play's title, cheers that Andre checked with an upraised hand. "*The Wonder! A Woman Keeps a Secret!*"

There were more cheers and laughter, which again Andre checked with a raised hand. He walked to the front of the stage while musicians came from the wings to set up their chairs and stands behind him. Tonight, instead of drama, the theatre was to hold a subscription ball for the widows and orphans of those who had lost their lives in the King's service. The benches of the pit had been pushed under the gallery to make way for dancing, while in the antechamber two Hessian officers had established a faro bank for the gamblers. It was a night for revelry, and Captain Andre thanked all who had paid to attend, raised laughter by imitating the preachers who claimed that the theatre had corrupted Philadelphia's youth, and enjoined each guest to an evening of celebration.

Applause followed his speech. "He did that remarkably well!" Sir William Howe clapped enthusiastically. "John's a talented fellow." He spied Martha on Lord Robert Massedene's arm and waved to attract her attention. "Amongst my other sins, dear Mrs. Crowl, do you see me as a corrupter of American youth?"

"Dear Sir William." Martha, splendid in vivid blue silk, gave the commander-in-chief her hand to be kissed. "Whom have you corrupted?"

"The clergy say everyone."

"They should be grateful for the business, should they not? Clergy need sinners like pork butchers need hogs."

And Martha, taking Sir Robert's arm, joined a quadrille. Christopher Vane, handing off one partner to link arms with another, saw that he must inevitably be drawn to offer a hand to Martha so, with an elegant sidestep, he left the dance. He stepped under the gallery, took a glass of wine, and saw Major Otto Zeigler standing gloomy and alone in the shadows.

"I'm drunk," the Hessian said in bald reply to Vane's greeting. "We should be fighting, not dancing."

"Indeed."

"You English don't know how to fight a war. You can dance, *ja*, but you don't fight. You are betrayed and you do nothing! Nothing!" He abruptly went into the antechamber where the Hessian officers ran their fast and profitable faro bank. Zeigler sat, took out a handful of coins, and joined the game.

Christopher Vane, the dancing suddenly forgotten, went into the antechamber and stood behind the interpreter. He watched for a while as Zeigler, drunk beyond caring, lost money fast. Faro was not a game of finesse but merely of luck, in which the players guessed the order in which the cards would be revealed. Zeigler consistently backed the Pharaoh itself, the King of Hearts, on which any wager was doubled.

Vane leaned down beside Zeigler. "What do you mean, Otto, betrayed?"

Zeigler searched his pockets for more coins and found two guineas. "My last funds," he said. "If I lose these I shall blow my goddamn brains out." A score of officers had killed themselves because of the winter's gambling debts.

"What do you mean?" Vane asked again. "Betrayed?"

"Who damn cares?" Zeigler havered between the Pharaoh and the Three of Diamonds, then, with the air of a doomed man, plumped for the lesser card.

Vane, smiling, took the two guineas from the Three of Diamonds and put them on the Pharaoh. "I'm feeling lucky tonight, Otto."

"For God's ..." Zeigler's hand shot out to move his money back, but Vane gripped the Hessian's wrist and held it firm until the bank began revealing their deck. Vane estimated there were sixty or seventy guineas depending on this hand, but only Zeigler's money was wagered on the Pharaoh.

Zeigler watched the cards turn. "It's my last money. If I lose that I have nothing. Only a bullet."

"I told you, I'm feeling lucky. I pay your losses, you keep your winnings."

The sixth card of the bank's deck was the King of Hearts. Money was scooped from around the table, doubled from the bank's hoard, and the whole golden pile pushed towards the drunken Hessian. "My God!" Zeigler stared at his fortune.

Vane scooped all the winnings into his handkerchief. "Now, come and talk to me."

"That's my money!"

"You can have it when you've talked to me."

Zeigler grumbled, but obeyed. He fetched himself a bottle of claret and staggered to a small table where Vane waited for him. "Donop," Zeigler explained when Vane repeated his question, "was betrayed."

Vane had to think for a moment before he remembered that Donop was the Hessian general who had led the attack on Fort Mercer in the autumn. The general had been wounded in the failed assault, captured, and had died three days later.

"They knew we were coming." Zeigler poured himself a glass of wine. "You do not have a glass. You need a glass." He turned and peered round.

"Why do you think Donop was betrayed?"

"You do not have a glass!" Zeigler said in drunken indignation.

Vane patiently fetched himself a glass, poured himself wine, and sat down again. "Why?"

"Because I was told it, that is why! You have my money!"

"I shall give it you. Who told you?"

Zeigler belched, then shook his head. "They shouldn't have beat us. We were betrayed, Kit, betrayed!"

"Who told you?"

"The rebeller prisoners!" Zeigler said indignantly, as if he had already explained the whole matter. "I talked to them to find out about Donop. One of them told me."

"What did the prisoner say?"

"It was a long time ago," Zeigler said wearily. "He said they knew! The rebellers were told! They were ready! They were waiting!"

"Fort Mercer was warned?"

"*Ja*! Here." Zeigler feverishly searched his pocket to produce a small notebook. He searched the pages. "A Lieutenant Lynch told me, there! You see? I make a note of it."

The note was in German and meant nothing to Vane. "What did he say?"

"He said they were warned! I want my money."

"And Lynch didn't tell you who brought the letter?"

"No. He was boasting at first, but then he became, how do you say, like the grave."

"Silent," Vane said. He felt the horror of Zeigler's revelations. Only a handful of officers, those closest to Sir William, had known of the attack on the forts. One of those officers had, at best, been indiscreet or, at worst, was a traitor. Vane frowned. "Why didn't you tell anyone earlier, Otto?"

"I did! I told Billy, didn't I? But Billy doesn't care. He said I should forget it. Four hundred men dead! And I must forget it!"

Vane looked sideways through the archway. Sir William was dancing with Martha Crowl, and the sight put a spasm of hatred through Vane's jealous soul. Forget treachery? That was typical of Sir William, who believed that a soft answer would turn away wrath. The rebel army had been at Valley Forge all winter, scarce three days' march away, yet Sir William had done nothing. Instead, he danced with Martha Crowl, who was allowed to flaunt her patriotism in the highest circles of the British command.

Zeigler gave a sour laugh. "The English aren't serious about war, Kit. I like Billy, truly, but you cannot be nice to the enemy." He put the bottle to his lips and finished the wine. "Where's my money?"

"Here." Vane pushed the handkerchief across the table, but palmed some of the coins into his own hand. "Is Lieutenant Lynch still alive?"

"Who cares?" Zeigler hiccupped, then rested his head on the golden pile of guineas. "I shall sleep."

Christopher Vane took the small notebook and tore out the page with the prisoner's name. The war was not lost yet. The French still havered, and there was yet a chance that the enemy could be brought to battle in the early spring. Crush Washington and the French would flinch from another beating, but not if the British were betrayed. And Vane, watching the widow glitter in the candlelight, was determined that, this time, there would be no betrayal to cheat the royal army of its victory.

WHITE CLOUDS SAILED across a blue sky. There was warmth at last in the sunlight. The nights were still cold but spring was bringing its green to the seaboard, and Philadelphia prepared for a new season of war.

Gunners practised their aim by firing at casks floated down the Delaware, the infantry ran with full packs to harden lazy muscles, and Sam exercised Vane's horses into battle strength. He took them to the Neck and pounded them across softening ground to put muscle beneath their pelts. Back in the stables he would bang their coats with bundled straw, then brush them till they gleamed. He trained Captain Vane's young stallion for war, firing muskets close to its ears, shouting at it, trying to scare it, yet always reassuring the horse that, whatever danger seemed to threaten, it could live and survive. Sam taught the stallion to rear and lash out with its hooves so that infantrymen, trying to attack its rider, would flinch away. Each morning the training went on, and each morning Sam would lead his string of horses past Jonathon's house and once, soon after the river ice melted, he saw Jonathon through a downstairs window, but Jonathon did not see him.

A month later, on the morning after the theatre's subscription ball, Sam was rasping down the hooves of the black stallion. He was alone. He had stripped off his red coat and donned a farrier's apron.

He heard the church's main door open and, assuming it was another groom, called out a rude reminder not to leave the bloody door open.

"You're just another arrogant Englishman," said a voice, "ordering us humble colonials about."

Sam let go of the stallion's fetlock and stared. "Jonathon!" He kicked the stool over and ran. "Just look at you! Pegleg!"

"Hello, Sam." Jonathon smiled with shy pleasure.

Sam had no shyness. He threw his arms round Jonathon, who had stumped in on his one good leg and one leather-tipped wooden peg. Two crutches gave him stability. "I told you!" Sam said triumphantly. "I said you'd be walking!"

"It's my first proper walk," Jonathon explained. "They fitted it two weeks ago, and I've been hopping round the house ever since." He leaned against one of the empty pews to take the weight off his stump, rubbed raw by the friction of the leather cup strapped to his thigh. "It's better than the old leg but it's awful sore."

"It will be. It takes time to settle a wooden leg, you know."

Jonathon still smiled. "I have to thank you, don't I? It was the beestings."

Sam shrugged the thanks away. "Caroline did most of that."

"She says it was you." Jonathon looked up the aisle towards the vestry door. "She said she'd meet me here."

Sam hid his sudden excitement.

"There is a guard on me." Jonathon spoke mockingly. "My uncle still thinks I'll run away, so I'm only allowed outdoors with a groom to keep me loyal. He's had enough of horses, though, so he'll not come in here."

"Then how does Caroline . . ."

"We write to each other." Jonathon's face was still thin from the illness, but there was colour in his cheeks and a brightness in his eyes. "One of the kitchen maids smuggles letters to Martha's house, and Martha sends them to Caroline." Jonathon looked up the aisle again. "She said she'd come in the back way." He heaved himself onto the crutches and began pegging and lurching towards the chancel.

Sam walked beside him. He saw the stallion's ears prick back and he knew someone had made a sound in the vestry. Then the door opened, and she stood there.

Jonathon hurried forward, but for a moment Caroline looked past Jonathon and stared at Sam.

And Sam, who had been so impatient for the ice's melting, suddenly felt tongue-tied. "Hello, miss."

"Hello, Sam," Caroline said, and walked towards Jonathon, and Sam turned away as the two embraced at the foot of the chancel steps. He stroked the stallion and tried not to listen to the joy of the reunion behind him.

But Jonathon would not let Sam be excluded from that joy. He bombarded him with questions. Wasn't Caroline looking well, wasn't this the happiest day, and wasn't it wonderful to be together again?

Sam was forced to look at Caroline, and he saw that nothing had changed. Nothing. He blushed. "It's been a long time, miss."

"Nearly four months, Sam."

Sam saw how his vision of her, which he had conjured in the long snow-silenced nights, had been so wrong. He had not remembered the life in her face, or the defiance and wildness and humour of those blue eyes and strong jaw.

"I've been busy," Caroline explained lamely. "It's calving time. But Jonathon wanted to meet me." She seemed to need to explain their sudden presence. "I said we should meet here."

"I'm glad."

Caroline took her hand from Jonathon's and walked to the nearest box pew, where she fondled Lord Robert Massedene's grey gelding. "We need your help, Sam." Her voice was strangely flat. She turned to him. "We're going soon."

"In three weeks." Jonathon bubbled with eagerness.

"You're going north?" Sam could hardly bear to look at her.

"By boat to Trenton," Jonathon said. "I can't do any fighting, Sam, but I can clerk."

"The difficulty," Caroline interrupted, "is getting Jonathon out of the city. He's still a prisoner, so he can't get a pass."

"I suppose not," Sam said. Sir William, in the last few weeks, had instituted a system of passes for anyone wanting to travel beyond the ring of British guardposts. It was intended to deter paroled rebel officers from attempting to rejoin Washington's army.

"But the sentries know you, Sam. If you were helping a drunken officer into a boat one night, no one would take any notice, would they? All we need is a uniform."

Sam wiped his hands on his leather apron. "Better be a naval uniform then," he said. "They're the only officers on the river at night. Going back to their ships, you see . . ." His voice petered out.

"Can you get me one?" Jonathon asked.

Sam nodded. "And the peg leg won't matter so much. There's a couple of navy fellows on stumps."

Jonathon smiled. "I knew you'd help, Sam." He glanced towards the main door, then looked sheepishly at Sam. "Do you mind if we go in the vestry?"

"It's a tack room now," Sam said.

Caroline had gone back to Jonathon's side. "Thank you, Sam."

Sam heard the farewell in her voice. "It was good seeing you again, Miss Caroline." The formality seemed strange.

"Could you take the uniform to Mrs. Crowl?" Caroline asked in the distant voice that hurt Sam.

"I can. I'll get it," Sam promised, and watched as Caroline helped Jonathon to the vestry. The door closed behind them.

Sam went back to the stallion. He rubbed its nose. "You shouldn't have dreams, eh? Daft things, dreams. Only let you down." Sam had waited for so long. He closed his eyes suddenly, as though he was afraid of tears.

Sam's eyes were still closed as the vestry door opened behind him. He listened to the footsteps, but dared not look in case he was disappointed.

"Hello, Sam."

He opened his eyes to find he was not disappointed.

Caroline gave a small, embarrassed shrug. "He went out the back way. He daren't stay away too long in case they get suspicious."

Sam tacked the horseshoe onto the hoof. "He daren't be seen with you?" Sam spoke without looking up from his work.

"He's frightened of his uncle. Frightened he might not get his inheritance." Caroline sat on the pulpit steps. "He'll be better when we reach Trenton."

"Where you'll marry him?" Sam tried to made his voice careless.

"I promised." Caroline spoke guardedly.

Sam patted the stallion's withers. "That's better, boy, isn't it? You won't be slipping and sliding now."

The stallion whinnied in answer. Caroline was silent. The sound of wagon wheels and of a whip cracking came from Race Street. "How are you, Sam?" Caroline broke the silence.

"Glad that the spring's come. Everyone is."

Caroline stood again, then climbed the chancel steps. The sunlight, coming through the broken window above her, glinted on her hair. "What's going to happen to you, Sam?"

"To me?" Sam laughed as though the answer did not matter, though in truth he had given the question much thought through the winter months. "I shall be all right."

"Tell me."

Sam hesitated for a second, then shrugged. "I cured the general's horse of the colic and his man reckons Billy might give me a job in his stables."

"Is that good?" Caroline's voice was bleak.

Sam led the stallion towards its pew. "It's certainly a lot better than carrying a musket."

Caroline nodded. For a few seconds she said nothing, then, her voice oddly quiet, almost inaudible, "I've been hoping that you'd come with us, Sam."

At first Sam thought he had misheard. "To Trenton?"

"That's where we're going."

For a moment Sam did not know what to say. He shrugged, half laughed, then shook his head. "You want me to fight my own side?"

"There's plenty of Redcoats who've changed sides, Sam."

"Aye. My brother wanted to, and look where he is now. I've watched them, miss, with blood dripping down their legs from the whips."

"You're frightened?" Caroline spoke with a hint of scorn.

"No, miss, I'm not frightened." Sam led the stallion into its stall. He did not tie the headrope, just latched the low door shut. "But I'm a bit like Jonathon, you see. Only one thing will make me run, and it isn't the liberty you go on about." Sam knew the moment had come to say the words he had rehearsed through the long weeks, but now that they should be said, he found the saying too hard and chose a circumlocution instead. "I kept waiting for the ice to melt."

Caroline answered with an evasion to match Sam's own. "We made Jonathon better, Sam."

"We did."

"And we knew what that meant."

"Aye, we did."

"I wasn't asking you to come for my sake, Sam."

"What for, then? Fifty acres of land and three hogs?" Sam's voice was scornful.

The scorn prompted Caroline to look at Sam again, and to put an urgent pleading into her voice. "It's a whole new country, Sam. A whole future, something for ever! Something good and shining. Can't you see that? We're going to make a new beginning, Sam, and it won't be rotten and corrupt. It will be clean!" All her passion and all her hopes seethed in her voice. "God's country, Sam. You could be happy, Sam, you could—"

Caroline stopped speaking because the main church door had banged open and a red-coated officer came into the church. His strident voice echoed down the aisle. "Sam! Sam! Sam!" Captain Vane strode between the horse-occupied pews. "Sam, you varlet! Have you finished? I have need of . . ." Vane's voice tailed away as he caught sight of Caroline. He stared, then swept off his hat to offer a low bow. "Dear lady. I don't believe we've met?" He was clearly in one of his more cheerful moods.

Sam's embarrassment was excruciating, but he managed to stumble out an introduction. "Miss Caroline, sir. Captain Vane, miss."

"Miss Caroline!" Vane stared shamelessly at her. "Are you Sam's mysterious kitchenmaid?"

Caroline was quick. She nodded. "Yes, sir." She edged towards the vestry door. "I have to be going." She nodded at Sam and almost ran out through the tack room.

Vane waited till the outer door banged shut. "My God, Sam! She's absolutely lovely."

"She's nice, sir."

"Nice?" Vane whirled on his servant. "Good God, boy! Men have killed for less! Is this where you meet her? No wonder you spend so long in the stables, Sam. So would I! If you ever tire of her?" Vane saw the irritation on Sam's face, and quickly shook his head. "Forget I said it, Sam. I apologise." Vane laughed, then fondled the stallion's nose. "How is he?"

"Footing properly now, sir."

"Truly?"

Sam smiled. "Stand away from him, sir." He waited till Vane had obeyed, then gave a short sharp whistle. The stallion whinnied, gathered itself, and jumped clean over the low door of the pew. It trotted obediently to Sam and lowered its head for his affection.

Vane laughed. "Teaching him tricks?"

"He's a good one, sir. The best." Sam led the stallion back into the stall and tied the headrope. "Did you want to take him out?"

"No, no. I'm just passing the time of day, Sam." Vane looked round the church's bare interior. "It's a dull church, isn't it? What was the name of the sergeant who so scared the tripe out of you?"

The last question was asked so suddenly that Sam could not gather his wits. "Sir?"

"The one who was married to what's her name? Sacharissa?"

Sam sounded horrified. "Scammell, sir?"

"That's it! Thank you, Sam." The captain turned to leave.

"Sir!"

Vane turned back. "Sam?"

Sam was alarmed. Since the night when Scammell had tried to hold Caroline against Maggie's return, Sam had neither seen nor heard of Sergeant Michael Scammell, and he would have liked that happy state to continue. "You're not going to report him, are you, sir?"

"Report him?" Vane was all innocence.

"Cos of what I told you? About the boy at Germantown, sir? The one he killed?"

"It was murder, Sam!" Vane teased. "But I'm not going to report him, Samuel, so calm yourself. My reasons are altogether more whimsical. I am informed that the beautiful Sacharissa has formed an attachment, Sam, and the officer concerned does not wish for any trouble from her husband. You follow me now? I have promised to square the man."

"He's a bastard, sir," Sam said warningly.

"Bastards will bring us victory. Those and good horses, like you, my friend." Vane patted the stallion's neck. "Thank you, Sam."

460

Sam watched the captain go and wondered why the skin of his spine was suddenly chill. Why could Maggie not have told her officer Scammell's name? Why did Vane need to seek it from Sam? Sam shivered, then, without really knowing why, drew his winter-blunted bayonet and sharpened it on a stone. Spring had come, and dark things stirred themselves for war.

Chapter Fourteen

Captain Christopher Vane met Sergeant Scammell outside a stone building which had windows disfigured by rusted iron bars. Vane, even though he had only glimpsed Scammell once, and that in the litter of a battlefield, recognised the sergeant instantly. "Sergeant Scammell!"

"Sir!" Scammell still bore a scar on his leg, gouged by a bullet on a winter night. He knew this officer was the master of the man who had inflicted that scar and because of that he was wary.

"My name is Vane, Captain Vane."

"I remember you, sir. Orders, sir?"

"To do nothing, say nothing, unless I tell you." Vane turned and tugged on a bell pull.

Scammell had been told by a puzzled Lieutenant-Colonel Elliott that Captain Vane had requested his help, and Scammell knew that such a request, because it was a request and not an order, probably did not presage trouble for himself. But he was curious. "Did Sam tell you about me, sir?"

"He told me you murdered a boy at Germantown." Vane was rewarded by a flicker of fear on the tall sergeant's face.

"I should have murdered more than one boy." Scammell spoke the challenge softly.

Vane ignored the words. He wondered whether he had given away an advantage by revealing so early his power over this intimidating man, yet the revelation should secure the sergeant's loyalty. And Vane needed that loyalty. He was ashamed of the need, bitterly so, yet ambition and jealousy led Vane inexorably onwards. A war was being lost because of hesitation, and it was time for someone to become brutal.

Vane rang the bell again and was rewarded by the door's opening. A British sentry admitted the two men into an entrance hall that twitched with a gibbering horde of lunatics. They waited as the sentry unlocked the iron grating that gave access to that part of the asylum which had been taken over as a prison for captured American officers. There was no heating in this part of the asylum; a single lice-ridden blanket was provided for each prisoner and a thin, fetid layer of straw put into each cell. Vane's nose wrinkled with distaste. The prisoners, those who had survived the bitter winter, were in rags. Vane, whose arrival was expected, was shown into a large stone-walled room where a table and chair waited. A sour-faced lieutenant, one of the jail's duty officers, ordered the prisoner James Lynch to be fetched.

While he waited, Vane took papers, an inkwell and quills from his sabretache and arranged them on the table. Sergeant Scammell watched.

The door opened and a prisoner dressed in a thin ticken jacket over soiled calico breeches was thrust into the room. The man had a face paled by long imprisonment, and uncut hair that he had pathetically tried to tie into a semblance of respectability. He shivered from the cold. "You again." The rebel prisoner spoke scornfully.

Vane did not look up. "Indeed it is. Good morning, Lieutenant."

Lieutenant Lynch inspected the sergeant, then turned back to Vane. "I want parole."

"So you said at our last meeting." That meeting had been four days before, in the early morning after the subscription ball, and the outcome had driven Captain Vane to seek Sergeant Scammell's help.

Lynch still insisted. "I have a right to parole! I'm an officer!"

Vane looked up at him. The winter's hunger and disease had nearly broken Lynch, yet there was still a feverish defiance in the haggard face. Vane shrugged. "You may have parole on the payment of one hundred pounds. You have a hundred pounds, Lieutenant?"

"You know I don't."

"Then you must stay as His Majesty's guest." Vane opened his inkwell and dipped a quill in the liquid. "Your name is Lieutenant James Lynch, and you were in the garrison at Fort Mercer. Is that correct?"

"You know damn well who I am. How many times do you need to ask me, Englishman?"

"As often as is necessary," Vane said mildly. He wrote Lynch's name on a clean sheet of paper. "You recall the Hessian attack on Fort Mercer?"

"I remember killing a score of you bastards."

"Who brought the warning of that attack?"

"No one."

So far the questioning had followed the course of Vane's first interrogation of Lynch. "You told Major Zeigler that you were warned. I wish to know who brought that message."

"There was no message."

Vane stood, walked to the small barred window, and stared into the courtyard where tiny shoots of new grass showed green beneath a dead, black tree. He turned, his boots scraping on the stone. "I know you were warned. You boasted of receiving the message when you were first captured. I have a record of your words."

"I lied. We weren't warned. We beat you square, Englishman, and we'll beat you square out of this whole country!"

Vane sighed and walked back to the table. "Sergeant Scammell!"

"Sir?"

"You might be more efficacious than myself at eliciting answers to my questions."

Scammell understood. "I might, sir. But I want a word first."

Vane turned, astonished at the sergeant's effrontery, yet helpless in the face of it. The orders he gave were illegal, and well Scammell knew it, so Vane could do nothing but nod and gesture to the door.

"Outside."

They were gone five minutes, leaving Lynch to contemplate his fate. They were five minutes in which Captain Vane made a pact with the devil, and Sergeant Scammell discovered the desperation for victory that burned in the captain.

At the end of that five minutes, the cell door reopened and Sergeant Scammell came in alone. He locked the door, then stared into Lynch's face. "You have one minute, bastard, to tell me everything."

"I am an officer and you call me—"

Scammell did not bother to wait the minute, but started his work.

Vane walked away from the sound. What he did was wrong, and he knew it. It was dishonourable, and that galled him, yet from the dishonour, and from the devil's pact he had made with the sergeant, could come one of the keys to victory. There was a traitor, and there could be no victory unless the traitor was stopped. And victory, Vane persuaded himself, justified any act, for victory would discourage France and crush an insolent rebellion. This spring, despite the vacillations that sprang from Sir William's hopes of peace, the army would have to make one great effort to trap and destroy the rebel army, but that effort would be in vain if it was betrayed. And so Vane vindicated what happened now within the bare, cold room.

It took twenty minutes, but at the end of that time Sergeant Scammell came out of the cell with the answers that Captain Vane had sought. "It was a bastard called Davie Logan, sir." Scammell's hands were bloodied. "He's a ferryman, sir, somewhere up the river."

Vane stared at the big sergeant. "He's not from the city?"

"Upriver, sir. A few miles."

"Damn!" Vane said it softly. He had hoped for the name of Martha Crowl, but now he was given a name that meant nothing, and a name which belonged to a man who lived out of Vane's reach. "Are you absolutely sure?"

"I'm sure." Scammell's voice was grim.

"How's the prisoner?" Vane's question was perfunctory.

"Dying, sir."

Vane's gaze snapped up. "*Dying?*"

Scammell, who had the measure of this officer now, gave a scornful grin.

"And what the hell else did you want? How were you going to explain one beaten Yankee?"

"I ordered you to frighten him!"

"I did." The words were implacable.

Vane moved to the cell door, and looked inside. "Oh, my God."

"I'll say he attacked you, sir." Sergeant Scammell was quite unmoved by the bloody and twitching thing on the floor. "We had to kill him, see? He went berserk, he did."

Vane could not speak. He had intended Lynch to be scared, he had wanted the prisoner to confess the name, but he had never dreamed of savagery such as this. He doubled over, gagging.

Scammell stepped past him and drew his bayonet. He stooped, and Captain Vane turned quickly away. Lynch's breathing, which had been hoarse and whimpering, suddenly stopped.

Scammell stood up. "There won't be no trouble, sir. He attacked you, fought like a bloody lunatic, and I had to kill him." Scammell wiped the blood from the bayonet and left the cell. He was in command now.

Vane nodded weakly. "Yes, Sergeant."

"And the money, sir? I'll come tonight?"

The sergeant's confiding and conspiratorial tone clawed at Vane's self-esteem. He straightened up, determined to regain mastery of this horrific relationship. "You'll get your money, Sergeant, when I discover whether you've earned it."

"Earned it, sir?" The sergeant glanced into the cell. "You wouldn't say that was proof?"

"When I discover whether the man told you the truth." Vane heard the whipcrack of authority coming back into his voice. "In the meantime, Sergeant, you'll tell no one."

"I ain't a choirboy like your Sam." Scammell's tone was scathing.

"No, you're not." Vane walked away from the cell, going to tell the lies that would explain murder, but also taking the name of Davie Logan that was the next steppingstone on this bloody path. Logan. Vane wondered how in hell's name he was to find the distant Logan. Yet discover the ferryman he must, for, just as Lynch had led to Logan, so Logan would lead to the next traitor, then the next, until the traitor in the city was at Vane's mercy and could never again betray the King's cause. In which cause Captain Vane had stepped on the path of horror; but he had done it willingly, for it could lead to victory.

THE FOLLOWING MORNING Sam returned from exercising the horses to find Sergeant Scammell standing in the kitchen. He was cutting a piece of cheese from a wheel. "Am I making your nice kitchen dirty, Sam?"

"What the hell are you doing here?"

"That's not nice, Samuel. That's no way to greet an old friend, is it?"

Scammell walked round the table, holding the cheese knife like a weapon. He pushed the blade into Sam's belly, but Sam neither moved, nor showed fear. Scammell laughed. "I ain't forgotten, boy. I owe you a beating."

"Any time, Sergeant."

"No, boy. In my time." Scammell shoved the knife hard enough to tear Sam's old coat and prick his skin, then he pulled it free and tossed it onto the table. "This your uniform?" Scammell fingered Sam's newer red coat, which was hanging by the hearth. Sam had cleaned it and pressed it because he had to be an orderly at an elaborate dinner party that Sir William was giving that day. "No," Sam said, "it ain't mine."

"Then it doesn't matter if it gets dirty, does it?" Scammell picked up a blackball from the table.

"Don't do it," Sam said warningly.

Scammell gently put the blackball onto the table. "How's that little whore of yours? Ain't seen her around. And I've been watching."

"She isn't mine."

"Perhaps I'll find her." Scammell gave Sam a sideways look. Then suddenly slammed to attention as Captain Vane pushed open the door from the hall. "Sir!"

Vane seemed embarrassed to see Sam. "You're back early."

"They didn't need much exercising after yesterday, sir."

Vane grunted. "I suppose not. Here." This last was to the sergeant and accompanied a bag that clinked with coin.

"Sir! Thank you, sir!" Scammell was suddenly very correct.

"That will be all, Sergeant."

"Sir!" Scammell about-turned and banged his way into the small back yard.

Captain Vane, obviously discomfited because Scammell had been discovered in the house, fingered Sam's hanging jacket. "You have to be macaronied today?"

"Yes, sir."

"I suppose I'd better hoist on the flummery myself." Vane paused. "And don't spill any wine at dinner."

Sam grinned. "No, sir."

It was a lavish dinner, needing six long tables joined in a horseshoe shape to seat all the senior officers who were invited and their aides. Admiral Lord Howe had come to the city from his battle fleet anchored in Delaware Bay, bringing a score of naval officers with him. Sam, with the other orderlies, poured wine and served cuts of beef and goose and lamb.

There was a reason for the dinner, but Sir William was loth to reveal it until the wine had softened his men's mood. Instead, he listened to the conversations about him and marvelled at the bellicosity of his command. The prospect of the French entering the war did not deter them one jot. "Let them come," a colonel growled. "It's what we English are good at, killing Frogs!" A great party should be held, to celebrate the opportunity of slaughtering Britain's traditional enemies. There was enthusiastic applause.

Massedene shrugged at Sir William. "Would you host such a party, sir?"

"To celebrate the imminent downfall of the French? It's a happy thought, but I won't be here to do such a thing, Robert. My resignation is accepted and Sir Henry Clinton will replace me as soon as a boat can bring him from New York. Might I trouble you for the gravy?" The request for the gravy was spoken in the same careless voice with which Sir William had confirmed the rumour that he was indeed leaving.

The gravy remained unpassed.

There was a silence round the table.

"Of course," Sir William pretended not to notice the shocked silence, "I shall stay on in America as a Peace Commissioner, but I think it would be monstrous unfair on Sir Henry were I to stay in Philadelphia. It will have to be New York, I fear. Never a town I liked particularly, but"—he broke off, reflecting that after all the years, and all the fighting, and despite their victories, the British were still pinned to three tiny enclaves on the edge of a continent—"there's not really a great deal of choice, is there? Might I beg the gravy, Robert?"

"Gravy, sir." Lord Robert Massedene passed it.

A chorus of protests inundated Sir William. It was to make this announcement of his imminent departure that he had arranged the dinner party, and he was troubled by the dismay it caused. Men who had been urging him to greater zeal now protested at his departure. Sir William held up a hand. "Soon gone, soon forgotten," he said, hoping it would not be true.

"But we shall not let you go, sir." Vane rapped the dinner table with a spoon, demanding silence. "We shall not let Sir William go," he started again, "without a farewell party that will be remembered for ever in these colonies!"

The proposal was loudly cheered. Sir William shook his head modestly. "You would celebrate my leaving!"

"Your triumphs, sir," Vane said firmly.

Sir William laughed. "It will be a very small party, Kit. What will you serve? Humble pie?"

"No!" Vane's protest was loud. He had a favour to ask of Sir William, and now launched himself on a well-rehearsed piece of flattery. "Since you came to America, sir, you have faced the enemy six times in open battle. Each meeting, sir, resulted in your victory. You have captured New York and Philadelphia. From Bunker Hill to Germantown you are unbeaten. I therefore propose a celebration to rival the triumphs of ancient Rome!"

"Seconded!" a naval captain shouted, and there was a roar of

466

approbation. The kindly Sir William's caution was forgotten in the flood of affection that surrounded him.

"I think, sir," Vane bowed to Sir William, "that the motion is carried. We shall celebrate your great victories in a fitting style."

Sir William gave Vane a rueful, though grateful, smile. "Perhaps we can celebrate peace instead, Kit?"

"Victory is peace." Vane stated his creed, and again a cheer echoed about the great room.

At the end of dinner Sir William took his customary walk in the garden. He liked to stroll alone, but this evening Vane begged for the privilege of accompanying his master.

"Gladly!" Sir William smiled, still evidently warmed by Vane's egregious flattery.

They paced the lawn in silence for a few seconds, then Sir William looked sideways at his aide. "When I appointed you, Kit, last summer after you'd been so very brave, what did you hope would happen?"

"Happen, sir?"

"Your ambitions, what were they?"

Vane was embarrassed. "To please you, sir."

"Your work does. Very much. You're very efficient, but in some ways I'm disappointed." Sir William offered Vane a kindly look. "You see the war, Kit, as a personal crusade, and it isn't. We're just the instruments of policy, nothing more." The commander-in-chief stopped his pacing and turned to face Vane. "So this evening you flattered me, hoping to soften me, and I fear it may be in aid of one of your personal vendettas. Who is it this time?"

Vane was horrified at the reprimand. For a second he was tempted to abandon his mission, but he had the scent of treachery in his nostrils and he was convinced that, by scotching whatever stank, he could tip the fragile balance of defeat and victory. "I don't know if it's a vendetta or not, sir. What I do know is that our attack on the river forts last autumn was betrayed. I also know who carried the warning to the forts."

It seemed he must have surprised Sir William, for the commander-in-chief appeared struck dumb. His only reaction was to flinch slightly, then rub his back, which had been giving him trouble in the last few days.

"I'm talking about betrayal, sir." Vane's voice was insistent.

"I suppose you are, yes."

"The man who delivered the warning, sir, must have confederates in the city. I want your permission to find that man and question him."

"A man, you say?" Sir William's interest seemed polite, rather than urgent. "And how did you discover this man's existence?"

"A rebel prisoner confessed, sir."

"Ah! So what did this prisoner confess to you?"

"He named the man who brought the warning to Fort Mercer, sir. A ferryman called Davie Logan. He lives upriver, has one eye and a broken nose."

The final details came lamely off Vane's tongue, but they amused Sir William. "And what do you wish to do about the one-eyed ferryman?"

"I've talked to the Rangers, sir, and they say we should be able to find Logan. They're enthusiastic, sir. I know that Logan himself isn't important, but we should know who gave him the information. If I can find that out, sir, we've found the person who betrayed all our plans this winter."

Sir William privately noted how the man who had evidently betrayed the attack on the forts was now held responsible for every setback of the winter, but he did not remark on such an expansion of Vane's argument. Instead, Sir William dug the point of his boot into the grass. "You talked to the Rangers?"

"Yes, sir."

"That was precipitate of you."

The words were said mildly, but Vane detected a further reproof in them. He offered Sir William a rueful smile and took refuge in a frank admission of the truth. "What I want to do, and what I need your permission to do, is ride north with the Rangers and find this man Logan. We can do it inside a day, sir."

Sir William, his hands clasped behind his back, walked a few paces in silence. "I fear you won't like this, Kit, but I must forbid you to pursue the matter."

"Forbid me?" Vane's astonishment was clear.

Sir William offered an apologetic shrug. "You mustn't get so excited about such things. The enemy have spies, yes. But so do we."

"But this treachery is close to you, sir. Too close for safety!"

Sir William's reply was checked by the opening of one of the doors leading onto the upper terrace. Lord Howe, resplendent in his admiral's braid, frowned at his younger brother. "Damnedest thing, Willie. Boat cloak and hat. Both gone! Your fellow Evans swears he hung them in the hall. I came to see if you'd borrowed them?"

"Not me, I fear."

"Bloody thieves!" The admiral growled his way back into the house.

Sir William, recovering the thread of the interrupted conversation, looked sadly at Vane. "Perhaps you do deserve an explanation, Kit."

"I'd be grateful, sir."

Sir William frowned to himself. "Otto Zeigler told me much the same news three or four months ago. He didn't know about this Logan fellow, but he knew enough to cause me some grief." Sir William shrugged. "I did nothing. I had particular reasons for doing nothing." Sir William stared at the pale grass which had been bruised during the frost months. "As you say, only a handful of people knew of the attack: all of them officers I trust implicitly. But I did tell one other person."

468

"Ah." Vane felt the acute embarrassment of a young man who was being shown the weakness of an older man.

"Indeed. Not that Lizzie's a traitor, that's nonsense! But she can be indiscreet, and she's become monstrous fond of Martha Crowl!" Sir William smiled ruefully. "I know you don't like the widow, but I like her. Indeed I do."

"Love your enemies? Do good to those who hate you?"

"What I especially like about Mrs. Crowl," Sir William said, "is that almost alone of my enemies she does not quote the Scriptures to me. But I have no doubt she would betray my plans to her friends."

"And you would leave her unpunished?"

"It was my fault, Kit. I betrayed my own confidence, and I cannot attach fault to an avowed rebel if she takes advantage of such foolishness." Sir William shrugged. "I dare say that if you found your one-eyed waterman and could persuade him to talk with you, he would lead you to Mrs. Crowl, but I cannot see what purpose would be served. She cannot betray us again, not unless I am indiscreet again. No, Kit, I must ask you to do nothing." He saw the disappointment in his aide's face. "Besides, Mrs. Crowl has been useful to me in the peace negotiations, indeed she has!"

"Useful?" Vane could not disguise his astonishment.

"It's most useful to have an enemy touchstone. Mrs. Crowl is most sanguine about the chances of a treaty. Her views encourage me, indeed they do."

"She would encourage you, sir," Vane said bitterly. "As long as we believe there may be peace, we're hardly likely to make outright war."

Sir William offered a tolerant smile which, far from placating Vane, only goaded him into an indiscreet outburst. "I must assume, sir, that Sir Henry Clinton might feel differently about these traitors."

Sir William's face showed instant anger. "Sir Henry has not succeeded me yet, nor will he until I see fit to relinquish this command. You will not correspond with Sir Henry on this matter, or any other!" There were times when Sir William was capable of a most royal and frigid hauteur. This was one of them. "Do not get above your station, Captain Vane! You will forget this matter! That is an order!"

Vane was appalled. This affable man, to protect his mistress and pursue his chimera of peace, was ordering Vane to ignore treachery. Vane pretended compliance.

"Yes, sir. Of course."

"If you disobey me, Captain Vane, I shall return you to regimental duty. There will be no advancement for you, none!"

A chill was there, a gulf fixed between men who had been so close when, in the hopeful days of last autumn, Sir William had believed that with the fall of Philadelphia peace and happiness would be restored to the colonies.

Peace had not come, yet still Sir William pursued his dream of amity. However, Sir William's dreams were not Captain Vane's, and Vane would not be so easily cheated. Sir William had mentioned the widow, and such a mention could only sharpen Vane's desire for revenge which, if it could not be expedited by a cavalry patrol on the river bank, might be found closer to home.

The Rangers had told him of one person who would know whom Davie Logan traded with. "If any man knows Logan's movements," they had said, "it's Becket's foreman, Ezra Woollard."

Sir William wanted peace, but Vane wanted victory, and he was determined to have it.

Chapter Fifteen

Abel Becket, dressed in his usual sober suit, was unnaturally loquacious as he walked beside the limping Jonathon on the quayside beneath the dark loom of a moored merchant ship. "She carried finished goods to the planters on Antigua. Clocks, chronometers and navigational instruments from London. Enamelled watchcases from Switzerland, French glass, and sword blades from Austria: luxuries, and all to Antigua! You mark that!"

"I haven't forgotten our business, sir." Jonathon stumped beside his uncle and looked up at the salt-streaked hull of the *Deirdre-Ann*, a merchantman now being loaded with a cargo from Becket's warehouse.

Abel Becket ignored his nephew's sardonic tone. "And from here she'll carry mahogany, walnut, oak and linseed to Europe. Trade, Jonathon, trade! It's the lifeblood of this coast."

"So you're fond of telling me, sir." Jonathon was inured to his uncle's propaganda now. He was staring towards the merchant ships which waited in the river, but he was not interested in those great movers of trade; instead, he searched for a glimpse of Caroline's shallop.

"You can negotiate the gangplank?" Abel Becket asked Jonathon in a rare moment of solicitude.

"I can, sir." Jonathon's stump was still an agony of soreness, but he had insisted on discarding the crutches and using a stick instead.

The gangplank was steep; Jonathon forced his way up, determined not to show any weakness in front of the British sailors who, under Ezra Woollard's wary gaze, lowered stacks of timber into the *Deirdre-Ann*'s holds. On either side of the hatches were cannons, testimony to the dangers of American privateers. Roundshot was stacked on gratings about the mast steps.

Woollard offered his confiding grin to Jonathon. "You're as nimble as a squirrel, Master Jonathon."

Jonathon suppressed his dislike of his uncle's foreman. "I try, Mr.

Woollard." He watched as burly men rolled hogsheads of ale up the aft gangplank, and great tuns of fresh water were lowered into the stern hold.

There had been times when such scenes had been Jonathon's bread and butter, but now he did not care. Yet he must needs pretend an enthusiasm for his return to work. It was only a front, for in less than a week's time he would be given the papers of his father's inheritance to sign. On that day, if Sam had found the naval disguise, Jonathon intended to leave Philadelphia and travel north with Caroline, north to the rebel army, and only when the battles were done and the great issue decided would he retrieve what, if anything, was left of his property.

Yet to admit such a plan to his uncle was to court disaster, for his uncle would permit no such thing. Thus, for just a few more days Jonathon must dissimulate, pretend a fascination with the purchase of hemp and tar and indigo and canvas and timber, when all he dreamed of was Caroline and victory.

Becket ducked under the break of the poop and, after a perfunctory knock, pushed open a high-silled and polished door. "Good afternoon, Captain."

"Mr. Becket! A pleasure, sir!" A tall, grey-haired man marked his place in the Bible he had been reading and held out a hand in greeting. "And this is your nephew?"

"Indeed it is." Abel Becket, at that moment, even seemed proud of Jonathon. "Captain Carroll, Jonathon, Master of the *Deirdre-Ann.*"

"A fine ship, sir."

"She is, too. Six years old this Whitsun and built of nothing but the finest English oak." Captain Oscar Carroll had a soft voice that contrasted strangely with his harsh face. He was afflicted by a tic which drew down his left eye in disconcerting spasms that seemed like batteries of confiding winks. His cabin was a comfortable and snug place. It was panelled in pale oak and bore paintings of sea monsters within each frame. The galleried windows looked onto the moored ships in the river and Jonathon, invited to sit down, stared longingly for a sight of the small, dark-canvased shallop. His uncle talked of London with the English sea captain, speaking of merchants who had their offices in Fish Street Hill and Pudding Lane. A steward brought in a can of hot sweet tea. "Have you been troubled by privateers?" Becket's question to the captain was anxious.

Carroll shook his head. "I've seen none myself this year, but I hear they took a fine Bristol craft in the islands a month back." The captain packed a small-bowled pipe which he lit from a shielded candle that evidently burned for just such a purpose. "But the northern route home is safe."

"And news of the French?"

"Watchful, watchful." Carroll, after this enigmatic reply, puffed a cloud of aromatic smoke that curled beneath the painted beams of his cabin. He

471

turned to Jonathon who, thus far, had sat silent. The captain's twitching face seemed to wink at him. "I hear you took that wound with the rebels, Mr. Jonathon?"

"Yes, sir."

"Foolishness in youth leads to wisdom in age, does it not, Mr. Becket?"

Abel Becket looked at his nephew. "You have learned your lesson, have you not, Jonathon?"

"I've learned not to close with infantry armed with loaded muskets."

Jonathon's quip was rewarded with a smile from the ship's captain. "At least there'll be no infantry to trouble you in London, that's certain."

The word hung in the cabin like the smoke from the captain's pipe. "London?" Jonathon's voice was a croak.

"You'll forgive us, Captain Carroll?" Abel Becket demanded.

Carroll nodded. "With pleasure, sir. With pleasure." He ducked out into the spring sunlight.

The door latched shut. The deck above was loud with men's feet and the creak of a windlass, but Jonathon, sensing disaster, was oblivious of everything except his uncle's narrow face. "London?"

"Did you imagine, for one instant"—Abel Becket used his harshest voice—"that I would permit you to take a proportion of my trade and hand it over, with its profits, to the rebellion?"

Jonathon was trembling. "London?" It seemed he was capable of saying nothing else.

"You are diseased, boy! Diseased with disaffection! Your sister carries the contagion, and that slut you write to—oh yes, sir, I know of your letters! You need quarantine and, by God, you will have it!"

"You can't—"

"I am your guardian. I'll do what is best for you." Uncle faced nephew over the cabin table. "Good God, boy, don't you know what a favour I offer you? London! The greatest city on earth! I never had such a chance, never!" Abel Becket produced a packet of papers from an inner pocket. "There is a draft of money, sufficient for a frugal life for a twelve-month, and a letter of introduction to a Mr. John Martin of Angel Passage, close to the River Thames. You will reside with his family and work in his counting house!" Abel Becket suddenly offered his nephew a rare smile. "Mr. Martin, a particular friend of mine, has a daughter. A not wholly ugly girl, I am told, and—"

"No!" Jonathon's protest was not just at the prospect of marrying a London girl, but at this whole fate which had been sprung on him with such abruptness.

"You will do as you are ordered." Abel Becket thumped the table. "You have disobeyed me once, sir, and you will not do so again. And you have been punished! The Lord saw fit to take your leg, and if you tread the paths of disobedience again I doubt not that he will take your life! You will go to

472

London, sir, and there, at the heart of the world's commerce, you will learn mastery of trade. There, sir, is your money, and there, sir, is your letter of introduction." The papers were pushed across the table. "Your dunnage was brought aboard an hour ago. I have enclosed a Bible in your bag that you will read each day —"

Abel Becket broke off as Jonathon abruptly flung himself along the bench towards the cabin door, but, before he had even cleared the table's edge, the door swung open to reveal a tall red-coated British officer. Jonathon froze.

Captain Vane nodded a greeting to Abel Becket. "The paper you wanted, sir." He held a document towards the merchant. "I didn't submit it to Sir William himself, but I think you'll find it will pass scrutiny." Vane looked at Jonathon. "You must be Jonathon?" Jonathon said nothing. "You're a most fortunate young man."

"Fortunate?"

Vane gestured towards the paper that Abel Becket now perused. "You are freed, Mr. Jonathon. You are no longer a prisoner of His Majesty's army, and are thereby empowered to pass beyond the city limits. I think you'll find everything is in order, sir." This last was to Abel Becket who, smiling, put the paper into his pocket.

"I thank you, Captain Vane."

Vane hesitated. "And Mr. Woollard..."

"Is ordered to tell you whatever you wish to know." Becket waited till the Englishman had gone, then looked at his nephew. "You heard Captain Vane. You're a free man now, but I doubt that either Captain Vane or Ezra Woollard will permit you to pass from the deck."

Jonathon stayed still.

"Mr. Martin will return you in one year, though if he judges you still to be of a traitorous sympathy he will, on my behalf, keep you in London." Becket leaned earnestly forward. "The Lord spared you for a purpose."

"I have no purpose in London." Jonathon's voice was miserable.

"Did you think I would let you marry that Fisher slut? Did you believe that all my work, all my profits, would go to her?"

"If I have to wait ten years, I will marry her."

"I am showing you favour, sir, favour! London and learning and opportunity!" Becket stood up. "You will thank me one day."

There were tears of rage in Jonathon's eyes as he stared at his uncle. "I will curse you."

"Your passage is paid. You have a gentleman's accommodation in the ship's stern. Pray use my London friends with politeness." Abel Becket picked up his hat. "You sail on the evening tide." He held out his hand. "Farewell."

Jonathon turned away. He was trapped. The gulls shrieked above hatches being battened down for sea, the wind freshened. Jonathon waited for the night during which, he swore, he would escape this ship and the exile that his uncle had so cleverly arranged. He would not go to London, he would not be driven from his country; he would escape.

CAPTAIN CHRISTOPHER VANE, after delivering the pass that had been Abel Becket's price for the help Vane needed, was forced to wait until the foreman had finished a discussion with the captain of the *Deirdre-Ann* which ended when Woollard handed the man a bag of money.

Vane, when Woollard was free at last, nodded to the foreman. "Mr. Becket suggested you would talk with me."

"He said you needed help," Woollard said bluntly, "and that you were paying for it by releasing young Jonathon?"

"True." Vane followed the foreman to the ship's starboard rail where, from between two salt-encrusted cannons, Woollard could watch the loading continue. "Do you disapprove?" Vane asked.

"Disapprove?" Woollard gave a humourless laugh. "If Master Jonathon's going to share this business, then the more he knows of trade the better. What the hell's that?"

The last question was directed at a naval longboat that was being rowed past the *Deirdre-Ann*'s counter. The boat, painted white, had been gilded above its gunwale, while a carved swan's head, unpainted as yet, reared above the bows.

"It's for the Meschianza," Vane offered in lame explanation. "There's going to be a parade of boats."

"The Meschianza?" Woollard had difficulty in pronouncing the odd word.

"A celebration for Sir William's departure."

"I wish you'd celebrate hanging George Washington." All Woollard's scorn for the city's high social life was apparent. Yet he had been ordered by Abel Becket to answer Vane's questions. "I know Davie Logan well enough," the foreman assured Vane. "We sold him his shallop four years back, and the devil's own job we had to get the money from him."

"Do you know where I'll find him?"

"Logan has a house up beyond Pennypack Creek, but he owes too much money in the city to risk berthing at a Philadelphia wharf. So, Captain, he's using a middleman." Woollard explained how the farmers of Pennsylvania found it difficult to trade with the city because their roads into Philadelphia were heavily patrolled by rebel forces. It was much easier, he said, for them to ship their goods to the New Jersey river bank opposite the city. That could not be construed as supplying the enemy, because the British had not occupied that bank. Once on the New Jersey shore of the river, the produce was sold to local people who, in turn, sailed it across the Delaware to Philadelphia's market. "The middlemen," Woollard explained, "make a profit out of our hunger."

474

"So Logan carries produce to Cooper's Point?"

"Near enough." Woollard sounded laconic.

"To any particular person at Cooper's Point?"

The foreman paused. "I don't like Davie Logan," he said eventually, "but he's a waterman on my river, and I don't want folks saying that Ezra Woollard betrayed a riverman."

Vane felt a flare of temper. "I have reason to believe," he said carefully, "that Davie Logan is an enemy of the Crown. I also believe that Logan delivers messages to Philadelphia on the rebels' behalf."

"Not Logan," Woollard said, "but his middleman." And for the first time since the conversation had begun, he gave a small smile. He turned, leaning on the rail to stare north towards the great bend of the river. "You see that small pier up there? Not the ferry pier, but the smaller one this side of it?"

Vane could just see a ramshackle timber jetty that prodded into the water from the New Jersey bank.

Woollard spat over the side. "If you watch, Captain, you'll see a fair-haired slut sail a boat from that pier. A young girl. She's called Fisher."

"Fisher?"

"Caroline Fisher."

Vane wrote the name down.

"She's a rebel. She's a flaunting, insolent devil of a girl, Captain."

"And she lives at Cooper's Point?"

"A half-mile south, with her grandparents, Caleb and Anna Fisher. They're farmers of a sort."

Vane wrote the names down. "Also rebels?"

Woollard shrugged. "Depends which way the wind blows, doesn't it? Davie Logan trades with them."

Vane closed his notebook. "I would be most grateful, Mr. Woollard, if you would keep the details of our conversation private."

Woollard offered Vane his second smile. "If my keeping quiet, Captain, leads to the punishment of that damned girl, then I'll keep silence till doomsday."

Vane heard the echoes of an old lust. He smiled. "I assure you, Mr. Woollard, that, if it is deserved, she will be punished."

Woollard nodded. "She hasn't been coming to the city much of late, but she's here today." He jerked his chin northwards. "You'll see her boat at Painter's Wharf. A shallop with a higher bow than most and a white sternpost."

"She brings produce to market?" Vane guessed.

Woollard nodded. "And to some private houses."

Vane drew a bow at a venture. "Mrs. Martha Crowl, perhaps?"

Woollard gave him a sharp glance. "Aye," Woollard spoke slowly, "she goes to the widow's house. That's where she met the cripple."

475

Vane knew now. Vane knew! The enemy lay revealed before him. He felt the soaring exultation of success, but hid it behind a calm, measured expression. "You've been very helpful. I thank you. Do you have time to show me Painter's Wharf?"

Woollard shook his head. "I have to stay aboard, Captain, till she casts off." He nodded meaningfully towards the cabin where Jonathon was immured, and Vane, understanding, walked down to the quay where the evening's shadows lengthened from bollards and cables.

He sauntered up the busy wharves. The northernmost quays were too small for the great ships, so it was there that the shallops and flatboats were crowded together in filthy docks. Baskets of fish were being hoisted from the boats to be spilt into barrels in cascades of silver. A woman offered Vane a sack of oysters. He paid her a shilling for the sack. "Which is Painter's Wharf, ma'am?"

"Second from the end."

Vane found the wharf and strolled to the dock's edge. A dozen shallops, their sails bent onto booms, jostled in the littered water beneath him. One had a limewashed sternpost and a high, flared bow. Vane knew he was seeing, in Caroline's neat shallop, a rebel weapon.

He abruptly turned away. At the very end of the wharves where a brick wall edged the northern shipyards, a British battery, protected by a crude parapet of undressed stone, faced the river. Vane walked to it. "Mind if I take the air, Sergeant?"

The sergeant in charge hid his chagrin at being disturbed by some strange officer. "Honoured, sir."

"I thought your men might like some oysters?"

"Thank you, sir."

An old battered spyglass, used for watching the fall of shot, lay on the firestep. Vane took it, slid the brass shutters from the outer lenses, and stared across the river. The land between Camden and Cooper's Point, Vane saw, was thickly wooded, but he could just see a handful of weatherboarded houses tucked into the trees.

Vane lowered the glass and settled comfortably into one of the gun embrasures. The wind was chill, but he was sheltered and happy to wait till dusk if it was necessary. The river flowed beneath him, its sound oddly comforting.

The shallop with the white sternpost appeared a half-hour later. Vane, lulled to a semisleep, did not notice it, but the sergeant, made familiar because of Vane's friendly behaviour, drew the officer's attention to the boat. "That one's worth a look, sir."

"Sergeant?" Vane was startled awake.

"Not the boat, sir. The doxy. A proper darling, she is."

Vane pulled the glass open and trained it. For a second all he could see was the dark red blur of the loose-sheeted sail, then he focused the telescope properly and edged it sideways until he could see a girl twisting a single scull over the shallop's stern. The freshening wind hit the sail as the shallop cleared the lee of the high wharves and Vane watched as the girl shipped the scull inboard and sat to the tiller.

She had to turn to sit, and the spyglass was suddenly filled with her face. Vane immediately recognised her, and hissed with astonishment.

"She is a little darling." The sergeant heard the indrawn breath and took it for admiration. "Keeps it to herself, though. Bleeding waste, if you ask me."

Caroline Fisher. Sam's Caroline. Vane stared. What, he wondered, was Sam doing with such a girl? She was not a kitchen maid at all, but a rebel who took her unsuspected boat in and out of a British garrison.

Vane collapsed the glass and twisted out of the embrasure. "Do you ever search the shallops?"

"Once in a while we root about the bilges, but you never find nothing. Wouldn't mind searching her, sir!"

To the south, from the bigger wharves, the *Deirdre-Ann* warped herself into the river. Vane saw the topsails drop to the wind and heard their great thump as the seamen hauled on the sheets.

Vane glanced once more at Caroline's shallop, but it was far off now, tacking towards the ramshackle pier below Cooper's Point. He turned to the gunnery sergeant. "You'd recognise the girl again?"

"Gawd, yes, sir!"

"I might ask you to give her a message, Sergeant."

The sergeant grinned. "Of course, sir."

"Her name is Miss Fisher." Vane ignored the insinuation in the sergeant's expression. "Until I tell you, I don't want her troubled. And when you do give her the message, you don't mention me. Understand? You say it's from someone called Sam. Just Sam." Vane handed the telescope to the sergeant. "I may not ask you to do it for some days, Sergeant, but there'll be a guinea in it for you. What's your name?"

"Pollock, sir."

"Goodnight, Sergeant Pollock."

"Goodnight, sir."

Lynch had led to Logan, Vane thought, and Logan to Caroline, and Caroline went straight to the widow's house. So now an insolent rejection could be balanced by revenge, and all Vane needed was the proof. And Sam, treacherous Sam, would provide the means. Vane went to that evening's pleasures a happy man.

THE *DEIRDRE-ANN* dropped downriver under topsails, staysails and drivesail alone. She would anchor at nightfall in the lee of Billings Island. Then, at dawn, she would be guided through the remains of the rebel obstructions that were still not entirely cleared from the river bed. "Open sea by noon tomorrow, Mr. Jonathon, and then you'll see her lean to the wind."

Jonathon, cloaked against the evening cold, rested on the barrel of a small cannon that was lashed to the poop deck. The American pilot stood by the helmsman, while Captain Oscar Carroll, smoking his pipe, stood with Jonathon. "Your uncle tells me you're not overjoyed about this voyage?"

"No, sir. I can't say I am."

"You'll be homesick, no doubt, but London's a grand city." The captain's tic distorted his face in a grotesque series of flickering winks. "There's temptation there, but it's a grand city, especially for a young man of means."

"I'm sure, sir." Jonathon was staring at the low, greasy shoreline that slipped past in the fading light. Duck punts were being poled in the shallows, while, closer to the merchantman, oyster boats loaded with rakes and baskets beat upstream past the battered and blackened walls of Fort Mifflin.

Carroll saw Jonathon's wistful expression. "Thinking of swimming, lad?"

"No, sir," Jonathon lied. He was determined to escape, and it had to be this night, for tomorrow the *Deirdre-Ann* would dip her bows into the open sea.

Carroll tapped out his pipe on the leeward rail. "You're no prisoner, lad, not on my ship. But there's not one of my men that'll stand by and watch as you try to drown yourself."

Jonathon wondered what kind of message was being delivered in these contradictory statements. "If I want to go ashore, will you let me?"

"I won't help you," Carroll said, "so don't ask."

"So I am a prisoner."

"You'll be my guest for supper, I hope. Perhaps we can have a game of chess afterwards?"

Night fell dark. The *Deirdre-Ann* was the last of a dozen anchored merchantmen that waited by Billings Island for the dawn passage. Captain Carroll offered a supper of bacon and lentils, followed by three games of chess, all of which Jonathon lost. At midnight Captain Carroll checkmated Jonathon for the last time, then peered into the darkness.

"Tide's flooding. Time for bed." He reached for his Bible. "Sleep well, lad, and count your blessings!"

Jonathon limped to his cabin, which was nothing more than a tiny cubbyhole in front of Carroll's more spacious quarters. There was no window, just a wooden bunk crammed beneath the poop deck's hanging structure. His dunnage, two sea bags, took up all the floor space. There was no light.

He undressed, but kept on his shirt and linen. Over those small clothes

he drew his topcoat. He did not unstrap his leg, but just sat on the bunk and waited.

He would not go to London. He was in love. Yet he sensed that the love was not entirely mirrored. He had imposed a duty on Caroline, and she had assumed it, but Jonathon was determined that he would earn her heartfelt love. Till now, he knew, he had achieved nothing. He had ridden with the rebel army for a few days and fallen at the first smell of action. This night he would prove himself worthy of Caroline. He would escape.

He waited till there was a period of silence outside the cabin. Then, taking his stick, he opened the door.

A seaman was standing by the ship's wheel. "Going somewhere, lad?"

Jonathon winced. "My stomach."

The seaman laughed. "Captain's broth, eh? You'd best develop a seaman's stomach, lad. You want a chamber pot?"

"I'll use the heads."

"You want help?"

"No, but thank you." Jonathon limped for'ard. His wooden leg thumped on the deck past the cannons and past the two men who kept a watch for rebel gunboats. At the ship's bows, where the great bowsprit reared up into the starlit darkness in a web of ropes, chains and netting, there was a low rail, beyond which, suspended over the flowing tide, were the heads.

Jonathon flinched with pain as he lifted his wooden leg over the rail. He gripped a rope and edged his one good leg out onto the spar, then, just as he was about to topple over, he sat. He saw that the seaman who had been standing by the wheel had followed him down the deck and was watching him.

Jonathon draped his topcoat about him, sat, and looked down to the black water. Beneath him was a spreading net, put there to save men who might fall from the precarious perch, while to his right was the full-breasted figurehead of the *Deirdre-Ann*. Beyond her, dark through the tangle of rigging, Jonathon could see the shoreline. It did not seem very far away.

The seaman, perhaps out of delicacy, turned to walk towards the galley.

Jonathon unbuckled the wooden leg. One strap was round his thigh, the second about his waist. The cold made his fingers clumsy. The leather cup stuck to his stump, but he pulled it away and dropped the leg, with the stick, into the net. One glance to his left showed that the seaman was out of sight. Jonathon shrugged off his topcoat, then grasped one of the bowsprit's shrouds, let himself hang for an instant, and dropped.

He bounced in the fouled netting. One tarred strand cut across his stump, almost making him cry aloud, but he bit the noise back as he found his wooden leg and stick. He struggled up the netting's side until he stared down at the black tide just six feet beneath him. The stick and wooden leg were in his left hand. He hung for a heartbeat, then dropped again.

The water was like ice.

He bobbed up against the rough hull of the ship. Sobbing with the cold, he pushed himself down the hull and trusted that the stick and stump would give him buoyancy. He had never swum in his life, though he remembered how Caroline had once told him it was as easy as walking. He prayed she was right. Dimly he heard a shout above him, and knew he had been missed.

He braced his good leg against the hull and thrust himself away, flailing with his free arm. A lantern was being held over the ship's side.

"Hey!" The voice seemed very close. "Hey, lad!" A rope suddenly splashed beside him and Jonathon kicked with his one leg and desperately dragged back with his right hand, feeling the surge of the tide lift and carry him away from the *Deirdre-Ann*.

He was swimming grimly now. He could hear bare feet running on the deck, then a shout as someone ordered the gig to be lowered.

The cold was eating into his flesh. He wore only a shirt. He fought for every breath. The tide was sweeping him towards the New Jersey shore, into the dark swirls of shoals and mudbanks. The thick bulk of the wooden leg was his salvation, and courage his inspiration.

480

He heard, faint behind him, the order to pull on the oars, and a last flicker of good sense made him stop his frantic beating of the water. He hugged the leg. The stick was gone. He floated, turning in the eddies, sobbing because of the cold.

The surging tide saved him. It was at the flood and it carried him landwards, to bump him against a glistening bank of mud. For a few moments, in the agony of his cold, Jonathon did not even know he was safe, then, with the blind instinct of a man on the very edge of death, he crawled towards the darker loom of the New Jersey shore.

He crawled in sticky mud that coated him black. He crawled through a creek and up onto another mudbank where, exhausted, he collapsed. He looked up to see the line of the shore stark against the stars, then he heard the creak and splash of oars behind him. He turned cautiously to see the gig's shadow on the water, and, like a wounded beast, he slithered down to the edge of the creek. He would lie there, hidden by the mudbank, till his pursuers were gone.

He did not know that he slept. He thought he was marching, with two sound legs, in a sweet-smelling meadow beneath a summer sun. Around him, victorious, were men who sang beneath a striped flag. Afterwards, he dreamed of a girl with golden hair, and he smiled as he thought of her arms reaching for him and of her smile rewarding him. Then the cold touch of the rising tide slithered him from dream into brute reality and his eyes opened to see, not Caroline, but the first flush of dawn touching the rippled ridges of the mud before his eyes.

And he saw two pairs of boots. Two men were standing just inches from his face.

Jonathon tried to raise his head to speak to the men, but one of the boots nudged his face sideways towards the water at the creek's edge. "Caroline!" Jonathon said. Then the water was cold in his mouth and nostrils.

There was only two inches of water, but it was enough. One of the men put a seaboot onto the back of Jonathon's skull and held his face under the salt water. It was as easy as drowning a kitten. Jonathon shivered and twitched for a few moments. His left hand clawed feebly at the mud, then went still.

Captain Carroll lifted his boot and saw that the boy was dead. "An ungrateful lad." Captain Carroll shook his head, sadly. "Offered the world on a platter, and he throws it away." He spoke to the gig's bosun. The gig itself was a hundred yards away at the end of the mudbank.

"It's a miracle he lasted this long." The bosun stooped and turned the body in a vain search for any valuables. "He said your name."

"The Lord alone knows why. I've no love for rebels." Carroll rolled Jonathon's body into the shallow creek, then turned to walk back to the waiting gig. "It was better this way," he said calmly.

481

"I'd have tipped him over the side," the bosun grumbled.

"Money's the same. And this way he'll be found and Woollard will know our agreement was kept."

The tide was almost at the full. The leading merchantmen were already hoisting their anchors to negotiate the cleared passage, but they had to wait as a naval sloop, sailing towards Philadelphia, warped past the obstructions first. Her sails were streaked and dirty, evidence of a long, hard passage. "Dispatches from London?" Carroll wondered aloud.

"Most likely, sir," the bosun agreed. Then he shouted for the gig's oarsmen to back their blades, and they brought the boat's transom close to the mud.

Two hours later the river was empty. Jonathon's body drifted on the tide in the eddies around the sunken obstacles. There his body snagged and stayed. Gulls found him and tore at water-whitened flesh.

But above him, and filling the sky with the glory of their wings, the geese skeined north.

Chapter Sixteen

Major General Sir Henry Clinton arrived at the city on a frigate from which, as the vessel edged past the old rebel obstructions in the river, a sharp-eyed topman saw a body lying caught in the stakes. The frigate's captain, unwilling to delay so important a passenger, refused to stop. Instead, a signal was made to a nearby sloop which lowered a boat as the frigate went on to the city.

Sir Henry was not welcomed in Philadelphia as Sir William's men had been greeted seven months before. In the dispatches from London came news that France had declared war and that consequently a small rebellion had been blown into a European conflict; indeed, more than European, for fortresses as far removed as Florida and India were being made ready for battle.

Sir Henry rode through gloomy streets. They were also filthy streets. Standards, Sir Henry thought grimly, had been left to slide. Fewer parties and more discipline would do Philadelphia a world of good.

Yet before he could impose his will upon his new command, the due ceremonies must be completed. So Sir Henry rode to the Centre Commons which were filled with the panoply of eight thousand paraded soldiers. There were dark-uniformed Hessians, red-coated British, and cavalrymen in their rainbow finery; and all paraded behind their colours, to be inspected by their old and their new commanders-in-chief.

"Fine! Very fine!" Sir Henry, trotting down the ranks of the 40th, complimented their colonel. If the city was filthy, then at least the men looked spruce. Sir William, he allowed, had not let all standards slip.

It was clear, too, just how popular Sir William was. Sir Henry must listen to the cheers with which each battalion said farewell to Sir William Howe, as the great parade began its march past: a Highland battalion, all tough clansmen who followed their hereditary chieftains to war; the 2nd Battalion of the New Jersey Volunteers; then the green-uniformed horsemen of the Queen's Rangers.

Sir William nodded towards the Loyalist cavalry. "The best horsemen you have!"

"But not mine yet. It might be more convenient," Sir Henry saluted the colours of an Irish regiment, "if you retained effective command until you leave?"

"That's most kind of you, most kind." Sir William sounded astonished at the offer. "I won't hesitate to accept, but are you certain?"

"I'm certain," Sir Henry said curtly, not caring to say that the troops' resentment at losing their popular commander might be lessened if Sir William retained effective command until the day he left. That way no immediate and odious comparisons could be made, and Sir Henry would be granted a breathing space in which he could judge the men he was to inherit. "Though doubtless your departure will be soon?" Sir Henry did not bother to hide his impatience.

"There's just the Meschianza to endure," Sir William said apologetically.

"Meschianza?"

Sir William smiled. "It's concocted of two Italian words. *Mescere*, to mix, and *mischiare*, to mingle. A very fanciful word to describe a small party which will mark my farewell." He waved at Lord Cathcart, who led the hussars into view. "Nothing too lavish, you understand," Sir William added modestly.

"Indeed." The word Meschianza summed up all Sir Henry's derision of Philadelphia's famous social life of the past winter. Sir Henry had encouraged no such frippery in New York.

"And I'm still a Peace Commissioner, of course, so I shall stay in America for as long as is necessary." Sir William's old enthusiasm shone through. "You heard the rebels have agreed to meet us? I thought I'd request the meeting in New York."

Sir Henry believed peace was as likely a prospect as pigs growing wings, but he said nothing on the matter during the parade, nor during the dinner which followed, as lavish as the one at which Sir William had announced his imminent departure.

After the meal the two commanders-in-chief retired to Sir William's study. "I fear," Sir William said, putting Hamlet on his lap, "that the news from France will make your task hard. Very hard."

"It may." Sir Henry paced the floor between fireplace and table. "London has ordered me to send eight thousand men to the islands."

"Are they sending you any replacements from England?"

"Two thousand, if they can. They're scouring Hanover as well, of course."

"Good God!" Sir William stared into the fire which, even though spring was warming the land, he still liked in his study. "One third of your troops going to the Caribbean!" His voice expressed the relief of a man who no longer needed to pick at the Gordian knot.

"Five thousand men to hold Philadelphia, and the same in New York. That should suffice," Sir Henry said brusquely.

"Indeed, indeed." Sir William was suddenly too tired to argue.

"And one savage blow at Washington before the French fleet can bring troops. If indeed it ever passes the Channel fleet!" Sir Henry, as he spoke these optimistic words, had walked to the table where a pile of his papers sat alongside Sir William's documents. "But it appears, Sir William, that any blow we do aim at the rebels is first betrayed?" Sir Henry found the paper he wanted.

"Betrayed?"

"Captain Vane wrote to me. I presume you saw a copy of his letter?"

Sir William closed his eyes rather than betray his bitter disappointment. He had expressly forbidden Captain Vane to communicate with Sir Henry.

Sir Henry scanned the paper. "He says he has proof of a rebel organisation within the city. One that has betrayed each and every one of our moves. He explains that you permitted its existence as a conduit for the discussion of peace?"

On hearing the accusation, which he knew would be reported to London and whispered in Parliament, Sir William sighed. "It was never quite like that."

"But the French are in the game now. It made sense to treat with the rebels before, but not now, Sir William, not now! Now we must strike at all our enemies." Sir Henry, still holding the letter, went to the window and stared at the State House roof. "I like the sound of young Vane!"

"I'm sure he'll be gratified to hear you say so."

"I shall make him an aide, of course, then let him end this defiance." Sir Henry remembered that he had already asked Sir William to continue in temporary command. "With your permission, of course."

Sir William shrugged. "The future command is yours. You must make your preparations for the year's campaigning as you think best."

"Then I shall ask Captain Vane to put his ideas into practice."

"He will appreciate that." Sir William tried to essay some small enthusiasm for his successor's eager plans. "The Loyalists will be gratified that you intend to stay in the city."

"They must be rewarded," Clinton said harshly. "For if they're seen to prosper then more of them may take up arms for our cause! Let the

Loyalists hold Pennsylvania and New Jersey," Clinton went on, "and I can punish the French in the Caribbean."

"Then come back and complete the pacification of the colonies?" Sir William achieved a tone of awed astonishment, just as if an answer, for which he had vainly sought through long and frustrating months, was suddenly, and too late for his own good, becoming clear.

"Exactly."

"It is gratifying"—Sir William paused to put Hamlet onto the rug, and groaned as another back pain stabbed at him—"that you have brought such eagerness to the war's prosecution, Sir Henry. We shall see you as Earl of Philadelphia yet! Now, will you forgive me? Hamlet does like a turn in the garden before dark."

Sir William walked through to the dining chamber where the orderlies were clearing away the tables. He smiled vaguely at them, then tried to open the garden door, but a stab of pain from his back made him fumble with the lever.

A red sleeve pushed past Sir William and the door was opened for him. "Sir," said a nervous and respectful voice.

"I do thank you." Sir William's back was suddenly extraordinarily painful, so much so that he had to clutch at the red sleeve for momentary support. "Do please forgive me. It's a passing thing. My father suffered from it, you know, and the doctors never knew how to treat it! Never." Sir William leaned on his helper as they went into the garden. Hamlet ran happily to the far shrubs, but Sir William was forced to hobble on the Redcoat's arm. He saw that his helper was one of the orderlies. "You're Vane's man, aren't you?"

"Yes, sir."

"Ah! Indeed." Sir William forced a smile. "It's really very foolish. I haven't had a twinge as severe as this for months. Perhaps there's wet weather coming?"

"That always seems to make it worse, sir, but a linseed poultice will have it beat."

Sir William's face lit up with a sudden and happy recollection. "Sam! That's your name, isn't it? You're the fellow who cured my bay stallion of the colic."

"Back in January, sir. Tom Evans fetched him to me."

"What on earth did you do?" Sir William, instead of being the commander-in-chief talking to a private, was suddenly an English squire talking of his favourite subject to an expert.

"Nothing much, sir. Just warmed his drinking water and gave him peppermint and honey."

"I must remember that."

"And some liquorice and powdered ginger after, sir."

"I think I could do with some powdered ginger myself." Sir William tentatively took his arm from Sam's and tested his back. "It seems to be passing. Why on earth are you in the infantry, Sam? I'd have thought a fellow like you would be a cavalryman!"

"Dunno, sir." Sam felt embarrassed.

Sir William saw the embarrassment. "But you'd like to work with horses, wouldn't you?"

"Yes, sir."

"You should, you should. The world's not so full of experts as you'd think. What will you do when you're back in England, Sam?"

Sam plucked at his good red coat. "I have no choice, sir."

"Of course you have! A man like you can name his price!" Sir William peered at Sam and decided that what he saw he liked very much indeed. "D'you want to come into my service?"

Sam was so astonished he almost stammered. "Your service, sir?"

"Racehorses, Sam. Fast!" Sir William was eager suddenly. "Something to make Newmarket jealous, eh? Well, you think on it, and talk to Tom Evans before the week's out. I'll say you were invalided out of the army." Sir William laughed. "There's always a way, Sam!"

"I'm sure, sir."

"I'll see that Vane doesn't make a fuss." Sir William added the last words rather grimly, then saw Lizzie Loring come onto the upper terrace. He waved her a welcome. "Talk to Tom Evans, Sam."

"I will, sir."

"And thank you, Sam. Thank you!" The words came over Sir William's shoulder, and Sam, astounded, knew that he had achieved the Redcoat's dream: he could go home.

ON THE EVENING BEFORE the Meschianza, and in a graveyard where rain spat from a grey sky, the Rev. MacTeague read the order for the burial of the dead. " 'Man that is born of a woman,' " he intoned, " 'hath but a short time to live, and is full of misery ...' "

"Murderer," Martha Crowl said aloud, as she had said the word aloud in the pauses of every prayer. She stared at her uncle as she spoke.

" 'O holy and most merciful Saviour,' " MacTeague raised his voice to drown the widow's interruption, " 'deliver us not into the pains of eternal death.' "

"Murderer!"

Captain Lord Robert Massedene took Martha's arm and drew her away from the grave. She went obediently. Martha had so feared her own violent reaction to the news of her brother's death that she had asked Massedene to bring her to the funeral, leaving Lydia in the house with Jenny. The priest's voice faded behind her and the thin late-afternoon rain beaded the black veil that hung over Martha's face. She was in her widow's weeds. "Jonathon didn't go willingly, Robert."

486

"I'm sure." Massedene spoke with gentle sympathy.

"Abel Becket is lying!" Martha cried the words in pain. "Jonathon was in love. He would not have gone to London if the very throne had been offered to him!" She led Massedene across the wet grass to where, beneath a broken pillar that marked an old grave, Caroline stood. The girl had sidled through the cemetery gate just a moment before.

"I couldn't come earlier," Caroline said.

"It doesn't matter." Martha embraced the girl. "I'm just glad the message reached you."

"What happened?" Caroline asked.

"They say he was going to London and that he stumbled overboard in the night." Martha's voice was scathing.

"They're lying." Caroline's voice was as bleak as the rain-soaked sky.

Martha drew Massedene forward. "I want you to tell Lord Robert Massedene what Jonathon planned to do."

Caroline hesitated. Massedene politely took off his hat.

"It's all right." Martha had seen Caroline's hesitation. "He's one of the decent ones. Tell him."

"Jonathon was going to run away, and we were to be married."

"I am so very sorry." Lord Robert Massedene did not know what else to say.

"He would never have boarded that boat willingly," Martha insisted. "Perhaps he tried to swim ashore, perhaps he was pushed, but it amounts to murder, Robert, murder!" Martha was vehement.

Massedene shook his head helplessly. "The ship's long gone, ma'am."

Martha began to weep. Caroline was weeping too. She was weeping silently and remorsefully, weeping because she had not loved Jonathon more. The priest's voice droned on.

A hollow rattling made Martha turn back towards the grave. Abel Becket had shovelled earth onto the coffin and now the sexton took the spade. "Wait!" Martha's voice rang loud across the graveyard. "Wait!"

She took Caroline's arm and dragged her towards the open grave. Ezra Woollard moved to block their approach, but Robert Massedene hurried ahead and the big man, not wanting a confrontation with a British officer, stood aside.

The sexton, his spade loaded with earth, hesitated, while MacTeague, his damp robes fluttering, stepped towards Martha, but Martha pushed past him. She opened her black cloak and took out a folded flag which she shook loose. Red and white stripes and stars on a blue field were bright in the drizzle. "He can at least be buried as he would wish to be buried," Martha said defiantly.

Abel Becket tried to snatch the rebel flag. "He had forsworn that nonsense! This is sacrilege!" He looked at Massedene. "Will you permit this? On British ground?"

487

Lord Robert Massedene stepped gently forward and took the flag from Martha. Sensing the widow's defeat, Becket and Woollard smiled.

But Massedene had only taken the flag so that he could arrange it properly. He found two of the flag's corners, then gave the other two to Martha. He smiled at her, stepped back, and the flag was stretched between them. Caroline reached out to touch the flag, then Massedene and Martha let it go and the bright standard fluttered down to rest on the coffin lid. Lord Robert Massedene took off his hat in formal salute. "God rest his soul."

"At least it will rest in a free country soon!" Martha stared at her uncle. "Thanks to the French. And where will you run and hide, you murderer?"

"It was an accident," Abel Becket said. "I wanted Jonathon to go to London to learn his business, nothing else. There was no unkindness in such a wish, none!"

"It was murder, Uncle. And you?" Martha turned on Ezra Woollard. "Do you say it was an accident?"

Ezra Woollard shrugged. "A ship's deck, darkness, and only one leg. Yes, I'd say they were the ingredients of an accident."

"And when," Martha asked in a loud voice that carried to every mourner, "do you purchase a share of the trade, Ezra Woollard? There's no nephew in your way now, is there?"

"You're mad, woman."

"Enough!" Abel Becket had no wish to stay in a damp graveyard to bandy words with a hysterical woman. He led his wife and servants away. Ezra Woollard nodded at the sexton and, with a last grim glance at Martha and Caroline, turned away.

"Murderers!" Martha shouted. She walked between Lord Robert Massedene and Caroline towards a walnut tree that offered shelter from the stinging rain.

Jonathon's body had been landed in the city the day before, just hours after Sir Henry's arrival, yet the corpse had not been named until this morning. "They buried him quickly enough!" Martha said vengefully.

"I fear they had to," Massedene murmured.

"I know. I'm told it wasn't pretty." Martha put an arm about Caroline's shoulders. "I tried to tell Sam, but Jenny couldn't find him."

Caroline shuddered. "I suppose I'll have to tell him."

"I will," Martha offered.

"He wants to meet me at six o'clock this evening." Caroline's voice was bleak. "He left a message with a sergeant on the wharf. I presumed he wanted to talk about Jonathon."

"Sam doesn't know from me," Martha said, "and I can't imagine who else might tell him. Will you go?"

Caroline looked at the grave. "I don't know if I should."

"It isn't your fault, Caroline. You didn't kill him!" Martha turned on

Massedene. "Why was Jonathon even on a ship, Robert? He was supposedly a prisoner, wasn't he?"

"He was released."

"By whom?" Martha's voice was dangerous. "Don't tell me, Robert. Let me guess. Captain Vane?"

Massedene shrugged. "I don't know. Truly. Jonathon's name was added to a list of people who were to be given passes, and there's no way of knowing who contrived it."

"And there's nothing I can do, is there?" Martha was close to tears again. "A brother dead, and there's nothing anyone can do because the murderers wear red!" She almost screamed the last word at Massedene, then, in tears, she shook her head. "I'm sorry, Robert. That wasn't fair."

Massedene said nothing. The sexton, his job done, walked away. Caroline, staring at the newly turned soil, broke the silence. "Sam wears red. I won't see Sam," she said softly. "Not today. Not after this." She was sobbing now and in a sudden rush of truth she clutched at Martha. "I wanted him to die."

"Oh, God, child." Martha hugged her.

"I used to imagine that he'd die and I'd be free." Caroline's words, racked by huge sobs, tumbled out. "I hated it, I prayed to stop it, but I still thought it. I was wicked. Wicked."

"No." Behind their veil, Martha's eyes were shut.

"I wish I'd never met Sam."

"No, you don't." Martha held Caroline tightly. "You're to go to Sam."

"Not today." Caroline pulled away and wiped her eyes on her sleeve. "I want to, but I can't." She gestured towards the grave. "It's not much, but it's something for Jonathon. I just won't see Sam today."

Martha understood. "Jonathon loved you," she spoke softly, "and whatever happiness he enjoyed came from that love. You never spoiled it, so I thank you. But you and Sam were made for each other."

Caroline sniffed. "I'm going home."

"God bless you." Martha watched the girl walk away, then she seemed to slump with a sudden tiredness. "Poor Robert." She took his arm. "So patient. Thank you for coming. It cannot have been very pleasant for you."

"I would have sought your company today, whatever happened." He walked beside her towards the grave. "I'm charged with a message for you, from Sir William. He desires me to tell you that Captain Vane has been given licence to seek out traitors within the city."

Martha stopped. "Traitors?"

"Someone warned Fort Mercer. Sir William thinks that Lizzie told you, and that you sent the message."

Martha gave a short laugh. "That wasn't what happened. Lizzie said nothing! Tell Sir William that!" She shook her head. "Robert, it was servants' gossip, nothing else, just servants' gossip!"

"But it was you who—?"

"Of course it was me! Are you going to arrest me? I shall deny the charges, of course, but I don't want Lizzie in trouble."

"She isn't in trouble. Nor are you, least of all from Sir William or myself. But in seven days, my dear Martha, we shall be leaving the city. Sir Henry will be in command then, and Sir Henry is already much impressed by Captain Vane."

Martha shook her head sadly. "I understand."

"And Sir William is eager that you be protected," Massedene said. "He feels keenly that he was responsible for your brother's fate, and he's fond of you, as I am, and so he has charged me with this." Massedene took a piece of paper from his sabretache. "It's a pass for you and all your household. It enables you to leave the city with two wagonloads of property." He held out the pass to the reluctant Martha. "Please take it."

Martha took it, inspected Sir William's red seal, then thrust the pass into a pocket of her cloak. "I really don't know why you're doing this. I'm your enemy, Robert."

"No woman is my enemy, you least of all." Massedene smiled. "Indeed, I value your friendship and would make it more than a friendship."

"Robert—"

"No, hear me, please." He was blushing as awkwardly as any school-boy, but he looked into Martha's face and said his piece. "I would offer you my own poor protection, my dear, in the only way I can. I'm a younger son, not wealthy, but no man will dare offend you if you are to be my wife. I know these are inappropriate words in a place and on a day like this, but they are sincere."

"Thank you."

"I hope I have not offended you?"

"My dear Robert." Martha walked in silence for a few paces, then offered her suitor a hopeless shrug. "Could you become an American?"

He thought about it, then offered her a wry smile. "I'm not sure I'm brave enough. England's the place I know, the place where I have my friends, or most of them." He gave her a swift smile. "It takes a brave man to surrender friendships."

"And a brave woman." Martha waited as Massedene opened the cemetery gate, then followed him into the small walk which went towards the city. "And one day, Robert, I'm going to see our flag up there." Martha gestured towards the State House spire. "I have no wish to live under any other flag. Not even with someone as dear as you."

Massedene sighed. "Do I assume, my most dear lady, that you have turned down my proposal of marriage?"

"Probably to your relief, yes."

490

"When this is over, my dear, and your new flag flies, I may try again?"

"I shall anticipate your return with pleasure." Martha spoke with genuine feeling. "But for now, you leave in a week's time?"

"Time during which you have Sir William's protection."

"Then I shall leave the day before you sail, and you will bring Sir William and Mrs. Loring to supper with me on the Friday night. Will you promise me that?"

"With all my heart."

Martha put her arm into his again. "I fear I won't see Sir William till that parting. Mourning has its duties."

"The Meschianza will be the poorer for your absence."

"But next Friday we shall part as friends." Martha looked again towards the State House and her voice was suddenly filled with a happy eagerness. "And one day, Robert, you will come back, and you will see my new flag in a blue sky, and you will know that I helped put it there."

"I think I shall." Lord Robert Massedene smiled at the thought. "I truly think I shall."

The minute hand of the State House clock clicked on to mark the new hour, six o'clock, and Martha wondered if Caroline had changed her mind about meeting Sam, and hoped, for the sake of love, that she had.

"IT WILL STOP RAINING," said Captain John Andre, "at midnight."

"I hope so, sir," Sam said loyally.

"Do not hope, young Gilpin. Trust me! I have spoken with the Deity, and he has harkened to my prayer. The rain will stop and tomorrow will be a day of the most sublime sunshine." Andre stared from the window across the wide lawn upon which, the next day, the Meschianza would blaze. "Plumes!" Andre said happily. "Plumes for the Knights of the Blended Rose and their sworn enemies, the Knights of the Burning Mountain. The hooves of their steeds will shake the very earth with their pounding."

Sam nodded towards the window. "But they won't get under those arches, sir. Not with plumes on their hats. Not unless they duck."

"Knights don't duck! And they wear huge plumes!" Andre's hands sketched his feathered fantasy in the air. "Enormous! Awesome!"

Sam laughed. Captain Vane had ordered him to Walnut Grove, a spacious house to the south of the city which was to be the setting for the grand Meschianza, and given instructions that he was to stay at the mansion to help Captain Andre with last-minute preparations. And grand it would be. The guests would come by water, serenaded by bands and escorted by nymphs of the sea-green deep who would be tastefully posed on the prows of decorated longboats. On shore the guests would be squired up the sloping lawn to where they would watch a grand tournament between the two bands of knights, and only then, when the tilting was done, would the doors of the mansion be flung open for dancing and feasting. "Perhaps, sir," Sam suggested, "the knights could carry their hats? Or they could hang them from their saddlehorns?"

"They'd fall off!" Andre, distraught at the image of tumbling plumes, stared from the ballroom at the two offending arches. The one closest to the river was dedicated to Admiral Lord Howe and was decorated with Neptune's trident and a model ship, while the closer arch, in tribute to the departing commander-in-chief, was festooned with unfurled colours, drums, piled arms, and was surmounted by the figure of Fame. "I think they're high enough," Andre said. "I think you just take joy in filling me with gloom, you wretch."

"They'll be trotting," Sam said darkly. "It'll add another two feet to their height, sir. Up and down!" Sam gently imitated a riding motion.

"I have ridden a horse," Andre said with dignity, then turned to scan the garden. "A horse! A horse! My kingdom for a horse!"

There were no horses in sight. There were sailors building the scaffold on which some of the Meschianza's fireworks would be arrayed, and soldiers who were carrying boards and trestles into the mansion, but there were no horses.

"I shall prove you wrong, you wretched Gilpin. Find me a horse! A large horse, mind! Find me a horse fit for a Knight of the Burning Mountain. Fetch two, and we shall rehearse this wondrous pageant ourselves!" Andre flung an imperious finger towards the rain. "Hurry, Gilpin!"

Sam hurried. He was looking forward to the Meschianza. Captain Vane was to be one of the Knights of the Blended Rose, in which obscure cause Sam had borrowed a cavalry breastplate, a dragoon's helmet and a shield on which was painted a heart pierced by an arrow. In truth Sam was fairly sure that a plumed Captain Vane, and all the other knights, could negotiate the two arches, but both he and Captain Andre wanted to play at tilting, which would mean Sam could spend the evening charging on Captain Vane's stallion with a lance couched in his arm.

The clocks in a watchmaker's shop told him it was twenty past six as he pushed open the door to the Lutheran church and clicked his tongue in his customary greeting to the horses. Their long faces turned towards him as he walked up the aisle. He took off the sling on which his bayonet was scabbarded and hung it over the stallion's door. Then he unlooped the stallion's headrope and stroked the white blaze. "You're going to be a knight's charger, boy."

The horse nuzzled him, then Sam turned to climb the three steps to the tack room. As he reached the second step he saw a movement out of the corner of his eye and instinctively broke to his right, rolled down the steps, and seized the first weapon to hand—an empty water pail.

Sam's quickness had spoilt Sergeant Scammell's attack. Stepping from behind the pulpit, Scammell had tried to stun Sam with a blow from a reversed musket, but instead Sam was crudely armed, and ready to fight.

"Stop!" The voice came from the back of the church.

Captain Vane appeared from behind the horse stalls. He closed the church door, then walked up the aisle. Suddenly the church was a place of strange menace. Vane, whose face seemed feverish in the dull light, stopped by the stallion's stall. "Where is she, Sam?"

"Who, sir?"

Vane did not answer. Instead he stroked the stallion's nose. "I thought I told you to stay with Captain Andre?"

"He wanted his horse, sir." Sam nodded towards Andre's mare. "And I was going to borrow yours, sir, because—"

Vane cut the explanation off with an impatient gesture. "Did you meet your girl today, Sam?"

"My girl?" Sam backed up the steps. "No, sir."

Vane smiled. "I don't think she likes you, Sam. She was supposed to meet you here a half-hour ago."

Sam said nothing, understood nothing. Scammell, below him, hefted the musket.

"Drop the bucket, Sam," Vane said softly. He waited. "I said drop it!" The wooden pail rolled down the steps. "Did you warn her, Sam?"

"I don't know what you're talking about, sir. I wasn't going to meet her, sir! I came to fetch the horses."

Vane stared at Sam as though he was seeing his servant for the first time. "No one can be that innocent, Sam, no one. You lied to me! You said she was a kitchen maid. She isn't. She's a rebel. Did you know that Miss Fisher was a rebel?"

"Of course I knew!" Sam said. "She never made a secret of it!"

"You knew she was a rebel, Sam, but you never saw fit to inform me?"

"Why should I? It ain't your business!" Sam paused. "Sir."

"But it is my business, Sam." Vane stepped closer. "Do you remember the attack on the forts? We were betrayed, Sam! Betrayed! And who carried the message across the river?" Vane pointed at Sam. "Your girl!"

"She wouldn't do—"

"Oh, shut up!" Vane snapped. "She wasn't your girl, and you know it! She was sweet on a rebel. So she used you. God knows what she thought you could tell her, but she used you! And whatever she learned, she told to her precious friends."

Sam shook his head stubbornly. "She didn't use me."

Vane scuffed some fallen oat husks with his boot. "You're a fool, Sam. I like you, but you are a bloody, bloody fool." Vane stepped closer to his servant. "Your Caroline's clever, Sam, too clever to be here tonight. Perhaps my message didn't work? Is there some special word you use when you want to meet her?"

"No, sir." Sam was indignant.

"But if she sees you at her farm tomorrow, Sam, she won't be suspicious, will she? She won't run away." Vane watched Sam's face. "You can help me tomorrow, Sam. I saved your life at Germantown, remember? You owe me loyalty and trust because of that. I want those things from you now. I want you to understand that there are some things in war which are hard to comprehend. That's why there are officers. Officers make those decisions, not men. Do you understand that?"

Sam stepped a pace back. "What were you going to do to her tonight, sir?"

"Just question her, Sam." Vane smiled reassurance.

"With him?" Sam nodded towards the sergeant.

"So instead we must question her tomorrow." Vane ignored Sam's question, and talked instead as though what he proposed was the most reasonable course in the world. "We have to discover where she collects her traitorous messages, and I want your help, Sam. I've earned it!" Vane smiled. "So, are you going to help me tomorrow?"

But Sam understood that Captain Vane did wrong. Vane would not need Scammell otherwise. The realisation startled Sam. It was evil that he felt in this desecrated church. He stared at Vane, seeing him for the first time, not as an officer, but as another young man, and a man, Sam thought, weaker than himself.

Vane, when no answer came, shrugged. "Sam! You have to trust me! I want your help tomorrow. Caroline Fisher has gulled you, Sam, but she trusts you. Now it's your turn to gull her. If you go to the farm, she won't run away, but go with you. And you can bring her, quietly and calmly, to where I'll be waiting. Will you do that for me?" Vane paused a second. "Not just for me, Sam, but for your king. For England!"

Sam was not thinking of England, but of an American boy whom Scammell had murdered before Germantown; and he remembered, too, his own pusillanimity when Sergeant Derrick had insisted the boy was a rebel. Nate had been brave then, and Sam, to curry favour with Scammell, had swallowed the lie. His decision now, Sam felt, would weigh in the eternal balance of his soul. He could choose good, or repeat the evil he had spoken at Germantown.

Vane watched the struggle on his servant's face, and sighed. "I shall ask you once more, Private Gilpin, and if you decline to help me, then you are no longer my servant. I shall return you to Sergeant Scammell's authority."

"I ain't your servant anyway!" Sam blurted out. "Sir William wants me to work for him, and I'm going! Going home!"

Vane shook his head. "Oh Sam! How little you do know of the world." He turned almost wearily to Sergeant Scammell. "I believe Private Gilpin struck you at Germantown, Sergeant?"

"Yes, sir, he did."

"And that offence remains unpunished?"

"Yes, sir!" Scammell was the very model of an efficient sergeant.

Vane turned back to Sam and his voice was still that of a reasonable and kindly man. "If you won't help me, Sam, then I fear you'll be under arrest on a most serious charge. I hardly think Sir William will have time to remember your existence before he leaves Philadelphia. So, Sam, will you help me tomorrow?"

Sam hesitated again, not out of indecision, but to choose the proper words with which to save his soul from perdition. "You can go to hell, sir."

Vane stared at Sam for a regretful second, then turned away. "He's yours, Sergeant."

"Dead?" Scammell's voice was toneless.

"I said he's yours!" Vane strode down the church aisle, but paused to loop the stallion's loosened headrope round a wooden pillar at the pew's corner. "You must do with him as you see best." Vane reached the church door and turned, his eyes suddenly very bright in the gloom. "Report to me in the morning, Sergeant."

"Yes, sir!" Scammell pulled back the flint of his musket. Sam, staring at Vane, appeared not to hear the click of the musket's lock.

Vane smiled. "Goodnight, Sergeant." He slipped out of the church and pulled the door shut, and Sam suddenly understood the click he had half heard an instant before. With the quickness of a cat he dropped, rolled, and scrambled towards the altar. The crash of the firing musket coincided with the banging of the church door, but Sam heard both. He had survived, and the bullet was buried in the choir stalls. The powdersmoke billowed as Sam climbed slowly to his feet.

Scammell chuckled. He drew out his bayonet, and twisted it onto the musket's muzzle. "Fast, aren't you, Sam?"

The attack was deliberate and slow. The sergeant backed Sam towards the altar, judging the moment, and the killing thrust, when it came, was a short hard lunge that should have driven the blade into Sam's left lung.

Except that Sam attacked first. A heartbeat before the bayonet was rammed forward, Sam twisted and leaped beside the blade. His right hand clawed for Scammell's eyes, while his left gripped the musket's barrel and tugged with sudden force just as Scammell jabbed it forwards.

Sam's tug and the sergeant's thrust combined to unbalance Scammell. Sam felt the elation of success. He hit Scammell with his right, then used all his strength to drag the weapon away from the sergeant. To Sam's astonishment, Scammell let the musket go and Sam tumbled backwards and the weapon fell to the floor.

Scammell followed hard. The sergeant was the more experienced fighter. He kicked Sam's kidneys, then his knee thumped into his belly and the sergeant was on top of him, fists flailing. Blood spurted from Sam's nose. "Bastard, bastard!" Scammell grunted, clawing with hooked fingers for Sam's eyes. Sam rolled right, heaved himself to his knees, and drove his right fist into the sergeant's nose. He felt the bone break, but feared his own was broken too.

Then a lance of pain seared up from Sam's groin, doubling him up, and Scammell grunted in grim laughter. Sam twisted towards the sergeant, reaching for a boot, but Scammell stepped back so that Sam fell forwards onto the flagstones.

Sam saw what was coming and could do nothing. Scammell raised his steel-tipped boot and hammered it down onto Sam's right hand. The middle finger snapped and Sam, on all fours, screamed with the pain. The horses, as though in sympathy, neighed in fear.

"I'll finish you, boy." Scammell's breath was coming in huge lung-racking gasps. He plucked the fallen musket from the floor, aimed the bayonet and drove it down at Sam's exposed neck. Sam, his vision blurred by the punches, did not see the attack, but he heard Scammell's grunt as the blade came down, and skewed aside so that the bayonet stabbed past him. It clanged on the floor and bent under the impact.

Sam rolled, stood, and kicked. Scammell was still unbalanced from the massive thrust and Sam's boot smashed into his knee. He followed with a hard, stinging blow of his left hand to Scammell's face. Scammell staggered backwards. Then Sam tripped on the discarded musket and Scammell used the opening to hit back. Neither man spoke. They stood like prize fighters, trying to punch the very blood and bones out of each other. Sam was rocked back and felt blood swill salty in his mouth. He brought up his right hand and slammed it into the sergeant's solar plexus. The pain from his broken finger was like a red-hot hook stabbing up his arm. He whimpered, but he knew he would die if he tried to protect the broken hand.

For a moment neither man could fight. Scammell was hurting, but Sam was hurting more. He knew that if he went down now, he would never rise. The sergeant, half dazed, stared from a blood-smeared face, then limped forward on his bruised knee to make one last huge effort. Sam let the blow come, then swayed back so that the fist hissed past him. He hooked with his left and the blow had just enough force to drive Scammell down the steps, staggering for support on the front pew where the frightened black stallion was tethered.

Sam leaned on the choir stalls. Blood trickled from his eye and mouth. His stomach hurt, his right hand was clutched to his belly, he did not want to move.

But nor, it seemed, did Sergeant Scammell. He was fumbling behind him, and Sam suddenly understood and despaired, because Scammell had seen Sam's bayonet hanging on the pew door, found it, and was limping forward with the new weapon held like a long knife in his right hand. "I killed your brother," Scammell said. "Now you, you bastard." Scammell slowly climbed the choir steps. "And tomorrow I'll have that girl of yours before I kill her."

Sam could not fight the bayonet, and he knew it. He backed away towards the altar, which had been draped with a tarpaulin, and pushed two fingers of his left hand into his mouth and tried to whistle, but his swollen and bloody mouth would not make the sound.

The sergeant came slowly forward, wary of Sam's strength, but confident. Sam wiped his mouth on his sleeve, put the fingers against his tongue again, and blew. The sudden whistle shrieked in the church and instantly the black stallion lunged at his headrope. Hooves clattered and banged on the pew door.

Scammell, hearing the noise, turned. The stallion, eyes white, was rearing and thrashing.

Sam whistled again and again.

Scammell turned back. "You're dead, Sam. You're dead!" He came forward, limping, and Sam gave one last piercing whistle that threw the stallion into a final lunge.

Its headrope snapped. It jumped, and Scammell whirled to face the new threat.

"Up!" Sam shouted. "Up! Up!"

The horse, as Sam had taught it, reared, bright hooves flailing, and the sergeant shouted, stabbing uselessly with the bayonet, and was forced backwards.

"Up, boy! Up!" Sam was staggering forward. The stallion, neighing and frightened, reared again as Sam picked up the discarded musket with its bent bayonet. The pain in his right hand had been translated into a scream in his body, making him moan. Scammell turned, sensing the new danger, but Sam had swung the musket in one last despairing effort and the bayonet's needle-sharp point, bent at right angles to the weapon's shank, hooked and tore into Scammell's belly.

Scammell staggered forward and probed with the bayonet in his right hand. He tried to speak, and then, as if poleaxed, dropped to his knees. He looked in pathetic appeal at Sam, then fell forward. The musket clattered as he fell moving and twitching in the sheeting blood.

Sam knew there would be no mercy now. He had tried to kill, and maybe had killed, and the army would demand his punishment. Sam instinctively twisted away from the bleeding, moaning man and called the stallion's name.

There was no time to find bridle or saddle. Sam led the beast down the aisle and dragged the church door open with his left hand. He was sobbing with pain.

Astonishingly, in the evening rain, ordinary people beneath drab umbrellas went about their ordinary business in the ordinary street.

Sam slowly and painfully climbed onto the horse's bare back from the mounting block beside the church door, then slashed his heels into the horse's flanks, and gripped a handful of black mane as the stallion surged forward.

Sam was running.

Chapter Seventeen

Sam fled the city. The alleys and courtyards would have offered a fugitive better hiding, but Sam was a country boy, at home where leaves gave shelter, and so he let the stallion take him through the western hovels, across the Centre Commons, and down towards the bare stumps where once the Neck had been so pretty with trees. He rode bareback, but he had learned to ride horses thus in his childhood and the stallion, trusting Sam, obeyed the pressure of its rider's knees.

Sam checked the stallion by hauling on the broken headrope, to take shelter among stakes that had been pushed into the ground to support the runner beans which soldiers had planted to supplement their meagre rations. He paused in this cover and tried to work out his future.

He could ride to the city and throw himself on the mercy of Sir William, or he could cross the river. His whole life, Sam thought, had led to this rain-soaked moment in a vegetable patch. Nate's moment had come on a battlefield, and Nate had chosen his freedom and taken a bullet in his spine as reward. That bullet was avenged now, but the vengeance meant that, unless Sam threw himself on the army's mercy, he would be a hunted creature for the rest of his life. He could go north to Canada where Redcoat rumour had it that ships' captains would offer a deserter passage home in exchange for work. But even if he reached his English village, his name would be posted in the church porch as a murderer and a deserter.

Sam stared wildly about the ruined landscape of the Neck, where ragged stumps, weeds and straggling vegetable patches had replaced the once gracious parkland. A few officers, braving the rain, exercised their horses, and Sam knew he must move before he caught their attention. Yet he feared to move. He was a stranger in a strange land, and the girl who could have drawn him into that wilderness was to marry another man. Sam, ignorant of Jonathon's death, thought he would be alone.

Sam yearned for the soft English countryside where the sun never sweltered and the snow never lay as deep as it did here. But Caroline was across the river, and Captain Vane would go to her home and Sam knew that what the captain would do there, in England's name, was wrong. And he did not believe he could stop the evil by going to Sir William, because the commander-in-chief, however kindly, could not listen to a private. The private must make his own decision and even if doing the right thing meant abandoning himself to loneliness in a strange wilderness, far from home, yet it must be done. Otherwise a man could not live with himself. Sam could betray his flag, or he could betray the girl he loved.

He turned the stallion's head towards the south and clicked his tongue. Sam would miss England, so much that he could weep for the loss, but England would survive without Sam, while Caroline would not.

The stallion smelt other horses close by and whinnied. Sam turned to see a group of mounted officers approaching him. They were suspicious because of the disarray of his clothes. One of them called for him to halt, and Sam, fearing all questions, gave the stallion its head.

The black horse galloped as though the Green Man himself were on its heels. It galloped with all the power and speed that Sam had put into it with long mornings of exercise, and left its pursuers far behind. Sam rode south of the guardpost at Gray's Ferry until he had reached the undergrowth which grew beside the Schuylkill, north of the Lower Ferry. There he slid from the horse's back.

He was half crazed with pain. He crouched among new leaves and took deep, calming breaths. Slowly he closed his left hand over the broken finger and jerked it straight. The agony bent him double, but at least the finger no longer stuck out like the bent bayonet that had hooked into Scammell's guts. Sam could feel the bone grating, but he took the kerchief from his pocket and, ignoring the pain, strapped the finger to its neighbour.

He could hear the voices of the young cavalry officers behind him now. He looked west and saw with relief how the light had faded from the clouded sky. A rent in the grey pall was edged with crimson and in the dying light Sam saw a scarlet bird flying across the river. Somehow that sight gave him hope.

The stallion shivered and Sam muttered for it to be still. He could use the horse no longer, for now there was a river to cross.

He slithered down the Schuylkill's bank to the water's edge and headed south. He had ridden the Neck almost every morning, and he knew where some engineer officers, quartered in one of the summer houses beside the river, kept punts for duck shooting. He prayed that the rain had kept the sportsmen indoors.

Sam clambered along the bank, slithering in the mud, forcing a way through brambles. Then he heard the cracking of twigs above him, followed a moment later by an officer's loud voice proclaiming the discovery of his stallion.

But Sam had made his own discovery: two punts that lay in a muddy cove of the river bank. The boats were chained. There were no poles or paddles, just the two empty, shallow vessels and their strings of crudely painted carved decoys with which waterfowl were lured to the marshes.

The chain was looped through iron fairleads, rings that were bolted through the prow of each punt, then locked to a thick stake which was sunk in the soil at the bank's top. Sam tugged the chain, but both stake and chain were secure.

He looked at the fairleads. One seemed loose. He slammed the heel of his boot onto it. He slammed again and again, but the bolts were stubborn and the fairlead stayed put. The chain jingled with every blow.

Hooves crashed through undergrowth above him. Sam, sobbing and gasping, ignored the pain in his right hand and seized the punt by both gunwales and, with all the strength left in his body, tugged it away from the stake.

"Stop!" A mounted cavalry officer burst through the low bushes six feet above Sam's head.

Sam pulled again, and the fairlead's bolts tore out of the wood so that he staggered backwards and fell with the shallow craft into the river, where the current caught it. Sam, with one last heave, threw himself across the punt's gunwale.

The cavalry officer turned in his saddle. "For'ard away! For'ard away!"

Sam had often heard that shout across the winter fields when a fox broke cover. Now he was the hunted fox, and the cry would bring the horsemen to the kill. Sam pulled himself into the boat and lay gasping on its bottom boards.

The officer drew a pistol from his saddle holster and pulled the trigger.

The bullet whipcracked over Sam's head and drove a splinter from the punt's gunwale.

There were whoops from the bank. A half-dozen officers had joined the first man, and seeing an obvious attempt at desertion they dragged pistols and carbines from their holsters. This was more fun than they had any right to expect of a rainy evening.

Sam knelt and wrenched free a low shelf in the punt's prow and drove it through the water like a paddle. The Schuylkill was fast, but the horsemen were faster, and their shots attracted more men from the houses on the river bank.

Bullets flecked the water. One slashed across Sam's back, tearing the red coat, while another cracked into the blunt bows, to let a trickle of water leak into the shallow boat. One of the decoy ducks, struck plump in its wooden belly, jumped and clattered on its tarred twine, but the laughter of Sam's pursuers faded as the current swept him faster and faster away.

Ahead now he could see the wide expanse of the Delaware, he could see the foam where the two rivers met to clash and break in tumbling waves. He pushed with his makeshift paddle, driving himself towards the great water. The cavalry officers had given up the hunt. Instead, in a splash of bright colours, they stood their horses by the battery at the Lower Ferry.

500

Sam knew what was about to happen. He paddled desperately, somehow keeping hold of the makeshift paddle, then he saw the billow of white smoke blossom from the parapet. Less than a second later the thunder of the gun crashed about Sam's ears, but the roundshot missed by a clear yard.

He paddled again. The current was driving him downstream, but holding him against the Pennsylvanian bank. He forced his way east-wards, struggling for the calmer waters that flooded from the wide Delaware.

Another pulse of thunder hammered his eardrums. The battery's second gun fired, but its barrel was cold and the gunners had overcompensated by elevating their aim too much. The two guns fired together. Their noise was like the banging of a door in hell, and the splash of water from the falling shot drenched Sam. But he was alive. He screamed a challenge for the joy of it, screaming that he lived, that he would win, that he would, God damn it, cross the river. He would not be beaten.

The current was carrying him south towards the islands where the British garrison manned Fort Mifflin, but Sam forced the pain aside to kneel and drag back with the paddle, and every stroke carried him across the currents, across the river, towards the low, dull muddy shore of New Jersey.

The gunners were losing him in the fading light. He felt the first elation of success, but he knew there could be neither success nor happiness unless Caroline was warned. Another young man on this same river had used the same girl as his talisman.

The guns fired for the last time, and Sam watched a black cannonball skip across the grey water like a skimming stone. He had been swept more than a mile downstream, far from Cooper's Point where Caroline lived, but second by second his frail boat closed on the New Jersey shore. He dipped the paddle for the last time and felt the bow of the punt bump onto land. For a second he remained motionless, then he collapsed over the low gunwale and let the cold river flow about his wounds. It was like the balm of Gilead.

He climbed to the top of the embankment. The dusk was thickening fast, making a blackness beneath the trees. He began to walk north. Scammell's body might already be discovered, and Captain Vane would guess where Sam would flee. Guard companies would be rousted from their billets and longboats ordered from the navy, and now it was a race between Sam and his erstwhile master to reach the rebel girl.

The last sunlight went, and the clouds lowered heavy above the river. Lightning stabbed at the far hills and thunder sounded in the distance before the rain began to drive into Sam's face. He faced a journey across miles of wet darkness, not for liberty, nor for a republic, but for love.

AFTER DARK THE RAIN became harder. The wind snatched at windows and doors, and flecked the river with hissing whitecaps. Somewhere to the west a sudden bolt of lightning revealed men gathering in the lee of a warehouse close to Painter's Wharf.

Two companies of light infantry had been ordered to the city's quays. A naval officer crouched by the quayside and watched the river for the promised longboats.

Lord Robert Massedene ran up the wharf. He was in dancing shoes and white silk stockings. His cloak was sopping wet and his wig was streaked with dye that leaked from his cocked hat. "Captain Vane! Captain Vane!"

Vane, sheltering in a warehouse doorway, stepped forward. "Here!"

Massedene swerved into the doorway where, in a rage, he snatched off his hat and wig and threw them onto the ground.

"What the hell's happening?"

"It's raining," Vane said, with calculated rudeness.

"You know what I mean! What have you done to Mrs. Crowl?"

At this moment, Vane despised Massedene. His lordship represented all that was most feeble about the British effort to crush a rebellion, and Vane could not hide the scorn in his voice. "I've done nothing to Mrs. Crowl. I searched her house for a murderer and a deserter. Is there some regulation that says rebel houses must be spared in such a contingency?"

"It was your servant who ran," Massedene said threateningly.

"Not my servant," Vane said airily, "but Sir William's. Or didn't you know that Sir William wanted him as a stableboy?"

"He fled across the river," Massedene protested. "You know that! There was no call to search Martha's house!"

"A man was seen to cross the river." Vane's voice was cold. "But there's no proof it was Gilpin. I merely searched where I thought he might have taken refuge. Moreover, I made the search on the authority of Sir Henry Clinton."

"And did Sir Henry order you to destroy her house?" Lord Robert Massedene's voice rose. "My God, Vane! Her house looks as if it has been plundered by savages! Floorboards ripped up, panelling torn away, the child terrified!"

"I was told to make haste," Vane said. "There was no time for the delicacy with which you wish to conduct this war." His anger suddenly erupted. "Gilpin killed a good man tonight! He did it because he's been seduced by some rebel woman to turn against his king. We can't love our enemy, Massedene! If we do they'll weaken us one by one. But not me! Not me, by God!"

"You're confusing vengeance with victory," Massedene said.

Vane laughed. "My lord, our attack on the forts was betrayed. It was done, I believe, by Mrs. Crowl, who communicates with a farm across there." Vane pointed through the seething rain to the river's far bank. "Traitors, my lord, traitors. You think I should let them be? I'll do whatever is needed to end this rebellion." Vane glanced angrily towards the river, willing the longboats to come. It was far past midnight, it had taken hours to roust the navy to their duty, and the Bluejackets had insisted that the expedition wait until the darkest hours were past before they would risk their men on the turbulent water. And every passing moment, Vane knew, would be taking Sam Gilpin closer to the Fisher house.

"You found nothing at Mrs. Crowl's," Massedene said.

"I'll find proof," Vane said. "By God I will!"

Lord Robert Massedene feared Vane was right, and he feared for Martha. If Vane found proof this night, then neither Massedene's affection nor Sir William's kindness could protect her.

"I'm crossing the river with you," he said.

"By God, you're not!"

"By God, you have no right to stop me!" Massedene shouted Vane down. "You'll not fabricate evidence this night, Captain Vane! I have Sir William's order to make certain of that!"

Vane's face was pale with anger, but a shout from the quayside announced the arrival of the longboats. Forgetting Massedene, he ran forward to hasten the embarkation. The boats, prepared for the Meschianza, were ludicrously disguised as swans and sea serpents but, however ludicrous, the four boats could take soldiers across a wind-torn river to find Captain Vane's evidence.

Massedene picked up his hat and ruined wig, then followed the soldiers down into the rocking craft. The eastern horizon was already edged with grey. Lightning flickered and a clap of thunder rolled its vast sound across the clouded sky beneath which, at long last, Captain Vane had been unleashed.

SAM GILPIN WAS SOAKED and chilled to the bone. He blundered through undergrowth and brambles that scratched his already bloodied face and sometimes caught his finger. His uniform snagged on twigs and thorns. The red coat was festooned with loops; the loops clutched at every bush. Sam ripped them off, but kept the coat for what small protection it offered against the weather.

He had turned off the river path into the deep woods to avoid the small settlements on the New Jersey bank. He heard the rain and the wind, the creak of huge boughs; then he was certain that a monstrous beast, green as the trees, dragged its huge limbs in pursuit of him. He forgot the pain and fled northwards, fleeing the Green Man that had come to haunt him in America.

He fled northwards, but he knew it might all be for nothing. Perhaps Caroline was already taken. Or perhaps Captain Vane was waiting at the farmhouse in the knowledge that Sam would run there. Perhaps tomorrow he would be stripped to the waist and tied to the tripod, and the whips would be dragged through fingers to loosen gobbets of Sam's bloody flesh from their lashes. He stumbled on. Love drove him through the wet darkness. Nothing else mattered; neither King, nor country, nor regiment, nor home; only love.

He climbed onto a shallow ridge of sandy ground where there were fewer brambles, and on which he could travel faster. He ran, stumbling and panting, tasting the blood that trickled on his broken lips. He feared now that he would not be able to find Caroline's house; he had only ever seen it from the city's wharves when Caroline had pointed over the water to it. He had no certainty that he could find the house in this rain-soaked darkness. He sobbed with the pain of his bruised body and because he feared he would be too late.

He came to the ridge's end and he saw the sky's first pale greyness in the east. Then, in the dazzle of a fork of lightning that slammed towards the river, he saw boats closing on the New Jersey shore.

He ran. Thunder cracked over his head, loud as a cannon's hammering, but Sam did not hear it. He forgot the rain, he forgot his fears, and he ran instead towards the place where, in the stark brilliance of the lightning, he had seen the wooden house. He ran as if his whole life depended on this one moment. He ran for Caroline.

He stumbled across pastureland, cannoned into a fence, forced himself onwards. There was enough light in the east to silhouette the soldiers who climbed from the river's bank. There was still time, Sam knew, but only a sliver of time.

504

"Caroline!" He shouted her name. "Caroline!"

A dog barked in the house as Sam climbed a last fence and staggered over a patch of wet grass. He hammered on the farmhouse door, beating his bloodied fist against the wood.

More thunder smashed the heavens above him and a streak of lightning seared into the orchard. Sam had an impression of soldiers beyond the orchard, soldiers who were already close, and he drove his fists against the locked door. "Caroline! Caroline!"

He shouted her name in despair, then suddenly the door was snatched open and a dog strained at its leash to snap at Sam. An old man, a blunderbuss in one hand, the dog's leash in the other, demanded an explanation.

"Soldiers!" Sam cut the man short. "Soldiers! Get out! Get out!"

Light flickered in the room as an old woman opened the stove door and blew the embers into flame. She lit a spill and in its bright light Sam saw Caroline standing at the foot of a wooden staircase. "They're coming to get you," Sam said. "Run!"

"Sam?" Caroline, swathed in a woollen robe, stared at the Redcoat. "Sam?"

"They're here! Get out!"

The old man turned. "The keep bag, Anna! Use the back door! Go!" The old woman snatched at a bag which hung beside a door on the far side of the room. In the bag, Sam knew, the family would keep its valuables. "Go, Anna!" Caleb Fisher shouted, then hefted the ancient gun in his right hand. "I'll teach them to wake Christian souls in the night. I'll—"

"Go!" Sam pushed the old man towards the other door. "Go! Leave me the gun. Now go!" Sam took the gun from the old man. "Caroline! Go!"

But Caroline had slipped round the kitchen table to drag at a heavy dresser which stood beside the front door. "There's a letter I need! Help me! It's hidden here."

"Damn the letter! Go!" Sam pulled her away from the dresser. He could hear the soldiers outside, then he saw terror flood Caroline's face. He whirled round.

"Don't move!" A sergeant, huge in a dripping greatcoat, filled the front doorway. Other men pushed in behind him. They had bayonets on their guns. The rain, Sam knew, could have turned the black powder in the musket pans into porridge, but he could not be sure. He pushed Caroline behind him and she pulled him towards the back door, edging him round the big kitchen table.

"Stay there, lad!" the sergeant cautioned.

Sam pointed the blunderbuss towards the Redcoats, watching the soldier's eyes, and when he was clear of the obstructing table he pushed Caroline towards the back door. "Run!"

"I think not."

Captain Christopher Vane suddenly stood in the back door. He had a drawn sword in his hand that he whipped left and right, as if to free it of water, and the steel made a hissing noise in the air. "Well done, Sergeant. Very well done." Vane had lost his hat in the darkness and the rain had plastered his fair hair to his narrow skull. He looked dangerous and tough. He also looked pleased. "Put the gun down, Sam."

Sam did not obey. He raised the blunderbuss and aimed it at Vane's mocking face. The sergeant, who had started to edge round the big table, checked. There was silence in the room. Two more men appeared in the doorway behind Vane and looked appalled at the great weapon which threatened their officer.

Captain Vane glanced at Caroline, then looked back to Sam. "You're a deserter, Sam, and a murderer, but I can find reasons for all you've done. Truly I can!" Vane spoke with the glib reasonableness that Sam knew so well. "Scammell persecuted you," Vane suggested, "and you were frightened. So you ran. I can explain all that, Sam, all of it! But if you pull that trigger, Sam Gilpin, then all the kindess in the world can't help you. You'll be a rebel, boy. You'll be an enemy. You'll be nothing."

"Get out of my way," Sam said.

"Don't be foolish." Vane threw a scornful look at Caroline. "She's trapped you here, Sam. So put the gun down." He paused, then snapped the words again. "Put the gun down, Private Gilpin!"

All Sam's old instincts were to obey. He was a Redcoat. He had been trained to obedience. But those chains of obedience had been broken by Vane. Sam, staring at the sleek face across the bell-mouthed weapon, did not move. Vane seemed to sneer at Sam's defiance, then he looked past Sam at the sergeant. "Take him, Sergeant. And his whore." Vane spat the last word, then sensed that he had made a mistake. He saw the sergeant open his mouth in warning, then Vane looked back to Sam just as the gun's trigger was pulled.

The recoil slammed at Sam's broken finger, making him scream, but the scream was lost in the blasting thunder of the gun which spat flame and smoke and its filthy charge of broken metal and bent nails at Vane. "Go!" Sam shouted, dragging Caroline behind him, and he did not hear the clicks as the flints fell on damp musket pans that did not fire.

He charged into the smoke of his gunfire and he saw one Redcoat lying in the doorway, another crawling into the night, and Sam had an impression of blood as though a man had been flensed alive by the screaming metal scraps, then he shoulder-charged the third man, sending him reeling, and leaped over the threshold. Caroline was with him. There were more soldiers in the farmyard, who now turned towards the fugitives. Sam knew that all was lost, but the madness of battle was deafening him to reason and he whirled the empty gun as though he would fight a regiment before he would surrender.

"Stand back! Hold your fire!" Sam heard the shout and thought he must have dreamed it. He was running hard, dragging Caroline with his broken right hand, sobbing with rage and pain; then Caroline twisted away, dragging Sam into the darkness of the shadows beyond the barn. Suddenly he was cloaked by night, and the rain was cool and blessed on his bloodied face. He stumbled, but Caroline pulled him onwards, and he realised that no one was pursuing them or shouting after them.

They stopped at the tree line. Both were panting, but Sam heard Caroline say his name aloud, heard her say it again and again, and he held her close in the greying darkness where he could not tell whether the wetness on his face was his own blood, or the rain, or tears of joy because, with a whole army set against him, he had not failed.

THE RAIN STOPPED. By full dawn the clouds were in ragged retreat from a blue sky in which the sun shone as sweetly as any man might have desired. The Meschianza was saved.

The crowds gathered early to watch the grand procession which, at half past three on the afternoon of 18 May 1778, launched the great event. The Meschianza, for which Sir William's officers, out of loyalty and love, had collected more than three thousand guineas, had begun.

A fleet of longboats carried the guests south from Knight's Wharf. A larger pinnace carried the two commanders-in-chief beneath a gaudy silken awning. The frigate *Roebuck* fired a nineteen-gun salute as the pinnace passed, and the spectators cheered the gallant sight.

The guests were landed on the wide lawns of the Wharton mansion. Seven young ladies, unmarried maidens all, were led to a pavilion which had been specially built on the north side of the lawn, and another seven were guided to an identical spired booth to the south. The girls, chosen for their beauty, were the ladies of the knights this day. Their white dresses, fashionably slashed to reveal silk petticoats, were encircled by sashes which each girl in turn presented to her chosen champion.

Those champions, at full gallop and with plumes erect, came safely beneath the twin arches. The Knights of the Burning Mountain challenged the Knights of the Blended Rose to a tourney to decide which pavilion held the most beautiful girls. Gauntlets were thrown down, lances raised, and the mock fight began.

It was all such happy fun. At the battle's end, happily without a drop of blood to mar the day, it was declared that each band of knights and each group of ladies was as brave and as beautiful as the other.

Sir William applauded the judicious decision, but his mind was far off. At last, at long last, the rebels had agreed to send Peace Commissioners to New York where they would discuss the war's ending and, while there were those who averred that the rebels merely played for time until the French forces arrived to tip the balance, Sir William was trying to persuade himself that peace could be attained. "Billie?" Lizzie Loring leaned towards him.

"My dear?" Sir William blinked.

"We're supposed to lead the procession, my dear."

"The procession? Ah, of course. Just so!"

The guests, now that the mock battle was done, walked in pairs between a hundred musicians and, as the day faded, entered a silk-hung hall lit by a galaxy of milk-white candles. Musicians played and guests danced.

Sir William surrendered Lizzie Loring to the arms of John Andre and walked with Lord Robert Massedene in the twilit garden. They strolled to the great arch which celebrated Sir William's triumphs. Sir William chuckled. "It's all nonsense, Robert, all nonsense."

"You did win the victories, sir," Massedene chided. "You've not been beaten here."

"True, I wasn't defeated, but I suspect that lady," and here Sir William glanced up at the goddess Fame with her outstretched laurels, "I suspect she won't reward victory over Mr. George Washington with undying renown. And victories or not, Robert, we still have our backs to the water, don't we?" Sir William looked towards the *Roebuck* moored in the stream. "Is Mrs. Crowl safe?"

"She is now, sir. Her house is damaged, but ..." Massedene shrugged.

"Houses can be repaired. And the papers you found across the water?"

Massedene shook his head. "There was merely a letter offering Mrs. Crowl's brother a post with the rebel army. Hardly a treasonable document, I think?"

"Not treasonable at all. But in the search for it, Robert, Captain Vane was killed."

"Indeed." Massedene's voice was quite toneless.

"Sir Henry says he must have a hero's burial." Sir William turned to his aide. "Sir Henry also says that you prevented his killer from being captured."

"He does, sir?" Massedene sounded faintly surprised.

Sir William smiled in the darkness. "One of the light-company captains says you ordered his men to hold their fire?"

"It was raining, sir. The muskets couldn't fire. Besides," Lord Robert Massedene shrugged, "it was dark. There was no way of knowing what damage might have been caused by indiscriminate fire."

"Quite so, quite so." Sir William began strolling across the lawn. "It was Vane's servant who fired the fatal shot?"

"I wouldn't know, sir."

Sir William appeared not to hear the disavowal. "Mrs. Crowl will be pleased. She told me she was rather fond of—whatever his name was."

Voices called from the house and Lord Robert Massedene gestured towards them. "I think your presence is needed for the fireworks, sir."

508

"Ah, yes, indeed! Fireworks for my victories! How very nice. And Lizzie will be pleased. And well done, Robert."

Massedene checked, astonished. "Well done?"

"That's what we're here for tonight, is it not? To congratulate ourselves?" Sir William smiled. "So, well done, my dear Robert, very well done indeed."

ROCKETS EXPLODED INTO STARS of crimson that fell like jewels into the river. Chinese fountains spewed white fire to make the night seem like day. Twenty separate displays launched their dazzling flames into the darkness to astonish a city.

Sam watched from across the river. He sat on a grass bank with his arm round Caroline's shoulders. He felt tears in his eyes. His brother, whom he had loved, had never found his American paradise, and Jonathon, whom Sam had befriended, lay dead beneath this soil. But Sam lived, and he must now live for both the dead men.

"What are they celebrating over there?" Caroline asked.

"Victory."

She laughed softly. "I never liked the city," she said suddenly.

"Nor I."

"I would have lived there, though."

"You'd have had to," Sam agreed. He held one of her hands in his left hand. Their fingers intertwined.

"I didn't want to live there." Caroline's voice was soft with regret.

Sam understood what she was saying. "You never let Jonathon down."

"I did in my dreams."

"That's what dreams are for. Things that aren't real. Things like the Green Man." He smiled because he had confessed to Caroline how scared he had been in last night's darkness.

Caroline looked at him. "Dreams can become real, Sam."

"We did nothing to make this one real."

"No." Caroline took comfort from that truth.

They had hidden in the woods all day. In the morning the soldiers had searched the Fisher farm, slaughtering the livestock for rations and taking away the precious stores from the barn. The farm had been plundered for food, but the family was safe. Caleb and Anna were now with neighbours, waiting to make certain that the Redcoats would not return, while Sam sat with Caroline beside a dark river.

Caroline leaned her head on his shoulder. "What were you planning to do, Sam?"

"After I'd warned you?" Sam thought for a moment. "Go far away, I suppose. Somewhere where no one could find me."

"And raise horses?"

"Like as not."

She smiled. "You can raise horses here, Sam."

"It's a good country for horses," Sam agreed. "And children."

"Yes." Caroline felt a surge of joy which was so strong that it astonished her.

"But children need peace."

Caroline said nothing. Their last exchanges, stumbling as they may have sounded, were declarations of love that would last their lifetimes, but Sam was a Redcoat, and she a rebel, and Sam had now hinted at the unasked question that lay between them.

"Children need peace," Sam said again, but this time more firmly, "so I suppose we'll have to fight for it."

Caroline turned her face up to Sam's. "We?"

"We," Sam said, and for a moment Caroline thought he would say no more. Then, to her surprise, he offered an explanation. "A man must fight for his home, mustn't he?"

"Is this home, Sam?"

"Home is where you love. And where you are loved."

Caroline stroked his hand. "This is your home, Sam."

The fireworks died. The music played on, coming thin over the dark water, but Sam and Caroline walked away. They walked home, and on the bank they abandoned the coat which Sam had spread on the muddy grass to keep the damp from Caroline's dress. It was his soldier's coat, his red coat that he had worn at Paoli's Tavern that night when he had carried a red blade to the killing. Now the coat was left in the mud and a new flag would dazzle Sam's eyes.

Because the Redcoat was free.

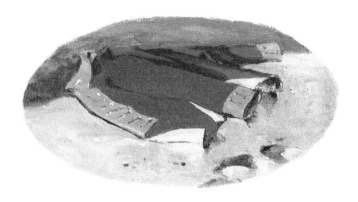

BERNARD CORNWELL

In his novels Bernard Cornwell's main aim is "to give the reader a cracking good story, whether it be historical or modern", and this he most certainly achieves.

Bernard Cornwell was born in London in 1944. After graduating from London University he taught for a while, before joining the BBC, where he worked for nearly ten years, mainly as a producer on "Nationwide". He then moved to Thames Television and worked on "Thames at Six". In 1979 he gave up his successful television career because he and his wife Judy had decided to go and live in her native America. "As I was unable to get a green card, I took up the only profession I could—writing," says Bernard Cornwell. He soon began to produce the series of bestselling novels about Richard Sharpe, fighting in the Peninsular War, which are currently being adapted as a serial for TV.

Redcoat entails a change of setting for Cornwell, and was based on research he did whilst living in New Jersey. He jokingly admits that he started researching the American War of Independence "mainly to annoy people at dinner parties". His American friends proudly boasted of the Rebel victory over the British at Philadelphia, but when he began delving into the archives, he discovered letters and records that showed that the British did in fact win an outstanding victory. At present Bernard Cornwell has no plans to write a sequel to *Redcoat* but he hopes it will soon be made into a film, as the rights have been sold.

Cornwell has just finished writing his next book, entitled *Wildtrack*, his first novel with a modern setting. The hero is an ex-Falklands sailor, awarded a third VC, who dreams of sailing away for ever on his boat. But on leaving hospital he discovers the boat beached and plundered, and gets caught up in a "perfect murder".

Bernard Cornwell can empathise with his latest hero's wish to sail away across the oceans, as he too loves the sea and spends much of his leisure time sailing on his ketch *Yankee Judy* round the coast of Devon, where he and his wife now live.